BRULES

AREA OF
BRULES'S TRAVELS

BRULES

HARRY COMBS

Delacorte Press

Published by
Delacorte Press
Bantam Doubleday Dell Publishing Group, Inc.
1540 Broadway
New York, New York 10036

Library of Congress Cataloging in Publication Data

Combs, Harry.
    Brules/Harry Combs.
      p.   cm.
    ISBN 0-385-31195-8
    1. Comanche Indians—Fiction.   I. Title.
[PS3553.04789B78   1994]
813'.54—dc20   93-37555
                                          CIP

Endpaper photograph © Bill Ellzey
Frontispiece map by GDS/Jeffrey L. Ward
Book design by Robin Arzt

Manufactured in the United States of America
Published simultaneously in Canada

June 1994

10 9 8 7 6 5 4 3 2 1
BVG

BRULES

THE OUTLAW

My name is Steven Cartwright, and I grew up in southwestern Colorado. Lone Cone Peak is a solitary mountain that stands out some fifteen miles to the west of the great San Juan Range near my dad's ranch. From its thirteen-thousand-foot summit you can gaze a hundred fifty miles out across the vast desert canyon country of northern Arizona and southern Utah. The immensity of this panorama is interrupted only by the sleeping mummylike silhouette of Ute Mountain to the south, the Mormon stronghold of the Blue Mountains to the west, and the snowcapped La Sals to the north.

Lone Cone Peak is my favorite mountain. I was born in its shadow in the spring of 1898 and spent my boyhood in the last days of the Old West wandering through the blue spruce and aspen forests that clothed its slopes.

Dad's ranch was a big one. To me it was a world of wonder and delight, from the evergreen forests of our upper summer range on the west side of the peak to the oak brush, cedars, and piñons of our winter forage.

I explored the ranch freely, as an eagle wings through the castles of the clouds, in tune with it all—the bright greens of the quaking aspens in summer and shiny gold in the fall; the white crown of winter snow on Lone Cone, standing starkly against the blue of the eastern sky; the dazzling sunsets of the desert country to the west; the shimmering mystery of the distant La Sal Mountains; and the rumbling of the San Miguel River, fresh-born from the rock springs of the glacial basin far above Telluride.

I sometimes heard my father talk of outlaws and their deeds, of Butch Cassidy and the Sundance Kid, of their hideout in the Hole-in-the-Wall country and their wanderings to Brown's Hole and Robber's Roost south of the Green River, only sixty miles west of us. I even remember my mother telling about the day the Wild Bunch robbed the San Miguel Valley Bank at Telluride in June of 1899, the year after I was born.

Of course, by my time all of the wild Indians were gone. The Battle of Wounded Knee, that last sad convulsion of the ghost-dancing Sioux, had taken place eight years before I was born, but I still knew, as a boy somehow does, all about Indians, and that the old cowmen I had met in the Four Corners country were the same breed of men as the early riders of the Chisholm Trail.

But the Wild West was fading, and even as a small boy I could see it. The long cattle drives were things of the past. The colorful processions of Indian tribes on the move would never be seen again. The railroads would soon reach our land around Lone Cone, and we would become the same as the rest—tame and unexciting.

So I was intrigued by the legend of the old man they called Brules. Father called him a mountain man, but mother used more uncomplimentary terms and told me to stay away from him, which only intrigued me more. All I knew for certain was that he lived in a cabin up on the southwest ridge of Lone Cone Peak—a place mother had warned me to avoid.

One day in the spring of 1909, I was riding my cow pony up from ranch headquarters to our summer range camp high on the mountain. I took a longer route by way of that southwest ridge, hoping to catch a glimpse of Brules's cabin. Sure enough, I spotted it, and there by the little stream running past it was the old mountain man himself, kneeling down, panning for gold. He looked up in a rather annoyed manner when I rode closer, but when he saw only an eleven-year-old boy, he went on about his business.

I got off my horse, stood to watch for a few minutes, and then asked, "Whatcha doin', mister?"

He stared at me for a spell before answering, "Son, I'm a-mindin' my own business."

After a few seconds of facing his cold-eyed gaze, I realized that I was unwelcome, so I got on my horse and rode away. But the memory of the old man with the hard, piercing eyes haunted me, and a few weeks later I deliberately rode back again. This time I found him sitting in the sunshine on the step of his cabin, cleaning an old rifle.

I rode up. "Howdy, sir."

His eyes shone with a glint of recognition. "Hello, boy."

I rode on, not daring to stop, but somehow I knew things would be easier from then on. I went out of my way several times during the rest of that summer to pass by the old man's cabin, never doing more than greeting him. But I sensed that I was cementing a relationship between an old man and a boy that might last. I desperately wanted it to, for I suspected that Brules knew things of the Old West that I yearned to know.

That fall when we drove the cattle down from the summer range, I hung back so I could cut away from the herd. I loped five miles to reach the little cabin by the stream.

The old man was out front and I casually rode by. "See you next summer, Mr. Brules."

He looked up, nodded, and went back to his whittling. As I rode away, I felt his eyes on me. When I reached the timber, I turned around and waved. He waved back.

In those days, there were no schools in the vicinity, so mother taught me herself. Learning with her was adventure and discovery, journeying through the magic medium of books to far-off lands and times gone by. My mother was a kind and beautiful lady and I loved her dearly, but when the occasion suited her she could be surprisingly stern.

It was during one of our tutoring sessions that I allowed a slip of the tongue and she learned of my visits to old Brules's cabin. Her quick intake of breath and shocked expression warned me of the gravity of my error.

"Steven, you know I've forbidden you to ever go near that man!"

"But why, Ma? He's just an old mountain man."

"Steven, that man is a thief and a murderer. He has a terrible criminal record and lives like a savage. I don't want you to go anywhere near him."

"But, Ma, was he ever in jail? If he's so bad, why wasn't he hung?"

"*Hanged*, Steven. All I know is what I've heard. People say he was a very bad man when he was young, and committed all sorts of crimes. I don't know if he was ever in jail. Perhaps he was too wild to be caught, but all the stories about him can't be fiction; there has to be some basis. You have disobeyed me; when your father gets home you're going to the woodshed."

That was in the summer and fall of 1909. As time passed, my curiosity rose to new heights. Over the next three years, some of my most treasured moments came during cattle drives to and from the summer range or when we were branding calves at the cow camp on the west side of the mountain. They were the times when, disobeying my mother's wishes, I could sneak away and visit old Brules.

I managed only four or five visits a summer during those three years, but each one was a precious adventure. During each visit to the old man's cabin I stayed on for longer and longer periods and began to feel more at home in his presence. He seldom said very much, but he showed me many things, among them how to make a fire from the spark of fire steel, how to make a figure-four bear trap, how to boresight a rifle, and how to braid a rawhide lariat.

I remember in 1912, when I was a boy of fourteen and he was an old man of sixty-three, he put on an exhibition of shooting at his cabin site, just to show me what he could do.

At that time he had a shock of beard and a rather distinguished head of white hair that he partially contained under a black sombrero of great character. It was old but obviously treasured, and it spoke of many things. In one stroke of style it said, Here is the plainsman, the Indian fighter, the mountain man, the hunter. Even at his age, his eyes were keen as fire and he moved with the speed and grace of a cat. His face, although weathered, was still handsome.

I have been around men with guns all my life, both before and since, and seen all kinds of shooting, both good and bad, but I never saw anything like Brules that afternoon. He fired many times at still or moving targets, with both pistol and rifle, and never missed.

He had an old 1873 lever-action Winchester. The stock at one time had evidently been badly cracked just back of the pistol grip, for it was bound tightly with shrunken buckskin so hard-used it appeared part of the wood. The stock itself was old and scratched in places, but the barrel was clean and bright and the lever action was slick and sound. His old .38 Smith & Wesson revolver was the same, worn with age and use but still smooth and clean in action.

Not only was Brules's shooting unsurpassed, but the speed with which he fired his weapons was unbelievable. He was so fast it was difficult for the eye to follow his movements. He complained that his reflexes had slowed and his eyesight had dimmed since his youth. That may have been so, but I have never seen any shooting comparable to what he showed me that afternoon. I believe he was the best gunman who ever lived.

When I reached the age of fourteen, my mother decided that she had given me all the education that she could contribute and wanted to send me away to complete my studies. My father, whose education was limited to his high school training and what he had learned on the job, respected Mother's wishes. In consequence, I was packed over the mountains to the rail station at Rico and from there I was shipped east.

I lived for one year with Aunt Beth, my mother's sister, in Granville, Ohio and attended the local high school. Then I moved on to the Phillips Academy in Andover, Massachusetts, to prepare for entrance into Yale University. My father always believed that the professional man had the greatest advantage in life and wanted me to become a civil engineer.

In 1914 a terrible war broke out in Europe. We heard a lot about it but it was far away across the ocean and didn't seem to affect our lives very much. I graduated from Andover in the spring of 1916. During the summer of 1916, as part of my training to become a civil engineer, a goal my father had pointed me toward, I worked on a survey crew in the Four Corners country of southwestern Colorado and northeastern Arizona. Our assignment was to survey the goosenecks of the San Juan River—then a very little-known country. I was only a rod and chain man on the crew, but I gained a great sense of independence and the feeling of being very much my own man.

When the survey crew broke up in September, I drew my pay and departed the gorge of the San Juan at Mexican Hat, where the wagon road to Monument Valley crosses the river.

On the north bank I came upon a young Navajo woman who was displaying several beautiful blankets of the Navajo weave on nearby bushes. Navajo blankets, with their striking colors and exotic designs, had always caught my eye, but there was one blanket in this group that stood out above all the others. It could only be described as stunning, and I knew I had to have it. I bargained fiercely with her, but the little Navajo lady was a shrewd trader and stuck to her guns. I finally had to pay her asking price.

I took the blanket and carefully rolled it up in my oilskin slicker and tied it to the back of my saddle, knowing that it would make an excellent bedroll—warm and comfortable in the cold of the high Rockies.

When I left Mexican Hat, I rode up to high ground and could see in the distance the snow-tipped peak of old Lone Cone, a hundred twenty miles away. It was a welcome sight that warmed my heart. I was coming home. I made the trip handily in three days, for both my horse and I were in top condition after a summer in the canyon country. When I arrived at the ranch, the cattle were still on the summer range. My father asked if I would like to join the hands at the high cow camp, where they were gathering and branding preparatory to the fall drive. I couldn't miss a chance like that. The joys and memories of my boyhood were too strong within me to be denied.

"Take old Paint," my father said casually.

I grinned. "Thank you, sir! Gee, that's great!" I exclaimed. Paint was father's favorite horse, and I'd never been invited to ride him before. I saddled up, lashed on my bedroll, slipped my old .30–.30 Winchester in the saddle scabbard, and headed for the high country. I made the trip to camp in quick order and renewed many acquaintances.

I enjoyed three wonderful days in camp before a strong force—something like desire, instinct, and curiosity combined—drew me to throw my bedroll on the back of Paint one afternoon and start down the southwest trail that led to Brules's cabin.

I cleared the edge of the blue spruce timber when the sun was low in the sky. The old man was sitting on a log in front of the door, whittling a piece of aspen wood.

When he heard my horse he looked up and shook his head, and a wide grin split his beard. "Why, hello, boy," he said.

"Hello, Mr. Brules," I replied, smiling in response. "Mind if I join you?"

He surprised me with the warmth of his answer. "Hell, no! Turn your pony loose in that horse trap over there. They's plenty of feed and water. I got some fixin's for supper—not much, but it'll keep you alive. They ain't much room in the cabin, but I see you got your bedroll. Ain't no reason why a prime young fella like you can't sleep on the ground."

I thanked him and got down off Paint, pulled the saddle, turned the horse loose in the corral, and came back to sit down by the doorsill of the cabin.

"Been missing you, boy," he said. "Where've you been these last three years? You sure growed some!"

That was all the invitation I needed to tell him what I had on my mind: all the things I'd done and, I guess, all the things I dreamed of doing. He listened intently, nodding his head and saying nothing.

Later, as the sun went down over the red rim of the La Sal Mountains and the desert below burned with the sunset that only that land knows, we built a campfire outside the cabin door. As the night came on and the stars began to shine, the old man fried up some venison and made biscuits and coffee, and we sat around the flames and ate together like old, old friends.

The flickering fire made shadows dance on the limbs of the blue spruce trees overhead and popped and sputtered warmth into the wind. I saw Brules's craggy features in the firelight—the lean face, hawklike nose, and crinkly crow's-feet above his beard, and long strands of white hair that flowed beneath the rim of the old battered black sombrero. They all told the story of a hard life on the plains and in the mountains when the West was young.

Most intriguing of all were his eyes. I have never seen a man with such eyes, not before and not since. Brules's eyes were slate gray, with just the slightest trim of light orange-brown edging the craters of the pupils, pupils that expanded in the dark and gleamed gray-green like those of a cat. Pupils that in bright sunshine narrowed into crosslike slits that seemed to squeeze the very secrets out of the light itself. Pupils set in fierce, piercing eyes—haunting, fearful eyes that appeared to hide the wounds of a badly scarred soul. I thought to myself with a delicious thrill that they were indeed the eyes of an outlaw. My outlaw.

An inner bravery prompted me to ask the question that I had long been wanting to ask. I turned to him. "Mr. Brules, were you ever an outlaw?"

The moment I spoke, I feared I had made a mistake. The old man looked up with a hard glint in those eyes. He turned silently to stir up the embers of the fire and spat before he spoke.

"Outlaw? Hell, young fella, I don't know what you mean by outlaw." His sharp cat eyes fixed me with a sideways look and I held my breath for an agonizing moment before he started to speak again.

"What's an outlaw, anyway? A bad man? A wanted man? Maybe some call me that. All I know is, that's the way a man sometimes has to work out his life."

He paused and peered out beyond the rim of the firelight as if he saw something in the distant shadows of the forest. Then he shook his head. "Well, come to think of it, seems like there was times when every man's hand was turned against me. I ain't too sure but what I was born unlucky. That may or may not be. I ain't complaining. But I sure gave it hell all the time. Rode hard. Hunted hard. Fought hard. Sinned hard, too. But I never asked no quarter from no man."

Old Brules pulled a pipe out of his pocket and lit it with a burning twig. I stayed very quiet and hoped he'd keep on talking. He didn't disappoint me.

This is the story he told me that night and over the next three days while we sat by the fire, or wandered around the slopes by his cabin, or leaned against the corral, or just looked out over the valley and watched the shadows of the clouds slide slowly over the meadows far below. I give it here in his own words. Some of these, like old Brules himself, are rough, harsh, even revolting. But, as I said before, he was my outlaw. I don't want to change him, and I tell his story the way he told it to me.

2
HEADED FOR TROUBLE

That evening in Hays City, Kansas, when I walked out of Mrs. Tatterback's boardinghouse, I had a feeling that I was heading for trouble. Maybe I was even looking for it, 'cause I hit right out for the Longhorn Saloon. I was fresh off a long, hard drive, herding a cussed, ornery bunch of longhorns up the Chisholm Trail.

In them days Hays City was a tough place. That was back in October of 1867. At that time it was the western railhead of the Kansas Pacific and a good place to sell trail-drive cattle at top prices. Hays City weren't too far from the Colorado line. You could tell by the way them railroad workers was laying track that it wouldn't be too long 'fore they'd be in sight of the Rocky Mountains. The streets was sloppy with mud that was ankle-deep and there was lots of activity and confusion, 'specially since the railroad'd come in.

I was a young fella then, just turned eighteen, full of life and energy. I figured maybe I was going someplace and might amount to something someday. I weren't afeared of no man and I was a right good shot. I'd learned lots about shooting from my daddy back in Kentucky, what they used to call "Cain-Tuck." He weren't no slouch with a gun hisself.

One of the things he taught me, which I found many times was plumb true, was never to be over-gunned. Them boys who was always shooting them two-gun six-shooters—most of 'em Colt .44s—they was way over-gunned. It ain't the power you got, it's your accuracy. That's what counts.

Now you take a .38 Smith & Wesson. That's one helluva gun. It'll kill anything you want it to, but you gotta shoot straight. You gotta hit something. It's no good nicking a man or shooting him in the leg. Try to drill him through the center of the head, which is messy, but it'll finish him for sure, and you don't have to worry 'bout the gun's kick. That Smith & Wesson is easy to handle. It's a light gun. It'll come out faster and shoot straighter than them big six-shooters—long as you know how to use it.

I crossed over in the mud and walked on the boardwalk, past that harness shop and the general store, and went into the Longhorn Saloon. My old friend Pedro Gonzales had told me all 'bout Lil Tucker's place, the Longhorn, so I felt like I knowed all the folks there already: the faro dealers and the men that tended the bar, but 'specially Lil. Pedro said she sure was a fine lady. She never did turn down a cowpuncher when he was in trouble, never give a sheepherder a bad deal, like putting him alongside a cowhand in a poker game. She always seemed to know what kind of action a man was looking for, and I was no different than the rest.

I'd been in the saddle for seventeen weeks, coming up that trail under the toughest trail boss there ever was, a bullheaded son of a bitch named McIntyre. He was the meanest man anybody ever rode for, and that particular trip we had lots of trouble.

We had to cross the Canadian and Red rivers when they was in flood on account of late rains. We had a bad time in Indian territory with them skunks taking potshots at us and trying to raid our remuda. Then Sammy, the cook, got hisself bushwhacked just as we passed over the Kansas line. That was some drive!

We got them longhorn steers through to Hays all right. In them days the Chisholm Trail used to go into Abilene, but McIntyre had reasons of his own not to go there, and besides, the railhead had moved on west to Hays during the year. You always got the best prices at the railhead. Out of fifteen hundred head we only lost sixty-three, and that's good driving. I'll say this for McIntyre, he knowed his cattle and how to handle stock, 'specially longhorns, but on the trail he weren't a man to cross. He'd just as soon kill you as look at you, and he had a mouth as foul as a two-hole outhouse. When he paid us boys off, it weren't a lot, but I felt too relieved to be rid of him and his tormenting ways to kick 'bout it. I'd made enough to have a helluva good time in Hays City, and that's what I was aiming to do.

Actually, I had two things on my mind, one of 'em real important. First, I was gonna find me a good-looking whore. Second, and most important, I was s'posed to meet old Pedro. He'd told me he had a job for us that'd pay well and I'd better look him up. That's what he'd said back in San Antone last spring. Said when I was ready to find him, he'd show up sooner or later at Lil's Longhorn Saloon. If Lil didn't know where he was, there wouldn't be nobody in the world that would. So that was my idea. Have myself one fine time, then tie in with old Pedro—my hell-raising friend who everybody called "Silver Pete."

When I was still a block away from the saloon, I could hear the yelling and hollering and the stomping and the music. That Longhorn Saloon sure had all the glories of sin in one spot. A fella could never get bored in a place like that.

Inside there was a show going on up on the stage and some of them fancy girls was dancing away. Some fella was up against the bar, singing songs that didn't have nothing to do with what was happening on the stage.

The bartenders was pouring drinks 'bout as fast as they could. They could pour whiskey faster and better than any men I ever seen, and they was working that cash drawer something fierce. Over in the corner, some real mean-looking characters was playing cards.

I went over to the bar, elbowed my way in, and paid for a couple of straight shots of whiskey. I tossed 'em down and ordered another. The whiskey warmed my belly and, after I stood there for a while, I got to thinking, by God, them men over at the card tables ain't as tough as they think they are. Bet I can make out all right.

I started over there and the biggest damn bouncer I ever seen tapped me on the shoulder. He wanted my gun and asked how I'd got in the saloon without checking it.

"Hell, ain't nobody asked me fer it," I told him.

But I weren't aiming to have any trouble with him. All I had was a .38 revolver tucked in my belt. If he was the one to keep it, he could have it all right. He wrapped it up in a piece of cloth and put it in a drawer along with some others in this old chest he had. Then he give me a paper and said when I wanted my gun I could have it, long as I was leaving, but he didn't want no gunplay in that saloon.

I went over and stood around the card table watching 'em play for a while. It was stud poker, and things was going mighty good. There was a gray-haired old man who looked like a rancher, a cowboy humming a little tune, and a city fella—a lawyer or a banker maybe. He weren't betting high, but he was winning.

I sipped another drink, wondering if I should ask for Lil and start tracking down my friend Pedro. The bartender asked me what I'd been doing, and I told him I'd come up the Chisholm Trail with McIntyre.

He laughed real smartlike. "By God, I never met nobody your age who made it clear through with McIntyre before. Thought he killed all his ornery young hands before they got here."

I scowled at him. He might've been kidding. I didn't know.

'Bout then the city fella got up from the table, picked up his chips, and took 'em over to cash 'em in. That left a place empty. I had a nice little roll from that cattle drive—almost a hundred forty dollars. I'd already had me a hot bath and some good whiskey, and I felt pretty cocky, not to mention handsome and lucky. I marched over there and sat down.

All three looked up at me and raised their eyebrows. They seen I was a young man and maybe figured me for a sucker. The dealing started right away and nobody said a word. They all anted up, so I done the same, just like I knowed what the hell I was doing.

I done all right the first hand, just lost my ante. Didn't bet nothing. Then I got worked up the next go-round. I had an ace turned down and I got another one turned up, back to back. The old rancher had two kings showing. He kept on going and I stayed right with him 'til the last deal. When we turned our cards over, he had three kings. My two aces weren't worth a damn. I started feeling more humble.

I'd bet twelve dollars on that hand, and I figured that was 'bout two weeks' riding half-broke broncs, swimming them rivers, camping out at night alongside mosquitoes, dodging bullets and waiting for them damn Indians to leave, eating lousy chow, and fooling around with them gol' durned longhorns—critters that give a man more trouble than he can think about.

I got a little mad at myself, and had decided to settle down and play some serious poker when one of them little dance hall gals come up and put her hand on my shoulder. She sure was cute—brown hair, pert nose, and real pretty. Something about her made her seem almost like a regular, decent girl. I wondered how she'd come to work in a joint like the Longhorn.

I was liquored up enough so that I dared to put my arm 'round her waist and give it a little squeeze. She giggled and held my wrist 'round her and looked down at me real nice. It was her eyes what give her away. They weren't the eyes of a whore. They was soft, gentle, sky blue eyes that spoke of love and pain and a deep sorrow that sent a shiver down my spine. But I was liquored up bad and I shook off the feeling and let my hand slide down over the curve of her ass.

Boy! That blowed the lid off! My heart caught fire and I couldn't have give less of a damn for that poker game. The twelve hard-earned dollars I was aiming to get back didn't seem like nothing much anymore. I had plenty of money left and, by God, I'd just found a better way to spend it than on that poker game. I throwed my hand down and pushed away from the table.

"Hey! Ain't you gonna finish this hand, partner?" the rancher asked.

"Hell, no," I shouted over my shoulder as I led the brunette to an empty table in the corner of the room. "Find yerselves some other sucker. I got me somethin' more interestin' here." They all laughed and went back to playing.

She sure was beautiful. I could see by the way she walked and the way her legs filled them lacy stockings that she had a trim little figure. Like I said, I was eighteen years old and full of fire—and whiskey—and we got to talking business right away.

She wanted five dollars. "Hell, no!" I said. "The goin' rate is two bucks. That's what they charged in San Antone, an' that's what I paid in Austin. I'll be damned if I'm gonna pay a nickel more."

She almost got up and left. I grabbed her by the wrist and set her back down again. We bargained for a while and finally settled on ten dollars for the whole night. That was lots of money back then, but she seemed like she might be worth it.

She took me up some rickety stairs into a fine room with lots of red wallpaper. There was a porcelain washbasin, a big old bedstead, frilly curtains, and everything. Boy! She was some gal, I'm telling you. I never spent a better ten bucks in my life. She told me she'd learned lots of things in St. Louis from some madam there who'd took her in, a big redhead she said had come from New Orleans and had learned the trade in France.

I don't know 'bout all that. All I know is that we had one helluva night. She was a dandy. About five o'clock in the morning, when I was plumb wore out, I fell asleep.

Seemed like real late in the morning when I woke up. I looked 'round that room, studied the washbasin and the stand, the old brass bedstead, the red-papered walls, and ruffled curtains. It didn't look quite as nice as it had the night before, but it was still fancier'n anyplace I'd slept for some time.

I looked 'round and seen that the little brunette was gone. I had a pounding head on me from that whiskey, but there was a smile on my lips. While I was lying there thinking and looking up at the ceiling, I heard a wagon train outside in the street. Men was shouting and cussing, bullwhips was cracking, and the oxen was lowing all at once.

I got up and pulled the curtains open. Bright sunshine lit up the street of Hays City. I watched a couple of wagons go by with a line of oxen pulling 'em along. One of the drivers was a big black nigger, stripped to the waist. He had uncommon muscles on him, and that dark skin of his was a-shining in the sun. He kept calling to the span and cracking a long black whip, making sounds like pistol shots.

I checked the room for my clothes and, sure enough, there was my buckskin britches hanging on a peg by the wall. The shirt I'd bought new in Austin was hanging there, too. Then I remembered my money. I'd put it in the breast pocket of that shirt and I thought, by God, I've been robbed!

I looked real quick. No, it was there all right, everything I had left after paying off that little gal last night. I decided right then that she was an honest woman.

Now, there's nothing better'n an honest whore. They really understand human nature. Know everything 'bout a man. Know how to please him, how to play it straight. They know, 'cause nobody ever give 'em something for nothing. I got to thinking what a fine woman that little brunette might be. The fact that she was a whore weren't nothing to hold against her. Hell, I was a roving son of a bitch myself, so I didn't have much to brag on.

Something on the chair by the bed caught my eye. It was a note that said, "I like you. Please come see me again. Don't forget." It was signed "M." I didn't know what that "M" stood for, prob'ly her first name, but I weren't sure. Didn't care. All I knowed was I'd had one helluva time with her the night before.

There was a washbasin, so I poured out some water and throwed it all over my face. Then I pulled on my britches, stuck my feet in my boots, took my shirt off the peg and slipped it on, and reached for my hat. Something was missing—my gun. I finally found the bouncer's ticket in my britches pocket.

I opened the door real easy, not knowing what I might be getting into. I looked up and down the corridor and seen there was a door with a window at the end of the hall. Sure enough, there was outside steps going down across the back of the place.

It was a bright, beautiful fall day and the sun was shining down warm. That made me feel better. The dust was blowing around a little bit, just lightly floating in the air. All in all, it weren't a bad time to be in Kansas.

I walked 'round front, feeling good and whistling a little. I run up the steps and into the saloon, where some old man was sweeping the floor. Otherwise, the place was plumb quiet, nothing like the night before. The tables and chairs was stacked around in different places. I gave the old man the claim check for my Smith & Wesson, and he left and come back with it. It sure felt good to have it tucked in my belt again.

I ambled on down the street, figuring I oughta get something to eat. Knowing that it was between meals at the boardinghouse, I crossed over to a Chinaman's joint. He was outta eggs, but he fried me up some ham, and there was plenty of black coffee and a loaf of bread that was a little tough, but it didn't taste too bad.

One of the things bothering me was that I'd spent more money'n I'd planned. The poker was a bad deal and the whiskey'd been okay, but that great little dance hall gal—well, I thought to myself, that particular ten bucks was worth it, anytime!

I finished thinking 'bout her and started worrying 'bout my horse, Piebald. I'd plumb forgot him. Now, Piebald was something else where horses was concerned. He didn't deserve to be forgot. He was extra special, a black and white Indian pony that I'd bought in San Antone with wages from my first cattle drive. I'd picked him out of a bunch 'cause he had a mean, bloodshot eye and was the best-muscled little stallion I ever saw.

Sure enough, that old mustang turned out to be one tough cayuse. He was the best horse a man could find in lots of ways—tireless, surefooted, not classy-looking, but ornery. That was Piebald. When you was astride him, you knowed you had something sassy and powerful 'tween your legs.

I used to get on him in the morning when he was still stiff-legged and full of oats, and he'd give me a real helluva bucking, just to see if he could off-load me. He didn't mean nothing personal by it, 'cause he was only acting sporty. As soon as he figured out that I was planning to stay right on him, he'd settle down and behave like one savvy cow pony for the rest of the day. My old Piebald, I sure did like him.

Back then I didn't use no stirrups when I mounted a horse. Didn't need 'em. I was a young man then, not stiff like I am now with rheumatiz, plumb wore out and sick of the world and all.

In them days, the skies shined bright and clear, clouds was always white, and the wind blowed plenty of nice smells. The women looked good and I felt like the king of it all. When I went to get on a horse, I took hold of the saddle horn, flicked 'round, and lit in the saddle. Some people called it vaulting, but to me it was the most natural way to get going. All I done was take hold and get up there. Then I could squeeze down real hard, 'cause I had legs as strong as steel bands. There was no getting rid of me with any ordinary, easy-going bucking.

I headed down to the livery stable to check on Piebald. As I walked past the stock corrals, damned if I didn't run into McIntyre hisself. He was sitting on the rails of a cattle pen in the rail yard, waiting for the next train to come in. He was perched up there big as life, playing God again like he had on the Chisholm Trail, jawboning with another cattleman. I tried to avoid 'em and pass on by. Besides, I weren't interested in him. I was interested in Piebald.

He spotted me and yelled out, "Hey kid! Get over here!"

I ignored him and he jumped down and headed me off. Then he spit a shit-brown stream of tobacco beside my boot. "Goddamn you, kid! Don't act like you didn't hear me," he yelled, loud enough for the other man to hear. "Ain't you s'posed to be saddled up and ready to go? Damnit to hell, we gotta load these cattle on the next train. Where've you been, you no-good bastard?"

I didn't cotton to his attitude, and I already had my pay. I was through working for that son of a bitch, so I looked him right in the eye. "Mr. McIntyre, they ain't no call fer ya ta talk ta me that way. I'm finished workin' fer ya."

"Goddamnit," he barked, "I'm gonna slap the livin' shit outta you, kid. You need correctin'."

He took one step toward me and stopped dead in his tracks. I don't know what I done, but it must've been faster'n a rattlesnake strike. That Smith & Wesson come outta my belt so quick that it surprised us both. It just slapped outta there cocked, and stared him right 'tween the eyes.

He got a real surprised look on his face, with his pupils crossed, and his hands shot straight up. "Now wait a minute, kid," he said. "I didn't mean no harm. Hell, I was just talkin'."

I knowed right then and there that I'd won. I could draw faster'n he could, even though he had the reputation of being a mean gunhand. He never had a chance to reach for them big .44s he was packing.

"McIntyre," I said, "back away 'fore I blow your fuckin' brains out. Keep your hands up an' your mouth shut, 'cause I've took all the crap from ya I'm gonna take."

He stammered, "Now wait a minute, kid, wait a minute. You got me all—"

"Shut up! An' don't call me no kid, neither!"

"Okay, mister," he said, his face almost pleading, looking sideways like he couldn't stand the direct gaze of my eyes.

"That's better," I said. "Keep on callin' me mister."

Just then his friend slid down off the rail. I moved my gun real quick, like a snake whip. "Keep your hands up, too!" I warned him. "If'n yore a friend a McIntyre's, ya ain't no friend a mine." I waved him over closer to McIntyre and stepped back a few paces. "I ain't lookin' fer trouble from neither of ya. I come down ta check on my horse. Just so's there ain't no misunderstandin', why don't ya both keep your hands up, turn 'round, and start marchin' down the street. Better not reach fer them guns, neither. Start marchin' now. That's right—one, two, three—an' keep on goin'."

I watched 'em for a ways to see if they'd try a quick turn-and-draw, but they didn't. Good thing. I would've killed 'em both. They went on down the street and into a store, then I headed over to the stable.

The livery man'd fed Piebald real good—his oat box was still wet where he'd licked it clean and he was munching on some dry timothy. He picked up his ears and nickered when I come up.

I grinned at him. "Piebald, ya ol' bastard, do ya wanta go fer a little ride?" He pawed and stomped the ground and acted like he knowed what I was talking about. I went to get my saddle and told the livery man, "I wanta take a ride 'round here. I'll be comin' back in a little while."

"Okay, mister. You don't need to pay me now." That livery man was all right. He knowed when he was dealing with a man that was square.

I went back and got me a curry comb. Piebald hadn't been groomed all the way from San Antone. He had some flecks of mud on his back and I figured he needed scratching a little bit. I combed down his back and rump and brushed the dust off'n him, talking to him real sweet in back of his ears and kissing him on the nose. I felt his belly and checked the backs of his legs, where I scraped off more mud. I patted him all 'round and finally scratched 'tween his ears. He acted real friendly.

Next I took a saddle blanket and throwed it on his back, heaved the saddle up, cinched the girth tight, slipped the bit 'tween his teeth, and buckled the throatlatch. Then I told the old man, "Open that corral gate, mister. Me an' Piebald's comin' out."

That paint stallion stood there plenty wary, like he always done 'fore I went to get on him. He leaned back a little bit, stiffening his front legs, then he give a snort and looked at me so wide-eyed his eyeballs bulged out.

"You ol' son of a bitch, ya know what yore gonna do?" I said. "Yore gonna give me a helluva buckin'. An' ya know what I'm gonna do? I'm gonna ride ya to a standstill come hell or high water. Now, here goes!"

With that I reached up and took hold of the horn, sprang up, and landed in the saddle. I didn't get time to put my feet in the stirrups, 'cause Piebald tore outta there like he was coming out of a bucking chute. We went sailing through that gate into the middle of the street like a cannonball. I commenced fanning him with my hat, hanging on with my knees. He kicked and bucked and twisted and bellered and had a good old time. I fanned him and yipped and hollered and stayed tight.

People on the boardwalk stopped to watch and cheer, but I was too busy to pay attention to 'em. When he quit bucking, he took out in a gallop and headed west, straight down the main street of Hays City. Folks kept stopping to look as we streaked through town, past where a crew was working on the railroad, then on 'cross the prairie. 'Bout five miles out, near the old Fort Hays cavalry post, Piebald stopped the galloping and snorting and started prancing and crow-hopping around, having a great time.

Then he settled down to a walk and snorted a little to get the dust outta his nose, and we got to talking. We understood each other real good, drinking in the bright sunshine of an Indian summer morning.

We rode on down to the Smoky Hill River for a short drink and a good look around 'fore we wound our way back across the prairie. Hays City didn't appear very big from out there. When we got back and went through town, Piebald was arching his head and his tail and I s'pose we looked real fine. In the back of my mind I was hoping I'd see the little brunette along the boardwalk somewhere and maybe she'd wave to me. I made Piebald prance sideways, but I never did see my girl.

That afternoon I took a nap. I guess I slept 'til near five o'clock. Then I got up and washed my face again. I always like to wash my face. A man can see better through his face if'n it's washed.

I dug my gun belt outta my gear and strapped it on with my little Smith & Wesson. She was deadly and I always felt better wearing her. Next I wanted to try and find Pedro.

Since it was so early in the evening, them swinging doors at the saloon didn't reveal near the noise and excitement they had the night before. I reminded myself that I was only going in to hook up with Pedro.

I went in and looked around. Four bored-looking characters slouched 'round one of the poker tables in the corner, idly fingering and tossing their chips. A couple of other men leaned against the bar. One was a cowpuncher. The other one was the city fella I'd seen playing poker the night before. The only women around were two old hags who waited on tables.

I went up to the bartender and asked for a shot. It was good whiskey, a little raw, but I drank it down real fast and ordered another one.

"You been in these parts long?" the bartender asked.

"Come in yesterday. I was in here last night."

"You was? Didn't see you. But then we was real busy."

"Yeah," I said, "I was, too. I enjoyed the comp'ny a one a them little gals that was here last night—the brunette."

"Oh, yeah. That must've been Michelle."

"I didn't catch her name, but she shore was cute. She was 'bout so high, had a turned-up nose and blue eyes, and brownish black hair that was pinned behind her head."

"Oh yeah, that's Michelle all right."

"But I ain't lookin' fer Michelle," I told him. "I'm lookin' fer a man. S'posed to meet him here—Pedro Gonzales. Folks call him 'Silver Pete.' "

"Sure, I know Pete. He's a friend of Lil's. He was in the day before yesterday. Then him and some other fellas rode out west of here. Said they'd be back in a day or so."

That set my mind a little at rest, so I asked, "Where's the little whore?"

"Michelle? She ain't here right now." The bartender twisted his mustache and smiled like he was reading my mind.

"Where'n the hell is she? Don't she live here an' don't she work fer Lil?"

"Hey, young fella. No use gettin' excited. Sure she works here. She's a businesswoman. She's got appointments to keep." He studied the way I was clenching my teeth and fists and smiled. "She's upstairs with a customer right now."

I could feel my blood really boiling and yelled, "What's she doin' up there, anyway?" Then I thought, ya knothead, Brules. 'Course she's entertainin' customers. She's a whore, ain't she? She's upstairs with some man doin' the same things she done with you last night.

"Sorry," I said to the bartender, who'd backed off. "Gimme another shot, buddy. Gimme a shot, quick!"

Whiskey always warms my belly. I couldn't blame the bartender for telling me the truth. "Thanks," I told him. "I didn't mean no trouble. Reckon I'll go over there an' see 'bout the poker game."

I started to amble across the room when the bouncer came up. "Hey, sonny, give me your gun."

I whirled on him and snapped, "Don't ya call me 'sonny'!"

"I ain't callin' you nothin'. Now hand over your gun or I'll have to ask you to leave."

I undid my slinger belt with my .38 and handed it to him. "I ain't lookin' fer no fight," I told him when he brought back a claim check same as the other night. I strolled on up to a table where a few boys was playing stud.

Before I could ask if I could get in the game, one of the fellas at the front tables called out, "By God, it's party time! Silver Pete's back!"

Sure enough, when I looked up at the door, there was my old amigo Pedro Gonzales. Of all the men I ever knowed, I liked Pedro the best. He was big for a Mexican, 'bout the same height as me—five foot eleven. He always wore black and silver: black boots, silver spurs, black britches, and black vest—both with silver trim—a black hat with a silver band, and a black belt with a big silver buckle. That was why folks called him Silver Pete.

Even his mustache was black—coal black—but when he smiled, his teeth flashed as white as the keys on a new piano. He was the best-looking Mexican I ever seen, kinda light complected like them high-born Spanish folks they call Castilians. His black eyes had a good, clear look and his smile was like the morning sunshine breaking through the clouds.

"Pete!" I called out.

He seen me and throwed his hat up in the air with a whoop. "Cat Brules!" he shouted. "*¡Hijo de puta!*" Then he run across that room and we stood hugging each other like we was both full of locoweed. Now, I never been much of a man for hugging, but with Pedro it was okay.

He made like he was real mad at me and pounded my chest. "*Jesucristo*, amigo, where in the hell have you been? I been lookin' all over for you, you damn fool gringo bastard." And then he pounded me on the chest something fierce and hugged me again.

We marched to the bar together and I announced, "I'm buyin' this round, ya crazy Mexican."

"Amigo, you say 'you crazy Mexican' to me, but look who offers to pay for the whiskey! You buy quick, no? Because I am very thirsty."

That whiskey sure tasted good. After Pedro and me got tired of cussing at each other, I told him, "I'm through with McIntyre. I come up the trail with that bastard, an' the only reason I signed on with the drive was 'cause I wanted ta meet ya here in Hays City. I won't ride no cattle trail again fer him nor any man. But hell, ya told me ya had a great job fer us. What—"

Pedro cut me off and whispered real low, "Hush now, amigo, come down to the end of the bar with me." I followed him there, and he went on in a quiet tone. "We gotta be careful around those other bastards with their big ears. You an' me is gonna be rich—all the money we'll ever need."

"Great," I said. "Now, how in the hell we gonna get that way?"

"Keep the goddamn voice down! You wanta tell everybody here?" Pedro looked hurt that I wasn't taking him real serious. "Brules, man, I'm talkin' about robbin' the bank."

"You *are* crazy, ya Mexican bastard. They got these Wells Fargo fellas just itchin' ta shoot our asses off in that bank."

Pedro widened his eyes in exasperation and poked me in the chest. "Shut up the big gringo mouth! We are not robbin' the bank in Hays City, you dumb son of a bitch. I know a better bank. We will rob the bank in Taos."

"In New Mexico Territory? Hell, man, that's eight hundred miles west a here."

"Jeez! You are one dumb gringo. Trust your amigo, Pedro Gonzales! I have a good plan, an' I know this bank. These stupid people in Taos have so much money that they are very careless."

I sobered up at the thought and he smiled at me.

"That's better. Soon you will be worth maybe twenty thousand dollars, maybe more. You like that idea, no? Have the faith in your amigo. Remember when we was in Laredo in that whorehouse an' you got into the fight with that big greaser, Malaga, an' I have to kill that son of a bitch to keep him from cuttin' your silly gringo throat? An' then we ride like hell from Laredo to San Antonio to keep the whole government of Tamaulipas off your ass? Who take care of you then, eh? Sure you no can doubt me now! Pay attention!"

And then Pedro began to unfurl a stream of thoughts that he must've had stashed away for a long time. I listened careful, for I knowed that Pedro weren't no ordinary Mexican. I knowed he'd come from one of them fine old ranchero families in Chihuahua, them big horse ranches that'd been passed down from father to son ever since the conquests of Mexico by that fella Cortez.

That night Pedro begun to tell me something about his background. It seemed his great, great, great gran'daddy, way back there somewhere, come with the rest of them conquistadores from the province of Estremadura or Andalusia in Spain. That was way back three hundred or more years ago, and when the conquest was done, Pedro said Cortez give to his captains great pieces of land all over Mexico.

His ancestor got hisself a piece of land up in northern Mexico that was near half the size of the State of Chihuahua. Of course, by splitting up the property among the heirs, that great big ranch was reduced in time to a number of small ones—that is, small next to what it once was. But they ain't small even now by our standards.

Pedro told me that his father had a ranch in Chihuahua that covered more than a million hectares—about two million acres. They raised cattle and mostly fine horses. I can sure believe the last of that statement 'cause Pedro rode a black stallion that was the finest piece of horseflesh I ever seen in my life. He was kind of affectionate towards him and called him Blackie. He could make that horse do things you couldn't believe. Them top Spanish horses was trained by the gentlest means, and was never rough broke.

Pedro used to talk to me for hours 'bout how that was done. He was the finest horseman I'd ever knowed. You couldn't ever tell from the way he acted what kind of pressure he was putting on either the horse's flanks or his withers or by the bit, but that horse would obey as if the orders come directly from Pedro's brain and without no physical movement.

I seen him time and time again have old Blackie rear up and stand on his hindquarters and pirouette real slow and make it almost clear 'round in a circle 'fore he had to drop his forefeet to get his balance again, and never at no time had I seen any kind of motions that Pedro was making to get that horse to obey that kind of command. 'Course they had to be somewhere, but only Pedro knowed the secret of it.

I reckon that old Blackie come from a selection of thousands and thousands of horses that was on Pedro's father's ranch, and Pedro got his choice. Naturally, the question that come to my mind was what was a fella who seemed like he had inherited half of the world doing messing around with a bunch of border bums like me and them other men that was in the Longhorn Saloon in Hays City.

Well, all men's got their own secrets and it weren't none of my business to go prying, but I sure was curious 'bout that side of things. I gleaned a little from what he'd say from time to time. I gathered that he was like the prodigal son that my mama read about to me in the Bible. Seems Pedro had an older brother that his father took most of a shine to, and it looked like his older brother was gonna be running things, and meanwhile Pedro was at loose ends about what his own future was gonna be. He had a great curiosity to see the world and, although he was prob'ly the favorite of his mother and sisters and had real favorable appreciation by his father, he still was gonna play second fiddle on the ranch with his brother running things.

This didn't exactly upset him too much, but it give him the idea that it oughta be a considerable while before he settled down. What he had to do now was to go out and see the world. I think what he was trying to prove to hisself and maybe to others was that he could damn well get along on his own without having to rely none on the family fortune and name.

Pedro knowed, too, that deep down in his family's feelings, as well as his own, the Mexican War of 1848 had been a robbery and that his people had lots of land and stuff stole from 'em by the U.S. government. He figured any act that he might commit north of the border weren't robbery nor any other kind of crime. From his standpoint it was merely getting even for the unsatisfactory conclusion of the Treaty of Guadalupe Hidalgo, where the United States took from Mexico a chunk of territory damned near as big as Mexico itself. There couldn't help but be some bitterness 'bout that.

I got to listening and thinking that maybe my young Mexican friend had a good idea after all. He knowed the whole situation at Taos and that bank—knowed the cashier, knowed the president, knowed many other things that was important for a man to know if he was planning a robbery.

The more I listened, the more I felt I oughta move in and be a partner in this deal. Pete had it figured out real slick. I allowed myself to start daydreaming 'bout going along, how I'd set myself up with the money, how going with Pedro might be lots of fun as well as an easy way to get rich.

'Sides that, robbing a bank eight hundred miles west of Kansas, there weren't much chance of folks spotting me when I came back to civilization. I was dreaming away about this when I seen a pair of pretty legs and a flouncy skirt coming down the stairway. It was Michelle, walking arm in arm with one of them damn gambling men.

My breathing started to hurt real fierce and my heart commenced beating faster, and I didn't hear another word that Pete was saying. He kept on talking, but all I could see was my girl coming down the stairs with another man. If I'd had my gun, I might've shot that man, but that's why they stashed away the guns of men coming into the Longhorn Saloon, so there'd be no easy way to do serious damage.

"What the hell," I told myself, "she's just a common whore."

I turned and tried to listen to Pete again, but all I could see was Michelle as she went over to mingle at the gambling tables. I couldn't stand it no longer, so without saying nothing to Pete, I walked off and left him talking to hisself. He must've thought I'd gone nuts. Considering what happened later, maybe I had.

I worked my way over towards the tables to see if I couldn't edge up next to her. She was in with a big crowd of fellas, laughing and carrying on. I looked at the back of her neck and seen how smooth it was, and what a nice way she'd done her hair, and I listened to the sounds of her laughter, and it all played on the strings of my heart. I finally got up close and motioned for her to come on over to the bar. She laughed and turned back to the gambling man who'd brought her downstairs.

I stood there frozen, with my knees shaking, when Pete come up and grabbed me by the arm. "What the hell is the matter with you, amigo? You got somethin' more important on your mind than makin' money? Or maybe you have no mind a'tall, no?"

I give him a sad smile. "Pete, leave me alone fer a little while. I'm with ya, so count me in, but there's somethin' I gotta work out fer myself 'fore we leave. I'll be all right in the mornin'."

That seemed to satisfy him. He just shook his head and joined some of the regulars eating supper up front. I walked over to the bar and started some serious drinking and thinking about things. Every time I tried to catch Michelle's eye, she'd turn away and get busy at the crap table. She kept laughing, and the sound of her laughter was the one clear thing I heard above all the commotion in that joint.

When she finally broke away, I hurried over beside her. "Hey, Michelle, we gonna get together again tonight?"

She kept on going. "Sorry, honey, but I can't work you in tonight," she said without looking at me.

I moved around to block her path. "Wait, Michelle. I gotta see ya again. I may be leavin' town tomorrow."

"Oh," she flirted, "you'd leave town without telling me good-bye?"

"I weren't aimin' ta, but if yore so tied up, what can I do?"

She put a hand on my arm. "Well, honey, I'd really like to talk to you more. I sure like you, but this is one of my real busy nights." She paused. "But I'll tell you what. Sneak up around five o'clock tomorrow morning. Come to my private room—number four. Maybe it'd be best if you come up the back stairs."

She smiled and squeezed my arm, and all I could do was smile back. Then she slipped off towards the stairway. As for me, I guess I got drunker'n hell. Then I went out in the street and walked up and down that Hays City boardwalk 'til I must've worn out half the lumber. I checked on Pedro a couple of times, but he'd lucked into a good card game and didn't wanta leave.

I remember walking out in the cold night air and looking at the stars. They was really swimming around. I stood there, out in the mud, looking up and listening to the noises of the town. Down the street a ways I heard a few shots, but they didn't bother me none. I was thinking what a helluv an interesting world this was and how, by God, I couldn't hardly wait 'til five o'clock in the morning.

Then it hit me. Five o'clock? By then, she'd have been with quite a few men. My blood run cold and I went back to the Longhorn and checked out my gun. Sure felt better to have it back within reach. I walked out towards the edge of town and kept on brooding about Michelle being with all them other men. There was a couple of drunks lying around on the ground. One of 'em got up and asked me to buy him a drink.

"Looks like you've already had too much," I told him. He started cussing at me and reached for something—prob'ly a knife or a gun. I cut loose and busted him in the jaw so hard I could hear his teeth chatter. He went down in the mud and never moved. I guess I hit him a lot harder'n I should've, but I was plumb mad at the world, and it didn't make no never mind to me. I kept on walking and headed out away from the town.

I've always enjoyed being out in the dark, and I'd known for a long time that I could see better in the darkness than most people. When I got out on the prairie, I noticed that the wind was blowing gentle and the air was nice and crisp. I looked up again at those stars and back towards the lights of town way off behind me. I could hear some dogs barking and the soft tinkle from a honky-tonk piano.

Seemed to me that it was a big world and all the troubles in that town was man-made. Maybe, I thought, if a man could get away from that stuff and get out on the prairie with a pack outfit and his bedroll, he could listen to the wind sighing through the grass and the coyotes yipping once in a while and the night owls hooting, and watch the stars for a spell—then things'd be better.

But back in that town where all hell was being raised was where Michelle was also. I shook my head to clear it and muttered, "Gol'durn it, I've gotta see her once more 'fore I go west."

I got to breathing deeper and started walking back real slow. I seen that it was getting a bit light on the horizon. Well, I didn't have no watch, but I reckoned it was close enough to five o'clock. Thinking 'bout how, real soon, there'd be a pink glow in the east reminded me of the wonderful pink and cream of Michelle in the lamplight there in that upstairs room, and I started moving along at my best, long-striding pace, already knowing how she was gonna feel.

When I got back to the Longhorn Saloon, there was still plenty going on inside. I could hear some of the boys gambling and the piano was still plinking although it had slowed down some. I went 'round the outside to the back stairs where I'd left the morning before and tiptoed up the steps real slow. A couple of times the stairs creaked, and I stopped and looked.

By God, I thought, coming up this way I ain't having to check my gun in. This time I got it with me. That's good business.

When I got to the head of the stairs I opened the door. The corridor was real dark, and even good as my eyes was I couldn't hardly see nothing. I left the door open a little to give me some light and I started easing down the hall looking for room number four. Just then, about twenty feet ahead of me, a door burst open. One of the gals come out, laughing and holding a cowhand by the arm. They started towards the end of the hall and turned down the stairway to the saloon.

I cozied up real close to the wall and they never did see I was there. I noticed there was a lamp still burning in the bedroom they'd left, so I stepped in, picked it up, and took it out in the hall so I could read the numbers on the doors. When I found door number four, I knocked and didn't hear nothing. I knocked again. Then I heard Michelle's voice, kinda sleepylike.

"Yes, who is it?"

"It's me, honey," I replied.

"Who's you?"

"It's me, honey. Come on, open the door."

I could hear her getting up from the bed and barefooting over to the door. The knob turned real slow. She opened the door and peeked out at me. I was standing there holding the lamp in my hand.

"Oh, it's you—you can't come in here now. It isn't five o'clock yet. It can't be. And even if it is, you can't come in here now. I gotta . . . I'm not ready for you."

There was a commotion behind her and I heard a man's voice. I knowed that voice and a mad rage started boiling up in me. Then I heard the bed moving and the noise of a hefty man getting up and thumping to the door behind Michelle. There come this ugly, bearded face peering over her shoulder, and I could see him real clear in the light—damn his blue guts if it weren't McIntyre!

"Why you lousy punk kid," he growled. "I'm gonna kick the shit outta you right now, coming in here bothering me at a time like this." With that, he stepped out with nothing on but his top shirt and made a rush at me.

The thought flashed across my mind real quick that McIntyre wouldn't rush me if he knowed I had a gun. He'd think I'd checked my gun 'fore I'd come in, 'cause he knowed that was the rule of the house. He'd seen how fast I could draw and it'd scared him some. No, he prob'ly thought I was unarmed and he had a chance to whip me. He would've had a good chance, too, if that were the case. I stood 'bout five feet eleven inches and weighed maybe a hundred seventy-five pounds. McIntyre stood six foot four or five and weighed two hundred forty if he weighed an ounce. He was as big and rough a man as I ever seen.

I threw up my arm to try to swing at him, but he hit me so damn hard I backed clear across the corridor and smashed into the wall. The lamp in my hand crashed to the floor and I lay sprawled on my ass trying to force some air back into my lungs. Coal oil was running all down the wall and the flames started to spread.

Michelle run over and grabbed McIntyre by the arm, screaming, "Oh, don't hit him! Don't hit him like that!"

Old McIntyre turned around and smacked her across the face as hard as any man ever hit a woman. The force of the blow knocked her clear back through the door and into the room, where she landed in a heap. She let out a hurt little cry and a dark stream of blood come pouring outta the side of her mouth. I was half-dizzy, lying right in the path of them flames as they was building up. I guess the heat of 'em and the light of 'em and the blue mad that I felt when I seen that big bastard hit Michelle was enough for me. When I got to my feet, there was cold-guts hate in my eyes and I didn't stop to think 'bout what I was doing.

My gun come out like a quick-striking snake and exploded with a roar. I shot that son of a bitch right through the front of his face. He gurgled and blubbed outta where his mouth used to be and then slithered down the wall to the floor. He lay there, the mortal life gone clean outta him.

In Trouble

Michelle scrambled to her feet and stuck her head outta the door. Her eyes looked plumb terrified. "My God, you've killed him. Run! Run!"

"Hell, yeah, I killed him," I shouted. "Ya better run, too. This whole place's catchin' on fire."

I grabbed Michelle, but she pulled away. "I gotta get my clothes," she said.

"Ya ain't got time!"

"Well, all I got on is my nightdress, and I'm barefoot."

"I don't give a damn! Yore comin' now."

I grabbed her by the arm and pushed her past the flames and down the hall. Then I dragged her down the back stairs and onto the street. We started running in the direction of the livery stable, but her poor bare feet kept slipping in the mud. Behind us, flames shot up through the roof of the saloon and somebody was yelling, "Fire! Fire!"

Somebody else was calling for water buckets, and people was running 'round outside that place something fierce. I figured the Longhorn Saloon was done for. Whenever you had any of them wood buildings in Kansas catch fire, there weren't enough water for miles around to get it stopped.

We got down to the stable and I busted in where the livery man was sleeping and shook him awake. "I want my Piebald an' I want him fast."

"Hey, young man, you in some kind of trouble?"

I whipped out my gun and shook it at him. "That ain't none a your gol'durned business. Here's ten dollars. Gimme my horse an' gear quick. I'm leavin'."

At that he jumped up and grabbed a lantern and opened up the tack room. I seen my saddle and my bridle, snatched 'em off the rack, and followed him on out into the corral. I give a whistle and Piebald come trotting over thinking sure as hell I was gonna give him some oats. Well, it was a bad deal for him, 'cause I sure as hell weren't about to. I slung them reins 'round his neck and slipped his bridle on real quick. When I grabbed the saddle, he yawed away a little and backed up.

"Steady boy," I said. "Steady now."

I clicked my tongue a couple of times to help settle him, then I throwed on the saddle blanket and saddle. I reached under his belly and grabbed the front cinch, then took two turns of the latigo and snugged it good before I buckled the rear tight enough so's he wouldn't put a hoof through it.

"Open that gate," I told the livery man.

"But I don't wanta lose these other horses."

"Damn yer hide!" I shouted. "Ya open that gol'durned gate! Ta hell with them other horses!"

I must've looked mighty fierce, 'cause he run right over to the gate. I knowed I was gonna have some trouble with Piebald for a few minutes and I couldn't get Michelle on right away. I grabbed the horn and leaped into the saddle. He started out bucking and kicking and jammed hisself in among the other horses.

When the livery man opened the gate, all of them horses went pouring out and Piebald tore out right after 'em, bucking and kicking. I hoped he'd get over it real quick, and he did. He got a little spooked when he come out into that street and seen all the fire and commotion. When he stopped short, I jerked him 'round and we come back into the corral.

There was Michelle, standing off a ways there kind of amazed. I could see her real clear in the firelight. I rode up and reached down and swung that gal up in the saddle right behind me and we started outta there at a dead gallop. I took one quick turn to the left, away from the fire. That way I knowed I was heading west on the Smoky Hill Trail.

We went outta that town hell-bent for election, but nobody seen us. If they did, they sure as hell didn't pay no attention—there was too many people running 'round and yelling 'bout that fire. It wasn't very long 'til we left Hays City far behind in the dark, but we could see that fire burning away back there in the distance. It kept fading away to a dim glow.

Michelle threw her arms 'round my neck and hung on. I could feel her real close and it sure was good to know that I had some company. Naturally, I was worried 'bout lots of things. If they caught me for killing an unarmed man, they'd string me up for sure.

Michelle kept hollering against my back, "Where're you taking me? Turn this horse around. I wanta go back." I realized then that I might have more trouble on my hands than I'd bargained for.

After we'd run 'bout four miles, I decided to give Piebald a breather. I drawed him down some and he jogged along. Then he settled down into that fast, single-foot shuffle that really eats up the miles.

"Now listen ta me, Michelle," I said. "Ya ain't crazy, are ya? Don't y'know that I killed a man back there? Don't y'know that them folks think yore part a the deal? Y'know damn well I let plenty of 'em know how I feel 'bout ya."

"Why, I don't think that's true a'tall," she said with a sniff. "Whatcha mean, how you feel about me? I didn't know—"

"Damnit, y'know damn well, else'n I wouldn't have ya with me now. Ya ain't goin' back there. Ya'd be an accomplice ta murder, that's what ya'd be. Folks'd think ya got McIntyre, my ol' trail boss, up there and rolled him. Then, when I come up there ta help ya out, he an' I got inta a fight an' I shot him."

I don't know if that was the wrong thing to say or not. Maybe she would've been in trouble, maybe not. Anyhow, it seemed good to have her hanging on to me, and for a while I forgot about her being a whore and thought about her as a real nice girl. She sure weren't wearing much, and from the way she was hugging me close I could feel her body lying up along my back and, I tell you, it made a difference.

Then I noticed she was shaking. There was a fresh prairie wind blowing, the sun hadn't come up yet, and it was plenty cool. I turned and said, "Honey, wait just a minute there. I'll undo that roll on the back a my saddle and put a slicker over ya." I kept my bedroll and my slicker all in one, with the slicker on the outside.

"That's better," she said after I got her all fixed up. "I ain't cold now, 'cept for my feet."

"Well, I don't know what we can do 'bout your feet. Maybe you can stick 'em in my boots."

She laughed. "Maybe that'd be a good idea. Let me see if there's room."

I could feel her toes trying to wiggle down in my boots, but that didn't work, so she slid her bare feet up beneath my pant legs and nestled the bottoms of her feet up against my calves. Her feet were icy cold, and still a little gritty from the mud, but it felt good. She put her arms back 'round my waist, and I could hear that slicker rattling in the wind. I could feel her warming my back and I knowed it was warming her, too. I kicked Piebald up to another good long lope and we went another four or five miles like that before I slowed him down for a breather.

By that time, the prairie was starting to light up. I'd been watching the stars and I knowed we was heading west, 'cause I could see that old North Star. My daddy, when he was sober, used to tell me 'bout that North Star and how to pick it out. He seemed to think that he was quite a navigator, thanks to all his riverboat experiences. He used to talk 'bout when he was a kid and how he used to sleep on the deck of an old paddle wheeler going up the Mississippi. Him and all the other boys liked to lie there looking up at the stars and naming 'em. You would've thought he'd sailed on the high seas the way he knew them stars.

By my reckoning, I figured that we was 'bout twelve miles out when dawn begun to break. Everything sure was beautiful. As far as you could see there was rolling prairie. It was first turning kinda gold, then to silver as the sun come up. I knowed it wouldn't be too long 'fore we'd be real warm. I slowed Piebald down again to that shuffle walk of his, realizing I oughta leave that trail soon. I was sure that any posse looking for me'd come along that trail to the west, since the livery man could've seen what way I'd turned. But I knowed the real reason I couldn't keep going on the Smoky Hill Trail: Sure as hell I'd run into somebody. If I did, they'd be going the other way and a posse'd come up to 'em and ask, Have ya seen a young hombre with a gal? Yeah, they'd say, we just seen 'em down the trail 'bout ten miles from here. That'd be the end of me.

I don't know how I'm gonna do it, I thought, but somewhere along here soon I'm gonna have to get off this trail and head south without leaving no tracks, and I'm gonna have to go 'bout a hundred miles south 'fore I hit the Santa Fe Trail. Then I can go west on it and take the Taos cutoff and meet Pete like we planned.

I hoped that Pete'd be able to figure it out. He knowed I hated McIntyre's guts. He'd hear what happened and see that Piebald and me was gone—and Michelle, too. Pedro weren't dumb.

I noticed that Michelle was acting awful tired. Well, it'd been mighty exciting, and I knowed that she hadn't slept much all night, anyway. I told her we'd stop for a rest in a short ways, as soon as the sun was well up. We come over a hill and there in the distance, crossing the trail, was a sandy creek lined with some cottonwoods.

The creek bed run on down to the south and that was the way I wanted to go when I got there. But I knowed I couldn't just turn right off the trail like some dumb greenhorn, or a posse'd be on our heels in no time a'tall.

Cottonwood trees is always a good camping place for the wagon trains and small freight outfits that pass along. There should be a way a man could turn off there without looking any different'n the rest of those campers. If there was somebody already camping there, I'd have to take my chances on being seen.

In another fifteen minutes we come right to the cottonwoods, and it was just like I'd thought it'd be. There was ruts where wagon trains had turned out when they'd camped. There was the remains of fires all around and a hole where somebody'd tried to dig for water in the sandy creek. There was horse tracks and cattle tracks and everything—just what a fella wants when he needs to turn off the trail and don't want nobody to know he done it.

We started south along them cottonwoods and I seen where campers'd spread all through there. A big train must've stopped there a couple of days before, 'cause there was plenty of fresh tracks stretching on down the creek for 'bout a quarter of a mile. Being the fall, them cottonwoods'd been throwing their leaves on the ground nice and thick. The chances of a horse going through without leaving tracks was real good. 'Sides that, if them cottonwood leaves got to blowing when the prairie wind come up, it'd cover them tracks.

When we got to where folks'd camped, there were quite a few more tracks from some cattle and a few stray horses that'd wandered on down the creek. I stayed along some of them tracks a ways, and then saw a big patch of leaves. I sashayed to the right in them leaves for quite a ways and then I said to Michelle, "We're gonna stop here."

I eased her down to the ground, and then I slid off. "Here, hold onta Piebald an' pet him a little. He ain't gonna act up none, he just come fifteen miles."

I left Michelle with the horse and went back and broke off some cottonwood limbs and used 'em to swish the leaves around. Then I went back up the trail for 'bout a quarter of a mile smoothing over leaves. Then I backed down again and stirred 'em up and let 'em blow with the wind. Sure enough, that's what it took to really cover our tracks. No one could tell that a horse'd been along there after I'd got through. When I come back I got up on Piebald and leaned down to hoist up Michelle.

"Can't we stay here?" she asked. "I'm tired, and I wanta go back to Hays."

I shook my head and pulled her up behind me.

"But I ain't got no clothes," she said. "What's a girl to do riding out here on horseback with nothing but a nightdress?"

"Now listen, honey, yore prettier in your nightdress than all a them rich ladies is in their fancy jewels. We're gonna be all right, so don't give me no trouble now. We're both hard-pressed—an' remember, ya can't go back."

She started to cry and the sound brought a cold, sick hurt to my belly. I patted her soft little leg. "Now listen, honey, there's no use cryin'. Ever'thin's gonna be all right. No need fer ya ta carry on like that."

"I'm real lonesome," she said, sniffling.

"Ya got me an' ya got my slicker, too. Ain't ya warm now?"

"Yeah, I guess. It's better now that the sun's come up, but you're riding in the shade of these scraggly old trees."

"Nah, these cottonwoods ain't got much shade on 'em. The leaves is all off now an' the sun's comin' through. We're ridin' along through 'em as far as we can. I reckon from what I can see they go 'bout five or six miles south a here. Don't ya worry none, we're gonna stop somewhere an' I'm gonna get ya some clothes."

We rode on. It was tough on Michelle—real uncomfortable for a gal who ain't done an awful lot of riding. Along 'bout the time the sun was past high noon she spoke up. "I'm tired and my behind is getting sore."

"Okay, let's stop here by this big ol' tree an' set fer a spell."

We got off and she said she was thirsty. Now she was beginning to be a problem. I tried to put her off. "Maybe down here a ways we'll come 'cross a creek that's got a little water, but there ain't none right now, honey."

"I'm hungry, too," she insisted.

The only thing I had was two old biscuits in my saddlebag. I reached in and pulled 'em out. Hell, they must've been at least four weeks old. I'd stashed 'em 'fore we crossed the Canadian. They was hard and dirty from being in the saddlebag, but that was all we had. I was feeling a little hungry myself, but it weren't too bad for me 'cause I'd sometimes gone two or three days without nothing to eat.

A man can do pretty good going hungry. It's a matter of keeping water in yourself. You gotta have water. I was worried 'bout that, but I didn't wanta tell Michelle. I figured we had to go south 'bout ninety miles to the Arkansas. That'd be the safest direction, and there'd be plenty of water there. I figured that Piebald could just 'bout make it. There might even be a couple of places where we could get water 'fore we reached the Arkansas. One of 'em was Smoky Hill River. I hoped we was gonna cross that 'fore too long, but I'd forgot my distances. I weren't sure whether we had to go all the way from the Smoky Hill to the Pawnee 'fore we'd get water again or whether Walnut Creek, which lay 'tween 'em, would still have any water in it.

I didn't tell Michelle any of that. All I told her was that I thought there'd be a spring over the next hill, but right then she'd better just eat them biscuits. She took one look at 'em and made a face. Then she tried to take a bite. They was so hard she couldn't hardly break 'em with her teeth. I picked up a good sharp rock, used a piece of cottonwood bark for a plate, and laid it down in the sand. Then I took that rock and chipped away at them biscuits 'til they was mostly crumbled.

"Now, little lady," I said, "reach down with them pretty fingers a yore'n an' take some a them crumbs an' put 'em in your mouth."

She did, looking real doubtful. She mouthed them for a minute or two and then spit them out. "That's awful. That's the worst thing I ever tasted. Damn you, what have you got me out here for? What am I doing here? I wish I'd never met you!"

"Well, I wish I could say the same 'bout you an' mean it, but I can't," I replied. "I'm real glad I seen ya. Yore a sight fer sore eyes."

Looking at her sitting there, by God, I begun to feel like making love to her right on the spot. Then I remembered there'd likely be a posse out looking for us and that cooled me right down.

To make it worse, she started to cry again, big gulping sobs, and tears come running down all over her face. My guts turned inside out. "Now hold on, honey, it's gonna turn out all right. I realize I ain't got a good supply a stuff. We left real sudden, an' I couldn't put a wagon train together for ya so's ya could travel 'round these prairies like a real lady."

"Don't try to make it into a joke," she sniffed. "I don't even know your name. Here we are out in this wild prairie, miles and miles from anywhere, and I don't even know your name."

I busted out laughing at that. "Look, honey, ya knowed lots a strange men an' ya never asked 'em their names. The proof a that is that I spent the entire night with ya the night 'fore last an' ya never did ask me my name."

"No, I didn't, but this is different. I'm stuck out here in the middle of nowhere with you and nobody else and I'd like to know your name. You keep calling me 'honey,' but I don't feel that fond of you right now. And my name is Michelle, I'm not your 'honey.' "

"Well," I said, "my name's Brules."

"Brules. That's an interesting name. Where did you get it from?"

"That's my real name—Brules. B-r-u-l-e-s."

"Don't you have no other name?"

She sure could worry a question to death, but, like I said, I liked her. And there was those eyes. Those sky blue, haunting eyes that seemed to say, there's a *real* woman in this body, not some money-grubbin' whore. So I told her, "Yeah, I have a first name, but I don't never use it 'cause it's the same's my ol' man's an' I don't care ta be reminded a him. Some folks calls me 'Cat.' They started it as a joke, callin' me 'Cat's-eye,' an' the Cat part stuck."

I looked at her real hard, and she took a good look at my eyes. Then she busted out laughing and run her fingers through my hair. "I guess you're not a cat," she said, "though you do have wicked eyes. You're pretty much all man—I can vouch for that. By the way, can I call you Cat?"

"Shore ya can, an I'll tell ya somethin' else," I said, "I'm man enough ta handle ya."

I give her a quick little kiss, and then broke the mood. "That really ain't important now. What's important is that we gotta find water. I reckon if we keep goin' down this dry sand creek, we'll hit a runnin' stream 'fore too long."

I pushed that horse pretty hard. When we come up on the Smoky Hill River, I was glad to see it was running—not much, though, only 'bout a foot deep. First thing, we got us a drink—me and Michelle lying flat on our bellies and sucking up wet, muddy water with our lips like it was the best champagne.

When we was through drinking, I stood up and looked for a way to cross. I knowed to watch out for quicksand, so I tried Piebald in two or three places. Once, we just backed out in time. Finally, I saw a place where I figured we could make it and, sure enough, Piebald went across there in good shape, although he didn't like it none.

I didn't like to leave my pony tracks in the sand along the riverbank real plainlike, but I figured if the men in a posse'd unraveled my leaf trick they'd be on my trail anyway. Main thing was to keep going. I wished we'd had something or other to carry water in, but I didn't have nothing.

When we got to a place that looked 'bout right, I decided to stop a while. We got down and I took off Piebald's gear so's to give him a good rest. I didn't have the heart to tell Michelle that we'd be riding all that day and all that night and part of the next day 'fore we got to the Arkansas. So I said, "I reckon it ain't too far 'til we get ta the Arkansas—it's just a little ways ahead, only a few miles."

Michelle had curled up in a sunny spot and was rubbing her bare feet. "What do we do when we get there?" she asked.

"We'll get some more water ta begin with."

"Water? I've gotta have some clothes!"

I had to laugh a little. "Never ya mind that. I'll get ya some clothes. But the one thing we don't need is ta keep comp'ny with some posse outta Hays City."

There weren't s'posed to be no Indians 'round that part of the country, and if there was, they was only strays, so it weren't gonna get tough on account of Indians 'til we got farther west. Lord almighty, if I'd only knowed how tough it was gonna get, I sure would've turned 'round and took my chances with a posse.

I figured it'd been 'bout twenty miles from Hays City to the campground in the cottonwood grove where we'd left the trail. By evening we'd gone 'bout another twenty-five miles. That made at least forty-five miles altogether, and it was getting towards dark. I allowed as to how Piebald'd prob'ly made that distance, even with the two of us on him, 'bout as fast as any ordinary horse could make it with only one man on him.

So, even allowing for the hour we'd took to rest, I figured that a posse'd still have to be quite a ways behind us. If they'd followed our tracks outta town and rode hard, they might've been able to close the gap to 'bout half the distance. I fell to calculating. It'd prob'ly take 'em, with all the excitement going on, the better part of 'tween half and three-quarters of an hour to organize any kinda posse and get saddled up in the dark and get outta Hays City. It'd more'n likely have took 'em a good hour. That'd give us 'bout a twelve-mile lead.

When they reached that turnoff they wouldn't be none too sure which way we'd went. If they happened to get lucky and figure out what I'd done, they sure was gonna have a helluva time plowing through them leaves and deciding which direction I'd took off in. That'd take lots of time, even though there was prob'ly a bunch of 'em and they'd have scattered out some. But then, I thought, they might have some of them half-breed trackers with 'em.

That made me think twice 'cause I might've just outsmarted myself and got too confident 'bout how I'd covered up my tracks. I poked old Piebald again and he broke into a trot. Michelle woke up and started complaining 'bout being jounced around like that, but I told her there weren't no help for it. "We're gonna have ta keep goin' 'til dark," I said. "After it gets dark we'll take it easy again, 'cause the chances of a posse comin' up on us in the dark is slim ta nothin'."

"Oh, no!" she said. "We're certainly gonna camp for the night, ain't we? I thought we was gonna rest and have a nice fire."

"Nope," I said, "we ain't gonna have no fire and we ain't gonna stop fer the night."

She started to cry again, so's I had to try and settle her down. "Now look here, honey, we ain't got nothin' to cook anyways. 'Sides, ain't ya thirsty?"

She sniffled. "I'm just as thirsty as I've ever been in all my life."

"All right, if yore that thirsty, ya'd better stay with me 'cause we've gotta find some water."

She spoke right up at that. "Yes, but you told me we'd find a spring over the next hill or so."

"Well, honey, I don't really know this country, but judgin' by the lay of it, they's a chance we could dig down in this sandy creek an' get some water. But that'd take three or four hours. I ain't gonna do that while there's a chance a posse's chasin' after us. Now, we know there's water at the Arkansas. We know it's a runnin' river. Once we get there, we got us some water."

"Okay," she said. "How much longer 'til we get there?"

"Oh, I reckon it'll be sometime after dark." I didn't tell her that it'd be long after dark, prob'ly the next day.

'Bout sundown we come up on Walnut Creek. There was a little water in it and it didn't look bad for quicksand, so we made it across and got us another drink. I reckoned by then we'd come some fifty miles and we'd have to go another forty-five to get to the Arkansas. Michelle said she was getting awful sore and riding back there was real tough. I took her up in the saddle with me and held her in my lap sideways—kinda on one leg—for a while. Then I let her ride in the saddle while I walked alongside, but that slowed us down too much. I finally got on behind, with her setting in the saddle, but it was still hard on her.

Since it was long past dark, we stopped for a little rest. The cottonwoods was beginning to thin out, so I chose the last good grove I could see.

After a short spell we mounted up and headed out again, still heading due south over the open range. There was rolling prairie covered with buffalo grass and no cottonwoods ahead, but I figured nobody'd see us in the dark.

The sky was just hinting at dawn when we come up on the banks of the Pawnee Fork. I could make out the cottonwoods in the dark against the stars. Since there was a good chance of somebody camping there, I eased down into the trees holding Piebald back. He was anxious to get down to the water, but I was worried 'bout quicksand and decided to wait until daybreak—'bout another hour, I judged.

The sun'd come up when I decided it was time to move on. I saddled up Piebald, put the bedroll back on the saddle, and then woke up Michelle. She was plenty tired, but I told her we had to keep moving. That was no kidding. I eased her back up into the saddle, then I led Piebald up to the edge of the Pawnee to see how chancy it was. I took it real easy, just walking ahead, taking it slow. I figured if I put my foot into someplace that I couldn't get out of, I could hang on to the reins and Piebald'd back me outta there. At least I'd have something to hang on to and drag myself out.

I found a place where we could get right up to the river's edge and give Piebald a good drink. The river had more water in it than I'd figured it would—a lot more'n the Smoky River or Walnut Creek—and I knowed we was gonna have some trouble. I dipped some water up in my hat and give it to Michelle 'cause she was too tired to get down. After we'd all took a good drink, I climbed up behind Michelle and nosed Piebald out into the current. It weren't quite deep enough to come up to his belly, so we made it across there all right, though there was a couple of times when my heart begun to pound a little bit when it felt like he was going into some shifting sand.

Piebald seemed to know that we had to cross, and he was bent on doing it. I'd picked out a place on the other side where the shore had a little rock and stone and thought it would hold pretty good. That's the way it was, so we made it 'cross the Pawnee just fine.

Then we had to hit out over the open prairies again towards the Santa Fe Trail and the Arkansas River that run along it. We rode all day, and that big, wide prairie kept getting bigger. We kept cool enough, thanks to lots of high, fast-moving clouds and a steady wind from the north. Michelle seemed set not to complain, so we rode in a peaceful silence. Shortly after sunset we come to another dry creek with scattered clumps of cottonwoods.

It begun to get cool. Then all of a sudden we heard an owl let out a low hoot. It liked to of scared Michelle to death.

"Cat! Listen!" she whispered. "That's Indians. They're hiding in them trees!"

"Naw, honey," I laughed, "that ain't no Injun. That's just one a them hoot owls."

"It sounds awful, like some ghost or something."

"Yeah, but that's all right. It won't hurt us none. It's prob'ly lookin' fer a prairie mouse fer supper."

"It still scares me, Cat. I never heard nothing make a noise like that before."

"Why," I said, "I thought everybody'd heard a hoot owl before. Ya must've spent mosta your time indoors."

"Of course I have. You know, I was born in the city."

"You was?"

"Yeah, I was born in St. Louis."

"My daddy used ta brag on his trips ta St. Louis," I recalled. "He rode the rafts down the Ohio and stopped in there ta have a good time."

She giggled. "Lots of them fellows used to come to St. Louis. I worked in a dance hall there for about six months. The river men was a bad lot and I didn't like 'em too much. You men out here in the West are a lot nicer."

"Well," I said, "I'm mighty glad ya feel that way. Right now yore gettin' a personal sight-seein' tour a the West—all free—courtesy a Cowboy Brules."

She sniffed. "Very funny. But I don't like it much. Besides, it's getting cold again."

I had her untie the slicker and put it on. Pretty soon she begun to get sleepy and just hung on 'round my waist. Piebald picked his way along and it got real dark. The clouds'd all blowed away and a few stars come out. We just kept plodding along that dry creek bed.

The stars shone down real bright and danced all around. I could see almost as good as if it was daylight. The prairie wind died off and the air carried a smell of sage and buffalo grass and, once in a while, a little whiff of the sun-warmed sand of the creek bed.

We kept on going for the rest of that night, all the next day, and all the next night, the three of us half-senseless for lack of water but dead set on pushing forward.

It was just a little bit 'fore dawn when we come up on the Santa Fe Trail. It was wide—maybe a hundred fifty to two hundred yards wide—and full of tracks: old ox wagon tracks and mule-team tracks and all kinds of horse tracks, tracks from pack-train outfits and handcarts and everything else you can imagine. It was like crossing a city street. You could hardly miss that trail, 'cept that there weren't nobody on it. We slipped across and when the sun come up we wasn't too far from the Arkansas River.

It must've been 'bout nine o'clock in the morning when we dropped down off'n the bluffs and into the cottonwoods along the river, and it was a pretty steep slope going down. Piebald was one damn tired horse. He shuffled along with that gait a tired horse gets when he's going down a hill—he'd let go with each foot 'fore he'd put another one down, like he was real reluctant to pick one foot up and put the weight on the other.

We worked our way down through the cottonwoods, and there

seemed to be quite a bit of grass. Near the river, I seen a place where we could set up camp outta sight. The first thing we done, of course, was to go right to the water and take us a long drink. I betcha that stallion outdone us all. He drank and drank 'til he was plumb full. Then he drank some more. We done the same thing. Michelle said her tongue was so swole up that she didn't know if she could drink a'tall, but she did, not even waiting for me to fill my hat for her.

The Arkansas was pretty muddy, but none of us paid no attention to that. Next I took my lariat and picketed Piebald so he could get a little feed. Then I fixed up a place where we could stay hid in the cottonwoods. At last it was time for some sleep.

I woke up first. The sun was right overhead. I had a bellyache and my skull felt too tight for my brains. I regretted being so free with that Arkansas River water, and for 'bout two hours I was awful sick. But it didn't seem to bother Michelle near as much.

Lying there awake them two hours in the heat of the sun, I started realizing what a mess we was in. I was gonna have to do something 'bout Michelle. Maybe leave her off at Dodge City so's she could go to work right away in one of them saloons or dance halls. 'Course it were possible that them people who'd seen her working in Hays City'd come to Dodge. Then it wouldn't be long 'fore the story leaked out as to how I'd escaped and which direction I'd took. Besides, how was I gonna get her to Dodge City 'cept in the dark? It must be a good fifty miles to the west, and of the whole outfit—me, Michelle, and Piebald—not one of us was in any shape to make it. So the first problem was to get food and then some clothes for Michelle.

I took stock of what I had: my horse, my saddle, my slicker, and my bedroll. I had some chewing tobacco, a knife, and my .38 Smith & Wesson with five shells in the cylinder and sixteen more in my belt. I had a couple of items I always carried in my pocket—a fire steel and a little whetstone for sharpening my knife, a big old red handkerchief that I used for lots of things, and a piece of string.

On my saddle I had my rawhide rope. There was some rawhide strings on the saddle, too. I used those to tie down my bedroll and my scabbard, only I didn't have it or my rifle with me. They was both back at Mrs. Tatterback's boardinghouse—along with the rest of my gear—and I weren't 'bout to go back to get 'em.

Most important, I had to figure out where we was going and what we was gonna do. I knowed I had to go west. I figured I was an outlaw in these parts, so I had to go on to Taos. Somehow, deep down inside of me, I kept feeling sure that Pedro Gonzales'd figure things out and meet me there.

I was trying to decide why in the hell I'd ever dragged Michelle outta the Longhorn and brought her out here. I realized why right quick—Michelle weren't no hand at keeping her mouth shut. Sure as hell she would've told 'bout me killing McIntyre. It was better that I had her along so's she wouldn't be talking to folks. 'Course there was still the livery man. He might be able to finger me somehow. That'd be all it'd take to get the town stirred up and a posse out after me. So having Michelle along for that reason didn't seem to count for much. The big reason, I finally decided, was that I was eighteen years old and full of beans. There weren't many women out on the frontier in them days as fine as Michelle, so a girl like her looked mighty good to a young buck like me. Maybe it was instinct more'n anything else that caused me to grab onto her when it was time to go—the instinct of a man wanting to keep his woman by his side. 'Course she'd made it clear she didn't think she was my woman. I aimed to change that notion.

4

I Weren't That Smart

We was camped on the Arkansas, and south of the Arkansas was Indian territory. Stories 'bout Indian fights and such got around real quick. We all knowed about the Fetterman Massacre up at Fort Phil Kearny, how Fetterman'd crossed Lodgepole Ridge, and how the Sioux'd massacred some eighty men along with him that previous December—almost a year before. They was told from one meeting place to another, 'round cowboys' camp-fires, in saloons and shops, everyplace people gathered. The news always traveled fast, so we all knowed 'bout it.

In the same way, we also knowed all 'bout what was going on south of the Arkansas. Even while we was riding, there was a helluva powwow going on at Medicine Lodge Creek fifty miles southwest of Wichita. Army officers and Indian commissioners was meeting with the whole confederacy of the Cheyenne, Kiowa, Comanche, Apache, and Arapaho tribes. Most of the big chiefs was there—Iron Mountain, Satanta, Kicking Eagle, and Ten Bears—all 'cept Quanah Parker and the Quohadi Comanches. The white men was promising to leave the land south of the Arkansas alone—to just let them Indians run wild and hunt buffalo if they'd come into the reservation and make peace.

Lately there'd been some stories going 'round 'bout how Chief Quanah Parker was raising hell among the Comanches and stirring 'em up to keep on fighting. Him and his tribe, the Quohadi Comanches, weren't 'bout to go into Medicine Lodge and sign no treaty. They said the hell with it and stayed out to roam the plains and to fight. Folks said it wouldn't be too long 'fore we was gonna have trouble.

Some of the trouble was on account of Dodge City. It was located north of the Arkansas in good buffalo country. For a number of years them buffalo'd been coming across the Arkansas every summer and the hide hunters'd had a field day. But the railroad-building at Hays City and other places'd slowed up on account of the railroads was running outta money. When the railroads couldn't pay the track-laying hands, the hands'd go out and hunt buffalo, 'cause that was another way to make a living. Some of 'em hired out as skinners for the buffalo hunters or wagon drivers or freighters on the Dodge City–Fort Larned Trail. They knowed they could work in the buffalo-skin trade and wait 'til the railroads got more money and then they could go back to their regular jobs.

It worked for a while, but then them buffalo quit coming across the Arkansas. By 1867 there weren't no buffalo hunting north of the Arkansas to amount to spit, and nobody could make a living on hides. Those aiming to hunt buffalo had to cross south of the Arkansas into Indian territory—and them Indians didn't like that one bit. They was raising plenty of hell.

Lots of them hunters got ambushed and killed. If Indians took a hunter alive, he faced a real tough go. It took lots of guts to go into Indian territory, and there wasn't too damned many men that'd do it. There was still some outfitters in Dodge City who'd get a bunch together now and then and swing down by the Canadian River, even clear down to Palo Duro Canyon, and right back through the heart of Comanche country. They'd come in with a load of hides, but it took lots of nerve, and most of them hombres, if you got 'em aside and knowed how to talk with 'em, would tell you that they was scared shitless the whole time.

I also knowed there was lots of traffic on the trail between Fort Larned and Dodge City. There was freighter wagons headed east with buffalo hides and going west with supplies—all kinds of stuff from the East that could be sold in the West. Rifles, yard goods, gunpowder, flour, coffee, horseshoes, nails, ammunition—all them things that we didn't have out on the frontier—come from the East.

The easiest way for me and Michelle to get some clothes and something to eat was to tie into some of that traffic.

First of all I thought I'd ride up there on the trail and find one of them freight wagon trains and see if I could barter with 'em. Maybe I could buy some food and stuff.

Then I got to wondering 'bout that. I'd have to find Michelle a hideout somewheres first. Even if I found one of those freighter outfits, would them men stop a whole wagon train to sell me something? They'd prob'ly wanta know what I was doing along the trail all alone and I'd have to dream up some cock-and-bull story. Then they'd say, Well, young fella, come on and join up with us. When we get ta camp tonight, we'll see if we can sell ya what ya need.

If I was to go along with 'em, I'd have to leave Michelle behind. What would she do in the meantime? Was I gonna ride back at night and pick her up someplace? Hell, that wouldn't do a'tall.

Now maybe I could tell 'em a big ol' story 'bout how we was man and wife and how our place'd been burned down by the Indians and they got away with our lot. Nope, that wouldn't work neither. Michelle didn't have no wedding ring. 'Sides, there was liable to be some wives along with them freighter trains. Quite a few settlers went out that way, and their wives went with 'em. They was hard-boiled puritans, and they'd see right away that Michelle was a dance hall girl.

No, I couldn't join up with no wagon train—either me alone or with Michelle. We couldn't go on into Dodge City. We couldn't go back to Fort Larned. We had to go to Taos. That was a long ride, and we was gonna need, among other things, another horse for Michelle. Then we'd need another one for packing, 'cause we was gonna have to carry some grub with us. Most important, if we was to try and live off'n the country, I sure was looking at a hard time doing it with just a revolver. I needed a rifle.

Come sundown, my mind begun to see clear. I started working out a plan. I piled together a few leaves and got a spark off my fire steel to get a fire going and added some driftwood sticks and stuff. Then I woke up Michelle. Right away she run off outta sight to heave up her guts. She come back looking real pale and sick. I told her there was only a few minutes of daylight left. That was good hunting time, so I told her to keep the fire going while I tried to get us something to eat to settle our innards after drinking so much muddy water.

"You ain't gonna leave me here all alone, are you?" she asked.

"Nope, I'm only goin' a couple hundred yards up the creek ta see if'n I can get a shot at a rabbit or prairie chicken or somethin'. Don't you fear none, honey. That fire can't be seen down here below the bluffs. They ain't likely to be nobody this far off the trail 'round here, an' the Injuns is all south a the river."

"Indians! Here?"

"Naw, I didn't mean ta say that. There ain't no use in your worryin' none. Now you tend that fire an' keep it goin' 'til I get back."

I went over to Piebald and moved his tether so's he could get more feed. I felt all over him and looked at his hooves. His shoes was holding pretty good. I dug out a little mud and some small pebbles jammed in his right forefoot: That's what'd made him a little footsore. He seemed to be coming along all right, but he was pretty ga'nt. He was a tired pony, but at least that muddy water didn't seem to be bothering him none.

"Ol'-timer," I told him, "get yerself a bellyful an' from now on we'll go real easy."

I walked on down the Arkansas for 'bout a quarter of a mile while the fiery sunset was lighting up the country, making it look real beautiful. That's the time when you see game. A rabbit run out from a willow bush, but it was 'bout fifty yards away and there weren't no way I was gonna get it with my revolver. I didn't see no sage hens, just some magpies and roadrunners. There weren't nothing we could eat. I turned 'round at dark and headed back towards the fire.

All of a sudden a hoot owl let go right over my head and my hat pretty near fell off when I jumped. I looked up and seen him sitting there on the limb of a cottonwood just looking down at me real straight, 'cause they can see real good in the dark. I didn't want him to see no more movement, so I took that Smith & Wesson out ever so slow. By looking real hard, I could see the barrel. I slowly drawed down on that owl and shot him off that limb cleaner'n hell. He come fluttering down and piled up in the bushes. Well, hell, I figured, at least we got us *something* to eat.

I made it back to camp in a hurry, and Michelle sang out, "Oh, I was so frightened. You've been away so long. What did you kill? Did you get us a deer?"

"Nope."

"But I heard a shot."

"Nope, I didn't kill no deer. I just killed this ol' hoot owl. Ya don't have ta eat none if ya don't wanta, but I am. I'm hungry."

I plucked all the feathers off'n that bird, took out my knife, slit him open, and snapped out his guts. Then I opened him up and stuck him over the fire on some sticks and started roasting. I didn't have no pot to boil him in and couldn't do nothing but hold him over the fire and let him sizzle.

There's only one thing to say about owl meat—it ain't no good. It just plain tasted like owl, but at least it was something. About an hour after we'd ate, we felt a little better. Later, the stars come out and the night wind began to blow real soft through the cottonwoods. We could hear the sound of the river just off'n the bank south of us.

"Ya gotta get some sleep now, honey," I told Michelle. "Sometime 'fore daylight we're gonna pull outta here."

"Pull out tonight? Where're we going?"

"I can't tell ya that, but first we're gonna get ya some clothes."

"Oh, that'll be good! That'll be so good," she said and throwed her arms around my neck.

"Yeah, I know. Lots a things is gonna be real, real good."

I reached around her waist and let my hand slide down to feel that cute little ass of hers. Slow down, Brules, I thought, better wait 'til ya get outta this jam yore in, then maybe ya can pay a little attention to this gal. Maybe she's in need of a little lovin'. Ya know you is, but now ain't the time.

"Lie down on that saddle blanket an' pull the slicker over ya," I said to her. "Ya can use the bedroll there fer a pillow and try ta get some sleep. I'm gonna be sittin' here. I'll wake ya up after midnight 'cause that's when we're leavin'."

"All right," she said. Then she give me a kiss as if she really liked me.

I kissed her back. "Now you lay down there an' go ta sleep," I said.

I thought it might be a good idea to put the fire out, so I did and stayed awake to keep watch. After a while I got to thinking 'bout Indians. I recollected things my daddy had told me and I remembered talking to two or three mountain men who'd come back through Kentucky when I was a little kid. They all said that Indians never did attack at night. They always come in on you at dawn. Well, we wasn't gonna be there come dawn, so there weren't no use to sweat that out.

When I reckoned by the Big Dipper that it was 'round midnight, I went over and come up real easy on Piebald and got his tether rope. I could tell by the way he was putting his feet down and how he held his head that he weren't feeling too sassy.

I sure hated to have to wake up Michelle, but I had to get the saddle blanket and bedroll. I eased her over and she murmured, but she kept on sleeping.

Once I got Piebald saddled and bridled, I talked to him and he stomped 'round a little more, but he took the bit all right. Then I went over to Michelle and shook her by the shoulder. "Okay now honey, get up, 'cause we gotta get goin'."

She protested. "I can't walk around here in the dark with my bare feet. I'll step on twigs. When are you gonna take me somewhere to get some—"

"Shush now," I said. "I promise ta take ya where ya'll be happy. Now, slide 'round back a me—that's the stuff—that's it. Hang on tight. Ol' Piebald's gonna settle down."

We come out on the prairie up above where the wind was blowing outta the northwest real gentlelike, ruffling the grass. There was stars all around and the air was fresh and cool. Michelle wrapped herself up in that old leather slicker and put her arms back 'round me. I could feel her up against my back, shivering some. I headed Piebald north and he eased along real smooth.

Then Michelle got to talking. "Is this horse always nervous this way? Was that why you made a great big bucking dash outta the corral there by the livery stable before you came back to get me?"

"Damned right. I weren't 'bout ta put ya on where ya could get hurt."

"Hmm," she said. "You know what I thought? I thought you was a show-off, proving how your horse could buck whenever you wanted him to. For a minute there I thought you was gonna run off and leave me."

"Maybe ya wished I had."

"No, I don't—not a lot anyway. I like being with you, but I'm awful cold, and that owl—ugh! Now, where're we going?"

"Up north a little ways so's I can get ya somethin' warm ta wear."

"How're you gonna do that?"

I give her a friendly pat on the leg. "Maybe I'll negotiate with some a the wagon trains that's goin' by."

She reached 'round and kissed me on the ear. That set me to tingling all over, and I got to thinking that maybe I weren't as tired as I'd felt a minute ago. Even Piebald perked up some.

'Bout another half hour traveling north and sure enough there was the trail—easy to spot even in the dark—wide and full of ruts. I figured to turn west 'til it got lighter so's I could find a good place to stop.

The sun come up behind us and the prairie looked pretty good. I kept glancing 'round to see if there was any dust and to see what was behind us. I didn't see nothing for miles and miles and miles, just that old trail stretching on out to the horizon, nothing but the nice soft wind blowing and the sun growing warm on our backs.

After a while I seen what I was looking for up ahead of us. There was a ridge that rose up by the trail, high enough to give a good view. Right below that ridge was a gentle draw full of cottonwoods that run south on down to the Arkansas. It looked just right. There was fine cover for hiding Michelle, and from the top of the ridge I figured I'd be able to see up and down the trail. I'd done plenty of thinking about all this. There weren't no gol'durned way I was gonna try and hold up a whole wagon train; hell, every one of the freighters had at least one rifle, and sometimes somebody else was riding guard. I had to find me a singleton, somebody that was traveling by hisself.

I rode Piebald up to the top of the ridge and looked west off into the distance. Far away there come a big old freighter train with wagons upon wagons like you'd never seen.

I pointed it out to Michelle. "Here comes somebody. Gotta figger out who it is. The first thing is ta get ya outta sight." I turned back east down off the ridge and into the cottonwoods. I found a nice place for Michelle, but she weren't real happy about it.

"So, whatcha gonna do? Why don't you keep me up there with you where I can see what's going on?"

"Listen, it ain't fittin' an' proper fer a young lady in a nightdress ta meet a whole wagon train—ya oughta know that. Ya better let me negotiate in my own way."

She wouldn't let me have the last word though, not Michelle. She flung herself down from the saddle. "Well, all right," she said. "You go ahead and do it, but I'm mighty tired of riding around these prairies half-naked and with no shoes and no nothing and hungry, too. That's right. I'm hungry, Mr. Cat Brules! Real hungry. You'd better find something quick."

I eased down off Piebald, then took the bedroll and spread it on the ground and told her to shut up and lie down on it. I put that slicker over her and suggested she go back to sleep.

"I can sure sleep all right," she said. "You're not going far away, are you?" She seemed to be cooling off.

" 'Course not. It ain't but four hundred yards up ta the top a the ridge—an' that's where I'm gonna be. Now ya take it easy and don't worry none 'bout nothin'."

She got up and took my hand. "Okay. But if you're going away, please give me another kiss."

I leaned down and give her a kiss. She flung her arms 'round my neck and pulled me close. Her bosom felt soft and warm against me. Boy, that pretty near fired me up. No, I thought, I'd better leave that alone. I got some serious business to attend to.

So I said to her, "Now Michelle, please stay here outta sight. They're gonna pass right by ya here 'bout a hundred yards off, but I want ya ta stay put. Don't wave at 'em or nothin', an' don't make no noise."

"What if they stop?" she asked. "I always like to say hello to people."

"This is one time ya can't do it. Ya gotta hide in these cottonwoods and yore just gonna have ta stay hid 'cause we'll be in real trouble if'n ya don't."

"How come?"

Damn if she weren't the one for asking questions! "Just stay outta sight or I'll spank your little bare ass!"

She grinned. "Oh, wouldn't you just love to do that!"

I couldn't lie and say no, so I smiled back at her and started off on Piebald. I rode up to the top of the ridge again and started watching. By this time the big freighter train coming from the west was a lot closer—only about two miles off. They was making slow progress. If I was lucky, one of the freighters'd be tagging along behind and maybe me and him could work some business. If I could outdraw McIntyre, maybe I could surprise a lone, tired teamster.

I figured to be riding west when the train passed, and if anybody asked, I'd tell 'em I was headed for Dodge City. I'd let on that I was going out there to look for some work in one of the buffalo camps. The only thing wrong was I wouldn't have no bedroll on my saddle, so they might think that I'd had to leave somewheres in a hurry. Ta hell with it! I thought. I'll have ta figger that out when the time comes.

Real soon, I could hear bullwhips cracking and mule skinners cussing their mules and yelling at the oxen. The outriders was yelling and hollering lots of things, too.

I was careful to stay below the horizon of that ridge, with only my head sticking up so's I could see. When they was 'bout a half-mile away I turned Piebald 'round and galloped east on the trail. When we'd gone half a mile, I turned again and started back west—like I'd been traveling all day outta Fort Larned. I'd planned it just about right, 'cause the first wagon team topped the rise after I'd turned 'round.

I rode along real casual-like. The first wagon was all covered, so I reckoned it was loaded with hides. That's 'bout all I could think of that'd be coming from Dodge City. I rode up and said, "Howdy," and seen the wagon boss riding alongside the lead wagon. I waved to him and tipped my hat.

"Howdy stranger," he said. "How are ya this mornin'?"

"Fine, sir. How're you? Ya comin' from Dodge City?"

"Yeah, we got a load of hides here and we're bound for Baxter Springs."

"That shore looks like a good outfit," I said with a smile.

He eyed me and let the wagons go on, but pulled up beside me. "Ya lookin' for work, son?"

"That's right. I reckon I'm goin' ta Dodge City an' see if'n I can get on there."

"Be careful," he said. "Most of the buffalo outfitters've gone south of the Arkansas, the damned fools. What kind of experience have ya had?"

"I ain't done so gol'durned bad on cattle drivin', an' I been up the Chisholm Trail a few times." I let on that I was all man 'cause I didn't like the idea of him thinking I was only a kid.

What he said next was something real unexpected. "I could give ya a job here. Know anything about drivin' a mule team?"

"Yessir," I said, "I've drove teams lots a times, but I'm mostly a cowhand."

"I'm short a man. It's a good job and it pays good wages—twenty dollars a month and keep."

"That sounds pretty good, but I'm headed west. I sorta got the yearnin' ta go that way."

Then I thought, I wonder if this ol' boy might sell me somethin'. He sure as hell ain't got no women's clothes. But maybe I could dicker with him fer a horse or a mule. I turned to him. "Mister, ya got any horses fer sale?"

"Hell no, man. With these wagons we need every one we got."

"Ya got a spare mule?"

"What do you want a mule for?"

"I just always had a hankerin' ta own one."

He laughed. "Well, there ain't no extra mules in this outfit. We need every head of stock we got. It don't make no difference what it is. When we was out in Dodge City, some of them hunters was beggin' to buy horses and mules off us 'cause some of 'em got their horses run off by the Injuns while they was out after hides. Horses are scarce, too. You'll have trouble findin' one."

"Thanks," I said, "but I always had me a hankerin' fer a mule—not a horse. I got me a good horse."

He looked at Piebald for a minute. "You may have yourself a good horse, but that horse is ga'nt."

"He's come a long way in the last few days," I said. Then I added real quick, "Well, mister, I'm much obliged. I shore thank ya fer the offer of a job, but I ain't lookin' ta head east just now. I'm set on Dodge City, so I'll be on my way. Thanks anyway."

He waved as I rode off. All them western fellas was like that. They tried to size you up right away, but when they got through they give you the benefit of the doubt. If you looked like you was gonna be all right, they'd leave you alone.

I rode right down the length of that wagon train, staying out on the flanks maybe fifty to a hundred yards to keep outta the dust as much as I could. After the train'd passed and they was over the hill, I drawed Piebald up short and figured that there was no need for me to go any farther. That train was run real businesslike, and I didn't see no stragglers, but I did get a few strips of jerky and some biscuits from another wagon driver.

When they was outta sight over the ridge, I rode back to where Michelle was and told her what I'd done. I handed her a couple biscuits and a strip of jerky. "Here's somethin' fer starters. But we can't risk nobody seein' ya. Climb on up here. I'm gonna take ya farther down this draw towards the river. Then if another wagon train comes up an' wants ta camp here, we'll be safe." I helped her get up in the saddle and started walking, leading Piebald.

When we reached another stand of timber 'bout half a mile down a sandy draw, I helped her down. "Here, ya can keep my slicker an' make up a nice, soft bed a leaves. Now, stay put, 'cause I'm goin' back an' give it another try."

I turned 'round and rode back up the draw, coming out on the trail just below the ridge. I rode up and took a look to the west. There was nothing coming from that way, but pretty soon off in the distance to the east I seen some more dust. I figured it'd be real late that afternoon 'fore that outfit got there and they'd most likely camp in them cottonwoods. I also figured I could tell 'em a good story.

It seemed like they took forever coming across there, making a long stream of dust that drifted away to the southeast towards the Arkansas. I started thinking of everything we needed and divided it into two halves. One half was stuff I could buy with the money I figured to get off'n the big wagon trains. We needed supplies, and I could buy 'em if I could get those folks to sell. We needed something to boil water in and I reckoned I could buy that, too.

Then I thought, I don't know how I'm gonna get any clothes without arousin' somebody's s'picions, an' I know those folks ain't gonna sell me no horse. I prob'ly ain't got enough money ta buy one if'n they would. I could shore use a rifle, too, but none a these men is gonna part with one. The horse an' rifle an' clothes come under the headin' of what I'm gonna have ta take with my Smith & Wesson.

By the time the wagons got to 'bout half a mile away, I could see there was ten or twelve in the train. Seven or eight of 'em were hitched to oxen, and there was 'bout four wagons drawed by mules.

I figured that them ox teams was a freighter train going from Fort Larned to Dodge City with some supplies. The four wagons drawed by mules appeared to be settlers working their way west—there was a couple of saddle horses tied behind each mule wagon. The settlers'd prob'ly joined up with this freighter train on account of the freighters knowed the way. Also, it was handy to be in a big train in case some trouble developed.

I figured to myself I had to time it just right. I had to watch myself, but I sure wanted to mingle with those folks while they was setting up camp. I figured I could do some business and negotiate for a little bit of flour or bacon and beans and some coffee.

I knowed I had to get my story straight. I couldn't say I'd come from Fort Larned 'cause I weren't headed in that direction. I couldn't be outta Dodge City, 'cause I didn't know enough to talk to them freighters 'bout it. And I sure as hell couldn't tell them folks that I'd come from up north on the Smoky Hill Trail, 'cause then they might connect me with Hays City.

I was in a real fix. If I couldn't come from the west and I couldn't come from the east and I didn't dare talk about coming from the north, there was only one direction left, and that was from the south. That was Indian territory, and that would've been even more unlikely.

When they was 'bout three hundred yards away from me, the lead wagon pulled off the trail to the south. Right away quick I knowed everything was gonna work out all right. I dropped down to the west below the ridge where there weren't no chance of being noticed. Then I turned south and went down 'bout three-quarters of a mile, to where I'd gauged I'd be a little bit below where I'd left Michelle. I come up over the ridge real gentle and slow, making sure the cottonwoods she was in shielded me from the wagon train. Then I dropped down into the sandy creek among the trees.

Sure enough, I come out right by Michelle. She was lying there half-asleep, and when I come up she let out a squeal. "Oh, gracious, you came from the wrong direction. I thought you went up to the trail."

"That's right, but I rode on 'round ta get back here, honey. Ever'thin's gonna be all right. They's a whole wagon train out'n them cottonwoods an' they're gonna stay there tonight. That's my chance."

"Great!" she said. "We'll go right in and see 'em."

"Nope, *we* ain't goin' nowheres. Y'gotta stay put an' let me handle it."

"I want to see somebody and pick out my new clothes." She stopped and took a good look at my face. "You aren't going away and leave me alone again are you?"

"Y'know I gotta, honey. It won't be long 'fore we're all set ta travel again—in style."

"What if it gets dark? You can't leave me here in the dark all by myself. The least you could do is make a fire for me."

She'd hit on something there. "That ain't a bad idea," I told her. "But

BRULES

I can't make no fire here. We'll go down the dry creek bed a little bit. I
think they's a good place there."

Farther down, the stream'd cut through in a narrow place. The
banks rose higher'n a man or a horse, and we had a lot of cottonwoods 'tween us and the train. I helped Michelle down and tied up
Piebald. It weren't long 'fore I had a pretty fair fire going.

"Now, we've got us 'bout two hours 'fore dark," I told Michelle. "Ya
keep gatherin' wood an' pile up a lotta it 'round here. That'll keep ya
busy an' we'll enjoy the fire together when I get back."

She didn't move. "I can't walk around here in my bare feet with all
these twigs and things."

"Shut up an' give me a chance. Ever'thin'll turn out okay."

"All right, I'll stay here and try to gather some wood, but please,
come back before dark, won't you? I get awfully frightened all alone."

I promised to hurry and I swung up on Piebald. When I got a little
ways off I heard Michelle call out, "Hey!" I pulled up, turned 'round,
and looked back at her.

"You're coming back here, ain't you?"

I laughed a bit. "Yeah, honey, I'm comin' back here fer shore. I'm
comin' back here an' make love ta ya by the fire."

She give me her sweetest smile. I swung Piebald 'round again and
worked my way out to 'bout half a mile south of the wagon train.
They'd be mighty interested in a stranger that was riding up from the
south—out of Indian country.

Just in case there was any trouble, I took a look at my Smith &
Wesson. All the chambers was loaded, so I checked to see if my knife
was loose and give the rest of me a quick going over to see if there was
anything to cause folks to ask strange questions. Everything looked
all right.

By God, Brules, I thought, the way yore inspectin' yerself, you'd
think ya was goin' ta take on the whole army. Hell, yore just comin' up
on a friendly wagon train.

A little closer, I started to hear camp noises. Some children was
hollering and playing and oxen was lowing. There was clinking and
jangling from unhitching harnesses, pots banged and clattered, and
men and women was calling back and forth. It sounded like a little
village up there in the cottonwoods.

I couldn't help but think, well, y'bunch a dunderheads, if'n there
was an Injun party comin' along, they'd be right on ya. Y'ain't got no

lookouts or nothin'. But then, Indians didn't go north a the Arkansas at that time, at least not very often. I got to thinkin' a little bit more 'bout them Indians an' the meetin' with General Harney an' the chiefs a the Kiowas an' Comanches an' Cheyennes an' Arapaho at Medicine Lodge. I figgered that could be part a my story.

I got to within three hundred yards of that campsite 'fore anybody seen me. A woman was standing at the back of a wagon, filling a bucket from a water barrel. She happened to look up and see me and she dropped her bucket right there. She run 'round to the front end, where I guess her husband was unhitching the mules. He come back, followed by a few kids and some folks from nearby wagons, and a bunch of 'em formed a raggedy line there.

All through the camp, the talking and the buzzing stopped and they stood 'round, silent, like they was all afraid to ask who this stranger was, appearing out here to hell and gone in God's country. There weren't s'posed to be nobody 'round, and I got within three hundred yards of the wagon train 'fore any of 'em seen me. I knowed I had to act natural, so I just come ambling up with Piebald looking plenty tired.

A big old boy stepped forward. He had a red beard and was wearing a set of miner's boots and an old hat, and his suspenders was bright red. Must've been the trail boss of the freighter bunch—rough-looking lot, them teamsters. I needed to be careful. I had two kinds of people to deal with here, freighters and settlers. What I said for one might not fit for the other.

The freighter boss who'd stepped forward spoke first. "Howdy, stranger."

"Howdy," I replied.

"You come a long ways?"

"Yessir."

"Ain't hard to tell, looks of your horse. What the hell you doin' out here alone, comin' up from the south like that?"

"Well," I said, "ta be right honest with ya, I had a little run a bad luck an' I need some help."

"Sorry to hear that. Just come on up. What can we do for you?"

I rode up and dismounted, and I seen him looking me over pretty good. He put out his hand. "My name is Johnson. I'm the boss of the freighters and this here is Sullivan. He's headin' up these settlers. They're goin' on through to Pueblo."

We traded greetings and Johnson invited me over to share some grub. I thanked him and asked, "First, could ya spare a little drink a water fer my horse?"

"We don't have too much water—we gotta ration it out, but we'll sure share some with a thirsty horse. There ain't no question about that."

Then he yelled out, "Ahab, come over here." A boy come running up and Johnson said, "You got any more water left, boy? You been waterin' the mules real scarce, ain't ya? This here stranger's horse needs some water. Now don't give him no more than ya do the mules. Just give him a little."

I knowed Piebald hadn't had a drink since midnight the night before, when we'd left the Arkansas. Now it was getting on towards sundown and he sure must've been one thirsty horse. The boy run back with some water in a bucket. I tied Piebald to a tree and pulled off his bridle and saddle to ease him. The boy set down the water and that old horse's head went right into that bucket. He was sucking and pulling for all he was worth, and he drained it in a couple of seconds.

Then old Sullivan, who'd been looking at me right friendly, spoke up. "I'll bet you're thirsty, too!"

"I'm so thirsty I can't hardly speak, mister."

He went over to a wagon and picked up a dipper. He stepped over to the tap of a barrel and filled it with water. It was brownish-looking and warm as hell but, by God, it sure was good. Poor Michelle, I thought, she's worse off'n I am. How'm I gonna get some water ta her?

I drained the dipper in one long pull. "You'd better have a little bit more," he said.

"Well, I don't wanta short ya none," I replied.

"Naw, it's not gonna short us. The freighter boss says we're gonna make it to Dodge City in two days and I got plenty for that. He says there's a water hole about fifteen miles from here."

I drunk down a second dipper full and stowed away the information 'bout the water hole. Sullivan kept talking. "You new in these parts, stranger?"

"I been 'round here a little," I told him.

He looked at me kind of quizzical again. "If ya'd rather not mix with them freighters, ya can join us for a bite to eat."

I decided it was a good time to get down to business. "I'm in no hurry 'bout food, but I shore could use some help."

"What kind of help d'ya need?"

"I need ta buy some supplies. I lost my packhorse an' ever'thin' with it."

"What happened? Did it run off?"

More questions, I thought. Being sociable was damn hard work. "Nosir. I done lost him crossin' the Arkansas."

"The Arkansas? That's in Injun territory."

"Yessir, I know that. It was quicksand. I lost ever'thin'."

I could see he believed me. He was hanging on every word. "That's a pity," he said. "We'd better talk to the freighter boss about this. Maybe ya oughta come with us to Dodge City."

"Nosir," I said, "I can't do that. But I got a little bit a money an' I shore would like ta buy some supplies off'n you folks."

"Hey, Johnson," he called out, "come here a minute. I want ya to listen to this boy's story."

"Mister," I told him real quietlike, "I ain't no boy."

He looked at me for a minute and his eyes twinkled a little bit. "All right, all right, I knows ya ain't no boy. Yore a growed man. A good hand. I can see that, but yore a little younger than I am and I didn't mean no harm by it."

Just then Johnson walked up. "Yeah, what is it, Sullivan?"

"It's this boy—er, this young man. He's had a tough time—lost his packhorse and needs to buy some equipment. I don't know if we can spare any."

"It ain't necessary for him to buy no supplies," Johnson answered. "He's welcome to join up with us. We can bring him along to Dodge. I could use another hand."

I turned to him and spoke up. "Mr. Johnson, I'm sorry, sir, but I can't go with ya ta Dodge City."

"That's too bad. We could use ya. Where ya goin'? Back to Fort Larned?"

"Nosir. I'm goin' ta Fort Wallace."

"Fort Wallace?" He threw me a sharp look. "Hell, that's way up north. Just what is it yore needin'?"

"First off, I need somethin' ta carry water in."

"We ain't got no canteens to spare, but—"

Sullivan cut in. "We could give him a jug."

"I'll pay ya fer it," I said. "I also need some supplies, like a little flour an' a slab a bacon or a little jerky, an' maybe some coffee."

"That's no problem," Johnson said. "And we won't take your money. But hell, I reckon it's three days' hard ride to Fort Wallace from here, ain't it? And that horse of yours is plumb tuckered out. Where'd ya come from?"

"Down south."

By this time, a couple of other mule skinners'd come up and was standing 'round listening to the conversation.

"Well, young fella," Sullivan said, "tell Johnson here what ya told me about how ya lost your packhorse."

"Crossin' the Arkansas—quicksand. I had two weeks' worth a supplies, a packsaddle—I lost most ever'thin'. What's more, I was fool enough ta tie my rifle scabbard on the pack."

With that there come a dead silence. Them men all looked at me, some of 'em chewing away on their tobacco, some of 'em looking real hardlike and others quizzical. I just stood there. Finally, old Johnson said, "Hmm, south of the Arkansas, huh? Injun territory. What in hell was ya doin' down there?"

"Mindin' my own business, sir."

"You was just mindin' your own business, huh? I don't mean to be interferin', but, by God, you ain't got no Comanches on your trail, have ya? They don't cotton too well to havin' a white man in their territory. We don't want no trouble here. I think ya better tell us what ya was doin' there. Was ya huntin' buffalo? Maybe you was tryin' to steal horses from them Injuns?"

"Well, sir, I already told ya, I was just mindin' my own business."

Old Johnson's face turned as red as his suspenders. "Now you listen here, mister. I'm gonna tell ya somethin'. I've been packin' this trail for nigh onto ten years, haulin' hides from Dodge City to St. Joe and back again with supplies. I know goddamned well that a man don't go down into Injun territory without some good reason. Now you ain't bein' trailed by no bucks, are ya?"

"Nosir," I said. "I swear they ain't no Injuns follerin' me."

"It's mighty damn s'picious, that's all I can say. So you was crossin' the Arkansas with a packhorse. What direction did ya come from?"

I was glad I'd thought out my story. "I come up Medicine Lodge Creek 'til I hit a height a land an' then I crossed over an' dropped down ta the Arkansas. I lost my packhorse down at the crossin'. He went clean under an' there ain't no use lookin' fer him. He just went down."

He scratched his beard. "Now, that's funny. How did your pack-horse go in?"

I was ready for that one, too. "I planned a stop on the edge a the Arkansas ta scout out the crossin'. When we come down off'n them clay banks on the south side, that packhorse was so damned thirsty he just started runnin'. He trotted out ahead an', by God, he got inta some thick stuff. I jerked up on Piebald—both a them horses was plumb crazy with thirst. Me an' Piebald just barely did get outta there."

Them folks was all watching me, hanging on every word. I didn't cotton to too much talking, but I had to tell 'em enough so's they'd believe me.

"I got off an' tried ta get up ta where I could get hold a that lead rope on the packhorse," I went on, "but Piebald headed fer the water, so I had ta grab him quick 'fore I had two horses stuck. I found a place ta tie him down an' went back ta try an' get that packhorse out. By the time I got ta him, it was hopeless. He was almost clear down, throwin' his head 'round an' screamin' like blazes. I didn't even dare ta get ta the panniers ta pull out my stuff. I got within fifteen feet, but the sand was quiverin' an' I was afraid I was gonna get stuck myself. It was awful."

"Whew!" Johnson said. "I've heard a lot of them stories. That Arkansas is full of quicksand. Ya gotta know what yore doin' an' when to do it. Yessir, you can lose your whole damned outfit—and your ass along with it, if yore not careful. I crossed that Arkansas quite a few times when I was freightin' for them buffalo hunters that was goin' down into Injun territory. That's 'fore the treaty an' all at Medicine Lodge. Say, didn't ya say ya'd come up from Medicine Lodge Creek? Was ya down at the powwow?"

"Yessir, I was."

"What in the hell was ya doin' down there?"

My mouth was real dry, and it weren't from thirst. I couldn't do nothing 'cept keep going. "I was ridin' jerk line on one a them wagons a trade goods that General Harney brought along fer that powwow."

The old boy looked at me real hard and I wondered what I'd said wrong. "What the hell you talkin' about?" he asked. "They don't need no jerk line on that run. That's all flat country. There ain't no turnin' or nothin'."

"Yeah, that's right," I answered real casual, "but they figgered they's a couple a canyons in there 'mongst the bluffs. One a them Injun scouts tol' General Harney they might be a windin' trail in them mud canyons, so they hired me on just in case."

"I see, I see. So you was at Medicine Lodge when the treaty was signed, huh? Well, I'll be damned."

Hell, I didn't know when the treaty'd been signed nor nothing 'bout it. I just nodded and let him keep talking.

"Did ya see any of them Comanche or Kiowa Injuns down there? Did ya see Black Kettle or Lone Wolf or Kicking Bird? How 'bout Satanta? Did ya see him? I always wondered what them Injuns was like. I hear that Black Kettle's the ugliest son of a bitch in the whole Injun territory. And they say Lone Wolf's the meanest."

He had me. He could've been testing to see if I was really there, so I changed my story a little. "Well, sir, I'll be real honest with ya, I never got ta see none a them."

"Never got to see 'em? I thought ya said you was there."

"Nosir." I tried to keep my voice real calm and earnest. "We was comin' inta Medicine Lodge when General Harney needed a dispatch rider—someone ta go ta Fort Wallace. I reckon they figgered I was the youngest an' they could afford ta get rid a me the easiest."

That brought a laugh from Johnson, Sullivan, and all the rest of them mule skinners, so I figured I'd broke the ice a little bit. But Johnson kept on after me.

"So now yore goin' to Fort Wallace. What're ya s'posed to do there?"

"Well, sir, I don't rightly know. I'm just carryin' the dispatch fer General Harney."

"Oh, a military dispatch, huh?"

"Yessir."

That seemed to satisfy him. His face relaxed into a big old smile and he clapped me on the back. "Yore a rough one, ain't ya? But yore all right. What we need to do is get ya fixed up. You got some saddlebags there so ya can carry a little grub—some biscuits and jerky. Hell, it's only about a hundred miles to Fort Wallace from here and ya shouldn't have no problems."

"That'd be fine. I shore would 'preciate that," I said. "An' please don't fergit that jug a water."

A few minutes later one of the freighters come back with a full water jug. Then Sullivan took me over to his wife. "Can we spare a few biscuits for a hungry stranger?" he asked her.

"Yes, but he's gonna stay here tonight and eat, ain't he?"

I shook my head. "I really gotta keep goin', ma'am."

Sullivan turned to me. "You oughta get some rest, mister. Besides, that horse of yours is wore out."

"Yessir, he is. Maybe I could buy a horse off'n ya, Mr. Sullivan."

"Listen mister, I can't sell ya no horse. We just got these here mules and my saddle horse there, and one for my boy. We ain't got no spares."

I was glad I had the excuse of carrying a military dispatch to Fort Wallace to get the hell outta there, so I thanked him and said I figured I'd make it through okay, but a little grub for the trail would sure be nice.

"Polly, fill up this feller's saddlebags with biscuits an' jerky," Sullivan said. "He's got to get north with an army dispatch and he's moving on tonight. Why don't ya throw in an old pot and some coffee, too."

Polly was a hard-looking old gal. She had long, bony arms, but they wasn't nothing compared to her face. She had eyes like a prairie hawk and her nose hooked down like a beak. If she'd knowed I had a damned-near-naked little gal hidden away less'n a mile from there, I'll bet the roof would've come right off'n that covered wagon.

The sunset was fading and it was getting dark when she come back. Most people was gathering 'round the fires, doing one thing and another. Johnson called me over. He give me a piece of fresh-roasted venison to eat and some coffee, and it tasted mighty fine.

I thanked him and all of them folks. Then I went over and said good-bye to Mr. and Mrs. Sullivan, thanked 'em for everything they'd done, and picked up my saddlebags. I saddled up old Piebald again, slipped on his bridle, and swung into the saddle real slow and stiff, like I'd gone a long ways. They all stood there watching me, and I eased 'round the wagon and passed the fire. I waved and thanked 'em again and headed out to cross the Santa Fe Trail like I was going north to Fort Wallace.

"Cat!" Michelle yelled, and tore out running to meet me when I finally got back to where I'd left her. I jumped down and she throwed her arms 'round me, hugging me and sobbing. "Oh, my God, am I glad to see you. I've been so worried. You been gone so long. Where've you been? Are you all right? Where've you been all this time?"

"Whoa now, honey, I've been out gettin' our grub, remember?"

"Oh, I almost died of fright. I thought there was bears and wolves and I heard Indians howling and yipping."

"All ya heard was some coyotes. Ya didn't hear no Injuns. I see ya kept that fire goin'."

"I just about burned all the wood out, but I kept a real good fire going. Oh, it got so dark!"

"Ya done real good," I said. "Now, look here at what I've got." With that I pulled out the biscuits and jerky. Then I lifted the jug off'n the saddle horn. "Here, honey, have a drink."

"Mm, I'm so glad to have some water." She took a big gulp and stopped. "It tastes funny, don't it?" She wrinkled her nose.

"Yeah, but just drink it slow, 'cause ya ain't had none in a while. Remember how sick we got down by the Arkansas, after all that time without a drink a water? Now just take it real easy."

I went off to get Piebald picketed, then I come back to Michelle. "I've got somethin' else good here," I told her, and pulled out a sack full of coffee and an old tin pot. We took the stuff and went over by the fire. It weren't long 'fore we had coffee to wash down the jerky and biscuits.

Michelle got to feeling better and we sat there by the fire looking at the stars. She moved up next to me real close and cooed, "Oh, Cat, I've been cold. Didn't you bring me some nice warm clothes?"

"No, that comes tomorrow. I didn't have the guts ta ask those folks fer nothin' more."

I told her all about Johnson, Sullivan, and how them wagons looked—and them freighters and old lady Sullivan. I told her how I thought Mrs. Sullivan would've acted if she'd found that I was keeping a half-naked dance hall girl down yonder in the bushes.

Michelle giggled. "It would've been funny, wouldn't it? But I wish you would've asked her for some clothes." Then she busted out laughing to beat all hell. "I got an idea, and it's a good one, too!"

I was s'picious of any real good ideas she got, but I said, "What's that?"

"You can ride up to the next wagon train naked and tell 'em—"

"Naked?"

"Yeah, you can tell 'em that the Indians stole your clothes."

"Listen. I ain't ridin' up ta no wagon train without no clothes on."

"Okay, you wouldn't have to be naked. You could just be wearing your underwear. By the way, are you wearing underwear? You could loan 'em to me."

"Honey, y'know damned well—"

"No," she said, "I don't. That was a long time ago. You know it's kind of cold tonight."

"Ya ain't gonna be cold long."

"Whatcha mean?"

"I mean we got us one bedroll and they's two a us, so's ya ain't gonna be cold fer long."

She leaned over and give me a nice kiss and put her arms 'round me. I was warm from the fire, and when I put my arms 'round her and began to feel her young body, my heart got to pounding and I was suddenly warm all over.

I fixed up the bedroll and took off my clothes. We crawled in together under the stars, and it was cozy warm. I slid my hand down and felt her bosom up against me, then I reached 'round and squeezed her cute little bare bottom. I felt the tenderness of how it was to have a woman way out there on the plains with the firelight dancing on the creek banks. Then she started kissing away and stirring me up.

I made love to her that night under them shiny stars. I made love more and better'n I'd ever made it with any woman before. I ain't exactly lived the life of no monk, but that was a bit of loving I never will forget.

When the red light of dawn appeared, it broke just like thunder in the East. The whole world begun to open up and sing. The sky turned from that gun-metal gray of first light to a blazing orange-red, and then into bright morning blue. The prairie wind was blowing smooth and the meadowlarks was singing and my heart was full of living.

I was on my way to Taos and I had me a gal. She weren't a whore no more. That night'd been pure man and woman loving—the best kind—and now we belonged together. Her past didn't make no difference to me, no-way. That morning as she slept there beside me, she sure looked wonderful. She was as pretty as an antelope on a prairie hillside.

I decided the world weren't half-bad after all. Y've got your work cut out fer ya today, I thought, so get the job done fast. Ya got lots a livin' ahead of ya.

I slipped outta that bedroll real easy so's not to wake her up. I pulled on my britches and boots, got the fire going again, and stirred up a little coffee.

After things got to going right, I got me a long stem of prairie grass and begun to tickle Michelle's face. She wrinkled her nose a little bit and rubbed it like it was bothered by a fly. Finally I tickled just right and she sneezed and woke up. Then she seen that it was me teasing her.

She sat right up, her eyes as shiny as the sky. "Cat Brules, you're the living end! You're the worst boy I ever seen."

She was so pretty and fiery, I didn't even mind her calling me "boy." I bowed. "At yer service, ma'am, yer royal majesty. Yer breakfast is waitin'."

She sniffed the air. "For heaven's sake. What have you done? Got the fire going and the coffee all set up?"

"Shore have. An' yore gonna have a real special menu this mornin'. A genuine prairie breakfast—coffee an' biscuits an' jerky. Ain't that grand?"

Right away, she slid outta that bedroll, her nightdress up kinda high, and in that early morning sunshine I seen how really beautiful her body was. She had long, shapely legs, and her hips was just round enough for a woman with a narrow waist. She was kinda modest, and turned away to pull down her nightdress. I had to remind myself there was work to do.

"Go ahead an' make yerself at home right here," I said. "I'm gonna be back in short order."

Piebald looked pretty near okay again. After I mounted up I let him give a couple of half-sporty little bucks, then headed to the Santa Fe Trail. By that time that wagon train'd be long gone, but there'd be something else coming along sooner or later.

When I reached them cottonwoods, I'll be damned if there weren't a wagon still there. I stopped while I was still pretty well hid. The way the water barrels was tied on the back reminded me of Sullivan's wagon. I wondered what was wrong. Maybe they'd lost a mule, or maybe one of 'em had gone lame. Or maybe they'd just left the wagon there. I kept watching, and then I thought I seen somebody moving 'round in front of the wagon, but from that distance I couldn't tell if it was a man or a woman.

I went back down the creek a ways and headed due west, where I could keep outta sight and get across the ridge. I trotted Piebald 'til I got up on the trail.

Sure enough, there was the wagon train to the west, 'bout an hour away. The whole train had moved out and left that one wagon in the cottonwoods. I crossed up on the north side of the trail, west of the ridge. After 'bout a mile and a half, I cut back over the ridge and come back down towards the trail.

Way off to the east, I seen the dust of another wagon train—it looked like a big one. Waiting for it wouldn't do no good, 'cause I'd be up against the same odds as before. The best thing was to go back and find out who was with that one lone wagon. If they wouldn't do business with me, then maybe my revolver'd change their thinking.

I crossed down into the cottonwoods where the wagon train had been camped. Skinny old Mrs. Sullivan was sitting there on a stool by the wagon doing some sewing. She looked up a minute and seen me, and she stood up real quick. I rode on up, took off my hat, and dismounted. "Good mornin', Mrs. Sullivan," I said.

She threw me a look as sharp as her chin. "I thought you rode north, young man, on your way to Fort Wallace."

I had my story all thought out. "Yes, ma'am, I did, but I had ta turn back."

"What do you mean you had to come back? What do you want now?"

"Well, ma'am, I had ta come back ta warn the train."

"To warn the train? What are you talking about? The train done left here at daylight."

"Thank ya, ma'am, I seen 'em, but then I spotted your wagon and thought I'd better come down here an' warn ya 'bout the Injuns."

"Indians?"

I knowed right then I'd hit the right string—got her good and worried. Them early settler women was plumb scared of Indians. You hardly had to mention Indians and they'd damned near lie down and die right there. They'd heard talk 'bout what happened to women that fell into the hands of the Indians.

"Yes'm, I crossed the fresh trail of a big war party—lots a pony tracks—'bout ten miles north a here. They was headed southwest, an' I figgered they might run inta you folks."

"Oh, Lord," she moaned. "That's awful, just awful. I've got to go find my husband right away."

"Where *is* Mr. Sullivan?"

"He's gone to get the mules and the mare. Our son's bay horse got loose last night and he's trailing it."

"If I was you," I said, "I'd get harnessed up real quick an' get outta here."

Mrs. Sullivan started shaking all over, trying to put everything together, and all the time she kept calling out for Sullivan. Pretty soon from across the other side of the cottonwoods, I heard him give a sorta "Halloooo," and she screamed, "John! Come quick!"

"I'm coming," he hollered back.

While this was going on, I got to eyeing things. She had the flaps of the wagon turned back and the wagon tongue was lying down so I was able to get close to it. There was a chest of drawers, a bed, and a stove in the wagon, and I figured, hell, they must have some kinda clothes. That kid of theirs was 'bout twelve years old, so his clothes should just 'bout fit Michelle. If I demanded some clothes and had my .38 to back me up, I'd prob'ly do all right. I could prob'ly get a rifle and some ammunition at the same time. Too bad their stock was scattered so I couldn't take a horse as well.

"Mrs. Sullivan, has Mr. Sullivan got a rifle?" I asked the old bag. "We may need it."

"Yes, he has. He has one of them new Winchesters."

"Does he have plenty a ammunition?"

"Of course. My husband would never go anywhere without enough ammunition. It's right there in the wagon."

"Well," I said, "I think ya'd better get that out an' get ready."

She come hurrying up carrying a shiny new hunting piece. "Do you know about rifles, young man?"

" 'Course I do, ma'am. I've handled 'em all my life. Let me see. Yep, that's shore a dandy."

That was no exaggeration. It was a brand-new shiny model 66 Winchester, a real honey. Sullivan must've bought it right 'fore they left. "Where's the ammunition?" I asked.

She pointed to the wagon. "Right in that wooden box there."

I levered the breech of the rifle and seen that there was nothing in the magazine or the chamber. "I'll tell ya what, ma'am, if'n ya don't mind, I know Mr. Sullivan'd want me ta load this rifle so's he'll have it ready."

"Oh, that would be fine. Are them Indians liable to attack us?"

"Naw, we'd see their dust first. But we'd better be ready."

She wrung her hands. "I wish Roger hadn't gone so far away. That horse of his, why it's been the worst kind of trouble."

"It looked like a good horse ta me."

"He may be, but he's all the time breaking his picket rope. We've had to stay behind more than once on account of that creature. And now there's Indians!"

I counted out them shells and started loading, and it took sixteen in the magazine. I shoved one in the chamber and let the hammer down with my thumb 'til it was against the safety. Then I set the Winchester down close by against the wagon tongue.

"You ain't got a rifle, do you, boy?"

"No, ma'am, I ain't. I just got a little .38. A six-shooter ain't much good at any kinda distance with Injuns. By the time they get close enough ta be hit, they're too close fer comfort."

She shuddered and looked all around. "I don't know what to do next."

"We'd better pack up the wagon here, an' as soon as Mr. Sullivan gets back, we'd better harness them mules."

"Oh, no!" she wailed. "We can't start without Roger."

" 'Course not. I'll ride out an' pick him up fer ya."

"Lord bless you, boy. I'm so glad you came back to warn us. Those Indians—I told John we shouldn't come this far west."

She dashed over to the fire pit where she had her pots and pans and begun to rustle 'em around. While she had her back turned, I dug into that ammunition box and put about six shells in each pocket. Outta the corner of my eye I spied a cartridge belt, but there wasn't no rifle bullets in it.

"Lookee here, Mrs. Sullivan," I called out, holding up the cartridge belt for her to see. "Mr. Sullivan's gonna want this belt loaded if'n we run inta them Injuns, so I'll take care a it."

"You go right ahead."

Then I heard old Sullivan coming. When he come out of the

cottonwoods, he saw Piebald standing there and he stopped dead in his tracks. Piebald whinnied and the sorrel mare Sullivan was leading whinnied back.

That's when I made a big mistake. I thought if he seen me with a rifle, he'd be mighty damned s'picious 'cause he knowed I'd lost mine. Like a damned fool, I throwed the cartridge belt over the wagon tongue and leaned the rifle up against it right where the tongue joins the bed of the wagon. I left it sitting there and walked out kinda smooth to where I had Piebald tied to the side of the wagon.

His missus run out to meet him, shouting, "Oh, John! Oh, John, there's Indians! This nice boy come back to tell us about the Indians."

He looked at me. "Injuns? What Injuns?"

"I turned back at daybreak today 'cause I seen Injun sign, Mr. Sullivan. They's a big war party 'bout ten miles north headed west a here."

He shoved his hat back on his head and wiped off some fresh beads of sweat. "How'd you know they was Injuns?"

"I seen their pony tracks."

"That could've been wild horses. We seen a lot of wild horses 'round here—seen a big herd outside Fort Larned."

"I been 'round long enough ta know the difference, Mr. Sullivan. A band a wild horses is mares an' a stallion an' maybe one or two young. But mostly mares, an' it takes a pretty good stud ta run a band a more'n twenty mares. These was stallion tracks mostly, an' there was a lot more'n twenty or thirty a them—they was nigh unto a hundred."

"How'd ya know it was a war party? It could've been just a peaceful bunch of Injuns movin' cross-country."

"Mr. Sullivan, ya don't know the Injuns 'round these parts like I do. They ain't just meanderin' 'round. They don't cross north a the Arkansas less'n they mean business. What's more, if'n it weren't a war party, it would've had squaws an' kids—an' there weren't no travois or foot tracks. This's a war party all right, an' they're travelin' fast!"

"It don't sound very good, us bein' alone here. Wait a minute, son."

"Don't call me 'son.' "

"Sorry, mister, but I just thought of somethin'. I seen a big wagon train up there off to the east about fifteen miles away. Did you see it?"

"Yessir. Maybe the best thing fer us ta do is head towards it."

"Or d'ya think it'd be safer to wait here?"

"We've got to wait for Roger!" Mrs. Sullivan cut in. "We've got to wait right here."

"Now wait just a minute," I said. "The best thing ta do whether we're goin' back or stayin' put is ta harness these mules an' get ready ta roll. I'll tell ya what I done, sir. I took the liberty a loadin' that Winchester fer ya, an' I laid it up there against the wagon tongue."

"But what about you? Yore not armed, are ya?"

I pointed to my side. "I got a .38 tucked away here. I think the thing we oughta do now is ta hitch up them mules, don't ya?"

"Let's get right to it."

The mules already had their collars and hames on 'em and the traces was dragging, so we backed 'em up and hitched 'em to the tongue and back to the whippletree. Then Mr. Sullivan tied the sorrel mare to the back of the wagon.

I followed him. "Have ya got a packsaddle, Mr. Sullivan?"

He looked at me funny. "Why?"

"Sometimes it's a pretty good idea, when they's Injuns 'round, ta saddle up one horse with a packsaddle. Ya can't never tell. Ya may have ta leave the wagon an' hit out fer safe hidin', an' ya shore don't wanta leave all your supplies back in the wagon. Put some ammunition an' some grub on a packsaddle if'n y've got it, an'—"

"Wait just a minute," he interrupted. "How'd ya figure that? We can't go off. Me an' Roger can ride, but what am I gonna do with Mrs. Sullivan? I can't leave her in the wagon alone."

"She can ride in the wagon while we're goin' down the trail here, but you an' me an' Roger, we'd best be on horses. If'n I was you, I'd take one a them mules outta the harness an' I'd put that packsaddle on the mule an' load him up with some supplies an' equipment. If we've gotta ride fer it, ya can put Mrs. Sullivan behind ya on the horse."

"Oh, no," he said. "I ain't gonna leave all my supplies and everything for no Injuns to plunder and burn."

"Don't ya think it'd be better'n leavin' your scalp?"

I could see that I had him a little agitated. He picked his hat off'n his head and run his hand over his skull, and I could see he was really sweating and his hands was shaking.

"I don't know," he said. "Maybe that ain't a bad idea. But I don't know how we'd handle the wagon with one mule shy."

"Well," I said, "maybe we can put the packsaddle an' empty panniers on one a them mules now an' have the things handy on the wagon box. If'n we have to unharness quick, we can throw it right in. Which is your best mule here?"

"Blackjack, the lead mule on the left. Y'know, that ain't a bad idea, young fella. Yore usin' your head."

We uncollared that mule and throwed the packsaddle and empty panniers on him. Then I talked Sullivan into putting some cups, a water jug, a side of venison, some flour, and extra ammunition into the panniers.

Then he took out his best saddle and some saddle blankets and rigged the sorrel mare up real good. Finally, he tied her up by the halter to the ring on the back of the wagon. She was a real gentle horse, and I thought, by God, she's just the thing fer Michelle.

I got to toting things up: a good mule with a packsaddle and supplies, a nice gentle mare with a full rig, and a brand-new Winchester with plenty of ammunition. What went running through my head real fast was how much was that mule worth? How much was that horse worth? How much was that rifle and them supplies worth? I reckoned the price of the rifle at eighty dollars and that sorrel mare about twenty-five dollars and the mule another thirty. It added up to a lot more'n a hundred dollars, and that was 'bout all I had. I sure couldn't pay for them and some clothes and supplies, too.

Hell, I thought, I wonder if he'd take sixty dollars fer the whole outfit—saddles an' all? I had to laugh at myself. There weren't no way he was gonna swap for no sixty dollars less'n it was at gunpoint. That was the way I was gonna have to go, and that was the time.

Sullivan was rummaging 'round in the wagon, so I took a big gulp to settle my breathing and stuck my head in there. "Mr. Sullivan, can I talk with ya just a minute?" I jerked my head for him to come out and step aside.

He come down off'n the wagon and I glanced over to where his rifle was resting beside the ammunition belt. I was standing 'bout five yards off to the right of the lead mule, looking the whole outfit over as if I was inspecting what we was s'posed to do with it. Mrs. Sullivan went back over by the fire on the other side of the mules. Old man Sullivan walked towards me and I lifted up my hat a couple of times as if I wanted to whisper something real important. "Mr. Sullivan, I wanta make a proposition. I wanta buy that mare off'n ya."

"Sorry," he said. "She ain't for sale."

"I wish ya'd change your mind, Mr. Sullivan. I've gotta go ta Fort

Wallace. I'm already twenty-four hours late 'cause I come back here ta warn ya 'bout them Injuns. Now if I ride back there ta them wagons with ya, it's gonna take another four or five hours."

I looked straight at him and repeated, "I'm twenty-four hours overdue an' Piebald here is plumb tuckered out."

Sullivan shook his head. "That's too bad, son. I agree your horse ain't in such good shape, but we can't very well spare you one. What was you figurin' to do? Trade him? He ain't much to trade with."

"Nosir, I don't wanta trade him. But I'll buy that mare off'n ya with good money."

He shook his head and waved me off. "No, I can't help ya, but ya might strike a deal with the folks in the rest of the train."

"Wait!" I said. "Another thing. 'Fore I make a ride through that kinda country, I'm gonna need a rifle. Sell me that new one a yours."

Now he looked a little peeved. "Kid, yore plumb crazy. Y'don't really think I'm gonna let go of that now, do ya?"

"The way I see it, Mr. Sullivan, ya pert near have ta, 'cause if I've gotta ride alone a hundred miles cross-country, I gotta have a rifle. I'll pay ya so's ya can buy another one, an' I won't leave ya 'til ya join up with that wagon train again. Seems to me ya owe me."

"Maybe so, but I've got a long ways to go and I'm not gonna give up no rifle." He paused to think. "I might sell ya that sorrel mare, but not the rifle."

I thought real hard, then asked, "How much ya want fer her?"

"Let's talk about that when we get back with the wagon train."

He took a few steps away and I raised my voice a little. "Oh no ya don't! I ain't escortin' ya clear back to that wagon train an' then have ya renege on the deal."

He turned back. "Whatta ya mean renege on the deal? I never backed out of a deal in my life and I don't—"

"Just shut up," I said, feeling a little dizzy as my mind raced and my heart pounded. "I'm carryin' military dispatches an' I've gotta get ta Fort Wallace. It's your duty ta sell me what I need."

He looked me up and down, real deliberate. "Well, that may be. I told ya that I might consider selling ya that mare, but I sure as hell don't have to give up my only rifle."

With that I knowed it was time, so I whipped out my .38 and pointed it at him. "Mr. Sullivan, I'll buy your mare, your saddle, your rifle, and what's more, I'll buy that lead mule."

His mouth dropped in surprise. "Why, you son of a bitch. How dare you—"

I cut him off. "Shut up an' don't make a move." I started easing 'round to where I could get to the rifle. I still held the gun on him while he stood there, mouth agape, 'tween me and the wagon. Just then he moved a little bit.

"Put your hands up!" I yelled.

Mrs. Sullivan called out from the other side of the camp where she'd been working by the fire. "What are you boys arguing about?"

Sullivan hollered back, "This son of a bitch wants to . . ." With that the damned fool whirled 'round and made him a run for the rifle. He didn't leave me no choice a'tall. But I was ready for it. He was gonna get that rifle at any cost and of course I seen it was my fault to leave it so far out on the wagon tongue that it tempted him. I felt real concerned 'cause I didn't wanta kill him. I could see him and Mrs. Sullivan was good folks and there weren't no use in causing a tragedy just 'cause that damn fool didn't know how to act when he was in an honest holdup. Sullivan was sure bent on making this come out wrong. That's the way lots of fellas gets killed. But when it come to shooting, I knowed I was good so I just bided my time.

Sullivan moved surprising fast and made the distance to the tongue in a matter of a second or two, reaching out with his left arm to grab the rifle. That's when I fired. I only nicked him on the upper part of his arm and tore his shirt a little, but he let out a howl as if he'd been mortally wounded.

Then it was my turn to do some yelling. "Y'damn fool, back up 'fore I kill ya! What the hell d'ya mean runnin' fer a gun when I got the drop on ya?" He was holding his arm and a small amount of blood was coming from the nick, but he whirled 'round and looked at me like a mad bull. "Get on back over there an' get your hands up, gol'durn it!" I shouted. "I don't wanta kill ya, but by God I will if'n ya don't do what yore tol'."

He stood there fuming and sweating, and I finally seen he needed more persuading. "Come on, put your hands up." He kinda lagged on that, and I let him have it again. My gun went off with a roar and blowed the hat right off the top of his head.

I wanta tell you that was one of the most comical things I ever seen in my life. That fat old fool had his hands halfway up and when that hat went flying, he reached up for where he thought it was and found only his bald head. It s'prised him cross-eyed and scared him plumb outta his wits.

Mrs. Sullivan begun screaming at me. "You devil, you! You devil! You're trying to kill my husband!"

"On the contrary, ma'am, I'm tryin' hard not ta kill him. I'm tryin' ta make him behave."

By that time, Sullivan had gone plumb docile. "Shut up, Polly. He's a wizard with that gun. He can kill us anytime he wants to, and I kinda think he's got that inclination. We'd better just keep still. We're dealin' with a crazy man."

"No, Mr. Sullivan, ya ain't dealin' with no crazy man, yore just dealin' with a buyer. I'm no thief. I ain't gonna steal nothin' from ya. I'm just gonna buy what I need at fair prices. Ya oughta know that out here on the prairies, tables turn pretty fast. Things is scarce lots a the time, an' a man who's got a horse, a rifle, or a saddle can ask what he wants fer it an' near get it. That's what's called a seller's market. But, ever' now an' then there comes a turn of fate. It changes things 'round just like them ol' Missouri traders always tells them Injuns. An' today things has shore enough changed 'round. This's become a buyer's market real sudden, an' I'm gonna buy your equipment an' your horse, an' I'm gonna tell ya the prices I'm gonna pay fer 'em an' you ain't gonna argue 'bout it one damn bit."

I reached in my shirt pocket and pulled out my money roll and peeled off twenty dollars. "This is fer the mule, an' I'll give another twenty-five fer the mare an' the saddle. I'm gonna throw in forty dollars fer the rifle an' the ammunition belt. Now, Mrs. Sullivan, I'm lookin' fer a few other things. I need a saddle scabbard, an' don't come out with no firearms or nothin' else that ya think ya can do some harm to me with less'n ya want ta see your husband deader'n hell."

Mrs. Sullivan just stood there for a minute looking at me, not knowing what to do. Then she looked at her husband. Pretty soon, Sullivan come to his senses. "Damn it, Polly, do what the man says. Hurry up, 'fore he gets mad. Get him the scabbard—that ain't nothin'."

Well, Mrs. Sullivan come alive like she was a young girl. She run into the wagon and come back in a couple of minutes carrying the saddle scabbard.

"Thank ya, ma'am," I said. "Now, Mrs. Sullivan, I'm givin' ya a dollar fer that scabbard."

Old Sullivan grunted some, but when I looked at him real sharp he just sorta smiled and didn't say nothing more. Then, still holding the gun on Sullivan so's he could see exactly what was gonna happen, I said to Mrs. Sullivan, "Ma'am, I'm in need a some clothes fer my kid brother."

"Kid brother? I thought you were riding alone."

"I am right now, but don't ask no questions," I said. "I've got a need fer some clothes fer my kid brother. I seen that ya got a dresser in that wagon. Kindly bring out the drawers and spread 'em here on the ground so's I can see what I'm needin' ta buy from ya."

She got a bit huffy about that. I guess she didn't want to show everything that was in them drawers—women's fixings and all. But I couldn't help that and Sullivan shouted, "Get on with it, Polly, get on with it!"

Then he turned to me. "Please don't kill us, stranger. Ya can have anythin' ya want. Just don't kill us."

"I won't kill ya if ya behave, but by God I want a fair trade an' I want it made fast."

Sullivan swallowed hard. "Polly, c'mon woman, hurry it up—the stranger here is in a hurry."

Mrs. Sullivan commenced dragging out the drawers of their dresser and I looked 'em over. I was trying to figure out what'd fit Michelle. There weren't no slim girl's styles, what with Mrs. Sullivan being as big as a horse and acting real embarrassed about all of them women's things that was in the drawers. I didn't give a damn considering who wore 'em, but I did see that there was a pair of buckskin pants and I realized they was for the boy. I thought they'd fit Michelle just right.

"Ma'am, I'll buy them pants fer two dollars. I also see y've got a blue shirt that'll be fine. That'll be another dollar." I looked a little more. "Ma'am, I see y'have a bonnet there, a lady's gray bonnet. My kid brother ain't got no hat. He'd prob'ly like a Stetson like Mr. Sullivan's much better, but it's all tore ta shreds an' I guess I'll just take that bonnet."

After she'd laid all them things aside, I said, "That's fine, Mrs. Sullivan. Now you just back off an' get over there by Mr. Sullivan. Sullivan, I want ya ta take five steps backwards, real slow—keep your hands up an' don't make a move." I went over and knelt down and picked up them clothes that'd been set aside and carried 'em over and stuck them in the mare's saddlebags, meanwhile keeping an eye on the Sullivans.

Finally I said, "Here's your money. I'm leavin' it right here under a rock so it don't blow away, but we got a couple a more things ta do. I don't want neither a you to be too damn anxious ta disrupt this deal, 'cause this's a good deal fer both a us. I got a fair price an' didn't get swindled, an' ya got a fair deal 'cause ya got paid an' didn't get killed."

"Mrs. Sullivan, I want ya ta take that rope. That's right, the one hangin' on the side a the wagon. And Sullivan, I want ya ta back up real slow. Just keep your hands in the air. I'll kill ya if'n ya make a wrong move. Now back up to that tree. Mrs. Sullivan, I'd be most obliged, ma'am, if'n you'd just move ta the other side a the tree an' stand with your back to it. I'm gonna tie ya up for a little while.

"Sullivan, ya got any more firearms in that wagon?" I asked. "Speak true, man, 'cause if'n I find ya lied ta me, I'll kill ya."

He kinda croaked, his hands still clasped over his bald head. "No, sir, I ain't got nothin'."

"Well, all right, yore just the luckiest man I seen in all my life. Now back up against that tree while I put this gun back inta my belt. I can draw it awful fast, so ya better keep your hands up. Mrs. Sullivan, don't bother me with no mad moves, 'cause I'd hate ta have ta kill your husband."

Mrs. Sullivan was plumb shaking with nervousness, and her lips was trembling. I didn't think I'd have no trouble with her. I took a rope and made a loop at one end. Then I made the Sullivans stand close to the tree and put their hands down at their sides. Then I run 'round the tree with the loop end of the rope and passed the rest of it through the loop and pulled it up tight, but not too tight, as I didn't wanta hurt 'em.

Then I walked 'round the tree five more times with the rest of the rope. When I got through they was really laced up. I hated to do it, but I sure as hell didn't want 'em raising any hell while I was on the way out. I needed plenty of time to get down to where Michelle was camped and get her into the clothes and get her on the mare and get outta there.

When it was all through, I said, "Well, there's your money. It's a fair deal, an' I'm leavin' now. I thank ya fer the transaction." With that I took off my hat and bowed to 'em.

FROM HEAVEN TO HELL

It didn't take too long for me to cover the ground to where Michelle was hid. As I rode up she called out, "Did you get any clothes?"

"I shore did."

"Well, where are they? I'm ready for 'em right now. By the way, what was those two shots I heard?"

"I had ta fire a couple a times ta let 'em know that I meant what I said."

"You didn't hurt nobody, did you?"

"No, nobody got hurt but, boy, y'know I had ta keep 'em at a distance there. They didn't look very kindly on my leavin' with all this stuff."

"Do you think they're gonna come after you?"

"Prob'ly, but it's gonna be some time yet 'cause they ain't got nothin' but some harness mules."

She laughed at that. "So you left 'em afoot, did you?"

"Yeah, I run off the other horses an' just left 'em the mules. They don't know where ta look fer me, neither, but we'd better get goin' just in case."

When I unrolled them buckskin pants and that shirt, she busted out laughing. "Oh, no! I thought you were gonna get me some dresses."

"Now, honey, it wouldn't be real comfortable fer ya ta wear no dresses. 'Sides that, I didn't know how ta get no underwear or nothin' fer ya." When she blushed a little bit, I added, "I figgered ya'd be better off dressed like a boy, anyway."

She nodded. "Well, that ain't a bad idea. Let me see them pants. I wonder if they'll fit." She held 'em up to her waist. "Oh, good, they're just about right."

She held the shirt up to her shoulders. "That's great," I said. "Now the thing ya gotta do is ta get inta them right away while I fix the mare's saddle. Looks like I oughta shorten them stirrups fer ya, too."

She walked over to pet the sorrel mare. "I sure hope this one don't carry on like yours does."

"Don't worry none, she seems real gentle. You'll have ta think of a good name fer her."

"Oh, she's a girl? Maybe I'll call her 'Taffy' to match her color. Is that okay?"

With that she went 'round behind the trees to change clothes. I couldn't figure it out. Women are funny like that. Why did she wanta be so darned modest and everything? I'd already seen her just as naked as the day she was born, and we'd had some good loving, but she didn't want me to watch her changing into them pants and shirt.

In a few minutes, Michelle come running out. "Well, here I am. How do you like it?"

I looked over at her standing there, and if it hadn't been for her hair hanging down, I'd have almost thought she was a boy. That shirt was a deep, sky blue color and it looked real fine with them buckskin pants. She sure was lovely, with her long brown hair waving in the breeze.

"Yore the prettiest little boy I ever seen," I assured her. "I noticed ya was startin' ta get sunburned, so I got ya this." I pulled out that old gray bonnet and Michelle busted out laughing.

"I'm awful glad to have these, but did you think to get me any shoes?"

I'd plumb forgot about that. "I'm afraid not, but I'll try ta do somethin' 'bout that soon. The important thing is that now ya got some clothes an' ya got a horse ta ride."

She made a pouty little face, then laughed and slipped on the bonnet, tucked her hair up behind, and tied the chin strap in a bow. The whole outfit looked real cute. I stood for a minute, admiring how her bottom filled out them buckskin pants and the way that little blue shirt strained across her full bosom.

"Yore lookin' great, honey," I told her. "Now, step over here an' let me swing ya up on this horse."

When she mounted, I finished adjusting the straps and patted one little bare foot. "I think them stirrups'll do just fine. And don't worry none, we'll get ya some shoes 'fore too long." I give Michelle's little bare foot a good-bye squeeze and swung back up on Piebald. I fastened on the lead rope of the mule and we started off towards the ridge to the west.

Just as we reached the crest, I looked back down that sandy creek. Way down yonder I seen a dark brown horse coming slowly back up the creek with Sullivan's boy riding him bareback. I figured that the boy seen us, 'cause he stopped and looked.

We had to get outta there. I pushed straight west across the prairie alongside the Santa Fe Trail, 'bout a mile to the south of it. I figured we'd go down into the Arkansas to camp just as quick as we could after sunset.

We must've rode 'bout ten miles 'fore it got dark enough so's people couldn't see us at a distance. Then I headed south. I let Piebald pick his way over the sand bluffs down by the edge of the river, and we worked along there in the dark 'til I spotted a place where I could make a little fire.

I pulled up and told Michelle, "Okay, honey, this's where we camp tonight. It ain't gonna be much of a camp 'cause we gotta start out real early. They're still apt ta be lookin' fer us."

For once it seemed like she was too tired to do much talking or arguing. She got down off that sorrel mare she'd named Taffy and handed me the reins. I got a fire going and started the coffee kettle and took a piece of venison and skewered it over the fire.

Michelle sat there with the firelight brightening up her face while she stared into the flames. After a spell she looked up. "How long are we gonna be running like this?"

"Just 'til we get past Dodge City. Once we get on the trail ta Santa Fe, I don't reckon we'll have no problems. I doubt if any posse'd follow us that far."

"I'll sure be glad when we don't have to hide out no more. How far away is Dodge City?"

" 'Bout thirty-five miles, I reckon."

She looked happier. "I'll sure be glad to get there and get me some nice things—and visit all the shops!"

There weren't no use talking 'bout it no more. We sure as hell wasn't going into Dodge City, but it wouldn't do no good trying to tell her that.

I took out the bedroll. "I reckon we'd better get us some sleep."

She pouted and didn't budge. "What am I gonna do? Sleep in these clothes?"

I didn't answer. After a while she come over and slipped into my bedroll to join me. She didn't have nothing on, but she was so tired that she went right to sleep.

I slept some, too, 'fore waking up and crawling out of the sack in the dark without disturbing Michelle. I pulled on my britches and boots and went out after Piebald, the mare, and the mule. When I had everything ready to go, I woke up Michelle. She was mystified 'bout leaving while it was still dark, so I told her I thought that was the safest thing to do. She didn't argue none. It was a little cold riding along there, and Michelle was shivering in just that thin shirt, so I give her my rawhide slicker again.

When the sun come up, Michelle stretched and said how good it was to feel warm again and how she wished she had something to eat. I reached for the biscuit in my pocket and we ate as we rode along. I stayed right in the bottom of the Arkansas riverbed, close to the sand bluffs on the north side, threading a curvy trail in and out amongst the cottonwoods and the creek alders.

The water was low and in places there was a little early morning ice in the sloughs alongside the river, but by midmorning it had all melted and the air felt nice and warm. The horses and the mule seemed to be doing all right. I knowed I should keep a real close lookout over all of 'em, 'cause we had six or seven hundred miles to go to Taos.

I reckon we rode nigh unto twenty miles that morning. Around noon we stopped in some cottonwoods. Michelle walked around slowly, rubbing a couple of tender spots on her rump and thighs. "How long are we gonna stop? This was a real short ride today. Are we gonna fix something decent to eat?"

"We're gonna lay up here the rest a the afternoon an' then we're gonna travel tonight. A little ways up, the trail comes close ta the river. As a matter a fact, Dodge City's right on the Arkansas. If'n we ain't careful, we're gonna ride right inta it."

"What's the matter with that?"

I figured I had to tell her. "Honey, we ain't goin' into Dodge City— we'd prob'ly be arrested in five minutes. Don't ya think a posse must've come from Hays City an' spread the news by now?"

Her face drawed up like a sudden rain squall on the prairie. I give her a little hug and led her over to where we could sit down on a clump of dry leaves and rest our backs on a fallen log. "Just 'fore dark we'll ride up the Arkansas another four or five miles an' when it gets too dark ta see what we're doin', we'll climb them bluffs out ta the river east a Dodge City. We'll ride north 'round the town an' strike the Santa Fe Trail again on the west side an' foller it 'til we're west a the Cimarron Crossin'."

"What's the Cimarron Crossing?"

"That's one a the trails ya can take ta go south. It crosses from the Arkansas over ta the north bend a the Cimarron River an' then up the Cimarron ta the south side a Raton Pass. Then it goes over Eagles Nest Pass an' inta Taos."

"Is that the way we're going? It sure sounds like a long way."

She shut her eyes wearily, and I went on. "Well, they's two crossin's. One is Cimarron—that's the Lower Crossin'. Then they's another one up by Chouteau Island that's called the Upper Crossin'. I ain't made up my mind which one we'll take yet."

"Let's go the shortest way. I'm tired of riding. I wish I could go into Dodge City."

"Sorry, Michelle, but it just ain't safe. Here, let me get the bed-roll so's ya can take a nap in this nice warm sun while I fix us some lunch."

I'd counted on her not asking why, as long as we was gonna cross the Arkansas anyway, that we couldn't cross the Arkansas right where we was, and keep south of Dodge City. There was a real good reason, and I was relieved when she didn't ask. South of the river was Indian territory, and I didn't wanta be there longer'n we had to. There was something else I didn't tell Michelle: I didn't tell her that even the Cimarron Crossing route was right through Indian territory and that lots of folks considered it a dangerous way to go, too. Besides, I figured there was so much traffic along the Santa Fe Trail going to Pueblo and Raton that we was apt to get recognized.

By then, word of McIntyre's killing must've spread throughout the territory. I was sure a posse had to be on our trail. It only made sense. The livery man'd prob'ly figured out it was me that'd killed McIntyre, and he knowed Michelle was with me. People was bound to be looking for the both of us. I figured our best chance was to cross into Indian territory, but I wanted to keep the amount of time we spent there as short as possible. I figured we'd do all right if we just minded our own business and kept going, traveling mostly at night and hiding during the day. I knowed we'd have to keep a sharp eye out, but I figured I was smart enough to make it across safe.

I got a small fire going and fixed coffee and venison. Michelle got up, and we ate and then lay down in the warm sunshine and slept like tired pups for a good part of the afternoon. When the sun got low, we was on our way, and we traveled along the riverbed 'til sunset.

While there was still plenty of light, I picked an easy way up the bluffs and rode just below the rim 'til dark. I didn't wanta be visible out in them prairies and I didn't know how far the Santa Fe Trail was from the bluffs.

We waited on the bluffs 'til it got real dark 'fore we topped out on the prairie, taking advantage of the blackness of the night. There was no moon. Nothing but the stars showed, and a cool, gentle breeze was blowing from the northwest. The stars give off enough light so's I could pick our way north 'til we come to the trail. It was easy to recognize, even in the darkness—all rutted up by wagon tracks and one thing and another.

The trail was less'n half a mile from the river, and 'bout five miles to the west of us shone a few lights that I knowed come from Dodge City. Just on this side of it I seen some campfires, and I reckoned a wagon train was camped out there. We eased across the trail in jig time and started north for a couple of miles 'fore turning west, keeping the lights of Dodge City on our left all the while.

'Bout that time the wind died down and the prairie got real quiet. We kept punching along for maybe three hours. By then I figured we'd covered a good fifteen miles westward, and the lights of Dodge was behind us. It was a gentle night on the prairie, and once or twice we stopped to listen and we could hear faint music coming from the honky-tonk joints.

One time Michelle rode up right beside me and drawed up the mare. I could see her looking towards the lights and could just make out the dim outline of her face as she gazed towards the town. It'd been a long time since that gal had talked to anybody but me. I knowed what was on her mind: She was longing for some company and human voices, and maybe she was wondering why she was out there riding along with me.

I wondered if hearing that music made her think that she could make a good living there. Being a new and pretty woman in Dodge City, everybody'd be glad to see her and chances were nobody'd ask her any questions. Any of them madams was sure to take her on in a minute. She'd get clothes and food and excitement and start making some money, instead of being stuck riding out there in the lone prairies with a hunted outlaw.

The scare of being hooked up with that fire and McIntyre's killing in Hays City'd prob'ly wore off by now. It chilled me to realize she might decide to take her chances on implication. She might just be thinking that if she turned me in, nobody'd even bother her about it. She could claim I'd kidnapped her or something. That was prob'ly the story she'd put up. Even if she didn't do that, sure as hell, if she ever got into that town, she'd spill the truth sooner or later.

I feared she was still a whore at heart, that when the chips was down she'd be looking out for her own hide 'cause she didn't have no special feeling for me. When I thought about it, I realized there weren't no reason why she should, nohow.

As we sat up there beside each other on our horses, I reached down and took hold of the sorrel mare's bridle rein just under the bit and jerked it out of Michelle's hand. Then I kicked up Piebald and started leading her horse off at a pretty good trot into the night. As much trouble as Michelle was, I decided I had to keep her with me 'til I could get far enough away so's she wouldn't do me no harm by talking.

We'd started off at a good clip. Michelle'd grabbed hold of the saddle horn and kept hollering, wanting to know what was the matter. I ignored her and kept going along at a good jog, trying to put as many miles as I could 'tween us and Dodge City 'fore we swung back to the trail.

Finally, it begun to get light. We come up over a slight rise in the prairie and in the first rays of the morning light, I seen where the trail run off to the west. There, 'bout half a mile south of it was the

Arkansas River all set about with bare-branched cottonwood trees kinda turned pink in the colors of that October dawn. From the top of that rise we could look back and just barely see the outline of the outskirts of Dodge City in the distance.

Then I stopped and saw Michelle looking back at the town with a wistful look in her eyes, and I seen the beginnings of some tears there. "That's a grubby town," I said. "That ain't no town ta be in. They tell me Taos is beautiful. They tell me they's a big ol' mountain up by it an' it's real pretty country an' the houses're all made a that Spanish 'dobe. You'll like Taos, I know ya will."

She turned back and looked at me with them beautiful, soulful eyes of hers. Even in that dawn light, they was a deep sky blue, and they was swimming in tears.

"You didn't need to tell me that. And you didn't need to take my reins away and lead Taffy all night. You didn't need to do that. I'm going where you're going, Cat, and you don't need to worry about me trying to run off."

A lump rose in my throat and I looked at her real hard. I'd never had no woman talk to me like that before. I didn't know a dance hall girl could ever talk straight like that. I wanted to lift her off that horse and hold her close and promise to always do the best I could for her. I wanted to kiss her so bad that it scared me. And when I'm scared, I get real careful. So I tried to laugh and act tough.

"Listen, baby, don't go tellin' me that yore in love with me, 'cause I'm no greenhorn ya can fool with. I'm playin' it safe an' takin' no chances."

She looked real hurt, then smiled as though I'd made a good joke. "Love? Me fall in love? I wanta see the West, and I wanta see Taos, that's all. So let's get started. One thing, though. I still need some shoes. My feet are almost froze off."

I looked down at her and for the first time I realized that she'd rode all night in her bare feet. She never did no complaining, never said nothing—but boy, I could see that her feet was almost blue.

I felt plenty ashamed when she said that, and I got down off Piebald and walked over to her and helped her down. I sat down and gently rubbed them poor little feet. "Baby, I'm real sorry. I feel like such a blockhead. I fergot all 'bout your bein' barefoot."

She sorta laughed. "I can't feel nothing no more. It don't make no difference."

"I feel kinda mean, ridin' all night an' you sufferin' like that. Here, take my boots."

"They'd be much too big for me."

"No, the way your feet are swole up now they'll be just 'bout right, an' they'll warm ya up." With that I pulled off my boots and carefully slid 'em up over her feet.

She stood up gingerly. "That makes 'em warm all right, but boy, they're beginning to hurt. Oh, they hurt terrible!"

I hugged her for being so brave, and I was burning to kiss her, but instead I lifted her back on the mare. Then I walked over towards Piebald in my stocking feet and realized how tenderfooted I was. I'd wore boots for a long time.

We headed out again, and even with the sun coming up I felt the cold sinking into my feet. What it must've been like—that girl riding all night that way! Hell, I guess I was just dumb. I hadn't been around womenfolk much. I'd mostly been all by myself. Never cared for nobody before 'cept for my amigo Pete. Never done no thinking 'bout nobody else.

We needed to get Michelle some shoes, and we was gonna get 'em damned quick. I got to thinking how we could do it. I had a rifle. Maybe I could kill an antelope, or a buckskin, or a buffalo, and make something outta the hide. Funny how if you don't have none yourself, you sure get to thinking 'bout it.

I pushed us pretty hard that morning. No sign of wagon trains or nothing. When we got within sight of some buildings up ahead— they looked pretty ramshackle from a distance—we cut over to the Arkansas and picked a path down to the riverbed and went along 'til we come to the crossings. There was tracks where wagons had gone across the river in a pretty good ford and, better yet, there weren't nobody around.

Fact was, the place looked real wild and forlorn and abandoned. To be right honest, I was a little bit disturbed to see that there wasn't no fresh crossings. It didn't look as if folks had been going across there much that summer. I'd heard talk 'bout Indian troubles south of the river—stories 'bout men who couldn't find no buffalo north of the Arkansas who'd gone down into that country and lots of 'em never come back. Some of the wagon masters felt the best and safest way to go was by the Bent's Fort ruins and on to Pueblo, the long route.

That was for wagon trains—visible for miles and miles. We was just a small party of two riders and a mule. We'd be pretty safe long as we traveled by night. We'd found us a nice safe ford to get over on the side where folks wouldn't be looking for us.

We stopped at the edge of the Arkansas to let the critters take a drink and didn't have no trouble crossing on over. I saw a good-sized grove of cottonwoods 'bout half a mile beyond the crossing and that's where we camped. It was early afternoon by then, and we sure had made one helluva ride since the evening before.

There was some good grass for the stock, so I decided to camp there for a couple of days before we hit across the open country towards the Cimarron River. Michelle fell asleep right away, and as soon as I secured the animals, I lay down close to her and don't remember moving 'til it was time for supper. We was so tired we just ate and got back into the bedroll, like we'd been on a two-day drunk.

When the sun come up we stretched ourselves and I checked the ponies over. They looked like they was in pretty fair shape. I couldn't see how I'd rode Piebald so hard and had him come right back, but it seemed like he was hardening up and doing right good. That's one thing 'bout that horse—he sure had a lot of bottom.

The sorrel mare was doing all right, too. 'Course she was in real good shape when I first got her, and Michelle couldn't have weighed more'n a hundred and ten or fifteen pounds, so she was packing light. The mule, old Blackjack, was doing fine. He was only carrying a few light supplies and half a leg of venison.

From what I knowed, I reckoned it was 'bout forty miles to the Cimarron. It might be that far 'fore we'd get to water, but I had two jugs to carry water in now and didn't need to be in no hurry. We sure could make that distance, 'specially if the stock got good water 'fore we left. I didn't see why we couldn't ride along and maybe find some kind of a hollow and make us a dry camp for the night, then head for the Cimarron the next day. We shouldn't have to push too hard. Besides, I wanted to get off into some game country—for food as well as Michelle's shoes.

Me and Michelle talked it over for a little bit. It seemed she was a little more used to the saddle and, thanks to the buckskin pants, wasn't feeling as tender as she had before. She was anxious to move on and said she really did wanta see Taos, so we decided to saddle up and start off that day. We climbed up out of the Arkansas and hit the old Cimarron cutoff out in the prairies.

There still weren't no recent traffic signs along there. It looked as if there hadn't been much along that trail all summer. It made me feel uneasy in one way on account of the Indians, but in another way I felt better, 'cause it was a damned-sure cinch that for the first time I was out of reach of a posse.

It sure was a beautiful day—a near cloudless sky stretched as far as the eye could see in every direction. We rode on across through them rolling prairie lands, with buffalo grass as far as you could see and not a single tree.

That was the beginning of about two of the best weeks I ever had in all of my life. It weren't long 'fore we got into a real game paradise, so we was never hungry. I could almost forget 'bout the things that'd just happened. It seemed like if we could avoid the Indians, our troubles was 'bout over. I knowed when I got out to Taos there wouldn't be nobody looking for me 'cept Pete.

Michelle was getting to be better company all the time. She'd got over worrying 'bout every this and that and seemed to be happy. I knowed we oughta begin traveling at night again, so's we could find some nice places to hide out in the daytime and get in some good lovemaking. It got to where I could hardly wait to snuggle up in the bedroll with Michelle. Looking back at it now, I can see it was too damn bad I didn't stick to that plan. But I didn't. Maybe it was 'cause the days was so bright and beautiful.

My first hunt was something else I'll never forget. We hadn't rode more'n ten miles into Indian territory when I seen a herd of antelope. I'd seen 'em before in Texas and up the Chisholm Trail, but I never could get over the way they run. A running antelope looks like a bird flying across the land.

There weren't no way to get a shot at long range if you tried to sneak up on 'em. But I remembered hearing how if you kept outta sight yourself and tied a bandanna onto your gun barrel and waved it, the sentinel of the herd would get so curious that he'd come within gunshot, looking to see what it was. I thought I'd give it a try.

The first bunch that we seen was 'bout a mile away. They blended into the prairie so well that their white rumps looked like rocks in the distance. By the time I spotted 'em, they'd had a real good look at us, and they lit out.

Michelle got all excited and hollered. "Look at 'em run!"

When we last seen 'em, they was maybe five miles away and crossing some hills in the distance.

Late in the afternoon we topped a little rise and I seen another herd feeding in a basin 'bout a mile and a quarter to our right. There was a stretch of grass that was greener than the rest, maybe from some underground water. There was a bunch feeding there, looking real easy, and I thought maybe I might have some luck.

We turned and cut back off the rise that we'd just crossed and started working upwind towards 'em. When I figured I was within 'bout half a mile of 'em I got down off Piebald, took out the rifle, and had Michelle hold the horses.

"Ol' Piebald won't give me no trouble when I shoot," I told her, "but I don't know 'bout that Taffy an' Blackjack. I wouldn't be a bit s'prised but what they might spook a little bit. Ya'd better hold 'em tight an' stay right there. I'll see if'n I can get us an antelope."

I kept in a running crouch just below the ridge and then got down on my hands and knees and peered over the crest. My heart give a big leap. I was within four hundred yards of the herd.

I lay there for a few minutes watching and thinking. I knowed I couldn't crawl down the slope and get to 'em. Most of 'em was feeding and they seemed to be undisturbed. The sentinel stood off to the right a little bit up a higher ridge. He hadn't seen me.

By God, I thought, there's our commissary for the next couple a days, if'n I handle it right. I didn't know how old Sullivan's rifle shot. In fact I wondered if'n that greenhorn had any idea how a rifle was properly sighted in. I just had to take the chance.

I took off my hat, put it on the barrel, held it up in the air, and let it rock in the breeze. Pretty soon that sentinel antelope swung 'round and looked my way. He stood looking and looking and looking and didn't give no alarm to the rest of the herd. I let the hat wave a little bit—back and forth, back and forth. That antelope must've stood there for at least ten minutes.

I kept thinking, is this gonna work? I figured if he gave the alarm and the herd started running, I'd be able to nick one of 'em 'fore they got out of range. I didn't know the range of that rifle, but I reckoned it'd be good up to four hundred yards if I give it enough lift. I'd be much surer if'n I could get that sentinel to come within 'bout two hundred yards of me. If that rifle was shooting right, I figured we'd eat royally that night.

After 'bout ten minutes of steady staring, sure enough that little animal took ten or twelve real quick steps in my direction with his head and his ears perked up. I lay real quiet. I didn't let the hat move none for a couple of minutes. Then I moved the rifle barrel back and forth 'til the hat got to rocking again.

Just like I'd hoped, that antelope took another ten or twelve steps closer. My heart was really thumping. He stopped and looked for a minute, and the rest of the herd stopped feeding and looked up, watching the sentinel. I moved the hat a little bit more and they all saw it and froze. Seemed like it was an age 'fore the sentinel took another quick run and stopped to look. His tail was twitching, and sometimes he'd stand with one forefoot off the ground, trying to sniff the air. 'Course I was downwind and he weren't gonna get no smell of me.

Pretty soon the sentinel come another twelve or fifteen steps towards me. I didn't move and I could hardly breathe. He took another few steps and paused and waited a long time. It looked to me like nothing was gonna happen. After a while, I rocked the hat some more and again he come closer.

There was a little shimmy of heat from the sun on the buffalo grass, and it seemed as if the image of that animal kept swaying like a mirage. It weren't quite clear, so I kept waiting and waiting. I moved the hat again, and he responded real nice. He'd move up some, then he'd wait. Then he'd put his head down like he was gonna graze— like he was trying to fool me, or whatever, a little bit. Finally, he raised his head and moved forward just one step at a time, real slow and steady. This time he didn't stop.

He kept coming on and on and on and on. I watched silently. When it seemed like he was in range, he stopped and looked again. I could see all the rest of the herd standing there watching him. I figured the distance to be 'bout two hundred fifty yards. He was looking straight at me.

He was stopped on a gentle swell of the prairie, and when he started towards me again, the main part of his body went down outta sight, but his head was still showing and I watched him keep coming on. Then he come up to the top of the swell, dead ahead of me at 'bout two hundred yards. He was walking real slow—ears pricked up high—and he started down the slope of that ridge and paused.

'Bout then I figured he weren't gonna give me no sideways shot, so's I'd better take what I could get. I slowly let the rifle down 'til the rim of the hat touched the ground. Then I eased the barrel out from under the hat and put my left hand underneath the barrel forward of the trigger guard. I laid my cheek on the stock and drawed the gun tight into my shoulder 'til the bead was right in the dead center of the notch on the sight. I could barely see the bead. Then I eased it up a little bit to allow for dropping at two hundred yards and beaded out just where his neck met his chest.

I squeezed off real slow, not knowing when the trigger was gonna pull, 'cause I'd never shot that rifle before. It went off with a roar and a kick, and that antelope leaped high up into the air and fell over dead. I let out a whoop and jumped up, and the rest of the herd lit outta there. They was gone in a cloud—they just sailed away.

I run up to that antelope thinking, boy! this rifle shoots better'n I figgered it would. 'Bout then I stepped on something that set my foot afire. I bellered and stopped to pull a couple of cactus spines outta my feet. Then I walked real slow and gingerlike up to where that little pronghorned buck was lying. He was drilled dead center of where I'd aimed.

I motioned to Michelle, who was waiting a good ways back, to come up with the horses, then I got out my knife and cut the buck's throat to bleed him, although it looked like the bullet wound'd pretty near busted the jugular. I bled him good, dressed him out, and had him pretty neared ready for skinning by the time Michelle got there.

She took one look and backed away.

I had to laugh. "Hey, honey, here's your new shoes—an' a feast fer tonight, too."

Silence. "Looks like this rifle's shootin' straight, anyhow," I went on. "That's the important thing. I wanta skin this thing out so's we've got the hide fer your footgear. We got plenty a food here, just the heart and the lungs was the only thing got shot up. The bullet didn't even get back inta the guts, so it looks like we ain't spoilt no meat a'tall. The hindquarters and back strap—that's these fine strips a meat along both sides a the backbone—is in real good shape, an' it looks as if the front quarters is all right."

Michelle stuck out one big-booted foot. "Footgear? Better make it for yourself, remember? I'm wearing your boots."

"Oh, no ya ain't. Not if'n I make ya a good pair a antelope booties. 'Sides, them boots is too big fer ya, the way I see 'em."

She tossed her head with a know-it-all smile. "Oh, I don't think so. Of course, I have to take three or four steps before they start moving, but they seem pretty comfortable. But I suppose I can let you have them back."

I skinned out that antelope in a hurry and butchered him, stacking the hindquarters in one side of the panniers on the mule, and the shoulders and the back strap on the other side. Then I stretched out the hide and looked over at Michelle. "I wish I either had some salt ta cure this hide or you was a good Injun squaw an' could chew it 'til it was soft."

She made a face.

I throwed the hide over the top of the packsaddle, hair side down, so's it'd dry in the sun. I told Michelle we'd keep going 'til nightfall and make a dry camp. When we got to the Cimarron the next evening, I figured we'd set up a real good camp.

It was late in the afternoon. We hadn't rode very long when I seen a grove of trees around what looked like a kind of spring. If there was water, there was likely to be a campground. I figured we'd better be damned careful so's we didn't just walk up on an Indian camp. I stopped and looked at them trees for nigh unto half an hour and didn't see no sign of life—no smoke, nothing in any direction. 'Course I'd been keeping a sharp eye out for any Indian pony tracks or something like that on the trail—like moccasin sign—and I hadn't seen nothing.

When we come up on the grove of trees, it looked like it'd been for sure an old camping place. I looked it over real careful. It didn't appear there'd been any Indians there since the early part of the summer. A little spring pool had seeped up by them cottonwoods and there was some kinda water grass 'round it. It weren't a very hefty spring, but it was prob'ly enough for us and the stock. I filled the coffeepot and our jugs again and then let the stock go at it. When they was through there was hardly any water left.

I made a fire and put on some of that antelope meat, then I put the mare on a tether rope and hobbled the mule and Piebald. I put the fire out when it got dark 'cause I figured it weren't smart to have a fire at night in the middle of Indian territory. I told Michelle it was on account of the fact a posse might see it.

We was up before daybreak again the next morning. We got a cold start and was in the saddle by the time the daylight broke. We made that twenty miles to the Cimarron easy and by midday we come in sight of the river. I knowed once we got to it, all we'd have to do was follow it right on up to its headwaters and cross from there on over the mountains to Taos.

When we hit the Cimarron River, I looked real careful for Indian sign, but I didn't see nothing. Things looked good, so I scouted out a nice secluded place to bed down 'tween some bluffs so's we could keep a fire going all night.

Then I set to work on that antelope hide. I rolled it 'round in the sand enough so's it was good and clean and soft, then I took a sliver outta one of the leg bones and made a big needle. I cut some strips off the edge of the hide for laces, and with my knife I drawed the outline of each of Michelle's feet on the hide.

I cut away the pieces like I figured they'd fold and made two sides and a tongue, and some more pieces for padding the soles on the inside and fastening the parts above the ankle. When I got through, I had some pretty fair moccasins. Considering that it was my first try at it, I don't think I done half-bad. They wouldn't be the pride of no Indian squaw, but they was something for Michelle's feet and, what's more, I could get my boots back.

I showed her how to put 'em on and stood back for a good look. Them moccasins come clear up to the calf of her leg and they laced all the way up and tied around in pretty good fashion. With her buckskin pants and her antelope boots and her blue shirt and her pioneer bonnet, why, she was looking all right.

We got to talking that night around the fire and I told her that we was gonna need some winter coats. It'd be into November or later 'fore we started crossing them mountains, and we might just get ourselves into a snowstorm. I told her to keep a sharp eye out for buffalo. I figured if'n we could knock us down a buffalo we'd for sure have something warm.

The next morning it was again a real beautiful day. We started up the Cimarron and both of us was feeling pretty good. Michelle was acting lighthearted, asking if every distant rock was a buffalo. But she was the first to spy two black specks over to our left, 'bout a mile away from the river. When we come up on 'em a little bit more, I seen they was two buffalo bulls. There was some cows farther off to the left, and some calves. We rode on and looked out over the plains, and it seemed there was a scattering of maybe several hundred of 'em. What's more, we seen more bands of antelope.

To keep outta sight, we kept going up the creek. A white-tailed buck got outta the creek bed and went crashing up into one of the dry draws, but I didn't shoot. I figured I'd rather get me a buffalo cow and a calf. They'd make good tender meat, and their coats was beginning to get ready for the winter. I left Michelle and the mule in a good spot and rode up to scout out the herd. They kept on grazing and paid no attention to me.

When I got within six hundred yards of 'em I ground-tied old Piebald and went forward in a low crouch 'til I finally got to a ridgelike place. Then I crawled on my belly to within four hundred yards of the herd. A buffalo is a big target—lots different from an antelope. I figured I could do all right at that distance. The rifle packed a good wallop, although it weren't no real buffalo gun. If I watched real careful for the nearest cow and calf and picked the ones I wanted, I'd wait 'til they worked their way 'round broadside. I hoped if I put down the cow, the calf'd stay with her for a minute—long enough for me to get another shot at it.

I drawed down real careful. From what I knowed 'bout the Winchesters I'd seen, I guessed I had 'bout a thirty-two-inch drop at that distance. There was a place on a buffalo right about at the shoulder joint that'd make for a real paralyzing shot. Otherwise, if I aimed a little bit lower, it'd be a heart shot all right, but the critter might run quite a ways.

I took careful aim and squeezed one off. When the rifle kicked I could see that buffalo cow jerk up her head real high, and I knowed I'd pasted one right into her. She didn't go down right away and, with the crack of the rifle, the rest of the cows and calves started trundling off. She started away with 'em, but only run a little way 'fore she folded up and fell over. Her calf done just like I wanted. He pulled up short and waited for her while I took real careful aim at him. I figured he must've been five hundred yards out, but I was gonna test that rifle. By God, it done right good with a forty-five-inch lift. It laid him right down.

Michelle come up with the horses and we went on down and

collected our buffalo. The cow was in good shape and so was the calf. Michelle, as usual, didn't wanta have nothing to do with the whole operation, and it took me mosta the afternoon to skin and dress out them carcasses.

Since we hadn't gone more'n four miles from where we'd camped before, we went back and set up again. We made us a nice fire and had a real pleasant time of it. After dark we sat around and watched the stars. Everything was going good and it didn't seem like there'd be no trouble a'tall.

The next morning, when we started out in earnest, we had a good supply of meat. Them buffalo hides heaped across old Blackjack made him look a little like a buffalo hisself. We went on up the Cimarron, making 'bout twenty miles a day, camping whenever we seen fit. It was beautiful weather and we seen herds of game on every side. We never lacked for nothing.

I kept a sharp watch for Indian sign and never seen a thing. Not a single sign—no tracks or nothing. I got the idea that the Indians'd left this country for good.

One morning when we was starting out I hollered at Michelle, "By God, honey—look!"

We brought our horses up short and sat there staring off to the west. In the distance we could see the snow line of a string of beautiful mountain peaks. "Them's the Rocky Mountains," I said. "Ain't they somethin'? Them's really the Rockies!"

"They look beautiful, but they got lots of snow on them. And they look awful high."

"Don't worry none, honey. They's passes through 'em an' we ain't goin' up in that high, snowy stuff. But they got pine forests, an' meadows, an' real nice streams with trout in 'em. It's gonna be great. There prob'ly won't be no buffalo, though, so's we'd better kill us another one 'fore we get outta here. We could always use another warm buffalo robe at night."

A good, happy feeling welled up in me. "Them's the Rocky Mountains, honey, an' we're on our way."

The country begun to change, and each day them mountains would stand in front of us, getting a little bit closer. We got out of the rolling prairie country and into a rougher land of broken mesas—them small, flat-topped mountains that look like tabletops.

When we drawed close to 'em we got into some scattered oak

brush and piñon pine. Some of them mesas had steep, rocky cliffs up near the top, with ribbons of different-colored rocks. It sure was pretty country. One morning I seen the finest band of elk I'd ever laid eyes on, spread out on the lower slopes of a mesa and over the plains a ways. There must've been three or four thousand head in that bunch. 'Course a man don't see nothing like that these days. It was a wonderment to behold.

They was all busy feeding and didn't pay no attention to us. I could've busted one of 'em if I'd wanted, but we was okay for meat and I hated to spoil the sight. Also, I was getting anxious to get up in them mountains, 'cause I knowed that the Comanche and Kiowa didn't cotton to that country. They was mostly plains Indians.

It was 'bout three o'clock that afternoon that I decided to get outta the creek bottom and ride up on top of a mesa that was running along to our right to have a good look around. It was a long mesa, and high—maybe three or four hundred feet higher'n the prairie—but we made our way up without no trouble. Way off towards the south a series of small mesas stretched out in the distance. Looking down there, I thought I seen some smoke. It was hard to tell. I sure wished I'd had some field glasses like them cavalry fellas used. I asked Michelle if she could tell.

"I don't think so. Why are you looking for smoke?"

I told her there must be some buffalo hunters down there or something, but I knowed there weren't. If it was smoke, it was more likely an Indian camp or maybe a small village. I never did see nothing more all afternoon. We dropped back down in the Cimarron Valley, and when I made camp that night, I set it up against one of them clay bluffs and made a real small fire.

Next morning early we headed on up the Cimarron. We rode along for 'bout four hours, and I kept looking out ahead. The river'd got kinda small up in that country. It stretched along the south side of a big old mesa on our right and wandered on towards them mountains that was looking bigger and better all the time. Maybe the Cimarron come out of a valley there in them mountains. I was sure anxious to get up there. I knowed that I'd feel better when I did.

Then, by God, I suddenly seen something. 'Bout half a mile ahead of us was a gentle riverbank that showed signs of recent traffic. When we come up on it, there was just what I didn't wanta find—recent tracks from a lot of unshod ponies. Chills run up and down my spine.

It was a bunch of Indians, a big village on the move: travois tracks and dog tracks—even some little foot tracks in the sand where children'd been running alongside. There was bits and pieces of litter—little chunks of rawhide and potsherds. Them Indians must've been moving cross-country at a pretty good clip. I reckoned that nigh unto two hundred had crossed there, and judging from the looks of the horse dung, not too long ago.

"Michelle," I said, "foller me, quick."

"What for?"

"I'll tell ya when we get there. Come on."

We trotted back into the cottonwood grove and I tied up our horses and unsaddled 'em 'fore I eased the panniers off the mule. Michelle waited 'til I was done and asked again, "Cat, why are we stopping?"

"Them tracks 'cross the river. We're gonna stay right here 'til it gets dark. From now on we're travelin' in the dark an' we ain't lightin' no fires."

Her eyes was big with fright.

"I think we'll be safe if'n we lay low an' don't show ourselves fer a spell. Them Injuns got eyes like hawks an' they can see any movement 'cross the prairie. We still got a good ways ta go 'fore we reach the mountains."

Her lips quivered. "I'm getting scared."

I told Michelle to sleep, but I think she mostly pretended. Anyhow, we lay there in the trees during the rest of the afternoon and waited for dark. Just before we saddled up and pushed off, I got out a few pieces of buffalo jerky for us to chew on while we was riding. We could get water outta the river anytime. Jerky goes a long ways if'n you eat it slow and drink a little water afterwards, 'cause it swells up inside your stomach.

We eased along the river during the night and I wanta tell you, if you ain't never rode through Indian country in the dark, you ain't never truly felt scared. Every bush, every little tree, every rock takes on a strange shape. Every minute you expect some war whoop or sudden rush at you, and even if you know it's all in your imaginings it don't help none to keep you from being jumpy.

We'd cross some open stretches for maybe a mile, then come up to a bunch of cottonwoods. I wouldn't know if there was Indians camped there or not, so I'd pick a careful way around to the next open stretch, and so we went on to the next one and the next one.

A quarter moon come up before dawn. It was a pale one, just a crescent in the eastern sky, but it lit the area a little bit and made them shadows even worse.

I kept checking my .38 in the holster and I carried the rifle on my arm, with sixteen shots in the magazine, a shell in the chamber, and the safety on, ready to go. I eased Piebald along real quiet and slow, and every now and then I'd glance back to see how Michelle and old Blackjack was coming.

Close to dawn, we come up on a good-sized bunch of cotton-woods. It looked like it might be a good safe place to hide. I figured one more night like this and we'd make it to the mountains. The thin gleam of moonlight on the bare trees looked like a hundred ghosts.

A hoot owl cried out in the distance, and I heard his mate answer close by. We come to a little open place with a big old tree and a pile of leaves and stuff right at the base of it, and I figured that was a good place for us. When we dismounted, another hoot let go. Both of us jumped, but then we snickered, 'cause it was just another of them old owls.

I really didn't wanta unsaddle the stock—I was afraid we might have to leave in a hurry. Hell, I thought, I ain't gonna outrun no Injuns. Not with a woman an' a pack mule. What I better make sure is that none a them horses breaks down.

I unsaddled Piebald and Taffy and rubbed 'em pretty good. I fixed up a picket line for 'em, then took our buffalo robe and laid it out on the leaves beside the horses. I got out the bedroll and we made ourselves comfortable.

I'm an old man now, and I know that was a mistake. Damn! I should've knowed that if they was Indians 'round they'd be looking for horses, and next to your horses was the worst place to camp. We should've left the stock there and gone on foot maybe a quarter of a mile and camped there. Then my life would've turned out a lot different. But when I was young, I weren't that smart. I only thought I was, which is dangerous.

Anyway, me and Michelle was lying there alongside that big cottonwood. I could see a few stars, and a pale crescent moon was sticking up through the branches. I was still a little edgy. I couldn't sleep none and I sure didn't feel like making love to Michelle. So I just lay there.

I got to thinking 'bout my shooting. Suddenly it come to me. I weren't a half-bad shot. I'd killed that buffalo cow an' that calf and that antelope all at a pretty good distance.

Then I got to thinking some more. How could I have done that good? I'd done some shootin', but I'd never compared myself to no one else. I hadn't realized that I was such a good shot. I thought back over how it felt when I fired my .38 revolver. It was then that I realized I could see a shaft of light stretchin' from my eye to the dead center of a target. An' another shaft from the gun to the target. Why, it made a perfect triangle! An' wherever the point a that triangle touched, that's where my bullet hit.

I've thought a lot 'bout that since, and it's true. Whenever I shot a handgun, I could see that imaginary triangle. Whenever I shot a rifle, I just squeezed the sides of that triangle down to one line and got the same results. I was a helluva shot—and fast. I never missed. That was what folks called a "dead gun."

I was thinking along them lines as I half-dozed away. Michelle was breathing kinda regular, but I knowed she weren't asleep. Then I felt her nudge me.

"What's that?" she said. "What's that?"

"It's nothin' ta worry 'bout, honey," I whispered. "Them ol' owls is hootin' up a storm tonight. Must be the sickle moon." Then another soft hoot come from across the clearing.

I started to shift and roll over and then . . . boy! The hair stood up on the back of my neck. Hoot owls don't answer each other at the same level of call. If one owl hoots, the answer comes back a note lower. The breath went outta my body. I felt cold all over and my mouth got dry. God almighty, it was Indians!

I listened real sharp for 'bout another ten seconds. Then I reached up and put my hand over Michelle's mouth. I put my lips up next to her ear and whispered, "Keep real quiet an' ease in under this bush with me."

I could feel her gasp and knowed that if I hadn't held my hand over her mouth she would've let out a scream. I could feel her trembling all over, shaking like a leaf. I eased in there real quiet and tucked her back in behind me. I had my rifle and revolver, and I took that Smith & Wesson outta the holster and cocked its hammer back and lay there propped up on one elbow, just listening.

It's at times like that when a man's eyes see uncommon well and his hearing gets better than it ever was before. I seen Piebald raise his head in the moonlight and turn and look to the right.

I kept listening and listening, and once I heard a faint sound. I couldn't tell if it was a little wind or whether it was something moving in the leaves and brush. It was just the faintest sound, nothing else.

Five minutes went by, then ten, then twenty. Finally it growed a tiny bit lighter, like the dawn was 'bout to break. I seen Piebald shift his hindquarters and move again and look. Then it was quiet. There weren't no crickets. No hoot owls. No sound of a breeze. I couldn't even hear the running water in the creek.

Then I seen it. Just a dim outline, moving like a snake—just one quick movement. I knowed then it was time. I drawed down right where I expected it was and squeezed the trigger, and that Smith & Wesson let out a roar.

Michelle screamed and a yell come outta the bushes. Then it seemed like there was a thousand yells, coming in from all sides. I thought I seen three braves—one on the left and one in the middle and one right behind us.

What got me—and I ain't never gonna forget it—was the way they looked as they rose up half-naked outta the grass in their buffalo-horned helmets with their faces painted black, their war sign of death. It was the first Comanche war party I'd ever seen, and in that dim light it was terrifying. Them bastards looked like horned devils from hell, and I soon found out that they acted like it, too.

I leaped up and killed all three of 'em in a flash. Then I spun 'round and gutshot another one that was moving off to my right. I'd guessed that there was maybe four or five of 'em, but that was a sad mistake. There was more like twenty, and they swarmed all over me. I went down in a heap under the whole writhing bunch.

CHILDREN OF THE DEVIL

Lots of folks've said at one time or another that one white man could whip two Indians. But I always figured it as most likely being the other way 'round. Comanche bucks in the wild was the greatest athletes you ever seen. Man, you don't know how quick and strong they was, how wiry and slippery. Them bodies of theirs was so hard and greasy, and God, how they could stink!

They took me down hard and it was like being held by a pile of powerful snakes. I could feel their arms and legs around me, and smell and hear their hoarse, hard breathing. I kept kicking and twisting and biting 'til I felt a whack on the head and then I seen stars and nothing else.

I don't know how long I was out. It must've been a while, though, 'cause it was broad daylight when I finally come to. I was lying face down in the leaves by the cottonwoods and I had a deep, dull pain in my head and real sharp pains in my arms. Then I seen that I was hog-tied. My arms was pulled 'round behind me, tied so tight I thought it was gonna tear 'em out of the sockets. Them rawhide thongs was wrapped from my wrist clear up to my elbows so tight, my hands was numb.

They had my feet tied up tight, too. The only thing I could do was bend my knees and move both feet together. I was to learn lots more 'bout it as time went on—that awful feeling of your arms going to sleep on you, your hands and fingers swelling up and getting numb, the agony of not being able to move.

Out of the corner of my eye I seen the moccasined foot and bare legs of one of them bucks. I looked up and seen a breechclout and a rifle and I realized he was standing guard just two feet from me. When he seen me try to move and twist my head and look up, he pulled back and gave me one helluva kick in the side of my ribs. He kicked like a mule, and it plumb knocked the air outta me and left me gasping.

As I was getting my breath, I heard them varmints talking and laughing, so I twisted my face around in the leaves and looked outta my right eye. There I seen something awful.

Four or five of them bucks was gathered 'round in a rough half-circle. Two big old bucks was holding Michelle. One of 'em had her hair twisted 'round his hand, and her head was jerked back so's she was looking straight up in the air with her mouth wide open. Her eyeballs was turned back so's just the whites of her eyes was showing.

The other buck was holding Michelle's arms in back of her real tight, forcing her hands almost down to her knees. They'd pulled off her blue shirt, and the way they had her bent 'round, her breasts was standing out real clear in the morning light.

They'd slid her buckskin britches down below her knees so's they was hanging from the tops of her antelope boots. The other bucks was laughing and poking at her, pinching and feeling her all over. One of 'em had his knife out and was making motions like he was gonna slit her throat or cut off her tits. Her whole body was shaking.

I thought for a minute they was gonna kill her right there. I felt so sick at that, I could hardly breathe. But I couldn't stop watching. Pretty soon the buck that was holding her by the hair give a big jerk and spun her 'round and let her fall down on the leaves. She let out a sob. Then the other buck who'd been holding her stepped over and give her a big kick in the back of her ribs. She rolled back and forth, screaming with pain while all of 'em laughed.

Another one stepped up and give her a kick. Then they all took turns kicking her back and forth, rolling her 'round naked in the leaves with them buckskin britches dragging down past her ankles, and all the time she was screaming a high shriek.

Real soon them bucks, tired of their fun, started to scatter. One stayed there by Michelle with his rifle in his hand and his foot on her head. Then two of 'em come over to me and grabbed me by the hair, jerking me to my feet. For the first time, I realized they'd taken away my shirt and stripped me to the waist. Half-rotted leaves and twigs was stuck to my belly along with the blood that'd come oozing out of my head.

I didn't get a chance to see much more, 'cause one of them bucks clapped a big piece of deer hide over my head and tied it 'round my throat so's my head was in a bag and I couldn't see nothing. The last thing I did see was Michelle reaching down to try to pull up her britches to cover her nakedness. The buck took his foot off her head. He had a leather horse quirt tied to his wrist and he took it and give her a helluva slice on her butt with the full force of his arm. She let out a scream. Then he kicked her in the middle of her back. That time she just groaned and lay real still. Then that bag come down over my head and I couldn't see nothing.

Somebody with a knife cut out slots for my nose and mouth in the buckskin hood so's I could breathe, but he weren't too gentle 'bout it and he sliced my lip. At least I knowed I weren't gonna suffocate.

He untied the thongs 'round my legs and prodded me forward with kicks and blows on the back of my head and shoulders with a stick. I figured they was gonna walk me off somewhere and kill me. Then I got a strong whiff of mule, and realized that I was standing by old Blackjack. Several of them bucks hoisted me up astride 'Jack and tied my ankles together under his belly.

I didn't know what they done to Michelle, but I heard some commotion and then I heard her sobbing, so I knowed she was still alive. I figured if they was fixing to do us any more harm right then, they wouldn't have put me on the mule. It looked like we was gonna travel.

It was only a few minutes 'fore I heard horses moving 'round, and one of them bucks rode up behind me and gave old 'Jack a cut with his quirt. 'Jack give two real hard jumps. When you're sitting on a mule bareback with your feet cinched underneath the belly and he takes a sudden jump, it feels like your back is broke.

I lost my balance and damn near swung down underneath the mule's belly, but just managed to keep from doing it. Then a new thought come to me: I remembered my daddy reading me the story of

Nelson Lee, and my fears was confirmed. We was in the hands of wild Comanches—the worst thing that can happen to any man.

Nelson Lee was a Texas Ranger. In the late '50s he got took by a Comanche war party on the Staked Plains in Texas. That's the region they called the Llano Estacado. Most of it was south of the Canadian River. The Comanches took Lee prisoner and traveled clear 'cross Mexico. He returned like someone back from the dead three years later and even lived to write a book about it.

Everybody on the big river knowed the story of Nelson Lee. It was common knowledge along the frontier, too, 'cause them folks that'd never read it'd heard others tell 'bout the god-awful things them Comanches done to Lee.

When they first captured him, they put a hood over his head and cut out nose and mouth slots—just like they done with me. Then they put him on a mule with his hands tied behind his back, him and the four other Rangers who was with him, each one tied on real tight with rawhide thongs under the bellies of their mules.

The party'd ride long distances during the day and them prisoners couldn't see nothing. When they'd go through rough country—piñon and oak brush and cedars—Lee told how, with the hood over his head, he couldn't see nothing, and when a bough'd crack him across the face or in the chest, he'd swing 'round under the mule's belly. The mule'd stop right quick. If he'd been tied on a horse and that'd happened, the horse would've kicked him to death and ended the fun. But the mule, being smarter, stopped moving. All of them bucks'd laugh and make fun of him. Then they'd get off and swing him back up again and on he'd go, waiting for the next bump.

Well, as soon as we got out of that cottonwood grove we'd be in open prairie and there wouldn't be no tree branches to knock me 'round. If I could lay low along the back of that old mule's neck 'til we was out of them cottonwoods, I'd have a pretty fair chance of not having my teeth busted in, so I stayed real low 'til it sounded like we was clear of the trees.

That was one helluva day in my life. There ain't no words to tell of a man's despair when he finds hisself the way I was, the captive of some cruel, stinking savages, not knowing where he's going, sure that they're just saving him for the torture.

It was in this state that I begun to hark back to everything I knowed or had heard 'bout the Comanche nation. As we was riding along, I begun to think. 'Course like all boys on the Mississippi, I'd heard tell of that terrible Indian nation far to the southwest—Indians that was called Comanches.

Comancheria, Comanche land, stretched in an almost thousand-mile circle from the Arkansas River on the north to the Balcones Escarpment down in south Texas, east to the lower Brazos, and west to the Rio Grande and some parts of Mexico. I heard tell that the Comanches'd occupied that territory for a thousand years and that, being as tough as they was—terrible fighters, cruel and ruthless—they'd even drove off the Lipan Apaches to the west and the cannibal Karankawas to the south.

One thing for sure, their presence'd blocked the advance of the Spanish people in Texas and Mexico for almost two hundred years, and when I'd come onto 'em, the advance of the American people at that time'd been blocked for nigh unto forty years—from the time that Texas'd become an independent republic in 1836.

During that time there was constant warfare and atrocities along the border. When I was in Texas in late '66, the folks there'd told me that for the last thirty years there'd been at least two hundred white captives a year took by the Comanches. The nation was made up of four tribes. Down south of the Balcones Escarpment along the Gulf Coast Plain was the Peichkas Teichas, the Fish Eaters. North of them was the Sata Teichas, the Dog Eaters. North of them was the Co-cho Teichas, or Buffalo Eaters.

The fourth tribe was the Quohadi Teichas, the Antelope Eaters. After the treaty of Medicine Lodge, the Antelope Eaters was the only tribe that was still out wild and raising hell on the frontier. It was their territory that I'd been stupid enough to come across with poor Michelle. Now we was in their hands.

It weren't no comfort to think back on what I'd heard happened to the captives. I remember hearing lots of stories when I was in San Antone, but I put them down to just frontier talk. It seemed like in them early days, from say 1836 on up to just 'fore the War of the Rebellion, Texans was so harassed by them bastard Comanches that they formed a military frontier force called the Texas Rangers.

The Comanches was a real power in them days—some said as many as fifty thousand—and they didn't think nothing of making big raids on the white settlements. If it hadn't been for them Rangers, there prob'ly wouldn't have been no Texas to speak of, for they was the real busters of the Comanche nation in the long run. But experiencing what the Rangers went through, you could get some idea of the kind of fiends that they was fighting for forty years.

I remember hearing tell 'bout Captain Adam Zumwalt's Ranger Company back in 1840, when he was trailing some Comanches who'd made a raid 'round Victoria. He found the body of a white man, and the soles of his feet'd been sliced off by his torturers. He'd been shredded real fine and tied by his wrists and made to run behind a horse on his raw, bloody feet for miles across cactus country before he fell, exhausted. Then them sons-of-bitching Comanches'd shot and scalped him.

In the mid-1840s, Chief Buffalo Hump and a thousand followers raided the frontier and circled the town of Victoria, then they went on down to Linville on the coast and drove off the settlers. They'd escaped by taking boats out to sea. When them Indians got through plundering the warehouses and was riding home wearing stovepipe hats and all kinds of ribbons and junk that they'd found and didn't know what to make of, they took with 'em a band of captives. What happened to them poor devils was part of the enragement of the Texas people.

One of the captives, Mrs. Hibbons, had been took with her whole family. Her husband and brother'd been killed and she'd been took off with their two young 'uns, a boy and a baby girl. The girl cried so much that a Comanche warrior took her by the feet and bashed her brains out against a tree. Then they took Mrs. Hibbons and stripped her naked and made her march along the banks of the Brazos River.

A bad sleet storm struck the band and the Comanches took shelter by the riverbank. They didn't tie up Mrs. Hibbons, thinking she'd never try to escape, naked as she was, in the face of a blizzard. But they didn't count on the courage of that fine woman. She slipped off in the night and run for miles down the riverbank 'til she come to a Ranger camp. They put clothes on her there and, after she got quieted down and weren't so hysterical, they got the story outta her. They rushed back and hit the Comanche encampment at dawn, killing some of 'em and rescuing the boy.

As I rode along on the mule with my hands tied behind my back and the hood over my face, I was sure longing for a company of Texas Rangers, but that was a hopeless proposition, for they was damn near six hundred miles to the south.

*   *   *

It was right after the Linville Raid that mosta the terrible things
happened that made the war 'tween the whites and the Comanches a
lasting proposition. The whites called for a meeting with the Comanche chiefs in San Antone so's they could work a trade for the
white prisoners they held. Them stupid Comanches only brought in
one white girl: the Lockhart girl. She was only sixteen, but she'd been
so bad abused that they come to make the biggest mistake in the
history of the Comanche nation. The poor girl'd underwent all kinds
of torture and sex abuse, but, worse of all, her nose'd been cut off and
she presented a hideous appearance. There weren't no doubt that she
was broke in spirit and that her life'd been ruined and that her
disfigurement'd never allow her to live right or happy again.

That'd made them San Antone whites so damned mad that when
they got the chiefs there for the powwow in a courtyard, they surrounded 'em all with riflemen and said that the only way they was
gonna free 'em was for them to give up all the rest of their prisoners.
Them Comanche chiefs, being wild dogs, started screaming and
hollering and wielding their tomahawks. There was a helluva fight
and the whole thing turned into a massacre, with most all of them
chiefs being killed along with quite a few whites.

That branch of the Co-cho Teichas, the Buffalo Eaters, never did
recover from the loss of their chiefs, but the revenge they'd took on
them white captives they'd still held—most of 'em young women and
children—was typical of what a bunch of bastards they really was.
They staked out them poor victims naked. Then one by one, they'd
begun torturing 'em to death with fire and knives. Them poor inno-
cents took a couple of days to die, screaming in the moonlight under
the bloody knives of them vicious Comanches.

The Lockhart girl's kid sister was one of the victims who died
crying wildlike with the rest. After that, there weren't never no peace
'tween the Texas people and the Comanches.

The fury of the Texans against the Comanches was so great that
there weren't no Comanche reservation in Texas. The Texans figured
that a dead Comanche was the only good one, and there weren't no
use making no provisions for 'em. In my present condition, I could
understand their point of view.

As far as I ever heard, the Comanche weren't much for ceremonies.

Men and women mated like animals when the time come, and burial ceremonies, so far as I knowed, just plain didn't exist. They sure as hell didn't seem to have no respect for their elders or the dead. Most Indian tribes had traditions, and some of 'em was quite noble. But the Comanche, to my knowledge, didn't have none.

Old people, when they become too weak to travel, was clubbed to death and left by the trail or, even worse, abandoned alive to the prairie wolves. Mercy was an unknowed quality in the Comanche nation. There weren't any of 'em that would've knowed what it meant or how to use it. Even worse was the Comanche's devotion to torture above all Indian nations—in fact, I s'pose, above all nations on earth.

Comanches always turned the squaws loose on a prisoner first. Them squaws was expert with obsidian knives. They'd been using 'em all their lives and they knowed how to cut so's to keep from hitting an artery or anything that'd kill a man—to keep him going for a long time. They was patient and knowing when it come to finding nerve endings that'd hurt the most and they went slow and easy to keep the prisoner alive, stretching it out for hours, even days. They'd torture 'til a body made its last twisting spasm of life and then think their job was well done. They weren't in no hurry. They enjoyed their work—seemed to get a mystic excitement out of it. I filled my mind up with protective hate, thinking of all the terrible things I'd like to do to 'em.

'Course as I've said before, most Indian nations had some form of torture for their captives but, in most cases, such happenings was carried on against warrior prisoners only and was conducted in a respectful way that honored their death song. But with the Comanches, torture was inflicted on all prisoners 'bout equal.

In some cases I'd heard of, though, squaws—outta jealousy— tortured female captives worse'n any of 'em. Fact is, them squaws seemed to get almost like they was sex-stirred by what they was doing.

Way back in the 1840s when the U.S. dragoons was working along the Santa Fe Trail as far as Bent's Fort, they was all kinds of people that'd come into contact with the Comanches—mountain men, fur traders, and the military. If them whites wasn't from Texas and was moving along the Santa Fe Trail, chances was they might get involved in a trading powwow with Comanche tribesmen without coming to blows.

Some white prisoners, mostly females, was ransomed that way. But lots of times the whites found that the Comanche captives wasn't for sale. The ones that was bought off bore testimony to the treatment that they'd had at the hands of their captors.

When a man's in a jam like that, he'll begin to think 'bout how it's gonna happen to him: how they're gonna slowly cut the flesh from him in long strips with their dull knives, how they're gonna cut out his eyes and cut off his ears and cut out his tongue and cut up his privates. He'll think 'bout 'em lighting a fire beneath him, a real slow fire, and keep him alive for a long time while they take turns searing his hide with firebrands.

It's one thing to read about it or talk about it. That's horrible enough. But when you're riding along like I was, and them thoughts begin to run through your mind, no matter how hard you try, you can't fight 'em down. Knowing it's gonna happen to you, you get a feeling of panic and you start sobbing like a baby, wondering what rotten luck it was that got you in the jam you're in. You get so scared you begin praying like you never prayed before.

Hell, I never did pray before, never paid no attention to it. But I was praying then, praying to the Lord God and the Lord Jesus Christ to save me. I kept on praying, even though I knowed it was hopeless. I knowed that those Comanches was gonna take me off to someplace in the Indian territory where I'd be hundreds of miles from any white man and I'd die some long, lingering death all by myself. Nobody'd ever know 'bout me, and my death wouldn't make no difference to nobody, just to me and the savages who was getting some fun out of it.

Then I realized I'd practically forgot 'bout Michelle, and thinking 'bout her took the terror off me just a little for a moment. I was the one who'd got her into this thing. If she was lucky, they'd make her a slave. Maybe someday she'd get rescued. I tried to think more 'bout her and not so much 'bout me. But in the end that didn't seem to do much good. The fright and fear of what was gonna happen to me chased out all other thoughts.

So we rode on 'til 'round midday, when we crossed the Cimarron. I could feel 'Jack cautiously finding his way 'cross the stones and the river's sandy bottom. We climbed up the riverbank and the sound of the water faded away behind us. I could tell from the sun on my chest that we was heading south. We kept on riding for a long time.

They're takin' us down to a village, I thought. It must be the village I'd seen the smoke from.

Judging where Michelle and me'd traveled the last four or five days 'fore we got took, I figured we was in New Mexico Territory. As we rode along, it seemed to get warmer and the late fall deerflies got to pestering me. I could feel 'em crawling 'round and biting where the blood'd dried on my chest and arms. My hands ached and my fingers was numb from the loss of circulation.

I started thinking 'bout the Comanche chief, Quanah Parker. He weren't all Comanche, he was part white. It was a story told 'round the campfires and the saloons and the other talking places of the West. Judge Parker and his wife was settlers in northwest Texas when the Comanches'd hit their homestead. They'd burned the place down and killed the judge. His nine-year-old daughter, Cynthia, was carried off along with the stock.

When a white girl was took captive by the Comanches, she was either tortured and killed or throwed right in with the Comanche squaws. That weren't no fit life even for a pig. A squaw was nothing but a slave herself, so a white woman ended up as the slave of slaves. The Indian squaws treated her like dirt and loaded all the toughest work on her—and the work of a squaw was plenty.

Comanches'd mess around with a newly captured white woman and do everything they could to make sport of her, but it seemed like once one of the braves took a shine to her, the rest of 'em left her alone.

'Bout the luckiest thing for a captive white woman was to get picked up by one of the braves as his third or fourth wife. Then she at least had some protection. If he happened to be a chief, she was real lucky. That was what'd happened to Cynthia Parker. She was young and pretty and got noticed by the chief of them Comanches, a warrior named Quanah. He took her into his lodge as his third wife, and when she'd lived with him for a year, she give birth to a son.

She named him Quanah Parker, half for the chief and half for herself, I reckon. That was way back in the '30s. That half-breed kid was raised in the Comanche villages and learned to ride with the rest of the braves—to hunt buffalo and to war with the Arapaho, Apaches, and Utes, maybe even the Cheyennes and the Kiowas to the north.

It didn't take long 'fore they found out he was a born leader. He was strong and he could run and ride a horse and shoot a bow and fight with a knife. He could do anything the other Comanche braves could do, only he could do it better.

What's more, he could give 'em new ideas when it come to their war tactics with the Apaches or the whites. He seemed to know how the white man was gonna react, and that made it easy for him to lay ambushes and all that kinda thing. His secret hideout was in Palo Duro Canyon, and he spread out from there.

He burned up a lot of wagon trains and raided a lot of farms and ranches in northwest Texas. He totally raised hell along the border, and woe be unto them buffalo hunters that got caught by Quanah's braves in that part of Indian territory below Dodge City, where they used to go after the last of the big buffalo herds.

When I was a kid, the old-timers used to tell that the Indians in Kentucky didn't only torture for revenge or amusement, torture was part of their religion. Seemed that causing pain allowed 'em to communicate with the spirits or some such thing, and there was a belief among 'em that a brave should die singing in the fire when he was in the hands of his enemies.

A white man don't have no such traditions to carry him through in times of torture. He ain't gonna sing in no fire when he's being burned to death. That was one thing the Indians didn't understand, so's they thought the white man was weak. I s'pose in that way a white man was. But it seemed to me that a white man could think better. The Indians was kinda like children. They could only think up to a point. Then they'd make some silly explanation 'bout spirits and let it go while they went off to amuse themselves with hunting or fishing or worrying 'bout something else.

Some folks've called Indians the children of God 'cause they wandered through the forests, over the hills and plains, and paddled on the lakes, living the simple life. That might be, but to me the Comanches was the children of the devil. They was the meanest, cruelest, stinkin'est bunch of hellhounds I ever knowed in all my life.

I remember towards the middle of the afternoon I heard someone coming up along the left side of me. I heard a swish and then it felt like a red-hot iron was laid across my back and shoulders. I let out a yell and shuddered all over with pain. One of them braves had cut me with his quirt, just for the hell of it.

It was right then that I begun to generate the slightest kind of a forlorn hope, and that hope centered 'round one thing. Before, I'd only been afraid of Indians and disgusted by 'em, but then I begun to develop a hate for 'em, 'specially them Comanches, and it started to well up in me like hot lava.

It begun to make a difference right away. I come to realize that if I could build up enough hate, it just might push out the sickly fear. If it done that, it was gonna be a welcome buddy. So I begun to concentrate on hating them goddamned Comanches. I made a practice of it—I mean a mental exercise. I started thinking and imagining and hating 'em and calling 'em all sorts of terrible names. I figured if I hated 'em enough it'd give me strength.

Along 'bout sundown we halted. I reckoned there was a spring or something, but they didn't give me no water and I was choking mad with thirst. The mule'd stopped and I felt a couple of them bucks— one on each side—untying the rawhide thong on my feet that run under Jack's belly. One give me a push and I fell off with a thud. Then they drug me along the ground on my back by the thong still tied to one leg. It scraped the hide off my back where they drug me through a couple of cactus patches and over some rocks. And that quirt mark on my shoulders'd left a mighty good welt that was even sorer'n the rest.

I kept kicking 'em with my loose foot. 'Course I couldn't see and my hands was tied behind me, so my elbows and fingers was getting skinned along with my shoulders, but I kicked at 'em the best I could with my loose foot. It didn't do no good. They was outta reach and all they did was laugh at me. They drug me what seemed like seventy-five feet 'fore they peeled the mask and britches off'n me. They spread-eagled me on my back and drove a stake into the ground by each arm and each leg and tied me down tight to them stakes. There I was all spraddled out just as naked as the day I was born.

Them Comanches knowed how to handle prisoners. They sure as hell weren't taking no chances on losing me. An older buck got his rifle and blanket and sat hisself down cross-legged 'bout two feet away from my chest. He sat there wearing a big buffalo-horned helmet, with his rifle hooked in the crook of his arm, looking at me, letting me know that in case there was any chance I thought about loosening them bonds, he was right there to see that it didn't happen.

The stakes was set out beside my wrists and ankles. The thongs was tied, but not as tight as they had been. The circulation started coming back a little bit in my hands and feet and they got to really hurting. At least then I knowed they was still there.

That first night they got a good fire going so I could see as far as I could twist my head. All I could do was turn it from side to side and lift it up 'til my chin hit my chest. I had a good view of my feet and what was going on up to fifty yards away in that direction. I strained to look up that way once or twice, but the buck that was guarding me give me a good smack across the face to make me understand that I weren't supposed to do that. Then all I did was look from side to side.

I couldn't see no sign of Michelle and I hadn't heard her voice, neither. I could smell something roasting over the fire and reckoned it was some of my buffalo meat or maybe something they'd got themselves. It smelled good, though what I really wanted was water.

I soon discovered how they were gonna feed me, and it weren't no gentle process. What they'd done was put a hunk of meat on the end of a stick and burn it for a few minutes in the fire. Then they brung it over, dripping with hot juices and fat, and held it over my chest to let them hot juices drip down on my chest and burn the hell outta me. To this day, fifty years later, I got the scars of them grease burns on my chest and belly. I was tied down, but that dripping fat still made me jump all over the place. They'd laugh and think it was the funniest thing, seeing me writhing 'round. Then they'd shove the meat at my face and I'd have to nibble it off the stick as best I could. Them devils didn't give me no water at all that night. I reckon they done it on purpose to put me through hell—and it sure did. Thirst is near as bad as fire, you can bet your ass on that.

I lay there stark naked and soon it started to get real cold. I begun to shake something terrible. It was the only time I seen that buck guarding me do anything nice. He went over and picked up a saddle blanket and throwed it over me. At first I thought he was showing me some kindness, but hell, all he was doing was keeping me from freezing to death that night. He was saving me, all right—for more torturing.

Nelson Lee'd escaped 'cause he'd had a silver watch that had an alarm in it, and them damned Comanches thought he was a witch doctor or something. They was afraid to kill a man who could talk to the spirits. I didn't have no silver watch, but I had my hatred, and that was gonna have to do it for me.

They changed my guard a couple of times, and along in the early hours of the morning I was so damned tired that I finally dozed off some. I'd been looking up at the stars and thinking 'bout my old home back on the south side of the Ohio River, down in Kentucky. I'd only known my ma for a few years, and I believe she could've been a real well-thought-of woman if she'd just lived longer. She used to try to keep the old man from licking me when he'd come home drunk. I might've had a happier childhood if she hadn't come down with consumption. She died when I was real young, so's I'd had to make out the best I could.

Come to think of it, the old man weren't too bad either—when he weren't drunk. I got to remembering the time when I was 'bout ten years old and he took me along on a lumber raft down the Ohio and the Mississippi to Natchez. It was a lot of fun. Later, the old man was always looking for some work and we kept drifting west. We'd moved from one ranch to another, and I worked right along with him. That's how I found out a little bit 'bout punching cattle. He died after a big drunk spell in San Antone when I was 'bout fourteen, and I went to work by myself on a ranch outside of there.

But then I snapped back to the present. There I was, a captive of the Comanches, waiting on a fate that made me nearly puke to think 'bout, and having no way out.

When it come daylight, the camp begun moving 'round and a couple of bucks come over. The sentry untied my bonds, jerked me to my feet, and kicked and knocked me towards the water hole. I knowed from how they'd treated me the day before that I wouldn't get no water after this. I was so parched from being twenty-four hours without it that I drank and drank and drank. I knowed I shouldn't, 'cause I'd pay for it by having stomach cramps later on, but I didn't see no other way. When I was filled up, they kicked and knocked me back towards where they'd laid my britches and hood.

I hadn't seen Michelle a'tall when I went to the water hole and I wondered where they had her. I don't know whether she seen me or not, but I must've been a sight, marching naked over to that spring. I knowed I was real bad beat up. My lip was cut and I'd been bleeding some more from the head. My back and shoulders was tore up where they'd drug me and quirted me, and I was limping and hopping on my sore feet across them rocks and cactus.

I hadn't had much chance to get the bearings of our camp, 'cause I seen it in the early light of dawn. We was out in the flat country, but there was some mesas in the distance. Off to the west I could just see the outline of the Rockies. We must've gone due south the day before, 'cause we hadn't got no closer to the mountains.

Them bucks didn't waste no ceremony on me that morning. Soon as I'd got my britches on they whirled me 'round and jammed my arms together, tying 'em tighter'n they'd done the day before. They clapped that damned hood over my head and pulled the drawstring up to where it near choked me, then they hoisted me up on the mule's back and tied my ankles same as before.

It was a tough ride that day. I could tell by the warmth of the sun on my chest that we was sorta heading south again, not in quite the direction where I'd seen that smoke, but more west. The day wore on, and two or three times I nearly passed out from being plumb exhausted. My head'd get down on my chest and then I'd begin to lean forward and get to swaying. I'd feel my head bending low, almost down to 'Jack's neck. Then some buck'd ride up alongside and give me a crack across my bare shoulders with his quirt. That'd sure revive me quick. There ain't nothing like one of them quirts on your back to make you come alive, no matter how tired you are.

Near sundown we forded a little stream, then we went through the same rigmarole as before. They untied my legs, shoved me off my mule so's I hit the ground with a thud, then yanked me over the rough ground 'til they found a place to stake me out. After they'd spread-eagled me down real rough and tight, they pulled the hood off'n my head.

I got the same treatment with the feed that night, too—more buffalo meat and hot drippings on my chest. Every time I'd twist and yowl, they'd laugh and shove the stuff into my mouth. A couple of times I wanted to choke so's it'd be all over with, but I couldn't manage it.

I was so danged tired I didn't stay awake long. I went off in a doze and dreamt a lot of bad dreams. When I woke up it was still dark. I seen the stars blinking bright up above and I could hear the coyotes howling way out on the prairie. Two feet from me, with his blanket 'round him and his rifle in the crook of his arm, was that damned guard. He didn't make no motion, just sat there outlined against the stars, with his buffalo-horned helmet making him look like the devil hisself. I tried to see his rifle and what kind it was. Couldn't tell exactly in the dark, but it didn't have no magazine, so I figured it was a single-shot.

When he seen I'd come awake, he leaned over and checked the thongs tied to my wrists. As he done so, his blanket opened and I could see he had a knife on his belt on the left side—the side nearest to me. I sure was hoping that I could get my hands on it and at least deny them devils the pleasure of torturing me, but there weren't no way to do that. I tugged my arms, but they was cinched down tight.

I couldn't go back to sleep. Just before dawn, what was left of the fading moon come up and there was a little more light. I got to thinking 'bout two nights before, when I was a free man riding along the river, worried stiff at every rock and tree. I knowed then I'd had good reason to be scared. I cussed myself for taking that Cimarron cutoff when I could've gone up 'round by the ruins of old Bent's Fort. I couldn't believe I'd took this terrible risk just to avoid a posse. Damn me! I sure wished I'd been picked up by that posse first. They wouldn't have done nothing more'n hang me.

I could see the face of the brave that was guarding me. It was the cruelest-looking thing I'd ever seen. Them beady eyes had the same look as something raised by a wolf, staring out from underneath them horns. There weren't no sign—not even the smallest glint—of any kinda sympathy or understanding. It was like I was in the hands of a savage animal with a heart of cold steel that was looking at something it was gonna destroy 'fore too long.

Then dawn broke and I got a good look at his rifle and seen that it was a single-shot Sharps. I also seen that there was a cartridge belt slung over his shoulder under the blanket. It showed when he bent over to check my bindings.

When it got a little lighter, them bucks come up and done the same thing they'd done the morning before. They unloosed my bindings, jerked me to my feet, and kicked and shoved me towards the running stream. I seen which way we was going and moved right along. When I got there I dropped into that creek stark-ass naked and just rolled 'round in it, drinking all I could and easing the pain of my cuts and bruises with that ice-cold water. It don't seem like a man in late October on the prairies'd get much enjoyment outta ducking in a stream of water that had ice 'round the edges, but it was a real relief.

Them stinking varmints sat 'round and watched me and laughed, then they come over and clipped me a couple of times with a quirt to tell me to get up outta there. I staggered back to where they'd had me staked out all night and dragged on my buckskin pants.

They grabbed ahold of me and spun me 'round to fasten my arms. Then I heard a whoop and a holler way out on the prairie and seen one of them Indians riding hell-bent for leather, yelling at our camp. Them bucks all stopped what they was doing and looked towards the rider real tenselike.

Some of the bucks in my party weren't wearing nothing but a breech-clout and moccasins. None of 'em had anything on from the waist up. Some of 'em had rifles and some of 'em just had bows and arrows and lances and buffalo-hide shields. Even in my misery I'd noticed that them shields and lances was decorated up with the colored feathers of eagles or hawks or some such, and there were some fancy painting on the shields. I reckoned they was s'posed to keep the evil eye away. If I hadn't been so damned miserable, I might've thought it was interesting, but the way I felt I just wanted to end it all.

It didn't take that rider long to get up to us. He pulled up short and started jabbering and waving his hands. Right away there was a lot of excitement and everybody went running for horses and one thing and another. A couple of bucks grabbed hold of me and yanked me down towards a cottonwood tree and run a rope 'round me about six times, good and tight about my chest and stomach, binding me close to the tree. Then they run it another six or seven times 'round my legs.

There was a little bit of wrangling among 'em and I reckoned they was deciding who was gonna stand guard. Finally, one of 'em come over and stopped in front of me for a minute or two, checking how tight I was bound. Then he spit in my face and went over and sat down with his blanket and rifle 'bout ten feet away. Meanwhile, all the rest of 'em was mounting their ponies and there was a lot of whooping and hollering. I reckoned that with whatever fun they was all headed for, maybe this one brave was peeved at me for being the cause of him not going.

I seen another buck on a dun horse start crossing the creek 'bout sixty yards downstream from me. He was leading a mule. My heart gave a mighty leap—it was Blackjack and he was carrying my Michelle. She was still bare from the waist up and her hair was hanging down to her shoulders, but I seen she had on them buckskin britches and antelope moccasins. I reckoned the Indians didn't know what to make of 'em. Maybe her feet was too small for any of them bucks to use her footgear, so's they'd let her keep 'em.

Anyhow, this buck headed off towards the southwest at a steady trot, leading my mule with my girl hanging on for dear life. She didn't give no sign she seen me. The rest of the bucks crossed that stream with a splash and headed off to the east. They was really riding wild. Them Comanches, I'll say this for 'em, they're horsemen. I couldn't make out what was going on, and I sure didn't want that damned guard of mine to put that hood back on my head. It'd been two days since I'd seen any blue skies or the sun or the green grass or the trees or running water, and I was soaking it all in.

It didn't take them Comanches long to disappear in the distance. I still couldn't see what they was after. It was hazy to the east with the sun just coming up, but when it'd rose a little, I seen a low cloud to the southeast. Then I knowed what it was—the dust cloud from a big buffalo herd. They was taking time out for a hunt.

I spent a long day standing there tied to that tree, but I didn't do no complaining. I watched the sun rising higher. From the distance of the dust cloud, I reckoned it was at least fifteen miles to the herd, and I knowed them varmints'd be riding in amongst 'em and killing as many as they could 'fore they come back. I reckoned they'd be gone quite a while.

I seen two big old birds circling 'round way, way up there in the blue, blue sky—floating with their wings spread all easylike. I kept looking and wondering whether they was hawks or, maybe, by God, they was eagles.

Then I seen their wing tips. They weren't nothing but hawks, but they sure was pretty. I envied the way they didn't have to do nothing, just idle with the current and flow this way and that.

Along in the early afternoon I seen some dust in the distance, and it was our band of braves coming back. The horses was tired and lathered, but them Comanches didn't give 'em no time for resting. They might've been great riders, but they didn't know how to treat a horse.

Our band crossed the stream and come into camp, whooping and hollering. Some of them bucks had blood on 'em and I knowed they must've had one helluva hunt. They whirled 'round again and come dashing by. Then they jerked their horses up quick and stopped 'em in the middle of the stream. By the way them horses went for the water, I knowed they really needed it.

The younger bucks started bringing up fresh ponies. I seen that one of 'em was Piebald, and he looked mighty good. I reckoned he hadn't had to carry no load the last couple of days, and he'd had that day to rest up and feed. He had plenty of that old spirit in him. A buck come by leading him and two other horses and Piebald turned his head and looked at me, but I didn't wanta say nothing. I didn't know what the consequences'd be, so I just looked at him and watched. I like to think he recognized me.

Them bucks saddled up real fast and brought over a moth-eaten old mustang for me to ride. They untied me real quick from the tree, tripped me up and knocked me down on the ground, then pulled my arms 'round behind me and tied 'em up real tight again.

Well, I'm lucky this time, I thought. They're gonna put me on that horse 'stead of a mule. If he gets ta actin' up, maybe I'll swing 'round under his belly. That'll be a quick, merciful way ta die.

They throwed me up on the horse and tied my legs underneath just like they'd done with the mule, but they didn't put no hood on my head. I reckon they'd figured I could keep my balance better if I could see where I was going. That mustang didn't act like much of a horse, neither. I reckoned his spirit'd been broke long ago and he weren't gonna be much trouble a'tall.

The buck holding the reins mounted his own horse and started off. We went 'bout eight or ten steps towards the creek and stopped. A bunch of braves was watching another young buck who was having a little trouble getting a rein on Piebald. They didn't use much of a bridle—just a kinda loop 'round the lower jaws. I seen that he was handling Piebald a little rough, and it looked to be an interesting contest.

The brave finally got his bridle on Piebald, but by then Piebald had a real wild look in his eyes. That buck took hold with one hand on his mane and vaulted right on, bareback. Old Piebald—God bless him!—didn't let me down. He started out real businesslike with his head down and his ears laid back and, boy, he went to sunfishing and twisting and bucking and kicking and bellering away.

The rest of them Comanches started yelling like hell and laughing. The brave lasted for a while, then he finally come off high in the air and landed flat on his ass in a patch of cactus. Everybody was howling with laughter, and old Piebald, that rope bridle still hanging from his mouth, tore off pitching and bucking across the prairie. A couple of braves headed out after him with a rope.

Hell, I was like the rest of 'em. When I seen that miserable redskin fall flat on his ass in the cactus, I laughed myself silly. That was a mistake. The brave that was leading my horse jerked back, showing his wolves' teeth. He lashed out at me with his quirt and hit me across the face twice. The blood started running down the bridge of my nose and it hurt like fire. I was lucky he hadn't put out my eye. I stopped laughing all right. He'd put the cold, black hate of hell back in me. I reckon my eyes was as wolfy as his when I looked back at him—only mine's gray.

The two braves brought back Piebald, but that first Comanche weren't quite as ready to ride him as he was before. I seen him walking up to Piebald with murder in his heart. He pulled a long shiny knife from his belt and made like he was gonna cut that horse's throat. But Piebald went to jerking like hell, turning and twisting to get away.

I believe that buck would've killed Piebald if he'd got to him, but the rest of them Comanches talked to him. I don't know what they said, but I guess they calmed him down. That buck went over and got one of the other horses and jumped onto him, and by that time the rest of 'em was ready to go.

They turned Piebald loose with the spares and I reckon by that time he was ready to go, too. Some life'd come back in my heart and I could've kissed Piebald for paying them dirty varmints back something of what they'd handed me.

The leader of the band of braves raised his lance up in the air and give a yell. With that, the whole bunch kicked up their horses and galloped outta there. We crossed the stream going south, with lots of spraying and splashing, then hit out over the prairie to the southwest—the same way I'd seen Michelle going on that mule with the Indian leading her.

It was a lucky thing I was a good horseman, 'cause it ain't easy riding at a dead gallop with your hands tied behind your back. With the help of that rawhide thong tied to my ankles, and by squeezing my knees real hard and getting with the rhythm of that horse, I could stay on him. But all I gotta do ta get outta this mess is lose my balance an' swing underneath an' this horse'll kick me ta death, I thought. It's simple as that. Two or three times I said to myself, "Well, now's your time. Now! Do it!"

But for the first time in three days, I could feel the wind on my face and breathe free. We was on a wild ride, and even though it was uncomfortable with my hands tied behind my back, and even though I was getting a lot of dirt in my face from the hooves of the horse in front, I felt proud to stay up and prove I was a good rider. Something in me wanted to keep on going—I didn't wanta turn in my chips just yet. Right then, I made the decision that I was gonna live as long as I could, and I stayed with it.

When we lit out, the sun was 'bout an hour above the horizon. We rode clear through 'til it was pitch-dark, then slowed some and kept on into the night. I was s'prised that we kept going.

We rode 'bout two hours at a jog in the dark 'fore we made camp. 'Course them bucks staked me out again like they'd done before, stark-ass naked and spread-eagled on the prairie, with a guard sitting by me all night.

It was the same old thing. That Indian guard, I knowed from experience, would sit there cross-legged 'bout two feet away, with his rifle crooked across his arm and a knife in his belt, real motionless, staring off across the countryside. Maybe I'd see his beady eyes looking into the fire. Maybe he'd be wearing his horned helmet and maybe he wouldn't. Maybe in the early hours of the morning I'd just see the faint outline of him underneath the stars. He was always there, real silent and still, like some kind of evil spirit that was watching and waiting for me to go to my grave.

The only time he'd move was 'bout once every half hour when the notion took him. Then he'd check the rawhide thongs that was on my wrists and ankles to make sure there weren't no looseness and that I didn't have no ideas 'bout getting away. 'Bout once every three or four hours another buck'd come and spell him, and they'd take turns guarding me like that. When one'd get up and leave so's the other one could sit down, the one that was leaving'd always give me a good healthy kick in the ribs to let me know there weren't no love lost 'tween us.

We was away by 'bout an hour after sunrise the next morning. This time they put the hood on me first. It seemed like we traveled on in the same direction and camped again early that night. The last time

I'd seen the Rocky Mountains, I'd reckoned we was maybe sixty miles from 'em. I figured we'd only come ten miles the day before and that day we'd made twenty miles, mostly due west. Soon we'd come into the foothills.

In the late afternoon of the third or fourth day, when I sniffed some piñon smoke, I heard a dog bark and then I smelled a camp. We was downwind, and I'll never forget that first stench of a big Comanche camp.

One of the braves jerked off my hood and, sure enough, in a little while I seen a glow in the night and lights from lots of fires. When we got closer to the village I heard people shouting and kids hollering and dogs barking. There must've been fifty or sixty tepees, all set up in rows, with fires 'tween most of 'em and everybody running around.

When we pulled up they all come crowding 'round. There was only real old squaws and kids in the camp, and they started pointing at me and making all kinds of gestures, like cutting my throat and skewering me, and even worse. I felt sick, knowing it prob'ly wouldn't be long 'fore they'd be more'n pretending.

A big Comanche come out of his tepee and everybody stopped and gathered 'round to see what he said. I reckoned he was the chief. He sure as hell was ugly enough to be. I knowed he weren't Quanah Parker, 'cause Quanah Parker had some white blood in him. This Comanche was all Indian. He was big and he was mean-looking, and he had his face all painted up. He gestured and jabbered, then they drug me into one of the tepees. They brought in a wooden pole, stretched me out on the ground beside it, and then tied me up to it. The buck that'd been leading me with his horse turned out to be my guard on the first watch.

For a while the kids flocked 'round to look at me, poking their heads in the tepee door to point at the white prisoner. My guard sat there cross-legged with his rifle in the hook of his arm, 'bout two feet away. Every time I'd look at him, I'd study the long knife sticking in his belt and wish I could just get my hands on it. Weren't no use thinking 'bout that, though, since my hands was tied behind my back real tight and I was strapped to that pole.

After a while I heard a new commotion outside—first horses, then a lot of younger women's voices. It sounded like the squaws was coming in. I could guess what'd happened. The buck that brought Michelle into the village must've arrived some time in the middle of the morning and told them squaws 'bout the buffalo hunt. The chief would've sent 'em out to tend to the skinning and butchering.

I hadn't heard or seen nothing of Michelle since that morning, and I didn't really know if she was still alive. I lay there expecting every few minutes for a couple of them bucks to come slipping into the tepee to grab me and take me out to the fire for the torture. There was lots of excitement and yelling out there, and after a while the drums started.

Then a smelly old squaw come in with some food in a pot. She give it to the guard and he ate 'til he was satisfied. Next she moved over beside me and started feeding me by hand. The food was some kinda corn mixed with buffalo meat. Didn't taste too awful bad, but the way she fed me was degrading.

She'd dip into the pot with her fingers and hold 'em up next to my mouth. When I'd open my lips to take it, she'd take the palm of her hand and smear the food into my mouth, like she was feeding a horse. I didn't expect no fancy service, though, I was just thankful to get something to eat.

The night drug on. I was real tuckered out from all the riding, plumb wore to the bone. I'd already called on all the reserves of my strength. I was low in mind and sick with fever from all my cuts and beatings. I lay there hearing them drums beat. I listened more carefully and noticed they was keeping up a steady rhythm. I could hear some low-pitched singing, but there weren't any wild excitement.

I hoped it was the kind of celebration they held after they'd had a good buffalo hunt, thanking the great Manitou that their brother—the buffalo—had come up outta the prairie to offer his body for food and all that, like them poetic Eastern fellas is always talking 'bout.

Well, I didn't see no poetry in it that night. But I took comfort in the hope that if they kept singing in that way it'd put off the torture for a while. Long past midnight, I finally went off into a fitful sleep.

I woke to a lot of commotion. It was daylight, and I could hear the squaws jabbering away. I could see a bunch of 'em through the tepee opening. Lying there watching them squaws, I heard a noise that felt like a needle stabbing clear through my heart. I heard the shrill laughter of a woman I knowed. There weren't no mistaking it. I would've knowed that laugh a thousand miles away. It was Michelle's laugh. At first I was glad to hear that she was alive, but then I couldn't figure out why she was laughing. I knowed what it was for a white woman to be a captive of the Comanches and the kinda work that'd be expected of her. I knowed how them squaws'd drive her just like they'd drive the beasts of burden that they'd hitched to them travois.

Then I heard some other laughter—men's voices, and a few of 'em sounded like they was young bucks. Then Michelle laughed again. It seemed outta place, like she was flirting and having herself a good time. I tried to twist around farther and look in that direction to see what was going on, but they was outta sight. Again I heard that peal of laughter that I'd heard so many times and that I'd grown to love.

I looked back at the squaws and seen an awful sight. Them squaws'd quit work and got their heads all turned in the direction of Michelle's laughter. The look in their wild eyes was like the look of a snake.

Then it got quiet and I couldn't hear Michelle no more. The group of squaws'd turned back and I could see 'em talking to one another—whispering and shooting sidelong glances in the same direction as they'd been looking. After a minute or two they started going back 'bout their work.

I wished I could warn Michelle that it might be hard for her with them squaws, unless she was picked up by one of the best bucks in the tribe to be his second or third wife or something. Then she'd be safe. Anyhow, at least I knowed she was alive.

There must've been an hour of sunshine left that day when they took me outta the tepee and spread-eagled me naked again. Along towards sundown, I saw some squaws coming into the camp. It was a group of young ones, and some of 'em was packing freshly butchered buckskin hides on their backs and some of 'em was packing the meat. As they passed by, I got a little idea of what was in store for me.

Three of 'em stopped beside me and pulled the skinning knives out from their belts. They looked at me with them beady eyes, common to all Comanche squaws. God, they had awful eyes! Wild as wolves and cold as snakes. They made some real understandable gestures and started laughing and licking dried blood off their knives. One of 'em pointed her knife at my crotch. I got the message real quick, that when they started carving me up, they was gonna cut off my private parts—like they done when they'd dress out a deer, only more so— and I was gonna be alive while they was doing it.

After them squaws passed by, there was all the usual sounds of campfires and commotion, and I thought maybe I heard Michelle's laughing, but I weren't sure.

It was along 'bout sundown that night when something real terrible begun that I wish I could forget. Right near where I was staked out, maybe thirty yards in a straight line from where my feet was tied, someone started a pounding that sounded like driving some big stakes into the ground. I raised my head up a couple of times, but not so far that the guard'd notice and hit me, and took a look. Sure enough, there was two eight-foot stakes that'd been drove into the ground 'bout four feet apart.

Things seemed quiet 'round the camp—just a low murmur of voices—and there didn't seem to be too much excitement. It grew late and they still hadn't brought me nothing to eat, although my guard sat by me just as motionless as ever—like a damn statue, never moving. I knowed something was strange. A couple of squaws brought some brush and started a fire a ways off from them posts.

I could feel the tension in the air, like before a thunderstorm. It kept getting more and more quiet, and I couldn't hear the usual noises from the children and squaws. The only thing I noticed was the crackling of the wood in the fire the two squaws'd set.

The silence lasted for what seemed like an hour after it got dark. All of a sudden I heard the gol'durnedest shriek, followed by hollering and screaming and a whole chorus of high-pitched voices. This loud, shrill noise kept coming closer and closer and closer. But I couldn't see past that fire, and I was afraid to look too hard anyway, else that guard would've hit me. My heart was beating fast and I was getting more scared by the minute.

Then, screeching like a thousand demons come this bunch of squaws, and they was dragging and kicking something along. They pulled up between the posts and I lay back and looked at the stars, promising myself that I could outhate 'em, no matter what they tried to do to me. Mine was one spirit they'd never break.

I glanced over and looked at my guard. He was sitting there with that motionless Comanche stare, looking towards the bonfire. The flicker of the flames on his face made him look like some evil spirit outta hell waiting for the brew to boil. Then them wolf teeth begun to show and he broke out in a real vicious smile. Slowly, he turned and shifted them beady eyes straight down at me.

With a quick motion he grabbed me by the hair and jerked my head up so's I could get a good look at what he was watching. Thirty or forty squaws was all squatted 'round in a circle, and back of 'em was standing a bunch of bucks—all of 'em watching with the same evil grins on their faces.

Hanging stretched and tied 'tween them two posts was Michelle, and she was as bare as the day she was born. I knowed she couldn't see me, 'cause I was in the shadows of the fire. I shut my eyes, but I could still see that awful scene—the firelight flickering and dancing and coloring her body almost red with reflected flames. That fire was a good twenty feet away from her, but it sure lit her up.

Somewhere back in the shadows I heard a drum start to pound with a slow, measured beat. The drum quickened and five of them young bucks jumped up and made a wild fast dance, circling 'round Michelle. They was wearing horned helmets and swinging their war clubs in front of her face like they was gonna chop her to pieces. They never hit her, but it must've scared the hell outta her, 'cause her eyes was bulging and she didn't make a sound. In a few minutes they stopped real sudden and sat down. The drum started again with that slow, measured beat. Then three of them young squaws jumped up and begun to shuffle 'round Michelle, their eyes shining with hate.

Each of 'em held a long obsidian knife. At a certain beat one of the squaws'd leap forward and quickly cut a slice into Michelle. She'd scream and then another squaw'd make another slice and Michelle'd scream again. Then each one made another cut and another, over and over. God! It was awful to watch. Next, one of 'em cross-cut a little and got hold of a piece of flesh and started jerking it loose and peeling it off. That poor girl kept up a constant screaming 'til, thank God, she fainted.

My buck held up my head, pulling my hair real tight. He wanted me to see the whole thing. I glanced up at him and he was grinning away and looking at me to see how I took it. He knowed that he was showing me what was coming my way 'fore long. I kept shaking my head and trying to close my eyes and ears, but that dirty buck kept looking at me and laughing. I could hear the other bucks laughing away at how them squaws was torturing and teasing a white woman.

When Michelle come to, they started in again. It liked to never end. I could hear Michelle's voice keep rising from a low moan up to a real shrill cry. Every once in a while there'd be a few minutes of silence, then a pitiful sobbing and she'd call out, "Oh, God! Oh, Mother of Jesus! Help me!"

All of a sudden the drum started a furious beat and all the squaws took up a high-pitched chant. One of them old cackling hags jumped up and run over to the fire. She come hurrying back, swinging a big old firebrand. I forced my head back and closed my eyes so's I wouldn't see what she done with it. Whatever it was, it brung out the worst screaming of all from Michelle.

I opened my eyes again after a minute or so, paralyzed with horror, and seen that the rest of them squaws'd got burning sticks and logs and throwed 'em in a big heap right underneath Michelle. The fire started curling up 'round her and she begun to twist and writhe in the flames, still screaming. Oh God! Her screams were unearthly. I closed my eyes again and muttered to myself, "Please, God, fer Christ's sake, let 'er go. Please, finish it off."

That was the only time I ever seen that buck put down his rifle. He lay the barrel across my belly and jumped 'round behind me so's to pull my head up again. Then he used his fingers to force my eyes open so's I had to watch. By then there was a good-sized fire licking away at Michelle's legs and thighs. Then the wind shifted and I could smell the stench of burning flesh.

I hadn't ate in twenty-four hours, but whatever the hell there was left in me come up in one gorging ball of bile that spewed out over my chest. I damn near choked on my own vomit. When that happened, the young buck dropped my head back on the ground and give me a good kick in the ribs. Then he spit in my face and turned away. I lay there all weak and trembling, sick to the core. At least I didn't have to look no more. But I could still hear her screaming.

The fire crackled and roared hotter and hotter. After what seemed like an eternity, Michelle give out a wild, shrill scream that run through me like cold vapor. Then come a merciful quiet, 'cept for the jabbering and laughter of them squaws and bucks. I lay there almost too sick to breathe, shifting my head back and forth to see if I couldn't shake out the awful sights and sounds that was still burning in my brain.

The morning sun was just beginning to peek over the top of old Lone Cone. I could see in the early light that tears were coming down the old man's cheeks. He had been telling me his story all night and he was obviously shaken. Indeed, so was I. Of course, all of the western people knew something about the Comanches and their reputation for terrible cruelty. Few people, however, knew the details. In fact, I had never heard anything as terrible as the description of Michelle's murder. I felt sick to my stomach and found myself empathizing with old Brules. I began to hate the whole Comanche nation with the same intensity that he displayed, and I remembered clearly once hearing one of the old-timers say that it was impossible to exaggerate Comanche atrocities.

I got up to stir the embers of the dying fire. It was plain that the old man needed to be left alone for a bit, so I fetched some water and started brewing up a fresh pot of coffee. After a while I told him what I thought.

"Yore right, boy," responded old Brules. "And it don't seem possible that no human beings'd treat one another that way. It was then that I decided them goddamned, stinking savages weren't human beings a'tall. They was nothing but wild wolves with the brain of a man and the desire to cause the kind of pain that no animal'd ever think of. The evil in their hearts must've come from the devil hisself. I hated 'em with a clean, white-hot hate that burned in my gut. I vowed then and there that if I lived I'd get revenge on 'em for what they'd done to my beautiful Michelle."

The old man leaned back and stared into the fire. I thought it would be a good idea to let him rest a while before fixing us some breakfast. Maybe after he'd slept a little and had something to eat he'd be in a mood to tell me the rest of his story. Obviously, he had escaped from the Comanches, but how? I was dying to know.

BRULES'S FORT

I didn't sleep that night, Brules said, resuming his narrative. After a while, the crowd broke up and things quieted down, but there was still the stench of burnt flesh and smoke hanging over that camp, and it lived in my memory for years.

In the morning, them bucks come over and jerked me to my feet just like they'd always done, and kicked me towards the stream. I was numb from sickness of mind and body during the whole ride that day. There didn't seem to be no rhyme or reason for nothing. Life was hell, and for sure there weren't no God. There weren't no way that, with a God in heaven, things like I'd seen would've happened. The steady jerking stride of the mule they'd put me on was like a dull, pounding throb that I listened to in a kind of half-dream. But, through it all, I could smell that burnt flesh and hear Michelle's screams.

It'd been so bad that somehow, in a way, it drove the fear of what was gonna happen to me outta my mind. I couldn't think 'bout it no more. I swayed along to the beat of the mule's hooves and give myself up to the passing of time and distance. It got real hot and dusty in the afternoon and I growed thirsty as hell, but somehow I didn't notice it too much. I was just numb.

Late that day when we stopped, I come to with a jerk and realized that we'd reached the edge of the mountains. There was a cool breeze blowing off the slopes and I could hear the sounds of the wind in the trees and a noisy running stream. They pulled the hood off'n me and staked me out. As usual they didn't give me nothing to drink—they just let me agonize with thirst all night. Only this time I could hear that running stream nearby and that made it even worse. Fact is, it was pure hell. In the dusk I could look up and see the long-timbered slopes of some high mountains, and up there against the evening sky I could see the gold of the sun hitting some snowfields that lay high along the peaks.

It was a beautiful sight, but something a poor suffering slave captive like me just couldn't enjoy. I ain't ashamed to say the tears was streaming down my cheeks. I figured that was gonna be my last night on earth, 'cause tonight they was gonna torture me to death like they done to Michelle.

It was in that sad state of mind that I turned my head slightly to the right and seen a sight that run a cold stab of fear through me. Coming straight towards me was one of them bitchy Comanche squaws carrying a middle-sized bowl in her hands. I knowed what that meant—I'd heard tell of it before. That bowl was full of red-hot coals and she was gonna dump 'em on my naked belly. At the worst, she'd be the "fire maiden" opening the torture ceremony. At best, she was just a squaw coming to have some fun with a helpless captive. Either way, it sent the fright right up through my brain. I watched the bitch coming, seeing that she was young and almost pretty, which I knowed added to the amusement of them that'd sent her. She was slimmer than the other squaws and moved kind of graceful, but that only added to the terror of her coming.

I closed my eyes, gritted my teeth, and writhed in my tie-downs, hissing and panting in anticipation of what them red-hot pieces of fire was gonna do to me. I reckon my heart was pounding like a war drum when I felt that hellish bitch kneel down beside me. She put one of her hands underneath my head and lifted it up slightly, then put the bowl to my lips. I guessed what terrible thing she was gonna do. She was gonna pour them red-hot coals right down my throat. My eyes was closed and my teeth was clenched. God, who ever made those hellish bitches?

Right there was the great crossroad of my life, for what I felt coming outta that bowl was something cold and wet that soothed my parched lips and went through my teeth into my swollen mouth. Suddenly I realized, God almighty, it weren't fire. It was water—the clear, cold water of the Cimarron that girl was giving me. I opened my eyes in wide surprise to look at her, and I seen the most beautiful sight of my whole life. The girl that'd been coming towards me—I seen she was graceful enough, but I didn't see she was so beautiful. She had the soft brown eyes of a doe. Her complexion was much lighter'n the other Comanche squaws. Her beautiful lips and teeth framed a kind, sad smile. I was gasping with relief and joy. She held my head up gently, so's I could continue to drink, and I took that cold, clear, delicious water in great gulps. If I live to be a hundred years old, there'll never be a drink like the one that Comanche girl give me on that hot, lonely, fearsome afternoon.

As I was gasping and drinking I kept looking at her and I seen her beautiful hair and eyes and face up against the sky. It was all that I could see of the world the way I was tied down. She crooned a little and I thought maybe she'd come outta the sky somehow—that she was the Sky Woman, a real angel of mercy. I don't know—a poor, ignorant man like me don't know much 'bout them things. I only know that this girl was the kindest, most beautiful creature in all the world, and somehow she was giving me a touch of life and tenderness. Yes, and even love like I'd never knowed before.

When I'd just 'bout drained the bowl, she took her fingertips and dipped 'em in the cool water and rubbed 'em on my brow and even on my cheeks and across my eyelids. All the time she was looking at me so soft and kind, I couldn't believe it. The world spun 'round and for a few seconds I was in heaven.

'Course it couldn't, and didn't, last. All of a sudden there was a yell from some of the guards who'd been a few feet away unpacking one of the mules. I s'pose they hadn't noticed the girl come up. When they seen her, they dashed over, grabbed her by the hair and jerked her up, slapped her four or five times, then turned her 'round and give her a kick to send her on her way. I seen outta the corner of my eye that she was running with her head down and her hands to her face, and I knowed she was crying. Then I suddenly sensed a revelation. She weren't crying 'cause they hurt her. She was crying for me!

Them guards picked up that empty bowl and throwed it as far away as they could, then they turned 'round and set to giving me a good bout of kicking. After each kick, I looked up at 'em thinking, why you goddamn, rotten sons of bitches. If'n there ever was somethin' decent in the Comanche nation, you'd a never let it be. What kinda damn animals are ya?

After a while they quit abusing me and went off to attend to their affairs. I lay there wondering what the latest developments was all about and thinking that there was indeed something on this earth above and beyond all the rottenness I'd seen 'round me.

Then I felt a brace in the air—and a pine smell different than the prairie—that, in a way, spoke of a new life and fresh beginnings. Maybe it was what I'd been through. Maybe it was some deeper strength I didn't even know I had. Maybe it was the change in the air. But somehow I think right then I stepped across the threshold into a different reason for living, and that's how I've felt ever since.

Just 'fore dusk, my guard got up from his squatting position on my right and stepped over to pick up his blanket. I don't know how I happened to do it, but I put a little tension on my right arm at just that moment—and my heart jumped. God almighty! I could feel that the peg holding my right arm was loose. In that fraction of a second I knowed that if I wanted to lift up my arm, I could pull that peg clear out real easy. Maybe we was on a little different kinda soil with more rocks in it, since it didn't hold so good.

Whatever, feelings of hope flashed through me like shooting stars. My heart started racing and I begun to breathe heavy with excitement. I knowed I had to play it just right—to pull my right hand hard towards me so's that stake had some pressure on it. That way, when my guard went to check it, it'd feel okay.

I glanced over as that brave wound his blanket 'round him. Sure enough, he had a knife there on his left side. He picked up his rifle again and come over and squatted down by me on the right. My heart kept racing even faster when I realized that for once he wasn't wearing his buffalo-horned helmet. He weren't on the warpath now, just peace—peace and torture.

I turned my head real slow and easy to the right. God was sure enough with me, 'cause lying there, just about eight inches from my hand, was a stone 'bout twice the size of an apple.

I took a minute to listen to that mountain stream. From the sound of it, it was moving a lot faster'n them streams we'd crossed out on the prairie. All 'round where I was lying was rocks from an old stream— bedrocks that had that gray granite look to 'em, the kind you don't see out on the prairie.

Since I'd seen an opportunity for action, I sure had to plan it right. I lay there in a nervous sweat thinking 'bout what my chances was. From all I could make out, we was camped in a small meadow, or park, as the mountain men'd say, at the base of some foothills. The elders of the band must've figured it was a good place to set up the village, and they was cutting down a lotta lodgepole pines to make tepee poles with. That was a good sign, 'cause if they was busy setting up the camp, the chances of 'em getting 'round to me that night wasn't near as good as they might've been otherwise. The chances of it being the next night was almost certain.

It was 'bout dusk when my guard leaned down and checked the stake holding my right leg. Then he got up on one knee, reached across, and checked the one holding my left leg. When he reached across to check my left arm, his blanket opened a little and I saw again right where his knife was. Finally, he eased back on his haunches and swung 'round to test that one mighty important right-hand peg. I was ready for him. When he pulled on it, I put a lotta tension into my arm, pulling hard crosswise so's that the peg'd seem real stiff. He squatted down again and grunted, satisfied, then hunched the blanket 'round his shoulders.

As usual, the fires'd been built far enough away so we was outta the firelight. I was looking at the stars, but I didn't enjoy 'em none. All the time, racing through my mind, was the idea that, dead or alive, I was gonna get free.

Several minutes went by and another buck walked over to where I was staked out. I panicked, thinking, God, there's gonna be two of 'em! That'd wreck my chances.

The buck squatted down next to my guard and started talking to him in a low voice. My heart was beating real wild and I was going through hell wondering what was being said. Their conversation lasted for 'bout ten minutes. Then the buck that'd come over got up and walked away. He weren't gonna do no relieving after all. My guard looked at me again and I figured it was 'bout time for him to check me. There was only one trouble—the other buck was too close for me to pull anything. He'd sure hear what was going on.

I went through the nerve-racking agony of having that buck check my right leg, my left leg, my left arm, then my right arm. Again I put plenty of tension on my right arm, pulling hard on that peg at right angles. He twanged on the thong, grunted a little, and settled hisself down again with his blanket, that old faithful rifle sticking up there in the crook of his arm. I had a new interest in that rifle then—one that buck didn't know 'bout.

The village was still real active—people was moving 'round and lots of fires was burning—and I wondered whether or not I should sweat it out 'til the middle of the night. No! I thought. I can't run through another check. It's too risky. I've gotta take my chance next time it comes.

Waiting that next stretch was the longest half hour of my life. I lived a thousand years, hanging 'tween the hope of freedom, or at least a chance to die fighting, and the certain hell of dying by slow torture. My stomach was churning and I could feel it half-pressing against my backbone. The sweat was pouring down off my face, although the night wind coming down off the mountains was ice cold. I couldn't hold back a shiver, and that buck grunted a little bit and went over and picked up a saddle blanket to throw over me. God almighty, I prayed, let it be lyin' just right when he gets done.

He threwed the blanket over me and kicked it up close against my sides with his foot. Then he got down on one knee and checked my right leg. Then he checked my left one. I tried to breathe normal.

Then he eased up the length of my body, holding his rifle in his right hand. Leaning on one knee, he bent across my chest and checked my left-hand binding. I smelled his stink. He was breathing through his mouth and his breath reeked like a hog trough.

A new thought crossed my mind. My right arm'd either been tied behind me or staked out fer days. Were my fingers gonna be able ta do the work? Would my arm move fast enough?

I didn't have no more time to think. He leaned over and I seen his blanket come open and the flash where his knife was. I raised my right arm and felt the peg pull loose.

With one quick movement I slipped my hand 'round the rock. The loose peg made a soft rattling noise and that buck turned his face sideways to look. I swung my arm like a club and hit him right across the side of the head with that rock. He hunched forward, holding his head.

He landed on my chest and rolled down my belly. I tried to reach his knife but couldn't find it, so I rolled him off me with my free right arm and exposed his chest. I stretched to grab the knife handle in his belt and, dear God, I could just barely reach it with my fingertips. I jerked it free. Then I reached over quick and cut the strands on my left arm.

I knowed he was only stunned, so I grabbed hold of that brave by the hair with my left hand and pulled his head back and cut his throat deep and clean from ear to ear.

"Fer you, Michelle, honey," I whispered.

He gurgled and choked as a fountain of his warm life's blood poured over me with a loud wheezing noise. It scared me plumb to death that somebody'd overhear, but I guess the rushing of that stream hid the noise, 'cause nobody come in my direction.

I reached down and cut my legs free. Moving as quick and quiet as I could, I reached for my britches and pulled 'em on, then stuck the knife in my belt.

I knowed exactly what else I was gonna need, 'cause I'd had it all planned out. First was moccasins. I jerked 'em off that dead Indian's feet faster'n lightning, slid my feet in, and pulled them bindings 'round real quick. Then I unbuckled the cartridge belt from 'round his shoulders and grabbed his rifle and blanket. I put everything, including the knife, in one hand and, crouching real low and moving as fast as I could, I headed right for the stream. I went slipping and sliding across, with the cold water pouring into them moccasins and the rocks pinching and gouging my feet, but I didn't give a damn. I was on my way.

I got to the other side and took me a quick look back. Nothing. It was all quiet over there. I made it into a patch of scrub oak and started climbing a steep hill. We was right at the foothills, and if I could keep my legs a-churning, I'd be in the high country 'fore daybreak.

I climbed fast and hard the first few minutes, shoving through that thick oak brush with lots of twisting and turning. Then I hit a stand of cedar and piñon and had to make my way up and 'round it. By that time, the stream was far enough below that I could still hear it, but I could also hear my own footsteps and the leaves and pine needles swishing and crackling as I moved.

I climbed that first three or four hundred feet just as damn fast as I could go. I finally slowed up a little but kept pushing. My legs was wobbly and I was weak from being tied up and from lack of food. My breath was coming in hoarse gasps, rasping my throat, and my lungs was fit to burst, setting my chest on fire.

There ain't nothing like them first few minutes of freedom. God! I was going, and going hell-bent for leather, 'cause I knowed that death was at my heels. I knowed that them Comanches was never gonna take me alive again—I reckoned I'd blow my head off with that rifle first. If that didn't work, I'd sure as hell stab myself with that knife.

I kept telling myself, "Don't pay no attention. Keep a-churnin', keep a-churnin'. Yore goin' uphill an' ya gotta keep goin'. By God, there ain't no rest fer a dyin' man."

I don't know how long I worked my way up that hill. I just kept steadily on. I come on several gravel slopes where the loose rocks'd slip and slide under my feet, and I had to drop to my hands and knees and crawl on up, grasping at bushes and little trees and limbs—anything I could get hold of in the darkness to help me up that mountain. I weren't never gonna quit. If I died on that run, that'd be a fair swap. I kept expecting to hear some yells or shots or some indication that them varmints had found out that I was gone, but I didn't hear nothing.

My mind was working like this: When them bucks try ta find me, they're gonna have a helluva time trackin' me in the dark. They can do it all right by torchlight, but it's gonna be tough goin' an' I got a good head start on 'em. They can't do no real good trackin' 'til dawn. By that time, I oughta be up on them slopes, way up on the side a the mountain where I can hide out an' get a shot at 'em first. I'll have ta check that Sharps over an' count my cartridges. I reckon they's eight or nine in that belt, but I ain't shore.

After 'bout an hour, I stopped for the first time for a quick rest and to rearrange things. I'd been carrying everything in one hand, gripped tighter'n tight. I put that cartridge belt over one shoulder, then throwed the blanket 'round me with the corners tied in a knot in front of my throat—the night was cold. I put the knife back in my belt and tied it with a piece of moccasin lace so's I damned well wouldn't lose it. That only took me a few minutes. Then, holding the rifle in my right hand, I kept on plunging upward in the darkness.

I was surprised at how good I could see just by the light of the stars. Pretty soon I reached some quakie-aspen groves. I didn't know they was quakies then—I'd never seen 'em before. They looked like birch trees. Once in a while I'd fall over some downed logs. Them aspen groves was plumb full of dead-falls, but I kept stumbling on.

I must've climbed up through quakie groves and small open parks for at least five hours 'fore I begun to see the country change. Then I went through a couple of stands of lodgepole pines and started getting into blue spruce. It was real dark in among the spruce and the light of the stars didn't come through as much, but it seemed like it was easier going. The slope'd got a little steeper and I slipped on the pine needles once in a while, but it was a little more open—there weren't no more brush around—and I kept ducking through and pushing ahead. Them pines sure smelled good.

The sky was still starry when I come out on a big open park. From there I could look far down the mountain to get some idea of how high I was. In the distance I seen the predawn campfires of the Comanche village.

Lights at night in that thin mountain air are deceiving. They look nearer than they really are. Still, it froze my heart to see how close that camp really was. Then, on the slope of the mountain, 'bout halfway 'tween me and the Comanche village, I spotted a light. Then I seen another one that was moving. I knowed then they was tracking me.

That sight put added fear to my feet. Although I was groaning and staggering with exhaustion, I turned to keep going on up that mountain. I figured by daybreak I could see to get myself in a good position to fight.

It was cold up there, but I wasn't. Not the way I was moving, no chance. The sweat was pouring off me and I kept chugging on. A funny feeling come over me. I noticed that all the stiffness I'd had with my wrists and my ankles from being tied up for so long and abused so much, it'd all oozed outta me. As my blood got to stirring 'round and my body got to working and I begun sweating, I felt a fresh new strength. It seemed like I'd got me a second wind. The piercing hurt of that gasping breathing passed outta my lungs and I begun to breathe easier again. The air smelled clean and sweet and I felt a surge of wild, pure joy at being alive.

When daybreak come, I was still climbing through the blue spruce. God, I hadn't never seen mountains like those before. The Rockies was something else.

'Bout half an hour after dawn, when the sun was just peeping over the eastern prairie, I broke out into another park covered with tall wild timothy that was blowing in the breeze. The smell in the air was like heaven itself. I looked way down across the valley and seen how high I'd come. I was pretty good at judging distances, and I figured I'd come maybe nine miles and climbed five thousand feet up that mountain.

I'd come upon a few patches of snow here and there, but there weren't too much of it—only 'bout an inch or so, 'cept on the north side of slopes and trees where it'd make maybe three- or four-inch-deep banks. I s'pose I should've worried a little bit 'bout hiding my tracks, 'specially across the snow, but I didn't have no time to be tricky, and I weren't real good at it then anyway.

I didn't have a plan. I just needed to find a place where I could get a good view and nobody could sneak up on me without me seeing 'em a long ways off. I didn't have no idea 'bout snow in the mountains and didn't know how deep it could get.

I finally hit timberline when the sun was 'bout an hour high in the sky. Then I seen that I was getting into deeper snow. It was three to four inches deep in most places, yet there was other areas where the wind had blowed the ground almost bare. I was at timberline, all right, and them spruce'd growed pinched down 'til they was just little windblown, stunted dwarfs. I kept working my way up a narrow open slope, trying to avoid the snowdrifts as much as possible.

As I got higher, them dry patches got fewer and fewer and the snow begun to cover the whole ground. My moccasins was slippery and my feet was tingling with cold. I rounded a little finger of a ridge and looked ahead of me up the grade to the north. What I seen gladdened my heart. A whole bunch of great big rocks and boulders lay in a big strip down the side of the mountain. They was real jaggedy and square, like toy blocks that a giant had throwed around.

I didn't know what I was looking at, 'cause I'd never seen a rockslide before, but by God, I only had to take one look to know that no horses was gonna make it over that dangerous jumble. What was better, that slide'd come right down off a big cliff that was hanging 'bout three hundred feet above it, so there weren't no easy way to get up and over. The slide went on down the mountain and disappeared into the timber, making it a tough obstacle to get around. I knowed that if I could find a hiding place right in the middle of that rockslide, I could sure hold out a long time and see anybody creeping up on me. They'd have to cross it on foot.

I jogged on over to the edge of the rockslide. When I got there, I was more pleased with it than when I'd been looking at it from a distance. Most of them boulders was as big as a kitchen table and some of 'em was damn near as big as a house. There was big holes and gaps and crevices 'tween 'em, and they was all on edge, tumbled topsy-turvy. No horse was gonna get across them things.

Not so for a man, but I had to get on my hands and knees 'bout half the time to work my way up 'tween the wedged rocks and slither my way 'round as best I could, slowly climbing up towards the base of that towering cliff.

I scrambled up high and took up a good position, wedged in there amongst some rocks where I could see in all directions 'round me. There weren't no way for nobody to get to me without my seeing 'em first, 'cept from the top of the cliff—and darkness'd come 'fore that time and I expected to be long gone by then. I could see to the edge of the timber where I'd come out, maybe eight hundred feet below. I figured that anything that was shagging me'd follow my tracks and come out right there where I could see 'em.

The wind was blowing, but the sun on that blanket felt warm on my shoulders. I sucked on some snow, then I took a good look at that Sharps rifle. It was a single-shot breechloader with a lever action falling block and side hammer for rimfire cartridges. I opened the breech and seen that there was a shell in it. I took out the shell and found it was as long as my hand. It was a buffalo Sharps, designed to kill at a thousand yards. I closed the block again, then yanked back the hammer and pulled the trigger a couple of times, aiming around at rocks and anything I could see at a distance, just to get the feel of the trigger pull and sighting.

It weren't near as good a weapon as that Winchester I'd got off'n Sullivan. The Sharps was heavy in the barrel with a real awkward stock, and it didn't come up to my eye good. The drop on the stock weren't enough for me. It must've been made for somebody a lot smaller or with a different build, like a shorter neck.

Anyhow, it was a gun, and I could pinch down on that rear sight notch and really draw a fine bead on something if I had to. I didn't know nothing 'bout the shooting characteristics of a Sharps, 'cept it shot about a 50-70 slug. All I knowed was it was used a lot on buffalo and oughta work just fine for Indians.

Then I looked at that rotten old cartridge belt. It was marked "U.S." and must've belonged to some cavalryman. It could be buckled 'round my waist, so I took it off my shoulder and refastened it. It'd once had a double set of buckles, but one of 'em was gone. The other was in good shape and I figured it'd hold. There was only eight cartridges in that thing, plus the one I'd put back in the gun after my dry firing it. I knowed I was gonna make every one of 'em count—and save the last one for me if it come to that.

I looked up at the clear blue sky. It was gonna be a real beautiful day, with not a cloud in sight. That sky above me was bluer than any I'd seen before. Behind and above, all lighted up by the rising sun, was that cliff. I reckoned it stretched for close to four miles in each direction along the rim of the mountain. The rockslide itself was 'bout six hundred yards wide.

On both sides there was a wide strip of loose gravel—like mine tailings—too steep to get much footing on without lots of slipping and sliding. Then the dry grass begun to show again. Them grassy slopes on either side run clear to the timber, but they was awful steep and partly snow-covered, 'specially up by the cliff. I reckoned a horse couldn't make it very far past the bottom of them open slopes.

'Bout a mile away to the south there was a long ridge that run out from the cliff base. It looked like there was a crevice or chimney at the bottom of the cliff where it just might be possible for a man to climb up through on his hands and knees, although it'd be tough going and he'd be exposed most of the time.

My real problem lay in how many warriors there was on my trail and how they was gonna react when they got to the rockslide. Even though I'd got myself in a real good position, I'd also put myself in a trap: If there was enough of 'em or if they wanted to stay long enough, they'd eventually get me.

Then I begun thinking that it sure seemed like a wonderful place to die. I looked from the rugged cliff reared up against the bright blue sky to the snow-covered peaks and down onto the shimmering blue spruce forest that faded out onto the yellow-brown plains and away into the hazy purple stretches of the great prairies.

I seen how beautiful the world really was and I got to feeling sorry for myself—thinking that it was gonna be my last day on earth.

Then I got to wondering where Pedro was. I reckoned that when he found out that I'd left Hays City, he would've figured out that I'd gone west. I'd told him to count me in, and he knowed my word was good. I reckoned by now he'd be somewhere along the trail to Taos, and I sure hoped he hadn't got hisself mixed up with the Comanches like I had. But I figured Pedro'd be lots smarter.

Then I thought 'bout Michelle. That was hard, and it hurt. What a great little gal she'd been. Lots a love, lots a charm, lots a understanding of what a man was all 'bout. What more in the world could a man want in a girl than that? Suddenly I knowed I loved her. But she was gone. I could never tell her how I felt, never whisper in her ear again, never squeeze her in my arms. No, Michelle was gone, she was a ghost. How in the hell could I ever make up for what I'd done? I'd kinda lied to her, pushed her along and got her coming with me into Comanche land. I'd be a helluva long time paying off that debt, but the whole Comanche nation owed her something, too—and I intended to collect that debt personally for her.

I looked out again at all the beautiful things that God'd made. There was the high peaks that was much closer now with their snowcaps shining in the bright sun. There was the blue, blue sky. There was the rock cliffs with their red color that stood out so clear. Then, farther down the slope was the tall beautiful blue spruce trees, and over their tips I could look out and see the great plains stretching away clear across the country that I'd come through in the last three weeks.

In the silence between the gentle whispers of the wind, I could hear the dripping of the melting snow in the rockslide and the sighing of the pines. I knowed I was 'bout ta die, and I thought again what a nice place I'd picked ta do it. Then I got ta thinkin' 'bout the love of other things, like God, nature, and what it was like ta be alive an' what it'd be like ta be dead. Right then I was alive an' I'd come ta 'preciate ever'thin' 'round me. How sweet an' delicious life was. I was lookin' at the mighty works of a God who could make the beautiful things a the world 'round me yet'd also made rattlesnakes an' Comanches.

Oh, Great Spirit, how could ya do so terrible a thing? Why'd ya create a creature like a wild Comanche an' give it the brains of a madman so's it'd think up horrible tortures that no animal'd ever dream of? Was ya angry beyond measure at someone? Maybe at me? No, not me, 'cause ya done it long 'fore I was ever on this earth. Oh God, why'd ya do this? What's the answer ta the mystery of all this terrible confusion?

Then I got ta thinkin' of the strange thing that'd happened ta me on the late afternoon of the day before, which seemed a thousand years ago. I got ta thinkin' of that beautiful face that I'd looked inta when I'd opened my eyes in grateful thanks fer the water that she'd brought ta me instead a the fire I'd been expectin'. Those soft brown eyes wasn't the eyes of a Comanche. Hell no, they was as different as night and day—they was soft as a doe's. That lighter color a hers, her expression, the sweet smile an' tenderness of her touch, those was things that never come outta no Comanche. No, that woman was a creature of God, and she had ta be one a the noblest of His works.

I called her the Sky Woman—that's what she'd looked like, framed there against the sky. She seemed like an angel, sent ta me outta the sky. How could she have got in that Comanche camp unless it was with wings? But she didn't have no wings, an' when the guards picked her up by the hair an' twisted her 'round an' slapped her hard, she was solid enough. She weren't no angel. If she had been, God would've struck them guards dead with a thunderbolt, but He didn't do no such thing, so she had ta be human. Maybe, fer the time bein', He'd turned His head away an' didn't see what happened, or maybe, just maybe, she was only an ordinary human bein' like you an' me. But where in all the world had she come from? How could she have been so different? Why'd she bother ta care fer me? She'd never seen me before. Or maybe she had, but only tied up as a prisoner. What was her reason fer doin' what she'd done? Well, I reckoned I'd never know, but I swore if by some slim chance I was ta see her again on this earth, I'd drop down on my knees an' kiss her feet, fer she'd brought me kindness an' help and perhaps a faint trace a hope when I was in the deepest part a my despair. If I didn't meet her again on this earth, perhaps I'd meet her some other place. But that was hardly likely, 'cause she'd certainly be in heaven, an' from the way I'd lived my life I figgered I had a better chance a goin' ta the other place.

Well, those was the thoughts I'd had—the thoughts of a man who knowed that he was 'bout ta die, but who was still livin' an' comprehended the wonderful things 'round him—and the evil things as well.

I reckoned I had quite a bit of time left, but just then, outta the corner of my eye, I caught a movement down among the blue spruce. I tensed up like a bowstring, ducked my head down, and barely peered over that block of rock, holding the rifle in my arm.

Soon I was gonna have a chance to put up an honest fight. What's more, I was looking forward to the chance of paying some of them varmints back. There was nothing sweeter sounding than when I'd cut that guard's throat and heard him gurgle, and now I was gonna paste a couple more of 'em.

I seen some movement again. And then, as fine as you please, 'bout eight hundred feet below and down to the right, three Comanches rode outta the timber. One of 'em was on an Appaloosa, another was riding a black, and the last one that come out was on a flashy paint. They was moving right along, making much better time than I'd figured—they'd overtook me fast. They could see my tracks in the snow, where I'd gone into the rockslide, and they was looking up towards the cliffs. I sat there sweating, trying to guess how long it'd be 'fore more showed up.

I wondered what them bucks was thinking 'bout. When they seen my trail going up into the rockslide, they knowed the riding was all over. Them Comanches was wonderful horsemen, but they was worse'n cowboys when it come to wanting to walk. They'd ride a horse right up to the last possible ditch 'fore they'd get off. 'Course when they did, they could move right fast and real stealthy.

The one that was on the paint motioned and pointed—first up towards the south cliffs by the crevice, then way over to the other side of the rockslide and back down into the timber. He paused for a minute, and it seemed they was talking amongst themselves. Then the leader threw back his head and let out the damnedest blood-chilling whoop I ever heard. The hunt was on, and like a two-legged bloodhound, he was announcing that they'd located their quarry. I'll never forget that whoop and the way it echoed across them cliffs.

Then far, far down in the timber I heard another whoop come back, real faint but unmistakable. Then there was several more distant yips. I knowed what that meant: Them three was the advance guard of a whole bunch of warriors, all out on a real spree, a hunting party, and they was after me. I was their whole focus of attention, and I wanta tell you, it weren't the kind of limelight I cottoned to.

If you wanta feel real sick, get yourself up on a mountain where there ain't no escape and get a bunch of Comanches crawling up the hill below you. Sometimes I wake up at night, even now, in a cold sweat from dreaming 'bout it.

All of a sudden them three Comanches split up and the one on the Appaloosa come straight up the trail I'd made to the rockslide. The one on the black turned south and went angling off, climbing his horse as best he could to the southwest. The one on the paint turned and went down into the timber as if he was following the rockslide. I took a keen interest in their movements, but I didn't move none myself, 'cause I weren't aiming to give away my position.

I watched that brave on the Appaloosa coming on up the track after me. He rode 'til he got to where my tracks disappeared into the rockslide and then he drew his horse up. That Indian was leaning forward to keep his seat—the hill was that steep. I figured he'd slide off his horse right then and take his rifle and start working his way into the rockslide, tracking me. If so, I'd have to meet up with him sometime and have it out, but at least I'd have an even chance.

He didn't slide off his horse a'tall, though. He stopped there motionless, 'bout five hundred feet below me and four hundred yards away, looking up that rockslide to try to see some movement. He had his rifle in his right hand, sticking straight up, with the butt resting on the withers of his horse. He was wearing a blanket poncho 'round his shoulders to ward off the cold and he had a feather on a stick of chokecherry wood stuck in his hair. He was wearing a breechclout and riding bare-legged 'cept for his moccasins. I could see his feet hanging down below his horse's belly. His speckle-rumped horse was looking up the slope, too, with its head up and ears cocked, and it seemed like it was looking right at me.

The way that Comanche stared, I felt like he could see right through them rocks and that I didn't have no cover a'tall. I watched him, and he remained stock-still for a long time.

Without turning my head, by just twisting my eyes 'round, I could see the Indian on the black. He was carrying a rifle, too. I thought that was why them boys was the first on my trail. Maybe they was the best trackers and the best armed.

Anyhow, they sure was the first to arrive. The rider on the black horse kept working along the dry-grass slope 'bout three furlongs away, south and to my right, switching back and forth to climb that hill. I didn't know how far up he could come, but it was clear he wasn't gonna do any walking when the horse could do it for him.

He could never get opposite my height, though, even on that grass slope. It was way too steep, and I reckoned he'd give it up 'bout three hundred feet below. He was slowly gaining and I watched him with interest.

I glanced back real quick at the Comanche sitting on the Appaloosa near the bottom of the slide, still waiting for him to slip off and start coming after me. The one on the paint horse had plumb disappeared down into the timber. I reckoned he was going back to hurry up the others. I cursed my luck at the thought that there was others on the way. There was a good chance I could handle them three, and I wondered how much more time I had 'fore any others got there.

The warrior on the black horse was putting his mount to the toughest kinda climbing for a horse. I hadn't got used to what them Indian ponies could do when they was hard-pressed, and some of that country he was covering I didn't think was passable. He was showing me that it was.

I noticed the real clever way that he chose his switchbacks—how he never hurried his horse none and how careful the horse was at feeling its way along through the snow on that steep, slippery slope. I couldn't help but admire his steady, determined horsemanship.

He was a long time in coming, and when he finally did get as high as he could go, he stopped and sat on his horse, looking out over the rocks. He'd done lots better'n I'd figured he would. He'd gotten to a level 'bout a hundred fifty feet below me, but he was off to the side. On his last zig, he'd come over as near as he could get to the edge of the rockslide. I reckoned that distance to be 'bout three hundred fifty yards.

He stopped there and sat, same as the warrior down below, not making a move. He weren't bare-legged but had buckskin britches and the same kinda blanket. He sat on his horse with his rifle in the crook of his arm, just like the guards who'd watched over me when I was staked out. His horse stood there motionless, too, its head up and its ears cocked, looking in my direction like it smelled that I was right there.

It was real spooky seeing them two Indians staring at me and not moving, one of 'em four hundred yards below at the base of the rockslide and the other damn near my level but farther out. The tension begun to build up and I debated whether or not to try a shot. My heart begun to pound. I didn't know how that Sharps'd shoot, but I figured that if the gun was designed to kill buffalo at a thousand yards, it oughta make mincemeat outta that black horse and rider, if I could just hit 'em. If I only killed the horse, there was a good chance its rider might get busted up in the fall on that steep slope. At least he'd have to fight on foot, and that might discourage him.

The more I thought about it, the worse the idea seemed. He was gonna have to fight me on foot anyway if he come into that rockslide after me, unless he wanted to sit on that horse for a week. If I planned to do any shooting, I'd better save the bullets.

The real threat was not from that Indian off to the right on the black, but the one that was way down below on the Appaloosa. If he slipped off that horse and started into the rockslide on foot, it'd be hard to see him coming uphill, the way them boulders lay. He might get pretty close 'fore I could get a clear shot.

They both kept sitting there and I figured they was waiting and watching 'til the rest of 'em come up. I wondered why they sat out in the open. Wasn't they worried that maybe I'd take a shot? They must've knowed I'd took a gun and cartridges. Maybe they was making a brave stand to try to draw fire, figuring that I'd miss. I didn't know what they was planning.

I didn't have to busy my own mind with any more thinking, though, 'cause just then something caught my eye off to the left. Down in the timber, just north of the rockslide, I seen a movement and then, sure enough, that buck on the paint come riding out into the open. He hadn't gone down in the blue spruce to backtrack and hurry up the other warriors like I'd figured. All he'd done was to go 'round the bottom of the rockslide through the timber and come up on the other side.

Then I got the idea. They'd knowed I was in that rockslide some-where, so now they'd left somebody near the bottom and somebody on both sides where they was sure to see me. They had me, and they wasn't gonna waste no time coming up through them rocks after me. They was gonna wait 'til the rest of 'em got up there for the fun. Then I figured they'd close off the circle real steady. It made me feel like a rat in a trap.

I watched that paint horse coming up on the grass and snow on the north side of the slide to the left. The more I watched that paint, the better I liked the way he handled hisself. Damned if he didn't remind me of Piebald, only instead of being black and white, he was tan and white. He was one helluva good horse, and it showed. He was surefooted and spirited, and that Indian rode like he was part of the horse. He made quite a sight working his way up the hill, zigging and zagging 'til he come to a place higher'n I reckoned he ever could. He stopped on a little level bench, not more'n a hundred feet below and maybe three hundred yards off to the north. That brave, too, just sat there staring in my general direction.

Then I watched the Indian on the black. When I'd look away at the others for a few minutes and come back to him, I'd see that his head'd moved just slightly and he was looking at a little different angle than where I'd left him before. I felt a little easier and stayed hid. This must've lasted for ten or fifteen minutes, with not a sound from 'em and nothing going on. The only thing I could hear was an occasional sigh of the wind and the water dripping on the rocks under the slide.

I was sorely tempted to shoot, but I didn't know which one of 'em to shoot at, what with all of 'em being 'bout the same distance away. I looked way out over them plains again. I could see for more'n a hundred miles—the mesas off in the distance that we'd been riding through that last awful week, then the cottonwoods marking the branch of the Cimarron that me and Michelle'd come up. I looked at the blue sky and them cliffs in back of me shining in the sun, and the brightness of the snow on the grass above timberline. I looked at them blue spruce trees and then way down below to where the quakie-aspens was all turned to gold and the oak brush run like a red skirt off the mountain and flounced on down to meet the yellow grasses of the plain.

Then I looked off to the right at the south end of the cliff where the mountain towered higher and higher up to a real sharp, jagged, snow-clad peak, and then off to my left to where, at the north end of the cliff 'bout a mile away, the slope seemed a little less steep and led on up to some unknown country beyond and to the west—a country I'd never seen. I felt too young to die and leave all them glories of the world behind. I figured that if I ever got outta that trap, I'd try going north over that high ridge.

I slowly swung my rifle 'round and aimed it down among the crevices of the rock, drawing the barrel up and seeing just how it looked. Then I lifted it all the way to my shoulder and drew a bead, but kept the barrel and my head outta sight from below.

I picked up a little piece of chipped rock and rubbed it along the bead to make it shine. Then I spit on my thumb and wiped away the dirt. I sighted the gun again and was real pleased to see that the bead showed up real plain now, thanks to the shine of the scratch angle and a little spit. That was a trick my daddy'd taught me back in Kentucky a long time before.

I looked over at the Indian to the north, sitting there on the paint, and judged his distance again. Then I looked at the one to the south and gauged how far he was, and done the same for the one down below. A plan begun to form in my mind. If it was to work, I'd have to move sideways without being seen.

I begun working along real cautious, staying hid while going north and maintaining the same level. The one thing I didn't have to worry about none was making noise. They was a loud, whistling breeze up there and no stones that'd make any sound that could be heard unless I kicked a real big one loose.

I went maybe ten yards at a time and then eased my head up real cautious to check each Indian in turn, and seen 'em still standing motionless. I covered maybe fifty or sixty yards to the north and then begun working my way downslope real slow. Soon as I got close enough, I raised up a little bit and studied each Indian. I tried my best to see what their rifles looked like. The thing I was most interested in was seeing if they was magazine rifles or single-shot. That was gonna make lots of difference in my plan.

The Indian on the black, to the south, was better'n four hundred yards away and he had his rifle down in the folds of his blanket, so's I couldn't see the barrel too good. But the Indian on the Appaloosa, down near the bottom of the slide, was 'bout the same distance from me as before. I was pretty sure I could make out an upper and a lower barrel, meaning that the rifle had a magazine, so I figured his gun must've been one of them sixteen-shot Henrys built back in '63.

I shifted my attention to the Indian that was on the paint to the north of me and seen that I'd closed the range on him to close to two hundred fifty yards. I could see him real plain and I breathed a sigh of relief, 'cause I seen his rifle was a single-shot. I reckoned it was like the one I carried. My plans all depended on that.

I kept working downhill real slow, easing myself from one boulder to another. I'd crawl a couple of feet and then look 'round real cautious, then crawl a couple more. I done this for maybe ten or fifteen minutes, 'til I'd worked myself down to where I was plumb on a level with that buck sitting on the paint horse. He still hadn't seen me, and I didn't think that the others had either.

By then I was 'bout halfway to my goal—a big block of rock that was sitting on the edge of the slide right next to the gravel slope, 'bout a hundred yards from the grass.

None of them Indians'd moved, so I went down a little bit farther and carefully judged my distance from the big rock. I reckoned it was still 'bout sixty yards away. I crouched way down then and real careful drawed out another bullet from the cartridge belt and stuck it 'tween my teeth. Then I worked myself down in short steps to within 'bout half the distance to that rock—maybe thirty yards. I stopped and come up to take a peek 'round and check on each Indian in turn. They was all still just sitting there, looking up above me in the direction where I'd been.

I reckoned I was gonna have to take my first shot then for two reasons: to give 'em an idea where I was located and to see how accurate that rifle was. I'd already made up my mind that I was gonna aim for the buck on the black, even though he was at least four hundred fifty yards behind me, but I had my reasons. I knowed that it'd be awful lucky, with a rifle I hadn't worked with, to kill him at that distance, but I figured I could for sure down the horse.

I took one last glance down at the Appaloosa to the south and got the scare of my life. That horse was standing there all alone. The buck'd slipped off his saddle and had to be making for my direction. The horse was looking my way and was prob'ly watching his master coming after me. I knowed he had a little angling uphill to do and four hundred fifty yards of rockslide to cross before he got to me.

Damn! I didn't have enough time to make it down to the big rock like I'd wanted to. If I was gonna try my plan, I had to do it then. Real careful, I eased the rifle barrel up over the edge of a sharp block of stone and drawed down on that distant black horse. I put that shining bead tight into the notch of the rear sight, then eased it up to where it lay right behind the withers 'bout on the saddle, since I figured that'd allow for the drop. With any luck, if the gun shot accurate, I'd take the Indian in the leg, as well as get the horse.

I held my breath, pressed down slow, and tried to remember them two dry runs I'd made with the trigger pull, knowing just where she'd let go. It come just like I'd expected, and the rifle went off with a roar. I seen real plain in that bright sunlight the spot on the shoulder where that black was hit. He flipped right up on his hindquarters and peeled over backwards. It was as clean a spill as I ever seen in my life.

Right away quick I knowed the gun was shooting a little high and a little to the right. I didn't wait to see if the buck got up from the spill. I started running like hell for that big rock and, sure enough, things started to happen like I'd hoped.

The buck on the paint horse to the north turned and started down the slope in the direction of the shot. I was jumping from rock to rock. When he seen me, he stopped short and took aim and fired. I could hear the bullet smack the rocks behind me, and I put on a burst of speed and reached the shelter of the big rock. It was as square as a kid's toy block and as big as a small house. I spun 'round the bottom end of it, and while I was running I jerked the bullet out from my teeth, snapped open the breech, pulled out the dead shell, and shoved in the new one.

Then I stuck my head 'round the rock enough to see where that Indian on the paint'd stopped to reload. He was just a little above me and 'bout a hundred yards across the gravel slope. I could've killed him real easy, but he weren't close enough to suit my purpose, so I waited there, crouched real low, to see if he made the move I hoped.

He didn't disappoint me. He clung real close to the neck of his horse and started working across the gravel slope towards the rock-slide. I seen right away that his horse was having trouble on that steep hillside, 'cause he slipped off and kept the horses's body 'tween where he must've guessed I was and hisself. He kept crouched low all the time, like he was waiting for some motion from me so's he'd have a chance to get off a shot.

He didn't know rightly where I was, 'cept that I was behind the big rock, and I could come out from either side. The advantage I had on him was that he was more exposed, but he was still hiding behind his horse. For me to kill that paint horse would've messed up my plan. I crouched there nigh unto two or three minutes waiting, to see what move he'd make.

I must say that he'd hid hisself real well, staying right behind the horse's shoulder and bending his legs pretty even with the horse's. Indians is real clever like that.

The hair on the back of my head begun to stand up a little bit. I realized I didn't have much protection against something coming up from behind—not the way I was hiding behind that boulder—so I crouched down as low as I could and waited.

Just then the Indian with the paint moved. The animal hesitated and pulled back a little on his rein, exposing the Indian's body. That was what I'd been waiting for and I raised up to draw a bead on him. It was almost the last aim I ever took, 'cause just then there was a helluva crash and a sharp splintering of rock stung my face.

I realized in a flash that a shot from behind me'd hit the rock. I whirled 'round in time to see that the buck who'd crossed that whole rockslide in jig time was now only 'bout thirty yards away. He was taking a quick jump to a rock, so he could get a plainer shot at me, and at the same time was working the lever action of his rifle to put another shell in the chamber.

There weren't no Indians 'round in them days that could shoot any faster'n I could. It only took me a fraction of a second to swing 'round and fire, and I didn't even bother to aim. I just shot from the hip. He balanced for a second, then tumbled off that rock with his rifle sliding down after him.

I got up and run as hard as I could—zigging and zagging and jumping over the rocks towards him. Sure enough, the buck with the paint horse cut loose from behind me. Thank God, he missed again. I made that thirty yards to the downed buck faster'n a wildcat. His body was wedged in a crevice 'tween them jagged boulders and I pitched myself down headlong on top of him.

I whipped out my knife and cut his throat real fast just to make certain he was dead, though I reckoned he was anyway. I quick took a look 'round and seen the repeating rifle lying there, jammed 'tween some rocks 'bout ten feet away. I unbuckled the dead buck's ammunition belt and grabbed that rifle with one fast jump.

My heart instantly filled with gladness: That weren't no Henry rifle, it was Sullivan's old Winchester! That buck must've been one of them that'd first jumped me. Better still, I had plenty of ammunition, 'cause I seen it was my old cartridge belt full of shells he'd worn 'round his shoulder.

I still had to take care of the Comanche with the paint horse, though. I dropped the old Sharps and took up the Winchester and lay down in a crevice, watching and waiting. I knowed that there was a shell in the chamber, 'cause I'd seen the buck cram it in when he went to shoot at me. The hammer was still cocked and somehow hadn't gone off when it'd slipped down the rocks.

I peered through a crack. That paint horse'd pulled off the gravel slope and was standing on the grass with his reins dragging on the ground, looking back like he was watching the Comanche coming after me, but I couldn't see no sign of movement.

Then that horse turned his head, put it down, and eased off down the slope in that half-float, half-shuffle that a horse uses for making his way downhill. It made my heart sink. I sure'd wanted that horse. Then something real nice happened, nicer'n anything I could've planned.

It seemed like that buck wanted the horse, too. When he noticed his mount was leaving, I reckoned he sure as hell wanted no part of walking back down that mountain. That weren't the kinda sport Comanches liked. I reckoned, too, that horse was a real good one and the Comanche wanted him bad.

All I can say is, he'd made a fatal mistake. He left his cover and started running hell-bent for leather 'cross the gravel slope, trying to catch up with his horse. I let him get out there a little ways to just where the going got good, then I shot him dead.

I was so used to that Winchester by then that I knowed right away how it'd shoot. He had better'n a hundred yards to go for the horse and he hadn't got no less'n halfway there when I nailed him. The horse took off at a good clip then, angling towards the north. I took a minute to look over the dead Comanche in the rock crevice and seen that he had a good knife, which I appropriated, and also that he had a kinda medicine pouch hanging from his belt. At least that's what I thought it was 'til I felt it, then I seen it was a bag with more cartridges for my Winchester.

I collected the cartridge pouch with a quick flip of my knife, and started hightailing it after that paint pony. I never went near the buck that I'd killed up on the slope. That would've required maybe a hundred feet of climbing and there weren't no dead Comanche worth that.

I didn't know what luck I'd have catching that horse, but I knowed I was gonna try. The paint jogged along and, when he got to the edge of the timber, he stopped. Then he turned and started heading back in the direction he'd come from. I half-run and half-slid straight down through the snow and the grass as fast as I could go. When I got to the timber, I seen that the horse'd stopped in a real small park where there was a little tall dry grass. He had his head down and was chomping away. Like all Indian horses, he was hungry. I reckoned he'd stay there for a few minutes 'til I could work downhill below him.

I done that in short order, as easy as I could without disturbing him, although he lifted his head a couple of times while he was eating and looked at me and snorted as I circled through the timber.

I put down the two rifles, the extra cartridges, and the blanket, and took it real easy sneaking up on him. He fed for a while and took a step or two away, then he raised his head. I spoke to him real easy, taking a step at a time, and moved closer and closer. If ever I tried to coax a horse, that was one time I done it. I was praying he wouldn't toss his head and bolt at the scent of me.

I eased up on him real careful, feeling pretty thankful that I'd had enough sense to come up on him from the downhill side. That pony'd been pushed pretty hard during the past four hours and he prob'ly didn't cotton to going uphill much anymore, least not of his own free will.

When I got 'bout three feet from him, I knowed that I was just 'bout three feet from life or death. I had to have that horse if I was gonna live.

I started to take one more step when he tossed his head and took off, so I made a dive for his reins and caught 'em. I prayed hard and hung on tight. He reared a little and snorted and tried to whirl 'round, but I managed to hang on. He backed off and then stood there spread-legged, trembling and snorting at me.

"Easy boy, easy ol' fella," I crooned. I reached up my hand and touched his nose and run my hand over on the side of his jaw and then up and 'round his neck. That seemed to quiet him down, and he just stood there shivering and shaking. Then I led him back to the edge of the timber to get ready to head out.

I seen right away that it was gonna be real awkward to pack both of them rifles. It didn't take me long to make up my mind which one I wanted. I took that old Sharps by the barrel and slung it down the mountain through the timber as far as I could. I slipped the extra blanket over my head, 'cause I knowed I'd need it in that high country. Then I walked 'round so's I was on the uphill side of that paint and, holding the rifle in my right hand, vaulted onto his back.

He crow-hopped 'round there a couple of steps and acted up a little, but nothing that give me any trouble. I headed him off into the timber and started to angle a little up the hill.

I was near startled outta my wits a minute later to hear lots of whooping and hollering. A party of braves'd come out on the slope on the other side of the rockslide behind me and was putting together the clues. I headed deeper back into the timber then, so's they wouldn't see me right away, and made my way along the side of the mountain, heading north as fast as I dared.

I knowed then that that paint was a real fine pony. Even though he'd had a hard ride for most of the night, he had lots of bottom left in him and kept us moving right along. I stayed in the timber 'til I come to where the cliffs ended—'bout six hundred feet above me. The mountain then went up in a gentle slope for another couple of thousand feet, so I left the timber and headed into the open country. What I wanted to do was to cross over the summit and head for Taos—to the country where the Mexican settlements was and where the Comanches didn't like to visit.

It weren't long 'fore I heard more yells and hollers from them Comanches on the other side of the rockslide. I looked back and swore there must've been twenty of 'em. They was milling 'round there, pointing this way and that, shouting and yelling. It didn't take 'em long to figure things out, and they headed on down into the timber towards the bottom of the slide to come after me. I figured I had maybe a mile-and-a-half lead on 'em.

I calculated the odds, all the time pushing my pony towards the summit. I was mounted on a good horse—prob'ly as good as theirs— and I had a repeating rifle. I proposed to outrun 'em and not get myself in no trap again. I kept churning on up that mountain and I s'pose it weren't much over fifteen minutes, but to me it seemed like fifteen years.

When I topped out on a high ridge, there was the grandest sight I'd ever seen. Behind me and to my right, the great plains stretched away to the east. Ahead of me, down the other side of the mountain, was the biggest valley I'd ever seen. It looked to be more'n a hundred miles long and maybe half that wide, rimmed in every direction by the high, snowcapped mountain peaks. I didn't know it then, but that was my first look at Colorado's famous San Luis Valley. I've seen it many times since, and it always takes my breath away. It was sure a welcome sight then.

I seen where I could head down the valley side of the mountain on a reason'bly gentle slope to the southwest and get back into the timber. From there, I figured I had a good chance of staying ahead of them Comanches. The ridge on my left rose kind of easy 'til it topped the head of them cliffs above where I'd been hiding. In the distance, 'bout a mile and a half behind me, the rockslide stood out like a gray gash on the mountainside. I've only been back to that rockslide once in the last fifty years, but I've always called it "Brules's Fort"—and a fort it sure was.

Right then I seen them Comanches riding in a long line outta the timber, following the tracks my paint pony'd made. I was pretty certain that I'd topped over the divide before they seen me. They was making pretty fair time.

Then I must've felt my oats some way or another, or I had more guts than brains, 'cause I done one of the damn foolest things I've ever done in my life.

I felt like a warrior his first time out on the warpath. I'd fought them devils and won. What's more, I'd discovered a taste for killing Comanches. The fear that'd been in me, fed and watered by my hate for them savages and the pleasure that come from seeing 'em die, turned to an overwhelming kinda confidence that seemed to rise up in me natural-like. I turned back and deliberately rode south, staying outta sight near the top of that ridge, taking advantage of where the wind had blowed away the snow, climbing all the time but still staying outta sight. I stopped when I got back to where them cliffs begun. I slipped off'n the paint and checked his bridle real good—it was strong and stout. Then I tied the end of the bridle rope 'round my left wrist real tight. I sure as hell weren't taking no chances on losing him.

Now I could look right down and watch that long line of Comanches coming outta the timber and following my trail to the northwest. They filed right by me five hundred feet below and still at least four hundred fifty yards away. I counted twenty-three of 'em and they was riding a whole assortment of horses.

It sure looked like an Indian parade, with all the colors you could imagine. Some of 'em was wearing horned helmets, and some of 'em had feathers on that stick of chokecherry wood they stuck in their hair. Some of 'em had on breechclouts with thigh-high moccasins and some of 'em was wearing buckskin britches, and most of 'em was bare from the waist up 'cept for their poncho blankets.

'Bout only five of 'em had rifles; the rest had bows and arrows. All of 'em carried long decorated lances and shields. They was moving along following my diagonal track in that thin snow as they worked up to the left towards the ridge that was now north of me.

I took a quick count of what I had in the way of ammunition. I unloaded the Winchester's magazine and seen I had seven shots there. Old Sullivan's cartridge belt still had twenty shells in it, and the pouch I'd took off'n the dead Indian carried eleven more. That give me a total of thirty-eight rounds—but I needed to save some of it, so I only had 'bout twenty rounds that I could use.

I was in a good spot there. Anyone looking up from below could only see a little part of my head. I had to hope my pony would stay put and not dance out to where they might do him some damage.

At that distance I had 'bout a fifty-fifty chance of hitting an Indian. I couldn't be too sure of making a fatal shot, but them horses was big targets and I figured I could hit some of 'em without no trouble.

Now, I love horses and don't like to see 'em get hurt on account of man's problems, but the truth of the matter is, a wild Comanche was pretty well discouraged without his horse and I couldn't afford to waste no ammunition. My idea was to discourage the hell out of 'em.

The Indian at the head of the column was riding a big gray. The first test was to see how my horse, Paint, was gonna behave, so I reloaded my rifle, took my time, and really squeezed down on that gray for the first shot. I knowed how that Winchester shot and where it'd lay a slug at four hundred fifty yards. Allowing for the slope, which was pretty steep off that cliff, I figured I didn't have more'n about a four-inch drop. At the explosion, Paint jerked back a bit and yanked my wrist that was tied to him, so for a second there I didn't see what happened. Then I took a good look down the valley and seen where that gray horse'd reared up and fell over backwards and his rider was struggling to get out from under it.

Things was a mass of confusion down there. They stopped for a minute and broke ranks, and all of 'em was hanging down on the offside of their horses to give themselves cover. I gentled old Paint and he steadied down, so I went back to work again. The next horse I picked was a bay, and it went down in a heap just like it'd been sledgehammered. I couldn't see what happened to the Indian. That time Paint didn't move much, so I went to work and fired all the rounds that was left in the magazine.

I killed a horse or wounded it bad every time, just picking 'em off starting at the head of the column. Four of 'em was down for good and the other three was hopping 'round in such a state that I didn't think they could be rode very far for very long. There was yelling, and horses screaming in pain, and blood all over the snow, and the unhorsed Comanches was crawling for cover. I reloaded as fast as I could. My next five shots killed five more horses, which put half the band on foot, and the rest of the mounted ones scattered down towards the timber. Some fired shots at me, but they never even come close.

Them bucks that was afoot run like hell for the timber, too, 'cept for a couple of 'em that jumped up behind other warriors and rode double. Two of 'em was still crawling 'round in the snow: Either I'd been lucky and hit 'em or they was hurt by a falling horse.

I felt like I was nine feet tall, like I'd put the whole Comanche nation to shame. I reloaded again, then eased back off the hill to where I was down outta sight. I patted Paint and told him, "By God, yore a damned good pony."

I'll say another thing for them Comanches—they sure trained them animals to stand up and not be gun-shy. That's most unusual, and that's the truth. After I'd spent a while with Paint I found out that you could shoot 'round him, over him, under him, and every other damned direction, and he didn't pay no attention. I reckon he jumped a little the first time I shot 'cause he weren't used to me yet.

Keeping on the west side of the ridge and outta sight, I rode back the way I'd come at a pretty good gallop, since it was downhill and fairly smooth going. We made it in nothing flat to where I'd first topped out on the ridge.

I didn't think for one minute that them Comanche warriors was gonna give up the chase just 'cause they'd lost half of their horses, but I knowed it was gonna slow 'em up and make 'em real cautious. I could stay there a little while and rest 'til I seen what they was gonna do.

I weren't long waiting. Them Indians must've regrouped and kept in that timber 'til they got right 'bout opposite of where I'd crossed over. Two or three of 'em come outta the timber almost directly below me and took a look at Paint's tracks where I'd climbed up out from the rockslide. Then four, and five, and six come out, and finally the whole bunch, and started working up that hill at a pretty good clip. Some of 'em was riding double and there was three or four more of 'em on foot. They was climbing along behind or hanging onto the tails of the horses. I reckoned they was determined to stay outta range of that cliff where I'd been 'til they could work 'round and trap me.

I waited 'til they got in range, 'bout two hundred yards away. At that distance I could start killing bucks instead of horses. I drawed down real careful and killed the man that was riding first in line.

There was wild confusion again, and while they was turning and looking 'round, I picked two more of 'em off'n their saddles, and them horses went tearing down the hill.

By then the others'd jumped off and got behind their mounts, so I had to start in on the horses again. I killed four of 'em as fast as I could pump the gun.

That Comanche advance weren't doing so good. They didn't all run, though. Some of 'em was lying in back of the dead horses and firing, while the others was scattered out in the snow trying to get some idea of what it was about. It didn't make no difference. I'd inflicted enough damage, and it was time for me to hightail it.

I crawled back and flicked onto old Paint's back. I headed him to the southwest and kept him at a good clip, going on down the hill and into the timber. I figured them bucks'd be taking their time getting to the top of that hill—what with the chance of me shooting at 'em again—if they didn't give up altogether and head back.

There weren't no use taking chances, though, so I kept right on moving as fast as Paint could go through the timber, fleeing like a desperate man—which is what I was—and working my way down the other side of that mountain. A couple of times I had my heart come up in my throat when we hit real steep places where no horse could get down, but we looked 'round and found another way to get through.

It weren't more'n an hour 'fore I broke outta that blue spruce and into the quakies. Them quakie groves was tough going with all the tall grass and deadfalls, so's I had to be real careful. You can tie a horse up worse'n anything if you get him stuck in a logjam in the quakies. I had to take it real easy, yet still hurry that horse for all he was worth.

At the time, I didn't know how lucky I was that day, but there was two things that was working for me. Many years before, Mexican dragoons'd crossed eastward over them mountains and knocked hell outta the Comanches a few times. Then there'd been a long period of peace 'tween the peoples. I didn't know it, but I was getting into Mexican country and that was one thing in my favor.

The second thing was how quick the weather changes in the mountains. When I'd first come over that ridge, there weren't a cloud in the sky. That big San Luis Valley was looking as beautiful and as clear as could be. But when I headed into the spruce there was a gathering of storm clouds to the southwest. I soon found out how fast one of them mountain storms moves. An hour later, when I was in the quakies, the clouds'd begun to gather overhead and a few flakes of snow started coming down.

I pushed old Paint as hard as I could, 'cause it wouldn't be no good to get caught in them mountains in a snowstorm. After another hour, I broke out into oak brush. I reckon I weren't no more'n six or seven miles from the valley floor and maybe two thousand feet above it. I could look way up at the top of that high ridge I'd crossed and see it sticking up way above timberline where the patches of snow and tundra was beginning to be swept by the shadows of the clouds.

Across the valley ahead of me it was snowing pretty heavy. It wouldn't be long 'fore it'd be on top of me, but I paused a minute to give Paint a breather and take a real close look to see if anything was following me. I had mighty good eyesight in them days.

A bit of sun was still shining on them upper snowy slopes and I seen a dark black line. I knowed what it meant—it was a small string of horses. I waited to see what direction they was moving in and then my heart jumped for joy, 'cause they was working their way back up over the ridge. It was that Comanche party—or what was left of it— and they was turning back.

GIVE UP FOR DEAD

I watched that dark line for nigh unto three minutes, then turned and started down. It was beginning to snow pretty hard, but I could make out the dim outlines of where I had to go—through an oak brush draw that was almost like a canyon.

I kicked Paint into a kinda trot, and dark come on us 'bout the time we got down into the draw. There was a fair wind blowing, but it was pretty good shelter in there. Besides the oak, there was some cottonwoods, but every time I'd hit a low-lying branch the snow'd drop off and soak me. I was sure grateful for them two blankets, and I throwed one of 'em over my head and held it with my hands as best I could. Even though I was shivering with cold, I weren't 'bout to stop to make no fire. I'd seen them Indians heading back, but there might've been a couple of eager bucks who'd took off on their own after me.

Nope, I'd made up my mind that I was gonna ride all night, by God. It was tough going and it was darker'n the inside of a cat. In daylight I could've made it through that draw in an hour, but I was all night long getting down that thing.

When the first gray light of day broke through, it'd stopped snowing. With a little better light, I was able to pick my way along pretty good. By daylight, I was out onto the valley floor. As far as I could see in every direction it was white. Low-lying clouds filled the sky and it was a bleak gray day. All that snow give the country a washed-out look, making a fella feel alone and forsaken.

Up the valley, maybe a mile away, I seen a small patch of trees. I took a good long look behind me to make sure I weren't being trailed and kicked Paint into a trot. When I got to the safety of the trees, I slipped down and shook the snow off'n me. Then I pranced 'round and got my legs to feeling a little better after the ride.

If I'd been on Piebald, I would've pulled off his saddle and rubbed him, but the way that Indian saddle was latigoed and tied on with rawhide, my frozen fingers never could've got it undone and back again. So I contented myself with giving Paint a rubdown to loosen him up. I looked him over pretty good and checked his hooves to see how they was doing. He seemed to be in pretty fair shape, although I could see that he was plumb tired. I put a couple of wads of snow in my mouth to quench my thirst, then hopped right back on that horse and started off again, heading due south. I kept looking back at our tracks stretching off across the valley in the bleak morning light, half-expecting to see some snowy ghosts of Comanches sniffing along.

I weren't exactly sure where I was, but I'd heard enough 'bout the country to know that I'd crossed the first ridge of the Rocky Mountains. There weren't no settlements to the north for pretty near six hundred miles—'til them army posts along the Overland or Bozeman Trail—and I sure didn't hanker going that way.

I figured if I headed south, the worst that could happen was that I'd hit the Rio Grande where it pinched up against the mountains at the south end of the valley. If I kept following it, I'd come up on something.

I was plumb tired and hungry as hell, but so was Paint. I figured as long as that horse'd keep going, I was willing to ride him. He'd been rode real hard two nights back, when he'd climbed that mountain after me, and then I'd pushed him along downhill all day and night. Now I was fixing on riding him all day again. He seemed to still have pretty good spirit, though. I couldn't help but marvel at them Indian ponies and how tough they was.

There ain't nothing like it when the sun comes out in our southwestern country. It can be cold as hell during the night and bleak at daybreak, but when them clouds begins to separate and pull away and that warm sun busts through, you see the whole landscape all laid out there like a fairyland of colors. The misty gray and white clouds works their way off them jagged peaks and all of them beautiful pine forests sparkle like jewels against the snow. The whole range of mountains stands out real sharp against the blue, blue sky. There's nothing like it, and life comes back into a man just from looking at it.

The southwest sun is a warm sun even in winter, and if it hits a man right, it thaws him out and he begins to feel pretty good. That morning it sure put life back into me—life that'd been froze up for a long time.

That valley was so big that I felt like I was stuck in the center of the whole blooming universe. The mountains appeared to stay put, and the only way I could tell that we was getting somewheres was to turn 'round and look at the hoofprints stretching back behind us.

'Bout noon, I got off Paint and walked a while to rest him and me both. I'd kept my eyes peeled for game but hadn't seen so much as a single rabbit track. I walked a couple hours, though them moccasins wasn't much protection against the wet snow. Then I mounted up and rode again.

When the sun was 'bout an hour above the western horizon, I seen some smoke rising from a patch of timber that stretched from the base of the mountains maybe five miles ahead. After my little visitation with the Comanches, I was s'picious of any smoke, but I figured that darkness'd be on me 'fore I got up there. Then I'd have a chance to take a closer look and make up my mind whether or not it was safe to let my presence be knowed.

By sundown I could see—kinda faint in the distance—what looked like some buildings. Old Paint's head was down and I could tell he didn't have too much left in him. To be right truthful, neither did I.

When it turned dark, I could see a steady kinda light ahead. So help me God, that light stayed right out in front of me there for hours. Seemed like that big old valley never ended.

Riding towards that light, wondering if I'd ever get to it, I slowly drifted off into a kinda frozen dream. I was woke up by some dogs barking and smelled piñon smoke. The single light become several, all shining through the tiny windows of a big Mexican hacienda. I rode right up to them adobe walls, and with what life I had left in me I took a deep breath and let out a "Hellooo!"

I didn't hear nothing but the barking of dogs at first, then finally I seen a light moving in one of the windows. There was an outer adobe wall clear 'round the place, and the house formed one side of it kinda like a fort. The door of the house must've been on the inside some- place, 'cause I seen a big old solid wooden gate in the adobe wall.

I started over towards the gate, figuring that was the way anybody'd be coming to answer me. Then one of them windows opened with a clatter and in the dim starlight I seen what looked like a rifle barrel sticking out.

"*¿Qué pasa?*" a voice said. I didn't know no Spanish 'cept what little I'd picked up from Pedro and in them whorehouses in Laredo, but I reckoned I'd better think of something fast.

"*¿Habla usted inglés?*" I replied.

"I speak English. What you want?" a man's voice answered.

"I'm American. I just rode 'cross them mountains. I got away from the Comanches. I'm starvin', cold, an' me an' my horse is plumb played out. I need some help."

"Why you come here? What you think we are, damn fools?" He laughed. "Go 'way 'fore I shoot."

Then I realized they'd prob'ly think I was a thief trying to get in. I reckoned it'd be easy for somebody to come up and tell some cock- and-bull story to get in the gates and rob 'em. It could be that needy strangers was welcome, but they was leery of strangers coming in the middle of the night—them being so far out from any neighbors.

At that point, from sheer exhaustion, I put my head down on my horse's neck and must've passed out and slid off in the snow. The next thing I remember was waking up in a big room.

I was lying on a mat on the floor under a buffalo robe. There was a fire in a kinda beehive-shaped fireplace in one corner, and a boy was sitting on a chair near it. Next to him, a rifle leaned against the wall, but he didn't act as if he needed to hold it or like he was expecting no trouble from me. I reckoned them folks living out there on them big ranches knowed they had to keep a gun handy and that's just the way it was.

The firelight made the shadows flicker on the white walls. It took me a minute or two to figure out that I weren't just dreaming 'bout it and that I weren't still staked out by them damned Comanches waiting for the torture fire. Then I closed my eyes and rolled over and went back to sleep. When I woke up again I seen that the fire was out and broad daylight was streaming in through the windows, but that boy was still there keeping watch over me.

I could hear women's voices out in what I guessed was the kitchen, along with the clattering of dishes and some laughter. I pushed off the buffalo robe and sat up. The boy looked at me for a minute with bright, curious eyes. I reckoned he was 'bout fourteen years old. He grabbed the rifle and hurried off with a grin and a wave.

Shortly after the boy left, another fella come in. "*Buenos dias, señor,*" he said. Then he switched to English. "You have sleep late. It is almost the middle of the day. You must be plenty tired, no?"

I grinned and nodded.

"You hungry?" he asked.

I didn't have to stop and think twice 'bout that. "Hell, yes, I'm hungry!" I rubbed my stomach to make it clear.

He went off in the direction of the kitchen, and right away an older woman come in. She was wearing a black dress with a white apron and some sandals. She took a look at me, and when I grinned she broke out in a smile. I seen that half her teeth was gone. Then she jabbered away in Spanish, but I didn't understand a word she was saying and shook my head. She kept on talking a mile a minute, then a young girl peeked 'round the door, looking wide-eyed at me. She was a real beautiful girl. When she smiled she had a whole mouthful of pearly white teeth that flashed like a burst of sunshine on a cloudy day.

The old woman scuttled back into the kitchen and come right back and laid some steaming-hot food on the table. I tried to stand up but almost lost my balance. Then I realized how tired and stiff and sore I was from that ride. But there was nothing wrong with my appetite.

I made it to the table, sat down in a big wooden chair, and just ate my heart out. It was a great spread and there was a big mug of black coffee that went along with all the rest of it. There was eggs and tortillas and chili and some tomato-flavored rice. I reckon I ate like a hog and the old lady seemed real tickled to see it. Then I stood up and done my best to show her I appreciated what she'd done by smiling and bowing to her. She looked real happy.

'Bout that time, the big studded wooden door opened and an old man come in, a real handsome fella. He was wearing leather boots and Spanish britches and a large, full-cut white shirt. The black hat on his head had a band of blue, red, and yellow Indian beads 'round it. He took it off and I got a look at his fine head of white hair. He also had a white mustache and a little white goatee.

He come over to me. "Well, amigo, you now feel better, no? You are back on the feet, no?"

I was surprised to hear that he too spoke English. I stood up. "Yessir. I shore am grateful to ya, sir. I was 'bout at the end a my rope."

"Yes, amigo. You have not had such a good time. Please, tell me what happened."

"I was captured by Comanches," I told him. "I got away from 'em, stole one a their horses, an' rode over them mountains inta your valley."

"You have come from the Comanches, you say?" He looked at me very keenly.

I figured that he was wondering if I was telling the truth, so I stuck out my hands from under that Indian poncho blanket that I was wearing and showed him where them rawhide bindings'd cut into my wrists on both sides. Then I pulled up my trousers and showed him where the same thing'd happened 'round my ankles.

"Yes, amigo," he said. "It is very bad. We have seen this last night when we carried you in here, and when the blanket fell away from your back, we have seen the stripes from the Comanche rawhide."

Now I hadn't had no look at my back. With all the rest of the problems I'd had, I'd near forgot the lacing I'd got every time them Comanches felt like laying a quirt 'cross my shoulders.

"We know you do not lie," he went on. "But then this rifle—where did you get this rifle? No Comanche has a rifle like that."

"That's right, sir, but that rifle's mine. They took it away from me an' then I got it back."

"Where did the Comanches get you?"

"I reckon it was over east a here. I was comin' up the Cimarron."

"Yes, yes—the Cimarron. That is a bad way. You are very foolish to come up the Cimarron. It would be better to go by Bent's Fort and the Purgatory, or better still, Pueblo, and then over to Raton Pass. But maybe even now there are some Comanches between Raton and the Eagles Nest Pass."

"I reckon it was a bad time ta come 'cross there." I said. "I lost my pack mule an' a real good horse an' all a my equipment. I was lucky ta get away after they captured me."

The old man kept looking at me with soft but understanding eyes. "What happened to the rest that was with you in the wagons, and the horses? Are you the only one that got away?"

"I weren't with nobody. I come alone." I realized then that I'd made a mistake, 'cause his eyebrows lifted and his eyes brightened up real keenlike.

"Why did you come across Comanche country alone? You run away from something?"

That old boy was coming so close to the facts that I didn't figure there was any use putting more truth into that discussion. "No," I told him. "I was buffalo huntin'. I didn't know no better. I figgered I'd get a few hides ta sell—an' I did get a few. I was 'bout ready ta turn back when they picked me up."

That seemed to satisfy his fears 'bout me. 'Sides, he could see that I was pretty bad beat up. He didn't say nothing more.

It was a real nice day outside, but I was too tired out to do nothing but go back and lie down on that mat and pull the buffalo robe up over me. The old man sat staring at me for a while, then he got up and went off towards the kitchen and I heard him giving the women some kind of orders.

Late in the afternoon, I woke up and started walking 'round to try out my legs. The women was in the kitchen and I could hear 'em clattering away with dishes and whatnot. I reckoned it wouldn't be good business to stick my head in there, so I went to the big old studded door and opened it up to look outside. The air was warm and it was a clear day. The sun was shining bright and most of the snow'd gone, but there was a steady dripping off the roof of the hacienda's porch.

I stepped out there in my bare feet and took a look 'round. The whole wall made a fort, with the house built at the southeast corner. There was a big solid wooden gate on the east wall and a small building in the northeast corner stuck up a little bit above the wall to make a watchtower. In the northeast corner of the wall was a corral. There I seen several horses, including my paint. There was another set of buildings in the southwest corner that looked like a bunkhouse alongside some sheds for stock. There was a big covered well sitting in the middle of the yard and some firewood was stacked against the wall. Some hides that looked like they'd been put out for tanning lay along the south side. Nearby was a pigpen, a chicken coop, and a place for a couple of cows.

I spent that night by the fire—only they didn't have nobody watching me, although I still didn't know what they'd done with my knife and rifle.

The next day the old man was real polite 'bout it, but he moved me out into the bunkhouse. It weren't too bad a place and I was feeling much better. They'd give me a fresh shirt, and I wore my Comanche blankets over that. They'd also give me some funny-looking woven leather sandals they called huaraches for my feet. It weren't so good walking across the yard of that hacienda in the cold mud in them things, but they was better'n nothing, so I didn't make no complaints. I shared the bunkhouse with an old peon named Pancho. We didn't neither of us have a bed—just mats on the floor. It was cold out there, but with that buffalo robe and blankets, I managed to keep plenty warm.

Winter was coming on and I was fine right where I was, but I needed to make myself useful. It didn't seem quite right, though, to just ask for my stuff back and then go on. 'Sides, I didn't know where the hell I was. At least I was getting something to eat and a fire to stand in front of a good part of the time. I figured pretty soon it'd be time for me to move on, but I wanted to do it right—get back my rifle and the horse that I'd got off the Indians, and I sure needed something warm to wear on my feet.

After a few days, when I felt a lot better'n I had in a long time, I eased up to the old man one morning and asked if it'd be all right to go out with Pancho and help work the cattle. He agreed, and during the next week or so I got a real good feel for the spread. Once, we left the hacienda and crossed a well-worn wagon trail 'bout a mile away. I learned that it run from Taos up to Fort Garland and over LaVeta Pass to Pueblo.

Them Mexicans that owned the ranch was wonderful people. I got to know 'em real well. Their name was Valdez. The old man's name was Fernando and he was the patriarch of the family. When he said "jump" they weren't no questions asked 'cept, "How high?" He was tough and mighty severe, but fair. He was a fine man, and it showed in his face.

I looked quite a few times at Valdez's real pretty fifteen-year-old daughter, but I decided I'd better behave myself 'fore I got my throat cut.

During all the rest of that November and well into December, I never seen much traffic on the trail from Fort Garland to Taos. I reckoned it was the wrong time of year. From what I could learn by talking with the old man, being as discreet as I knowed how to be, I found out that we was maybe forty-five miles north of Taos and 'bout thirty miles away from Arroyo Hondo. I seen a couple of wagon loads of stuff going from Taos up north, but I reckoned they could only go as far as Fort Garland, 'cause they sure wouldn't try to negotiate LaVeta Pass during that time of year. I didn't have no hankering to go spend a winter at a cavalry post, so I just kept minding my own business, trying to make myself useful 'round the Valdez spread.

When they didn't have nothing for me to do, I always tried to find something useful and I reckoned that made me all right with 'em. Things went along that way for quite a while. We had a couple of snowstorms, but it cleared off real quick when the sun'd come out, and on them days I rode out with Pancho. Some trips we didn't find no strays, but after some snow'd fall, we'd have good luck tracking 'em.

I guess 'tween him and me and them other vaqueros we must've gathered three hundred head that otherwise would've been spread out all over the ranch and maybe got holed up and froze stiff in the winter. This went along for quite a spell—me getting my strength back and beginning to enjoy the life and at the same time coming to really like the people.

Then one day I took the mule and the cart and headed off east to the piñon slope for more firewood, just to keep from being idle. I was beginning to feel restless and I asked myself how long I intended staying with the Valdez family. Somehow or other I had to get my equipment back and get on my feet, but how to do it puzzled me. Them Mexicans was good at keeping somebody in debt, and I'd heard tell of some fellas that'd gone to work as vaqueros on Mexican ranches and ended up owing the boss. They was prisoners of that old peon system that'd worked for so long.

There'd been a lot of talk 'bout Mariana Jaramillo, who'd broke up the peon system that summer of '67 on the ranches 'round Taos.

When she was a young girl her old man'd tried to sell her into slavery to pay a debt. She'd refused to go and the case finally got to court. The peon system'd been 'round for a couple hundred years in them parts, but since the Mexican War some Anglos'd got into that country. The judge who was sent in to clean up the mess after Governor Bent got murdered was an old whiskey pusher named Benedict, and he had strong ideas of right and wrong. When that little girl come before him, damned if he didn't throw the case outta court and spend a lot of time seeing to it that the custom was stopped for good.

I didn't really have to worry 'bout nothing like that, but if I kept on and there weren't no offer of wages or nothing and all I could do was work for three squares a day, I might be almost as bad off as them peons. I sat on the front of the cart, letting the mule amble on, burning a lot of brain material trying to figure the best way outta my fix.

When I come up to the Fort Garland—Taos trail, I seen a lone horseman coming from the north. He was riding a fine-looking black, and even though he was quite a ways off in the distance, I seen he had two pack mules with him. Being real curious like I am, I loitered 'til he come closer.

There was something 'bout that fella that seemed familiar, but I couldn't figure what it was 'til he got 'bout three hundred yards away. Then, by God, just as clear and plain as you please, I seen a sight for sore eyes.

There was that old familiar black sombrero and that old black jacket with them silver trimmings and black pants and black boots and that wide grin that you could see a mile away under a black mustache 'cause them teeth looked like a damned piano keyboard.

I let out a whoop and the horseman stopped and looked over at me. I let out a yell again. "Pedro Gonzales, gol'durn your hide! What're ya doin' in these parts?"

He looked at me real funny, since at three hundred yards he likely couldn't make out who I was. He wouldn't expect to know some peon on a cart, so he kept his hand near his holster and didn't say a word. He stared at me a minute, then kicked his horse into a slow walk and come on real curious—leaning from one side of his saddle to the other, peering at me 'til he got within fifty yards.

Then he exploded. *"¡Jesucristo!* Cat Brules! What is going on here? Damned if you don't look like you come straight from hell!"

He galloped up and dismounted and at the same time I jumped

down off that cart. He reached out and grabbed me 'round the shoulders, shaking me and punching me and crying. "Where in the hell have you been, amigo? You goddamned crazy bastard—you lousy gringo! I have give you up for dead!"

I wanta tell you there was a few tears in my eyes, too. I never was so glad to see anybody in my life.

Finally Pedro stepped back and shook his head in pretended admiration. "Amigo, I have worry many times 'bout how much brains you have. Now I see you are just a peon. You are going after wood with the cart, no? You are sure stupid, but you are now where you belong. You are finally achieving the aim which in your life was the highest. Now you have no other place to go. I am glad that I have seen you and that you are so happy. Now I know there is nothing more that any man can do for you because you have riz so high in all the world." He grabbed his hat and made a grand bow.

"Pedro, damn your black soul!" I hollered. "Don't you rawhide me. I'm doin' the very best I can. Considerin' the bad luck I've had an' the life-threatenin' circumstances, I think I'm doin' right well."

Pedro took a long look at the sad-eyed mule that was waiting patiently in the harness of that rickety old two-wheeled cart. "Si, my frien'. We have much to talk about. But tell me, what is the matter with Piebald? How come you are not ride him?"

Now that really made me feel bad, and I could hardly speak the word that stuck like bile in my throat. "Comanches."

Pedro looked long and hard at me in sympathy. "You don't say! Comanches, eh? Run off with your horse? You have to walk a long ways, no?"

"No. More'n that. They picked me up, too."

"¡Santísimo!" He whistled between his teeth. "They capture you an' you are still alive? I don' believe."

"Yessir. You'll believe. Lookit this." I showed him the scars on my wrists and ankles and then pulled up my shirt and showed him what was on my back.

He looked long and hard and then suddenly turned away. He picked up a blade of dry winter grass and begun running it through his teeth while he stared off towards the Sangre de Cristo Mountains to the east.

Then he turned to me with a film of tears still in his eyes. "You know, Brules, you are one lucky man. Only once before have I hear of a man who get away from the Comanche, and he have one plenty sad story to tell. Them Comanches, they is like the devils outta hell. I know. Chihuahua is where I lose my oldest sister and her husband and two cousins to them devils. My father, he rather kill Comanches than watch the bullfight. How you ever get away?"

We sat down on the back of the cart and I told him the story of my knifing the guard and running to freedom. He listened real quiet 'til I finished. Then he said, "*¡Madre de Dios!* You are the luckiest man I know. They were sure fix to burn you in the fire."

Then another thought hit him. "What happen to your little whore, Michelle? She leave you somewhere? Dodge City maybe? Somewhere else? She was *muy bella!*"

Then I really had a tough decision. I didn't feel like talking 'bout it, but I had to tell my one and only best friend. So, I looked him hard in the eyes. "Naw, she never left me. They burned her."

"*¡Dios mio! ¡No!*" Then he spat.

I ain't never seen a man spit with the kinda hate he had in him. I guess all the way from Chihuahua to Taos the Mexicans hated them goddamned Comanches. They'd had two or three hundred years of bloody wars with them bastards, ever since they'd lost their horses to 'em.

The Indians weren't much problem 'til the Spaniards'd come north from Mexico City into the state of Chihuahua and started them big horse ranches. I'd heard tell in San Antone 'bout how them early conquistadores'd come up there and start them horse ranches, and how they used to have a law saying that they wouldn't turn no horses loose to no Indians. Any man that'd trade a horse to an Indian was as good as dead, and he died the hard way.

There was a story 'bout one of them Spanish dons who at one time lost a few horses to some Indians that'd stole 'em, and he rode damn near a thousand miles to pick 'em up again. They knowed that when the Indians got horses of their own, they'd be tough enemies, and of course that's what happened.

It weren't possible to keep the horses to themselves forever. What with strays and such, they fell into the hands of the Indians, and the Comanches was among the first to get 'em. When they got hold of their own mounts, they turned into real horsemen and it changed their whole way of life.

'Fore they'd had horses, Comanches weren't nothing better'n varmints living in wickiups in the desert and the plains. But with the horse, they got the freedom of all the world laid out in front of 'em. It changed their whole culture, 'cept for how they stunk.

Pedro didn't say nothing for near five minutes, he just kept chewing on his sprig of grass. Then he finally turned on me, and it was the only time I ever knowed him to give me a cussing, 'cept for when he was kidding with me.

"Amigo," he said, "you are my amigo always, but this time I think you are the biggest damn fool I ever know. What the hell is the matter with you? You was a damn fool to ride alone with a woman across the Cimarron cut-off for Eagles Nest Pass and Taos. You have got to have the mind of the monkey.

"Y'know same as me that Quanah Parker and his Quohadies never went into Medicine Lodge like the other chiefs—he still out wild. They is crazy for blood, and the place where the Quohadi Comanches go is at the head of the Cimarron for the buffalo hunt in the fall. They is going to kill all the white men they can find—both Spanish and gringo. They will kill him, kill him, and kill him. What is the matter with you, Brules—you not know that? So you go through the Comanche country just to offer your head for to get it scalped, no?"

I hung my head and let him rant.

"Look, my frien', when I hear you was gone after the saloon fire, I come after you fast. I know you run away from Hays City, but I did not know why you run. I track you across the Smoky Hill, across the Pawnee Fork, and then I lose you on the Santa Fe Trail. There was too many tracks and I cannot follow Piebald's hoofprint all of the time. I hoped you was going to Taos, so I start out to Taos to find you, but I am not such a goddamned fool as to go near the Comanche."

I nodded, hoping he was finished, but he had some more on his mind.

"Now, y'know, amigo, I am for sure no coward. But I am not damned fool enough to think that one man alone is going to fight the whole goddamned Comanche nation! No sir, I pass by old Bent's Fort. I go to Pueblo. I go to Fort Garland over across LaVeta Pass. I spend a little time in Fort Garland, to take the money away from them soldiers that are playing poker, and then I come down here on the road to Taos, and what do I meet along the way? My amigo here—looking like a goddamned peon riding in the wood cart! You are the biggest damned fool I ever know—and the luckiest, too."

Finally I said, "Pedro, yore my best amigo, an' I had that cussin' comin'. But hell, man, I was runnin' from a posse. 'Sides that, I tried ta buy a gun off'n an hombre on the Santa Fe Trail an' I ended up havin' ta rob him."

Pedro looked at me real sad. "Amigo, I love you like my brother, but sometimes I think maybe you are one bad-luck man. Maybe you are born under some star that is not so good. Did your mother tell you that maybe the coyotes or wolves howl when you was born? Or that maybe your father's best horse, he lay down and die the day you come from your mother's womb? What you mean you run away from the posse? There was no posse."

That was like hitting me with a ton of bricks. "Whatcha mean, no posse? Y'mean there weren't no posse outta Hays City after I killed old McIntyre?"

Pedro looked surprised. "No! So you killed McIntyre, eh? We all thought he die in the fire."

"Fer Christ's sake, Pete, didn't they hear my shot? What happened?"

"I was playing poker and sure I hear a shot, but there was lots of shots outside and no one pays no attention. Then we smell the smoke, and quick the bartender he run up the stairs and it is a roaring furnace up there. So everybody get the hell out and that place she burn down fast. There was no way to get water. Nobody knew you was up there."

Nobody'd seen me a'tall! I'd took Michelle out the same way as I'd come in and nobody'd seen us 'cept the old livery man—and he hadn't recognized Michelle!

Then I asked, "Well, how in the hell did *you* know that I'd took Michelle? Ya said ya all thought she was killed in the fire."

"I look all around the town and you are not there. I thought maybe you was there when the place burned and maybe not—how do I know? The fire was so damned hot that there was nothing but some bones left. Also, they find some doorknobs and pisspots and spurs and a .44 six-gun, and they think maybe it belong to McIntyre, but Christ, there is nothing left."

He picked up a fresh piece of straw. "Then I go back to where you was staying and that old landlady tell me, 'You mean that no-count?

He did not even come in to pay me for last night." So then I try the stable and sure enough, that goddamned Piebald is gone, and the stable man he say, 'Hell, he come in here like a wild man and he tell me to get the horse ready damned quick, and boy, I didn't argue."

I nodded, kind of imagining how it was. "He also thought maybe you have a woman with you. So right away I know you had gone and took Michelle. I say nothing, and they think maybe she burn in the fire with McIntyre. They say, 'Poor Michelle,' and they have the funeral service that last 'bout fifteen minutes for everybody in the fire, which they think is McIntyre and Michelle, and maybe some old drunk that somebody saw in there. There is no posse."

For a few minutes I couldn't say nothing. I kept looking down at the ground and feeling like the whole world was swaying out from under me. All that trouble. All them Comanches. And Michelle's dying and me robbing Sullivan. All that stuff needn't never have been. But how in hell was I to've knowed there weren't no damned posse behind me?

Then old Pedro started to talk again. I reckoned he could see how low I felt. "Y'know, amigo, I stop back by the boardinghouse to see Mrs. Tatterback. I tell her that you have to go to Independence to ride another cattle train. And she says, 'Well, that's funny. He left his rifle and his belt and some of his clothes here.' She feel that you are not trustworthy since you have not paid for the room. She say she keep the rifle 'til you pay the board."

That snapped me out of it. "Jesus Christ! Keep my rifle fer the damned board? Hell, that rifle was worth more'n any—that was a good Henry rifle!"

Pete looked at me. "Hey, just because you, amigo, are a damned fool does not also mean that Pedro Gonzales must be stupid, no? The old bitch, she soak me for two nights, so I give her fifty centavos and I pick up your rifle and your clothes. The clothes is on the other pack mule there, and your Henry rifle is too. With your ammunition."

I always knowed that Pedro Gonzales was the greatest hombre in the world, but when he told me that, I could've throwed my arms 'round him and kissed him. So I reached over and punched his shoulder. "You son of a bitch. Yore the best no-good bastard I ever knowed in my life." And I couldn't stop the tears that was coming outta my eyes.

He grinned at me. "You, too, 'cept for you are one very stupid gringo. I call you Comanche Brules from now on. But tell me, for what are you driving this cart? Where you steal this from, eh?"

"This belongs ta old man Valdez. That's who I'm workin' fer, so don't go accusin' me a stealin' nothin' this lousy."

"Valdez? Fernando Valdez? ¡Jesucristo! That is where I always stop for the night. Let me tell you something: Pedro Valdez, Fernando's brother, he is the first cousin to the man that marry my father's sister in Chihuahua. I tell you, I know this Taos. I know everybody!"

"That's great," I said. "If I'd knowed ya was related ta the Valdezes, why I'd a had ya 'range me a written introduction. Fact is, there ain't nothin' I'd a rather had than fer you ta set me up with a nice job—get me my own remuda a horses an' extra double wages just on account a knowin' you—whose brother's son's first cousin is the second in line ta the king a Spain an', fer all I know, your uncle!"

"Shut up, amigo. Come on, Comanche Brules, you lucky son of a bitch. You goddamned peon. Get back on that cart and we go to the hacienda. I speak right quick now to tell Fernando that he has found the most expensive vaquero from the Rio del Norte to Chihuahua and I have come looking for that famous cowboy."

When Pedro Gonzales come riding up and they all recognized him, I thought the place was gonna explode. I'd always figured that Pedro Gonzales knowed his way 'round, but I didn't know how popular an hombre he really was.

Pedro jumped down off his horse and he and old Fernando Valdez hugged each other, and Señora Valdez come running up with tears in her eyes and throwed her arms 'round him. Even that good-looking fifteen-year-old come out and curtsied to him. The boys went to pounding him on the back and everybody tried to hug him, while old Pancho took off his big ragged hat and went 'round there bowing and smiling with that toothless grin of his.

Soon's things quieted down some, Pedro pointed at me and started rattling off some Spanish. I don't know what he told 'em, but it sure changed things 'round. Right away, old Fernando come up and hugged me. Then all the boys hugged me, and finally the old mama hugged me. I was disappointed that the fifteen-year-old didn't hug me, too—but she smiled a shy, admiring smile.

Then the old man announced that he was gonna throw a big fiesta that night in honor of Pedro's return, and he sent riders to all the neighboring ranches to spread the word.

They finally ushered old Pete into the house just like he owned the place, and me right behind him. Right away they fixed a bed for him in a big bedroom and rushed out to get my buffalo robe and stuff. It seemed nothing'd do but to move me outta the bunkhouse and in with Pedro like I was a member of the family.

I was real glad to move inside where it was a lot cleaner and nicer, and I'd a damn sight rather stay in the same room with Pedro Gonzales, my amigo, than that old peon. 'Course I liked Pancho, but I was tired of hearing the old bastard fart in his blankets and smelling that damned onion breath of his for half the night. I reckoned it was five o'clock in the afternoon by the time we got the room arranged the way they wanted it.

I went out to help get the plunder that was in Pedro's packsaddles and hauled it to our room. I had more in mind than just accommodating him. I plumb longed for some clothes of my own and, since he'd brought 'em, I sure wanted to have a good hot bath and climb into my own duds 'fore that party the Valdezes was fixing to have.

The clothes that I'd left behind weren't much, but they was a helluv an improvement over what I'd had with me. First place, there was my extra shirt that I'd bought down in San Antone and that was cut to fit me. Then there was my extra belt with the big buckle that I'd bought from that tanner at the Wichita agency. I'd plumb forgot I had it. Most of all, there was a clean pair of Levi's.

Some folks've done lots of arguing 'bout what was the greatest invention for the West. Some say the railroads, some say the repeating rifle, and some say the telegraph. Far as I'm concerned, it weren't none of 'em. It's something thought up by Levi Strauss when he was in the California goldfields.

Oh yeah, I know it's kinda realistic-like to be seen wearing buckskin pants same as them mountain men, but I can tell you, leather don't work worth a damn. It's hotter'n hell in the summer, and when it gets wet, it clings to you something terrible. Then it shrinks. That buckskin takes the hide right off'n you lots of times when you're riding, or it'll crease up on you, and when it gets dirty it's harder'n hell to clean. It's damn heavy and don't allow much knee action. But them Levi's is damn near as tough as leather, only you can wash 'em. They're real light and easy to handle, and after a while it seems like they grows to fit your body. So I was glad to see 'em.

But best of all was my old pair of boots. I'd been wearing my best boots when I went to see Michelle that last night in Hays City, and the Comanches had 'em now. But my old boots was real comfortable, and with a little saddle soap and polish, they'd do just fine.

Pedro went out and had 'em start 'bout four buckets of hot water steaming up on the stove. Then they carried 'em out on the back patio and dumped 'em into two old tubs. By that time the sun'd gone down and it was feeling mighty sporty outside. I tell you, when you get outta a hot-water tub into below-freezing air, it peps you up real quick. I felt as sound as a new silver dollar.

I even shaved, using Pedro's knife, and I was plenty glad to get rid of a two-month beard, although I felt like maybe I was losing some of my dignity. Pedro didn't think so. He said that when I shaved it made it easier to tell me from an ape, but then Pedro never was no diplomat.

The next day was bright and plenty nippy, but it weren't too bad in the sun. Me and Pedro took some time to catch up on what'd happened since we'd parted in Hays City. Our heads was both sore from all the drinking we'd done the night before, and Pedro had some Bull Durham makings, so I rolled up the first smoke I'd had in damned near two months. I'd got outta the habit, and that smoking made my head swim.

While we was sitting out there in the sun by the corrals, I told Pedro the story of my Winchester model 66, how I'd got it and then lost it and how I'd got it again off'n that buck on the rockslide. Then how I'd throwed away that old single-shot Sharps. While I was talking, that was the only time he said anything.

"That was too bad, amigo. I wish you could have brought that gun even if it's no good to use for yourself. Sure, the barrel is too heavy and it is awkward, but you could have sold it in Taos. But that's no matter. I have some money. We will do okay."

"Pedro, it was either my scalp or that gun, an' I decided ta throw the gun away. I had runnin' ta do an' I had the Winchester repeater. Y'know there's nothin' better on the frontier." Then I told him 'bout how Valdez'd taken it away from me and that I reckoned he didn't trust me.

"Oh, he has forget," Pedro said. "I will speak to him. He will be embarrassed, like he did not think that you wish for it right now or something, but you do not worry."

Then it was Pedro's turn to tell me all 'bout what'd happened to him since the fire. He said he'd left Hays City looking for me two days after the blaze. He told me how he'd followed Piebald's tracks the morning of the fire and seen where right away I'd headed off way up to the north and stayed away from Fort Hays. Then he'd seen where I'd crossed the trail going south and figured how I'd covered up my tracks with the leaves.

He said he'd been able to follow our tracks to where we'd come to Sullivan's wagon train, but then it'd got too confused. Too many folks'd gone through there and Pedro said he'd lost the trail.

He'd went on to Dodge City and started asking 'round, but of course no one'd seen us. It was clear to him that we was running hard and had gone on west. He had some money and he got hisself a couple of mules and loaded up. He was a right fair poker player, and he done good when he hit Pueblo.

He'd got across LaVeta Pass just 'fore the first snowstorm and hit the canteen by the cavalry post at Fort Garland. He spent a few days 'round there taking more poker money away from the soldiers.

After he'd found out I hadn't been through there neither, he'd begun to worry. He figured I might've missed everything and then turned south from Pueblo and gone through Raton. Even that was dangerous, but he thought I'd sure as hell have more sense than to ride right across to the Cimarron straight through Comanche country. That never entered his head, him being 'bout three degrees smarter'n me.

"Amigo, even though you is the stupidest gringo in all the whole frontier, a no-good bastard, a loafer, and nothing but Comanche bait, I am real happy to see you," he finally allowed. "I thought I never see you again, 'cause maybe you go far away or maybe you die. Now, you are here." His face split into that famous grin. "You are a damned big nuisance and for you now, I must be responsible."

"Ah, shut up, ya miserable greaser. Right now I'm goin' back ta the house."

When I pushed open the door to our room I seen a welcome sight. There on the little bed that was mine lay my Winchester rifle with the cartridge belt and them cartridges that'd been in the Indian's medicine bag. It was laid out there like somebody'd forgot it, or had seen it somewhere else in the house and just remembered that now, since I was moving into this room, maybe I'd like to have it. Nothing more was ever said 'bout it, but I sure was glad to have that rifle back.

Pedro took one look at it and whistled. "Amigo, you have two fine rifles." He dug 'round in them packsaddles of his and pulled out my Henry rifle. I'd bought it off a Yankee trader that'd come into San Antone from Natchez the year before, and it'd cost me a heap.

'Fore the Winchester 66'd come out, that Henry was the best rifle on the frontier. It was made by the Henry Arms Company, which later changed its name to Winchester. Old Henry hisself designed it in early '62 and them rifles was all over the frontier by late '65 and early '66.

The Henry handled a .44 rimfire cartridge, carried fifteen shots in the magazine, and if you used a flat-nosed bullet you could crowd in up to sixteen. You loaded the magazine from the front end and it had a slot down the underside where you could see the cartridges and check how many you had and how they was riding.

There was only one thing wrong with that Henry. The slot in the magazine weakened the tube, and once in a while if you was lying down shooting from a rest, dirt and grease'd get into that slot and work their way into the chamber with the cartridges. Then you'd have a jam—and a jammed rifle on the frontier was bad medicine.

But that Henry was a helluv an improvement over anything else around, like them old muzzle-loaders or even a breech-loading Sharps that'd been converted to shoot a cartridge. If you took care not to get your magazine dirty, it'd serve you well. That rifle was real accurate up to 'bout three hundred to three hundred fifty yards. It begun to fade bad after that, though.

As a matter of fact, there never was a real good long-range repeating rifle on the frontier 'til Winchester put out its model 73. It had more power and better balance and was the greatest rifle in the West.

When Pedro handed me that Henry rifle, I took it and laid it down beside the Winchester and begun comparing 'em. Both was lever-action repeaters and shot .44-caliber rimfires. They had round barrels, although you could get 'em with the octagonal barrel if you wanted to haul that extra iron around. Both of 'em had 'bout the same range and shot 'bout the same.

The model 66 Winchester had a big advantage over the Henry

besides being seventeen shots. The magazine was all solid, and instead of loading it from the end, you fed in your bullets through a slot in the side of the breech. That was one helluv an advantage. It kept the dirt away and kept it from jamming. The only thing was, you couldn't tell for sure how many shots you had left in the magazine if you hadn't kept count.

The Winchester 66 had a wooden forestock that run along the barrel and the magazine 'bout halfway. You could get the barrel hot and still not worry about putting your hand on it—something to reckon with. This rifle was made in late '66 and'd got out 'round the frontier by '67. I reckon that's why Sullivan'd picked it up in Independence. Being a greenhorn, he'd wanted the very best. The storekeeper'd prob'ly sold it to him at the highest price plus. It was new and the latest thing, and he'd the money to buy it.

I was real grateful that both of them guns was rifles and not carbines—they come in both lengths. The carbine barrel was twenty inches long to the rifle's twenty-four inches. That made carbines easy to handle on a saddle and in the scabbard, and the cavalry used 'em a lot in later years. But I didn't give a damn for 'em, 'cause they lost a lot of their accuracy with them four inches took off'n the barrel. It seemed like that extra-length barrel give the gun that much more reach—not only in pushing that bullet farther, but also in adding that much more twist to it. It was a little less handy on the saddle, but it was worth it.

Right then I was feeling real grateful to Pedro. "Amigo, yore always shootin' a handgun an' ya throw knives an' ya don't seem ta give much of a damn fer a rifle, but ya should have one. So's I'm givin' you this Winchester. It's the best a the two guns, an' I want ya ta have it."

Pedro looked at me for a minute. "No, amigo. Both of these rifles, they belong to you and I am not very good with the rifle at all, so I think maybe you keep them both."

"Now listen here, I can't shoot two rifles at once, so I can't use 'em both. Ya take one. If ya don't know how ta shoot it, I'll damn well teach ya. I'll make ya a deal: Ya teach me ta throw a knife an' I'll teach ya ta shoot a rifle."

"All right, amigo. You mean what you say. You wish for me to have a rifle. It is easy to see that the Winchester is best and therefore it should be yours, but I will take with heartfelt thanks the Henry if it is your wish. I will always keep it with me and I hope I can use it well with you many times. For sure I will teach you to throw the knife. Tomorrow we ride off to Taos and there we will spend the rest of the winter maybe."

Then he reached over in his pack outfit and picked up a small sheath. He drawed from it the wickedest-looking knife I'd ever seen. It was shaped like a bowie, but smaller. It had edges like a Spanish bayonet and there was slight carvings on the ivory handle and some metal points. It was a beautiful thing to see and looked like a deadly weapon.

He took it by the blade and with a kinda ceremony handed it to me across his arm, handle first. "If I accept the rifle, amigo, you must accept this knife. We will teach each other the best use for both."

I pulled off my belt and run it through the top of the sheath and back through my pant loops. Then I went down in a crouch and whispered, "I am ready, amigo. Where do we go first?"

I pulled out the knife as fast as I could and Pedro busted out laughing. He laughed so hard he fell over on his bed and rolled 'round and gasped, "Now I have seen everything. Now I can go into the arms of Santa Maria. I have no further curiosity for this world. I have seen a gringo pull the knife and now I have seen the clumsiest thing in all the whole world. Brules, your throat would be cut four times before you get that knife out! You have much to learn, my frien', but I will teach you. Now, for Christ's sake, let us go and get some sleep, no? Tomorrow we ride to Taos."

A man has many days in his life—some of 'em he can remember and some just goes by and is long forgotten. Every once in a while there's a certain day that stands out so bright and clear that he feels that everything in his past life seems to fade into no account.

I ain't never going to forget that ride we made to the end of the San Luis Valley. The Sangre de Cristos to the east of us was a mighty mountain range, as I can well testify. As I took in the beauty of it all, I couldn't help thinking that it sure weren't no use for a man to hold hisself too grand or too low, 'cause the wheel of fortune was always correcting itself one way or t'other. And whichever way it was, a man could always count on one thing for sure: It wouldn't last long.

So it was with glad hearts and the whole world ahead of us that me and Pedro rode on down the valley. Everything I'd been through in the last few weeks'd made me older and smarter. I'd stopped kidding myself, or overrating myself, on either good luck or skill. The main thing was, I kept appreciating being alive.

'Long 'bout sunset we come up on the Indian pueblo of Taos. The winter sun was going down behind the frozen hills and that old pueblo was lit up with a golden light. I could understand just by looking at it what old Coronado was thinking when him and the rest of the conquistadores come into that valley nigh unto three hundred years before. If they was looking for gold, Taos sure showed 'em the way in the afternoon sun.

Folks say it's been standing there for a thousand years. There was really two settlements, one on each side of the creek. The way the road run by 'bout a mile to the west of 'em sure made for a great sight. Behind 'em to the east stood them high mountains, with their pine forests and their snowy peaks. That mountain right back of the pueblo that them Taos Indians hold sacred looks just as mighty, I reckon, as it did when them Indians' ancestors'd built there a long, long time ago. The Mexican town of Taos itself was 'bout a third of a mile to the west of the pueblo. It was an exciting and beautiful place.

I was real took with them narrow winding streets, them adobe houses and thick walls, and them great big old cottonwood trees that must've been growing there back when the Spanish'd first come. There was an old Spanish plaza in the middle of town, and a whole crowd of colorful and happy folks was gathered 'round there. It sure was a sight for a young man coming back from the dead.

When we rode in there in December of 1867, Taos was mighty changed from what it'd been thirty years or so before, back when it was the wintering place of them mountain men like Kit Carson, James Ohio Patty, Jim Bridger, and Charlie Bent.

In them days, the trappers used to come down from Green River and the Tetons and spend their winters in Taos, drinking that "Taos lightning" and making love to them Taos girls. It was all Spanish then. As far as them Yankees that went there was concerned, they was beyond the reach of the law. It was that way all through the '20s and the '30s, but after the Mexican War things'd changed mightily.

I 'spect it had to change, 'specially after them Mexicans didn't take to being conquered and went plumb crazy and murdered old Governor Charles Bent, the man that General Frémont sent down from Bent's Fort to govern the new Territory of New Mexico. The Indians and Mexicans murdered him right there in Taos, and of course that called for a big bunch of U.S. dragoons to come down there to clean up the place.

After that, it never was the same. Seemed like Yankees moved in everywhere. Some Mexicans still resented 'em, but they'd finally settled down to getting along with 'em. I don't mean that there weren't plenty of the old Spanish flavor running everywhere, 'cause there sure was. There was lots of good-loving, dark-eyed girls and flashy vaqueros walking 'round the streets and Indians from the pueblo aplenty, wearing them blankets over their heads. Everything 'round was Spanish, all right. But there was also the wagons of Yankee freighters. Americans now run some of the harness shops, livery stables, blacksmith outfits, a few stores, and a trading post, where in the olden days it'd all been Spanish.

Wherever the Americans goes, they stir up action. A lot of the time they don't fit very good into the country or in with the people they're working alongside, so they just tear the hell outta things as they go. When a Yankee goes to building a railroad, he bores and blasts the hell outta everything. He dams up rivers and builds bridges and runs tunnels clear through mountainsides and generally tears up stuff. 'Course in them days the closest railroad was a long ways away— clear back in Hays City, Kansas. Them folks in Taos'd never heard a whistle blowed or seen an engine puffing along.

Anyhow, that was the first impression I had of Taos. It was a mixture of Americans and the old Spanish, along with the original Pueblo-type Indians. There weren't near as many Yankees as there was Mexicans, but it seemed like what Yankees was there made more commotion. As for the Indians, I have to say that the first time I seen a Taos Indian I near reached for my gun. For a minute I thought he was a Comanche. But then I got to looking real close and seen that there was a helluva difference.

Them Taos Indians was damned-near civilized. They'd been living in their pueblos, or towns, for a thousand years I reckon, while them Comanches'd been roaming the plains like wolves.

When we got to Taos proper, Pedro seemed to know right where to go. He rode through the square and kept winding along one of them side streets 'til he come to a house that had a big old gate. He told me it was the home of a friend of one of his father's relatives in Chihuahua. It always seemed that old Pedro was close friends or relatives with everyone from Taos to central Mexico. His ancestors'd been in that whole area roaming 'round it and breeding and chewing it up for three hundred years, so it weren't as if he'd just broke out on the new end of things.

The people's name was Ruiz. The señor and señora was plenty old, but they was real glad to see Pedro and to have us 'round. They acted like Pedro was their long-lost son. Me, being his amigo, was treated like I was one of 'em, too. They didn't know a word of English, and I sure as hell didn't try none of my Spanish on 'em, worrying 'bout what I might say without knowing no better.

There was a well outside the door of the house in the courtyard, and some sheds there for the horses kinda like at the Valdezes' hacienda, only much smaller. Everything in Taos was a lot more crowded and pinched together, being in a town, than it was out at the Valdezes' open spread. We stayed there at the Ruizes' house clear on through Christmas and 'bout three weeks into January of '68, and that was sure a good place to be. They treated us real fine. I got to know Taos by wandering 'round and seeing the town and the countryside and figuring out what it was about.

I knowed I was gonna need some money sooner or later, and I found out I could get a job driving a freight wagon just as soon as I wanted one. A few times, when I was out walking down one of them little old dirt streets, I had to get outta the way of a bunch of freight wagons coming through. Usually, the wagon boss'd slow up his horse and lean over and ask me if I knowed anything 'bout mules and was I interested in joining his outfit.

Considering the way I was fixed with the Ruizes and with Pedro, I reckoned I'd stick around a while and learn something 'bout Taos and the country 'round about and think things over. I was anxious to make a little money, but I figured that moving too fast could be a mistake. In the back of my mind was the thing that old Pedro'd been talking 'bout in Hays City. He hadn't mentioned it again, but I sure remembered it.

There was one little old bank in Taos and it seemed like it was doing real good. It was run by a Mexican family and I reckon Pedro knowed all about 'em. I don't think the bank'd been there more'n fifteen years, 'cause in the old days in Taos 'fore the Mexican War, when the mountain men was in there and the Indians used to come over the mountains and camp all 'round for the Taos fairs, why there weren't no such thing as money. All trading was done by barter. You swapped beaver skins for blankets or blankets for a horse, a rifle for a woman or something. But after the Yankees took over the territory, money come into the picture and then they'd had to have banks.

Thinking 'bout Pedro's plan for robbing that bank made me a little uncomfortable. I reckon that most men's 'fraid of things they don't know 'bout, and I sure didn't know nothing 'bout banks. The idea of robbing it seemed awkward, but at least the bank didn't look none too secure. It was a little adobe house with some small windows, a counter, and a big old iron safe in the back. There was some tables and chairs around and a swinging gate in the counter that had a hook on it, so's the fella who was cashiering could lock it whenever he went in and out. The thing that worried me was how good things was going for us and how we might be foolish to spoil it.

That was a wonderful winter. Me and Pedro mostly hung 'round a few of them cantinas and picked up all of the local news—Pedro listening in Spanish and me turning an ear towards the freighters and the post riders and anybody else that spoke English that I could understand. We went to a few dances and it didn't take Pedro and me very long to pick up a couple of girls to go with. Depending on what kind of families them Taos girls come from, some of 'em was easy with their favors, and me and Pedro didn't suffer none from no lack of loving.

I also got used to that Taos lightning, if you can say that anybody ever got used to it. It's a special mixture. Small quantities of it is likely to blow your head off, and you don't know you're in trouble 'til it's too late.

There was lots of fiestas—big festivals, 'specially at Christmas and for the New Year. There was dances and music everywhere. Sometimes, when the moon was shining that bright silver light and the outline of them snowcapped mountains to the east stood out against the stars, I'd sit and listen to them soft Spanish voices singing to the strumming of a guitar. Then I'd think back—clear back to San Antone and when I'd started out on the Chisholm Trail—and wonder how my life might've gone if I'd done some things different. It seemed like a long ways away and a long time ago.

One morning towards the end of January, I stopped by a harness shop where a freighter was mending some mule harnesses. Freighters didn't haul over the mountains during the winter 'cause the snow was too deep, but there was good traffic 'tween Taos and Santa Fe and Albuquerque and even clear on down into Chihuahua.

Two or three of the wagon bosses was standing 'round watching the fella mending a harness. They talked 'bout the trail south, and the names of a few interesting places got to itching on my young ears. It weren't very long 'fore one of 'em come up to me and asked what I knowed 'bout mule skinning. He wanted to know whether I'd sign up to go to Albuquerque and maybe on to El Paso. I told him I'd talk it over with my amigo and see whether he had any hankering to go south. The wagon boss made no bones 'bout the fact that if I had a friend and he was any hand with mules, he could sure use us.

I mentioned it to Pedro and he seemed real interested. "Amigo, you know we come here to Taos to rob that damned little bank," he said. "But now is not the good time for that. There is not much money changing hands in Taos now, like there will be in the summer when the traffic with the freighters is coming. Besides, amigo, when we rob the bank, we are going to have to do some long, hard riding into the mountains, and I don't want to do that when the snow is ass-deep to a tall squaw."

"I feel right naked without a six-shooter, an' there ain't one fer sale 'round this town that suits me," I replied. "Maybe they got somethin' in Santa Fe or Albuquerque. I'd like ta make a little money an' see them places."

Pedro throwed me a wink. "I had enough money for the two of us when we got here, but the girls are using it up a little more faster than I plan. Go on and tell that wagon boss that we'll sign up maybe as far as Santa Fe. We can ride back here from Santa Fe one hard day if we make a push, okay? Or maybe we go on from there. Who can say?"

We left town the next morning after telling the Ruizes good-bye and leaving Pedro's mules with 'em. We was driving a wagon with a six-mule team. Our bedrolls, saddles, and rifles was all throwed in the back and our horses was tied to the rear. Mules is different from horses when it comes to handling 'em in rough country or on real windy canyon roads. When you got a big wagon and a six- or eight-mule team, you gotta use a jerk line for making most of your turns. That's where me and Pedro showed up good, 'cause we both knowed what we was doing. The trip from Taos to Santa Fe took us 'bout five days, down through some real fine canyon country.

While we was laying over in Santa Fe waiting for the wagon boss to get his business took care of and his load shifted, I visited every gun shop in town, but I couldn't find me a Smith & Wesson .38. I reckoned maybe I was gonna have to settle for a bigger gun, but that thought irked me.

We collected wages at the end of each week, and after we'd been in Santa Fe for two weeks, we had enough to get drunk and make love to a couple of them señoritas and still have a little left over. Otherwise, me and Pedro slept in the freight wagons every night, so we didn't have no extra expenses.

Things being so easy, we agreed to go on to Albuquerque and maybe points south. We was 'bout four days making it to Albuquerque and had us a good look at that town. It didn't seem like they was anything special there, 'cept I did find a gun store with a Smith & Wesson .38.

I was careful not to act happy. I talked with the old boy that owned the gun shop and I run that .38 down aplenty. I told him it didn't have enough punch to do much good and that the ammunition'd be hard to find, which was true, and that 'bout the only thing you could use it for'd be a rabbit gun. I reckoned he'd heard enough of the same talk from other passersby that didn't really appreciate the value of a .38, and I 'spect he was tired of having it in his stock. In any case, he sold it to me for twelve dollars and throwed in three boxes of shells. Then I got me a holster made up at a harness shop just the way I wanted it— one that tied down to my right thigh so's I could make a slick, fast draw. I also found a cartridge belt that fitted me comfortable, and that fixed it.

We stuck 'round Albuquerque for almost three weeks. Seemed like there was always something that had to be repaired on them freight wagons. We didn't ask no questions, since we was drawing wages all the time. All we had to do was see that them mules got fed and watered once a day and help out with any repairs we could.

While we was there I spotted the best saddle that I'd ever seen in my life and really got my heart set on it. It was a slick-looking Spanish type made of black leather with some silver trimmings on it. The man wanted a damned fortune for it. I couldn't afford it right then, but I figured that when I had some more dough I'd come back and get it. I remember wishing I'd still had Piebald to put it on.

Pedro also begun teaching me how to throw a knife.

If'n there was anybody could teach a man to throw a knife, it was Pedro. I'd first seen him in action more'n a year before, when we'd rode down from San Antone to Laredo, just for the hell of it. We'd wound up in a Laredo whorehouse where we'd had us a helluva time. There was a man there playing a honky-tonk piano, and all them pretty Mexican whores was gathering 'round. We was singing away, and old Pedro, standing up behind the piano player, his teeth flashing, was singing louder and better'n anybody else. He had a gal on each arm and was enjoying hisself no end.

There was lots of them no-'count greasers 'round, of course, and they was jealous enough of Pedro, but they was even more jealous of me, being a gringo. Maybe they figured I had more dough and prob'ly would beat 'em out of their whores somehow.

I weren't paying much attention when a beautiful, dangerous-looking whore come up to me. It seemed like she had some Indian blood in her. She started hanging on my arm and making eyes at me. It wouldn't have made no matter normally, but a few minutes before, I'd seen her sitting over in a booth with a great big greaser who'd been hugging and kissing her and pinching her tits. Now I seen him sitting over there looking real mean.

Me and Pedro'd already been upstairs in that cathouse for five hours and had got plenty of exercise. 'Sides that, I weren't too eager to get crossed up with any of them folks. I was just there for a good time.

I emptied my glass, give the whore a pat on the butt, and wandered over towards the bar for another drink. When I come back, the greaser got up and stepped 'tween me and the piano. The piano player stopped playing right 'bout that time and everybody realized there was gonna be some trouble.

It got real quiet and this greaser looked me in the face and snarled, "Gringo!" in a manner that give me the idea it weren't no compliment. Then he puckered up and spit in my face.

Now, you know I ain't taking that from no man. I reached over and put my drink down on the piano. Then I turned back 'round and quick like a flash I cracked him in the jaw. He spun 'round, hit against the wall, and slipped down to the floor. I thought I'd hit him just right, but I reckon not, 'cause he worked hisself 'round and got up on his knees. When he stood on up, I figured he'd come at me again and I'd deck him a little harder, but then I seen the flash of a knife.

He let out a yell and come at me with his teeth bared, flashing that blade. I jumped aside real quick and tripped him so he piled up again on the other side of the floor.

A big roar of laughter went up, and that sure didn't do his self-respect no good. He come up on his feet again faster'n I expected and this time I seen the knife real clear in his right hand. It was a wicked-looking blade and I figured that if he got close to me I'd have to get my hand on his wrist real quick or he'd carve me to pieces.

But he weren't figuring to get close to me a'tall. His hand went back with a flick and there was no mistaking what he was planning.

Now I ain't slick enough to catch no knife in the air or even duck it. A knife throwed right comes at you awful fast. I thought then and there that I was prob'ly in real bad shape. But then I saw a spinning flash with my left eye and heard a kind of ku-chunk sound. That greaser got the damnedest look on his face I ever seen, and there was four inches of knife handle sticking outta his throat. His mouth fell wide open, his eyes popped out, then he gurgled a little bit and the blood come running outta his mouth. Then his legs bowed and sagged and he slithered down on the floor and lay there with his eyes rolled back. It was the slickest thing I'd ever seen. Pedro's knife-throw'd killed him dead.

Right away all hell broke loose. The whores started screaming and people was running 'round every which way. Pedro stepped out from behind the piano, took three long strides, and reached down real calm and pulled the knife outta the neck. He wiped it clean on the greaser's shirt and put it back in the sheath. "Now, amigo," he said, "it is necessary that we get the hell out of here!"

I didn't need no more advice. I'm here to tell you we moved. Our horses was outside, and we come flying out the door, jerked the reins loose from that hitching post, vaulted into the saddle, and tore off through town at a dead gallop. We kept on going hard 'til we crossed the Rio Grande at a place where Pedro knowed it was safe. When we got to the U.S. side we made our way back deep into Texas. Pedro never said nothing to me on that ride. He didn't have to. He'd killed a man to save me and I knowed I'd never have a better friend in the world.

So while we was there in Albuquerque, he set out to teach me how to throw a knife, and I knowed there weren't no better man in the world to do it. Near the corrals was an old shed that had wooden sides to it. Most of the buildings was made of adobe and weren't no good

for throwing knives at, but that wooden shed'd do just fine. We got
'bout twenty feet away, and Pete took a knife outta the sheath on his
belt. Like all of his knives, it was a wicked-looking one, but it didn't
have no fancy handle or nothing.

"We use the ones with fancy handles for dress," he said, "but
when it comes to throwing the knife, the looks are not the important
thing. It is the balance. You must have the balance. You have seen
people throw the knife lots of ways, but there is only one right way.
Some they hold by the blade and throw. Some they hold flat in the
palm of the hand and they throw like this—underhand. But that is
no good.

"There is just one way you throw the knife. You throw by the
handle. You draw the knife from the sheath, with the handle, so you
must be able to throw like that. You have no time to change the knife
position. If you want to make the fast throw, you must throw as soon
as you have the knife free of the sheath and this means that you throw
with the handle.

"Then it must be that the handle and the blade are of the same
weight. This is most important, 'cause when you throw the knife, the
knife will turn like a wheel in the air and you must know that when
the knife hits the target, the blade is to come first.

"Now, when you take the knife like this and you throw, you must
always throw with the elbow and the wrist in a straight line, and
always throw with the same force exactly. It makes no difference
whether you are close or far away. You always throw with the same
force. The same snap of the wrist. The same snap of the elbow. You
train the arm always to use the same force. Why? Because the knife
must spin end over end exactly the same speed every time.

"The knife is good for maybe twenty feet away. Sometimes I have
seen a knife thrown maybe thirty, maybe even more, at the most
thirty-five, but this is not good.

"You must know the distance exact. If you know that, you know
where the blade will come forward in the spin—like so. You must
figure one and one-half strides is good for one whole complete spin of
the knife. So, if you are one and one-half strides away, you throw the
knife, and he will stick with one revolution. I show you."

Pete measured one and one-half paces from that wooden wall, then
stepped back and real quick flashed the knife. It stuck, quivering in
the wood, so I figured that I could do it real easy—from that close.

"Now look," he said, "I show you. We go one and one-half more strides. Now the knife he take two revolutions. You watch and see."

He slung the knife and it stuck hard as hell, quivering there in the shed wall. I noticed how slick and fast the movement was and how his wrist put the snap at the end of the throw.

He showed me a couple more times, then let me try it. 'Course I didn't do no good a'tall. He told me that there was a little difference 'tween each man, like a bit different speed in the arm, or shorter and longer strides. With me, I found it weren't too bad when I was 'bout one and a quarter strides from the wall. I could put the knife in most times from there, but when I got out 'bout twenty feet away, why, the knife was hitting handle first and blade crosswise and every other which way. I'd sling it and it'd clatter to the ground, and Pedro'd give me hell.

We kept working away at it that afternoon 'til I got so's I could stick that knife in at any certain distance once in a while.

Pedro finished up that first afternoon by showing me special tricks he had. One I sure remember. He put two knives in sheaths, one in each boot. Then he showed me how, when he was squatting down by a fire or maybe just resting on his heels and he had a reason to throw them knives, he could draw 'em out in one motion.

It was really wonderful to see, like a snake striking. Them knives'd come out and twenty feet away they'd both stick quivering in the side of the shed in a space no bigger'n a silver dollar.

Then he hung the two sheaths from the back of his neck on a cord hid by his shirt collar. It was real clever the way he done it. Less'n you looked careful, you couldn't see the knives was there. The idea was that if a man was to point a gun at him, he could put his hands up like he was going to surrender. If he could get his thumb and forefinger to the collar of his shirt, that guy with the gun was dead. Pedro could pull out them knives just 'bout as fast as an ordinary man could pull a trigger.

"Now, amigo," he said, "you pretend that you are to hold me up. Do not worry. I will not throw the knives at you. I will throw at the side of the shed."

So I sidled up and drawed on him real quick and said, "Get yer hands up!"

He started to put up his hands. He worked 'round real slow and I couldn't see what he was doing. All of a sudden them knives was out and spinning, and stuck close together in the wood.

Of all the things he showed me, I picked the one that I thought was the easiest, which was the one in back of the collar, but I couldn't hide the knife right, and a couple of times I come close to cutting off my ear when I drawed it out. I was mad that I couldn't get it right in one afternoon, but I went back there and I practiced almost every day while we was in Albuquerque, and improved some. Pedro laughed at how clumsy I was, but it didn't make no difference, 'cause I knowed that knives'd never be my long suit.

There finally come a time when our freight outfit was ready to go on south and me and Pedro went back to driving mules. We headed down the Rio Grande to Socorro and then to El Paso. It weren't a bad drive, with the mountains stretching away on both sides, but we kept getting into drier and drier country.

It was 'bout a three-week trip, and we camped along the river every night. That river in them days had lots of marshes 'round it, with cattails and tall reeds and thousands and thousands of waterfowl—ducks and geese and other birds that was coming down from way up in Canada, fixing to go south to Mexico for the winter. There was feeding grounds and some nesting grounds and lots of life along that river. It sure was a beautiful sight to see. Whole flocks of them geese and ducks was flying in the distance, and it looked like smoke that kept curling and uncurling as the lines of the flock moved across the sky.

One evening, when we'd camped early along the edge of some cottonwoods near the river, we heard some honkers close by. I reckoned they was coming out of the reeds in the riverbed to do some feeding somewhere. There was a couple of them Indian pueblos along the route and them geese used to go out into their cornfields once in a while.

Anyhow, we seen this bunch of geese coming, and off to the side of 'em was a loner. It was a real still evening and we heard 'em honking from a long ways away. I stepped into the wagon, jerked my Winchester out of the scabbard, and slammed a shell in the chamber.

I sighted in and waited 'til after that goose passed by. I reckoned he was 'bout eighty yards away when I drawed up and shot him dead. He come tumbling outta the sky and hit the ground with a thud. It was the first time that any of them mule skinners'd ever seen a man kill a bird on the wing with a rifle. It just weren't done much, and none of 'em used shotguns in them days. The only bird-shooting done was usually sitting ducks on the water, or something of that kind.

Pedro got a big kick outta that and laughed and danced 'round and sorta bragged me up to the rest of them wagon drivers and jerk-line boys. After that I had a real fair reputation as a dead gun. We roasted that big bird over the coals that evening and really had ourselves a feast.

One day, Pedro got to telling the boys more stories 'bout how good I could shoot and some of 'em wanted to see some more tricks. I said if they'd supply the ammunition, I'd be glad to show 'em. They was willing, so I put on a couple of mighty sharp exhibitions. I knowed I was a helluva good shot, but I never made no mind of it. But after them men got to oohing and aahing 'bout what I was doing, I reckoned I was just naturally a better shot than any man they'd ever seen.

That give me some confidence. I settled down some then and tried to figure out what it was I really wanted to do. All that long freight trek down to El Paso, I'd been thinking 'bout that beautiful Mexican saddle in Albuquerque. Somehow I had to get me some more money. Pedro never seemed to be outta funds, him being a good poker player and all, but I didn't seem to have the knack for the game.

In a way, I was itching to get on with the job of robbing the Taos bank, like Pedro'd suggested, but I knowed he was right 'bout our having to get away across them mountains to the west. We didn't want them deep snows, so we'd have to wait 'til late spring to give it a try.

Then, too, the more I got to thinking 'bout robbing the bank, the more nervous I got about it. Not exactly nervous, but a feeling that there was something wrong with it, and I couldn't put my finger on what it was. Anyhow, it weren't no use to think 'bout it then.

I figured there had to be a way to get a little extra money from somewhere. There weren't no way any kinda holdup was gonna work out in El Paso, Albuquerque, Santa Fe, or Taos during the winter. It was too hard to get away. I was keeping my mind open for any chance that might come my way, 'cause I knowed that opportunity always comes one way or another.

IT AIN'T RIGHT TO KILL KIN

I don't know how El Paso is now, 'cause I ain't been back in fifty years. But in them days it was only a little frontier town with lots of customs officials going 'round trying to pick up bribes. It hadn't progressed much from what it was like when it was all owned by Mexico. There was 'bout three good saloons and a couple of whorehouses. 'Course there was lots more going on in the Mexican town of Juarez just across the Rio Grande.

Juarez hadn't been nothing more'n a crossing place on the river in Mexican days, but after the Americans'd taken over the north side of the river, Juarez'd grown in importance on the Mexican side. Some of the best whorehouses was over there. I never did get to go over though, 'cause I'd got kinda busy.

Pedro was real anxious to go down to Chihuahua to see his folks and he wanted me to come along. He kept telling me that he'd show me one great time on his family's big horse ranch. His folks, his brother, and three very beautiful younger sisters'd sure give us a grand welcome, he said.

I could really believe it, seeing as how I'd watched people take him in all along the route. Everybody knowed Pedro and everybody liked him. Noting his high-society good looks, I could just imagine how beautiful his sisters was and I really did have a hankering to go.

While Pedro kept on talking 'bout going down to Chihuahua, I kept telling him it looked like we was gonna be freighters for quite a while less'n we could figure out some kinda way to make us a quick dollar. So's we was both feeling a little outta sorts.

One night in the saloon I got to talking to a buffalo hunter that'd come in from Adobe Walls. He near set my mind on fire, telling 'bout how there was some fella up at the trading post there on the Canadian River who was buying buffalo hides. This trader had a contract with the English to collect several hundred thousand of 'em, and the hunter give me an idea what kinda profits a fella could make outta buffalo hunting.

He had some other tales that was real rough, 'bout how the Comanches treated the buffalo hunters they caught in that country. I didn't give him no signal that I knowed what it was 'bout.

I figured if me and Pedro could go out east from Albuquerque in the mid-spring, we'd have a chance of making a real fortune collecting buffalo hides, and we might be able to get outta there without crossing with no Comanches. If we run across any, well, I figured I had a score to settle, and someday or other I was actually hoping to face up with 'em and get it straightened out. That balanced my fear of going out there and let me focus in on the big profits we was gonna make.

I told Pedro how much the trader was paying for buffalo hides, and his black eyes gleamed. He thought 'bout it for a while. "I think we need wagons and skinners and some money to pay them when we first go out, but if we had the money for such an outfit, amigo, maybe we could do good. Maybe after we come back from Chihuahua we can go to Albuquerque or Santa Fe and fix the buffalo-hunting outfit—what you say, eh?"

That was good enough for me. I figured he'd gone along with my scheme and now we just had to play for time and get some money. I really weren't keen on riding two hundred miles across that desert to Chihuahua real soon, but if I had to do it to stay with Pedro, I was willing.

The next evening I was in that same saloon watching a big ugly bastard named Waldo playing poker with a bunch of cowpunchers and a few hunters and freighters. I plain hadn't liked that hombre when I'd first met him. He was big and thick lipped, with squinty snake eyes that gleamed through little slits in his face. I watched that game for near an hour and marveled at the way Waldo was winning.

Then I seen he was cheating. It was a nice slick deal—he throwed the cards out to cut 'em, but he always seemed to come up with the right cards in his hand. I was standing by the bar and, kinda like by accident, I dropped a silver dollar on the floor. When I leaned down to pick it up, I looked over and seen that when he stuck the cards forward for somebody to cut, he was keeping two of 'em hid up in his hand, and after the cut was made, them cards come right out on top just like he'd stacked 'em. I didn't see no use telling nobody 'bout it and I sure weren't gonna play myself.

Then I got to looking over his armament. They never did take the guns away from you in El Paso like they done in Hays City. He was carrying the usual holsters on each side with .44 Colts in 'em. From the way he handled the cards, I knowed his fingers and his hands was fast. He was prob'ly as quick on the draw as he was with them cards. But I knowed that I could pull out a .38 faster'n he could ever get them two cannons out.

It must've been near five o'clock in the morning when Waldo finally cleaned out the other men at his table. He picked up quite a pile of cash—and a few IOUs along with it. I reckoned he had near eight hundred dollars cash—enough, I figured, to make a good start on buying a buffalo-hunting outfit.

A couple of minutes after he left, I eased out through the saloon doors real natural-like. Walking out in the cool late winter air, I looked up and seen what looked like a thousand stars shining. It was in early March then, but even in El Paso it was chilly at that time of morning. There was what I'd call a quarter-moon, but it didn't seem to dim the stars none.

Nothing much was going on. A couple of honky-tonk joints was still open and the lights from the bar doors shone out in the dirt street. Laughter was coming from down the street at another joint, and someone was playing a slow melody on a piano that sounded like it hadn't been tuned in many a year.

Looking far down the street to the west, I seen a man walking off towards the livery stable. I reckoned it was Waldo. Even from that distance I could make him out as being a real big man. I seen how he walked down the middle of the street and didn't stay close under the buildings on the boardwalk. And I knowed why: It was on account of carrying all that money. He weren't taking no chances on being jumped. I reckoned if he was worried, that was gonna make my job tougher.

I leaned up against one of the posts of the bar, looking down the street and picking my teeth, 'til I seen him disappear in the shadows. I reckoned he was headed for the livery stable.

After a while, I eased off the porch, feeling real self-conscious with all the noise that my jingling spurs was making as I went down them wood steps. I took it easy and walked real natural down the board-walk in the same direction he was going.

I heard some noise by the livery stable and seen a man lead a horse out the door. I crouched down and seen that he'd headed his horse back towards the east, so I savvied where he was going.

If he'd headed west, he could've gone up to Albuquerque alongside the river or crossed over and gone on west to Tucson. Going east, he had three choices: He could be taking the Fort Worth Trail back to central Texas, or maybe he was gonna turn south and cross the Rio Grande into old Mexico and get lost back in that country some way, or maybe he was gonna turn northeast when he got outta town and head up towards the Sacramento Mountains. He could've been working at a mine up there or some such.

When I watched him ride by, I seen it was definitely Waldo mounted on a big powerful-looking roan, and he weren't headed for Fort Worth. He didn't have no pack outfit, only a bedroll, so he couldn't be traveling that distance. He had a rifle on a saddle scab-bard, but I couldn't make out what kind. Anyhow, he clomped off down through the lights and shadows of the town and headed off to the east.

When I knowed he wouldn't be able to see me, I hightailed it up the street to the livery stable myself. I caused quite a commotion by hurrying up that livery stable man to get me old Paint, not stopping to visit with him none. He kept grumbling 'bout how everybody was taking out in a hurry.

I took it sorta easy leaving town, just ambling through the streets like any old body just moseying along minding his own business. When I got out in the darkness, I spurred up and rode like hell for 'bout a mile. I figured that dawn was gonna break pretty quick and I wanted to be close enough to that card cheat to see him on the trail ahead but not so close as to spook him.

When the light started rising, the whole prairie lit up and I could see the trail stretching away in front of me. Sure enough, there he was, 'bout a mile and a half ahead, riding his horse at an easy lope.

I kept my pony at about the same speed as Waldo, so's not to gain none or lose none on him. I figured that after a while, like any other horseman who was aiming on riding a considerable distance, he'd slow his horse's pace.

In 'bout fifteen minutes, he pulled his horse up into a trot and I kept on at a lope to close the distance. It weren't 'til he slowed down to a walk that I started gaining on him in real earnest. He must've been 'bout half a mile away when he first knowed I was coming. Whether he'd heard me or happened to glance behind, I couldn't say. Anyhow, I seen him rein his horse up real sharp and turn sideways to look towards me. I couldn't make him out too good with the sun directly in my face, but he could see me real plain.

When I seen he was looking at me, I reined in old Paint and kept on at an easy trot. He sat there on his horse watching me 'til I was 'bout two hundred yards away. Then he reached down and drawed out his rifle from the saddle scabbard. I gentled Paint down to a walk and kept on coming at him, real slow.

He sat there motionless on his horse, with his rifle laid 'cross his knees behind the pommel, looking at me with a stonelike stare, and let me come up 'til I got to 'bout a hundred yards. Then his rifle come up with a nice easy swing to his shoulder and he laid his eye dead down the barrel. I found myself looking at the business end of a buffalo Sharps.

I come to a complete halt and raised my hands above my head, my right hand holding the reins. There was just a fraction of a second there when I didn't know whether he might let fly without saying nothing.

Waldo was a mean-looking man, and when he talked, his voice sounded like a war drum booming. What little I'd heard him say weren't very kindly—and it sure weren't this time neither. He didn't convey no warm welcome nor no desire for companionship. I could hear him real plain 'cross that hundred-yard gap 'tween us, and his voice seemed like it come right down the rifle barrel.

"What the hell y'want?" he asked.

"I don't want nothin'. Just some comp'ny. I heard maybe ya was goin' down Fort Worth way—that's where I'm headed—an' figgered maybe we could ride t'gether."

"Well," he said, "ain't that real thoughtful. Damnit, if I'd have wanted any company, I'd have asked for it. I ain't hankerin' to travel with no man—certainly not the likes of you. What's more, there's lots of people found out that it ain't exactly healthy to follow me. I don't cotton to no boys ridin' up behind me like that."

"Nosir," I said, real pleasant. "Ya got me wrong, mister. I don't wanta make no nuisance of myself, but I figgered that two's better'n one ridin' on the Pecos Trail ta Fort Worth, 'specially goin' through Injun country."

"Where'd you hear tell of where I'm goin'? Seems maybe y'know more about my plans than I know myself."

What a fool I'd been! I'd already figured he weren't going to Fort Worth. He was either gonna turn north to the Sacramento Mountains 'fore he got too far out, or turn south and cross the Rio Grande into old Mexico.

Either way, he didn't wanta be followed, which meant that poker playing prob'ly wasn't his main business. Whatever it was, it prob'ly wouldn't stand no examination from no ordinary men. All I could hope for was that he wouldn't take the notion to blow my head off. It looked to me like my best chance was to ease off and hightail it back to town. The only thing 'tween me and hell was a little more pressure on that trigger finger of his.

Those was the unsavory thoughts that run through my mind as I sat there with the sun in my eyes and my hands raised above my head. I felt real foolish, like I should've figured it all out ahead of time.

I didn't get very long to think 'bout it, though, 'cause down that rifle barrel come the boom of his voice again. "Go on, get the hell outta here 'fore I blow your goddamn head off."

I didn't dare drop my hands down none. I held the reins high in my right hand and jerked Paint's head 'round and started back up the trail at a slow walk. Seemed like I could feel that Sharps burning a hole through my back, but I didn't dare look behind me.

Right away quick his voice come a-booming again. "Wait a minute, stranger. You ain't goin' back that way. You said you was headed to Fort Worth, so's you'd better get goin' in that direction. I don't like them that rides behind me. I want the likes of you out in front where I can see you. Now turn that cayuse of yours around and head back this way and keep your hands up. If you make any kind of wrong move, I'll ventilate that hide of yours."

I could feel the cold sweat running down the back of my neck as I eased 'round real slow and come up looking at that Sharps again. It was pointed at me from 'bout a hundred ten yards away. It hadn't moved none and its barrel shined in the sun.

Then Waldo's voice boomed again. "That's it, you done right. Now don't you make no wrong move. Just come on slow and easy towards me 'til I tell you to halt."

I pressured Paint a little with my knees and he moved forward at a slow walk, his ears cocked, looking at Waldo's big roan. My mouth started to get dry and I could feel a sick lump in my stomach. It looked to me like I was riding to my own death and making it real easy for Waldo. As I got closer, it seemed like the mouth of that gun wanted to eat me up.

When I got to within 'bout thirty yards, I seen him take his left hand off the barrel and point to his left with an easy motion. "Now swing outta the trail there to the south a little. Keep an even distance and don't you make no wrong moves. That's it. Just keep easin' around."

With the hairs raised up on the back of my neck, I swung off the trail a little to the south through the clumps of sage. Old Paint's head was raised high and his ears was cocked. He went sashaying sideways a little 'round the strange horse.

That old boy Waldo sure had easy pickings. If he'd blowed a hole in me then, he'd have had him an extra horse, not to mention the Winchester repeater that he couldn't help seeing in my scabbard.

I decided right away what to do. A rifle gives a man a mighty big advantage at a distance, and if his target moves, he don't have to move the barrel much to cover it. But at close range it's a different thing. If the target moves when it's in close, the barrel's gotta swing considerable to stay with it. It was on that very notion that I aimed to stake my life.

Like a flash, I dug my spurs hard into Paint's flanks. At the same time, I flung myself forward to meet the arch of his neck as he come up for his first jump. At that instant the Sharps roared and I felt a hot flame across my back.

I grabbed the mane on Paint's arched neck as I pitched forward, Comanche style, outta Waldo's sight just to the right of my horse's withers. As I went down, I whipped out my .38 like a striking snake. I felt the pressure of Paint's windpipe on my right forearm as I reached under his neck and got off two quick shots. Then I spurred away at a gallop, hanging from his neck, with my left heel on the saddle and my left hand gripping his mane.

In the curl of dust behind me, I seen how old Waldo's head slumped back and his whole body wheeled and pivoted as he fell off his pitching horse. I jerked Paint to a stop and slid off on his east side, using him for cover. I pulled the Winchester outta its scabbard, slammed a shell in the chamber, and knelt to finish off Waldo.

I held the rifle on him for the better part of a minute. Then I decided that maybe it weren't necessary to do nothing. I stood and come up on him real careful and steady. He never moved.

When I got to 'bout ten yards away, I could see by the puddle of blood rolling out in the dirt near his face that the job was finished. There was a big hole in the back of his head where the bullet'd come out. I stepped up and rolled him over on his back with my boot tip. I wanted to check my aim, and what I seen made me right satisfied. One bullet'd entered at the bridge of his nose and gone out through the back of his skull. The other bullet'd hit dead center in his chest.

Waldo didn't have nothing that I wanted but money. I'd seen him leave that saloon with eight hundred dollars and I aimed to have it. It was in a money belt that was strapped 'round him like a shoulder holster. There was eight hundred ninety dollars in currency and some IOUs for 'bout a hundred dollars more. I reckoned that the IOUs wouldn't do me no good, so I tore 'em up and buried 'em. Then I strapped on the money belt under my shirt.

I took my rope off Paint and slipped a loop up over Waldo's feet. Then I mounted up, took a turn of rope 'round the saddle horn, and drug him off the trail and over beside a dry arroyo. I buried his weapons in the sand and pitched his body into the dry gulch, which was 'bout five or six feet deep, figuring the coyotes'd get rid of him for me. Then I kicked some dirt over the bloody spots with my boots so's nobody'd see 'em. Taking some sage branches, I brushed over where I'd drug his body to the arroyo.

I got back up on Paint to see where Waldo's horse'd gone. He was 'bout half a mile away and starting to feed between the sage. I eased up on him and got close enough to sling a rope, then I led him back onto the trail again. I would've liked to've kept the roan for a spare to take buffalo hunting, but too many folks was likely to recognize him as Waldo's and start asking questions. Best thing was to take him a good ways off the trail and shoot him. That'd be too bad, 'cause he was a real good horse, powerful-built with long legs. He had the nicest white markings—a big white star on his forehead and tall white stockings on all four feet. He sure was a horse you'd remember seeing. I figured that Waldo must've cheated him off'n somebody in one of his poker games.

I turned north off the trail towards the Sacramento Mountains and rode a couple hundred yards to where there was some cactus and sage that made for good hiding. With a little digging in the sand, I buried Waldo's saddle and rifle in its scabbard. I marked the place as best I could, planning to come back there again some time. His saddle was one of them silly-looking army rigs, but maybe I could use it 'til I got back to buy that black and silver one.

I figured that once I got rid of Waldo's horse, as far as anybody'd be able to see I'd been out for a ride in the desert. Only thing, I was eight hundred ninety dollars richer.

I didn't harbor no guilt 'bout killing old Waldo. He weren't nothing but a mean son of a bitch. 'Sides that, he'd had the draw on me, and I'm sure he'd meant to kill me. The money he'd had on him he'd got by stealing from others. Just 'cause he stole it with a pack of cards didn't make no difference. I reckoned nobody'd feel sorry 'bout losing him.

On the other hand, I felt a little guilty 'bout having to shoot his horse. But what else could I do? Anybody that seen me come into El Paso leading that white-stockinged roan'd know for sure it was Waldo's.

I tied Paint to a good-sized clump of sage and led the roan off over a rise into the sandy gulch and 'cross to the other side. He kinda nickered at leaving Paint behind, then he nudged me on the shoulder like a big old dog wanting to be petted.

Damn him! Why'd he have to go getting personal right when I was fixing to kill him? It threw me off and somehow I couldn't bring myself to reach for the Smith & Wesson.

"Okay, ya big handsome son of a bitch," I told him as I took off his bridle. "Ya get outta here now an' don't make me do somethin' I really don't wanta do. So, get! Hee-yah!"

I busted him over the rump with the reins and then jumped up and down, shouting and waving my arms to send him running. He trotted off a few steps, then stopped to turn 'round and look at me, kinda puzzled. I run at him, swinging the bridle like a slingshot, and let it go flying through the air to land smack up against his shoulder. That spooked him, and he went galloping off with his tail lifted up and his head held high.

Then he stopped a safe distance away and watched me walk over to pick up the bridle. He tossed his head up and down and nickered, and when I just stood there, he come trotting back over and shoved his forehead up against my chest, almost knocking me down while he showed he didn't have no hard feelings.

It was plain to see I weren't gonna run him off that easy. I could try leading him away toward the mountains, riding Paint, but judging by his actions he'd go following me back, and with them long legs of his he could keep up with Paint easy if I tried to leave him behind.

Maybe it was 'cause I'd killed that no-good bastard who'd been riding him, and he was trying to show his appreciation. I had to smile at the thought.

I felt plumb sick 'bout it as I slipped his bridle back on and cast 'round for another likely spot where I could put him down, some-place outta sight of the trail where nobody'd find his carcass 'fore me and Pete had time to get clear of the area.

There was another good-sized gulch up ahead. It looked deep enough for the job, and I led him down into the bottom of it. "I hate ta kill ya, ya big friendly bastard, but it's your life or mine."

He kept trying to rub his head on me while I got him turned 'round down there. What I knowed I had to do seemed real unfair and I near choked up. I scratched him a little behind the ears, the way I used to do to old Piebald. Then, slow and reluctant, I slipped out the Smith & Wesson and raised it up to below his ear, cocking the hammer with my thumb. Right then that overgrowed nuisance decided he wanted some more ear scratching and went to rubbing on me again with his head.

"Gol'durn ya, hold still!" I hollered. The thought of killing him was almost more'n I could take, and it seemed like all the sick, sad feelings I'd ever had welled up inside me and tried to burst outta my throat.

I let out part of a breath, the best way I knowed to keep rock steady, and real soft I said, "This is it, boy. One, two. . . ."

All of a sudden he jerked his head in the direction of the trail and flicked his ears, stopping me again. I heard something, too—the sound of a horse galloping real furious along the hard dirt surface of the trail. I really started shaking then, 'cause I knowed that somehow, somebody must've found out 'bout me and Waldo.

Damn! I remembered I'd left Paint picketed out there in plain sight, too far to get back to. Thinking real fast, I clamped a hand over the roan's nose to keep him from neighing while I slipped the revolver back in my belt. The thought come to me that my instinct had barely saved me from shooting down my handiest way outta there—right on the back of that big, fast roan.

I was ready to run, but I sure was curious to see just who, and how many, was after me. Since I'd only heard one horse, I edged the roan over so's I could raise up and get a good look. There weren't nothing, just a few specks of dust coming off the trail and leading into the first gully.

The plunging head of a big black horse come up outta the gully, and there on his back, wearing fancy black duds and a shiny black mustache, sat Pedro. I stuck my gun back in my holster, then led the roan up the steep bank beside us and stood there, waiting, as he rode up. I busted out laughing at the funny look Pedro had on his face.

"Brules, you lousy, stupid gringo bastard!" he sputtered. "Are you trying to make your good frien' Pedro die of fright? *¡Jesucristo!* The livery man say you have gone after the Señor Waldo. I know this man. He is one very bad hombre—a professional gun and one of the worst killers in all of this country."

"Well," I told him, "he ain't the worst killer no more. He's lyin' out there in the desert now, an' he ain't fit fer nothing better'n coyote feed."

I pulled out Waldo's money belt and tossed it up to Pedro. "Here's the little bankroll that's gonna get us started makin' our fortune. I was just fixin' ta shoot Waldo's horse ta get rid a the evidence."

Pedro sat there, looking stunned. "*¡Ay, Virgen!* The money, the horse, and you have escape with only a big stripe on your shoulders, like somebody has slash you with a bull's whip!"

I'd forgot 'bout Waldo's bullet. It'd sure enough ripped the back off'n my shirt. Pedro shook his head. Then a little smile crept up on his face. "Come, amigo, let us ride back and pick up your horse and you tell me what is happening this morning."

I vaulted up on the roan and give Pete a quick rundown on how I'd killed Waldo. Pete said that I didn't have no business going back into El Paso nohow, torn shirt and roan horse, besides. The livery man'd spread the story of me taking out after Waldo, so if I showed up alive, the game'd be up.

"We must think of the new plan," he said. "First of all, I am tired of seeing you riding on the Indian saddle. I know this Waldo had a good one, and you say you have buried it—and a buffalo Sharps!"

"I ain't too shore 'bout that saddle, but I don't s'pose I'd have no trouble findin' where I hid it. It shore was funny lookin'—didn't have no horn or nothin' much else."

Pete's white teeth flashed in that big grin of his. "It is what you call a cavalry saddle, the McClellan. There are so many of them 'cause every cavalry post has them, and some of the soldiers steal them and sell them. Now those saddles are all over and no one can say where you get it. You will like it much better than that silly thing you have from the Comanches."

Pete headed back to El Paso to pay our bills and buy me a new shirt, planning to let on like he was doing a favor for a dead friend of his, but without really saying much. I dug up Waldo's gear and switched 'round the saddles and rifle scabbards so's I could ride Paint and carry my Winchester and have the roan carry the Sharps.

I decided right then and there to name the roan "Lucky." Leading him and riding Paint, I went off in the desert and hid out there in a big arroyo to wait for Pete. I knowed he'd remember the place where we'd left the trail and pick up our tracks.

It was 'bout midafternoon 'fore Pedro come back, ambling along and singing out loud, and I knowed everything was all right.

He rode right by as if he didn't see me a'tall, but I knowed right well he weren't that stupid. Then he throwed up his hands and squealed in a high, funny voice, "Oh, don' shoot! Don' shoot! Have mercy, Mister Comanche Brules, on this poor traveler."

"Ya damn greaser!" I shouted. "What's the matter with ya?"

He turned and made a praying motion with one hand. "Ah, I am in the vicinity of the greatest gunman in the whole of the southwest and he is the shootingest fool. He is liable to shoot anything from a jackrabbit to an innocent hombre like me."

"Well, that may be, but I ain't gonna shoot no jackass—an' I knows one when I sees one all right—'specially all done up in black an' silver with a big mustache, an' brayin' like a mountain canary comin' 'cross the desert."

Pete laughed and become normal again. "Si, that is one for you, amigo. I tell you, we are in good shape. I have paid the livery stable and the boardinghouse. I have tol' the story that you have gone east and I do not expect you back, and so I am paying your bills because I am your frien'. Nobody question that you were not coming back because they all know you took out after Waldo. They know that when a man goes after Waldo, he never come back. So everybody give it the shrug and take the money and there is no problem. Now, as far as El Paso is concerned, you are the dead man."

We checked over the Sharps. "I tell you what, amigo," said Pedro, "this is a good buffalo rifle and I think it is time we go on the buffalo hunt. I am putting off the invitation to Chihuahua, where you will meet *mi madre* and *mi padre* and see my sisters. But now, amigo, we have much more important business. We go north again to Albuquerque or maybe Santa Fe to buy the wagon, the horses, and the mules, and we got to hire the skinners. We must buy the ammunition, but most of all we must go pronto!"

We traveled hard and rode all that night, trading off mounts to give all three horses a little rest. We made a circle 'round north of El Paso and cut trail along the Rio Grande.

It took us fifteen days to come down the trail from Albuquerque to El Paso, and only five days to get back. Actually, it was five hard nights of riding, since we holed up days in the cottonwoods along the Rio Grande. That Lucky was a good horse and friendly as a hound dog, but he sure didn't have the easy gait and fighting spirit of Paint or Piebald.

We knowed all the good campsites from coming down, so we avoided 'em. We stopped at some good places so's the horses could graze. It was rough going and we didn't have many supplies, but Pedro had some flour and beans, and Waldo'd been thoughtful enough to fill the bags on the McClellan with some coffee and pemmican.

The first time I ever tried that pemmican I hated it, and I can't say as I ever learned to enjoy it, but I sure appreciated what it'd do for a man. It weren't nothing but jerky—dried venison pounded up in a powder and packed away in a bag like a tobacco pouch with some berries added for flavor and some fat to make it hold together. It didn't weigh much, and when you took it in your fingers and dipped it in a little water, you could make a little ball and munch on it for a while and then swallow it slow. It tasted like hell, but it carried lots of nourishment, and your stomach felt full after you ate just a little bit.

When the Indians thought up the idea of pemmican, they made a helluva contribution to a man traveling cross-country packing his own supplies. Even a man on foot could carry the equal of two or three weeks' worth of grub, and if he could get some water, he'd be in pretty good shape.

It helped when I killed two geese early one morning with my Winchester. It was a little foggy on the river, but we could hear a bunch of 'em calling. We'd been riding all night and'd stopped just before dawn. 'Fore we had our fire going good, I heard them two honkers calling to each other as they was coming up through the fog. I let 'em come in close and then dropped 'em within forty yards of where we was standing. I sure enjoyed the big burst of clapping and laughter that Pedro give out when them birds come tumbling down. They made several good meals for us and we carried 'em along 'til they was all ate up, although I must admit they'd got a little ripe by that time.

While we rode up the Rio Grande we planned how our outfit was gonna be made up. We decided against them big Conestoga wagons—the ones with six-foot wheels that weighed three hundred pounds apiece and'd carry 'bout five thousand pounds of goods. We figured they was too big. It'd take a whole span of oxen to pull one of 'em, and the whole outfit'd prob'ly cost too much.

We talked a lot 'bout whether we oughta use oxen or mules. We knowed that to find any buffalo we was gonna have to go into Comanche country, due east of Santa Fe and Fort Union, maybe out there by Adobe Walls. There we figured we'd run the chance of coming 'cross Indians and having our stock run off.

Pete argued that if we had oxen, them Indians'd never run off our transport, but I objected to oxen on the grounds we never could make no distance with 'em. They was way too slow and we'd be all year getting out there and back again. We needed a smaller wagon, one we could handle with two pair of mules, one that'd pack 'bout three thousand pounds.

A buffalo hide'd weigh 'bout thirty-five pounds if it was fleshed good and dried in the sun. That meant a wagon'd haul 'bout ninety hides. Them hides was worth 'tween twelve and fifteen dollars laid into Santa Fe, maybe something like twenty to twenty-five dollars at Independence—if we wanted to go all that way.

Seemed like an awful freighting job from Santa Fe to Independence, so's we'd have to figure the difference of the worth of them hides against the cost of hauling 'em. That didn't look too practical. Seemed like the best way was to let some others in that Santa Fe– Independence trade do our hauling for us. We'd just keep our outfit for hunting.

We figured we'd need two wagons that we could fill in a week's hunt and take back to Santa Fe, or maybe we could store them hides in Fort Union to make the trip a little shorter and go back out hunting again 'til we made a good collection. Anyhow, each wagonload'd pay for the outfit if we handled it right. We'd have to pay outright for just the mules. We might be able to get them wagons on some kinda share.

We also figured we'd need 'bout three skinners. A skinner could skin 'bout five buffalo a day, if'n he kept his knife sharp and we didn't kill them buffalo too far apart from one another. With three skinners we could count on 'bout fifteen hides a day. That'd be 'bout how we'd do on the average, less'n we got us a stand going.

I figured we could get Mexican skinners for 'bout twenty dollars a month and keep. Two wagon drivers'd cost us another fifty. I figured we'd work it in relays, keeping one wagon with us out on the range. As soon as we got a wagonload, one of us'd go back while the other stayed out hunting. We could make it from the Adobe Walls country 'round the Canadian to Fort Union in a matter of a week or ten days.

If we had good hunting and kept at it for three months, we could bring in 'bout eighteen wagonloads worth maybe a thousand bucks apiece. We sure'd pay for the outfits fast on that basis, and have plenty of dough left over. But we was gonna have to hustle to do it. The hardest part was that we didn't have quite enough money to get started. We needed something to pay crew wages with, although we reckoned them bastards could wait 'til we got some money back from hides.

We was gonna have to buy ammunition and prob'ly another Sharps rifle. I weren't too sure 'bout how much better them Sharps was than my Winchester. Pedro kept insisting that all good buffalo hunters had them heavy guns.

I reckoned I was a better enough shot than the average man to where I could make a Winchester count, and that maybe the one Sharps'd be all we'd need. Besides, I always had the idea in mind that if I could get a buffalo stand going with my Winchester, it wouldn't take me long to put a dozen or so animals on the ground.

Anyway, the way I figured it, we was gonna need 'bout fifteen hundred dollars. On top of Waldo's eight hundred ninety, I'd saved up 'bout fifty-five outta my freight wages. That was nine hundred forty-five, and Pedro'd made 'bout a hundred sixty-five at poker. Altogether, that only come to 'round eleven hundred. It looked like we was 'bout three to four hundred short. Well, we knowed from past experience we had ways of getting things together. 'Sides that, we might be able to get the wagons on credit.

We spent damned near ten days in Albuquerque trying to get things done right. We couldn't find no small wagons worth the money, and there weren't no outfits 'round that'd talk 'bout letting us have anything on credit. The best hope we had was to find one of them freighting outfits in a slump so's maybe we could make a deal with 'em for their wagons. Trouble was, as soon as spring come, them freighters was planning to hit the trail to Kansas again and use every wagon.

We bought two teams of mules off'n a Mexican friend of Pedro's, and they was good ones. They come with harnesses and all, and we give two hundred fifteen dollars for the four of 'em. Pedro's friend agreed to pasture 'em as part of the deal 'til we was ready to leave.

'Course we was green as hell 'bout buffalo hunting, so we tried to ask as many questions as we could 'round the bars. Naturally we used up some of our money, but we gained a helluva lot of information. One thing we found out was that we was for sure gonna need some spare horses. They was a damn sight cheaper'n mules—if we handled it right we could buy a good horse for thirty-five dollars.

Another thing we found out from some of the men who'd gone out before was that they hadn't gone very far east. Most of 'em wasn't too anxious to tangle with the Comanches, so's they hadn't gone as far as the Canadian. Some of their expeditions sounded like sorta half-sickly deals anyway. We picked up a few supplies from 'em. We did find one hunter who'd gone all the way out. It didn't make us feel very good when he told us he'd nearly shit his pants most of the time worrying 'bout Comanches and seeing their tracks. He said he didn't stay out there long enough to fill a wagon, 'cause he was too worried 'bout getting home with his scalp on.

We kept sticking 'round there in Albuquerque, gaining information and looking to buy mules and wagons at a bargain price. Like every outfit that's getting started, we spent some money on whores, and that didn't help our fortunes none, neither.

There was one part of our stay in Albuquerque that done me good for the rest of my life, and it didn't have nothing to do with buffalo hunting. It had to do with them Sandia Mountains that lies east of Albuquerque. In them days there was a couple of haciendas that lay along the foot of 'em, particularly on the southwest and southeast sides. Pedro knowed everybody, so of course he knowed one of them ranchers—a fella name of Valencia.

We got drunk with him one night in a bar and he told us to come out to his place the next day to go hunting. He had him a pack of hounds that he used to hunt mountain lions, and there was lots of lions in the Sandias in them days. He kept bragging 'bout it so much when he was drunk that Pedro and me decided to take him up on it.

Next day we rode 'round to his girlfriend's house, got him sobered up enough to get him on his horse, and headed out. Señor Valencia didn't sober up enough to go hunting that afternoon, so we spent the night in the hacienda and fixed to go the next morning. That night, his wife fed us the hottest Mexican food I reckon I've had anywhere. The stuff made my nose run and my eyes water and the sweat pop out on my head, but it sure tasted good. Me and Pedro slept out in a shed by the wall of the hacienda. It was a cold, clear night and we wrapped our blankets 'round us tight, but I didn't sleep no good on account of that hot food still burning my innards.

We left 'bout daybreak and started up the slopes of the Sandias. There was still patches of snow 'long the foothills, and every time we crossed one of them patches Valencia'd stop and look for lion tracks. When we got up to where the patches was frequent, we didn't climb no farther, but kept skirting the range and following the contour line 'round at that height. I could see that Valencia was quite a hunter hisself, and them dogs was trotting 'round sniffing like they knowed what they was doing, too. It hadn't snowed for maybe two weeks, so we seen lots of old tracks from all kinds of game—mule deer, elk, and even a big old bear.

It was still early morning when we come up on the paw prints of a big cat that was reason'bly fresh and heading 'round the range to the south. The rancher and Pedro talked a lot of Spanish and then Pedro turned to me. "Valencia say it is a big tom and he knows this cat. The sign is two days old, but we will follow 'til we see something better. What you say?" I was having a good time, so I told him it was okay with me.

The track was stale and the dogs only give occasional tongue. After 'bout an hour, seeing where the cat'd laid down a few times and gone wandering along at a slow pace, we got into what looked like fresher tracks.

The hounds started acting different, 'specially the two lead dogs. They was giving tongue every now and then, putting out bays that sounded woeful as hell. By noon the baying was coming a lot more frequent, and the dogs was acting more excited, with their tails all a-wagging and their noses close to the ground.

We followed them tracks for at least six miles. It was slow going, but by late afternoon they was getting clearer and we could see fresh lion sign in the snow.

Then we come up on a big buck that'd been killed the night before. There was a lot of it left. It looked like that lion'd ate what he'd wanted and went on, and there was blood and scuff marks all 'round where the buck'd gone down with his neck broke.

I was real amazed by the strength of that lion. He'd tore a whole foreleg off'n the carcass—it looked like he'd give it one big wrench and jerked it loose. Then there was a spot where the lion'd lay down to eat 'fore he'd wandered on, this time heading uphill. The dogs took off, baying loud, and Valencia got excited and yelled at us to hurry up.

'Bout five minutes 'fore we come up on that dead buck, I'd noticed old Paint's right forefoot was bothering him a little bit and I worried that there was something wrong. When Paint got to limping I knowed it was time to stop and check his hooves. I hated to lose track of the hounds and hear 'em going off in the distance with Valencia and Pedro riding like hell behind 'em, but there weren't nothing for me to do but to stop.

I got a stick and scraped out Paint's right forefoot where the snow'd balled up and froze hard. It took a bit of doing 'cause he weren't used to having his feet fooled with much. I must've been fifteen or twenty minutes easing him 'round and getting all his feet cleaned up. I'd picked a dry place where there weren't no snow on the ground, up by the edge of a cliff that faced to the west-southwest. The cliff was part of a long red sandstone ridge that run up to a point and then turned off away. That cliff was near vertical and went up in a series of ledges or steps. The height 'tween them ledges was maybe fifteen feet. I remember that there was three tiers of 'em and a bunch of big boulders on the top.

When I quit fooling with Paint's hooves, I straightened up and tossed the stick away. I looked up at them cliffs and seen a sight I ain't likely to ever forget. It was way late in the afternoon by then and the sun was low and shining fiery red in the west. The sunlight made them rocks glow red and them shadows stand out real plain. Pedro and Valencia and the hounds'd long gone outta hearing distance and there was a soft sighing wind in the trees.

I don't know how it happened, as it's kind of unusual for a man's eye to catch that kinda movement, but I reckon I didn't have ordinary eyes. I saw a flick of motion 'bout fifty yards from me on the first ledge of the cliff. When I took a good look, I seen something that thrilled me clean through.

I used to watch house cats when I was a kid. We kept 'em for mousers, and I remember how graceful they was. A house cat could jump real easy to a cupboard shelf that was four and a half feet off the floor. That's the same as jumping three times its own length.

If a man that was six feet tall could do that, he'd be jumping eighteen feet. That gives you an idea of the difference 'tween a man's muscles and cat muscles. Now, a mountain lion standing on his hind legs will measure almost six feet tall, and by God, he can do just that thing that a man can't. He *can* jump 'bout three times that far. When he does, I'm here to tell you, it's a sight to see.

After I noticed that motion on the ledge, I seen it was a big cat crouching real low, and I reckoned he hadn't seen me, 'cause he was looking at the ledge above him and gathering hisself for a spring. I ain't never seen nothing like it. He was jumping off'n a real narrow ledge of rock where he'd been hunched up. The ledge above him was all of fifteen feet high, but he flowed up to that ledge as if he was a puff of smoke. He didn't have no trouble landing and kept his balance well in hand.

Then I learned that he was a damn sight smarter than I'd give him credit for, 'cause the minute he landed, he crouched low, turned his head, and looked right at me as if to say, Buddy, I seen ya. I seen ya fer a long time 'fore ya seen me, an' I know right where ya are. Now, what is it yore fixin' ta do? Then he lay there and stared at me.

I got this real keen sensation while I was watching him. I could've drawed out my Winchester and knocked him off'n that ledge plumb easy, but I didn't do no such. I reckon I was fascinated. I kept looking at his eyes and, even though he was fifty yards away, I could see 'em real plain. They shone like big yellow moonstones, glowing as they looked at me. The pupils was formed in crosses.

As I looked at that big cat's eyes, the hair slowly stood up on the back of my neck. I couldn't take my eyes off'n him. It seemed like he and I was trying to talk to each other, like there was something going back and forth 'tween us through our eyes. He stayed there real motionless. For once, that horse Paint never moved. He must not've spotted the lion or smelled it, 'cause if'n he had, I don't think he would've stood still.

Then that big cat started to move, keeping low on the ledge, creeping along real easy. It looked like his body flowed towards me like water along that uneven piece of rock. He moved slow and steady and cautious, and he never took his eyes off'n me. Somehow I knowed that he meant me no harm and that he was just coming to get a better look.

My heart kept beating faster. He got to within thirty yards, lay down, and stayed absolutely motionless. I didn't move neither. I felt something akin to that lion.

'Bout then, way off in the distance, I heard the sound of the dogs again, coming back my way. Then I knowed that the lion'd doubled back and passed overhead of 'em, fooling 'em all the while. The lion heard the dogs, too, and turned his head real slow to look behind him. He didn't seem disturbed. He just waited and watched. We must've stayed like that for ten minutes. Meanwhile, the baying of them hounds was getting closer all the time.

Suddenly the baying got real loud when they rounded the point of the cliffs 'bout a mile to the northeast. I couldn't see the dogs just then, but I could see the two horsemen coming 'round the shoulder of the hill. The lion seen 'em, too. He lay down flat against the rock and watched 'em as they come closer. When they got to 'bout half a mile away, he saw his chance.

They went down into a little draw outta sight for a minute. That lion gathered hisself up and made another spring to a ledge above him and then leaped up to a second ledge, then to a third and a fourth. In a matter of seconds he was lying 'bout sixty feet above where he'd been before. From where I was standing, it looked to be the top of the cliff.

Then he crouched down real low again, put his head on his paws, and just lay there, his pale yellow eyes with the cross-hair pupils looking towards where the riders'd come out—towards where the sun's slanting rays'd keep 'em in plain sight.

If I hadn't knowed exactly where he was, I couldn't have spotted him, the way he blended into those red rocks. The rays of the dying sun high-lighted that scene plenty—the color of the lion blending in with the shadows and colors of the cliff. It seemed like he could see everything that was going on, but nobody could see him.

Right away, them dogs come howling and baying with their tails going and the horsemen behind 'em with their ponies all lathered. They come galloping up like they was carrying the mail, 'til they got to the place where the lion'd started up. Them dogs was stopped at the bottom of the cliff and they looked up and started a woeful baying.

The riders stopped, too, and looked up at the cliff, trying to spot where the lion was. I was still 'bout fifty or sixty yards from 'em and hid by some piñon trees. I just watched the show and thought it was a sight worth seeing. I knowed they couldn't spot the lion, what with the way he blended into them rocks, although the dogs told 'em he was up there.

That scene lasted 'bout five minutes while the sun went down. Then I seen, like a moving shadow, a motion in the dark that slowly disappeared over the hill as that beautiful cat seemed to walk away real indifferent. He knowed them dogs and horses wasn't coming up the face of that cliff, and they'd be a long time picking up his trail, going way out 'round and climbing that mountain to find him in the dark. For the rest of the night, anyway, he knowed he was safe. I stood there in a trance and realized that I was quivering all over. I couldn't say nothing.

I finally crawled up on Paint and rode outta the piñons towards Pedro and Valencia and the baying hounds. They seen me when I come outta the timber and Pedro begun yelling and pointing up the rock and saying, "Amigo, the lion has gone up the rocks. He is up there right now!"

I knowed then for sure they hadn't seen that lion walk away. I didn't tell 'em that I'd been watching that lion for the last fifteen minutes. I didn't tell 'em 'cause they'd have asked me why I hadn't shot him, when it was such an easy shot. I didn't say nothing, 'cause I didn't want to have to tell 'em that I'd passed up that chance on account of how I felt 'bout that lion. Me and him'd shared some deep, mysterious secret.

That ain't all. I've hunted and rode and robbed from the Big Bend of the Rio Grande to Clark's Fork of the Bitter Root, and I've killed men and animals. I've killed grizzly, black bear, mule deer, elk, white-tail, bighorn sheep, wolves, coyotes, and Indians a-plenty, but I ain't never killed no mountain lion.

Lord knows I've seen my share of 'em—and some I could've killed easy—but they always looked at me with them eyes the same way I looked back at them. I never so much as drawed a bead on 'em, let alone ever fired a shot, 'cause somehow it ain't right to kill kin.

I know there're lots of folks who'd say that's crazy talk, and I 'spect in a way it is. No man can rightly be kin to no animal. All I know is, every time I seen them lions and they looked at me and I looked back at them, I knowed what they was thinking and they knowed I wasn't gonna harm 'em and I sure weren't afraid of 'em. What drawed me to 'em was the way they walked and watched from on high, kinda stealthy and shadowlike, the way they lay amongst the rocks and blended in amongst the sandstones like they wasn't there.

Anyway, it took some time 'fore Pedro and Valencia got the idea that the lion'd give 'em the slip, and we headed on back to the ranch house. While we was having supper, the two men got to talking 'bout how we was gonna track down that lion in the morning. It made me plumb uneasy. I finally told Pedro that we'd better get on into Albuquerque and put the rest of our buffalo-hunting outfit together or we'd miss the spring hunt.

Next morning at daybreak we hit out for Albuquerque and spent the rest of the day trying to round us up some more mules and find something that'd suit us for wagons. It was tough business and we didn't do no good. Seemed like everybody was getting into the freighting business. Ever since the war there'd been lots of folks coming west and needing supplies. Them Spanish folks up and down the Rio Grande bought American goods, and there was lots to be made in the freighting line in them days by those that could keep the Comanches from plundering their outfits. We finally reckoned that Albuquerque was too small a town, so we rounded up them two span of mules we'd bought and jangled on over to Santa Fe with our harnesses tied up on their backs.

I figured we could do better at Santa Fe, but even there the going was hard. It took us near two weeks to buy two more pair of mules, and we'd had to give two hundred fifty dollars for 'em. Pedro bought a horse for forty dollars. It was the sorriest-looking Appaloosa I'd ever seen, but I reckoned he was a traveler.

We looked everywhere for wagons. We stayed with Pedro's friends again and done real good, not spending no money unnecessarily in the bars 'til one day Pedro run into one of his old girlfriends on the plaza. She sold Navajo blankets and silver jewelry and other stuff in the little shop that her and her husband run. Her husband was a Navajo trader who'd go out for a month's stretch in Navajo country and bring a load of goods to town to stock the shop.

When we run into her, her husband'd left and was fixing to be gone for at least three weeks, so Pedro moved in, all smiles and graceful gestures. I moved in, too, and slept in the kitchen.

That didn't slow us up too bad. It didn't stop us from looking for wagons, but they was scarce. We finally bought us a used-up Conestoga off'n an old Spanish Jew 'cause it was the only decent thing available. He had to build us a new tongue and one rear wheel and axle, and even at that it cost us better'n four hundred dollars. We were damned near outta money and still hadn't hired us no skinners. It looked real unlikely we'd be able to get another wagon, even if we'd had the money to pay for it.

I told Pedro that since we had eight mules and a Conestoga wagon, we could carry near five thousand pounds in it. I figured we might as well try to run the outfit with one wagon. Maybe the hunter that stayed behind on the plains could pile up the hides somewhere and wait for the wagon to come back.

We argued 'bout that for a spell 'til things was decided for us late one night when Pedro's girlfriend's husband come home real unexpected, pulling his mule team up by the side of the shop. I reckon Pedro's girl had a good ear for her husband's voice when he was cussing his mules. She woke up, kicked Pete outta bed in a hurry, and throwed his stuff out the window and him after it. Then she come into the kitchen where I'd been sleeping and pushed me out the side door. I met Pedro coming 'round the side of the house, and me and him hightailed it down the street in the dark, him cussing away in Mexican and me madder'n hell to be woke up sudden and barely able to get out with my boots and rifle, all on account of Pedro's bad arrangements.

We both agreed it was 'bout time we got outta town, so at daybreak we hitched them mules up to the Conestoga, with the spares and horses tied on behind. I'd ride Lucky and we fixed it so's we'd change off riding horses and driving the wagon as we went.

We almost looked like an outfit—a damned small one. We'd already loaded the wagon with some supplies we was fixing to use, including that Sharps rifle plus enough ammunition for both it and our repeaters. We had some other stuff too—an old tent, a stove, an ax, some cooking equipment, a few skinning knives, salt for the hides, some bedrolls, and some odd clothes. That was 'bout all. It was a sorry outfit compared to some others, but from the outside it didn't look too bad.

We left town 'bout five o'clock, just as dawn broke, but you'd have thought we was going on the wildest expedition the West'd ever seen. Pedro started shouting and cussing and hollering away, cracking his whip and waving his hat. I reckon you gotta know Spanish to drive a big team of Mexican mules, 'cause it takes a special kinda cussing to get 'em up against them collars and pulling together. Pedro sure knowed how to do it. He was one of the best mule skinners that'd ever come up the Rio Grande. Them mules took off at a trot, sending the dust spinning off the wheels. I was riding alongside, trying to keep from busting my gut laughing.

After we'd gone 'bout a mile or so, I yelled at Pedro to slow up. "I reckon we'd better save them mules, 'cause we got us a long ways ta travel. At the rate yore goin', they'll burn up 'fore we get ta the Pecos, let alone out ta the Canadian!"

Pete shot me a dirty look. He must've still been riled up 'bout being tossed out by that gal.

We kept on the Santa Fe Trail 'til we crossed the headwaters of the Pecos at Fort Sumner. We stopped there for a couple of days to get ourselves straightened out and to try to pick up any last bits of information we could from any hunters that might've been out in the prairies towards the Canadian.

We didn't do no good as far as information was concerned. Them that was hunters'd already gone. The loafers we talked to 'round the fort didn't know nothing, and it was a damned sure cinch that them cavalry soldiers didn't know their ass from their elbow 'bout buffalo hunting.

We done mighty good overall, though. We picked up three skin-ners: a half-breed Frenchman named Dubeck and two Mexicans that I only knowed as Jose and Emanuel. They smelled bad enough to be good skinners, so we hired 'em on. We had to buy a little tequila in a canteen from the fort 'fore they'd agree to go out there into Comanche country, though.

We bought some more grub and a couple of water barrels, along with some spare harness parts and whatnot. Finally, we hit out 'cross them great rolling prairies east of Fort Sumner and kept our weather eye cocked for any dust clouds that'd mean buffalo—or anything else.

10

THE BUFFALO IS A STRANGE CRITTER

That was great country. It was all sky meeting prairie, as far as you could see, with the grass rolling away forever. There weren't nothing else to the south or the east. To the north and northeast there was some big mesas and then some small ones, and behind us to the west and a little north stood the great snowcapped peaks of the Sangre de Cristos.

I remember as we was working our way east across them prairies, with the dust clouds curling up 'round the wagon and the mules nickering the stuff outta their noses, I'd swing 'round in the saddle and look back over the canvas top of that old Conestoga at them beautiful mountains that we was leaving behind. The snow-clad peaks with those beautiful forests of blue spruce and ponderosa cloaking their slopes was a sight to gladden a man's heart.

The country due east was a rolling sea of endless prairie. It didn't look near as inviting or beautiful as them glorious mountains. But we knowed that to the east was a fortune, if we was smart enough to get it.

We kept going for nigh onto ten days, long after the mountains'd disappeared behind us. Though we was south of the Canadian River, we didn't see no buffalo, not even any fresh sign, and no Indians neither. Seemed like our little wagon was nothing but a speck way out there in that vast rolling sea. It sure gets spooky when for miles 'round—as far as you can see, day after day—you don't see no life.

I reckon this's a good time to tell 'bout the buffalo herds and what they was like in them days, how they acted and why we was looking for 'em the way we was.

In the early days 'fore I come to the frontier, the old-timers used to say that there was four big buffalo herds: the Texas herd, the Arkansas herd, the Republican herd, and the Montana herd, named according to the areas where they roamed.

Now, the buffalo is a strange critter. He ain't like a cow. He's got his fur coat up front covering his shoulders and withers and all over his head. His hind end is thin haired, that's why the buffalo always grazes into the wind. Nature made him that way as a protection for when it got to storming. He'd turn his woolly face into the icy wind and it never bothered him none. He might bunch up some in a real blizzard, but he'd face right into it and never get into no trouble.

Now, cattle—they'll drift before the wind, turning their rumps to the sting of the snow and sleet rather than face into it. When they get to drifting, they'll pile up in some arroyo or against a cliff where the snowdrifts will plumb smother 'em 'fore the storm is over.

But nature equipped the buffalo to do better, and I reckon that's why he survived in such great numbers out on the western plains 'fore the white man come along and messed it all up.

Yessir, the buffalo was a great animal, and he sure enough was the supply depot for them Indians. He furnished the Indian most everything he needed—hides for his tepees, buffalo robes for his sleeping and comfort, meat for his belly, and even hair for making ropes for his horse halters and lassos.

Funny thing 'bout the buffalo, though. When the gentle prairie wind was blowing and there weren't no storms, he'd graze real slow into the wind. In the springtime the gentle breezes and Chinook winds'd come outta the northwest, so the buffalo'd begin meandering in that direction. Then, as it got on into summer, them winds'd swing 'round to the north and the buffalo'd keep eating and heading into the wind, working his way north.

In late August, them winds'd swing 'round to the east, and the buffalo'd keep eating and grazing that way. Finally, in the late fall, the winds'd come outta the southeast and the buffalo'd follow that. When he got through, he would've covered a great big circle. It took him a year to make it, but that circle was prob'ly twelve hundred miles 'round.

It seemed like nature thought of everything, 'cause when one buffalo herd was in its summer range, it was fertilizing the winter range of the herd that was to the north of 'em. That's the way the prairie grasses growed and how they supported them big herds. 'Course when the white man come along and broke them trails like the Santa Fe and the Smoky Hill and the Overland, all the commotion split up them buffalo herds. When the railroads come, the real destruction begun. There was all kinds of men coming out on them trains, fanning out and shooting them buffalo in every direction. Lots of 'em done it for sport, and then there was the hide hunters, too.

By the time I'd come along the Arkansas with Michelle, enough damage'd been done so's there weren't no buffalo north of the Arkansas to amount to nothing. They tell me that you had to go clear up into northern Wyoming and southern Montana Territory 'fore you picked up any herds again. They had to be far enough north of the Overland Trail not to've got messed up.

Even in my day there still was lots of buffalo down there in the Comanche country south of the Arkansas. I reckon that spring of 1868 was prob'ly the last time them critters could be found in real big herds, and by big herds I mean that when you come on one, as far as you could see there was buffalo.

I s'pose there's been lots told 'bout the buffalo. I must admit, I didn't know when I was hunting 'em in the spring of '68 that the buffalo weren't gonna last more'n six or seven years in that country, and that they'd all be shot out even in Montana Territory fifteen years from then. Yessir, the last of them buffalo was cleared out 'long the Milk River in Montana in 1883. After that, the Sioux dancers and Comanche witch doctors could beat their drums and do the buffalo dance and call on the Great Manitou to bring their brother the buffalo up outta the ground, but the buffalo herds never appeared again, and there weren't nothing left but open space that the cattlemen soon took up.

That April, when me and Pedro was working our Conestoga wagon east towards Adobe Walls on the Canadian River, I didn't have no idea that the buffalo was gonna go that fast. I just kept looking for the steam cloud. That's what all the buffalo hunters looked for when there weren't no buffalo around. They looked for the cloud that you'd see early in the morning from the heat of all them bodies when the prairies was cold. That was the telltale sign that told you you was coming up on what you was looking for.

It got lonesome out on them prairies. Ten days out of Fort Sumner we still hadn't sighted no buffalo, and we begun to worry plenty. You usually think of that part of the country as being full of game, and when it ain't you're puzzling all the time. The spaces was so vast on them prairies that no matter how many animals there was, you couldn't always find 'em. I later heard old Indians tell 'bout how people went starving 'cause they couldn't locate game, although three weeks before, the same place where they was hunting was thick with it.

On the tenth day out we seen some cottonwoods in the distance, and that meant there was water ahead. Although we'd had our own water in barrels, we was damn glad for it. When you was buffalo hunting, you hit right over open country, not like when you was traveling the trails along the riverbanks like them pioneer outfits. Hunting buffalo, you was really on your own in wild country, and you hoped you'd hit the headwaters of some creeks or find some springs somewheres so's you could water your stock and fill your barrels again.

We was all day getting to them cottonwoods, and 'bout four in the afternoon we come up on 'em. Sure enough, there was a spring bubbling out and a little creek running from it down to the southeast. Them last two miles our mules was getting frantic, they was so anxious to get to the water.

Funny how stock is. When you'd travel several days and there weren't no natural water so's you had to water 'em out of your barrels, they'd get plenty nervous. They seemed to know that if you didn't find water ahead, they'd traveled too far to make it back.

When we hit that cottonwood patch we made camp, the first decent camp since we'd left Fort Sumner. I'd been wondering all the time how we was gonna get along with them skinners, but they seemed like right good fellas and they didn't complain none. The Mexicans rode in the wagon and the Frenchman, Dubeck, rode his own horse. It was the damndest-looking dilapidated old mouse-colored gelding I'd ever seen. He looked like he was leftover from a Mexican bullfight, patched up and turned loose for the last three weeks 'fore he cashed in his chips. But the Frenchman didn't seem to mind. He rode along off to the side of the wagon where he weren't getting the dust and spent his days singing songs. Some of 'em I'd heard already, 'cause they was the same ones them French boatmen'd sung on the Missouri and the Mississippi when I was a kid. They was great old songs, and somehow they fit the prairies. It reminded me of the fact that them Frenchmen was out on those prairies exploring and trapping long 'fore any of us others ever seen that land.

Dubeck was good when it come to making camp. He knowed the right things to do and was handy at unharnessing the mules and seeing that they was took care of. He was real good at spotting harness sores, pulling the collars and the hanes off'n the mules, and checking for any places where the rig might've been rubbing too hard. That was another thing 'bout that country—off in the open prairie land, you'd damn well better look after your stock. It don't take long to figure out that without them horses and mules, you ain't going nowhere. Any man that thinks he can walk back is crazy.

That night when we set 'round the campfire among them cotton-wood trees, me and Pedro hashed things over. We figured it weren't no use in going much farther. Ten days east of Fort Sumner must've put us within a few miles of the Canadian somewhere near Adobe Walls.

It wouldn't pay none for us to go up that way. There was bound to be hunters from the Arkansas there, and we'd only run into their doings. We reckoned the best thing was to wait 'round and see what was going on. There weren't no doubt that we was in buffalo range, 'cause we seen plenty of sign, but it was old—real old. It'd been there since the spring before, so we knowed it was spring buffalo range, only the buffalo hadn't got there yet. The only thing to do was to sit and wait.

'Sides, if we was to go much farther, it wouldn't have been practical for us to make four or five trips back to Fort Sumner with our hides. As a matter of fact, we even debated turning back maybe two days' worth, just to be a little closer in, but then we remembered that there weren't no good campsites and we was better off right where we was by that cottonwood spring with its little sandy creek so's we could keep our water barrels full.

Only old-time buffalo hunters knowed what it was like to wait for a herd. It's the most monotonous damn thing a man can do. For a thousand miles 'round, it seemed, there weren't nothing going on. 'Course there was the prairie wind, and it tried to tell you a thing or two. Then there was the dawn and the heat of the day when you was glad for the shade of the cottonwoods. There was also the sun setting with fiery red streaks in the clouds to the west. But that's 'bout it, day after day.

You had to pass the time somehow, and every man does a little something different. Pedro, being a gambler, had a deck of cards, so's we pitched in for a little easy poker with the skinners. We done that for a few afternoons, but I got tired of it real quick. Them Mexican skinners and old Dubeck didn't seem to think there was anything in the world more fun than gambling. 'Course they was dead meat for Pedro. Like I said, I'd never seen Pedro cheat and I never heard of him cheating, but he was the best poker player 'round, and them skinners soon found it out. By the third afternoon, it looked like they was gonna work the first month for nothing, 'cause Pedro'd won all of their wages and then some.

Pedro'd laugh a little bit and let 'em win once in a while, just to keep 'em in the game, but he sure did take 'em to town. When that kinda stuff wore off, Pedro'd give us some exhibitions of his knife-throwing. It sure drawed the respect from them boys.

I didn't have nothing else to do, so I practiced a lot throwing a knife and it helped some. I got so's I could throw a knife and figure on it sticking most of the time, but I wasn't no sure shakes like Pedro. Dubeck was right good, too, and them Mexicans done all right. I reckon they all was as good or better'n me, but none of 'em even come close to Pedro.

I would like to've had a little shooting contest—maybe give 'em an exhibition. I knowed damn well I could do it. If anything, my shooting was getting better. We had some whiskey with us, but we'd been using it sparingly, 'cause we didn't know how long we was gonna be out. Y'know how sparing I mean when I say we was out for over fifteen days 'fore we had two empty bottles. I knowed that 'cause one day, even though it was plain to all that we had to watch our ammunition, I just felt like showing off. Pedro throwed them bottles up in the air for me with a full underhanded sweep of his knife-throwing arm. They flew up into the blue sky, turning over as they went and spreading apart 'bout two yards. I busted 'em both all to hell with that Winchester with two quick shots, just as they reached the top of their arc. That raised the eyebrows on them skinners, but they didn't say nothing. There weren't no buffalo, and all we was doing was blasting away in the sky at whiskey bottles. That ain't much of a buffalo hunt.

We camped by that place for two whole weeks. By that time we was getting plenty discouraged 'cause there still weren't no sight of nothing.

We never did sleep in the tent or the wagon on them clear nights. We slept out under the stars by the campfire with blankets wrapped 'round us and our saddlebags for a pillow. I usually slept sound, but once in a while I'd wake up in the early hours of the morning and look at them diamonds of stars in the black sky overhead and get to wondering 'bout the making of it all and how I fit into the scheme of things. Then, ever so faint, to the east would come a finger of light— the first sheen of dawn. Slowly, them stars'd fade and the whole world'd light up and the prairie grasses'd shine like silver in the rising sun.

It was on such a morning that I woke up feeling uneasy 'bout the earth. Seemed like the land was trying to tell me something and I had a faint humming in my ears. Then I knowed what it was. I was hearing a far-off rumble. I sat up in my blankets to take a look and I felt a slight tremor in the earth, and that was all it took. I kicked off my covers in a flash. Two strides and I was booting Pedro outta his blankets. "Get up, ya damn greaser, the buffalo's comin'."

Pedro come up like he'd been shot out of a cannon. He could feel the earth trembling, too. So could the horses—we could tell by the way they was looking with their ears perked up. I knowed by the sound that it was a big herd.

We slung our saddles on, tightened them cinches 'bout as fast as you can make it 'round, and run for the ammunition box in the wagon. We filled our pockets and ammunition belts, and Pedro took the Sharps. That big rifle wouldn't fit in his scabbard, so he jumped onto his black and held the gun straight up in the air like a lance. Behind me, Dubeck was mounted on his mousy dun carrying more ammunition. I tossed him the Henry rifle and yelled at him to stick close.

We headed out towards the rumble at a dead gallop. You'd have thought from the noise that the herd was right on us, but in the early light we couldn't see it yet. The weather was too warm for a steam cloud to show, but there was no mistaking the direction. We covered three and a half miles in 'bout ten minutes, and it was getting light enough to see good.

If you see a buffalo herd in flat country like the panhandle, then you can see it all at once—stretching as far as the eye can reach. If you hit it in rolling country, it can be two miles away and you can't see none of it. It's that effect that used to make the Indian think that the buffalo come up outta the ground, and that's what he used to pray to the great Manitou for—to see his brother, the buffalo, come outta the ground every spring.

Sure enough, when we seen that herd, it seemed to rise up that way led by a few cows and calves coming down through some draws here and there. We reined up our horses and took a good look. Then we seen more, and more, and more—coming on like a big avalanche—a mass of dark brown bodies that was heaving and thundering along, coming right at us.

We was 'bout half a mile away, so we spurred on. We must've come within two hundred yards of the advance ranks 'fore they spotted us and tried to pause to look us over. I could see what'd happen next: A whole line of 'em'd stop, then the pressure from behind'd build up and push 'em towards us. I reckoned they'd get to within a hundred yards 'fore they'd break off to the sides and try to go 'round.

I brought Paint to a shuddering stop and bailed outta the saddle, yelling at Dubeck to hold my horse and keep that Henry handy. My heart was pounding like a war drum. It weren't just that it was my first real buffalo hunt and my first sight of a big herd. I could also see my fortune out there in front of me, if'n I could just settle down and shoot straight.

They was 'bout a hundred fifty yards from us when I drawed down on a big bull in the lead. I squeezed off a shot and he rolled over and piled up on the ground like he'd been poleaxed. I shoved the lever action fast and squeezed off on a cow that was maybe twenty yards to his left. She went down likewise. Then I turned to a bull on the right, and another cow on the right, then a bull dead ahead, and kept on working in that way.

When I'd emptied the magazine of that Winchester, the barrel was hot and there was sixteen dead buffalo lying out in a ring in front of me, from sixty to a hundred fifty yards off. I tossed Dubeck the empty rifle for him to reload and grabbed the Henry and went to work again.

By this time, the herd's movement towards us'd stopped and they was milling 'round in confusion. We didn't have no stand going, a stand being where they stood real still and you could work on the outer edges and keep shooting your way in 'til you finally laid 'em all down. It weren't like that a'tall. They was confused and upset by the firing, but they hadn't yet begun to stampede off. I kept on shooting and emptied the Henry.

When I stepped back to get the Winchester from Dubeck, I seen that he hadn't got the magazine full-up yet. That'll give you an idea of how fast I'd emptied the Henry. Every now and then I could hear the roar of the big .50 when Pedro'd cut loose. The only trouble was, every time he'd let drive, he'd cheer while he'd watch his animal going down, and I was worried that all his yipping and yelling'd stampede the herd and we'd lose the chance to make a big kill.

I emptied the Winchester again real fast, but there was only seven shots in it. When I went back for the Henry again, I seen that Dubeck hadn't done no better with it, but I didn't have time to argue. I fired six more shots and then all hell broke loose. Snorting and bellowing, the whole herd turned and thundered away at a helluva clip, leaving behind a rolling cloud of prairie dust that looked like the earth'd done shook open. I run and give the gun back to Dubeck and jerked my Winchester outta his hand. In another second, I was on Paint and heading after the herd, loading as I rode.

It's a trick to load a magazine rifle from your belt loops when you're at a dead gallop, but I could slide them cartridges into the slot without looking at what I was doing. I soon come up on the laggards—not the big bulls, but cows with their calves.

For real accuracy, it would've been better to dismount to shoot. That weren't possible in a buffalo hunt, but with a good horse you could get up close enough to where even a lady with an umbrella could damn near hit what she wanted.

I followed that herd for 'bout three miles 'cross the prairie 'til I was outta ammunition and had another twenty animals on the ground. I pulled Paint up, 'cause he was plenty blowed. He'd run three and a half miles to get to the herd and'd had only a few minutes' rest, then another three miles, and he weren't doing it at no lope, but at a flat-out run. A horse'll ease off and save hisself once in a while, but if he's got the spirit and you put the spurs to him, he'll damn near pull his heart out while he's catching what you're after.

I set there while he was heaving and sweating, watching the herd fade away in the distance and then counting 'round to see what our profits looked like. Them buffalo looked big and shaggy where they lay like furry mounds in the prairie grass. I counted more'n sixty of 'em. Then I seen Pedro over to one side counting away, too.

Pedro looked like one of them old conquistador ancestors of his setting there on his big black horse all dressed up with that broad-brimmed black leather hat with a mule deer tail stuck in the band, holding the Sharps like it was a lance. He seen me look over his way and waved his rifle high and let out a yell that them cavalry boys must've heard clear back at Fort Sumner.

We made quite a haul our first go-round, but with them sixty buffalo down, we had more'n four days' work for our skinners. In four days, even in cool weather, the hair on them hides was sure to slip. There weren't no choice but for me and Pedro to pitch in and help skin, and that's damn dirty work. It was plain that Pedro hadn't thought 'bout that yet, the way he was grinning.

While the rumble died away in the distance, me and him rode back together them three miles, slow and easy, recounting the carcasses as we went. I broke the sad news to Pedro 'bout having to help the skinners if we didn't want them hides to slip, and he got real down in the mouth.

When we got to where we'd made the first kill, Dubeck was already at work skinning out the first buffalo. 'Cross the prairie come the others with the wagon. When them Mexicans come up, we all fell to skinning with a will, and worked through the heat of the day 'til near sundown. By then we had more'n thirty hides off the carcasses but hadn't fleshed none of 'em. Dubeck collected a few buffalo chips and started a fire. We stayed up a good part of the night by the firelight, fleshing what we'd already skinned, so's we could salt 'em and leave 'em out to dry in the morning sun.

We got a little sleep and at daybreak was up and at it again. A good skinner could skin and flesh 'bout five hides a day, but me and Pedro was a little slower. It took us all of the next day to peel the rest of them carcasses. Along towards the second afternoon we wasn't only getting wore down ourselves, but them buffalo was beginning to swell in the heat. They'd growed stiff from being long dead, and skinning got to be a tougher job. We had to stop and sharpen our knives a good part of the time, then go back to working away, trying to pay no attention to the buzzing flies and the stink.

We fleshed the rest of them hides all through that night. 'Bout an hour after sunup we had 'em all salted and spread. We collected the hides that'd growed stiff and dry in the sun the day before and stacked 'em in the wagon, then we crawled into the shade of that Conestoga and went to sleep.

The stock'd long since been picketed and grained, them not being able to make much of a living on the prairie grass at the end of the picket line. We was plenty tired and slept on through the afternoon and most of that night. Come daybreak, we collected the rest of the hides, stacked 'em in the wagon, hitched up our mules, lead-roped the spare mules and extra horses, and hit off up the wide trail the buffalo'd left behind 'em.

I'd took a good look at the herd and made an estimate of it. It sure weren't as big as the ones Carson and Bent used to hunt along the Arkansas. The herds'd been thinned down considerable. It definitely weren't the biggest herd I'd ever seen, and it weren't near as big as I'd thought it was gonna be when I'd first heard the rumble. I remember looking at it and figuring that it was running in a stream 'bout half a mile wide and maybe two to three miles long. There must've been well over ten thousand head in the herd, which was big enough to provide plenty of hunting.

We knowed our best chance was to follow 'em. I figured they'd run maybe twenty miles from where we'd done our shooting and then slacken up and commence to feed, so chances was that once they started grazing, the herd'd spread out and move kinda slow.

We couldn't go as fast as we wanted to on account of them two span being slowed up a little by that two-thousand-pound load we had in the wagon, so it was almost five days 'fore we come up on fresh sign again. We still couldn't see no animals, but I knowed they wasn't too far off.

Me and Pedro rode out ahead, catching sight of the herd 'bout sundown. We was getting into flatter country, and when we first seen 'em they was 'bout eight miles away, spread out good and feeding. Lucky for us, the wind was out of the northwest and that was the direction that we was trailing 'em from. Less'n the wind shifted, we wouldn't spook 'em if they didn't see us, so we waited 'til sundown and moved up on 'em in the dark, close enough to where we could start shooting at daybreak.

Me and Pedro'd never stalked no herds at night, but we'd heard lots of old hunters tell how they done it. They liked to work up on a herd in the moonlight, 'specially in flat country where there weren't no strange shadows cast and where no strays from the herd might be lingering where you might s'prise 'em. You always had to figure that them strays, on account of their being away from the herd, was apt to be the most nervous. When a buffalo gets jumpy he ain't no different from no other game. He spooks real easy at the slightest sound, smell, or sight of anything that ain't familiar.

When we'd seen the herd at sundown, long shafts of sunlight was coming down from where the sun was setting in the west 'tween a couple layers of clouds. Then darkness come on and them clouds turned black and drifted towards us like they was carrying one of them spring rains that brings the green to the parched grasses of the Llano Estacado—the great Staked Plains that was so flat that the Spanish'd drove stakes in the ground to keep their direction.

We figured that the strong wind coming along with the rain'd hide our whereabouts. That way we could not only work upwind close to the herd, but if the wind kept blowing good and the rain started falling, the sound of our horses' hooves wouldn't carry very far. On top of that, we'd smell the buffalo if we got near enough.

We could've lost our direction easy that night if it hadn't been for the wind. We could count on it to keep blowing steady from one direction 'cause it weren't a thunderstorm. With thunderstorms, the direction of the wind is apt to change mighty fast as the storm passes over, but with one of them warm spring rains, the breeze'll hold steady. We knowed that, so we kept riding into it.

After what seemed like more'n two hours to me, Pedro drawed up and said in a whisper, "I think we have come close enough, amigo. Maybe now we dismount and listen for the sound of the herd."

We got down off the horses and stood there cupping our ears into the wind and the light rain, trying to hear that herd. The wind was blowing light and steady and you would've thought the buffalo noises'd come to us easy, but there was quite a rustle of the prairie grass and the popping sound of the rain, and that was all we could make out.

Then I got a bright idea. "Which way was them buffalo facin' when we last seen 'em, amigo?"

"Why, they go facing every different way."

"That was 'fore the storm. Them critters always face into a storm an' they likely been grazin' right towards it. I reckon they's another mile upwind."

"*Si, si.* I think maybe you have for once in your life just a faint trace of the brain."

We kept easing upwind in the dark and the rain, staring and straining our ears. We didn't get nothing but the sound of the wind and the patter of rain and the clomp of our horses' hooves and the creak of saddle leather.

"The night she is dark," Pedro said. "So damned dark I cannot see the hand from my face."

To test that I turned to Pedro and said in a soft voice barely above the wind, "Can ya see me, amigo?"

"No, you bastard, I cannot see a thing. But I can sure hear you, you loud-mouthed son of a bitch. I know right where you are."

I didn't say nothing. Ain't it strange? I thought. Pedro says he can't see me a'tall, but I can see him. I can see the outline a that black stallion he's ridin'. I can see his hat, his face, his legs, his spurs, the silver on his saddle harness, an' his bridle. Oh, not like in daylight, but I can see it all an' he can't see nothin'.

While I was musing along like that, I swung my eyes away from Pedro out ahead of my horse and 'round to the right. Then I almost jerked old Paint back on his hindquarters. There was something big and dark and different 'bout thirty yards away, bordering on my right side.

I'd seen it too late, for just as Paint reared back with a snort, that black thing moved off in a flash in the dark. When Paint's front legs touched the ground again, he done so to the tune of my cussing, 'cause I knowed we'd done sprung the works. Yessir, we'd rode up on one of them strays 'fore we'd knowed it.

Both of us stopped our horses and sat there listening to the hooves of that critter pounding in the wind. I hoped we was so far out that he wouldn't spook the herd, or that maybe he'd stop running.

In a minute I knowed that was wishful thinking, for outta that wind and rain there come the rise of a steady rumble, and it rose almost like thunder, high above the wind. Then it begun to fade away.

Me and Pete damn near lit up that night sky with our cussing, but it didn't do no good.

There weren't nothing to do but sit there and wait out the dawn. When it come, the storm'd died away and there was some clearing skies to the west, but there weren't no buffalo in sight. We rode along their tracks 'til the middle of that day, lay down and got us some rest 'til midafternoon, and then rode on. By dark we still hadn't seen nothing.

The rain'd soaked the plains so's there weren't no dust clouds rising from nothing. We was getting back into rolling country by then, and we'd knowed we was gonna have to rely on trail sign. The sign was still fresh, but our horses was near wore out. The best thing to do was stop and rest and wait for the wagon to come up, so we made us a fire outta buffalo chips and settled down.

It was noon the next day when we seen the wagon top a rise behind us 'bout four miles to the south. In another hour they was with us and we told 'em the sad news. There was plenty of cussing, but more stirring 'round and cooking some meals. Pedro and me hadn't had nothing to eat since we'd left the wagon. At a time like that, coffee and beans taste like they was made in heaven.

I decided right then that from there on I was always gonna carry some pemmican, like I'd done before. Dubeck said that the next buffalo we killed, he'd cut jerky so's we could grind it and make our own pemmican.

Late on the second afternoon we seen the buffalo again, and that time we done our work well. The stars'd come out that evening, so we kept our direction and moved up real careful. When dawn broke we wasn't close enough to shoot, but we was within half a mile of the herd and we hid from sight in a dry arroyo. The buffalo was grazing slowly west by northwest. If we didn't move too fast up the arroyo for 'bout a mile, we'd come within two hundred yards of the herd and still be outta sight.

We had the sun mostly at our backs and the wind was coming steady and gentle from the northwest. We rode away from the wagon with Dubeck along to help load. You can damn well bet we was real careful and didn't make no hasty motions. Time was running out on us and we needed to get several wagonloads of hides to Fort Sumner if we was gonna make any money. We sure as hell wasn't getting paid to be tracking all over the Llano Estacado.

When we got in close, me and Pedro slipped off our ponies, give the reins to Dubeck, and had him walk slow and easy behind us. I whispered to Pedro to lay up against the bank of the arroyo and ease his gun and head up real slow, and not to let fly with that big .50 'fore I started to shoot.

When I got into position with the Winchester cocked, Pedro swung his gun 'round real slow towards a big old bull that was on our far left. I picked out another one on the far right, at the edge of the herd, and drawed down real careful. I held my breath, squeezed off the shot, and watched that bull go down in a swirl of dust.

Funny thing 'bout buffalo. You'd think as spooky as they was when you rode up on 'em at night, that with the first sound of gunfire there'd be snorts, a whirl of flying tails, and they'd be off in a stampede. But it didn't work like that. When I fired, ten or fifteen of the closest ones put their heads up from feeding and begun looking 'round. Farther down the herd they wasn't even stopping their grazing, so I started pumping and squeezing off shots just as fast as I could.

I must've shot six times and put down as many animals 'fore I begun to get real excited. I thought for a minute there that we had us a stand going, but that ain't the way it worked out.

'Bout my seventh or eighth shot, the animals nearest us begun to get a little restless. I kept right on shooting and I could hear every now and then the roar of that big .50. Pedro was loading that single-shot as fast as he could. By the time I'd got off my twelfth shot, the animals was starting to mill 'round and I sensed a restlessness running through the herd. When I'd emptied the sixteenth shot from that Winchester, the whole herd took off, snorting and bellowing, looking like a big, dark, shaggy blanket rippling over the prairie.

I got the loaded Henry from Dubeck and shoved the Winchester at him, vaulted into the saddle, and was off at a dead gallop. I weren't long pulling up on the herd and I emptied the Henry and had a full magazine's worth of animals to show for it.

Dubeck done lots better that time, me having instructed him some. He didn't lose no time passing over that loaded Winchester to me in exchange for the Henry at a high gallop, sailing along in the dust of the herd. The horses was getting wore out but I got off ten more shots 'fore them buffalo was out of range.

We had enough for a day-and-a-half's worth of skinning for all of us, and I figured that'd fill the wagon. Around the campfire that night, we kept fleshing the hides we'd skinned, and we decided on lots of things. We'd only brought along two barrels of salt to cure them hides after we'd fleshed 'em. At the rate we was using it, we needed a bigger supply if we was gonna do this buffalo business right.

When we got to figuring out how long it'd take the wagon, even with an extra span of mules, to make it back to Fort Sumner and return, Pedro come up with a better idea. He said we oughta head northwest for someplace like Fort Union on the Santa Fe Trail, rather than keep going southwest to Sumner. Then we might be able to ship them hides direct, or at least find somebody to store 'em for us. It might be we'd later on have to take a trip to Independence or Freeport Landing ourselves to sell 'em. The main thing was to get them hides off the prairies to someplace where they'd cure good, then get ready for another load.

Pedro'd had another idea, too, and at the time I'd agreed with him. Many long years now, I sure been sorry I listened. What he said was we oughta operate in the most efficient style. One of us oughta drive the wagonload of hides back to civilization while the other stayed out with Dubeck and the skinners and killed buffalo.

The question was, who was gonna drive that wagon back to wherever it was going? We couldn't spare the skinners or Dubeck. Oh, they'd get the wagon there all right, but arrangements'd have to be made to protect our interest in them hides. They'd have to be stored with some trustworthy person or be sent with a reliable shipper. You couldn't leave that up to no hired help to handle.

It come right down to the fact that either me or Pedro had to take the wagon. He figured the best thing would be for him to take it, 'cause I was the best shot and could keep producing hides while he run the ones we had back to civilization. On the face of it, it didn't seem to be a half-bad idea, and we come to the conclusion that the morning after next, we'd load the wagon and Pedro'd start out for Fort Union. We spent the next day finishing our work and loaded them hides during the night. They was heavier'n I'd reckoned and when we finished, that wagon was fair groaning. It was gonna be slow, even using the third span of mules rather'n keeping 'em in reserve.

If Pedro just kept heading a little west by northwest, he'd strike the Santa Fe Trail in something over a week's time, and with his negotiations and all, he oughta be back in sixteen or seventeen days. Meanwhile, we both reckoned that I'd have to move north following the herd or maybe even look for another one, and it'd take Pedro some more time to pick us up. What he'd do was come back to our old campsite and pick up our trail. I was s'posed to leave good sign for him at every camp we made.

Now, that's tough business, leaving messages in the wild. Always seems like things goes wrong and something you mark that seems real plain to you don't make sense to another man when he comes up on it in different circumstances. But Pedro was a good enough man in the wild and a good tracker, and he knowed how I thought.

I seen to it that Pedro had plenty of ammunition and water and supplies. The rest of the stuff he left with us in a hopeless-looking pile sitting there on the prairie. He had his black stallion tied on a lead rope to the back of the wagon, all saddled up with the rifle scabbard empty, and he carried his Henry rifle on the wagon box. He'd wanted to leave most of the ammunition with me to do the hunting, but I wouldn't hear none of that and seen to it that he took plenty with him. I also made sure that he took that Henry rifle, 'cause a repeating rifle was awful good medicine to have. We give the big buffalo Sharps to Dubeck to see what he could do 'til Pedro got back.

The morning Pedro mounted the wagon box to head out for Fort Union, he was wearing his black and silver outfit and that piano-keyboard grin of his, waving his black hat and acting like he was going to a fiesta.

I stepped up to him 'fore he left. "Now listen, y'damn greaser, you make it back here pronto with that wagon. I don't want ya spendin' my money on no señoritas."

He laughed that healthy laugh of his, 'cause we both knowed that as long as his pardner was out on the prairie, waiting for him to return, there wouldn't be none of that stuff. Pedro'd get back as fast as any man alive could make it.

He turned to me. "You know, you are the most stupid gringo I have yet to see. You think that I am going to be so foolish as to go into Fort Union and spend Comanche Brules's money? You have lost the mind. I am not loco! I tell you what. Do not worry about Pedro. I will get back. I bet you now that I will be back before you get another wagonload full of the hides. You keep that Winchester hot and make the hides all over the place. I will be back before you have time to miss my singing! Adios, amigo. Good hunting!"

With that he give a yell and a whoop and a crack of the whip and them mules leaned into the collar and that old wagon started groaning away. The mules finally got it rolling good and settled down to a steady pull. Pedro waved once more at us, the dust curling up 'round the wagon and that black stallion trotting along behind, shaking his head like he felt abused at being given last place in the procession.

I turned back to our camp and started thinking things out. We had my horses—Paint and Lucky—that dun of Dubeck's, and Pedro's spare Appaloosa. We could use Pedro's spare for a packhorse.

We had some water bags and quite a bit of grub and ammunition and other stuff—more'n one packhorse could carry. We'd have to load that Appaloosa with as much as he could take. One of them skinners'd have to stay with the camp while the other skinner rode Lucky, leading the packhorse and following us. Me and Dubeck could go off ahead and fan out looking for buffalo.

When the packer had gone 'bout eight miles, he was to unload the packhorse and go back for another load. We figured it'd take 'bout three loads on the packhorse to move the whole camp, so we figured we'd make 'bout eight miles a day. It sounded like a good plan.

We busied ourselves getting packed up, me not wanting to see that wagon with Pedro in it fading away to the west. We got things in order and moved out with our first load, heading due north towards the buffalo herd. I mounted Paint and looked off into the distance, and there was that covered wagon, real small now, topping a far rise in the prairie. There was a little stream of dust coming out behind it like smoke. We started off on our trail northward. When I looked again, the wagon was gone over the horizon.

Me and Dubeck rode out in a fan for maybe thirty miles, looking for buffalo, then returned to where the camp'd been moved. We done this day after day for the better part of twelve days 'fore we seen any fresh buffalo sign. After two weeks of moving 'bout eight miles a day, I figured we'd come 'bout a hundred miles from where Pedro'd left us. I remember it well, 'cause that was the day we sighted the buffalo herd again. By then we'd knowed a little bit more 'bout hunting 'em and done a better job. We moved slow and easy and got into a good position just at daybreak, with the sun behind us and the wind in our faces.

I done a real careful job of shooting, picking off the stragglers on the outside of the herd. I kept working with the Winchester on one side and Dubeck had the big .50 on the other. It was the only time that I seen that quiet Frenchman get excited, but his hands started shaking when we got a buffalo stand going. Conditions was just right and we was both shooting mighty good that morning. We put down thirty-five animals 'fore the herd got our wind and stampeded off.

After that we had to go back almost fifteen miles to move the skinners and the camp up in three stages. It was a big job: We'd had skinning ahead of us that was more'n four men could handle in two days, but we stayed with it 'til we got them hides fleshed, salted, and piled. We figured we wouldn't do no more traveling 'til Pedro come up. There weren't no way in the world that we could move them hides without the wagon, and to go off and desert 'em was like ignoring money in the bank.

Sixteen days'd gone by since Pedro'd left and we knowed that we oughta see him coming anytime. Every day we rode 'bout three miles to some cottonwoods where there was water and brought it back to the camp. Otherwise, it was real tedious, just sitting there on the prairie day after day, waiting and watching by that pile of hides.

A strong sense of loneliness come over me. I sure missed Pedro. Dubeck and them two skinners weren't no company compared to him. When you're sitting there on the prairie not knowing what's going on, your mind gets to imagining lots of things. I couldn't figure what was delaying Pedro, and I kept wondering 'bout it.

Maybe he'd got to Fort Union and couldn't do nothing with them hides. It was our understanding, if that was the case, that he'd backtrack along the Santa Fe Trail clear to Santa Fe if need be, where we knowed he could warehouse 'em. If he'd done that, he was sure to be gone for lots longer'n we'd figured.

Each day I'd mount old Paint and ride out to a high roll of the prairie and sit for hours looking to the southwest for any sign of that wagon. A couple times I seen what looked like a wagon, but the light changed and I seen that it was just a distant mesa. Sometimes my heart'd leap when I'd spot a little bit of dust in the distance and figure that it was what I was looking for. I'd watch and hope, but every time it'd turn out to be nothing but a dust devil, and my spirits'd sink.

I was lonely and bitter, and each night when I'd come back to the campfire and see them skinners playing cards with them old dirty pieces of pasteboard and laughing and having a good time, I really got down in the mouth.

Then, too, there was the idea of Indians. You can say what you like 'bout being in Indian country and forgetting 'bout 'em, but way back in your memory somewhere, you ain't never forgetting that there's Indians 'round and that it ain't too healthy to come up on 'em.

I gotta admit that one time the thought crossed my mind that maybe Pedro'd got too greedy and run out on me. He sure could've sold them hides and took off down to Chihuahua with the money. But I didn't give it a second thought. I reckoned I could bet my life on that Mexican—and live a long time on the winnings. I just had to sit tight and wait.

There ain't a man alive that, after a while, don't feel the strain of being in a spot like that. It comes in different ways. Folks get irritable 'round the camp or they goes to staring away into the distance. It plumb wears you down, and I could see them skinners'd started getting restless.

Pedro'd left in early May. I kept track of the days, and by the twenty-eighth day, I couldn't stand it no more. I didn't sleep most of that night and worried through all the next day. I made up my mind and the next morning I told the gang to pack up. We was gonna have to leave anyhow, 'cause we was 'bout outta supplies.

A BITTER TRAIL

We piled up the hides along with the goods we couldn't carry and built a brush pile to protect 'em 'til we could come back. I told the two greasers to ride double on Lucky, then I loaded the Appaloosa with all the supplies and ammunition we was taking, along with them water bags filled from the spring. Then we started backtracking. It took us two days to get back to where Pedro'd left us. His trail was almost a month old and getting kind of faint, but we started following it and checking his campsites.

It was like reading a book. We traveled fast, making thirty miles a day, and we could see where he'd squatted by a buffalo-chip fire and where he'd watered his stock from out of the barrels. We seen one place in some cottonwoods where he'd dug a water hole and watered his stock from that. We also seen lots of other things—like where he'd got bogged down in a sandbank and'd had to half-unload the wagon to get it through. Now that ain't no child's play for one man to unload seventeen hundred pounds of hides.

Judging by the distance 'tween campsites, I figured he weren't making near as good time as we'd hoped. He'd had lots of tough going. The country was rougher'n the smooth plains of the Llano Estacado, and I could see right away that we'd made a mistake not to have him head back towards Fort Sumner.

There was one camp where he'd stayed two nights—I reckon to rest his mules—and another place where he'd broke a harness and'd had to take time out to repair it. I could tell that from the scuff marks he'd made and the fresh-cut leather chunks lying near 'em. Me and Pete'd figured he'd make the Santa Fe Trail in seven days, but I counted where he'd camped eleven times 'fore he'd even come up on some running water. There was tracks where he'd took the black stallion and rode up and down that creek for miles to find a good place to cross where there weren't no quicksand.

Then we seen another sad sight. The place where he'd chose to cross was the best, but it was still so tough he'd had to half-unload the wagon again, move across, unload the other half, and come back for the load he'd left.

I made a study of it, and I could read Pedro's campsites real plain—where he'd laid his bedroll, where he'd made his fire. Then we come to a place where he'd made a dry camp with no fire, even though there was plenty of buffalo chips around.

When I didn't see no sign of fires at his next two stops I got real uneasy. If he hadn't built hisself a fire, he must've figured he'd had to hide from something. First, I thought maybe he'd come on some Indian sign, but I hadn't seen none on the trail. Then I figured maybe he'd seen something in the distance that'd bothered him. But it couldn't have been ahead of him, 'cause he wouldn't have kept going in the same direction. Aside from a couple of roundabout tours of dry arroyos and rock ridges, he'd kept working steady towards the Santa Fe Trail, so's he must've seen something behind him off to the right or left. It couldn't have been no Indians, 'cause I seen that the stallion's hoofprints stayed right 'tween the wheel tracks. That meant he'd been lead-roped to the rear of the wagon, and whatever'd bothered Pedro weren't enough to worry him into untying his stallion so's he could be ready to make a getaway. It meant he'd kept staying right on the wagon box and driving them mules, prob'ly keeping his eyes peeled all the time.

The country kept getting rougher, and I could see that his progress was slower. That was only one of the troubles. Rough country also meant that if he was heading towards any Indians, he wouldn't have been able to spot 'em a long ways off.

I could see two or three places where he'd gone into a shallow creek bottom, prob'ly so's he could get outta sight of the tall ridges of volcano rocks. Every time he'd started into one of them hollows there was marks where he'd brought his team to a halt and got out to walk to the top of a clump of nearby rocks. He must've wanted to take a good look 'round 'fore he'd entered them valleys.

Then we come to a dry, sandy creek bed crossing and I seen where Pedro'd gone to climb up on top of the rocks and then'd come back. The stallion's tracks went off to the side of the wagon when Pedro'd continued on. That meant just one thing: He'd been worried enough 'bout something that he'd seen to untie the stallion, mount him, and take the lead rope of a mule and pull the team 'cross the gentle swale of the creek bed and up a rolling rise of ground for maybe a mile and a half.

When he'd got up on top of the rise to where he could see maybe twenty miles in every direction, the sight must've eased him, 'cause after that the stallion's tracks was back to running 'tween the wheels. I tried to tell myself that maybe Pedro'd just felt like riding old Blackie again for a while, but I knowed that weren't so.

We got into rougher and rougher country and there was more of them little volcanic rock piles here and there. To the north, more little mesas was starting to show up, and in the far distance I could see where there was a few big mesas. It reminded me of the country I'd rode through when I was a captive of the Comanches. I thought 'bout Pedro driving that heavy load through there all by hisself, and my heart started beating faster.

I kept on trying to figure out what Pedro'd been up against. He'd seen something and it weren't too close, but he'd been watching all the time. It might've been smoke or Indian ponies running loose. If he'd seen an Indian on the horizon, either on foot or on horseback, Pedro wouldn't have took no chances. He would've mounted that old black and kept leading the team.

If it was a bunch of Indians coming his direction, he would've waited 'til they'd got unfavorably close and then left the wagon and hightailed it outta there. That black stallion stood 'bout sixteen hands high and was one of the most powerful horses I'd ever seen, as well as one of the fastest. Indian ponies is tough, but they'd never've kept up with that black, let alone catch him. 'Sides, chances was that Indians would've wanted what they thought was in that wagon rather than just one white man's scalp, so they would've left off chasing Pedro.

Maybe a bunch of wild ponies'd put up a cloud of dust in the distance. Pete might've stopped to watch 'em for a while to see if there was any Indians herding 'em or if they was near a big camp.

When you read trail sign, you gotta think 'bout all the things that're going on. Otherwise there ain't nothing but a mess of tracks and you'll miss getting the truth—even if it's right in front of your nose. If you're a good tracker and really know what you're doing, you can read the signs if you keep eliminating the possibilities 'til you get down to what's really going on. That's why I'd finally decided that it was smoke he'd seen and that it had to've been off to his right rear quarter. Off to his left rear, the country was much flatter and run away clear down to the Llano Estacado. Pedro'd been avoiding something and it had to've been smoke—lots of it—from an Indian village or something like that that'd kept him so apprehensive and always checking. But out there on the Llano Estacado was no place to find an Indian village or a big camp. No, them villages was all s'posed to be up north, and that would've been to Pedro's right rear. That's why I'd come to decide that he was keeping a close watch on some smoke he kept seeing back in that direction.

At one of them volcanic cones, he'd unhitched the stallion and rode up to the top. There the stallion tracks stopped and faced north and northeast, so I was right: What Pedro'd seen way off in the distance, to his right rear quarter, must've been smoke from some big village. Towards the northeast it was getting more and more broke up with mesas and you couldn't see as well as you could in real flat country, so it had to've been a column of smoke that he'd seen and it had to've been high enough so's he could've kept on seeing it for two or three days' travel.

I figured he'd rode up to the top of the cone 'cause he'd got far enough west to where he couldn't see the smoke when he was down on the flats in the wagon. He'd been watching it over his right shoulder for a long time, and that was prob'ly why he'd been real careful not to light a fire. It'd been a big enough column of smoke for him to see for two days, and when he'd got outta sight of it, he'd rode up to the top of that cone to see if he could get a better view. It was plain that he weren't too worried when he'd come down from there, 'cause he'd hitched Blackie to the rear of the wagon again.

We was traveling lots faster'n Pedro, so I seen his last two cold camps in 'bout five hours of our travel. Then, towards the late afternoon, I come up on something that shook me real bad. I seen where Pedro'd turned the whole team and wagon real abrupt—turned 'em almost at a right angle to the left and started heading southwest for no apparent reason. There weren't nothing in the road ahead of 'em. As a matter of fact, the going'd improved a little and there was big mesas all 'round.

The stallion'd still been hitched to the wagon, so Pedro hadn't seen no Indians or got spooked enough to unhitch that horse and mount him. It also seemed that he hadn't been hurrying the team none, 'cause the tracks indicated they'd just kept walking. We followed them tracks to the southwest 'til it got dark.

Then, since I'd got this feeling that I can't hardly explain, we made a cold camp that night. We ate a little pemmican, unsaddled our horses, keeping 'em on long ropes tied to our wrists, and lay down in our blankets. All through the night the horses kept waking us by jerking at one time or another when they'd come to the end of the rope, but it was better to know you had a horse and miss a little sleep than to risk being without a means of escape. We had everything ready to go at a minute's notice.

All through the night I'd been lying in my blankets staring up at the stars, trying to figure out what it was that Pedro'd seen. He wouldn't have done what he'd done if there hadn't been a real good reason. Yet it was something that didn't excite him, so's he couldn't have run into no band of Indians, and he hadn't seen nothing against the skyline that'd shook him up.

There was only one thing I could think of: Way off in the distance to the northwest he must've seen a smoke signal. He might've seen it climbing in a column against the sky and he could've watched the puffs. They'd have been different than just a big cloud of smoke from a village. As a matter of fact, when I recall thinking back on the trail where he'd turned, I'd seen where he'd stopped the wagon and them mules and stood for a while. He must've been watching something ahead of him or off to his right. If it'd been off to his left he wouldn't have headed southwest, so it either had to've been ahead or to his right front.

Anyhow, whatever it was, he'd been thinking enough 'bout it to ease out of its way. The fact that he'd been easing instead of hurrying meant that he didn't think the situation was dangerous.

At daybreak we took off again and followed Pedro's tracks for quite a ways towards the southwest. The country was stretching out and the going was getting a little better, but I knowed he hadn't turned just on account of it being easier going. I knowed what kind of distance he'd been making every day—maybe twenty miles—so I knowed where to expect his next camp, but we kept going and going and never did see no sign. He must've been worried enough so that when nighttime come, he'd kept traveling on. From the way the mules'd been scuffling their hooves, shortening the length of their stride, I could tell that they'd been getting mighty tired and moving lots slower.

Then we come to a place where Pedro's tracks appeared 'longside the trail. At first it looked like he'd been walking beside the mules, but when I went back and studied the trail I seen that them mules'd been standing while he was walking. That meant just one thing: He'd walked up ahead of that tired team to see if there was any bad draws or stone piles. That meant not only had he been traveling at night, but he'd been worried 'bout getting stuck.

For another thing, he must've been getting awful low on supplies. He couldn't have had no fodder left, so's they'd have to've made a living off the prairie grass. They hadn't been getting much chance to do that, traveling day and night. I reckoned that Pedro might've been a little short of water, too, but there was one good thing: I hadn't found no spent shell casings, so it were plain he'd had plenty of ammunition, 'cause he sure hadn't been doing no shooting. Also, I reckoned he'd been smart enough to save whatever oats he'd had left for Blackie, 'cause it was that stallion that was gonna have to get the job done if them Comanches come into the picture.

'Bout noon that day we come to a point in Pedro's trail where I knowed that after traveling all night he'd kept on traveling in the daylight. I didn't see no man tracks where he'd been getting off the wagon box and walking ahead of the animals. That meant that he could see just fine from where he was. I also seen from the mules' short strides that they were still mighty weary.

Then I come up to a place where the stallion'd been unhitched again and his tracks started leading to the northwest. I stopped to take a good look at 'em and felt better when I seen that they was going at a gentle trot. The mules'd stood there for a long time where he'd left 'em. They must've been too tired to move.

I followed the stallion's trail towards a small bunch of cottonwoods and bushes at the foot of a mesa 'bout two miles off. When I got there I seen a sight that really give me some worry. Pedro'd been digging in the ground, apparently looking for water. He'd used the stallion to go over there to look for water rather than push the mule team.

That was bad. If he'd kept heading northwest, he would've come across some stream coming outta the mountains 'fore too long, but the way he was going he might've had to go clear to the Pecos, at least seventy-five miles to the southwest. Them mules couldn't have made it that far in the condition they was in.

He'd gone back and mounted the wagon box, and they'd set off again. The stallion's tracks was trailing behind the wagon where he'd been hitched, and I knowed what'd been in Pedro's mind. He'd been balancing how long he could push them mules 'fore he'd have to leave 'em and take the stallion and head for water.

That stallion hadn't been carrying no load, and he was a strong animal, so's his chances of making it to water would've been better'n the mules'. But that would've meant leaving the wagonload of hides, that even if Pedro did find water and get back to the wagon, in all probability them mules would've been dead. 'Course he could've unhitched them spans from the wagon and turned the mules loose 'fore he'd headed out. Chances were that the animals'd find water quicker'n a man, provided they didn't have too far to go.

I kept hoping I'd come up on a sign like that, 'cause by that time I didn't give a damn 'bout them hides—I was more worried 'bout Pedro. But I never seen what I'd hoped for. He must've had lots of grit and stayed right with it, 'cause he'd kept going mile after long mile, headed southwest.

Then my spirits rose plenty when we come up over a little swale in the prairie and I seen where he'd turned his teams to the northwest again. He'd traveled maybe a mile from the top of the swale when he'd turned. It was a good place to turn and it meant that he'd gone far enough in his estimation from where he'd seen that smoke signal to where he was outta danger. I could see he'd had some trouble turning them mules. They was thirsty and didn't understand why they had to go in another direction from the one they'd been heading in.

Not too far after that, one of the mules throwed a shoe and started limping. From the lack of mule droppings, I could tell that them mules was plumb near starved to death.

Then my heart almost jumped into my mouth when we come up over another slight rise. Off in the distance was a dark object on the ground. As tired as our horses was and as tough as it was for them skinners who'd been riding double all of that way, I yelled at Dubeck and spurred up. We rode hard 'til we come up on it.

I'd had all kinds of misgivings that it might be a mule that'd give out, but when I got 'bout a quarter of a mile away I seen what it was: a pile of hides where Pedro'd had to lighten the load. After three or four more miles we come to another pile, and it went that way for 'bout the next ten miles. At that point Pedro'd finally stopped and made camp. He'd hobbled and picketed them mules, but they hadn't moved much. They must've stood with their heads hung low, ga'nt and plumb wore out from the trip.

Right nearby was the biggest pile of hides of all. Pedro must've worked half the night to get them hides unloaded. The way I reckoned it, he must've had less'n half his load left. He must've figured he'd still make it with that, get a little money, and try to come back and pick up what he'd left. He must've been keeping some water for hisself or he wouldn't have been thinking along them lines. A man that desperate thirsty would've gone and looked for water on his own.

We was working our way up a slow rolling rise of prairie with me riding on ahead, leaning down off the saddle watching the ground every step, trying to read the trail. All of a sudden my heart stopped, 'cause I seen where the mules'd begun jumping and plunging and making big lunges 'tween their tracks. I figured right then and there that Pedro'd been jumped by Indians, and them mules'd been frightened and'd took off. Still, as we got towards the top of the rise, the stallion tracks was running 'tween the wagon wheels—which meant that he'd still been hitched, and although them mules was running like hell, it didn't seem like Pedro'd left the wagon.

When we topped the rise, I seen the cause of it. In the distance was some trees and close by 'em, a half-dry water hole. It looked like an old buffalo wallow near a spring. The mules'd scented that water and they'd gone almost frantic. It looked like Pedro'd had all he could do to hold 'em down, tired as they was. Well, our animals perked up the same way.

After we got to the water hole, we seen it weren't much—just a dirty mudhole with some rainwater left in it. I'd hoped there'd be a real fresh spring, but there weren't. That water was right stinky and mighty foul—so bad that we couldn't drink none of it, and although our horses did, they didn't drink with no enthusiasm.

It must've been different with Pedro's mules. It didn't look like it made no difference that they was in harness. The front mules must've stopped first and them rear mules didn't figure to take no backseat and forged on ahead, twisting things all up. It must've been a helluva mess.

It looked like there'd been more water in the hole then. By the time we got there it weren't more'n ten feet across and three inches deep, but I could see from where the wagon tracks'd stopped that it'd been a lot bigger.

Well, anyway, it'd been enough water to satisfy 'em. Pedro'd camped and mended some harnesses, by the looks of things, and then started out again, heading towards the northwest.

I reckon that normally Pedro would've stayed by that water hole for several days, 'cause there was some feed 'round there. It was a little scant but all right for tired mules, and he would've stayed 'til them mules was back in shape, then backtracked and picked up the rest of them hides. They was too valuable to be left behind. But he hadn't rested very long, and I knowed there was a good reason why.

Pedro'd been on the wagon box and the stallion'd still been hitched to the rear. 'Bout a mile from the water hole, Pedro must've figured that he still had too much weight and had off-loaded some more hides, which showed that his mules was mighty weak—near the give-out point.

I started looking for the wagon, 'cause I figured that somewhere along there Pedro had to've made up his mind to abandon the whole load and hit out fast for the trail.

I guess I didn't reckon right in estimating Pedro. He had more guts'n a government mule, and he weren't 'bout to let go of that load if'n he could help it. It was a matter of pride with him that he was gonna get something through.

We found his next camp and it'd been another cold and dry one, but he'd kept pushing on. By that time I could see he'd had good reason to think that he was gonna make it. Rising slowly outta the western horizon was the snowy peaks of the Sangre de Cristos. He'd been in sight of them mountains, and 'tween them and hisself was the Santa Fe Trail.

He could've estimated his distance to them peaks at 'bout eighty miles, meaning he'd had 'bout another sixty miles to the trail. That was two days' haul with a good team, but for him it must've looked to be three. It was plain that he had to find some water somewhere, and his chances was getting better as he got closer to them mountains.

The going weren't no better, and I could tell from the tracks that the teams'd been giving out. For that reason, I weren't too s'prised when I topped the rise and seen a dark object off in the distance. When I pointed out what I'd seen, Dubeck and them two greasers couldn't make it out, but it was real clear and plain to me.

You could smell the stink from a quarter of a mile away, and when we got close, our horses acted plenty spooked. Sure enough, when we got there a mule was lying near half-rotted out, and the coyotes'd been working on a good part of it. I asked Dubeck if he could recognize which one of the mules it was. I wanted to find out if it was a wheel mule, one of the leads, or one of the middle span, but it was so bad rotted out that even Dubeck couldn't recognize nothing of it.

Later on I seen that it didn't make no difference which mule it was. Pedro'd had to cut the harness loose and then start over again. From the tracks, I could see how he'd had two mules in span and then one on the whippletree in the lead in the middle. That was the only rig he could put together with what he'd had. I expected it wouldn't be too long 'fore we found another one.

Sure enough, 'bout four and a half miles on, there was another downed mule—and beside it was another big pile of hides. No doubt the four remaining mules, although at the wearing-out point, had still been able to pull the wagon.

'Bout two miles beyond that, Pedro'd made a cold camp. This time it weren't a dry one. He'd stopped along a little sandy creek and there was trickles of water coming through in potholes along the adobe banks. I could see where he'd watered the mules and the stallion, then pushed on the next day.

Then he'd gone back to his old trick of stopping to climb up and get a good view from a rock pile or high mound. Such things was easy to come by—we was getting into the real jagged mesa country that lies east of the Santa Fe Trail in New Mexico Territory.

Each time I seen where he'd done that, I'd follow, taking in every sign I could. He'd always turned to face the northeast. He must've been watching something real continuous, and I reckoned it had to've been them same smoke signals that'd caused him to change his course.

Anybody second-guessing Pedro would've said that the smart thing to do then was to get onto that stallion, turn them mules loose, and ride like hell for the Santa Fe Trail on his own, but Pedro was game right down to the roots of his toes.

We was on a real smooth stretch of country, and I was leaning off the saddle looking at the trail when I almost jumped outta my skin. I'd seen an unshod pony print crossing the wagon track from the south! First there was one and then, a hundred yards on, two more. They was crossing the track heading north and they'd passed after the wagon, 'cause they was printed over the wagon ruts. They was Indian ponies, but they could've crossed a long time after the wagon'd went by.

I followed 'em off to the side real quick for maybe a hundred yards, and then I knowed they hadn't passed too long after Pedro'd gone by. If they had, them tracks would've turned and followed the wagon tracks for a ways. That was the Indian's way. If an Indian come on the tracks of a wagon that he hadn't seen, he'd go following them tracks outta curiosity to see what they meant, where they was going, and if there was any chance for him to pick up something.

Them pony tracks didn't tell no such tale. They crossed over and headed into the rough mesa country to the northwest. They must've seen the wagon and figured they didn't need to follow its tracks. They must've been going somewhere either to get word to more of their tribe or to get themselves into a position to do something.

I really started to sweat, and I hugged Paint's withers as I studied the signs. I knowed that Pedro hadn't been asleep 'cause there weren't no camp sign, and 'fore long he'd stopped and not just walked but trotted over to one of them volcanic rock piles and climbed up on it.

His tracks going back to the wagon was all made with just the toe of his boots, and the distance 'tween each step was right far. Pedro'd been running like hell. Then I could see the prints of the stallion's hooves backing and moving all 'round like every spirited horse does when you go to get on him.

Then the stallion's tracks was trotting 'longside of the wagon. You could see that the horse and mules'd all set off at a good trot. Soon they'd broke into a gallop and run as fast as they could. I could see right away where Pedro'd been headed. 'Bout two miles away was a big mesa, but there was lots of uneven ground between, rolling in swells with some dry, washed-out draws.

I didn't say nothing to Dubeck, but he seen a little of what I did and picked up my nervous feelings. Them greasers was talking away in Mexican like mad so they must've knowed something 'bout it, too.

The stallion'd been sidestepping a little bit and prancing and bouncing and lunging, but them mules'd held to a straight gallop. That meant the stallion'd been spooked and knowed he could go a whole lot faster, but Pedro'd kept reining him in and hanging tight to the rope of the lead mule. The sight'd made me sick to my stomach. I didn't think them wore-out mules could last long at that rate.

When we got to the top of the next rise, I seen what I'd been afraid of—the charred remains of the wagon. The bunch of ribs that'd once held a white canvas top was now lying on its side like the skeleton of a great dead whale. I put my spurs to Paint and rode down there with my teeth biting at the wind, saying to myself, "Oh God! Oh God, no!"

The story was plain. The mules'd been tearing along in a helluva rush when they'd come to a dry gulch. The stallion'd gathered hisself and jumped the gully, which was maybe seven or eight feet across and six feet deep. The mules and wagon hadn't had that kind of luck. The left-hand lead mule'd stumbled and smashed against the opposite clay bank, busting his harness traces loose. The rest'd carried right on at a rush, dragging the wagon side-ways 'cross there and breaking both right wheels.

The whole thing'd piled up 'bout thirty or forty feet on the other side of the draw, where it lay on its side. There was deep gashes where the lead mule'd clawed his way up and outta that clay draw. He hadn't made it very far. The dried black circle of his blood told all 'bout how bad hurt he'd been. The rotted carcasses of the other three mules was lying by the wagon, still in harness, and one of 'em had an arrow in him.

I galloped to the side of the wreck, yelling at Dubeck to stop his horse. The greasers was still trotting along behind us, and I told Dubeck to stop 'em there. I didn't want nobody tramping 'round the place 'til I'd read all the sign. I tied up Paint to what was left of the wagon tongue and started walking 'round real careful, taking in everything.

First thing I done was find the tracks of that stallion. I could see where he'd took off at a dead gallop, heading almost due west towards the mountains. There was a series of mesas and breaks, but it didn't look like an impossible route. From the jumps the stallion'd took, it seemed like he'd still been in good shape. I was glad to see that

Pedro'd prob'ly been all right, just riding like hell to get away from them Indians.

Then I walked back to check them mules. The arrow in the one animal hadn't been shot into it when it was lying on the ground. It was too far forward for that, and an Indian don't do no mercy killing. That mule'd been hit at a dead run.

I looked for how the other mules'd been killed, and kicked 'round their mostly dried but still stinking carcasses some. It must've been bullets, but I couldn't find nothing in them decayed remains. There sure weren't no more arrows. I pulled out the one and looked at it real careful. I was really lucky to find it. Normally, an Indian'd cut out an arrow and use it again, 'cause they was right hard to make and took lots of time. But when that mule'd gone down it'd cracked the shaft, so the Indian hadn't bothered. From the feathers and the paint rings, I seen that it was Quohadi Comanche, and I knowed we was dealing with Quanah Parker's Quohadi Teichas—the Antelope Eaters.

I took a good look 'round at the trail sign in the area. It was easy to read. Them Comanches'd come out from behind a ridge of volcanic rock where they must've hid as the wagon went by. Then they'd started riding in to head it off. That was when Pedro'd had them mules up to a run. Them Indians'd swung parallel with the wagon, which meant they'd been chasing but not gaining on it. I kept looking for empty shell cases, to see what kinda guns them Indians'd had, but look as hard as I would, I didn't see none.

I looked all 'round there to see if Pedro'd fired that Henry, but I didn't see no empty cartridges from that gun, and I was thankful. He hadn't been damn fool enough to waste any ammunition.

I knowed then there was just one thing left to do—follow them galloping stallion tracks and see what'd happened to Pedro. I'd noticed six sets of unshod pony tracks out maybe ninety to a hundred yards to the south going at a gallop, and there weren't no pause, so there'd been at least six of 'em after him. But I figured that Pedro knowed how to take care of hisself, being the kinda rider he was.

You heard them stories everywhere 'bout how some white man— Buffalo Bill, Kit Carson, Davy Crockett, or somebody—had rode off and left them Indians in the dust, but when you had real, live, bloodthirsty savages riding tough ponies at a dead gallop with only one intention—to take your scalp—it's a helluva feeling. I know.

There ain't a man alive that's ever been out-numbered by Indians that won't tell you he got cold shivers up and down his spine and was so scared that he felt plumb sick to his stomach.

I kept right on riding Paint at a jogging trot, stopping every now and then to examine the track. At first, while I was riding along in the late afternoon sun looking at them tracks, I felt my hopes kind of rising. I was betting on Pedro to do all sorts of things to come outta that mess smelling like a rose—like he usually done when he was in trouble. I was hoping to find the bodies of three or four dead Indians and see where the rest of 'em'd run off. Then I'd know that old Pedro'd made it outta there.

But that was foolish. In the first place, Indians never left their dead, so's there weren't no chance of finding their bodies like that. Second, I knowed deep down that Pedro weren't quite that good a shot. His best chance was in his riding. He was a helluva good rider and well mounted. That led me to think that Pedro would've made it to the Santa Fe Trail. He'd prob'ly gone on into Fort Union and told his story and tried to get some money and some supplies to come back out. Maybe he'd gone on to Santa Fe if he hadn't had no luck there. I didn't even care if he'd gone out and got hisself drunk and forgot all 'bout us, just so's he was still alive.

But I knowed that weren't like him. He would've come back with some packhorses or something. At the least he would've come back by hisself to warn us 'bout them Indians. The more I got to thinking, the more downhearted I become.

I kept watching along the trail for a shining piece of brass, a shell case from Pedro's Henry. That more'n anything else would've showed me whether them Indians'd been getting close or if Pedro'd been spooked and lost his head.

I was real proud of my buddy when I seen that he'd used the right judgment. He'd been either far enough away from them Indians to have a good head start on 'em and not need to shoot, or he'd held his fire, knowing that nobody could do a decent job of shooting from a horse. At any rate, old Pedro hadn't wasted no ammunition. I kept looking on the ground just dreading to see one of them shell cases and was sure happy not to locate none of 'em, 'cause it meant he hadn't been too hard-pressed at that point.

The tracking was tough. The stallion'd gone west at a dead gallop up over a rocky ridge. For a while I lost him where the ground was hard. But I went back to where I'd tracked him last and cast 'round a little bit. If I was Pedro, where would I go? I thought.

There was a gradual slope off to the northwest—I would've rode down there if I'd wanted to shake my followers. I took a chance and went on down. Sure enough, there in the soft dirt I picked up Blackie's tracks again. By the way he was landing and the distance 'tween his fore and hind hoof marks, I could tell that Pedro'd been running him flat out.

I cast 'round to the side and it didn't take me long to pick up the tracks of the Indian ponies. They'd come 'round on the other side of the ridge and'd begun closing in at an angle. Pedro'd rode out onto a real big open plain, dotted here and there with volcanic rock piles. There was some mesas in the distance just ahead and to the right, but there weren't no draws in sight—no place were he could've forted up.

I could see by the pony tracks that them Indians'd been pushing 'em as hard as they could. Their jumps was big, but not as big as the stallion's. Pedro must've been gaining on 'em with every hop, and I figured all was well.

The sure sign that the stallion was outdistancing 'em come when I seen where the Indians' pony tracks finally converged with Pedro's tracks and begun covering 'em up. That meant that they'd swung in behind him and was likely far back. I kept watching and didn't see no shells from any Indian guns.

I kept looking for the place where I hoped I'd see that them Indians had reined up their ponies and give up the chase for good, but I sure didn't see it.

Even though Pedro'd been gaining, with his powerful Blackie drinking the wind, it was a mighty big span of prairie that he'd been riding 'cross. He wouldn't get outta sight 'til he reached one of them mesas or maybe hit a big volcanic ridge, and there weren't none of them ahead for many a mile.

We must've gone the better part of ten miles 'fore I could see where the Indian ponies, tough as they was, started to tire a little. The jumps they'd been taking was shorter, and their front hooves'd made a better print'n they had before.

That's a sure sign a horse's tiring. He lands harder on his front feet than he does when he's sailing good. When a running horse is blowed, he flounders a little bit. He gets his head down and hits hard with his shoulders, taking the full force of his withers on his front legs. Maybe it takes the load off the tiring hindquarters that's doing all of the driving. I don't know.

When I seen that, I got down off my horse to examine all the tracks real careful, hoping to find the stallion's horseshoe marks. I didn't have no trouble finding 'em, even though they was mixed up in places, and I put the points of all four legs together to see how he'd been holding up. That old Blackie seemed to have the same stride that he'd had before—he'd been putting his front feet down no harder'n he'd been doing for the last ten miles. I reckoned them Indian ponies was in for the sad part of the race.

The trail continued like that for 'bout another three miles 'cross the open plain, then led up to a small mesa that was off to the right. I knowed then that the stallion'd pulled a long ways ahead, 'cause the tracks of the Indian ponies'd spread out more'n they was at first. That was a sure sign that the pursuers was losing the race and their horses was tiring.

The funny thing 'bout a horse that's blowed his wind is that he seems to have the instinct to move out away from the horses beside him. He acts entirely different'n he does when he first starts out in a race. Then he ain't afraid of bunching up and jamming his nose out in the wind ahead of the horses on his right or on his left.

Them Indian pony tracks was spread out as much as forty to fifty yards on either side of the stallion's trail. Maybe they was opening wide out in case Pedro might try to turn one way or another—that way they could gain on him by cutting 'cross the curve. But Pedro'd been too smart to do that. He must've knowed he had the fastest horse, so he'd kept right on charging dead ahead, trying to outdistance 'em.

I expected to find where them pony tracks pulled up and turned off to quit the race. Sure enough, when we got to within a mile of the mesa, the two on the right-hand side'd suddenly swung over and crossed Pedro's tracks, heading towards the southwest almost at right angles. I felt good all over, 'cause it looked like Pedro'd give them Indians the slip.

I kept following the pony tracks to see where them Indians'd joined together and pulled up with the other bucks. I kept looking for 'em to intercept the tracks of the ponies on the left of Pedro's course, but as the ponies kept on galloping it didn't seem like their tracks crossed a'tall. That puzzled me.

I kept along them pony tracks for a ways as they headed to the southwest, then rode over to my left 'bout a hundred yards and picked up the other set—they was going in the same direction. Oh, God! I thought my heart was gonna jump into my mouth 'cause that meant Pedro'd turned and headed southwest, and them Comanches'd set out to cut him off.

Then I went back and picked up the stallion's tracks where he'd been originally going northwest and started riding as fast as I could without losing sight of the tracks. I seen that Pedro'd suddenly reined up and Blackie'd really checked hard on his haunches. Stopping like that takes lots of energy out of a horse when he's been traveling at a good gallop for twelve or thirteen miles.

Then I seen where Blackie'd wheeled on his hind legs and headed off hard to the left, running as tight as he could go. There weren't no doubt that Pedro'd seen something else that'd stopped him—and that something could've only been more Indians.

I didn't waste no time trying to pick up other sign. I kept right on the stallion's trail. From the looks of his tracks, I could see that Pedro'd been pushing him hard. If anything, his jumps was longer. I couldn't help but admire that horse.

As I rode along at a trot, I seen something from almost fifty yards away shining there in the afternoon sun. I jerked Paint to a stop and picked it up. It was a .44-caliber Henry cartridge case, and it hadn't been lying there long enough to tarnish, though the shortage of rain'd helped preserve it.

For a minute I hoped it might be a shell from one of the Indian guns, but there weren't no tracks nearby, 'cept the stallion's, so's it had to be Pedro's. He must've begun shooting. He wouldn't have if they hadn't been desperate close to him.

I couldn't help clucking with my tongue and talking as if Pedro could hear me. "Ah, c'mon, Pete. Don't do no shootin' now. Don't fire from a runnin' horse. Save your ammunition, amigo, 'til ya can get down off'n your horse an' take steady aim. Save it fer that deadly execution ya gotta use in a tight fix like this."

The shell'd landed 'bout four or five feet off to the left side of the stallion's tracks. Pedro'd likely been turning in his saddle and shooting at something to his right, 'cause when he'd ejected that shell, it'd gone over his shoulder in the other direction.

I followed along a little farther, going real careful now. Sure enough, I seen another shell—and then another one. Pedro'd had sixteen shots in that Henry, but he'd managed to waste three of 'em. Chances was he hadn't done no damage, less'n what he'd been shooting at was real close.

I jumped on Paint again, turned northwest at right angles to the stallion's tracks, and rode straight out to see what it was that Pedro'd been trying to shoot down. I hadn't gone more'n twenty-five yards when I come on a whole mass of running pony tracks. There was so many I couldn't separate 'em to count. A soft whistle went out through my teeth. There must've been thirty or forty ponies, and from the way they was traveling I figured it was a war party riding like hell.

I looked back to where them pony tracks'd come from and let out all the cusswords I knowed. That big bunch of bucks'd been waiting behind that little mesa outta sight, watching the horse race from a long ways off. They might've picked up the dust in the distance, and with the keen eyes them Comanches has, it wouldn't have been no trouble for 'em to see that there was one lone horseman riding out ahead of some of their kind.

Maybe it was all planned. I don't know. Pedro'd seen something that'd kept him from making fires, and I sure as hell think it was smoke signals. Maybe it was Pedro's hard luck that he'd took off in the direction he did, or maybe the Indians'd planned it that way. I don't know and it didn't make no difference noway.

I followed along behind the trail of them ponies. They'd really churned up the ground, so there weren't no doubt that they'd been riding fresh horses and trying to close in fast. I begun to see empty Winchester shell cases, which meant that some of 'em'd had repeating rifles. I also seen a few empties from an old buffalo Sharps and a couple of musket cartridges that must've come from some piece made during the Mexican War.

I followed that bunch of Indian pony tracks for almost a mile and a half and noticed that they never did come up and join with the stallion's tracks. That meant they'd been riding out to the side a little and squeezing Pedro up against them other bucks.

I cut back across to pick up the stallion's trail again. That stallion's front feet was coming down real hard. That meant he was beginning to wear out, or maybe he'd been hit. I looked on both sides of the trail for blood, but I didn't see nothing.

I cut over to the left and seen the tracks of them bucks that'd first jumped Pedro coming in close. After following a ways, I seen two empty shell cases. They'd closed in on Pedro and begun shooting at him from both sides.

That got me all choked up and feeling terrible. God, how I wished I could've been there with Pedro. One more gun—'specially a dead gun—would've done lots of good right then. I would like to've took a crack at that band of Comanches. I'll bet I could've had fifteen of 'em down, shooting as fast as I could work that lever action. That would've dampened their war medicine plenty.

It was hard for me to keep down the welling hate for them Comanches that'd been simmering in my guts all those months and was fanned to a blaze when I'd seen our burnt-out wagon. Ever since I'd been their prisoner, the smallest thought of Comanches'd send my insides to curling like raw flesh under a branding iron. My jaw'd tighten up 'til the muscles ached. Sometimes, when I got to remembering them devils, I'd notice that my fists was clutched together so hard that my fingers'd turned white.

I cut back again to Blackie's tracks and seen that his front hooves'd been digging in real hard and that he'd begun stumbling in places, so I strained my eyeballs looking for other sign—blood or something. All of a sudden I seen it.

There in a patch of dirt, 'tween the tufts of buffalo grass, was some dried blood mixed with a green spot of bile. Blackie'd been gutshot! That wouldn't have killed him right away, but it meant that big beautiful stallion couldn't have kept going much farther.

While I hung over Paint's withers following Blackie's tracks, I kept talking to Pedro as if he could hear me. "Pedro, fer God's sake, your Blackie's gutshot! He's hurt bad, ol' buddy. He ain't got far ta go. Don't run him out. Pull him up now! Pull him up quick, get off an' kill him. That's your only chance, Pete. Ya gotta put down that stallion! Shoot him an' fort up behind him. Them bucks'll soon be comin' at ya from every which way. If'n ya lay low, they can't hit ya from their runnin' ponies. Ya can hide behind that dead black an' just blast the hell out of 'em."

I was almost begging, feeling desperate sick. "Listen ta me, Pedro. Stop ridin'! Don't ride that horse 'til he spills. Get down! It's the only way, amigo. Fer God's sake, Pedro, haul in that stallion an' do like I say! Damnit, man, don't keep ridin'! He's gonna go down an' that'll be the end of ya, too."

Nobody was there to hear me 'cept the prairie wind. Dubeck and the greasers'd dropped back a good ways behind me, easing their horses along at a gentle walk. I was real thankful that they was outta sight when I topped a sudden rise and seen three hundred yards ahead of me what was left of Pedro's big Blackie, half ate up by varmints and rotting with maggots there in the sun.

Right then I'd had to grab a handful of Paint's mane to keep from falling off while I heaved my guts out. Shaking all over and feeling sick to death, I got off Paint and walked over towards that carcass, staring at it like I was in a trance. I didn't wanta get up close, but I had to.

As I moved, I started feeling like a machine—no pain and no hope, just a thinking machine—walking up slow and steady to learn some more secrets from the gates of hell. I got closer and closer and walked slower and slower 'til at last I stood ten feet away from that sorry-looking mess that'd been Pedro's magnificent black stallion.

I cast my eyes 'round for some sign of Pedro, but I didn't see nothing. Then, outta instinct, I begun to read the clues as I circled 'round, taking in everything I could. Broken arrows was sticking into the carcass like porcupine quills. 'Course the beautiful saddle that'd been Pedro's pride was gone. Lying there so still, with closed and sunken eyes, that once proud and silky black head looked real ashamed that it hadn't won the race. I imagined Blackie saying that he'd let his master down, feeling sad and crying big horse tears while he went racing through the clouds of horse heaven.

I retraced his tracks back 'bout ten yards and read the story. I seen where Blackie'd gone down. He'd stumbled first and must've somer-saulted and Pedro'd been pitched off. There was a real plain mark where Pedro's body'd landed and skidded along. I looked 'round in the dirt and buffalo grass and found what I'd hoped I wouldn't— dried brown stains on some of the shoots of grass. It was blood, and it had to be Pedro's. Either he'd got hurt in the tumble or he'd been hit.

Dubeck and the greasers come up and stopped a little ways away and sat staring at that terrible sight. The decaying, arrow-filled body of the black told the story. I couldn't say nothing, so I just led Paint over and handed his reins to Dubeck.

I went back to try to find out what'd happened to Pedro. There was moccasin tracks all 'round the horse, and in some places I seen the marks of where gun butts'd been placed on the ground while the

Indians'd leaned on the barrels. I s'pose they'd been looking at their captive's dead horse and bragging 'bout how great a job they'd done.

"Ya think yore brave warriors, ya stinkin' skunks! You was fifty ta one—a lone white man, an' him downed on a gutshot horse. Ya cowardly yella sons a bitches." I was almost sobbing. "Ya done took my little girl away an' tortured her ta death, an' now, ya goddamn hellhounds, ya took my buddy Pedro fer the same reason."

I didn't have to cast 'round much to see where they'd all mounted up again. They'd wheeled their ponies towards the west and headed straight in the direction of the shining peaks of the Sangre de Cristos. A sudden burning rage of hate flamed up in me and I made up my mind that I was gonna follow them Indians all the way to hell. I didn't stop to really study their tracks—it was a plain, wide trail and easy to follow. One thing I knowed, though, them Comanches weren't fixing to go clear up into them mountains. They weren't mountain Indians. I knowed that from watching 'em the time they'd followed me.

I also figured they'd captured Pedro, 'cause otherwise I would've seen his remains. But there weren't nothing there but the stallion. So they must've taken him away. If he'd been dead they wouldn't have hauled his body away, him being an enemy. They would've mutilated his body and left it to rot so's his spirit couldn't go to the white man's happy hunting ground. The only hope for Pedro was that he'd been wounded so bad that he'd died 'fore they could get him back to their village. If he hadn't, I knowed from raw experience what that meant.

When I climbed back up on Paint, I couldn't see nothing but them Comanche warriors' pony tracks. I couldn't see Dubeck, or the greasers, or the vast stretch of prairie rolling away in front of me. There was only one thing that I was living for then: to get revenge on them Comanche bucks.

I started Paint off at a slow walk, 'cause there weren't no real hurry. I had all the rest of my life to find 'em. I weren't gonna hurry, 'cause I knowed there weren't no use in it. I wouldn't make it in time to help my buddy. Only God hisself could help Pedro at that point.

Dubeck and the greasers followed along. I figured they knowed that when I looked at 'em I didn't see 'em, so they didn't ask me no questions. They must've read the signs of death and vengeance in my eyes and decided there weren't no use trying to figure on anything but keeping their distance and waiting for orders.

It was a cinch to follow them Comanche tracks—that bunch left a trail like a buffalo herd. I sat on my saddle and eased along to the rhythm of old Paint's gentle walk. I squeezed my eyes down to a catlike half-slit and let the wind blow while my thoughts boiled. I must've gone almost a mile 'fore I noticed that the trail'd been winding back and forth, like they'd been twisting up a rope or weaving rawhide into a pattern.

I looked more careful and noticed a strange smooth mark running along through all of them pony tracks. My first thought was that it might've been something that'd eased off'n a travois—maybe the bag of a teepee or some such Indian belongings. Then I quick checked myself on that. It weren't no travois. They was for squaws when villages was moved. To get mixed up over something like that showed how addled my brain was from the shock.

I could see by the tracks that the Indian ponies'd been going along in a good lope. For the life of me, I couldn't figure out why they'd be pulling something. They sure wouldn't ruin a prize like Pedro's saddle by bouncing it along in the dirt. Maybe they'd been dragging something as a spirit sign of victory. I got to thinking that's what it'd been. It was some kinda symbol of the Comanche religion, some sign of victory. It sure puzzled me, but I kept on thinking that way.

The trail led up across the center of one of them prairie swales. 'Bout half a mile ahead it went over a ridge of volcanic rock, then down outta sight. When I topped that ridge, I seen a stretch of brown streaks and patches on the prairie grass and dirt just ahead. It was a good thing that I'd turned into a hate-feeling, Comanche-stalking machine, else I'd have been too sick to look 'round. The brown was blood and the drag marks was from a body—and that body was Pedro's. If he'd been dead they wouldn't have dragged him, 'cause that wouldn't have been no sport.

I rode back over that ridge hanging down over Paint's withers and seen where them sharp rocks'd took chunks of flesh and bone and hair. There was pieces of teeth and signs of blood and bile and oozing innards. I followed the trail of brown stains and it weren't far 'til I found Pedro—what there was left of him after them Comanches'd cut him loose and the sun'd dried him and the wind'd dusted him and the coyotes'd fed on him.

The rib cage on the right side of his back was plumb gone. He didn't have no face left—nothing but scraped and broken bone. His scalp was gone and so was his right leg from the knee down. 'Round the ankle bone of his left leg was the piece of rawhide rope they'd dragged him with. It lay there with some frayed strands that pointed towards the west, sort of like accusing fingers. There was a few moccasin tracks mixed up with pony tracks where them red devils'd got off their ponies and stood 'round to see the last of the fun.

I didn't have much to work with 'sides an ax and my bare hands, but I set out to dig Pedro's grave. Dubeck and the greasers offered to help, but I looked at 'em just once and they backed away. I laid Pedro so he could see the sunrise. His head was pillowed, if you can imagine it that way, at the foot of them snow-covered Sangre de Cristos. He'd loved them mountains, and I reckoned he'd find some peace there.

I gathered some stones from the rocky volcanic ridge—them stones that'd helped put my best friend outta his misery—and laid 'em on top of the earth where he was buried, in the hope that they'd serve him some more and keep the coyotes and wolves away. I piled 'em up so's that someday, someone, if it ever mattered, would know that a man—a real brave man, someone's friend—had died and was buried there.

That pile of rocks also served to mark a new life for Cat Brules.

When I got through, I took off my hat and stood there for a spell facing the setting sun. I don't know quite why, but it seemed the fitting thing to do. Then I walked over and took Paint from Dubeck, who was still holding him. I mounted up and didn't say nothing. I didn't need to—they'd seen the expression on my face. I turned west towards the Santa Fe Trail, 'bout forty miles away, and give 'em a farewell salute. Then I headed due north alone, following that Comanche pony path as the sunlight faded. They didn't attempt to follow. They just stood there and watched me go in the gathering dark, and then they turned and went west. I reckon they made it to Santa Fe, 'cause I never seen or heard of 'em again.

GOING A LITTLE LOCO

I rode along, keeping my eyes on that big Comanche trail, and I kept 'em there all night. There was a blackness in my heart like the stored-up poison of a cobra. I hated Comanches. Oh God, how I hated 'em! Not only had they tortured and killed my girl and intended the same for me, but I'd seen where they'd dragged the only friend I really ever had to a horrible death. I hated the living guts and soul of 'em even more for that. All sorts of thoughts was pumping up inside my brain, and my heart was on fire with a mixture of hate and a growing thirst for one helluva revenge.

I could see that trail by starlight real plain. Along 'bout daylight I come to where the trail crossed one of them few prairie streams that bubbles up here and there. I seen where the Comanches'd watered their ponies and themselves and then rode on at a walk. By the looks of the pony droppings, I reckoned that the trail was 'bout four or five days old. They wasn't in no hurry and neither was I. I'd never be less'n a few days behind 'em, and I sure planned on gaining. I rode all through the next day, getting off once in a while to walk to keep old Paint from getting footsore and me from getting too stiff in the saddle.

The trail led back from wide-open grass plains to the beginnings of the mesa country up Raton way. Them table mountains stood out like monuments, with lava-streaked slopes running up to cap rocks—

sheer hundred-foot cliffs like the top layer of a cake. The tops are all the same level and flatter'n pancakes. It's a country all its own and a big relief from the monotonous grass plains, but it weren't the best horse country. In fact, in some ways it was better for traveling on foot.

It got pretty warm the next day, but I rode and walked and kept going right along. In the late afternoon I stopped at a place where a spring come up at the head of a sand creek. It was good, sweet water. There seemed to be a little green feed around and Paint showed he was mighty hungry by the way he went after it. I hobbled him up and lay down in the shade and got a little sleep.

I reckon it was almost midnight when I woke up. The stars was out and an early crescent moon was going down in the west. I slung the saddle on my horse, pulled the hobbles, and we was off again in the night. As long as there was a faint light from the stars I was all right. I could see good and follow the trail. When dawn broke, I seen that I was beginning to swing back towards the northeast, into some more mesa country. It didn't take no ghost dancer to figure out that party was heading back towards something, maybe to the village whose smoke Pedro'd seen.

'Bout midday, I come to the banks of another small, seeping streambed and seen where them Comanches'd camped for the night. Their ponies'd ate out the range on all sides and left some fresh droppings. I seen from their trail that they was traveling slow and easy.

I kept doing the same thing with Paint as I'd done the day before— riding a little and walking a little, never moving him faster'n an easy jog. When we'd come to a stretch of real good prairie grass, I'd get off and sit down, put him on a long rope, and let him feed. I kept speaking to him confidential-like, telling him to take his time, 'cause we had a long, long trail ahead. I didn't tell him, but I reckoned that 'fore we was through we'd ride right through the gates of hell.

Now, that poor pony couldn't have knowed what I was talking 'bout, but sometimes he'd quit munching on his grass and look at me with his ears cocked and his eyes real puzzled, as if he'd knowed that the man sitting there was going a little loco.

The following night I only camped for three hours, then I rode out most of the rest of it. By daybreak, I'd come through the best part of that mesa country and was looking ahead at the open plains. Down 'cross the prairie ahead of me, I seen the sandbanks of a good stream 'bout four or five miles away. All of that time I'd knowed I was in the heart of Comanche land—at least in the heart of their summer range. I knowed they'd come north for their buffalo hunting, following the herds. I guessed that the whole country must be full of Comanches, but I was just riding along watching the trail with a blackness in my heart that told me that the happiest thing I could do was to find me some of them skunks.

As I rode up on a big stream, I got to mulling my recollections over in my mind and decided that it must be one of them creeks that flowed from the south to the Cimarron. I reckoned that maybe I'd come that far north. It sure looked a lot like the stream I'd been on when I was tied up to that tree. That day seemed so far away, almost like a dream. I used to have a fear in my heart when I thought 'bout my captivity with the Indians. I'd wake up in a sweat at night, dreaming that I was a prisoner again. But I didn't have no fear left.

I s'pose the odds of me getting killed was real good, but I weren't interested in my life anymore. I was interested only in settling my score with the Comanches. I didn't feel much of nothing. No hope, no joy, no fear, no nothing. I felt like I had something to do. I weren't the least bit excited 'bout nothing, or worried 'bout nothing, or in any kinda hurry. I was traveling for a purpose, with the sign of death looking outta my eyes.

By noon I'd come up on that stream and found the leftovers of a big Indian village. It looked like the village'd been took down and moved only a couple of days before. The pony tracks of my band of warriors run right straight into the camp. From there they was all mixed up with the rest. There was a lot of tepee rings and dead campfires, and I noticed that stink that always goes with a Comanche village and lasts six months after the filthy scum've left the place. For a couple of miles 'round, the prairie grass was all ate up, so there must've been a big band of ponies moving along with that village.

It weren't no trick a'tall to follow the trail that headed off 'cross the stream and out over the open prairie. That trail led off strong, wide, and silent towards the northeast. It was a couple of hundred yards wide and full of all kinds of Indian fixings—the tracks of travois, odd bits of rawhide, occasional pieces of colored cloth, and some trashlike pieces of basket weave and broken pottery that some squaw had throwed away.

I could damn near hear the shrill cries of the squaws and the laughter and screaming of the children and the barking and growling of the village got on the move. I could see the dust kicking up from the pony herds that the young bucks was driving ahead, and hear the yipping and hollering of them painted devils as they rode down that long trail in search of buffalo.

I took a little time out to water Paint and let us both get rested. That bunch'd be traveling northeast real slow, and by my best reckoning I couldn't put 'em more'n thirty miles away. I knowed that it weren't gonna take too long to catch up with 'em then. I figured I'd spend the rest of the afternoon watering and feeding Paint and taking in a little pemmican for myself.

I rested by the stream 'til it was real dark, then saddled up old Paint again. He didn't look too bad, considering all the traveling he'd done. I reckon he felt my mood. He knowed there weren't no hurry, so he didn't wear hisself out.

It weren't 'til I seen the smoke of the village that I begun to realize what I was doing. 'Fore then, I was just following the tracks of them Comanche bands on instinct. I'd been going along, hour after hour, aiming to kill and never giving no thought as to how I was gonna do it.

Out there was flat country, or mostly flat, with enough roll so's I couldn't see the village, only the smoke of it. I'd have a tough time hiding from them varmints out there. So, as the haze from the morning sun faded away and I rode towards that village smoke I seen rising in the emptiness of that vast prairie, I begun to work out my plan.

I turned back and rode a mile and a half to where I'd crossed a dry arroyo. Down in there, outta sight, I hobbled old Paint and curled up under the shadow of a clay bluff and went to sleep. I knowed my pony was gonna be plenty restless with no water, but that couldn't be helped. I told him that we'd have water after sundown that night. There was a little bit of fresh grass he could poke his nose into, and that'd keep him comfortable 'til we was on the move again.

Funny how it was with me, but I could roll up and sleep most anyplace in them days and I knowed how to do it, just like a cat napping. I remember I slept mighty good that day. I'd had to shift a few times when the sun'd outrun the shadows of the cliff and I'd found myself broiling hot. 'Bout sundown I got up, scraped off the dust, unhobbled Paint, mounted him, and started off at a walk in the direction of the Comanche village.

I reckon it was a couple of hours later that old Paint quickened his pace. He'd sniffed some running water and sure enough, in another half hour we come up on another one of them small creeks running north to the Cimarron.

I watered Paint at the creek and had a little drink myself. Funny, I thought, I been without water all day an' I ain't doin' too bad. Then I forced myself to drink a little more, even though I didn't want none. I told myself it might be a long time 'fore I'd have any again. Old Paint, he guzzled away like it was his last chance to put his nose in the cool of a stream.

We eased on. I walked for a while 'fore I mounted Paint, then rode along hearing the faint murmur of that prairie stream. I was moving east, down towards the village, and the wind was quartering outta the north. Then, as I rode, it swung to the northeast. It was still the late spring of the year, and there weren't no way to tell which way the winds was gonna blow less'n you got a warm chinook.

I was grateful that the wind'd swung 'round when it did, 'cause I'd be coming up on that village from upwind, so's them yeller dogs that the Indians always had eating scraps 'round their tepees wouldn't pick up my scent too quick and set up a yowling. Thanks to that wind, I knowed I was coming up on the village long 'fore I got there. Like I said, there ain't no stink like a Comanche village.

Every Comanche stinks, but when you got three or four hundred of 'em together, it was awful. Comanches weren't clean in their habits. Lots of Indians'd go a long ways out of the village to relieve theirselves, but not a Comanche. If he got a little ways from the tepee, that was good enough. When you put lots of 'em in a village like that, it didn't take long to put a real ring of stench 'round the place.

It was all to my good. First I smelled that village, then, as I got closer, I heard the usual yapping of dogs. But there weren't no increase in it or nothing, so I was sure they hadn't noticed me.

When I could hear the sound of their camp comings and goings, like the shrieks of children and squaws, and when I could smell the dust and droppings of some pony herds, I knowed it was time to hobble Paint and make my way on foot. I was 'bout a mile from the village when I set out in the night, leaving old Paint to make the best living he could off'n what buffalo grass there was.

I remember that first hunt real well. I carried my Winchester with the magazine and chamber loaded—seventeen shots in all. I had another twenty-five rounds in my cartridge belt and four extra rounds in each pocket of my shirt. I also carried a knife, which I kept loose in its sheath. There never was a time when that knife wasn't as sharp as a razor. I seen to that, believe me. I carried two pieces of rawhide cord tied 'round my waist, and that was all the equipment I took with me.

I moved smooth and quick and easy towards the camp, carrying my rifle in my right hand. It weren't no trick to pick out the little trails in the grass coming and going to the village. I eased up over a slight prairie swale and seen the light of their fires half a mile away. Twenty minutes later I was lying down in the grass a hundred fifty yards outta the circle of light from their twenty or thirty fires. I could see all their comings and goings—people passing back and forth 'tween me and the fires, squaws and children and dogs. The warriors was mostly squatting on their haunches in front of the flames and smoking their pipes.

Just watching an Indian village with all its sights and sounds and smells at night is an experience. I felt the excitement building up in me that any hunter feels when he's getting close to his prey. I didn't have no exact plan, but I knowed an opportunity would present itself. All I'd have to do was be there and act right when the time come. It was a question of waiting, and I had all my life to wait.

I'd been in that patch of grass for maybe an hour when I heard the whuffing and tromping of a band of ponies on my left. They must've worked downwind from me and smelt something 'sides Indians, so they'd begun to snort and caper 'round a little. Right soon, there come a brave heading out from the village. I reckoned he was one of them young bucks that was in charge of the horse herds. He passed 'bout thirty feet from me in the dark.

Real silent, I rose up to follow and slowly closed the distance. He was going along humming some funny, high, singsong Indian tune, and I kept moving 'til I was within five yards of him. Real swift I laid down my rifle on the grass, slipped the cord from 'round my waist, and took 'bout five quick jumps to come up behind him. He never heard a thing. I throwed that cord 'round his neck and twisted him down to the ground 'fore he could get out a gurgle. I turned the cord tight—real tight—'til he quit struggling, then, holding the cord in one hand, I pulled out my knife with the other and stabbed him five times.

It was the first cold-blooded killing I'd done, and I reckon I done a butcher's job. I could've just as easy put the blade through his heart once and been done with it. The way I done it, though, I cut out 'bout half his guts. It was a waste of time and energy, but I weren't worried 'bout that. I had lots of other things to do and I still had a little time to do 'em. It'd be a while 'fore somebody'd come looking for that brave, and then they'd have trouble finding him in the dark.

I picked up my rifle and waited 'round there a little bit longer to see what'd come outta the camp that'd be easy prey. Sure enough, after a while, I heard some laughing and cackling, and the shadows 'cross the campfire showed me that there was a couple of squaws coming out my way. My first thought was that they was coming to look for the brave, but they wouldn't have been laughing and giggling if they'd been worried 'bout something. So I sat there in the dark cover of night and listened to 'em coming closer and closer. Then I heard 'em stop.

It didn't take me long to know what they was doing. They'd stopped 'bout ten or fifteen yards from me. I heard 'em puddling and could see 'em squatting together down there. I glided over and come up behind one without either of 'em having the slightest idea I was there.

I could've garroted 'em easy, nothing to it, but right then and there I hesitated, something you never should do in a situation like that. Somehow I suddenly had a bad feeling 'bout killing women, even she-wolf Comanche bitches. It was a mistake, 'cause a few seconds later them two squaws rose up and started back to the camp. They hadn't gone ten paces when one of 'em stumbled over the body of the dead warrior. When she looked down and seen what it was, she let out a scream like you never heard before. Then, grabbing their skirts, them two squaws run like hell for the firelight.

The usual noise and confusion of the camp quieted down right quick. It seemed like everybody was listening. Then some dogs begun to bark and some figures started making their way outta the campfire light in my direction. Of course that was my time to leave. Moving as fast and quiet as I could, I hurried back to where I'd left Paint. I pulled the hobbles off'n him in one jerk and was in the saddle and off into the night.

The thought kept running through my mind that when they heard my horse running off they'd think there was some renegade bucks from the Utes or the Arapaho or southern Cheyennes trying to run off their horses. That'd be reason enough for 'em to mount up and scour

'round. It wouldn't take 'em too long 'fore they'd find the body of that
young buck. Then I could sure as hell count on a good follow-up.
Horse raiders they might follow for a day or so, but I reckoned if they
was after somebody who'd killed one of their kind, they'd stay on that
trail for a month.

I didn't mind that, but I sure was disappointed that I hadn't had
time to kill more of 'em while I was at it. Seemed like I'd botched
the job. If I'd handled it right, I could've killed half a dozen or more
'fore they'd got wise to me. At this rate, they'd breed faster'n I could
kill 'em.

I got to thinking what I'd done wrong. When them two squaws was
squatting together out there, I should've had a club and killed 'em
both 'fore they could've made any outcry.

I headed back along the way I'd come, 'cause I knowed a little bit
more 'bout the country. I rode all through the night, changing from a
lope to a trot to a walk and back to a lope again. 'Bout midnight, I
pulled the saddle off'n Paint and rubbed him down good with the
saddle blanket. I checked his feet and felt along his haunches and
withers, and it seemed like he was real sound. I saddled him up again
and we was off.

When dawn broke, I was back in mesa country, at least forty miles
from the village. I reckoned it wouldn't be too long after the sun rose
up in the east that I'd see the dust of them that was following me. I
didn't make no attempt to hide my trail, figuring it was tough enough
for 'em to track me in the dark. With it being daylight, I figured I was
gonna have to do something special. I looked 'round to see what was
available in that land of wide distances.

The mesas rose maybe three or four hundred feet above the plain
with a few ridges of volcanic rocks 'tween 'em. I'd rode far enough
towards the west during the night to see the snowy tips of the Sangre
de Cristos poking up above the horizon. While the dawn was lighting
up, turning the world kinda silver and sending up some fingers of red
in the clouds, I got to thinking of my present position and what a poor
job I'd done for a whole night's work.

"Brules, there ain't no use in cussin' yourself," I muttered out loud.
"Yore new at this game. Ya messed up the first evenin's work 'cause ya
didn't know no better. With a little s'perience, your methods is gonna
improve an' it ain't gonna be too long 'fore ya get ta be real good. Right
now, ya gotta keep ridin' along with your eyes open."

I looked at the mesas and the occasional piles of volcanic rock all 'round me and begun to figure what I'd best do with a vengeful war party of Comanches coming fast on my trail.

I figured I could go up against one of them mesas and get on the back side or up against a cliff. For a while I could stand off a few of them bucks, but it wouldn't be too long 'fore some of 'em'd come over the top or 'round the side somewhere. Then, when I was raising up to shoot, one of 'em'd pick me off. That weren't part of my plan.

No, it'd be better to go to one of them lonely volcanic rock piles and hole up. Then I'd have a clear range to shoot all 'round and nobody could sneak up on me without being seen. The only trouble with that was what to do with Paint. He'd be left standing out there as conspic-uous as a preacher in a whorehouse. He wouldn't serve no purpose 'cept to lead the Comanches right to me. Then they'd just run him off or, if I'd hobbled him, they'd kill him.

A real strange thought come over me then. In that rock and mesa country, a man might do better without a horse. Maybe a horse is just made for the open prairie. If a man had the right walking gear, not boots like I was wearing but good Indian moccasins or some such, he could keep working in them rocks and not hole hisself up in a position he couldn't get out of. As it turned out, I was to think more on that subject as time went by. Just then, though, I didn't take it too serious.

The sun'd been up for pretty near an hour, and the haze'd gone off in the east. When we come up aside the next mesa, I pushed old Paint uphill into the oak brush to them steep cliff walls, and turned and looked back to see if anything was following me. I weren't disap-pointed. There was a dust cloud 'bout ten miles away. I reckoned there was thirty or more horsemen. At that distance I couldn't tell that they was Indians, but it sure couldn't have been nothing else.

I seen with some satisfaction that their night tracking'd been tough. They'd only started 'bout a mile behind me, but they'd been traveling lots slower and I'd gained plenty on 'em. Since daylight they'd started making up for it. Judging the dust, they was holding their horses to a good run.

I reckon that a year before, or maybe even three months ago, if'n I'd seen a band of Comanche warriors following my trail, I would've been so scared I'd prob'ly have messed my pants. But back then *they* was the hunters. *This* time, *I* was the hunter.

I suddenly got a bright idea. I was going to do what I'd been begging old Pedro to do when I was tracking his gutshot Blackie— something I'd knowed deep down in my heart that Pedro couldn't do, but something I damn well could. I kicked up old Paint and went down through that oak brush in a real hurry, off the side of the mesa, and we headed due south, back towards that trail that I'd come up a couple of days before tracking them Comanches to their village. I didn't pick up the old track right away, but after another two hours of riding I'd wove through them mesas and come back to where I run into my own tracks. I backtracked right on that old trail, heading south towards the open country where I'd left Pedro sleeping in his grave.

It was getting on towards noon and Paint was beginning to show signs of wearing out. I couldn't hardly blame him, considering that he'd done lots of traveling in the last four days, but I reckoned there weren't nothing I could do 'bout that. I kept looking back, and I had to admit that dust cloud was gaining on me. Them Comanches was real strong on avenging their blood kin, so I knowed that they wasn't gonna let go easy.

By early afternoon I was looking out over them plains that'd seen the long, hard race of Pedro on his Blackie and'd witnessed him being dragged to his death. I knowed that Paint was giving out all right, but I had a plan, and I'd rode him hard to get in a position to make that plan work. To the north the plains was broke up with them mesas, and to the east there was some rough country where bunches of volcanic rock plugged through. Far to the west was them snowy peaks of the Sangre de Cristos. Right where I was, coming up on Pedro's grave, it was as flat as anything in this world could be. There weren't no place for nothing to hide, less'n a man could get down behind a blade of grass.

I rode along, feeling old Paint gasping from weariness. My nerves was cold as ice, and there weren't no fear in me, no panic. Them yipping devils that was riding back there in the dust behind me was closing the gap fast, but there weren't nothing to be afeared of. This was the meeting that I'd been looking forward to, and it was gonna be sweet revenge.

I was ready. I felt Paint floundering along under me. I reached forward and patted him on the neck a little bit and told him, "Paint, ya done a helluva job. Now I'm gonna have ta do somethin' that don't seem fair or right, but it's gotta be done. I can't say that ya served me bad. We just gotta go 'bout another half a mile an' your troubles'll all be over."

Sure enough, 'fore long I seen the pile of rocks marking Pedro Gonzales's final resting place. As we got closer, I slipped my Winchester out of its scabbard and swung my right leg 'round so's I was standing on my left leg in the stirrup, ready to dismount and land running when the time come. I kept urging Paint on—from three hundred yards, then two hundred yards. Then only a hundred more yards. Paint weren't gonna quite make it to the end.

When we got to thirty yards away, I knowed it was time. I jumped off and landed running, still holding the reins. Paint stumbled to a standstill, his sides heaving, his legs shaking, sweat pouring down off'n him, and his nostrils blowing bloody froth—a horse plumb wore out.

When I got off'n him, I was on the east side. As I held the reins, he staggered 'round so's he was facing west, with his nose turned towards me, and I took two jumps 'round so's to stand close behind his head. I let go of them reins, drawed out my .38, and shot him dead.

Paint collapsed as if he'd been poleaxed. He fell right where I wanted him to, with his feet stretched to the south and his head to the west so's I could drop down behind his belly, forted up. I was ready for them yelling devils that was less'n three-quarters of a mile away. I just had time to take a .38 shell from my cartridge belt, draw the empty outta the cylinder, slide the fresh one in, and slip it back in my belt.

I slammed the Winchester open and levered one of the shells into the chamber. Then I reached down to my belt and pulled out a .44 shell and eased it into the magazine slot. That give me seventeen shots, plus six in the Smith & Wesson.

I remember thinking how funny it was that I could be that cool, saying to myself, "I got sixteen shots in the magazine an' one in the chamber—a total a twenty-three, countin' the Smith & Wesson, an' I aim ta make ever' one of 'em count."

Yep, I'd had it all figured out. I nestled down 'tween the legs of old dead Paint, feeling the warmth of his belly. I laid the rifle along his ribs and drawed down on that band of Comanches coming up on me. I had plenty of time to get a good look at the situation.

Outta them thirty or so bucks that'd been rawhiding it, riding like hell to catch up with me, 'bout ten of 'em was out in the lead. The rest of 'em was strung along behind, spaced out maybe forty or fifty yards apart according to the speed and stamina of their ponies.

There was pretty near a third of a mile difference 'tween the leaders and them that was bringing up the rear. That was the kind of spacing you'd expect after a good, hard, thirty-mile chase. By the way their ponies was running, even at that distance, although they wasn't beginning to flounder, I could see they was weary and had been hard put to it, running their guts out for the last ten miles.

I knowed that a good, fast thoroughbred horse'd take a furlong in 'bout twelve seconds, and 'bout a quarter of a mile in twenty-two seconds. Those ponies was gonna be considerable slower, and I estimated that they'd do a furlong in something like sixteen to eighteen seconds. I reckoned I had better'n twenty-two seconds for them to cover three hundred yards, which I considered my maximum range. I knowed too, at that distance, that my drop on the Winchester was 'bout eighteen inches.

Now, it may sound funny to you that an ignorant cowhand like me would've spent that much time figuring out things like that. But I can tell you, when your life depends on it, you knows your rifle and you knows what it can do.

I knowed one other thing, 'cause I'd practiced it often. I could get off a shot with that Winchester, working the lever action with the gun at my shoulder, 'bout once every two seconds. But that didn't count for drawing down careful—it took another second for that. That meant that if I opened fire at three hundred yards with them Comanches coming at a dead run, they'd be right on top of me by the time I got off my sixth shot.

Still, that weren't so bad. I knowed that some of them bucks was carrying rifles, but I reckoned there'd be more of 'em carrying lances. In them days, there still weren't near enough rifles to go 'round. Maybe in the first bunch, not more'n four or five of 'em'd have rifles, and the rest lances and bows. Them lances with their feathered collars could be picked out easy from five hundred yards away.

I knowed I had to be awful careful to kill the man and not the horse. If I shot a horse and the man went down unhurt, that varmint'd come crawling towards me. Worse'n that, he could fort up behind his dead horse like I done.

'Sides all that, I remembered what my daddy'd told me 'bout when he fought on Missionary Ridge. He said that there weren't no troops in the world that could stand losses of one man outta three. Any attack that's coming at you, if you kill one man outta three, the others is gonna lose their enthusiasm and swing off to the side to think 'bout another plan for getting you.

As I watched that cloud of dust from them hard-riding horsemen, I figured I was gonna have a chance to prove everything that I'd planned on. That first bunch of 'bout ten braves was down to less'n a quarter-mile away and coming fast. Six of 'em carried lances, so's the other four must've had rifles. One of them four was out in the lead, riding a white horse.

Now, a Comanche charge of more'n thirty warriors, whether they come at you in bunches of ten or all at once, is a damn terrifying sight. I've knowed of good plainsmen that was dead guns who'd lose their nerve when a Comanche charge come thundering down on 'em. They'd start shooting crazy, waste ammunition, and not hit a thing.

With me it was different. I was just cold. I didn't give a damn 'bout nothing but killing a Comanche every time I pulled the trigger, and I was plumb dedicated to that proposition.

Snuggling down on Paint, I laid my eye down the barrel of that Winchester and leveled the bead with 'bout half of the stem showing above the notch. I picked out a patch of grass three hundred yards away and waited. I kept the sights on the leader as he come, and seen he was carrying a rifle in one hand and quirting the hell outta his horse with the other. Even at three hundred yards, I could see his black war paint—the "color of death." It give me something to sight on.

Now, one thing you gotta remember is when a horse and rider are coming flat-out straight at you, they seem to be bouncing up and down. You think you're looking at a moving target that's gonna be damned hard to hit, but if you look again you'll see that if the rider is leaning way forward on the withers of his horse, which is usually what he's doing, his head and face'll hardly be moving up and down a'tall, 'cause his knees and the rest of his body is taking the horse's motion. In other words, he's damn near a still target. If he's wearing black war paint on his face, it helps even more: It makes a nice bull's-eye! To a good gun, he's well exposed coming head-on. Also, it ain't natural for a man to ride straight on to something and not look off to one side or the other of his horse's head to see where he's going. That was all the target I needed.

I seen they was closing fast, and it seemed like there was a thousand legs churning up the dust, bringing them red devils in for the joy of cutting me to pieces. A couple of minutes before, I'd heard a burst of their yips and hollers when they'd seen that my horse was down and prob'ly figured I was easy prey.

That was the kinda deal they liked. I got some grim satisfaction outta thinking 'bout what a big mistake they'd made and how I was gonna teach 'em a lesson that wouldn't be forgot for a long time in Comanche land.

The lead horse was closing the range, so I drawed down tight. I squeezed off the shot just as he passed the three-hundred-yard mark. I declare, it was the sweetest thing I'd ever seen in my life when that rider flung up both hands and cartwheeled outta that saddle. He plowed up the prairie with his chest while his pony took an extra jump when he realized he was loose from the weight and pain of his quirting rider.

I slammed in another shell and drawed down again, dropping the bead just a bit. I seen the next rider's face real good, even at two hundred fifty yards. He had on that same black war paint that makes 'em look like death skulls. Funny how you can see things real clear and vivid in times like that and call to memory the details for years to come. That one was riding an Appaloosa. I remember thinking how that war paint sure didn't match his horse. He would've looked lots better riding a white or a black. But it didn't make no difference. When I squeezed off the shot, he humped over some and then slithered down off the side and bounced a little in the dust.

I heard a yipping, wild cry as I slipped another shell in the chamber. I reckoned that the yardage'd closed to almost two hundred. Them six lancers was out in the front by then and I knowed that I had to let 'em come on at me. The danger was in them that had the rifles, but I hadn't counted on no riflemen lagging behind the lancers and making it tough for me to pick 'em off.

I didn't have no other choice then but to kill a lancer, which I done at 'bout the two-hundred-yard mark. At that, they split apart a little and I could see a rifleman coming up, and in the background maybe forty to sixty yards behind was the other Indians bringing up the rear in a swirl of dust.

I took my time and eased down to where I only saw the bead with no stem. I killed that rifleman at a hundred twenty yards. At eighty yards out, I took aim at the last buck that had a rifle, and I could sure tell he had it, 'cause I remember to this day seeing it spit fire at me as he rode up. He was trying to shoot from a running horse, and even though he was only eighty yards away, he couldn't aim worth a damn.

'Course he couldn't shoot straight traveling that fast. Maybe he liked to hear the gun bang. By the time he reached that eighty-yard mark, the last chance he ever had in his life to do any good shooting was all over, 'cause my bullet went right through his skull.

There was still five of them six lancers left and they should've been getting discouraged, but they didn't seem to none. I shoved another shell into the chamber of the Winchester and felt the barrel getting hot. I remember watching a lancer coming at me on a big bay horse, and I reckon I got more satisfaction outta that one shot than any I ever made 'fore or since. I remember the feeling of pressure on the trigger and the kick of the rifle when I seen that buck's features just spoil right in front of me. That buck didn't roll off'n his horse, he jack-knifed back over his rump. The force of a .44 Winchester at that close a range is something to see.

That done it, 'cause them lancers broke apart at that point and swerved away and only one of 'em kept on coming in tight. He was tearing along right at me and only 'bout thirty yards away. There was lots of noise and yelling, and I reckoned he was doing some of it, 'cause I seen his mouth wide open with his teeth snapping and gnashing as he slung his lance. If I hadn't rolled away and shot at the same time, he would've ripped my back open with that long blade.

His horse jumped clear over Paint and me. As it was, he missed me, but my bullet went straight in under his belly and up through his chest, coming out the upper part of his back. I turned for a second to look behind me and seen that he'd lasted through two more jumps of his horse 'fore his carcass hit the prairie.

The other lancers passed by off to the side with lots of yipping and yelling, letting go some arrows, and then they whirled their horses out in a big circle to the right. Paint's carcass had four arrows sticking in it. I weren't scratched, but I didn't have time to think 'bout it.

I rolled back behind Paint's belly and started working on the stragglers that was coming up. Them that was real close behind didn't like the looks of the losses they was taking. Just like my old daddy used to say, "They become real disenchanted with the action."

They whirled outta range off to the sides, which give me a chance to work on those that was coming up from quite far behind. After that first bunch, they'd lost the momentum and I never did have another lancer get as close as the ones that'd just come up. There was lots of dust—lots of action—and I kept firing that Winchester as fast as I could. When I say that, I mean as fast as I could and still make a dead shot.

When I was through, there was fourteen Comanches lying dead out there on the prairie. I don't rightly know how many Comanches was after me all that time, but when I seen the rest of the band whirling 'round in a circle, most of 'em carrying lances, I got the impression that there was only 'bout half the number that'd come after me to begin with. They didn't ride 'round like you'd mostly think, trapping me. They rode off to a safe distance and gathered theirselves for a powwow.

It was a typical damn-fool Indian stunt. I reckon that white men would've pressed their attack in spite of their losses and wouldn't have give the enemy no time to reload. When them Comanches galloped off 'bout four hundred yards away to parley, I took some shells outta my belt and started shoving 'em into the magazine slot.

Then, as I felt 'round my belt, I seen I didn't have too many shells left and it was time to dig out the spare ammunition in my bedroll. I reached up 'round Paint and untied that blanket real fast. I had 'bout thirty rounds wrapped in an oilskin cloth, and I filled the empty rings in my belt. I knowed that it wasn't all over and we was gonna have to have some more sporty shooting, but I was sure enjoying it. I kept looking over there at them Comanches as I was tending to my ammunition, studying to see how many riflemen was left.

I was right pleased when all I could see was two bucks that wasn't carrying lances. They'd been churning 'round on their horses and pretty soon one of 'em drawed his horse up and begun shooting at me. Well, he could do a better job from a standing horse than he could from a running one, but I lay real close to my horse's belly and only remember one shot that come close. It plowed into Paint's spine just forward of his rump. I heard the thud and felt his body shake a little, but that was all. Them bucks started yelling and hollering and galloping back and forth, but they didn't come in close. I decided that if that Indian could stand off there at four hundred yards and shoot at me, I could do the same.

I took my time and lined up that bead on his chest, then held more'n half the stem of the bead above the crotch of the rear sight. I squeezed off, holding my breath to keep steady. For a minute I didn't think I'd hit him. He sat there on his horse motionless, but then he slowly wheeled 'round and fell off under its belly. The horse shied away a little bit and trotted off.

One of the lancer bucks let out a yell and rode over there. He jumped off his horse and run towards the buck's body. He was fixing to pick up the rifle. Since I hadn't gone to all that trouble to kill a rifleman with the idea of somebody else using his gun, I quicklike jammed in another round. When that buck made the mistake of stopping and kneeling down, I killed him dead in his tracks.

That kinda got to the others and they decided that if I could bite 'em hard at that distance, they'd better ease off to a safer range. They left at a slow canter, looking back all the time. I debated some whether or not to try to plant a shot 'tween the shoulders of one of the trailing bucks, but decided against it. I might miss, and that wouldn't help none to conserve my ammunition.

A rising joy took hold of me and I started cussing at 'em and telling 'em some things that I'd sure wanted to say for a long time. "You goddamned, red-skinned sons a bitches! Now ya know what it's like ta be up against a dead gun 'stead of a helpless prisoner, don'tcha? There was a whole big bunch a ya after me an' ya thought ya'd had me cold, huh? Ya no-good, lousy, stinkin' bastards. Half a ya is lyin' out there dead now, an' the rest a ya ain't got the guts ta come in again."

I stood up and shook my rifle at 'em. "C'mon, ya sons a bitches, lemme give ya some more a my hot steel! None a ya ugly varmints knows how ta shoot. C'mon back here an' let's finish it out. What's the matter with ya, ya yeller-bellied shit eaters? C'mere an' let Cat Brules kiss ya with his Winchester. When I get through with ya skunks, your guts is gonna be spread out all over this prairie, an' that'll be good riddance."

That sure made me feel better. 'Course them bucks didn't know what I was talking 'bout, but they heard me shouting and turned their ugly faces in my direction, and then they'd begun their parley all over again. That time they didn't go riding their horses 'round and yipping and yelling. They just stood there real quiet, talking it over. I lay back down and got ready.

One thing that irked an Indian more'n a white man could ever know was to leave a war brother's body lying out there to be scalped. It's all their fashion to scalp their enemies and to mutilate their bodies, so's they can never find a home in the spirit land. Since that's the case with their enemies, they gotta try to save their own kin from the same fate.

To do this, they'd make what we'd called bravery runs and go out and pick up their dead friends. It was quite a piece of horsemanship, if you ever seen it. They'd take off riding at a dead gallop and reach down on the run to pick up the body by hooking it under the arm. The amount of strength it takes to do it at that speed, and the special kind of riding, made you take your hat off to 'em.

When the first one started off at a gallop, I thought he was coming for me in a suicide run, but he swung off to the north towards one of the bodies that was lying out there in front. I kept watching him and watching him, holding the bead close to where he was hanging way down on the side of his horse for protection.

When he got to his buddy, I watched him lean way down, and in a flurry of dust he grabbed that body at a gallop and jerked it up from the ground. It spun out and the legs kicked a little, and I seen him hunch his back up as he lifted the weight of it.

That was all the target I needed. I put a bullet just under his lungs and through the back of his shoulder blade. Then there was two corpses, and they rolled off real clean under the horse. It sure made a pileup.

Lots of angry whoops and hollers come from them other bucks. They was swirling 'round and waving their lances and yelling and cussing at me. I guess they was saying that what I was doing weren't fair. It sure was a nice feeling.

I yelled back at 'em. "Ya wanta talk 'bout bein' fair, do ya? Ya bastards! Ya didn't think a that when ya was rawhidin' my bare back when I was tied on that mule blindfolded. Ya didn't think a that when ya was burning up a poor little naked girl tied ta a couple a posts, did ya? Now, I'll show ya what's fair! C'mon, who's next? I ain't even got started yet. Ya don't know how ta use a repeatin' rifle, but I do. It's a rifle that makes twenty men outta one. Ya ain't never seen it used in the hands of a dead gun, have ya? All ya ever seen was some a them ol' farmers comin' 'cross the plains in their wagons—them with the women an' children—nice folks that ya scums was always comin' in and pickin' on when there weren't nothin' there your size. Now, ya dirty red bastards, yore up against someone better. It ain't no fun, is it? C'mon back an' let ol' Cat Brules kiss ya again!"

I spit in the dirt and wiped the dust off my lips with the back of my hand. That was quite a speech for me. I don't usually say that much, but I guess I'd been getting rid of some heavy poison. A man gets a little dry when he's fighting Indians. It ain't too bad if you don't get your wind up. I reckon that was one time I weren't scared, just alert.

I remember thinking, after I'd got through cussing an' felt better an' a little relaxed, that maybe I hadn't better indulge in too much a that. It might give me a big head. A man that's got him a bunch a wild Comanches hangin' 'round has got serious business, an' he never knows when somethin' unexpected's gonna come his way. Some a them Comanches might get a lucky shot through him an' that wouldn't be no fun. Or maybe his rifle might jam. . . . That thought made me shudder.

I calmed myself and got back down close to Paint's haunches with nothing but the tip of my head showing above him and my chin planted right down flat on his flanks. My shirt was wet with sweat. There weren't no clouds and things was plenty hot. Add to that a little excitement with the Comanches and a gentle wind kicking the dust back and forth from all of the scrambling, and I had to admit I was getting dry.

I unhooked my canteen off'n the saddle horn and took me a sip. That water tasted like it'd come straight from the snows of the Sangre de Cristos. I'd really got it out of a water hole near the Cimarron the night before.

I kept watching them Comanches and seen that they was hesitant. I was lying down in back of Paint, ready for anything, but they stayed out 'bout a thousand yards. Every now and then the rifleman would stop and take careful aim and fire, and I'd hear the bullet whine or I'd see some dust spit up, but I didn't reply none.

While they was off in the distance, sitting 'round on their horses and talking it over, I got to doing some consulting with myself. I knowed that at least five of them Indians that I'd put down'd had guns. I didn't know what kinda guns they was—maybe Sharps, maybe Spencer rifles, maybe old Spanish muskets, or repeating Henrys. I had no idea.

I wondered if maybe one of them Indians that I'd put down was carrying a .44 Winchester. Might even be that he'd have one of them old .44 singles. Anyhow, there was a good chance that he'd have some ammunition. I sure needed anything I could get. I took a good look 'round and seen that there weren't nothing else in all of that broad expanse of prairie for miles 'cept them Indians out there 'bout a thousand yards away.

Judging from his past shooting, that last rifleman couldn't do me no harm at that distance. I looked 'round real careful at all of them bodies. I knowed I'd better check 'em again and see if there was any movement, indicating that one of 'em might just be hurt and playing possum.

As a matter of fact, I'd been so confident of my shooting that I was sure they was all dead, but the best shot in the world can mortally wound something that don't die right off. Grizzly bear hunters has learned that, to their sad experience.

I took real good care to look 'em all over, even them last Indians that I'd killed out there at four hundred yards. I didn't see no sign of movement and I watched 'em all real careful—concentrating on each body for as much as four or five minutes. Then I reckoned it was safe enough for me to go take a look. The nearest dead Indian with a gun was lying straight in front of me, out 'bout eighty yards.

I decided to walk slow rather than run. I didn't wanta give them bucks any idea that I was in a hurry or excited. I figured that when they seen me walking they'd know that I was plenty calm and ready to shoot just as deadly as I done before. So, real casual-like, carrying my rifle in plain sight, I rose up on one knee, then stood on the back of old Paint's carcass.

Them Indians was looking at me, with their ponies all spread out in a line. They might've been thinking I'd been wounded, and I was anxious to show 'em that there weren't nothing wrong with me a'tall. Then I whistled my way straight out 'cross the prairie in the direction the first charge'd come from.

I went by a lancer lying facedown and continued on twenty yards to the next man. Though he was a rifleman, I was disappointed to find that he didn't have nothing but a .44 Sharps. He had a cartridge pouch hanging from his breechclout so I jerked it loose and pulled it open. The .44 Sharps shells he had in there, even though they was the same caliber I needed, was too long to fit the chamber of my Winchester, so's I had to throw 'em away. I scattered 'em out good while I was at it.

I looked 'round and wondered if it was worth my while to keep walking farther out. I didn't wanta get too far away from Paint's carcass. I s'pose I could've lied down behind a dead Comanche, but them skinny bastards wouldn't give a man no real protection. I much preferred the horse.

Them devils out there just sat motionless on their horses, like they was fascinated with me. I decided to go on to the body of the next Indian, who was thirty yards farther away. That put me 'bout a hundred thirty yards from Paint. When I got fairly close, I was real let down to see that he was lying there with a lance still in his hand and wondered why I'd wasted a shell on him.

Then I remembered that he was the lancer that'd crossed in front of the Indian that was carrying a gun. I'd had to kill him to get him outta the way. Then I looked out nine hundred yards 'cross them flat, flat plains to where them living braves was still staying put on their horses. I decided it was a good chance to stop and count the living ones, so I stood right there beginning from the left to the right, and counted as best as I could.

When I got through, I had seventeen. There I was, Cat Brules, standing out in the broad prairie with a bunch of dead Indian bodies 'round me, walking along real slow and making a head count of seventeen armed Comanches—all sitting on their horses nine hundred yards out, still hesitating to attack one lone white man. Somehow I got to really enjoying that late afternoon walk, poking 'round among them bodies.

I took a look as I passed by the body of the Comanche with the lance and started a gentle stroll towards the next one—twenty-five yards farther out—that had a gun lying by him. It was an old musket—prob'ly come from way up at the Hudson Bay Trading Post at Assiniboine. That's where most of 'em come from. I picked it up and throwed it away.

Seeing me do that, them other braves let out a helluva yipping and yelling and started milling 'round again, shaking their lances in the air. I was sure agitating the hell out of 'em. Finally, one of 'em let out a long, wild whoop and started coming at me at a dead gallop. I reckon that he got so mad seeing what I'd done to his dead buddies that he couldn't control hisself. He was gonna show the rest of 'em that he had the guts to finish me off.

I took my time getting back to the cover of Paint's carcass and dropped down behind his belly like I'd done before, only this time I noticed that the old horse was getting stiff and cold. Lots of time'd passed and I remember thinking that when he got hard and tough like that, he'd stop bullets better.

I worked the lever action of the Winchester real slow and deliberate, looking down and watching the brass shell go sliding into the chamber as nice as you please and seeing how sweet that hammer looked, cocked back and ready to go. Then I snuggled down against Paint's carcass and laid my eye down 'til the barrel pinched that bead up real tight in the notch of the rear sight, and waited for the Comanche's horse feathers to keep coming.

I reckoned that I didn't have no reason to kill him 'til he was right in close, so I waited and watched real careful and seen him grow in size over the bead of the rifle as he come towards me. I remember looking at him and thinking lots of things—like how fancy he looked with his war paint, his horned helmet, and his shield and lance, and how that lance must've had lots of feathers tied onto it, 'cause it was trailing along in the wind. His buffalo-hide shield stood out all fancy colored, painted with some mystic or superstitious signs that them varmints thought so much about—like an evil eye or something—that kept the harm from 'em. I wonder if them charms a his is gonna work, I thought.

The sun was sinking low in the western sky and it seemed like he was coming right outta the prairie sun. I got interested in the picture and let him come up real close. When he got to 'bout a hundred fifty yards, I started squeezing down on the trigger. As it cut loose and I felt the shock of the recoil, it was real satisfying to see him cartwheel off the horse and bust his ass on the ground. It was pretty as could be, seeing that riderless pony swing by on a big curve to the west of me with all of his war fixings—a white hand painted on his neck and some stripes on his rump.

I looked over at where that buck was lying on the ground to make sure he weren't making no unnecessary movements. I wanted him stone-cold dead, 'cause he was within eighty yards of me and it weren't gonna be too long 'fore it started getting dark.

Then I heard a fresh batch of yipping and yowling from the rest of the warriors that was back there. When that last buck'd gone down, it seemed like their fury overcome their judgment and the whole kit and caboodle come roaring towards me, screaming all kinds of wild yells that give me to understand they wasn't feeling too kindly 'bout me.

I sat up a little bit and took four shells outta my belt and slid 'em into the slot of the magazine to make up for the four I'd already used. I levered a shell into the chamber and slipped another in the magazine to make up for it. Then I settled down to wait 'til they got close enough.

I started shooting when they was 'bout three hundred yards out, and by the time they got a hundred fifty yards closer, I had four of 'em down. The fire got too hot for 'em and they started splitting up, 'bout half of 'em to the right and half to the left. I didn't have no time to count. Then I seen what they was up to. They was gonna spread out and start riding 'round me in a circle.

I still made out only one rider with a gun. He'd gone off to the right. I drawed down on him and dropped him at a hundred yards. I thought he was the last one with a rifle, but I was mistaken, 'cause one on the left started firing. He must've kept his weapon hid away all that time. Anyway, I heard the twang of a bullet hit ten or fifteen feet away.

I had to slither 'round Paint's rump to keep something 'tween me and that brave, and I still had to keep watching all the rest of 'em while they was milling 'round. I kept watching for the brave with the gun, and when I finally saw him shoot, I knowed what pony was his and how it moved. Every time he'd come 'round the circle on one side, I'd slip over and get on the other side of Paint's carcass.

For a while I didn't do no shooting, 'cause every one of them bucks was hanging down on the far side of his horse. From the way they was tightening the circle, I could see that one of those times they'd turn and come charging in on me from all sides, and I wouldn't get enough shots off 'fore they'd get to me. With them hiding down behind their horses, I was gonna have to take the lesser of two evils and start killing horses.

I reasoned I'd better kill a lancer's horse first, 'cause it wouldn't be no danger to me for a lancer to hide down behind a dead horse, and it was a cinch that he wouldn't charge me on foot at a distance of a hundred yards. If he did, he'd be awful sick from a bullet in his chest by the time he got halfway to me. On the other hand if he stayed put, he wouldn't be forted up very long 'fore another Indian'd pick him up.

I drawed down on the lancer that was riding right in front of the Indian with the gun and shot his horse out from under him. It was a direct fatal hit, 'cause the horse just dropped his head and somer-saulted, and that throwed the buck quite a distance out into the prairie grass.

It must've stunned him for a minute, 'cause he didn't get up very quick. Finally he stumbled over to pick up his lance. One of them other bucks cut outta the circle and swung by to pick him up. He hopped on and they broke from the circle and started riding away. Couldn't either one of 'em hide behind the horse's withers riding double. It made a real easy shot, so I took careful aim and put one bullet through the both of 'em. I laughed like hell, cause it was the first time I'd got me a double in Comanche land.

One of them lancer bucks on the other side of the circle seen what'd happened and turned to come right at me. He got too close for comfort and wasn't more'n forty yards away when I killed him. Then the rifleman cut outta the circle and come straight for me, shooting all the while. That was what I'd wanted. I drawed down on him and fired the only bad shot I made during the whole fight.

I reckon by that time I was getting tired and maybe a little worked up. He was lying low on his horse's withers and, although he was riding straight towards me, only part of him was exposed. I must've held just a bit too much to the left, 'cause I shot his horse. They both went down in a big somersault sixty yards out in front. That Indian went through the air and hit the ground on his hands and knees, still holding his rifle in his right hand. He hit awful hard in that prairie dust, but he rolled and got up.

I guess it addled his senses when he hit. What he should've done was made a big dive for that horse's carcass, but he didn't. He run three or four steps towards me and then knelt down to shoot. He never did get his shot off. A man kneeling at thirty-five yards is a cinch target, and I killed him 'fore he ever got a chance.

I can't tell you why, but that seemed to do it. A howl went up from all them that was circling, and they rode off in a cloud of dust to the northeast. The hoofbeats of them Indian ponies was fading away in the distance and I watched their dust cloud for a couple of miles 'til I seen that they was really pulling out.

Then I wondered what they was fixing to do next. Although they didn't like to fight after dark, they might try to come back and sneak up on me at dawn. On the other hand, they might be giving up, having had a bellyful of my Winchester. They sure lost an awful lot of warriors trying to take one white man, and that was the kinda defeat that'd really nettle 'em. I figured they'd try to do something to even the score. I imagine it would've been awful hard for them bucks to go back to their village and tell the elders and the squaws that one white man'd killed more'n twenty of 'em. That kinda thing just didn't happen. Only it really did that afternoon on the flat prairie, sixty-five miles east of the Santa Fe Trail and south of the Cimarron cutoff.

As the evening shadows gathered I realized how tired I was. I took another swig from the canteen and for the first time felt real bone weary. I hadn't slept the night 'fore to amount to nothing. I'd rode hard all morning and then been busy 'til dark, so I just lay there for a while against old Paint's stiff, dried body, watching the stars. I run through my mind the things that was ahead of me.

The night prairie wind was getting on the chilly side. I couldn't stay by Paint no longer, 'cause if I did, sure as hell some of them Indians might come back and find me. I reckoned I was gonna have to travel at night and get moving real soon.

Like I said, I'd reloaded my rifle and had 'bout five cartridges left in my belt. That give me twenty-two, counting the one in the chamber. I still had six shots left in my .38 and four more shells for it in the pocket of my other shirt. I also had a knife, a small batch of pemmi-can, a fire steel for starting fires, and an oilskin cloth that I could tie 'round my waist.

Most of all, I started to worry 'bout the kind of footgear I was wearing. Cowboy boots was good for riding, but I didn't reckon to walk in 'em too damn far. I done some cussing at myself for fancying up when I was back in Santa Fe and not being more practical; I sure as hell didn't need no cowboy boots and spurs now, what with being afoot.

After doing some more thinking, I got up. It was real dark, but I didn't have no trouble walking right to the last buck I'd killed—the one with the rifle. He was lying there in the prairie pitched facedown with his gun 'bout half a foot away from his stretched-out right arm.

I picked up the gun, and I could sure see its outline real easy. When I run my fingers down along the bottom of the magazine, I felt the open slot of a Henry. I'd knowed right then that I could use the extra shells if he had any. I worked the action and ejected one shell from the chamber. It was spent, but I kept pumping. There was three more in the magazine.

I felt all 'round the buck's body 'til I found a shell bag, and there was six rounds left in it. That give me nine more rounds that I stuck in my belt. As I was feeling over the still-warm corpse, I found another thing that really caught my fancy. Hanging over his shoulder on a leather thong was a war club. The handle was 'bout sixteen inches long, with a rough stone ax blade, all bound with drawed rawhide at the business end.

I appropriated that item, too. There was one more thing that I could do. I went back to Pedro's grave and stood there a minute talking to him. "Pete, s'posin' ya consider this headstone temporary 'til I get somethin' better. I ain't near finished the job a revengin' ya yet, pardner, but I shore've had some open sport this afternoon. I only wish ya could've been with me. From now on, this is gonna be knowed as the Battle of Pedro's Fort—the fort bein' a dead horse, an' the battle bein' the one where one white man killed twenty Comanches an' walked away, all in honor of his friend."

I went back over to Paint and picked up my rifle and the oilskin cloth, then headed out north to look over them Indians' bodies. I kept working from one to another, feeling for moccasins. Some of 'em was barefoot, and some had wore-out footgear that was as useless as none a'tall. I visited 'bout nine bodies, every time looking for a gun or ammunition, and checking to see what kind of moccasins was on the feet. I found one more buck in the dark that had a gun by him. It was a Spencer musket and the ammunition was useless to me.

I'd picked up 'bout four pairs of moccasins, so I sat down and pulled off my boots and tried 'em all to see which'd be the most comfortable. They was regular Comanche moccasins that come up near to thigh high and had some good strong rawhide thongs that wrapped 'round your legs. Two pairs of 'em fit real good. I wore one set and put a spare pair in the oilskin and tied it 'round my waist. I hated to leave them new boots and spurs, but I didn't have no use for 'em and I figured they'd just be a dead burden.

Then I picked up my canteen, oilskin blanket roll, and bag of pemmican and, using the North Star as a guide, headed out due west, leaving old Pedro behind with only a thumbs-up gesture and a muttered salute from me.

THE GREATEST HUNT OF ALL

Most horsemen would've took their bridle and spurs with 'em, even though they might not've tried walking far in cowpuncher's boots, but my plans didn't take a horse into consideration.

There weren't nothing for me to do but travel real light, just like I done. Indian moccasins was easy and nice for walking, real quiet and smooth and comfortable. They'd been tanned outta elk hide, so they was tough. Some squaw'd chewed 'em 'til they was soft and pliable to really fit your feet and the action of your ankle when you was moving along.

I traveled west for 'bout five miles. Then I turned due north. The tiredness went outta me as I kept walking, facing into the prairie wind and moving out at a good clip. I didn't worry much 'bout coming on no Indians in the dark. I figured I could see better'n they could and I'd sure notice their horses or smell 'em 'fore I got too close. What I'd really been aiming for was that mesa country to the north, with all them volcanic ridges where a man on foot could go right along and a horse'd have a tough time.

I kept moving all night. Sometimes I'd run for 'bout twenty minutes to half an hour, then I'd walk again. I was as hard as nails in them days, and even though I'd put in a helluva day and a night before, I still had lots of reserve. As I traveled, the stiffness eased outta me and I felt better from getting up a sweat and stretching out. I couldn't say how many miles I covered that night, but when dawn broke I was where I'd wanted to be—coming up on the base of one of them big mesas that lay to the north. By the time it got light enough to see anything at a distance, I was crawling up the side of the oak brush slope.

When the sun come up, I'd reached way up under the cliffs of the cap rock and found me a nice shelter along one of them rock ledges. Couldn't nobody see me from above, and if I stretched out on the ledge I could see off to the sides and below and far out over the plains for miles 'round. It was a real good spot, and I reckoned I had plenty of cover.

I figured them Comanches'd go back for reinforcements and come back a day later to pick up the bodies of their kin, recover them rifles, and hunt me down. I reckoned they wouldn't have too much trouble tracking me 'cross that prairie grass, still soft with the spring moisture, but I'd traveled over lots of rocky places wherever I could during the last hour of my running, and I was hoping it'd make it tough for 'em to follow me. I didn't see how they could get back and take care of their friends and track me down by late afternoon, and I didn't intend being anywhere near there by that time. I figured I had enough time for 'bout five hours of sleep, then I'd get on the move again.

I lay down in the shadow of that ledge and slept real hard all through the morning and a couple hours past noon. When I wanted to wake up at a certain time, I could do it, no matter how tired I was. When I woke up, I took a swig outta my canteen and then spent quite a long time looking out over the prairie to see if there was any movement along the path I'd took from the south. I decided to rest as long as I could and then travel again during the night.

'Bout four o'clock in the afternoon I seen some dust in the distance. I knowed only too well what it was. They was a good many miles away—too far to even make 'em out—but I knowed that I couldn't stay where I was any longer. I got up and stretched, drank some more water, and then picked up my rifle and worked 'round the east side of the mesa, staying under the cap rock all the time. Moccasins don't make much of an imprint on cap rock. I knowed I wouldn't have to travel many miles 'round the shady side of the mesa 'fore there'd be no trace of where I'd gone.

By seven o'clock that night, the sun'd set and I'd worked 'round to the north end looking out at a dozen more mesas to the north and east. I waited 'til it was real dark, then dropped down and crossed over to the next mesa. I reckoned there was 'bout two miles 'tween 'em. I traveled as fast as I could at a comfortable, steady run. Where there was rock, I stayed on it.

The country to the north was big and complicated, and I found another good place to hole up not long after dawn. I figured I could keep 'em plenty confused and they'd never catch up with me. I lay down and kept watching and finally I seen a little patch of dust way out on the prairie, down south of the mesa land where it was all flat and there weren't no place to hide.

I knowed it was my Comanches. Maybe it weren't just the band I'd whipped, but some others that they'd either met or gone back to their village for. They was riding, and riding hard, kicking up them dust clouds that look like birds flying 'cross the prairie. They was coming from the place that I called Pedro's Fort, where at least twenty of their brethren was lying out there on the prairie, kissed to death by my Winchester.

They might've seen where I'd crossed dry arroyos, places where I'd climbed steep banks and'd had to dig in my toes a little, or where I'd covered some soft ground and the wind and the rain'd left a little of the adobe that made an impression or two. They was following pretty good—they'd looked up ahead at them mesas and knowed somehow that I was headed up in there. They knowed also that I was afoot and figured that with their being mounted, it wouldn't take 'em too long to come up to me.

Well, I was comforted by the thought that nobody could ride a horse up to where I was, lying up there on a ledge under the cap rock. Below me was a wide rockslide of small, slippery flat rocks. Down below that was lots of thick oak brush. Not only was they gonna lose my trail somewhere down in the brush, but they was gonna have to walk up to me. If they did, I'd see 'em real clear, so I figured I was safe. What I was fixing to do was to gather my strength.

There was some of them long, thin wisps of clouds, and over yonder on my right and far to the southwest, I could barely see the snowy Sangre de Cristos. Far, far out to the southeast was them open panhandle plains of Comanche land. To the north of me spread more of the series of mesas and volcanic rock that I needed for a good hiding place—a place where a man with a repeating rifle could give hell to any horseman that come after him. That was where I was fixing to hide.

I was kinda hungry, so I reached in my pouch and took out a handful of pemmican. I held it in the palm of my hand and poured a little water on it from the canteen. I squeezed it into a ball and then real slow I started nibbling on it, my Winchester at my side and me on my belly propped up on my elbows, looking far out over the plains.

I was fascinated with watching that little cloud of dust that was coming my way far, far out on the panhandle. I felt like a cat lying in wait for a mouse. Every now and then I'd squeeze that lump of wet pemmican in the palm of my hand real tight so's it'd get a little hard. Then I'd nibble some of it and look around out there real slow and calm, wondering how many Comanches I was gonna catch.

While they was still a few miles off, I give up the luxury of such thoughts and eased up and moved on. I was careful to stay under the cap rock, where I wouldn't leave no traces, and I moved 'round to the end of the mesa on the east. Then, in the shadows of the late afternoon sun, where there weren't no chance of any of them Co-manches seeing me, I moved 'round towards the north 'til I come out two miles ahead on the north end.

Off to the northeast there was another mesa. I dropped down and crossed over to it, 'bout a mile and a quarter away. I took good care to step on stones everywhere I went, but I knowed it was impossible to make it perfect. I traveled on during the night clear 'round to the north side of that next mesa. I reckoned it was eight miles from where I'd been looking.

Then I done something that I'd thought about for a long time. If you cast 'round below where them rockslides are, you can find any amount of flat stones. They're 'bout an inch thick and a foot square. Wherever there was bare ground, I'd put one of them stones out ahead and jump across using it so's to keep from leaving footprints. Them mesas got closer together the farther north I went, so the going weren't too tough. The ground was pretty gravelly, so's them flat foot stones, even with my weight on 'em, didn't leave a single mark.

When I got up to the cap rock of the next mesa—a big, lone one— I found a place to hide out and nap 'til dark. Then I stuck to that bare rocky part and traveled all night along that mesa. When I come to the next crossing, it was near daylight.

I kept working along the northeast side 'til I reached a big overhang with heavy brush all 'round and no chance of anyone seeing me from any direction. I curled up there and slept through the day. 'Fore I went to sleep, and after I woke up, I done the same thing as before—a little pemmican in the palm of the hand, a little water, give a little squeeze, and then eat the lump. I know it don't sound too tasty, but in a ball of that stuff the size of a chestnut, there's enough food to last a man for a day. Water swells it up in your stomach and gives you the feeling of eating a full meal.

I didn't even think 'bout making no fire. That would've been suicide, and what's more, I didn't need one. Them rocks held the heat of the sun. I was outta the wind and tucked right up in there, and there weren't no way for 'em to track me.

I moved the same way the next day and night, and traveled 'til mid-morning, when I come up on a little spring feeding outta the side of a mesa. I found it by spotting a patch of green down in the oak brush.

I climbed down there and seen the water coming out from under the rocks, gurgling as clear and nice as anything you'd want. I drunk 'til I didn't have no thirst. Then I pulled off my shirt and freshed up a little, throwing water all over my face and hands and splashing some on my chest and back. It sure made me feel good. I soaked my shirt in the spring and put it on, knowing that it'd keep me cool as it dried during the day. Then I filled my canteen and hit out again, heading towards the northeast.

'Bout three o'clock in the afternoon I suddenly stopped and sniffed the air. I smelt something. It was the smoky odor of burning piñon wood. When I sniffed it, the hairs on the back of my neck stood up. My heart got to beating and my mouth went dry and I started licking my lips.

I felt the excitement of the hunt. Boy, there weren't nothing in the world like hunting Comanches. Now, any other hunt is exciting—it's man's nature, whether you're coming up on elk, or deer, or bighorn sheep, or grizzly. You get keen of sight and taut of muscle and your nerves set up on edge. Your breath comes fast. It's them thousands of years of your ancestors' hunting that comes out in you.

I kept thinkin', don't move 'til ya look real careful, Brules. Where ya gonna put your foot? What's your balance gonna be? Ya ain't gonna stumble an' have ta grab at a branch or twig. Ya ain't gonna knock a stone down the hill an' attract attention. No, ya ain't. Yore gonna keep your balance. Yore goin' along there real smooth an' quiet. Then real soon yore gonna smell that Comanche smell.

That's how I worked along 'til I got close enough to smell the sour, greasy stench of a Comanche camp. Oh hell, there ain't no stink like it. Grizzlies smell like you're coming up on fresh dog shit. Elk smell halfway 'tween cattle and something wild. But Comanches, they've got a stink all their own. It's a nasty smell like stale grease and rotted fish mixed all together with sweat and human droppings. All wild Indians smell bad, but Comanches smell the worst. Anybody that's laid out split-assed waiting to be tortured by them bastards ain't never gonna forget their smell.

"Take it slow an' easy, Brules," I said out loud to myself. "When ya get in there real close, drop ta your knees an' start crawlin'. Stay up there in the cap rock. Don't move no pebbles. Keep ta the shadows. Take it easy. Work along 'til ya come out 'round the edge ta where yore lookin' right down on the camp. See! There's the tepees! There's the spring water! There's the fires! There's the squaws goin' back an' forth haulin' wood, workin' their hides, an' cooking. Off a little bit farther, there's the horses. Some of 'em are on a picket an' the others is out grazin'. There's a bunch a kids foolin' 'round, an' a few dogs in the village."

Ya gotta watch them dogs, I thought. They can smell a white man real easy. When an Indian dog smells a white man, it's a real different scent an' gives 'em the clue. Ya gotta watch that. If yore watchin' all them squaws workin' an' some a the girls go down to a stream ta swim bare-assed, an' all a that, don't go gettin' excited. That ain't fer you. Yore killin' Comanches.

Sometimes you can look 'round and see a few bucks—maybe an old chief and some of the other elders. They'll gather 'round the fire, squatting down and shooting the breeze. They ain't doing nothing. They ain't gonna work. They're too old to hunt, but they're smoking the pipe and telling all them lies 'bout when they was young and out buffalo hunting or killing white folks and all that.

Then you know it ain't gonna be too long 'fore more bucks come in. They're gonna be coming in from the hunt or from some warpath, and the squaws'll wanta know how many scalps they got and what kinda battle they had. Some of them squaws'll wanta know whether their bucks was killed or not. If it turned out so, then they'll get to keening. There ain't no weirder cry than the keening of a Comanche squaw. It's a high-pitched trill that lasts a long time and then fades away. It sends chills all up and down your spine. They sure do howl when they hear their bucks is gone.

Best of all, them squaws likes to see prisoners come in; that sure does fire 'em up. They know that there's gonna be lots of fun with the torture, and there ain't nothing that them squaws'd rather do than sit 'round and watch a prisoner die slow. They sure like to take part in the torture—'specially them that's lost a buck in the fight. Them squaws'll stop their keening and go right to work on a prisoner, if'n the elders'll let 'em. Yessir, they get their knives red-hot and go right to cutting and carving with a vengeance.

Many's the time over the years since, that I'd lie up on a cap rock and look down on a Comanche camp, like I done that late afternoon. It was always the same. Sometimes the bucks wouldn't come back a'tall. Mostly they'd come in from the hunt. It was just on rare occasions that they'd have a prisoner. In all the years I hunted Comanches, I only seen the torture maybe a dozen times, but that was enough. Hearing the bone-chilling cries from some poor devil begging to die while the squaws was patiently unraveling him was sheer hell.

Up on the cap rock on a moonlit night when all the rest of the world was beautiful, looking down on the fires of a Quohadi village, smelling the stench and hearing the screams of the victims and the laughter of those enjoying it, was like looking into a little piece of hell, stuck in the middle of our wide, splendid world.

You just couldn't help knowing that them Comanches was the worst animal that ever lived—an evil, ferocious animal with the brains of a man. There weren't nothing else like 'em in the world and never had been.

That afternoon while I was lying there looking down on a Comanche camp, for the first time I felt like a leopard watching his prey and I knowed that I was satisfied, real satisfied in my heart, to be a Comanche hunter.

I looked far out over the plains to see if I could pick up a speck of dust that'd mean some bucks on their ponies was coming in from the hunt or a fight. All the time I kept observing the habits of the camp, counting the dogs and seeing how they was acting, counting the fires and tepee circles. One thing that was most important was to see where the Indians went out of the camp. The bucks went in one direction and the squaws went in another. Then I took a look at the brush cover and how far it was from the tepees, looking for the best route down from the cap rock to creep up on the camp without being seen. I seen how I could leave when I had to, and what direction to travel.

Once in a while a boy'd go out and check the picket line of the horses and look over the rest of the remuda, or a squaw'd go out to catch a horse and harness him up to a travois like she was working on it to fit the pony. Anyhow, it all added up to the normal life you'd expect to find in an Indian camp—much the same as it'd gone on for hundreds and maybe thousands of years.

Right then—as I was lying up there looking down on this little Comanche village with fifteen tepees, a few bucks, and twenty or twenty-five old men and boys and maybe twice as many squaws—I could get an idea how many bucks was out on the prairie and away.

You could figure lots of things by studying a village like I done. I could tell by the number of hides that was laid out for tanning in the sun how good their hunting'd been. I could tell by the nature of them hides whether they'd been killing buffalo or elk or antelope. I could tell by the piles of wood remaining how long they was fixing on staying, and by the number of ponies whether they'd been on horse raids or whether they was just working the string they had.

The other thing I done was to count the dogs. I fixed it so's I knowed every dog in the village—watching 'em and learning 'em and seeing how they went. Them dogs might give me away if I weren't careful. While I was looking at them dogs, I was mindful of the wind. I could tell by the direction of the smoke from the fire and the prairie grasses which way it was blowing down there.

The wind on my cheek didn't mean too much, lying up there on the cap rock, 'cause the wind up there was different than it was down in the valley. Truly, the wind could pass by you and then go on a ways, swirling down into the valley, and cut back to come right in over the Indian village and give them yellow curs a whiff of you. Then all kinda howling'd go up.

Whatever the case, it paid you to be careful all the time. A good

Comanche hunter didn't take no chances. He watched every angle all the time, from every direction. You never knowed when your luck'd change. Some little shift of wind, some little change of light, just the wrong movement that could loosen a rock or snap a twig, or a slight turn of your face in the rays of the sun, and you could be discovered.

No, a Comanche hunter had to lie high up on the mesa along some ledge, hardly breathing or moving, keeping his eyes focused like the eyes of a cat on his prey, always watching with the intent of a hunter—cold, perceiving, and carrying sudden death. You didn't have no time to think 'bout how bad off you might be. You spent your time keeping from getting bad off.

Sure, you knowed there was danger, plenty of danger, something to chill the guts out of a man, but on the other hand, the excitement was so great that you could never keep yourself from it. As for me, besides the thrill of a dangerous hunt, there was always that deep-set pleasure in the back of my mind as to how I was not only gonna kill Co-manches, but I was leaving the sign of the Cat so's that others'd know that Cat Brules'd passed that way.

I lay there for the rest of the afternoon, watching all the time for any sign of them bucks coming in, but I never seen a thing. The plains to the east was as free of dust clouds as if nothing'd ever moved across 'em. Also, I didn't see nothing coming from the southwest. I reckoned that bunch tracking me was still milling 'round and circling 'bout the mesas where they'd had so much trouble following my tracks.

'Long towards evening there was lots of activity 'round the camp-fires, and just 'fore dark, two bucks come out from the camp and I could hear 'em laughing and singing 'tween themselves.

That was my signal. I eased up in the gathering shadows from my ledge I'd been hiding behind and slipped down through the rockslide like a shadow, moving rapid but sure. By the time them braves got to the place where they was gonna do their business, I'd reached the oak brush and was working through the openings here and there where the rockslide penetrated. I got up real close. I remember hearing their laughter as they was coming towards me.

I picked a big stand of oak brush to hide behind and they come out there as nice as you please. I seen 'em step out in the fading light in front of me and felt my fingers tighten 'round my war club. I'd slipped it off'n the thong on my belt and had it swinging real easy. All the time, I was carrying my rifle in my left hand.

I slid 'round that brush quiet as a cat, took two steps, and whacked the first one with the war club. I swung and hit the other one on the side of the head 'fore he ever moved. Both of 'em tumbled forward without making a sound. It was as nice and clean a kill as you please.

I took 'em both by the hair and drug 'em off into the bushes. Then I sat there and waited. I knowed they'd be missed in the camp, but I didn't think there'd be any fuss raised for a while, and there'd prob'ly be some more bucks arriving. I weren't wrong 'bout that, 'cause ten minutes later two more of 'em come along.

They didn't stop quite as close to me, but they had their backs turned to me, same as the others. I took 'bout ten steps to get to 'em. I whacked 'em both the same way—as clean as before—and drug 'em on in with the others. Then I slipped back 'cross the rockslide as fast as I could, moving silent and quick, and worked my way towards the north side of the camp, way below that ledge where I'd been watching 'em from.

There was a gentle hum of voices in the camp, and it begun to rise some in tone. I guessed there might've been a little concern over the fact that four bucks'd left quite a while ago and hadn't come back. There hadn't been no alarm set off, but I reckoned that some of 'em'd got stirred up.

A couple of voices called out from the fireside. When there weren't no answer, there was another hubbub of conversation and then it died down again. I couldn't see from where I was, but I guessed that maybe two or three of 'em went out a ways in the darkness on the south end of the camp to look for the missing warriors. I didn't know if there was any squaws going to look for 'em or what, but if so, I expected I'd hear the screaming when they found the bodies.

From where I was crouched I could see dim outlines through the oak brush 'round the fire where two more men and a boy'd got up from the fire and headed my way, the boy following at a little distance behind. They come out and stopped in a small clearing in the oak brush. Although there weren't no moon—just the light of the stars— I could make 'em out real plain and clear.

I held the club real straight in my hand and moved in as close as I could without making a sound. The backs of all three of 'em was turned towards me. I considered that mighty convenient and moved as quick as I could to get within range.

It took me 'bout ten seconds to ease out from under the oak brush and move real quiet to where I was right behind the first man. I was ready to rise up on my tiptoes and use my full force to swing that club through his brain when there come a bloodcurdling scream outta the darkness.

Them two bucks stopped still right then and one of 'em said something. They stood there listening. I knowed that the bodies of the others'd been discovered, so I moved fast. There was a swish and a thump as my club broke into the skull of the first man. He sank to the ground with a groan. The other man started to move, but too late. I caught him on the side of the head with a smash.

The boy turned at the sound. He must've knowed that something was happening and that the men was in deep trouble. He let out a yell and started running like a wild hare towards the fire. He was a small boy and couldn't move as fast as Cat Brules, but I let him go.

By that time, all hell'd broke loose in the camp. There was shouting and yelling and the sounds of Indians crashing up through the brush towards where the kid'd been yelling. I guessed there'd be quite a few of 'em going out the other end of the camp to where the squaw'd let out her yip. I slipped up through the oak brush to the rockslide.

I peered down at the tepees below me and seen all sorts of confusion. There was one group gathered 'round a fire and they was all looking out in different directions. There was others running back and forth 'tween the tepees, calling in the darkness. Some of 'em'd gone out and the rest was milling 'round by the big fire in the center of the camp, trying to figure out what was going on and maybe getting ready to run.

Indians is mighty superstitious, and when something happens like that squaw screaming without any enemy war whoops sounding with it through the night air, they don't know what to make of it. If it was an attack, that'd be one thing, and I reckon that was what they'd expected at first. When it didn't come, they must've had all kinda wild ideas 'bout spirits and other stuff that them savages is always dreaming up 'bout the darkness.

I picked up a big rock, swung it back in my hand like I was throwing a spear, and flung it way out in the night air and down in a nice clean arc towards the camp. It landed quite a ways from the campfire near one of the tepees. Them Indians that was gathered 'round the fire didn't see it coming 'til it hit, and then they all jumped as if somebody'd fired a gun. Two or three of 'em run over to see what it was. That was what I'd figured on. I whirled a second rock 'round and let it go, putting it way over on the other side of the circle. When it hit the ground, they all whirled 'round and run over in that direction. By that time a third rock was in the air and then a fourth. I didn't sling 'em quite as hard and they both landed near the fire.

It all come as a helluva surprise to 'em. First they was milling 'round and shouting and yelling. Then they looked up the hill towards where the rocks was coming from, but they couldn't see nothing. They all just stood there looking horrified, and that was what I was waiting for. I slid right down onto a big boulder and snuggled my Winchester into my shoulder while I picked me out a big buck right in the center of the mob. I drawed back the hammer of that Winchester with my thumb and then real careful-like squeezed off a shot. The rifle crashed and echoed in them rocks and that Comanche went down in the light of the fire, his feathers fluttering like a dying ostrich.

After that shot they all started yelling and hollering and begun scattering. Some of 'em went running for the tepees and others was hunting for guns. A few of 'em tried to get off in the dark, away from the fire, and I kept right on shooting, looking for the biggest targets, knowing that they was the men.

By the time them Comanches'd all got outta the firelight, there was nine bodies lying on the ground 'tween the fire circle and the tepees, and none of 'em was moving. I reckoned that was all the shooting I was gonna get for the night, so I picked up my war club and headed up to the cap rock.

I seen a motion off to my right and slipped into the shadow of the nearest rock. It didn't take long 'fore I seen a buck climbing with a rifle in his hand. He was working his way right to where he'd seen the flash of my gun.

I moved 'bout twenty feet away in the shadows, knowing where he'd last seen me. He fell for the trap just as neat and nice as anything you'd wanta see. Crouching low, he crept up real stealthy to where I'd been lying on that rock. He couldn't have made it more convenient, and it was real easy to kill him with the war club.

When he fell, his gun went down with a clatter on the rocks and I heard a different noise off to the right. I seen it was another buck. By that time I knowed my position was give away. That buck was looking 'round real careful in the darkness, ducking his head and shoulders this way and that, trying to peer 'round the rocks and see what there was to work on. I gathered from the way he was acting that he didn't have a rifle—maybe just a lance.

In any case, he'd made the mistake of looking to check out the situation once too often, and I killed him too. He weren't more'n twenty-five feet away, so I didn't have no necessity of raising that Winchester to my shoulder—I just let him have it from the hip. He give a big gasp, and 'fore the echo of the shot died away he slumped over among the rocks and I heard the clatter of his spear.

Then I knowed for certain that the time for old Cat Brules to pull out was at hand. Real quick, I fastened the war club under my belt and, taking my rifle in my right hand, I made it on up through the rockslide. In another hour I was off that mesa and crossing to another one. I must've traveled ten or twelve miles 'fore daybreak. It would've normally been my custom to hole up during the day and let things take their course, but dawn come early that time of the year and I hadn't made enough mileage to satisfy me.

Using all the cover I could, I kept on at a steady jog, ducking and stepping from stone to stone and trying my level best not to leave no track. I was in condition and as hard as a marble slab. I was sweating a little, but I had lots of distance left in me, and I'd developed a swinging gait that I could keep up all day and all night.

I don't know if them Indians ever did pick up my trail, but I never seen any of 'em or even any dust of their following. I traveled all through that next day, crossing from mesa to mesa with as much caution as I could muster.

By late afternoon I could see them old Sangre de Cristos sticking up there in the blue spring sky and I knowed I'd made maybe forty miles. Just 'fore sundown I reached the rim of the big open bowl that looks out northwest towards that long tongue of mountains and mesas that make up Raton Pass. I knowed then I weren't too far from the Santa Fe Trail. When nightfall come, I holed up under a piece of cap rock and watched the last traces of the light of day sinking behind the western mountains.

I'd stopped for a couple of reasons. One, I wanted to do some thinking and planning and also to rest myself a little. And two, I didn't wanta move out 'til right 'fore dawn. I had enough pemmican to last another week or ten days, and them Comanche moccasins was doing fine—I reckoned they'd hold up for a long time. But I was getting low on ammunition.

I had two ways to go. One was to try to circle 'round maybe two hundred fifty miles to where I'd left the cache of buffalo hides when we'd begun tracking Pedro. There was a whole case of ammunition there, half of it Winchester and the rest for that Sharps, but it might not still be there. Them piles of hides sure would've been seen by roving Indians at some time or other, and if they'd gone over to examine 'em, they was sure gonna help theirselves.

No, I reckoned that there weren't nothing for me to do but go pick up the Santa Fe Trail and take the Eagles Nest cutoff to Taos. I reckoned I could get myself replenished there somehow.

It was dark, and far off in the distance to the northwest I seen a flickering light, and then later another one almost due west—campfires on the Santa Fe Trail. They was ten miles apart from each other and a good twenty miles from me. They marked where some wagon train—maybe freighters, maybe settlers—was camped for the night. I figured I'd avoid 'em and cut 'cross that Santa Fe Trail to pick up the cutoff to Taos. I'd go right on up the headwaters of the Cimarron, over Eagles Nest Pass, and down into the valley of Ranchos de Taos. I could do that all by myself, and instinct told me that was the best course of action.

The stars was out and sparkling in the dark night sky when I got up. Although I felt a little stiff from the cold night wind that was blowing, it didn't take me but a few minutes to get warmed up again and loose. I headed out and didn't jog no more, just kept striding at a steady pace, aiming to hit the Santa Fe Trail 'tween them two camps, with 'bout five miles of clearance on each side.

When it was light enough to see 'bout a mile ahead of me, I spotted them wide ribbons of wagon tracks—maybe a hundred to two hundred yards wide and all rutted from the passage of wagons over the last forty years. What suited me best was that there weren't no wagon trains moving nor any horsemen going up and down on the trail as far as I could see. The trail run north and south in that country, angling a little towards the southwest. Traveling northwest, I crossed the trail at a right angle. To the north, I seen some smoke from one of them campfires that I'd seen the night before. I marveled at the way them ruts'd increased since I'd crossed the trail the year before. That meant lots of white folks was heading out west.

At 'bout ten o'clock that morning I picked up a fork of the Cimarron that come running down outta the mountains. It was along that creek that the branch-off trail to Taos run, so I knowed there might be a little traffic. When I come to one of them dry draws 'bout midafternoon, I left the creek and went up it a ways 'til I come to where some clay bluffs pinched together. I dug a hole in the bank, pulled some tumbleweeds over me, and went off to sleep.

I stayed along the creek the next morning, moving in and out of the oak brush a little ways off the trail. When I got in close to the mountains where the creek got to gushing and running sparkling clear, I kept to the south side, away from the trail. I didn't want to meet nobody. I wanted to travel them mountains alone and slip into Taos and have time to get my bearings.

Maybe I'd been in the untamed country too long by myself. That does strange things to men. It makes 'em so's they don't trust their fellow man too much and don't care to mix with 'em. I reckon I was a little wild anyway by that time, and if I'd had the ammunition, I would've stayed out in them prairies.

On a couple of occasions, I heard the sounds of freighters, some of 'em going towards Taos and some the other way. I could hear the bullwhips cracking from a long ways off, then some of the teamsters cussing and hollering. It seemed to me like they was spoiling the wild country, almost confusing nature. I must say that the Indian's ways is better'n ours when it comes to traveling in the wild. 'Cept when he's yipping and yelling, driving buffalo, or riding down an enemy, an Indian don't disturb the country.

Seems like a white man's gotta make noise wherever he goes—even where he ain't tearing up the country with his outfits, building his fences and roads and houses and things like that. A white man in the wild stands out like a sore thumb. If he don't have time to do much real damage, then he tries to stir up nature by yelling and hollering 'round and by leaving a mess behind at his campsite that's ten times as bad as an Indian's. Indians may stink bad, but they don't leave stuff that'll stay on the ground a long time. A white man leaves wagon hoops and other metal things. An Indian leaves tools of leather or sticks or stones or wove baskets—stuff that'll rot away.

I kept in the timber and none of them wagon trains ever caught sight of me. I could hear 'em all right, even above the rushing of the creek, and I could see their dust rising 'cross the stream.

I decided to get higher up so's I could see better through the openings in the timber and get away from the sound of rushing water. That's a pleasant sound all right, but it sure ain't good if you think you might be trailed.

If you're hunting something, it's good to find it by a running stream. Your quarry don't hear you and you can work right up to 'em. But the same goes when somebody's hunting you, so I moved up higher on the hill to where the sound of the river was just a dim and faint whisper in the valley below.

It took me two more days to get to Taos. The first day I got to the headwaters of the river and broke out into the broad valley of Eagles Nest. On the second day, I was looking down into the south end of that beautiful San Luis Valley.

After sunset I slipped down to the road and begun walking into Taos. It'd been a long time since I'd been in a town—more'n three months since I'd left Albuquerque—and I reckon I was a little bit itchy 'bout coming up on people, not really knowing how to act but determined that I had to get back amongst other folks. I had to get some more ammunition if nothing else and maybe attend to some other things.

I remember coming up to the far edge of town and seeing them adobe walls and them tile-roofed houses and hearing the sound of people's voices. It was a dark night with no moon, but I could smell the smoke of the piñon fires. Once in a while I'd pass somebody on the road, first a man leading a donkey, then a family going by—the man and boy riding a donkey and the woman walking beside 'em with a shawl over her head. Then there was a couple of mule-drawn wagons and once an ox team, but nobody said nothing to me.

I was busy thinking my own thoughts, a little stirred and dreaming 'bout what I was gonna do my second time in Taos. I knowed then that it was a good thing we hadn't robbed that bank like Pedro'd been suggesting. I would've been a real wanted man in that town instead of finding me a friendly place to rearm.

I got to thinking on them early mountain men and how in the twenties and thirties them buggers'd come down all the way from the Trappers' Rendezvous up on the Green River or the Teton country to spend the winters in Taos. They knowed that no matter what they'd done or how bad they was wanted all over the West and the Northwest, they was welcome down there in that Spanish town.

That's the way I felt. Nobody'd be looking for me there. Taos seemed more like a home to me than anyplace I'd ever been before. Although I didn't have no place to stay, and I'd only met a few folks when me and Pedro was there in the winter, it seemed like them adobe walls brought a comfort, and them big cottonwoods and mesquite that lined the streets was reaching out their limbs to take me in.

I didn't know exactly what to do at first. I still had twelve American dollars on me, fastened up in the pocket of that buckskin shirt I was wearing—the same twelve dollars I'd left Albuquerque with. Neither the money nor the shirt'd been off'n me in three months, 'cept when I drunk from that mesa spring, and for a few minutes one time down there on the Canadian when we'd washed up a little and laid our things out in the sun to dry.

When I thought 'bout Pedro and remembered him kneeling out there in the middle of some stream, throwing water over his broad shoulders and turning 'round to laugh at me, it sure made me feel bad. Losing him cut a big hole in my life. As I was walking along them dark streets on the outskirts of Taos, my thoughts rolled back. I could hear Pete laughing and kidding 'round the way he used to do when he was riding alongside me on his stallion, all fancied up in his dress outfit, sitting proud in that saddle of his with its silver trimmings. He got lots of joy outta life, had lots of guts, and he was a true friend.

I tightened my jaw and kept on trudging down the street—not speaking to no one, with my head down and looking right in front of my feet. Then I lifted up my eyes a little and looked 'round me. I weren't gonna spend no more time than was necessary to get a supply of ammunition. Then I was going back to pay them Comanches another visit—a visit they'd never forget.

When I rounded one of the street corners I looked up and seen some light coming out of a cantina. I heard a guitar playing and then some laughter floated out to where I was standing in the darkness. For a few minutes the wildness went outta me. I seen the warmth of the light flooding out on the street and listened to the happy sound of them people's voices. Maybe I'd still be able to mix with my own kind.

Real slow and gentle, like I was looking back into the good memories of the past, I stepped into the light coming outta that door and walked into the cantina. There was lots of laughter and singing and some of the girls and men was dancing over on one side. I could just make 'em out—clapping and stomping—by the light of them colored lanterns that hung from the roof and the candles burning on some of the tables.

A lot of folks was crowded in there—some prospectors and mule skinners, and I seen the uniform of a soldier or two. There was a few buffalo hunters and some surveyors the government'd been sending out.

Mixed in with all of 'em was them pretty Mexican gals. They had their cheeks painted rouge red and some of 'em had lacy shawls on their shoulders and jeweled combs in their hair. Others was running 'round barefoot and plain-looking. They all looked good to me. The only women I'd seen for three months was Comanche squaws. There was warmth and laughter, yet somehow I felt shy and fearful 'bout what to say and do.

Several of them folks 'round the tables looked up and seen me in the doorway and stared. I remembered that maybe I didn't look quite like I did before. I hadn't had a shave in three months and my beard was stained and dirty. My buckskin britches and shirt was blotchy with grease and dust, coated with a lot of old buffalo blood and a little Comanche blood that was more recent.

What was left of my old leather hat hid some of the dirt on the top of my head. My hair was tied in the back with a beaded armband that I'd took from one of them first dead bucks so my hair wouldn't go drooping down in my eyes and spoil my shooting. Though I hadn't seen myself in a mirror for a long time, I reckoned that band stood out real bright above my shoulders.

When I seen 'em run their eyes down and stop, I also remembered I was wearing them Comanche moccasins. There was a pause in the murmur of conversation and the guitars eased off as I stood there in the doorway, but it all started up again when I moved over to a table against the far wall and leaned my rifle in the corner.

I'd no more'n lighted when one of them pretty señoritas come hurrying over and said something to me in Spanish. What little I'd learned of the language had gone outta my head in the last three months, and maybe even if she'd spoke English at first I wouldn't have understood much of what was said. It took a little time to get my brain cranked up to understand her.

As soon as she'd seen I couldn't speak no Mexican, she started talking English, asking me if I'd care for a shot of Taos lightning. I got the idea of that and told her tequila was just what I was looking for.

She brought me a whole mug. I upended it quick and that stuff damn near burnt my throat out. Then I fiddled 'round trying to get my shirt pocket open where it was all stuck together. I finally worked it loose and come up with them twelve dollars. You could tell they was United States currency, but just barely. They was the worst-looking, hardest-hit twelve dollars I'd ever seen. Considering all they'd been through, it weren't surprising. As a matter of fact, I remember thinking that Washington made paper money that sure held up good.

I got a dollar loose from the rest and she took it, so I reckoned it still passed for money. She was back soon with the change in pesos and I had me a couple more shots. I sat there taking in the smell of sweat and perfume, watching them dancers and listening to the guitars and the talking 'round me. I heard voices, but I didn't seem to be able to connect them up with much. It made a nice noise in the background, but I didn't care, 'cause I felt like I was sitting 'round amongst my own kind. The sights and sounds and smells got me outta the mood I'd been in, and that Taos lightning glowed warm in my belly.

If I'd just finished the Chisholm Trail and come into a cantina like that a year ago, I'd have sure been wild and raring to go. I would've been fixing to take me a piece of ass off'n one of them Mexican gals, and I might've even cast 'round and tried three or four of 'em 'fore the night was out. I would've got drunk for sure and got in some fights and had myself a helluva time. But I didn't feel like that no more.

There I was, only nineteen years old, and I felt like an old man. Not in the body, but my spirit was down. I'd seen so much. Like so many of them boys that'd come outta the war feeling much the same way— young fellas that'd left the farm at sixteen or seventeen, seen Shiloh and the second Battle of Bull Run and the like, and when they'd come back at twenty, they was old men.

Well, I was dreaming along like that and didn't pay no attention to the señoritas who come up and tried to make conversation. I sat there and poured down the Taos lightning, peeled off another one of them moldy dollar bills, and drunk some more.

Now, in them days, if you drunk two dollars' worth of Taos lightning, your soul filled up with fire. It weren't no different with me. The room went to swaying 'round and things blurred out to where I weren't worrying too much 'bout nothing, just enjoying myself sitting dreamy quiet over there in the corner, sipping tequila and sorta edging my hip up against the wall so's I could feel the Winchester rifle tight against my thigh.

After a while, my eyes come back into focus and I realized that there was somebody standing in front of my table. When I looked over I seen it was a big man, wearing them blue britches of the U.S. Cavalry. My eyes traveled on up and I seen the buckle of his belt and then the collar and cuffs that marks a trooper. He was standing there swaying, a big-boned Irishman with a ruddy red face and cheeks, a stub nose, and squinting eyes. He had the head of a big pig, all soft and puffy, even though he must've spent lots of time in the saddle. He weren't no recruit. He just stood there weaving back and forth and staring down at me, holding a whiskey bottle in his hand.

It disturbed me a little bit. I reckon it was 'cause I hadn't had a human being look at me for a long time—leastwise not real close up. I shifted 'round a little bit and thought, this bastard reminds me a that no-good varmint McIntyre. He'd acted like him, too, standing there with his feet wide apart, staring down with a sneer on his face like he was telling the whole world what a miserable son of a bitch I was. I couldn't figure out why he was interfering with me. I sure didn't know him, so there weren't no reason for him to be like that.

He leaned down and put his face close to mine. I still remember the greasy sweat on his face and the nasty stink of his breath.

He blinked his piggy little eyes and reached over and slurred out, "Well, if'n it ain't an old tweaky-beard mountain man hisself." Then he give my beard a good jerk and started laughing like hell.

What he'd done was like setting the fuse to a barrel of dynamite. Everything happened so fast that even now I can't recollect exactly how it went. All I know is that I come up outta that seat like a coiled spring. My fist shot out like a cannonball, and everybody in the room could hear his jaw crack.

He hadn't no more'n hit the floor when I picked up the table by the legs and smashed it over his head and shoulders. It was one crash following another. The whole place went crazy. Women begun to scream, and outta the corner of my eye I seen some more troopers get up and head for me.

Then that .38 of mine come out so fast you couldn't see it. I stood there, crouching like a tiger ready to spring. I didn't say nothing. I just looked at them boys and they stopped in their tracks. Then a hush settled over the place. Everybody stood still, looking at me. I eased over to pick up my rifle and kept my eye on them troopers. They knowed from my look that if they'd made a move, they was dead men. When a man draws as fast as that, it's a signal.

Then, holding the .38 on them blue-coated flatheads, I eased my way towards the door and stepped out into the dark. Right away I run down the street a ways and ducked off into a side street. I'd come into Taos to rest up and get my bearings and some more ammunition. I sure as hell weren't looking for that kinda fun, but there ain't no man alive that can lay a hand on me in an insult and get away with it. But I'd squared matters up and I weren't looking for no more trouble.

I figured I'd better hike on outta there, so I moved fast. In fifteen minutes I was back outta town in the open, looking up at the sky. It was a cool night, the stars was bright, and there was a gentle wind. I walked around considerable—maybe an hour or two—'fore I cooled down.

Along one of them dirt roads south of town I seen in the starlight where there was a small hayfield. Although things was hazy, I remember crawling over the fence out into the field, and lying down in front of a haystack and looking up at the stars. The next thing I knowed, I woke up with the warm sun shining on my face and my head was near to busting. The knuckles of my right hand felt sore and swole up, and I was puzzled 'bout it at first. Then I remembered the sound of that trooper's jaw cracking and I felt some better 'bout my whole condition.

I took stock of things. I had my rifle with me, and my small bag of pemmican was still hanging from my belt along with the war club. I felt 'round real easy with my fingers and there was that Smith & Wesson .38 sticking in my holster. I reckoned everything was just fine. I went over to the irrigation ditch and got me a little water and mixed it in the palm of my hand with some pemmican. I kneaded me up a ball and sat there chewing on the stuff, slow and easy, just munching away in the sunshine and thinking.

I weren't feeling so old as I had the night before. Things was brighter and better, and although I was dirty and my beard was just as long, I still felt like a new man—like I'd broke through into civilization again and that things was gonna be fine. After all, it ain't no fun getting back to civilization if you can't get drunk and have a good fight.

I got to thinking 'bout the Ruiz family. I reckoned I'd go back to Taos and stop off at their house. They needed to know 'bout old Pedro, although I sure hated to tell 'em. They'd been real nice to us when we'd been there that winter, and they'd treated Pedro like a son. They'd know how to get the word to his folks in Chihuahua. 'Sides that, they might be able to put me on to some work so's I could buy me some more ammunition.

Folks was coming and going in every direction and nobody seemed to pay much attention to me. So I come on back into town, avoiding that cantina, and made my way through the narrow streets 'til I come to the Ruizes' house.

I knocked on their door. The old señora come and opened it a crack and looked at me puzzledlike. Ain't no wonder she didn't recognize me, what with all that beard and dirt and me looking like general hell.

Then I said to her in English, "Ma'am, it's me—Cat Brules—Pedro's amigo."

Then she throwed open the door and held her hands up in the air and started talking in Spanish. I couldn't understand nothing she was saying. Finally, she grabbed me by the arm and asked me to come in. She could speak a little English, and her husband was right good at it when he wanted to be. She called out something, and from one of the back rooms come Señor Ruiz hisself. I thought what a fine old couple they was: Them folks never acted like I was anything but the best, as if I was all dressed up like a gentleman and no questions asked.

She brought out some coffee and right away I felt it was time for me to raise the subject of how I was dressed by way of explanation. So I started apologizing, but they wouldn't hear none of it.

The old señor told me, "No, amigo, you did not need to apologize. You are the nobleman of the plains. I see that you and Pedro have been hunting the buffalo and have been so successful. I see from the way the clothes look on you that you have done well. You and Pedro must have many hides and you make a lot of money, no? Ah, he is a fine man, that young Pedro. He like you so much, he really like you, and he say you are the best shot in all the Southwest. So you kill a lot of buffalo, no? I bet you kill a lot. Our Pedro, now tell me, where is Pedro? He come in a few minutes, no?"

It was with a heart like lead that I had to look the old boy in the eye and say, "Señor and Señora Ruiz, Pedro ain't comin' back. He's buried out there on the prairie."

I ain't never seen nothing like it. Them two old folks turned plumb pale. Then the old señora let out a shriek and held her hands up to her mouth, trembling all over. You'd have thought that Pedro was her own child. Then they both looked at me with so much hurt in their eyes that I reckoned they had to know, so I told 'em slow and plain what'd happened, everything from beginning to end.

Through it all, the old woman held her hand over her mouth as if she was in shock. The old man sat there, nodding with them sharp eyes, taking it all in and understanding all of it. His eyes was brimming with tears.

I didn't describe everything—there weren't no need to. There weren't no secret 'bout what happened when the Comanches got you. There ain't nothing a Mexican hates much more'n a Comanche—not even a rattlesnake.

When I got through they just sat there in silence, the old woman sobbing and holding a handkerchief to her face and the old man silent, with fresh tears running down his face. 'Course I told 'em I'd killed a lot of Comanches in revenge and I was headed out to get more as soon's I could lay my hands on a little ammunition. But it didn't do no good, and finally I just sat there fumbling with that old leather hat of mine.

I seen that there weren't no use in staying. Them folks was too hard hit to think 'bout anything else. I got up, mumbled a few excuses, then eased towards the door while they watched me go. When I swung it open they both stood up. They never said nothing, just looked at me. I eased on out, closed the door real slow and quiet, and walked off down the street.

I didn't have nowhere to go. I walked past all the hurry and bustle—the teamsters and the mule wagons, the ox teams, the bull-whackers cracking their whips and cussing, the women scurrying 'round in the marketplace in the plaza—and I kept on walking. I walked north on outta town, and it was a long time 'fore I realized that I was on the road to Fort Garland.

The year before, when I'd come up the Chisholm Trail, I'd never dreamt of going anywhere without a horse. But I'd sure come to realize how much more flexible and independent a man could be when he's on foot, how much quicker he could hide and how much easier it was to cover his trail, and how he could travel without no noise and less chance of spooking game. Most folks don't travel much on foot, 'cause they need to take too much gear. They need a bedroll, a bunch of camping supplies, water, extra clothes, and other things.

Now, when I come outta that Comanche country it was different. All I'd needed to carry was my rifle, a little ammunition, my revolver, pemmican, water, my knife, that war club, and fire steel. When I needed to sleep I could roll up in a bunch of leaves and brush and tuck myself under some adobe bank. I was free as the breeze—freer'n an Indian even, him with all his spirits and customs and troubles with other tribes. I didn't need to get tied up in no obligations with no man.

With Pedro gone, I didn't really owe nobody nothing. I seen in some ways that getting tied too close to a human being could be a drag on you. Take that old Ruiz couple. Then I decided that even though I was still a young man with my whole life spread out ahead of me, I'd seen enough to know that life weren't gonna last forever. The more entanglements you got into, the tougher it was in the parting.

I figured I'd live alone for a while and see what happened. I could look at the sky and the clouds and the mountains and drink from the streams and eat off the game on the land. I wouldn't follow no laws 'cept the laws of nature, and when it come time to die, I'd go back into the earth like I'd come out of it—with nobody grieving. As long as no man or woman meant anything to me, I wouldn't be hurt in the leastwise.

I'd run the course of my life like them animals that took to the ways of freedom on the prairies and in the mountains. Ain't none of 'em sad. When they're afraid, they run off from man or other enemies. They ain't none of 'em doing any mourning nor any thinking 'bout what's gonna happen to 'em. They live and enjoy living, and they're a part of the scheme of things. Only man, trying to get hisself something permanent, trying to fight an impossible battle, is the one that saddens his own heart. I didn't aim to do that. So I kept right on walking, trying to get as far away as I could from Taos and them tears of grief.

I'd took the Fort Garland Trail just outta instinct. Maybe in the back of my mind I thought there might be something up that way—somewhere's I could get me some more ammunition. Or maybe it was that I was out for a good long walk.

In the early afternoon I come to the Valdez hacienda. A thought struck me and I turned aside to give 'em the bad news. I wondered at myself for turning into the Valdez place after the upset I'd give the Ruiz folks. Maybe this'd be the last act to separate myself from any real close association with humans.

When I trotted up to the walls of the hacienda I couldn't help thinking how different it was from the night I'd come off the mountain that fall before. The dogs barked again all right, but it was daylight and old Señora Valdez looked out and seen a man coming at a steady jog, carrying a rifle in his hand and wearing buckskin clothes and Comanche footgear.

She stepped out the door and called to old man Valdez over by the corrals. He come to the big gate to meet me. Neither of 'em knowed who I was 'til I got right up to 'em and give 'em a greeting. Then the old man hurried out to give me a big hug, took me by the arm, and brought me over to the old señora. Soon the Valdez boys and that young señorita with the bright eyes that I'd been looking at so much when I was there before come out and started milling 'round and giving me the big greeting.

That's the way it was with folks them days, 'specially towards somebody that looked like a mountain man. They seemed to open up their hearts to 'em—like they was some kinda hero or something. I reckon that's what I'd looked like, with my heavy beard and that old buckskin shirt and Indian footgear and rifle and that old hat and a band tying back my long hair. The whole West, back to the days of Daniel Boone, had been opened up by mountain men. Most of 'em looked the same—dirty and grizzled and weather-beat, wearing buckskin clothes that'd seen lots of wear, and carrying a rifle, a knife, maybe a war club, a small bag of pemmican, and a keen, hard look in their eye.

I guess that's what it was that fascinated both the men and the women, and in fact all ages. When a man'd been out on the prairies or the mountains by hisself living off his own wit, there was something 'bout him, some kinda atmosphere that seemed to catch on. His eye was keener and fiercer, he weren't give to too much talk, and when he did he had something to tell of far-off places. When them mountain men come in, the menfolk'd gather 'round and listen real jealous to the stories 'bout the roaring waters of the Columbia, or the geysers of the Yellowstone, or the snowy ranges of the Sierras or the Rockies, or their countings of buffalo on the open plain and their tales of the Indians from Pawnee country to California.

That was how the frontier folks got their information as to where the trails was, where the water holes was, and what to look for when they was traveling with their slow wagons. They knowed the value of listening to the mountain man's experiences. But there was more to it than that. In many ways, in every man's soul there's a grinding and a yearning to be off on his own. I seen it lots of times when I was a kid, when them genuine mountain men'd come back from the West and all the folks'd gather 'round while the men'd question 'em 'bout this and that.

You could see in the men's eyes that they was wishing they'd guts enough to be free as the breeze and on their way. Then they'd look back at their families and they'd sigh and realize they was yoked up for life.

The mountain man, he was free. He traveled from tribe to tribe and covered the country from one end to the other. The frontier folks knowed this—both the men and the womenfolk—and the women thought of the mountain man as a hero. They'd look at him and see how puny and scared their husbands was compared to this fierce man who'd come outta the wild country, traveling all on his own. They all knowed it was dangerous. They all knowed that a man had to have wits and eyes and savvy and strength or he weren't coming back. The mountain men was the legend of the opening of the Old West all the way from the Alleghenies to the Pacific. The legend was still alive and real strong even as late as that summer of 1868, though of course I weren't no real mountain man then.

"Ah, amigo," said old man Valdez, "come in the hacienda. Say how you be. How the buffalo hunt, eh? We hear from Santa Fe you go for the buffalo. You are with Pedro and you two do fine? I see you have killed many buffalo, no? Where is Pedro now? I s'pose he come along quick too, no?"

So it was to be the same again. I was slow to answer. It weren't 'til I got in and sat down and the old señora give me a cup of that strong coffee I remembered so well that I'd the guts to tell 'em what'd happened to Pedro. I talked and the señor translated.

'Course they was terrible shocked at the news and started asking me questions 'til I told 'em what happened. When I got through, there was a long silence. I didn't feel like continuing on to say what I'd done by way of avenging his death.

The old man spoke first, and he let out a loud, "¡Madre de Dios!" followed by a long stream of cussing in Spanish that give us to understand what he thought of them Comanches. He walked to the door of the hacienda and throwed it open and spit, like he was cleaning the bitter story outta his mouth. The old señora sat there with her hands crossed in her lap, looking down real sad, and I could see the young señorita, her eyes wide open, watching me in wonderment. The two boys just sat there, too, and I could see the hate in their eyes.

Then the señor inquired as to what, if anything, I'd done about it. They was all familiar with Comanche ways. I reckon they thought right away that there weren't much one man could do. They prob'ly took it that I'd left the scene of Pedro's death and come away with the Frenchman Dubeck and them greaser skinners—that I must've come back to Fort Union or Santa Fe and then on up the trail.

'Fore I could answer, one of the boys asked, "Where is your horse? Did you lose him to the Comanche, too?"

I nodded.

"Ah," said the old man. "You lose the horse, but I see you gain the Comanche moccasins, no? Maybe you make to the Comanche a little payment for Pedro's death, no?"

I nodded again, but I didn't think it was worthwhile giving him no details. "Señor Valdez, Pedro was my only real friend. There ain't nobody—white, black, or red—that could've done Pedro harm 'thout crossin' me, too. Them Comanches killed my amigo an' I aim ta make 'em pay. I done some good so far—killed nigh unta twenty-five of 'em—but I got lots more score ta settle, an' I'm headin' back inta Comanche country quick as I can get me some ammunition."

At that, old man Valdez raised his eyebrows, looked at me for a long time, and then he spoke soft. "Ah, amigo, I see you tell the truth. It is a very real thing you feel about Pedro, and he had the same feelings for you. He tell me when he was here that you are the finest frien' he ever know, like a blood brother. This is strong. Sometimes they say, you know, the feeling of a man for a woman may be a wax and a wane, like maybe the moon, but the feeling of a brother for a brother is a steady one, like maybe the stars. Now I see by the fine eye you have, that you mean what you say when you want to avenge Pedro. My heart is with you, but I must tell you, young hombre, in my head it tells me that maybe there is enough killing, and that maybe you should go on somewhere to the west and make your home. Leave the murderous Comanches to the hell and the devil that will claim them someday."

He stopped and looked at me to see the effect of his words, but I didn't wait much as I knew my answer. I shook my head. "No, Señor Valdez, I 'preciate what yore tellin' me. Yore a man that knows a lot more 'bout life than me. But every man has a right ta live his own life, an' I intend that mine is gonna be lived avengin' Pedro an' Michelle. 'Fore I'm gone, many a Comanche buck is gonna leave this world ta serve in hell. It ain't no use in talkin' ta me no more 'bout that. I done made up my mind an' I'm on my way."

The whole family sat there in silence staring at me. While I was looking hard at the old man, he shuddered a little and broke away from my glance. I seen the boys staring at me with open fascination and the old lady still sitting there in her chair with her head down, kinda pale and not daring to look at me. In the corner, the little señorita huddled with pinched cheeks and an almost frightened look on her face.

Well, there weren't much to talk about after what I'd said. They invited me for the evening meal and I accepted, then they offered me the courtesy of the bed and room that me and Pedro'd slept in before, but I reckoned I'd spent too much time in the open by then to feel comfortable in any man's house.

When we finished supper I thanked 'em for the food and said my best good-byes, first to the señora, next the children, and then the old man. With that I clapped on my old hat, took my rifle from where it was leaning up against the wall, and went outta the hacienda and through the gate.

EQUAL TO TWENTY MEN

I hit up a good jog and made fif-
teen more miles towards Fort Garland that night before I curled up in
a dry wash by the trail. I couldn't help but think that I could've asked
Valdez for money to buy ammunition.

Then I thought about it twice and figured that it weren't a good
idea. I'd just be getting myself into debt by asking for anything. I'd
have to get what I wanted by myself without no asking.

I didn't have much hope of finding no .44 ammunition for sale at
the fort, though, 'cause them cavalry outfits still had single-shot
carbines. That was my frame of mind when I come into Fort Garland
and went to the sutler's store. Although there weren't many buffalo in
the San Luis Valley—prob'ly not any—you could always see buffalo
hunters that'd come from Pueblo way, so there weren't nothing
strange 'bout my coming in and asking for .44 rimfire ammunition.
The storekeeper told me that he didn't have none there at that time.

I was real disappointed, but I did see a box of .38 shells, and I
bought it in a hurry. I spent three bucks of the ten I had left for twenty
rounds. It was expensive, but that's what ammunition cost on the
frontier in them days. The storekeeper give me a good steer though,
telling me that a freight outfit'd come through that morning, and he'd
heard tell that one of 'em was carrying ammunition for some stores

down along the Taos-Santa Fe run and it was possible that there might be some .44 rimfire.

I hurried down to where the freight wagons was parked. I knowed how them freight boys liked to talk, having been one myself, so it didn't take me long to get next to the driver of the wagon that had all that ammunition. He told me he couldn't sell none of it, 'cause it was all consigned to a merchant in Santa Fe. When I asked him why he'd come over the Fort Garland route, he said they'd got orders outta Fort Larned and routed the train that way on account of some Comanche trouble on the Santa Fe Trail below Raton.

That bit of news made my mind tingle a little, learning that there was Comanches closer'n I'd figured—and not too damn far away. If only I could get me some ammunition!

I took a hard look at the driver and made me a plan. I told him I was looking for .44 rimfire and he said he didn't know if he had any of that in the shipment a'tall. It was all in cases, and anyhow he couldn't sell none of it, as he'd said before, so I'd have to see the merchant in Santa Fe. I told him I'd already figured that, and that I reckoned I'd have to go farther up the San Luis Valley and then come back to that Santa Fe merchant to get me some ammunition from him. But I sure didn't want to make that long trip if there weren't no .44 stuff available.

He said he'd talk to the other drivers and ask if they remembered loading any. One of 'em reckoned there was a case of .44 rimfire cartridges he'd loaded back in Independence, but he couldn't swear to it. Anyway, they was too busy taking care of the mules and one thing and another to go looking through the wagon for me.

I said that was fair enough and pitched in to help them boys with their mules. When they got through, I invited 'em down to the cantina for a shot of tequila. That broke the ice. We went in there and had us a few shots. The boys mixed it up a little bit with the Mexican whores who was always hanging 'round them army posts in the Southwest. I'd been a long time on the road and them gals looked mighty inviting, but I'd more important business on my mind.

I kept buying the boys drinks 'til I'd spent most of the seven dollars I had left, and I got the driver of the ammunition wagon drunk enough to where he figured we was real tight buddies. He swore he'd do me any favor I wanted. If he had any .44 rimfire ammunition, he'd give it to me. I could pay his buyer later. He was being real generous with the other man's money. 'Course I told him what a helluva fine fella he was and said I never would've made it without him—which was true. It was getting late and it didn't take very long for me to talk him into going back to the wagon and taking a look at what he had.

There was enough light to see what we was doing. I stumbled 'round and crawled onto his wagon. It was all battened down with ropes and canvas. We was in the spirit of don't give a damn, so I took out my knife and sliced 'round them tie-down ropes and the tarp that was over the ammunition. I cut a hole here and there to take a peek, peering through all them cables on the outside of the wooden cases.

It took lots of slicing and hacking away, but I finally found one case that made the night worthwhile. Right there, real clear it said, "Winchester Arms Company, .44 rimfire, 280-grain lead bullet." 'Tween us two drunks we worked that case out far enough to where I could get a pinch bar on the side and jerk off the end panel. I slipped out ten packs of twenty cartridges each—two hundred rounds. It was heavier'n what I wanted to carry, but I reckoned I'd better be long than short.

We patched up the load as best we could, and by that time the wagon driver was 'bout ready to pass out, so I didn't have to argue none with him. We shook hands like old buddies making a deal and then he collapsed. I found a piece of tarp and throwed it over him. I cut off the corner, got some rope and made a so-so pack out of it, and put my ammunition in it. I picked up my rifle and headed off as the sun was coming up over the mountains.

I cut south of LaVeta Pass, climbing high into the Sangre de Cristos. By midday I was above timberline 'round twelve or thirteen thousand feet. Maybe ten miles ahead of me was a ridge I knowed real well. It was the one I'd rode Paint over when the Comanches was dogging me, after I'd left my fort on the rockslide. 'Round late afternoon, I topped that ridge and worked my way over to the eastern side, just following along at the edge of the timber.

When I come up on the rockslide, I had to stop and take a long, hard look at them big blocks of rock where I'd holed up. I didn't take the time to go up the hill to see if there was any of them horse skeletons still left, and there weren't no use looking for no Comanche skeletons. I went down into the timber and slipped 'round the bottom side of the rockslide and kept heading down off the mountain to the southeast, going back down in the general direction that I'd come up so desperate when I was making my escape—only this time I weren't desperate. I worked on down, and by sunset I was out of the blue spruce and into the quakies.

'Fore dark I come up on a doe in a small park. Her big mule ears was turned and listening to something she'd heard coming down the mountain. I stepped out in the clearing and she stood there and looked at me while I shot her through the head with my Winchester. I dressed her out and built a fire and had a real nice meal. I sliced up most of her back strap so's I could make jerky out of it.

There was a pile of old quakie deadfalls right nearby with last year's leaves under 'em, so I rolled up under that brush and got me a good night's sleep. It'd been two nights since I'd done any sleeping, and having traveled a good fifty miles and got drunk besides, I figured there weren't no reason why I shouldn't take a little rest.

I woke up at first light and seen a handsome scene. As the morning sun grew brighter it became harder to see real details at a great distance in the haze, although I hoped if I looked real hard I might see any distant smoke—maybe seventy-five or a hundred miles away—or perhaps a cloud of dust that might mean buffalo or something even more important, but I still couldn't see nothing stirring.

Then I picked up the jerky that was fairly well dried and put it in the canvas bag along with the ammunition. Carrying my rifle, I hiked towards the southeast, angling down off the mountain. It weren't long 'fore I was in the oak brush and down to where I could look out and see that small valley and the tiny creek running off'n the Cimarron where them Comanches'd staked me out that night I'd escaped from 'em. I kept on going downhill easylike, keeping my eyes open and taking care to be quiet.

I reckon I'd gone 'bout half a mile when I jerked up quick. I smelt smoke. Sure enough, smoke is something that a lone man comes up on mighty cautious. Could be that it was trappers, or a hunter, or a camp of prospectors, or a wagon outfitter. Even better, it might be an Indian camp. When I thought of that, my heart got to pounding. So I took it easy, following the scent real careful. I crawled up to peer over a ridge, and 'bout four hundred yards away I seen that thing I like to see most—the top cluster of a tepee's poles.

I stayed right where I was, dead still for the better part of an hour, and the smell of the smoke begun to fade. Seemed like the fire'd gone out. Peeking down through the oak brush to the clearing below, I could see the tips of one set of poles. If I was ever seen, Comanche hunting would go all to hell for that day.

It weren't no trouble for me to lie absolutely motionless. I didn't hear the sounds of no voices or nothing. As the sun got a little higher, I looked 'round to see where I could get a better view without exposing myself. There was a little knob off to my left that was clean in line with the sun, and I got to it without being seen.

It looked like there was only one tepee. I figured the distance to be right at three hundred yards. It sure was a nice place to camp, and I realized again that it was the same clearing I had sick memories of. It made me shudder to think how close I'd come to supplying them slime with amusement.

I spent most of the day in a slow crawl. By four in the afternoon, I'd got to 'bout a hundred fifty yards from the tepee and was in a good position to see the layout. It sure was a fine campground, with good water and lots of grass for ponies. The fact that there weren't no ponies staked out in the meadow near the cottonwoods was sure puzzling. The grass was tall and green, it being well into the middle of June, and as the sun kept working 'round to the west and giving me a lot better look at things, I seen that the camp was deserted.

But out in the meadow beside the trees, I seen a sight that curdled my blood. There was a couple of wooden posts, half-charred by fire. I seen with horror that they was the kinda posts that Michelle'd been tied to when they'd burned her alive. Whatever skeleton was there was gone now, thank God, and I didn't go no closer. I looked 'round the deserted camp real mystified, and then suddenly it all come to me. This was a sacred place to the Comanches. The tepee was a medicine lodge. The shaman, or medicine man, had prob'ly been there a few days making medicine and then left a few hours before. He prob'ly wouldn't be back for some time.

Inside the tepee was a little ground corn, a few strips of jerky that looked like antelope meat, some blankets next to a lance, and a quiver and some arrows over against one wall.

Then I seen something that I decided I'd really like to have—a necklace of bear claws. It sure was nice. It'd come off'n a big grizzly and the nineteen claws hanging on it was strung on a piece of rawhide with some turquoise beads 'tween 'em. I reckoned the medicine man'd got it off'n a grizzly he'd killed and somehow or other that grizzly'd been missing one claw. That's usually the way it is by the time a grizzly gets big enough to grow claws like that—he'd been in lots of fights and maybe a trap or two. Anyway, he must've been a big one, 'cause them claws was better'n three inches long.

I slung the bear-claw necklace over my head so's it hung down 'round my neck and fondled it with my fingers. It was 'bout the only vain thing I'd ever done in my life. Since I didn't see nothing else in the tepee that interested me, I figured maybe the best thing to do'd be to fire it. Then I thought 'bout taking a piece of burnt wood and painting the sign of the Cat on all sides of the tepee and let it sit there for a Comanche party to come along and find. I chuckled at the thought. They'd know then that old Cat Brules'd paid a visit.

Then I seen a piece of hide lying on the ground that I hadn't paid much attention to. It was just what I wanted—elk hide. I took out my knife and cut a nice slice big enough to make two more soles for my moccasins. I figured I'd be doing lots of walking, 'cause I planned to spend most of the summer in that high country and out on them mesas looking for Comanches I reckoned'd be up there hunting buffalo.

I figured I'd wait to get me a horse 'til the leaves fell off the trees in the late fall. When the winds was blowing and the buffalo'd gone off on their big circle south, then the Comanche travois'd head out in long strings, towards the Llano Estacado and down 'cross the Canadian River. That'd be the time to get me a horse.

I took one last look 'round the clearing. If Comanches should find my sign of the Cat, they'd go crazy trying to figure it out. It just weren't the Comanche way to come along and paint the sign of the Cat and never leave no horse tracks or disturb the tepee.

The sun'd gone down behind the hills when I lit out along the stream, angling a little southwest, gaining altitude on the side of the mountain. It weren't my intention to camp that night, but to keep traveling. That was another good thing 'bout going on foot: I could make good time at night in the rough and not leave much trail. Following a man in moccasins when he's been thinking 'bout how to hide his tracks is impossible at night even for an Indian, and in daylight only the best trackers can do it.

I'd got clear up through the quakies to the edge of the blue spruce when I found a real steep ravine filled with a lot of brush. I crawled down into it and holed up for some sleep just as day was breaking. One thing I'd knowed for sure was to hide out in some thick brush—

so thick that nobody within ten yards could see you. You couldn't see out of it, of course, but anybody getting to you'd have to make lots of noise.

I slept 'til noon and then eased out of my hole and made my way diagonal again, this time southeast and downhill. Pretty soon I come across a small stream and mixed a little of the pemmican I'd made with some water and started nibbling.

I was a ways south of Raton Pass, and I figured it wouldn't be long 'fore I'd come up on the Taos cutoff. I wanted to cross the Santa Fe Trail south of there and I sure didn't wanta spend any more time than I could help in the open basin country that separated the mountains from the mesas. I reckoned I'd work on south in the timber 'til I crossed the Taos trail, and then in the night I'd make for the mesas.

I was pushing as fast as I could. The sod was still soft from the melting snows of spring, so I was able to move real quiet along them quakie groves. When I was maybe five miles from the Taos cutoff, I come up over a rise and was looking down a ravine and 'cross to the timbered hill on the other side when I seen a flash of color and movement. Real quick, I faded behind a fallen log and hid there watching. Sure enough, I seen it again. And then more of it. There, weaving in and out among the quakies that was still greening with spring leaves was a long line of Comanche warriors. It was a war party all right. They was all decked out in their brilliant paint and feathers and was riding every kinda horse you can imagine—paints of black, tan, and white, Appaloosas, and bays and blacks. Some of 'em was carrying lances and shields and a few of 'em had guns. From that distance, I couldn't tell whether they was rifles or smoothbore, but they sure as hell made a handsome sight, wearing their buffalo-horned helmets, all riding stripped to the waist, brave and proud on as fine a bunch of ponies as I'd ever seen.

Like always, when I come near Comanches, the blood rose hot in me and the instinct to kill growed strong. But there was something in the back of my mind that held me cautious. Hunting Comanches was prob'ly the most dangerous game a man could play.

I'd realized how, in my hands, a repeating rifle was equal to twenty men, but I'd also had sense enough to know it had its limitations. I'd took on a war party near this size out in the open prairie, banked up against a horse's belly, but it wouldn't be the same story here in the depths of the forest. There was too much for 'em to hide behind and it was too easy for 'em to get up on me. I could kill a couple of 'em, but then they'd be coming at me from every direction like a swarm of hornets.

I lay low and kept watching. It sure was a fascinating sight—that line of Indian horsemen winding 'round the hillside like a beautiful, many-colored snake, and I reckon it was a hundred times as dangerous. I could see glimpses of it here and there gliding in and out of the timber and marveled at the quiet as it moved along in single file. It reminded me of a long line of elk heading out to the high country in back of their leader, 'cept instead of 'em being that soft tan color, they was sharp patches of red and white and yellow and black and brown.

I watched 'em as they curled up over the hill 'til the last warrior passed outta sight. Then I stayed there for a long time waiting to see if something else was coming. I was real surprised to find a war party that close to the settlements, and it seemed fair obvious what they was doing. They'd had to cross the Santa Fe and Taos trails to get to where they was, so's they weren't just wandering. They must've been headed out for a purpose. They was either going to attack some of them ranches 'round Taos or they was fixing to waylay a wagon train of immigrants or freighters.

When I was sure it was clear, I left that fallen log, pitched on down the hill in a hurry, and went on up the other side to have me a good look at their tracks. I seen what I expected—all them horses' hooves was hide covered to make 'em move silent and easy and smooth through the forest. They weren't figuring on no hard riding but rather to lay ambush, and I reckoned that meant they was gonna hit a wagon train. I could've gone down to the Taos Trail and tried to spread a warning, but I weren't in the business of playing scout for no freighters or settlers. I had my own game to play, and I reckoned I'd move on and mind my own business.

I kept on due south and 'fore long I come up on the Taos Trail. I seen it through a break in the timber and looked in both directions to check if there was any traffic moving along it. By that time it'd become my instinct to stay hid when I could, moving silent, like a wild thing, and staying outta the way of all men—at least 'til I was ready to strike.

I didn't see nothing coming, so I slid 'cross and down through the timber to where the headwaters of the Cimarron was gurgling and churning over the rocks. I filled my canteen and crossed the stream, then headed up over the other side and southeast along a ridge of timber. I reckoned that when I got to the end of it, I'd be able to see clear 'cross the big basin and the Santa Fe Trail to them mesas in the east.

'Fore sundown I was on a high part of the ridge where I could see through an opening in the timber and look off to the west. The sun was going down in back of them snowcapped peaks and the long shadows was stretching away 'cross the blue spruce and quakie mantle of the foothills. Off in the distance I heard some firing, and a little later I seen a column of smoke rising 'bout ten miles away to the northeast. There weren't no mistaking that the war party'd hit something—maybe a wagon train, maybe a ranch, maybe one of them relay stations along the trail.

Well, whatever it was, it was done. I reckoned that while them bloody bastards was burning and pillaging along the Taos Trail—and maybe as far as the San Luis Valley—I'd be paying 'em back in the heart of their own nation, punch for punch.

I hiked back over to where I could take stock of the trail situation, and seen one long column of dust a little bit to the east. It was a wagon train making for a grove of cottonwoods. That'd be the logical place for 'em to camp. Otherwise, there weren't nothing moving.

I didn't pause to rest or eat but just trotted down off'n the ridge. By the time it was real deep dark, I'd moved out into the open sagebrush flats of the basin and was headed towards them big mesas ten to twenty miles to the east. All night long I kept up an easy jog, swinging my rifle first in one hand and then the other. 'Long 'bout midnight I crossed the Santa Fe Trail for the third time in a year, then I climbed up the nearest mesa to where the oak brush met the cap rock. As dawn broke, I holed up in a good hiding place and slept the day through.

At sundown, I ate a little more pemmican, took a swig from my canteen, and started southeast along the string of mesas. I traveled all through the night, moving right along, picking my way to find the easiest going. The excitement kept mounting in me as I got close to a Comanche campground I'd visited before.

When the next dawn broke I judged I was only fifteen miles from that campground. I s'pose it would've been best if I'd slept all day, but I was too keyed up. After 'bout three hours lying under a pile of leaves and brush, I was ready to go on. It was midmorning, but the oak brush was thick and I could stay right along the cap rock and keep well outta sight. So it was that 'long 'bout noon, perhaps a little after, I come 'round the north side of the last mesa, moving real cautious, and eased forward 'til I could peer down into the campground where I'd seen them Comanches twice before.

It was a great place, with a spring pouring out good water and lots of grass feed for miles 'round. The big old cap rock of the mesa shielded the camp from the west wind and there was plenty of places where big blocks of rock'd rolled down from the top and settled in the lonely oak brush—places where a tepee could be pitched and be outta the wind from most any direction. It was a natural place. If there was any Comanches in the country, that's where they'd be camped.

It was a great disappointment when I eased my head up over the edge of a big flat rock, looked down below, and seen that there weren't nothing there a'tall. I lay there for a real long time. That's always a good idea when you're out on the frontier. If you got a good view, you take your time to look it all over and not show yourself 'til you know what the situation is. So that's what I done.

First I looked 'round the spring and seen that the tracks was old. I looked where them tepees'd been pitched and seen where the traces of 'em was still in the grass, although it was midsummer and the grass was coming up good. Indians always set their tepees with the opening facing to the east. That protects 'em from the prevailing west winds and also makes it so's when they turn the sides of the tepee back in the morning, the sun fills the inside and warms them that's in it. Then, too, in the afternoon in the summertime, when the sun is real hot, the tepee facing east shades them that sits in front of the opening. I looked far out over the plains to the north and to the south and didn't see no Indian sign—no tepees, no horses, no travois, no clouds of dust—nothing but the shadows of them great big clouds drifting by high up in the blue sky.

The grass was standing tall right 'round the area of the camp-ground, so there hadn't been animals of any kind grazing 'round there in some time. There was at least a thirty-day stand of grass, and there weren't no signs of nothing having crossed through the country, even for an overnight stop.

That puzzled me plenty. It sure was a natural place. On the other hand, maybe the buffalo'd been late or maybe them white buffalo hunters'd been working out deep in Comanche country, by the Canadian and the Red, and'd chiseled down them buffalo herds during the last winter more'n I'd figured.

I told myself that maybe the hunting'd been a little tough and them Comanches'd moved out. I reckon for an ordinary man it would've been natural, after looking over everything, to wander on down and check 'round the campground. But I knowed better'n that. I knowed the ways of the prairies and the mountain country and I knowed what it was like to be cautious.

There weren't no way of telling if there was Indians 'round up on some of them other mesas to the south. Some of 'em had sharp enough eyes to catch the movement of even one lone man on foot out on the open prairie. In any case, I weren't taking no chances. I lay there summing up the situation and figuring that something'd happen to give me a clue.

'Round five o'clock in the afternoon when the sun was starting to sink in the west but was still a long ways from sundown, I seen the shadows of a big cloud moving off far out over the prairie. Watching that shadow move, I seen some black specks. It seemed like there was only a few of 'em at first, but as the shadow of the cloud moved on I begun to pick out more and more and more, and it weren't no trick to figure out what they was. I was looking at a good-sized herd of buffalo maybe twenty-five miles away.

They was scattered and grazing easy, which meant that they hadn't been worked recent. It was puzzling that I hadn't seen them buffalo when I'd come up there at noontime, but that was often the case—I'd seen this happen when I was hunting. The conditions of the sunlight directly overhead or the shadows of some clouds can make it so's even the best man, with the keenest eyes, could miss the whole herd at that distance if they weren't moving and stirring the dust, or if they was just spread out feeding or maybe lying down in the heat of the day. Then along towards evening it seems they appear outta nowhere. That's the way it is with a lot of animals—in fact 'most all of 'em. I don't care whether they're elk, deer, buffalo, or wild horses. There's a period that you don't see anything moving—like the whole world is dead. Three hours later, when the cool of the evening starts, them animals get up and move 'round and you begin to see all sorts of things—whole bands of 'em in places where you'd bet your scalp there weren't nothing.

Judging by the way those animals acted, they hadn't been hunted in a long time, and that meant that there weren't no Comanches in that area.

Much later in the afternoon, when the shadows'd stretched out, I stayed in 'em and worked down off the mesa's east side, careful to keep to the oak brush 'til I come out on the campsite. By that time the sun was going down behind the ridge, so it cast a deep shadow. I reached the spring in the center of the campground—a beautiful little spring that bubbled out from underneath the rocks of the mesa and formed a little pool, then overflowed and lost its way as it trickled off over the prairie.

I cast 'round that campground for some sign of why they'd pulled out. It seemed like they had plenty of grass and water, and there was buffalo in the area. Then I thought maybe there'd been an enemy war party come along—perhaps some Sioux—although it weren't hardly likely that there could be any Sioux that far south, maybe only the southern Cheyenne. I recalled they'd both been confined to their reservations by the Fort Laramie Treaty, but they could've broke outta the reservations. Them damned Indians was always doing something like that. But then, it weren't likely that even a good-sized band of southern Cheyenne'd give too much trouble to the Comanches in the middle of their own hunting grounds.

No, it had to be some other reason. Maybe they'd followed the herds on out to the east and the north, whichever way them herds was moving that time of the year. With the coming of the railroads and all the traffic on the Santa Fe Trail and so much hunting along the Arkansas, the whole traveling habits of the buffalo was getting changed. And yet there was them buffalo grazing real peaceful and looking like they hadn't been hunted for a month.

I wondered if there'd been some kinda peace treaty signed by them Quohadi Comanches, but I reckoned that something like that'd be knowed up and down the frontier if it'd happened, and that war party I'd seen a few days before didn't look or sound like it was peaceful. Surely some men at Fort Garland would've heard 'bout it and I would've got the news from them. Everybody liked to go out and hunt buffalo.

If there'd been some easing off of Comanche pressure, the word would've been passed all 'round and there would've been lots of white men down in there, but I hadn't seen no sign of a white man since I'd crossed the Santa Fe Trail.

I didn't have nothing to do but keep looking, trying to see if I could pick up any sign or clue as to which direction they'd gone. There was some old tepee poles lying there in a pile and also a little travois throwed aside, and in one place a kind of dump where they'd throwed animal bones and other junk, including what was left of an old moth-eat blanket. But, aside from that, there weren't nothing.

I worked on 'round to the face of a steep rock bank—the one I'd crawled down to as I was hunting them bucks when I'd visited that camp the last time. Then it'd been a busy place with dogs barking and squaws shrieking and kids hollering.

I crawled up and scratched me a big old cat's-eye sign right on the rock face. Maybe pretty soon them damned Comanches'd figure out that Mister Cat Brules was gonna bring 'em all the kiss of death and send their very souls to wander forever in hell.

While there was still enough light, I looked 'round to see if'n I couldn't come up with the direction them varmints'd gone. Sure enough I found where the travois and the ponies'd gone out towards the southwest, 'round the south side of the mesa. I'd come in on the north side, and that's why I hadn't picked it up before. I started out and must've moved six miles along 'tween the mesas, following the old track and knowing it couldn't go nowhere else.

I reckon I covered another thirty miles that night. When I seen that it weren't gonna be long 'fore dawn, I found me a good hole against the side of the cliff where I hid and rolled up in some leaves. Hugging my rifle with my head against the stone and my right ear cocked to the wind, I tumbled off to sleep and I slept all through the day. Towards late afternoon I broke outta them leaves and took me a look 'round. It always was a good time to look. In the early morning, it ain't so good, 'cause there's a haze. But by late afternoon, the sun's heated up the prairie and the air is lifted, and most times there's been a rainstorm or two, so everything is real clear and the shadows is long, marking out objects so's you can see 'em at a long distance.

If there's gonna be any campfires, they'll likely be in the late afternoon or towards the evening when the campers—white men or Indians—go to cooking up their evening meal. If there's anybody traveling, like a wagon train or a band of Indians, the dust'll churn up all gold in the afternoon like a stream in the air 'cross the prairie.

That afternoon when the sun was still an hour from going down, its long, sloping rays lit up the prairie and small broken mesas that lay to the southwest. I crawled up on a boulder that'd broke off from the cap rock and lay down up there where I could get a good look at all the surroundings. The sky was still blue and there was a couple of them big old thunderheads tumbling and growling along their way far to the south and southwest on the prairie. From under the flat clouds, a curtain of rain curved in the afternoon breeze and swept like a slow brush across the face of the earth. The rest of the air was clear and it seemed like I could see for almost a hundred miles.

I kept watching and waiting, knowing that it wouldn't be too long 'fore I'd see some sign of action. Sure enough, 'bout four miles away beside a dry sand draw, I seen a flash of the white butts of antelope. There was quite a few in the band, maybe forty or fifty.

I smiled to myself, 'cause I'd been looking there ten minutes before and hadn't seen nothing. They'd got up from the tufts of grass where they'd prob'ly been lying all day and was starting to move about for their evening feed.

Up in the blue sky I seen two eagles wheeling 'round, sailing and drifting towards the southeast with the wind. It weren't much later that a lone coyote trotted across the sand draw 'tween my mesa and the next one. His long, bushy tail trailed behind almost like a fox. He kept turning his head this way and that, looking for something to supply his evening meal. Way off to the distant south, almost on the horizon, I thought I seen some dark specks that might be buffalo, but I couldn't be sure. I strained my eyes and worked at it hard, but I didn't see nothing to make it positive.

I waited there a long time watching one thing and another. Once, a jackrabbit hopped across the pan basin in front of me, and down below I seen two mule deer move outta the oak brush and into a park to start feeding. I looked out towards the southwest and judged that the last mesa 'fore the open panhandle was at least forty miles away. I figured I'd have to travel all night to get there, so I decided I'd best move along and get started if'n I was gonna cover that distance and hole up 'fore dawn.

I took one last look 'round and my eyes lit on something that made me tense real sudden and tremble with excitement. Far out on the prairie to the south was a faint, waving, curling stream of golden smoke in the late afternoon sun. I knowed what it was. It was the dust of passing horsemen maybe fifteen miles away.

I squinted hard and looked down to where I'd first picked it up. There was times when the dust'd fade out, then it'd come back a little stronger 'fore it faded out again. But I kept watching and waiting.

Judging by that dust, they was moving from south to north and it looked like they'd cut 'cross my route of travel somewhere eight or ten miles ahead. If they was what I hoped, I had a promise for some good hunting tonight.

I marked it well where I'd last seen 'em and quickly dropped off that boulder, pitched down through the oak brush, and started 'cross one of the open park ledges that was halfway down the mesas. Then I hit out at a steady trot, heading southwest. Right then I didn't know if they was Indians, but the chances was awful good. It'd be real doubtful to find white men riding out there so far away from the Santa Fe Trail and not in a big rush. If it'd been a cavalry troop, the smoke and the dust would've been many times as big. Less'n they was white buffalo hunters, they had to be Indians.

I kept up that steady trot for twenty minutes. Then I picked me a likely spot and topped out on a small knoll where a pile of rocks made a good lookout place. Sure enough, when I looked over the top of them rocks, the dust trail was much closer. I reckoned the range to be only 'bout seven miles. I spent a few minutes watching 'em careful, but they was still too far away to figure out who they were. It was a small party of horsemen—maybe only three or four—and they was moving along at a steady gait. It looked like they'd cross my trail 'bout a mile ahead. The country was fairly open, with some small distant mesas way behind 'em, but they was crossing a big pan basin heading either towards the mesa that I was on or, more likely, the next one to the west.

Close in, there was a maze of flat mesas, all of 'em with oak brush and cap rock and winding canyons 'tween 'em. If I was to lose them horsemen at dusk, I'd have a helluva time coming up on 'em again.

I watched 'em for a few minutes. Whether they was Indians or white men, it sure weren't no family party—they was moving too fast. If they kept up that pace and I didn't intercept 'em somewhere, I'd never catch up with 'em on foot after they went by.

There was a good-sized pile of rocks 'bout a quarter of a mile ahead with reason'bly smooth going 'tween there and where I was standing. I made up my mind real quick to sprint for it. I covered that distance as fast as any man could've done it and I arrived breathing hard.

I stuck my head up real slow and easy and my heart leaped with the thrill of the hunt. A couple of miles away, three horsemen was coming at a fast lope, and I could see the color of the feathers on the shields and lances and the white spots on the paint horses. I was looking at my natural prey. I judged where their path'd take 'em and seen that there was a real green clump of cottonwoods lying at the base of the mesa ahead. The grass 'round it looked greener and even some of the nearby oak brush'd took on a brighter color. There had to be a spring there and that was what they was headed for.

It was getting on towards dark and they prob'ly wasn't aiming to ride all night. Maybe they'd make camp by that spring. It didn't appear that they was war partying but rather buffalo hunting, 'cause I seen buffalo-horn headgear on only one of them Indians. If it was a hunting party, they'd be pushing on, trying to get to their village and get the squaws out after the meat—assuming that the hunt was successful. If it was a war party, God only knows what plans they had. Anyhow, it was all guesswork. The only way to know was to watch 'em, and that was what I decided to do.

They was gonna cross my path too far ahead for me to intercept 'em and I sure didn't wanta expose myself by making a false move, so I lay real close in amongst them rocks and watched. If they was to pass on without stopping, that'd be the luck of the hunt. They was coming on in a nice steady lope, dust trailing out behind 'em. From the way their horses was holding their heads down and putting lots of weight on their forefeet, I reckoned they'd come many a weary mile.

One buck was carrying a rifle and the other two had lances. Although they weren't showing their horses no mercy, it didn't look like they was pushing too hard or trying to run towards something or away from something. They was traveling like them young Indians always travel: They never walk a horse, they always keep him at a good, hard, steady gait and 'fore they've owned him very long they either kill him or make a real tough horse outta him.

Then I seen the cause of why they was stirring up so much dust. Two of 'em was leading a couple of spare horses. So, with five horses all told, they was bound to cut up some dust and that's what I'd seen so far out on the plains. I lay there and watched 'em heading towards that green clump on the south side of the mesa. 'Fore long, they disappeared in the oak brush and was gone. I didn't make no move, 'cause I was too experienced of a hand to get caught out there in the open. If they was to pause and camp, I had the whole night to come up on 'em.

I waited and watched for quite a spell 'til the sun'd gone down behind them snow-clad western peaks. I was thinking 'bout moving out again and examining their trail, perhaps following it along through the night. Then, as if I was getting my reward, over there in the faint light of evening near that green clump of trees, I spied the long, curling blue smoke of a campfire rising into the evening sky on the windless air. I was gonna get some real hunting done, and it was gonna be fun!

When it turned dark enough, I headed out and picked up their trail where I'd last seen them horses. I didn't have no trouble finding it, even though it was in the dark, and I kept following it slow and easy.

Like I said, there weren't no wind: The campfire smoke'd been rising straight up when I'd last seen it in the fading twilight. I waited for a while, knowing that after dark the night breeze'd spring up and I'd have a good chance to come in upwind and not spook their horses.

I figured that night wind'd most likely be coming down off the mesa. It always happens that way in the mountains. The wind comes off the cool peaks and slides downhill in the evening, taking the place of the hot air rising outta them sun-baked prairies. The Comanches prob'ly knowed that, too, and most likely they'd picket their horses where they could give 'em the best warning of any surprise. Those was things I'd learned roaming 'round Comanche land, and I wish to God I'd knowed 'em when I was working my way up the Cimarron with Michelle.

The Comanches wouldn't stake their horses too far from where they was camped, 'cause horse stealing was a regular pastime for all the plains Indians. It was a test of skill, a matter of a young buck showing what a great fella he was by getting out there and stealing somebody else's horse—maybe facing death and other consequences. It was part of the tribal warfare of the plains. They all expected it and took all kinds of cautions to keep from losing their horses to their thieving neighbors. But most of the time, Indians didn't worry too much 'bout getting jumped theirselves. They knowed that most of their enemies' expeditions'd be for horse thieving, and if the raiders could get away with the horses, they wouldn't bother the owners.

The night had that chill it always gets in the mountains and plains when them breezes get to blowing. The stars was out bright and cold, so I could make out my path real easy. I seen with satisfaction that the wind weren't dead ahead but quartering to my right, which meant I could ease 'round to the left and not cut the wind and spook them horses.

I eased off down towards the southwest and come up in a nice easy quarter-circle, always mindful of that wind and of the location of the camp as I'd seen it 'fore the sun went down. I could guess that them horses'd be picketed upwind from the camp 'bout a hundred yards. I hadn't traveled too far 'fore I seen a flicker of light through the cottonwoods.

I worked forward real cautiouslike, and finally got into a position where I could see the firelight near steady, 'bout a quarter of a mile away. I crouched real low and traveled to within 'bout a furlong and then snaked the rest of the way on my belly, just easing along, careful so's not to make no noise, watching out for the breaking of a twig, the noise of leaves, or the sound of a gun barrel touching rocks. I'd pulled the rawhide string on the collar of my buckskin shirt real tight so's to keep my bear-claw necklace from rattling, too.

Any little thing like that'll spook your game. It don't make no difference whether you're hunting elk or Comanches. The most successful hunters are the ones who move the quietest, always trying to keep everything that might make a sound buttoned up. I couldn't understand them men that wore fancy belt buckles. You can't do no silent crawling with a belt buckle in the way. A piece of rawhide rope is the best belt you'll ever have, and it can be useful for lots of things 'sides holding your britches up. It ain't got no metal to nick on anything and give you away. It was the same way with my big knife: The sheath had a piece of soft buckskin that folded over the bone handle, and the rawhide tie kept it protected from weather as well as from making noise.

A lot of Indian war clubs is made with a piece of hide sewed over the knob. I reckon it was for the same reason. Anyhow, that's how mine was when I took it off that Comanche, and that's the way I always kept it. I could knock somebody's brains out just as well with a soft, hide-covered club that wouldn't make no noise when I was moving through the brush as I could with an uncovered one that'd rattle 'round. Cartridge belts is another thing. It seems like they're a necessary evil, but at least them cartridge loops keeps the brass cases from rapping against anything, and I always put a soft leather flap on my belt that laid over the cartridge rims and done a right good job of protecting 'em.

Anyhow, it didn't take me too much longer to work myself close enough to that Indian fire to get a good look. The sight of them three Indians moving 'bout in the firelight made me tingle all over. They weren't wearing nothing but breechclouts and I could see their muscles shining in the firelight. Being a little bit quarter-wind from 'em, I couldn't smell 'em, but right then I weren't thinking 'bout that. I was trembling all over with excitement.

One of them bucks stood up and walked out into the darkness to get some more wood for the fire. When he come back and throwed it on, there was a burst of sparks and the fire crackled and rose, lighting things up so's I could see 'em real plain. They was young bucks in the best of shape. As much as I hated 'em, I sure admired the way them Indians was built strong. All them muscles rippling under their oily skin showed through like snake hide. They wore side braids and scalp locks, with them chokecherry wood spikes stuck through their hair and fixed with feathers—all 'cept the one with the buffalo-horned helmet. I couldn't help thinking that they would've been fine-looking specimens if they hadn't been so squat and bowlegged and had them half-ape faces.

I slipped my rifle forward, brought it up to my shoulder, and sighted down at the standing buck. He was turned sideways to me and I could've shot him through both ears just clean and nice as could be. I eased the hammer back into a cocked position. I looked down the sights and laid that bead down on the side of his head. It sure was a temptation to squeeze the trigger and send that big bastard to eternity.

But I slowly lowered my rifle, letting the hammer back down gentle to the safe position, and took a deep breath. I lay there in the darkness and knowed I was perfectly safe as long as I kept still. There was hardly a chance in a million of them coming out that far from camp and stumbling on me. The only thing that might give me away'd be if the wind shifted to where them horses could sniff me. I knowed that my success and safety depended on the wind, so I kept a sensitivity for any change in it.

Meanwhile, I was trying to figure out how I could get me all three of them Comanches. I thought maybe I'd wait 'til two of 'em stood up, and if I could line 'em up right, I might try to get 'em both in one shot like I'd done with them two on horseback. But that plan had its drawbacks, too. In the first place, you couldn't ever be sure of the accuracy or the deadliness of a bullet once it passed through one body and then into another. You never knowed how it was gonna be deflected by some bone or how much force it might lose making its way through. I've seen both animals and men killed in twos with one shot, but more often than not the second animal or the second man is only wounded and gets away, and I weren't aiming to have no such misfortune. What I wanted was three dead Comanches, and right then they was plenty alive and hard to corner.

Thinking back on it now, I'm real surprised at the cold guts I had in them days. I even thought 'bout waiting 'til them Comanches was rolled up asleep in their blankets and crawling in to knife or club 'em right there where they slept. That'd be a real undertaking, but I didn't shrink from it none a'tall. Looking back at it from old age, I can see what a foolish risk it would've been and how dangerous, too, but at that time, me being young and full of energy and hate, it didn't bother me none.

Anyhow, it seemed like an impractical scheme. I couldn't kill all three in their sleep without any of 'em waking up. One or two of 'em'd take off running and if they ever got away from the firelight, chances were I'd lose 'em.

The only sure way I was gonna get 'em was to gun 'em all down, and I couldn't allow 'em any darkness to escape into. I finally come 'round to begrudging that I was gonna have to wait 'til first light. I waited and watched careful for a quite a spell. Then I seen them Indians roll up in their blankets right near the fire. I knowed I had a long wait 'til daybreak, but I figured I could amuse myself in the meantime by crawling closer to 'em.

The firelight was beginning to die down and there weren't no movement nor sound to show that them Comanche braves was doing anything but dreaming 'bout squaws or buffalo hunting. Meanwhile, I crept forward inch by inch, careful to always hold my rifle up so's there weren't the slightest sound, and keeping downwind of the horses. The stars was out bright overhead and the cool, sharp breeze kept coming down off the mountain. By then the firelight weren't nothing but a low glow and them Comanches slept sound as could be. Once in a while one of 'em'd turn in his blanket, but it was only a slight movement and I'd held my breath 'til things'd quieted down again.

The first streaks of light appeared when I was within twenty yards of the camp and still in good cover. I reckoned I was near enough. Soon, them Indians begun stirring. One of 'em rolled over and sat up in his blanket, stretched, and looked 'round. The others moved a little but was still lying prone.

I kept as still as stone while that buck was glancing about. Then, when he rolled slightly to stand, I eased my rifle up. The hammer come back, automatic-like under my thumb, smooth and natural, and cocked noiselessly. I timed it just right. The Indian'd reached an upright position and was letting the blanket slide off him when the calm of the morning was shattered by the explosion of my rifle.

He must've been balanced just perfect, 'cause it was almost comical to see his knees buckle as he spiraled back into a squat and fell over. I was watching him outta the corner of my eye while I worked the lever action for my next shot.

Like I said, it takes at least two seconds to get reloaded and fire, and that was one and a half seconds too long. When the sound of my first shot exploded, them other two Comanche bucks'd busted outta their blankets and disappeared into the oak brush like a flash. I was a little disappointed, but I knowed what they was gonna do. They was gonna make a run for the horses, 'cause that was their nature when trouble was brewing. They wasn't gonna stand and fight 'cause they didn't have no idea how many there was that'd ambushed 'em. No doubt they was thinking they'd got into a horse-stealing ambush.

I weren't exactly standing still myself. I started running, too, zig-zagging through the oak brush looking for them horses. I knowed right 'bout where they was from the sound of their stomping during the night. Them two bucks'd had 'bout a twenty-yard lead on me and I knowed that I'd have to sweat to get a jump shot at 'em 'fore they got to the horses.

While I was running flat out I seen the flash of one buck just ahead of me. I cut to the right to get some clearance and seen another flash of him as he come wheeling like a running antelope 'round the edge of a big clump of brush. In the same second, I glimpsed the hindquarters of a paint horse jutting out. I knowed that was the picket line.

The Indian rounded the clump of oak brush, really churning smoke, but he never did make it to the horses. I shot him right through the back. The other buck'd gone 'round the other side of the oak brush and grabbed at the rear of a plunging horse. I was running and jamming another shell in my gun when I come 'round the turn just in time to see him vault onto a fine Appaloosa gelding while he cradled his rifle in his arm, then turn and cut loose two of the other horses that was picketed.

The way that Indian mounted one horse and turned the other two loose so fast, I couldn't help but admire his skill. He didn't ride straight away from me, but instead started circling off at an angle with that horse kicking and jumping at every step. He used that angle to give me a bad target as he slid Comanche style down behind the withers of his horse, clinging to the mane and hooking one of his heels over the backbone.

I didn't have no choice but to kill the horse. By the time I drawed down on him and made sure of my shot as he was dashing away in a long curve, that horse must've been the better part of a hundred yards away. I squeezed off and he piled up and rolled over in a big cloud of dust. It was a bad fall, and the buck jumped up from the ruckus, grabbed his gun, and made a dash for cover, mostly hopping and dragging one leg. I had me a wounded Comanche down in the bush, and he was more dangerous than any wounded animal. What made matters worse, he had a rifle with him. I didn't have a chance to see what kinda gun it was, but I knowed it weren't a repeater—the barrel was too long. So I reckoned it was a Sharps.

It promised to be a real exciting day. In fact, I welcomed the opportunity to pit my skill against that of an Indian. I figured it was gonna be a good hunt, 'bout as fair a game as a man could expect—hunting down a wounded Comanche in his own country and him armed near as good as me.

I knowed enough to duck outta sight myself, 'cause he didn't have nothing to do but wait for my approach. He had one chance to live, and that was to wait real quiet 'til he could get a shot at me, presuming by that time he'd worked it out that he was only being hunted by one man.

If he killed me, he could make it back to the spring. He could live by that spring for a number of days and hope that somebody'd come by and pick him up, although that weren't hardly likely. He prob'ly couldn't catch no horse in his present condition, with maybe a broke hip or leg, and he couldn't do no traveling. On the other hand, he had to kill me to get to the spring and he had to figure that I'd prob'ly be hid somewhere by it to ambush him.

I had two choices. I could either go back to the spring and wait for him, or take the riskier course of hunting him down. Being the impatient kind, I chose the last. 'Sides, I figured it'd be better sport. I reckoned I could do as good a job of tracking and ambushing as any Indian, and I wanted to prove it to myself, so I never give another thought to returning to that spring.

The first thing I done was to stay real quiet for the best part of an hour. I figured he might try to move—maybe to get sight of me, maybe 'cause of his pain from that injury or 'cause he'd start getting thirsty, but I couldn't expect no action on that last 'til late in the afternoon. 'Course he was playing the same game as me, just lying low and waiting for the first move.

It passed through my mind that maybe he hadn't got hurt in the fall, but that my bullet'd somehow struck him in the leg after it went through the horse. I thought 'bout that and then give it up. Shooting a buffalo Sharps, that might happen, but not with that Winchester. By the time a bullet went through the horse, it wouldn't have enough power left to do no real damage to nothing else.

No, what he'd done was bust hisself up in the fall. It was too bad, 'cause if he'd had a gunshot wound, he'd prob'ly bleed and get a damn sight thirstier than he would just lying there with a broke leg. I knowed it'd be plenty painful and I might hear him moan. That'd give me a direction, so I stayed real quiet.

Finally I got the idea of tossing something to get his attention. Keeping my eye on that scrub oak, I picked up two rocks and throwed 'em, hoping that when they landed he might move quick and that'd expose him. But there weren't no sign nor motion. There was a chance he'd been hurt so bad that he'd either fainted or maybe died, but that was what he'd want me to think.

I knowed where he'd first hid, back of that brushy clump, but I couldn't be sure he was still there. If I moved any, it'd give my position away, and then he could work up on me. Maybe he was doing that already. Them Indians can move silent as snakes and pour all over the ground when they want to. I was gonna have to be mighty careful of him.

It was dead calm in the early morning, but as the sun begun to work up and the heat of the day gathered, a slight breeze rose and made it even tougher to hear anything. It was a real deadly waiting game. I had to figure that he was just as anxious to get a shot at me as I was him.

He was sure thinking 'bout something, and the best way to deal with an animal or man that you're hunting is to think like they think. If I was that Indian, the last thing I'd do'd be to stay behind the same clump of brush. The enemy that shot my horse would've sure seen me dive for cover and figure I was right there. No, I'd crawl off someplace and think 'bout the situation.

He'd been almost due west of me when he went down. From what I could judge by looking at that hillside, there weren't no way that he could go south to my left and not be seen, 'cause it was open ground. He either had to go straight on backwards to the west or perhaps work up 'round to the north.

There was also the possibility that he might try to work out 'round me and get to the spring first. I considered that highly unlikely. It'd take lots of maneuvering, and he might figure that I'd be right near the spring waiting for him. No, his first job was to hunt me down and kill me, and he couldn't come straight towards me without my seeing him. Most likely he'd make a big circle and come in on me real quiet. If I stayed where I was, he could circle 'round and come in to kill me 'fore I knowed what it was all about. Or maybe he figured that if he waited me out, after a while I'd jump up and walk on into the open where he'd get a good shot.

While I was thinking this way, I done the only thing that seemed smart to me. I eased up and headed north myself, moving quiet, keeping alert all the time, but not traveling as slow as I'd done in the night when I was crawling up on their fire. If he was going north and I went north, we'd be the same distance apart later on in the day, but if he circled 'round towards the east to take a potshot at me, chances were he'd cross my trail and come up on top of me. If I was real careful I might get a shot at him first. The question was in knowing how far to go.

It's instinctive for a wounded animal to hole up in the thickest bush, and that was where he'd be going if he was working to the north. On top of that, while he was working towards the north he'd be climbing higher up the slopes of that mesa. I'd do that, too, if I was wounded. I always liked climbing up high, 'cause it meant that I could look down and see lots more from above.

I couldn't move straight west towards him any more'n he could move east towards me, and it wouldn't have done no good for me to retreat back east any more'n it'd done him to retreat to the west.

Neither one of us could go south on account of it being out in plain sight. It was a matter of us going north and him turning towards the spring at some point. If I kept going on, he'd have to turn sometime and he'd cross on down below me, 'tween me and the open prairie. If he picked up my trail, which he was sure to do, he'd know I was above him and he'd either hightail it for the spring, or come on after me, or turn back towards the west and hide out.

All three of them choices was gonna be fatal to him. The only thing that could go wrong with my plan was for him to think the way I was thinking, work towards the north, and keep staying with me. I knowed an Indian was cunning, but I didn't give his reasoning powers much credit. I didn't think he'd go far enough to outthink a white man. What he'd do, he'd do by instinct, being as he was long accustomed to the ways of nature. If I knowed what them ways was, that'd be his downfall.

The only thing that bothered me some was the matter of timing. How long was that Indian gonna take to make his circle? Two hours? Three or four hours? Or was he gonna take all day? I had to guess that one. I already knowed he was gonna take longer'n an hour. I'd waited for that long already and hadn't seen no sign nor heard nothing.

As for taking all day, I didn't see how he was gonna do that, being as thirsty as he must've been if he was still alive. No, it looked to me like he'd take the middle course of 'bout three or four hours. If that was the case, I could guess the distance he'd be able to crawl in that time and the size of the circle he'd expect to make. A man, even an Indian, crawling real silent don't make very much distance in an hour's time. In three or four hours, 'bout a furlong and a half'd be all that was possible. He'd crawl 'bout two hundred yards to the north of his position in the first hour and a half, work a hundred fifty yards east during the next hour, and then he'd move real slow and quiet and it'd take him the best part of two hours to make it back to where he figured he last seen me.

He might even take longer. He wouldn't be sure he was right and he'd go casting all 'round looking for sign and trying to keep from being ambushed.

In the next hour and a half I crawled 'bout two hundred fifty yards northwest. Every so often I'd snake up alongside a rock and ease up to look 'round, listening for sounds. Towards the middle of the day I got to the place where I reckoned I oughta be. By that time the plains was beginning to shimmer in the heat. Far out over the flat stretches I could see some dust devils turning and spinning in the late morning sun.

I found me a nice place jammed in the wedge 'tween two rocks where I could ease up and look 'round. I was protected from three sides and only had to keep an eye or ear to the east. I didn't make no move 'cept a slow one. It took what seemed like forever to ease my head up over the ledge to look 'round, then I held real still for 'tween a quarter to a half hour, looking at everything 'bout me and trying to see a sign of anything. Crouching there in the sun, my mind begun to give me a bad time. I got to thinking 'bout all sorts of possibilities. Maybe that buck was lying down in back of the bushes dead or maybe he'd been winged by my shot after all and'd bled to death.

I decided he must've had a hip wound considering the way he'd drug his leg. If it'd been an injury to the lower part of his leg, his knee would've been bent. But it weren't—it was straightened out and he was hopping along, dragging his leg like he didn't have no control from the hip down. My bullet might've smashed his hip, but I didn't see how that was possible the way he'd been riding. His body was far down on the withers of the horse. Then I remembered which leg I'd seen him drag—his left one. He was riding away from me on a long curve to the right, so his left leg had the deepest protection.

No, he'd hurt that leg in the spill, and there weren't no chance that he was dead. Anytime you think you got a dead Indian, you're the one that's apt to be dead soon. The only way to make sure is to check 'em firsthand, and you'd better be mighty careful or it could be the last check you'd ever make.

As the time wore on I got to worrying. He'd either crossed on down below me where I hadn't seen him, which meant he was a smarter Indian than I'd figured, or he was making a bigger loop than I thought and was working up above me. That idea made my scalp crawl and didn't do no good for my heartbeat, so I stopped thinking 'bout it. Either he'd crawl up close enough to shoot me and I'd never know what hit me, or I'd see just a flash of him and have to make a jump shot, or I'd catch him crawling slow and easy at quite some distance and'd have to make dead sure of my aim to squeeze off and finish the job.

Any way I figured it, I'd have to be on my toes and ready for whatever come. Thinking like that sharpened my senses. You'd be surprised what it can do to make a man see things real clear. When I was in a situation like that, I could count the ants crawling fifty yards away. There weren't no twig, or leaf, or bush that weren't glowing in the sun, lit up to show everything I needed to see. It seemed like I could see clear through things when I needed to, and my ears tuned in to all kinda sounds. I could sort 'em out even when they come at me in a dozen different ways. Seemed like my sense of smell was extra clear, too. Don't wanta never underrate that. Humans think they ain't got no sense of smell 'cause they watch a hound dog working in a way they never could. But man don't wanta put his sense of smell down too far just on account of that. No, he can't smell as good as no hound dog, but there's lots of times when he can smell well enough to save his life. He can smell buffalo or elk or grizzly bear real easy when he's tracking 'em, and I could sure smell Comanches.

Noon come and went and I kept watching for signs—a little movement of birds or the scurrying of a rabbit or maybe a coyote jumping outta his lair, or any sign that'd give me a clue as to where that buck'd gone.

The sun'd started moving into the afternoon, and I had to do some recalculating. A three- or four-hour program for that circling buck weren't a good guess no more. He'd either stayed right where he was or he was moving in a bigger circle. Whichever it was, I couldn't take the chance of staying—I had to move on up the mesa.

Lots of people believe that Indians does all their attacking at the break of day. That's true in many cases, but there's frontiersmen and pioneer folk that's met their end right in the middle of the day, 'cause it was the least likely time that they was thinking of being bush-whacked. A man gets dull in the heat of the day. Oft'times it's right after the noon meal, and he gets a little sleepy, and his senses ain't up to tune.

The same idea works for hunting game. You go out and spot game in the early morning when they're alert like you are. If you watch careful and see where they go under cover and then take the noon hours to work up on 'em, there's many a time you'll find your hunt successful. Animals stay bedded down 'til you're right up on 'em and then they jump up sluggish or act surprised that you'd come and disturb 'em. I figured it weren't gonna be healthy to lie down and get sluggish in one place, 'specially not with a wounded Comanche hunting me.

I stayed belly low like a snake and inched through the oak brush and on up the slope of that mesa, watching each move real careful. As I was working my way up 'round a rocky ledge, I heard a slight noise. My heart jumped and I snapped my cheek against the butt of my rifle and froze solid trying to figure out where that Indian was and how he could've loused me up. Then I almost laughed when I seen a big camp-robber jay bird go hopping up over the ridge and outta sight.

I relaxed a little then. I'd worked up near four hundred yards, and less'n all my figuring was wrong, that buck had to be below me. I was staking my life on that judgment, but I didn't see how else it could be. Even if he'd started crawling right away after I shot his horse—even if he'd been crawling while I was lying up there in them rocks—he still had to be below me.

The sides of the mesa was getting too steep for easy crawling, 'specially for a man with a broke limb. If he'd kept on going farther north, the going would've got mighty tough in the rockslide that lay beneath the cap rock of the mesa. I was several hundred feet above the open plain and better'n halfway up to the top. If he'd circled back to get me, it wouldn't have served his purpose to go that high.

If he'd crossed lower and moved earlier, I sure would've crossed his tracks coming up. It bothered me some that I hadn't. Well, maybe he hadn't moved 'til later than I'd figured. But if he'd done anything like I'd figured, he must've crossed my trail by then, and he wouldn't have had no trouble reading the signs. I hadn't been able to stick to rocky places, so he sure would've noticed the soft dirt, the odd leaf, the twisted twig of a bush—all the things that'd tell a good Indian tracker where his enemy'd passed.

It had to be one of two things. When he did cross my tracks he decided to follow it up slow and easy and was tracking me with the idea of getting a shot, or else, being in bad need of water, he'd headed for the spring.

There was one way to find out. I made a fifty-yard circle out and down the hill and come back a hundred yards below in real good position to wait and see if he was coming down my tracks. I'd wait 'til the sun worked down to past the midafternoon and then I'd make another circle to come up on the uphill side of the spring. I stayed there watching and waiting and listening for something like two hours.

I decided then that I'd misjudged my Comanche. He'd headed for the spring after all, regardless of the risk and knowing that he was prob'ly walking into a certain ambush. I didn't like the idea much. It didn't seem Comanche-like, but I couldn't see how I could escape the conclusion. I figured I'd best make one big loop to the east and come down on the spring and see if I could pick up his tracks and follow him and kill him.

I started to move out, then I stopped. It just didn't fit. There weren't no Comanche alive fool enough to cross his enemy's trail without tracking that enemy when he knowed his life depended on it. It didn't make no difference how thirsty he was hisself; savages was used to suffering. Yet the afternoon was waning on, and if that Comanche was alive, he had to be moving somewhere. I guessed the only way was towards the spring.

Yet my instinct said to wait, stay a minute. Something's wrong. Them ain't Comanche ways. He's doing something you ain't figuring on.

I felt too uneasy to stay put, so I pivoted 'round on my belly and started to work towards the spring. I'd crawled maybe ten yards when it hit me strong that I weren't doing the right thing. Instinct told me to crawl back and take a last look. To keep from feeling too foolish, I didn't crawl back to the same place, but looped down and come out on a little rise 'bout ten yards below where I'd waited before.

I looked everywhere for motion but couldn't see nothing but two big old vultures swinging 'round high, riding them currents off the cap rock, circling round and round, maybe a mile away to the northwest. Nothing else stirred. No sign of any wildlife—no elk, no deer. I didn't see antelope out over the plains or even a rabbit or chipmunk close by. It was in the dreamy, sleepy part of the late afternoon and all of the wild folk was slumbering—lulled asleep by the humming of the bees.

I run my eye all over the country again and studied where I'd come up the side of the mountain. There still weren't nothing moving. I give a sigh and started turning away. Then I froze. I had seen something— just a slight motion below and to the west. Maybe it was a bird or a squirrel but something *had* moved.

I held tense as a bowstring. I didn't move a muscle and my breath stayed as good as gone outta my body. I waited a long time and then started to breathe again. I thought maybe I was imagining it, but I knowed that weren't right. I'd sure as hell seen something move, maybe fifty yards to the west and down the slope.

I waited stone still for ten minutes, telling myself that it was time to turn and go, and my instinct telling me, Ya find out what that was. Ya ain't movin' 'til ya do.

Then I seen it again. First just a small tuft of black. Then something light-colored and long-sided. Then the dark, old-copper look of something that was round and shiny. It moved again and I clearly seen what it was—the chokecherry stick and side braid and the back of an Indian.

It was my Comanche. My eyes was concentrating so much, it seemed like I had a built-in pair of them field glasses like the cavalrymen had. I watched the slow, easy movement of that buck on the trail that I'd made, dragging hisself along like a snake—a smooth, oozing snake.

From the way that Indian was crawling—moving slightly, maybe three or four inches at a time and holding his head in such a way as to make no motion but give his eyes a chance to look up 'round—there weren't no doubt that he was working up on my tracks with the sure-as-hell idea he was gonna get a shot at me.

My rifle come up nice and slow and easy and the hammer went back without a sound. Then that bead drawed down in the notch and went to working in a very small circle, 'tween the back of that Indian's shoulders and the back of his head. His head moved again and raised a little, and when my breathing quieted down, the bead rested dead against the back of his neck.

The pressure of the trigger eased and the gun went off with a crash. His head slumped forward, then he just lay there. I watched him for five minutes and was sorely tempted to put in another shot, but his head never turned and even from fifty yards away I could see that there weren't no breathing.

Still, I didn't rise up right away. I crawled forward with my rifle ready, watching him. When I come up on him, I seen that my caution weren't necessary. My bullet'd gone in the back of his neck at the base of his skull. I rolled him over. It'd come out through the front of his face, which weren't there no more, and I noted—amused—that some of his teeth was lying 'round. Then I took a good look at his upper legs. Like I thought, his left one was broke high up, so bad broke that part of the bone was sticking out through the flesh. When I'd shot his horse out from under him, he'd prob'ly jammed against some rocks as he went down.

Funny thing, he was one of the few Comanches I ever killed that I really admired. He'd plenty of guts. He hadn't allowed no quarter, lying there and wounded hard. He'd had a one-shot rifle and was coming up on me, who he knowed weren't wounded and had a repeater. He'd done the only thing that a very smart and desperate animal could do, and he took his time doing it.

I saw then that my plan'd been the right one. I'd moved up the side of the mesa and he'd been circling nothing. When he'd crossed my tracks he found that out. Then, instead of losing his guts, with all his pain and thirst, and deciding to head for the water, he'd done the warrior's thing. He'd turned and started up the mountain, following my tracks with the idea that he was gonna put a bullet through me 'fore he looked after hisself.

For all of that, I weren't sympathizing over no dead Indians. They weren't nothing to me but so many snakes stamped out against the face of the earth.

His rifle was an old Spencer single-shot, just like I'd figured, and he had a beaded band 'round his upper right arm. I took it off, wiped the blood off against some grass, and strung it 'round my belt. I'd out-hunted that Comanche and I didn't have no feeling but pride in my achievement. It was my trophy showing I'd outdone an Indian. By then I'd knowed I could outmatch 'em anytime—wits and skill.

It was late afternoon and I was a little drowsy. I set down by the bush that the Indian'd been hiding in, ten feet from his dead body, took out a little pemmican, and gnawed on it. After a while I got more sleepy, leaned back, and begun looking up at them tall white clouds in that blue, blue sky. They was drifting and sailing by high up there and it seemed like they never did have no worries. I wondered what it'd be like to be a cloud.

Then I closed my eyes and dozed off.

When I woke up, the sun was pretty far down towards the western horizon, but I felt real fresh and clean. As the shadows gathered, I dropped down off that mesa. By the time I reached the floor of the plain, the sun'd gone down. There was a nice cool wind coming off the hill. I swung by the spring to fill my canteen and had me a good enough swig from the spring itself to last for a long time. I couldn't help thinking 'bout that Comanche buck up on the side of the mountain and how bad he'd wanted to make it to that spring, 'til I'd come along and interrupted his plans. There was two things you had to say 'bout an Indian. He could sure stand lots of suffering, and when he got on the trail of an enemy he was a deadly tracker.

I went back to where them other two dead bucks was lying—first the one I'd killed as he was running 'round towards the horses, then the other one there in the camp. I cut my cat's-eye sign in the bark of the tree nearest the fire to let the next visitor know whose territory he was in. Then I lay down in the middle of a thick bunch of brush and leaves and, as tired as I was, it weren't no problem going off to sleep.

The sun'd almost broke over the eastern horizon when I woke up. It'd been daylight for maybe half an hour, and I cussed myself for not being up and going early. It weren't like me to get a late start and it weren't a healthy thing to do in Comanche land.

I jogged along, working out my thoughts as I begun to get back into the mesa country again in real earnest. The oak brush was getting thicker, and off to the north was the kind of country that I'd been footing over for the last half year. I picked out a mesa off to the right and decided to head for the cap rock. I didn't have me a plan, but I figured it wouldn't be a bad idea to get a little altitude. Maybe I could look out over the country and see what was happening.

I couldn't help thinking with a smile that it was a different Cat Brules that was running 'round them mesas from the greenhorn kid that'd come up the Arkansas with a sassy little whore less'n a year before. I hadn't known what I was going to do then, but I sure as hell did by that time.

My mind was amusing itself like that while I climbed up four or five hundred feet of mesa to the top of the cap rock. I come out on a great big tableland, beautiful as anything you'd wanta see. It was a big place up there, with lots of pine and some big, open parks. I sure did think it was grand country. The rains'd been good that spring and the grass was knee-high. I wandered along enjoying myself and kept my eyes open, looking for something that'd interest me. I was willing to take a look at most anything but hoped I'd see some Comanches first. After that I figured I'd look for any other game.

It's a funny thing. When you start out looking for game, sometimes you don't see none a'tall. You can travel for hours and even days and cover many long miles and see nary a thing, and then sometimes when you ain't hunting a'tall, the game's all 'round. It was the same way with Comanches.

I kept moving along the top of that high cap rock all day and then made me a cold camp right where I was. I struck out at daylight, again moving through them big parks and occasional stands of timber. 'Bout noon I come up on a sinkhole that'd had some rainwater left, so I filled up on that and put some in to top off my canteen. I kept on 'til late afternoon and then crossed the mesa to where I was looking down on some real interesting country to the north. Another series of broke-up mesa tops stretched as far as I could see, both to the north and to the east. To the west there was the big basin south of Raton Pass, and west of that them snow-clad Sangre de Cristos.

I decided to work 'round to the north and east, passing through all the mesa country in that direction to see if I could make me another loop and watch for Comanche trails. My plan'd give me something to work on as I kept swinging more and more towards the east. Finally I picked up a view of the open plains again and I thought maybe I'd spot some of the buffalo herds. I dropped on down off the cap rock, crossed over the valley and climbed up on the next mesa, and made camp for the night. I picked up a little fresh water from a spring and, with the pemmican I had with me, made out all right.

The third day, coming down off'n one of them mesas, I jumped a big buck in the sagebrush and put him down. I didn't bother to bleed him or gut him out, but just cut me out the back straps and saved a piece for my evening meal. The rest I laid out in strips in the sun to dry and work into jerky.

I hung 'round that spot 'til I got the job done, and that meant camping overnight. But I weren't in no hurry and it was good business to make sure of everything I was doing. I sat there after dark in front of a little fire I'd made, hid away in among the rocks where the light couldn't be seen from no other direction. I cooked me a chunk of venison and had the first fresh meat I'd had in quite a spell. I roasted some piñon nuts and they went along with it just fine.

Brules stopped talking. It was as if a waterfall had suddenly dried up and an ominous stillness was all that was left. It was another one of those clear, cold Colorado nights with thousands of stars twinkling in the heavens and the light of a three-quarter moon bathing the mountainside all around us.

I looked up and saw Brules's eyes shining in the firelight. Those incredible haunting, piercing, soul-searching eyes that had thrilled me through all my boyhood years had become inscrutable again, hiding who knows what treasures of frontier lore, what scenes, what legends, what mysteries!

Suddenly, Brules rose and walked slowly to the cool, shady north side of the cabin. A screened locker was nailed against the cabin wall and obviously served as a good place to keep fresh meat away from flies and small predators. He opened the door, reached in and pulled out a piece of meat, walked around the side of the cabin, and picked up an old wire grill. He brought it over and laid it on the logs of the fire and threw the meat on it. Fat bubbled up and dripped into the fire. Flames spit and I saw by their light that the slab was a back strap, and the delicious smell told me that it was venison. The meat sizzled and popped pleasantly while Brules poked it and turned it repeatedly with his knife.

"That sure smells good, Mr. Brules."

He grinned and looked at me. "Well, I reckon yore pretty hungry, son. Looks to me like it's done now."

He carved the meat into thick slices, then turned and picked up two sticks. He skillfully carved the ends of both into sharp points and drove one of them into a piece of sizzling meat, handing me the impaled morsel as if he were the maitre d' of the most exclusive gourmet restaurant in Paris. I laughed and took the offering.

"Be careful," he said, "it's hot."

I blew on it a little bit and when I finally put it to my lips I decided that it was the most delicious piece of meat I had ever tasted. I told him so and he nodded and grinned again. He seemed pleased. He took a big piece for himself and went at it heartily, the juices dribbling down both sides of his ample beard. He savored it for a few minutes and then pointed his knife.

"Son," he said emphatically, "there's something I want to tell you, something I believe is important to your health and will be good for you for the rest of your life. Ain't much I can give you, though I'd like to, but this piece of information may be the best thing you'll ever know.

"Now, you remember the Bible says that man must eat the meat of the cloven hoof. That means something very simple. It means that he should eat meat like what comes from cattle, deer, elk, or moose, or the like—animals that have been feeding on grass—'cause that's the meat that'll agree with you. You can eat that kind of meat for a long time and it won't hurt you none.

"What you can't do is eat the meat of clawed animals for any length of time. You can't eat bear, 'coon, or even dog or coyote, as their meat is too strong. Them animals has been living off other animals and that complexes things a mite. Their meat is too rich and if you eat it as a steady diet, you'll break out in boils and all kinds of bad things. Do like the Bible says. Them ol' Bible patriarchs had it figured out.

"You may wonder how I know this. Well, I learned it when my daddy and I come down from Independence to St. Louis on a raft on the Missouri River. We'd been rafting on the Mississippi all along, of course, but rafting on the Missouri was another thing—that ol' Mo was always full of mud and sandbars, and there wasn't near as much water in it as there was in the Mississippi. You had to watch out all the time. But we did float a load of buffalo hides down on a raft along with an old-timer, an old mountain man that had come down from the Montana Territory with the hides. My daddy was so impressed by that ol' boy that his eyes was just a-shining when he was asking him all kinds of questions 'bout the Northwest. He treated that man like somebody who'd come from another world. Matter of fact, that was 'bout what the fella'd done, 'cause he come from three thousand miles up the Missouri and that was wild and unexplored territory in them days.

"Well, the old mountain man got to talking and told me just the exact same thing that I just told you. It's plain that the Indians must've believed the same way, 'cause they never made pemmican outta nothing but venison, elk, or buffalo meat. They never used no beaver, bear, or that kind of thing."

Brules stopped talking and finished attacking the meat on his stick. Somehow I felt relieved. When he was done, he wiped his sleeve across his mouth and stood up. The firelight was bright enough so that you could see several of the horses in the corral. The old man watched them for a while and then his gaze softened. He stood there looking at the animals for a few more minutes and then he leaned over and put his hand on my shoulder.

"You know," he said, kind of quietlike, "I didn't think no horse could really ever love a man, but if there was one that ever did, it was that Blackie loving ol' Pedro. I reckon that had something to do with Pedro not wanting to kill him and get down behind him when the Comanches was coming up fast. It prob'ly cost Pedro his life, although I s'pose the real truth of it was that Pedro weren't a good enough shot to stand off a bunch of Comanches like I'd done. What we know for sure, he just didn't have it in him to kill that horse.

"That ain't s'prising, considering that Pedro's daddy, his granddaddy, and his great granddaddy before him used to raise horses, so it run in his blood. He told me how careful they was with a colt when they first took charge of 'em. They'd rub 'em down and feed 'em right and train 'em with special bridles that only had a knot under the chin. They used gentle pressure to lead 'em before they'd mount, and they'd mount 'em real careful and ride ever so slow and gentle so's to let 'em know the feeling of being rode. Them colts grew up knowing the smell of their master, and the touch of his hand, and the sound of his voice. I reckon it made for a special bond 'tween 'em.

"Pedro's old granddaddy took pride in all them horses they had on the ranch. I'm sure sorry now that we never made it down to Chihuahua to see 'em. They was a breed of horses that'd been brought over from Spain a long time before by Pedro's great, great granddaddy. The horses them Comanches had—in fact all them Indian horses—come from the same strain as the horses them conquistadores brought over from the Old World. Ol' Pedro never called it Spain; he always said 'Andalusia' or 'Estremadura,' and I remember one time when I asked him what the hell he was talking 'bout."

Brules shook his head and chuckled. "That really tickled ol' Pedro's funny bone. 'You damn gringo, you ignorant bastard, Brules,' he said, flashing that old piano-key grin and laughing. 'Andalusia and Estremadura are Spanish provinces where the finest horses of all the world are raised. That's where the real fighting conquistadores came from. They was tough and different from other Spaniards.'

"Y'know, son, memory's a funny thing—like I can almost hear his voice now telling me how them Spanish horses was bred when them Arab horses come to Spain with the Moors and got crossed with the cool-blooded European horses. He told me how you could always tell the difference 'tween an Arab horse and a European horse. I cottoned to that real quick. A European horse, ol' Pedro explained, has five of them big vertebrae bones in his back, and the Arab's only got four. The Arab horse has an arched neck and a spoon-billed nose with real wide nostrils made to drink the wind. He's quick and light-limbed— fast and wiry and tough, hot-blooded and bred for the desert. Them European horses is big and heavy and bred for carrying bigger loads.

"Pedro told me that them Andalusian horses was made up of a cross 'tween the European and some other kind of horse that Pedro called a Barb. I never did see exactly what the difference was 'tween the Arab and the Barb, but Pedro seemed to know, so I was willing to listen without interrupting none so's I wouldn't break his train of thought.

"He said that them Andalusian horses, when they was crossed 'tween the European and the Arab Barb, come out with four and a half vertebraes in their spine. That's the way you could tell which of them horses come over to the New World with them Spanish knights that conquered Mexico. I reckon they was men with plenty of guts and it was plain that ol' Pedro was real proud to have 'em in his family line.

"Pedro told me how they brung them horses over on sailing ships, putting the stallions in slings on the decks so's that when the ship rolled and wallowed in the heavy sea, the horses always stayed upright in the sling. Them Spanish dons, even though they was born lords and rich men and had servants to look out for 'em, would stay on deck, feeding and caring for them horses in the rough seas. Them voyages took a long time and sometimes some of them horses would get so seasick they'd die.

"Pedro said that the mares seemed to take it better'n the stallions. Worst of all, though, was when one of them dons'd lose his stallion. It made even a strong man like that bawl like a baby. I guess those men lived for their horses and liked nothing better, leastwise that's what Pedro told me.

"He told me the story the way it'd been passed down to him from his daddy, who heard it from his daddy before him. He said that when the first load of them horses come across the ocean, they was so weak and skinny that when they put 'em ashore in Mexico, they could hardly stand. It only took a few days for them stallions to get over their sickness, and they rallied and got to prancing and ripsnorting around once they had some of that good fodder that growed so lush and plentiful. Them mares brightened right quick, too. Their hides got all slick in a hurry and they started to run around like they hadn't experienced no travel trouble a'tall.

"Pedro said that them conquistadores rode up and scared the hell outta the Indians in Mexico. When they finally conquered the country, they realized it was the horses that'd done it. Pedro's ancestors went way the hell back, so far back that even he couldn't follow the line all the way, although he seemed to know lots about 'em. I reckon maybe he hadn't wanted to embarrass me with a lot of details 'bout his family, 'cause he knowed if I started talking 'bout mine, I wouldn't have much worth saying."

The old man paused and fingered his beard, staring up at old Lone Cone Peak in the moonlight, lost in thought.

"How did Pedro's family get that big spread in Chihuahua you mentioned they had?" I finally asked.

"I think it was his granddaddy's great granddaddy or some such. Pedro said that one of them ancestors of his was with the conquistadores and the general that conquered all of Mexico. I forget his name now, but it was Pedro's ancestors who was with that general, serving as one of his captains, and he was rewarded with a big ol' parcel of land. That ol' boy turned it into a giant horse-raising spread. I can't recollect how many thousands of acres Pedro said it was, but he bred the finest horses in all of Mexico, and I reckon that folk come from all over to get horses from him. They was trained real fine and looked damn good, Pedro said, coming as they had from top-grade stock."

Brules's mention of how the Indians had been scared by the horses made me wonder why it was that they got so many for themselves, so I put the question to him, thinking that he might know the answer. I wasn't disappointed.

"It was pure envy," he said with a chuckle. "There weren't no horses in the New World 'fore the Spaniards come, I hear tell. So, naturally, the Indians at first figured that them conquistadores was some kind of monsters or something. When they dismounted it seemed that they didn't fight so good, but a running armored horseman swinging a broadsword could still raise hell with them Indians.

"It didn't take them Indians long to figure out that the horse was powerful medicine, and they got to really craving some of 'em for themselves. Pedro said that his ancestors used to spend a lot of time fretting 'bout their horses getting stole by the Indians. They didn't want no horses getting into their hands, 'cause that would've made things too damned equal. But there weren't no stopping that from happening. Them horses bred real well out in the open grasslands and they made easy pickings for thieving Indians.

"Pedro said he had one ancestor who, every time a band of Indians'd come around to steal some of the horses and head out north across the Rio Grande with 'em, he'd track 'em and try to get his animals back. Sometimes he'd travel for weeks on end, up to a thousand miles or so, 'til he'd catch up with 'em and kill 'em, to get his horses back.

"He had the right idea, but there just weren't no way to enforce it in all of Mexico. Them horses was breeding like hell, and them stallions'd run a remuda of mares around and get 'em all pregnant and within a year there'd be foals running all over the prairie. 'Fore you knowed it, them horses'd expanded clear up across the Rio Grande through Texas, New Mexico, and the Indian territory, and on into Kansas and Nebraska. As far as them Indians was concerned, why hell, there weren't no way to stop 'em from getting horses.

"It only took a few generations 'fore the plains Indians discovered it was a helluva lot better to ride a horse than it was to walk. And then, too, when it come to moving a village, they could rig up a travois on a pony and carry lots of stuff. 'Fore them horses come along, there weren't no real way to carry no big loads. The Indians was going everywhere on foot, with only dogs to help tote their stuff. They'd pack them dogs and when the dogs wore out, they'd eat 'em.

"Them plains Indians was a miserable scrawny lot 'fore they got horses. But once they got 'em, they was a force to be reckoned with. They could hunt buffalo and ride all over hell with lots of speed and power to burn. Anyway, that's the way they got 'em, and it sure changed their lives. They got to living real good when they got them horses—all thanks to the early Spaniards."

The wind began to pick up and I felt a chill run down my spine. The old man looked tired—he'd been talking all through the day and it was now nearing midnight. I finally suggested to him that we ought to curl up in our blankets by the fire and get some sleep. I figured that there would be plenty of time to pick up the story again after we had rested.

ON THE PROWL

Strange as it may seem, continued
Brules the next morning, I went damn near six weeks after I killed
them last three Comanches 'fore I seen another Indian. There was
times when I thought maybe I'd better give it up and go back to the
Spanish settlement, but I passed that idea outta my mind. I weren't
about to go back and quit. I weren't ready to face civilization. I was
out where I liked it best, wandering in and out of Comanche land,
living off'n anything that come 'round, hunting for my intended prey.

But for more'n a month I hadn't seen no signs of them devils and I
was getting plumb discouraged. The first thing that broke the monotony was a mule deer I seen. He was a big old racking buck, all turned
red with summer. I spotted him standing clear 'cross the valley on
another mesa. He'd been resting in the oak brush in the shadow of the
cap rock for most of a warm August afternoon.

I knowed, 'cause I was napping on the other side of the canyon,
kinda sleeping lazy myself. I'd been traveling since dawn and hadn't
seen nothing. Towards the late afternoon I looked up at the wall of
this cap rock on the mesa 'cross the valley nearly eight hundred yards
away. I couldn't see nothing move. When I looked back, all of a
sudden I seen this buck standing there in the afternoon sunshine. His
hide was slick and his rack was grand but still in the velvet. He stood

there like a monarch surveying the valley below. I seen the strength and breadth of him and how high he was holding his head. I could even see the shadow he cast.

He was a long, long ways off, and I didn't wanta waste no ammunition. I also had that pride that says you don't shoot without making a kill. So I thought considerable 'fore I decided to draw down on him. Like I say, I'd reckoned the range to be near eight hundred yards.

Now, anybody'll tell you that a model 66 Winchester ain't got that kinda range. A Sharps, yes, but not a Winchester. That gun is good up to three hundred, sometimes four hundred yards—but not no eight hundred, not accurately. Yet, the more I thought 'bout it, the more I figured I could do it. I knowed the bullet'd carry that far and it'd kill if I give it enough lift. After thinking 'bout the ballistics of the model 66, I speculated it'd still hit with enough punch if I could just place my shot right. At that distance it'd be damn near a fifteen-foot drop—a real sporting shot.

I calculated the distance again and raised my rifle to my cheek. I lifted that sight up, way up above where that buck was standing, then put the gun down again and took another look. I must've done that 'bout three or four times. Then I aimed again, and when the situation looked right to me and I could see the whole thing in my mind's eye and trace where the bullet was gonna travel, I let go just for the hell of it.

When the gun roared and I seen that buck collapse, it was one of the greatest thrills of my life. I let out a war whoop and stood up and danced 'round and then run down off the face of the mesa and 'cross the valley and up the other side. When I come up to him I let out another whoop and held my rifle up high and went dancing all 'round.

To be real honest, I don't reckon I could do it again. It was a scratch shot and there had to be lots of luck in it, but I'd done some calculating and my calculating'd turned out right. I drawed my knife and cut that buck's throat real quick and seen that the quivering weren't nothing but an after-death reaction. There weren't no heartbeat nor nothing left.

I leaned my gun up against one of them oak brush bushes and took my knife and made three or four quick slashes to get me some back straps. I straddled his big, broad back and leaned down there slicing them pieces, thinking what a fine batch of jerky they was gonna make. The flies'd come buzzing 'round and I straightened up and used the back of my knife hand to brush 'em away from my eyes.

Then I happened to look 'cross the next valley. I'd been so tickled to kill that buck that I'd gone off whooping and hollering, like it weren't never my custom to do, carrying on like I was the only man in the country. When I looked 'cross the valley I got the shock of my life, 'cause there spiraling up in the afternoon sunshine was the nicest curl of smoke you ever seen. It was a little north of me and 'round the edge of a hill, so I hadn't seen it before. The source was situated in a crevice on the north side of the mesa where there was prob'ly a spring and a real good campsite.

It sure made me feel foolish to think that I'd been dozing ever since noon on the other side and hadn't smelt no smoke or whiffs of Comanche. Then I'd made a rifle shot and gone whooping and hollering 'cross the canyon and up the side of the hill I was on. It made me downright ashamed to be that careless. For a few minutes I felt something like fear. I hadn't felt fear for a long time. I hadn't reckoned on getting careless, and that's just what I'd done.

If that was a Comanche fire, they'd sure heard my shot. How many of 'em had watched me yelling and whooping and hollering as I'd gone 'cross the canyon? I felt plumb embarrassed. It was a damn poor piece of workmanship and I knowed it. What's more, I knowed that if'n it was a Comanche camp, and it had to be, my life was in real danger. They must've been maneuvering 'round in good shape by that time.

I left them back straps right where they lay and run down into the brush, then started moving slow and cautious, keeping an eye on everything I could see. I'd move a little and then look clear 'round me and watch and listen. Then I'd move a little farther and do the same thing. I was working downhill on a diagonal course that'd bring me plumb opposite the fire, maybe five hundred yards away, 'fore nightfall.

The first thing was to find out how many Indians was in the camp. The second was how close they was to me and if they was coming for me. I had to work into a position where I could look back at the mule buck and see what come to find me there. I stayed real quiet for 'bout fifteen minutes, looking 'round for a spot that'd be the most likely point to move to. I weren't long in finding it—a clump of oak brush on top of a little knoll 'bout forty yards to the north.

From there I reckoned that I could see 'cross the valley, up against the cap rock of the mesa I was on, and back to where I'd dropped the deer. I knowed I couldn't see the animal itself, 'cause there'd be too much oak brush in between, but I reckoned I might see some movement. Best of all, I could see that there was a line of thick oak brush 'tween me and where I wanted to go.

I moved real cautious and was awful glad that the foliage was still green so's I could move well without being seen. I'd almost got halfway when I seen a movement off to my left. I froze in a low crouch and held my breath, easing back the hammer of my rifle.

I watched for the motion and I seen it again. Then it was clear—the back, shoulders, and head of a Comanche moving forward slow and cautious in a crouch, staying behind each piece of oak brush and traveling from one to the next with the stealth of a snake. He was stripped to the waist, wearing a breechclout and moccasins like I had. He was carrying a gun of some kind, but there weren't no magazine along the barrel, so I knowed it was a single-shot of some kind.

I lay real still and watched that Comanche. He was moving right 'cross the path ahead of me, 'tween me and the place I was making for. Sometimes I could see all of him and other times just part of him. I turned my head ever so slow and scanned as far as I could 'round the sides of my head to see if there was any others with him.

I didn't see no motion, so I sat there and watched that Comanche brave pass within fifteen yards of me without him ever knowing I was there. I could've killed him easy, but not knowing how many others there was, it would've been damned foolish.

A minute later I made out another Indian moving slow and cautious through the brush. I looked in the direction where the first Indian'd crossed and seen another motion. That made three—and there might well be more'n that. I soon found out I was right when I seen a fourth one a little bit off to my left.

That oak brush was infested with Comanches, all of 'em moving in, real deadlylike, hoping to catch me dressing out that deer. It wouldn't be long 'fore they'd come up on the place where the buck was and they'd see where I'd ducked into the brush. No matter how cautious I tried to be, they wouldn't have no trouble following my tracks right down to where I was.

My only hope was to keep outta their way 'til it got dark. I sure weren't in no position to fight 'em off, not knowing how big their numbers was. I eased on a few yards at a time, silent as a cat, hoping and looking and listening and watching as I went. I'd made maybe a hundred yards when I heard a yell behind me that meant one of them Indians'd come up on my kill and found where I'd dropped them back straps. I reckoned it to be 'bout a half hour 'fore sundown, so it'd be a good hour 'fore darkness'd cover me. With them braves gathering fast on my trail, I couldn't afford to be cautious no longer.

Instinct told me to make a run for it. I crouched and lit out for safety, but I had to go into the clearing for a ways to do it. I zigzagged 'round a big bunch of oak brush and kept working along, bent low but running at a real good clip. I went along like that for a couple of minutes, gaining speed all the time.

Then I raised to my full height and stretched out my stride. I heard a yell off to my left and at the same time I felt a stabbing pain in the side of my neck and heard the crash of a rifle. I didn't know how bad I'd been hit, but I weren't down and I was still running.

Though I was ducking from one clump of oak brush to another, I was moving faster'n any scalded cat you ever seen. There weren't no more shots right away, but I heard lots of war cries behind me, like they was coming from a bush on every side.

I reckoned I'd got me into a hornets' nest of Comanches, and I cussed the hell outta my stupidity. How could I've been traveling in Comanche land all that time, thinking I was so good at keeping silent and hid, then expose myself to this kinda mess? The only thing that'd kept me from being afraid was being so mad at myself.

I've heard men talk 'bout running, and you have, too. They usually refer to things like "running a hundred yards," or "running a mile," or even "running five miles," but don't many of 'em talk 'bout running 'til dark. It didn't make no difference how far I went. The only chance I had to stay alive was to stay ahead of them Comanches 'til it was damn well night.

I looked up at the sun. I'd have to keep running as hard as I could for more'n an hour. It may not seem possible, but when your life depends on it, there ain't hardly no limit to your strength and endurance. So I kept on ducking in and outta the oak brush and working up the side of the mesa towards the cap rock where the hiding was the best. All the time I was running I was thinking.

I knowed some of 'em was gonna head for their horses, and if they done that it wouldn't do me a bit of good to get out into open country—they'd overtake me there in a hurry. My aim was to get up underneath the cap rock to where the brush was the thickest. I could cross some of them rockslides and that'd sure fix a horse. I also knowed I couldn't afford to get out into the open any more'n I could help, 'cause I didn't know how close they was behind me or when they might get another shot.

I could still feel the burning in the side of my neck and I thanked my stars that I'd just felt a sharp, red-hot burn instead of the shock of shattered bone. That might teach me a lesson to keep my eyes and ears open in Comanche country.

I went jumping from one oak brush clump to another, skipping over the tops of the rocks at high speed and all the time gaining altitude. The oak brush was getting thicker and the rocks I come on was larger and rougher. That's the way I wanted it. Them Comanches weren't far behind. Every now and then I heard a yip and knowed that them devils was encouraging each other to hurry up and help their-selves to my scalp. That was one of their plans I weren't figuring to oblige.

When I'd been running fifteen or twenty minutes and the sun was getting awful low, I come to the end of the oak brush. It broke off 'cause there was a real rough rockslide that come off the cap rock. Millions of years ago something'd let loose and the big jumble'd slid down the side of the hill. It was maybe seventy-five yards across with small blocks of stone resting on loose rocks and gravel.

I took one quick glance and knowed I didn't have no choice but to start across. My only hope was that I could make it to the other side 'fore any Comanches come to the clearing. I ducked and twisted and jumped and bounded 'tween one sharp jagged block and another, watching my footing all the time and praying that I wouldn't feel another bullet.

I tried to give myself as much cover as possible, but that weren't easy, as most of them chunks was only 'bout the size of a powder keg. So when I was running, at least half of my body showed from time to time, and sometimes all of it. A careful shot would've had a good chance of spilling my guts out right there.

I don't know how long it took me to cross that seventy-five yards, but I reckon it weren't any more'n fifteen or twenty seconds, and the last couple was on the fly, diving into a clump of oak brush. I whirled and jerked my rifle up and levered a shell into the chamber.

I was puffing and blowing, and any accurate shooting was gonna be tough.

Then one of them bucks come running right out into plain view. God, he was a beautiful sight! His face was painted up with war paint and he had a red feather tied to the chokecherry stick in his hair. He was naked 'cept for a breechclout and them big Comanche moccasins. He had a cartridge belt strung diagonal 'cross from his shoulders to his waist and I seen a rifle in his right hand as he swung up his arm to check hisself.

He'd seen his mistake at once. He'd busted out into the open without knowing it. He started to duck back, but it was too late for him. My rifle went off with a crash that echoed along the mesa, and that buck pitched backwards. The bullet went through the front of his chest, tearing out part of his backbone, and his rifle clattered as it slid down the rocks.

A second later another buck broke out 'bout ten yards to the right and stopped so's only his head with all that war paint showed. It was the first and last time it ever showed there. Cat Brules weren't missing no target the size of a man's head at seventy-five yards. The buck's face kinda disintegrated as his head snapped back.

Suddenly I felt good all over. Although I was breathing ragged and had just been cussing myself for being a fool, I was enjoying the thrill of the fight. Cat Brules was speaking the way Cat Brules should, from the business end of a Winchester.

There come over me the same feeling that I'd got in many a fight. It's something hard to explain. It was a calm and deadlike steadiness which told the story of all my shooting. I knowed I couldn't miss. If an Indian showed hisself, I'd kill him. It'd take a long while for somebody to come up 'round behind, and the more them varmints showed any part of their bodies, the more I'd ventilate 'em.

There was a dead silence. The shooting'd spelled caution for the rest of them bucks. If they weren't real close and hadn't seen it, they wouldn't have knowed what'd happened, 'cause both them bucks'd died without making an outcry. For all they knowed, I'd missed my shots, so they'd still come up with their curiosity all bubbling. More power to 'em. What I needed was more Comanche targets.

In a little while I heard a thumping and crashing—it was horses running in the brush. To a Comanche hunter there ain't no dearer sound than them skunks coming in close on horseback, 'specially when yore packed away in a nice fortified place. Them bucks prob'ly didn't have no more idea than I'd had that they was coming up on that rockslide. The noise drawed a little closer, and then three of them riders busted into view just as nice as you please. Then they'd seen the rockslide, checked their horses, and wheeled 'round for cover.

Well, I done some fancy shooting in my life, but I reckon I never done any fancier'n that. I took two of them bucks off their horses as fast as I could work the Winchester's lever action. Then I got a parting shot at the third one as he disappeared back into the oak brush. I weren't dead sure, but I reckoned that the point where I'd let drive was four or five feet inside the brush from where I'd last seen him. A minute later a riderless horse flashed 'cross an open space, so I knowed I done some good.

The last bit of fancy shooting seemed to put the stopper on the bottle for a while. They quieted down quick. I must say I preferred to have 'em yelling and showing theirselves. I didn't like them long quiet spells with Indians around.

It was getting on towards dark and I figured I'd made 'bout as much of that rockslide stand as I could expect. It was time to hightail it. I eased back in the brush, turned northwest, and kept plugging on, ducking in and out of the stuff and moving in silence.

Maybe half an hour later, when it'd got real dark, I'd covered enough distance to where I could catch my breath and do some thinking. I dropped down to a steady walk and begun to take stock of the situation. I could still feel some burning on the side of my neck and there was a little blood. I weren't losing enough to make a difference, but without a little bit of luck I would've lost all I had. I'd come close to being finished off by the very game I was hunting. That bunch of Comanches owed me something for scaring me and disturbing my peace. I was going back to collect. The more I thought about it, the better it seemed.

What'll they expect me ta do? I thought. Keep on runnin'? Get the hell outta the country an' save my scalp? Prob'ly. What'll they least expect me ta do? Why, I figgered, they'll least expect me ta double back an' come up on their camp.

I started down off the mesa, dropped through the oak brush, and made my way out to the open prairie. I got my bearings and swung back to where I reckoned their camp was. I knowed they wasn't 'bout to leave their dead, so they'd be lugging them five bucks in on their horses, and that'd keep 'em busy for a little while. I didn't know but what I might come up on 'em in the dark, but I reckoned I'd hear 'em 'fore they heard me.

I had all night to cover the distance, and I moved cautious but fast. In 'bout an hour and a half I seen what I was looking for—a speck of light on the side of the mesa right 'bout where I'd figured a spring'd be.

Real soon I smelled the fire, and stopped to take stock of things. I needed to figure out where their horses'd be. I checked the wind and didn't like it—it was at my back. I thought about climbing the mesa to come 'round over the top from the other side, but I give up on that idea. Even if I found a way up through the cap rock, which was unlikely, I might have had a tough time getting down after I got 'round to the other side of the fire. No, I reckoned that the best thing for me to do was to head out into the prairie and keep the campfire on my right all the time. Then I could work my way back upwind.

All that time I never seen or heard nothing of any of them Indians that'd took off after me. I didn't know whether they was coming back to the fire or still looking for me. But I knowed where their fire was and that there was a few more Indians there and likely some horses. It was nigh unto midnight by the time I'd worked myself close enough to the fire so's I could get some idea of what was going on. I'd circled clear 'round and had the wind in my face and'd prob'ly be able to hear them horses if they was 'tween me and the fire.

Just to make sure, I worked my way up towards the cap rock of the mesa, it being most unlikely that them Comanches'd stake their horses there. Getting a little elevation helped, 'cause I could look down and get a better view of the group 'round the fire. It was a war party for sure—there weren't no tepees around. From time to time, figures passed back and forth in front of the fire, and soon I knowed there was only three bucks attending the camp. If there was any others around, they was off in the shadows asleep.

One buck kept squatting down by the fire, facing towards me. I could see his war paint and how unholy his face looked in the flickering flames. He reminded me of some damn spook or idol that you see them artist people painting. Finally all three of 'em squatted 'round the fire. They stayed that way for some time and seemed to show no inclination to roll up in their blankets. I thought that was odd. Every now and then they'd glance off into the dark like they was waiting for somebody.

Finally one of them bucks jumped up and cupped his hand to his ear to listen. Then I seen him conversing with the other two and they stood up, too, and begun listening. Soon I heard what they was hearing. It was the sound of horses' hooves. In another few minutes two bucks rode into the firelight, each of 'em leading extra horses. There was something draped over each horse—the bodies of them bucks I'd shot. I tell you, it was a real happy sight.

I crawled forward and closed the range to 'bout seventy-five yards. I got me a good place to watch—a nice round rock that stood up above the brush. I lay there real quiet and watched the show with interest. There was lots of talk and lots of explaining, and I looked real careful in the flickering firelight to count the bodies. There was five of 'em. Seeing 'em made me feel real good and give me lots of confidence—until I felt the side of my neck.

The first thing the Indians done was to unload the bodies and roll 'em up in some blankets that they fetched. I reckoned they was the blankets that them braves'd left when they'd heard my shooting. Less'n there was others that I didn't know nothing 'bout, there'd been ten in the party and I'd cleaned out half of 'em.

I wished that I'd knowed some Comanche talk, 'cause every now and then above the soft sigh of the wind I could hear their voices. They was making signs and gestures with their arms, and standing up one after another and being kind of dramatic. I knowed that they'd been plenty upset and they was trying to express things.

Maybe they'd decide to stay up all night and ride away in the morning or maybe take turns keeping watch. I'd have to wait and see. It sure weren't easy to lie there on that rock and look at them bucks in the firelight and make plans on 'em.

How was I gonna finish up five Comanches and make sure of it? If I could start shooting then, I figured I could get two of 'em, and if I was fast enough I might get three, but that was doubtful. They moved like lightning when they was spooked.

Well, there was a way, but I had to get lots closer'n seventy-five yards.

Them Comanches acted plenty shook up 'bout bringing in their dead compadres and they weren't in any mood for no sleeping. They was still sitting 'round the fire, making motions and talking, and it looked like they was gonna keep it up all night, then hit the trail in the morning to take the bodies of their fella warriors back home, wherever that might be. I had some satisfaction in knowing that even if I didn't get 'em right then, they would come plowing into their village with half their number sacked over the back of their ponies like bags of potatoes and there'd be lots of keening among the squaws. That keening wail was music to my ears, 'specially knowing I was the one that'd killed their bucks.

I was there for the most part of an hour 'fore I come to a conclusion. The soldier books all says that when you ambush an enemy at daybreak, you'd best get yourself in a position where the sun is coming up behind you. Then you can see clear to do your shooting and the enemy has the handicap of facing into the sun. That's all fine for book learning, but it weren't worth a damn for handling Comanches. In the first place, when the first streak of dawn come up over the edge of the eastern horizon, them bucks'd go packing up and be off, with none of that waiting 'til the sun rose.

On top of that, if I come in from the eastern side to get the sun behind me, I'd silhouette myself and make a real good target. Even more important, most of our winds was out of the west and it weren't no exception that night. Them Indians was sitting on the upwind side of the fire with their backs to the west, facing east, and if I come from that direction, I'd be looking at 'em head-on.

I was going to have to take 'em from behind while looking straight into the rising sun, or, if I was lucky, just a little 'fore that, when I could see 'em out there good. It was 'bout three hours before dawn, and I had to crawl fifty or sixty yards to get in close. I figured I'd need all that time since I'd have to move real slow so's not to make noise. I crawled down off that rock and lay real careful and quiet beneath the oak brush. I felt it out with my hand ever so slow and easy to see if there was any twigs or leaves or anything else in my way. When I'd made sure it was all right, I lifted myself slightly off my belly and eased on forward 'bout six inches. Then I repeated the deal.

It was a long, tedious night, but I couldn't afford to be seen or heard. I kept working towards a point that was 'bout ten yards west of the firelight, and although I moved as quiet as a cat, every now and then there'd be the slightest, faintest rustle of leaves and dirt. I'm telling you, it sounded like an avalanche to me. I'd lay still for ten minutes or so to see if there was any change in the voices of them bucks, but they kept on in a low, melodious tone.

I took all of them three hours making that crawl. When I was through, I was only ten yards behind three of them bucks sitting 'round the fire. Crawling in and outta the oak brush and losing sight of the campfire every now and then, I hadn't been able to keep track of 'em all. I was a little disturbed when I seen that all five of 'em weren't there—just the three with their backs to me. I waited a little and soon seen another one when I heard him snore. He'd rolled up in his blanket 'cross from the fire in the shadows.

I was trembling with excitement. I had to see every one of them Comanches 'fore I stood up and started to shoot. I couldn't afford to have even one of 'em hiding out in the darkness. All I could do was wait.

It weren't fifteen minutes 'til the first streak of dawn begun showing on the eastern horizon. It seemed like fifteen hours. I kept waiting for the other buck, knowing that when dawn broke, the ones in front of me'd start getting up and moving 'round and then the whole show'd be a mess, and I wouldn't know where any of 'em was.

Very, very gradual from the east there come a faint light. I waited a little longer and I could see real clear. Just like I'd expected, them bucks'd been sitting a long time in silence. One of 'em was smoking a pipe and the others was gazing in the firelight. The one that'd been smoking leaned forward to shake the ashes outta his pipe and made as if he was gonna rise.

Then I got a break. The Comanche I hadn't been able to spot appeared in the firelight from the east. Guess he'd been lying out there in the darkness. I couldn't see for sure what he had in his hand, but it looked like a long stick he was putting in the fire. At the same instant, one of the bucks with their backs to me—the one who'd put out the pipe—rose slowly from his cross-legged position and stood up.

I rose right with him. I had it fixed in my mind exactly where they all was. I had never intended to use my rifle that close up. You can't swing a rifle barrel or reload the chamber with the lever action fast enough to do that kinda job. It was Smith & Wesson work, all one slick motion—real oily smooth and fast.

I leaned forward in a slight crouch on my toes, my balance just right and my left hand free. It was as if someone'd been timing me and'd said, Go! That's when I let drive.

I started fanning that old .38 with my left hand so fast that there was a continual roar of the gun firing. I got off five shots 'tween two and three seconds, and the results was a sight to see. It seemed like the shooting was all over 'fore anything'd happened. I'd took each Indian in order. The buck standing in front of me buckled at the knees and pitched into the fire. Them two that was sitting cross-legged on either side of him wheeled over flat onto the ground. The one facing me 'cross the fire took a shot 'bout head-on at his jawbone, and I seen later that the bullet'd passed right through the back of his neck and broke his spine. He snapped back outta the firelight like he'd been hit broadside with an ax. The one in the blanket was half-rolled out and'd started kneeling to stand up. He took it in the chest.

I weren't never gonna forget that scene, 'cause that was the best and fastest shooting I'd ever done in my life—and the most effective. One thing that stood out in my mind for a long time was the sight of that buck who'd come out of his blanket with his copper body glistening in the firelight, half-kneeling and rising with his left arm on the ground and his right arm holding his chest where he'd been shot. Like in all them war parties, he was naked 'cept for a breechclout. His body was a mass of rippling muscles and in perfect shape.

He'd stayed in that position for three or four seconds, his wild eyes gleaming at me while he held the wound in his chest. Then he'd started coughing and spitting blood, and it come in a torrent. He rolled over and the life went outta him with a hoarse sigh. It was a beautiful sight.

I stood in the firelight as dawn rimmed the horizon, and 'round me was five more dead Comanches. My revolver barrel was hot. I felt like letting out a war whoop and hopping up and down, dancing 'round my victims, but I kept quiet. I'd learned my lesson.

It took me a minute to calm down and begin to look 'em over. I rolled each one 'round to see if he had anything I wanted. The Indian in the blanket had an old Spencer rifle, but it didn't look much good to me. I figured he was groping for it as he'd come sliding outta his blanket when I commenced shooting.

The Indian that'd stood up with his back to me had his head in the fire. I pulled him out by the heels and seen that he had a necklace made of bright-colored stones. It sure was a nice thing, and I took it for my trophy. One of them bucks had a good pair of moccasins. They looked a mite better'n the ones I was wearing, so I decided that even though I had an extra pair still tied 'round my waist, I'd take 'em. I changed those for my old ones right there. I didn't see nothing else on none of 'em that I wanted.

For a while I stood looking at 'em as they was lying 'round the fire there and then over at the other bunch that'd been brought in and rolled in their blankets the evening before. I cut my cat's-eye mark deep into the ground where it couldn't be missed. Then I eased on down towards where the horses was picketed. I couldn't see 'em, but I could hear 'em stomping a little.

I didn't have no trouble locating 'em, and when I come up I seen there was 'bout eight horses picketed and maybe twelve more grazing 'round. They looked like a fine bunch of animals. When them Indian ponies was in the wild, they sure looked good. Only time I ever seen 'em look real bad was after a hard winter, or when one of them war parties'd come back from a long raid where they'd nearly rode 'em to death. But that rich grass on the prairie was full of good feed and them creatures was born to that country, so in no time they'd look great.

I reckon if you took 'em to some eastern stable and put 'em beside some of them nice racehorses from Kentucky, they wouldn't have looked like much, but out there on the prairie, with the wind blowing through their manes and their hides shining in the morning sun, they was a handsome sight. I walked down the picket line and them horses, knowing me to be a stranger, went to rearing and twisting and snorting and kicking up dust. I liked that, 'cause it showed they had plenty of spirit.

I was looking for the best horse and sure as hell I found him. He was a young Appaloosa stallion as big as a mountain. He had a broad, powerful chest and round, muscled hindquarters. He had a slim, arched neck and snorty nostrils, and his eyes was fiery and wild. The way he pulled on the rope and twisted his head 'round, I could see a glimpse of his teeth. They looked good. I reckoned that'd be the horse for me.

I went up and down the line again and didn't see nothing else. Then I looked over them that was out ranging around. I picked me a nice bay mare and a white gelding that I figured'd be good backup horses.

I'd done some more thinking. The next thing I wanted to do was to find that old hide cache that me and Pedro'd left and stock up on ammunition. It weren't gonna be easy. The country north of the Canadian was wild and open. To try to find anything in it was like looking for a needle in a haystack, yet that's what I aimed to do. Just in case some of them hides was still okay and hadn't slipped, I might load 'em on and take 'em back to Fort Union. Even if that weren't possible, I knowed I'd need a couple of good horses to haul the ammunition, assuming nobody'd got to it first. Lots of it was big .50 Sharps stuff, and I couldn't use it in my Winchester, but it was worth some money and there weren't no use leaving it out on the range if I could help it.

16

COMANCHE LAND

While I was standing there thinking 'bout them buffalo hides, I got to looking at the horses that'd been grazing in the open stretches of grass nearby. All of 'em had their heads up and their ears cocked and was watching off northwest towards the mesa on the other side of the valley. I didn't wait long to hide myself behind some rocks where I could take a look. Then I seen what they was staring at.

Coming out of the oak brush on the other side of the valley was two horsemen. It was plain to see in the morning sunlight that they was Comanches. Each of 'em had a gun in the crook of his arm and they was moving along at a slow jogging pace, looking down at the ground and pointing every so often. Then I got the chills, not from seeing them two horsemen but from realizing what kind of a bad situation I'd almost got myself into.

Them Indians was following my trail. They was backtracking me to this Indian camp. I couldn't understand why they weren't coming at a wild gallop, since they must've heard my shooting. But then maybe a revolver don't sound as strong as all that, 'specially from four or five miles away, which they must've been at the time. If they'd heard something, they sure wouldn't be expecting nothing like the results they was gonna find.

I debated some as to what to do. It weren't no use to try to take them horses and leave. I was gonna have a little trouble with that Appaloosa stallion, I could see that. Maybe we was gonna have a little bucking contest 'fore I got him quieted down, but there weren't no time for that. I sure as hell didn't wanta leave without him, so I decided to hole up and watch for a little while to see what happened.

I wanted to make sure what the odds was. A low whistle escaped my lips when I thought how easy it would've been for them two to've come back a little earlier while I was shooting up the camp—they might've spoiled all the fun. It was sure fortunate for me that they'd took so long to pick up my tracks, but I was cussing myself again for being such a damn fool and s'posing them Comanches would've dropped my tracks completely just 'cause I'd busted five of their members. They was real stubborn Indians.

I guessed that last night when two of 'em brung the bodies of their compadres back to camp, them other two'd been following my trail. It'd been tough going, 'cause darkness'd come on, and I don't reckon they never dreamed that I would've doubled back during the night. They'd prob'ly kept on slowly working towards the northwest, and at daylight'd found that they'd lost the trail. They must've scattered 'round some 'fore they picked it up again. If they'd heard the gunfire a'tall, they must've figured it was their buddies doing the shooting and expected when they got there that they'd find a white man all trussed up on a spike ready for cooking.

One thing I reckoned I'd have to do 'fore I took more liberties was to make sure there weren't no more of 'em coming. I watched them two horsemen crossing the valley for ten or fifteen minutes and managed to satisfy myself that if there was any other bucks out hunting for me, they was a long ways off. I figured I could hightail it back to camp then and be there in time to form a reception committee for 'em.

I guess I misjudged the distance, or luck weren't with me, 'cause it sure would've been nice to've got to the camp ahead of them bucks. I could've picked 'em off clean as a whistle as they'd come up. Maybe the great Manitou figured I'd busted enough of his Indians for that day and weren't gonna give me no more chances. However it was, them bucks got to the camp just a minute 'fore I did. Then I heard the damnedest shrieking and hollering going on and I swore under my breath, 'cause I figured they'd be lying there waiting for me.

Right then the thundering of hooves stopped me in my tracks. I froze, but realized that they was going the other way. I couldn't understand that. I thought they'd at least examine the camp, if not mill 'round looking for my tracks leading out of it. I was afraid I might stumble onto an ambush or something, but my curiosity was too much. I went jogging through the oak brush and busted out at the campsite. The campfire was still burning and the dead bodies hadn't moved none. Nothing'd been touched.

Off to the southeast, headed down the valley and out to the open plains, was two Indian horsemen riding hell-bent for something. They was whipping their ponies and going like the wind. I looked 'round and tried to figure it out. I finally guessed that they just couldn't believe seeing their compadres dead with my cat's-eye signature nearby, and thought it must've been some evil spirit that'd done it. Indians was plumb scared to death by the supernatural, so they'd lit out for home. I couldn't help laughing and thinking that Pedro sure would've enjoyed that sight.

I turned 'round and headed back up towards them Indian horses. It was time to go on 'bout my business. When I got to the picket line, things'd calmed down some. That being the second time they'd seen me, them horses didn't carry on too much, and I hummed to 'em in a low voice, keeping my eye on that big Appaloosa stallion. I thought he'd have a chance to whiff me and wouldn't be so spooked, but I had another think coming. He didn't want no part of me or nothing connected with me. He had a wild look in his eye, and when I got close, he reared and plunged and twisted. He sure looked like a lot of horse. The more I seen him, the more I liked him. It was just a question of time 'fore I'd calm him down.

I got hold of that picket rope and eased along to try to get my hand on his muzzle. When I got close to him, all hell broke loose. He reared and struck at me with them front feet, slacking up the rope good. I jerked it sideways and throwed him off and saved me from getting my skull crushed.

I looked over the rest of them horses on the picket line again and decided there weren't any of 'em I wanted. What I needed was a piece of rope, and one of them picket ropes'd do fine. There was a small paint gelding who was the most likely to let go. I got up to him easy to get my hand on his neck, and he was trembling some, but he didn't act near as spirited as that Appaloosa had.

I undone his picket rope and let him loose. He went galloping out over the prairie, looking to join the other fellas. It sure was fun to see. The other horses all had their heads up, so I studied the white gelding and the bay mare. They looked to be the best of the bunch, so I kept an eye on 'em.

I took the rope that'd been 'round the little paint and gathered it up in a coil to make a lariat. I knowed I had a real job ahead of me training the Appaloosa. I reckoned he'd been a one-Indian horse. It rankled me to think that there was a young Indian who could ride that magnificent animal, but at the same time that horse wouldn't have nothing to do with me. He'd soon learn that I was the new boss, having already proved myself better'n his master.

I had the lariat ready and come 'round on him, quartering from the rear. He whirled and pulled against the picket rope, then he made a sashay at me to give me them hooves again. Slick as hell I shook that old lasso out and snagged his forefeet. Then I jerked hard and he went down with a crash, throwing up a bunch of dust. He was snorting and thrashing and tugging, but I really leaned on the lariat and kept him down. Thanks to that, plus the picket rope 'round his neck, he weren't going nowhere.

He done lots of struggling that must've lasted five minutes. Then he sunk back exhausted with the dust all settling 'round him. I pulled hard on the lariat to keep them forefeet pinched up, and passed 'round to his back. Then I eased up and put my hand on his neck right above his withers. You would've thought my touch was a hot iron. He jerked and heaved and tried to turn 'round and bite—all the time doing the damndest amount of snorting and coughing I'd ever heard. It could've been terrifying, 'cept I was determined to ride him and knowed that if I ever got him gentled down he'd be the kind of horse a man'd need for making a quick getaway.

I come 'round over his back and made a half-loop with the rope 'round one of his rear legs. Then I took another turn 'round his forefoot and drawed 'em up together, buckling him down to where he could barely move. That's the way I aimed to keep him 'til I could get his attitude straightened out.

I untied the picket rope and come back to take it off his head, and he took a swipe at me with his jaws. I was mighty glad I was outta his reach—them teeth looked dangerous. I reckoned he could take your arm off.

After I reworked his picket line to make a jaw rope out of it, I got close enough to tempt him to have another try. When he did, I slipped the rope through his mouth and drawed it up tight 'round his lower jaw. Then I worked 'round by his withers and really leaned into that jaw, just to let him know that I had some leverage. I pulled his neck down to a tight curve with that jaw rope 'til I was pulling his mouth wide open. I wanted him to know that there was gonna be plenty of tugging there 'fore I let him up. He weren't gonna be running off free 'cross the plains like he'd like to.

I eased 'round and put my hand on his mane. He was quivering all over and his neck was bowed like a coiled spring. When I was kneeling a-straddle of his withers with one knee on the ground and the other right along his shoulder, I eased the pressure on the rope that I'd used to hog-tie his legs and give it a little flick.

It took a second for him to kick a little bit and realize that his feet was loose. He let out a deep grunt and leaped to his feet with me solid tight on his back, barely pausing to get his balance 'fore he started trying to unload me. That horse begun rearing and plunging and pitching and bucking, all the time snorting like a bull.

His breath come outta his throat like a deep-toned trumpet. His hind legs snapped and kicked and his forelegs worked like whirling pivots. He pitched—and bang, he'd come down stiff-legged and hard with a twist, jarring my guts. It seemed like my teeth was coming out.

I had legs that could clamp as strong as a bear trap, so there weren't no shaking me loose. I didn't try no fancy riding or fanning him, I just hung on tight to his mane and hauled back on the jaw rope every time he jumped, jerking and twisting him and giving him some competition to let him know I was still there.

I don't know how long he kept bucking, but soon his pitching started to line up in a single direction and he headed out towards the prairie, still snorting and fighting and jumping. Finally, his jumps got longer and longer and settled into a wild, furious gallop.

The way he'd stretched out and run, I knowed I had a real horse underneath me. It'd been several months since I'd been on horseback, and I got a great feeling that I was flying, seeing the way that prairie land swept by on both sides and feeling the thrust and jump of the horse every time he took a stride.

I eased off on the jaw rope a little and let him roll. In fact, I kept urging him with my knees at every jump and kicking him in the ribs as he tore along. I kept calling for more speed, asking him to give me all he had. His ears was laid back and his nostrils flared big, drinking in the wind. The breeze sailed through my teeth so strong I had to turn my head sideways to catch my breath.

I don't know how long he kept running. It was a long, long while. I reckon he covered seven or eight miles 'fore he showed any inclination to ease off. When I seen he was weakening a little and slowing up, I started urging him on even more to let him know I could stay with him and was ready for more if he had it in him.

Then I begun pressuring on the jaw rope a little to the left, easing him 'round in a great circle, and after a while I had him turned clear 'round and headed back. Every time he'd ease off a little bit, I'd keep urging him on 'til he finally run hisself out. When I seen he was ready to quit, I pulled back on the jaw rope and helped him settle down. He come to a quivering halt, shaking all over.

Then I begun to talk to him real gentle, patting him along the neck and the withers. Every time I'd touch him he'd jerk a little, but real soon he got used to the feel of my hand. I eased off on the jaw rope and he started walking. He was still gasping and blowing, all foam flecked from the run and covered with dust. His eyes still had a wild look in them and he kept tossing his head and blowing foam from his nostrils as he walked, but the real bucking and pitching was over with and it was plain to see that he'd got it through his head that the man riding him was gonna stay put. "We gotta think of a name fer ya, big fella," I told him.

'Fore I'd got on him, I'd took my rifle off my shoulder sling and laid it up against a tree. But then I was anxious to get it back. I nudged him for more speed and he broke into the prettiest ground-eating single-foot gait you could ask for. It was as smooth as riding a rocking chair or drifting with the prairie wind. I thought 'bout that for a minute, then cussed him a little, and patted his sweaty, speckled neck.

"You've got lots a fight in ya, horse, an' I'm gonna use it plenty. Yore a warrior. Yeah, that's it, that's a good name fer ya—Warrior."

Once or twice on the way back he tried to turn and go some other direction, but I clapped him on the side of the head to remind him who was in charge, and he headed back towards the picket line. It weren't too long 'fore I seen them other horses. Some of 'em'd run out on the prairie with us during the bucking contest, but they'd got tired of it all and stopped to feed. They raised their heads when they seen us coming in, and as I rode by they begun to join up and follow.

Them horses still tied to the picket line raised their heads, too, and whinnied. Warrior snorted and whinnied back, as if he was saying to 'em, Well, I done my damndest. I put up a helluva fight, but I still got this man on my back. I guess I'm stuck with him.

When we come back in close to the picket line, the quiver'd all gone outta him and I spoke to him real easy. He was still blowing a little bit from his hard run, and he was sweated all over. It seemed like he knowed and understood just where his place was.

I kept my hand on his neck while I was talking to him and then slowly slid off'n him and stood beside him. I stroked his muzzle and run my hand up 'tween his ears. Then I scratched the under part of his jaw and run my hand down his withers, along his back, and over his rump, talking to him in a low, steady voice all the time.

Then I reached for his muzzle again and held my hand alongside of his jaw while I breathed a long breath into his nose. He snorted and tossed his head, but didn't move much.

I took hold of his mane again and eased myself up onto his back. He stood there trembling a little, then I touched him with my heels. He give a start and then walked off. I turned him this way and that and walked him back and forth, talking to him all the time. We kept that exercise up for most of an hour, me getting off'n him and back on, talking to him and handling him. Finally, it seemed like everything was all right.

That's how I got hold of one of the best horses I ever had. In some ways he didn't have the nimbleness of Piebald, and he weren't so smart, but he had as much strength, if not more, and every bit of the fight and heart that Piebald'd had.

When I thought he'd quieted down enough, I went back and picked up the lariat and coiled it up. I showed it to him and let him smell it, then I swung it back and forth in front of him to get him used to what it was all about. When I eased myself back up on him, he stood real quiet. Meanwhile, I swung the rope back and forth along his withers and up by his jaw and then over on the other side of his back. He flicked his ears and give it a wild eye, but he was willing to go along with anything that the man on his back was wanting to do.

Then, picking out the bay mare, I eased him off in a slow walk towards her. When she seen I was coming in close, she quit grazing and raised her head and stared at me. I got up almost within roping range 'fore she turned and started walking away easy.

I nudged Warrior up to an easy trot and she started trotting, too. When I eased him into turning on a little more speed, she done the same thing. It finally got to a flat-out race, but she weren't no match for the stallion. I drawed up on her steady and it weren't long 'fore I tossed the loop over her head and jerked her to a halt. She put on a mighty good rodeo herself, but she weren't nothing compared to Warrior. I didn't have no trouble snubbing her with a little twisting and turning. After we got back to the picket line I turned one of them other horses loose and used its rope to tie her up with, then I went on out after the white gelding and done the same thing to him. He done a little sashaying 'round of his own, but he was child's play.

What I really wanted to do was travel fast across the countryside to that buffalo hide cache and recover what I could from it and get out. I turned the rest of them horses loose and watched 'em run off a ways. Then I gathered up the picket ropes and tied 'em up 'round the gelding and mare, and I fashioned their lead ropes so's I could bring 'em along pack-string style. By the time I had everything ready, the sun was almost down. I watered my little caravan and hit out into the open prairie, heading south-southeast.

It give me a funny feeling to leave that mesa country and head out into the flat Comanche land north of the Canadian. Putting out to sea in a ship must be like that. When you got away from the mountains and the mesas, there weren't no landmarks, and the prairies stretched broad in every direction 'til they met the sky. A man really had to keep his sense of direction and had to have lots of faith in where he was going.

I had to make for water somewhere out in that vastness 'fore too long, 'cause out there in them dry prairies, you could run out of it real easy. I was heading out from a point on the mesas where I'd never been before and, as far as I knowed, neither'd any other white man. Going southeast, if I went far enough I'd hit the Canadian, but that'd be near ten days' hard riding.

The kind of riding that Warrior was up against for the next couple of days was gonna be real tough. I figured he'd prob'ly run hisself out that day—at a hard gallop we made a good fifteen miles that afternoon—but that horse done just fine. He had more bottom to him than any other horse I'd rode.

One good thing was the way I was set up. I weren't carrying no heavy saddle gear like a cowboy, but riding bareback with nothing but a jaw rope. Then, too, I had them other two horses to trade off on. I kept navigating by the stars all through the night, sometimes walking and sometimes going on at an easy jog, figuring it was better to take it slow. I knowed we just might have to travel forty-eight hours 'fore we hit any water.

It was late August by then, and it'd been a hot summer. Most of the creeks'd prob'ly be dry, but that was a chance I had to take. I stopped 'bout midnight to rest the horses and then kept on going. When dawn broke, I looked back and seen I'd traveled far enough to sink them mesas clear outta sight. There weren't nothing but wide prairie in every direction.

I put the lead rope on the stallion, then put the jaw rope on the mare and rode her all through the day just walking and jogging. By late afternoon it was getting too hot to do anything but walk. All the while I kept a sharp eye out for anything moving. I thought I seen some Indians in the distance, but it turned out to be tufts of bear grass shimmering in the heat. I was wise to them things, having been out in the flat country before. I knowed what kind of tricks your mind could play on you.

By dark them horses was getting fairly frantic from thirst. I give 'em a taste outta the canteen by jamming the spout in their mouths and letting 'em have a little gulp. It didn't seem to do no good—just made 'em crazier for water.

I changed to the white gelding that evening and kept right on going, but by midnight he showed signs of giving out. I rode him a little more and then got back on the stallion and found out he still had lots left in him. By that time all them horses was choking mad with thirst. From the way they was tossing their heads into the breeze, I could tell they was trying to find water. But there weren't no sign of it.

Towards dawn they perked up a little and quickened their steps, sniffing the wind in the direction we was going. That was a hopeful sign. When it got light enough to see, I reckoned I knowed the reason. I seen a faint, dark line in the distance, twenty to thirty miles away. I watched it for a considerable time, 'til the sun was high enough—then there weren't no mistaking it. There was a long line of cottonwoods and that meant we was coming up on a creek. Even if it was a dry one, there'd be a chance to dig for water.

Out in the open sea of prairie, distances is hard to judge. They seem like they ain't got no limits. I seen them cottonwoods at daybreak and we kept our pace up 'til noon. By then it was scorching hot and the cottonwoods was still a great ways ahead of us. The horses was so frantic they was damn near unmanageable. They kept breaking into a trot, then loping, and then falling back into a trot, but always sniffing and tossing their heads and looking towards them cottonwoods in the distance.

By two in the afternoon, the water in the canteen was gone and I was as choking mad with thirst as them horses. My tongue was dry and parched and thick in my mouth, blocking the back of my throat. Seemed like every time I drawed a breath my throat was being scraped by sandpaper. The mouths of them ponies'd been flecked with a little foam and it was all dried and caked. Their nostrils was wide open, and although they still had some spirit and was holding their heads up, their gait was a little stiff and their breath was coming much quicker.

Late in the afternoon it seemed like them cottonwoods was right in front of us, yet it was almost sunset when we finally come up on 'em. They was along a dry creek bed. When we got in close, thank God, I could see a little seepage against the banks in one or two places. I pitched down off'n Warrior and started digging a hole in the sand right along one of them seeps to gain a little more water, but them horses beat me to it.

I never seen anything like it. They dug in the sand with their forefeet and churned up enough moisture to get to drinking. They'd make a hole big enough for their muzzle and then stick it in and drain it. Maybe that was nature's way of controlling how much they drunk. Sure as hell if they'd come to a full spring where they could've got a bellyful of water, it would've killed 'em. The way it was, they worked hard for little sips here and there. It was the same way with me. That water was alkali and tasted like hell, but it was as refreshing as some of the sweetest stuff I ever drunk.

We stayed in the creek bottom 'til long after sundown—nearly three hours. I didn't give no thought to lighting a campfire. I just figured to make a cold camp and have a hard look around in the morning. I took the extra rope and made hobbles for each of them horses, then tied a long line to the stallion and fastened it 'round my wrist. I weren't taking no chance of being left on foot out there.

The night passed real easy and I was only woke up twice by the stallion jerking at the end of the line. I didn't mind it a bit. It was a welcome pull and I was glad to know that old Warrior was still there.

When dawn broke I had a look around. I reckoned we was still a little west of the north-south line that'd lead to the cache of buffalo hides. I pushed on down the streambed for another day's ride. There was seep holes all along it, 'bout the same as they'd been at the first place we'd hit. We didn't lack for no water, although once in a while we had to dig some.

I hit a stretch where the creek bed swung northeast, and decided to camp for a while in the cottonwood groves and push on at night, when it'd be cool and we wouldn't need so much water.

When it got cool and dark, I used the stars as a guide and hit out due south. I figured that way'd bring me out on a line near where I'd left the cache. If I couldn't see it anywhere, I'd travel clear through to the Canadian and then work back upstream and find where we'd crossed and try to follow our tracks on back.

When dawn broke, it seemed like I was riding along in the middle of a lost world. There weren't no cottonwoods in sight in any direction, and the land was flat all the way to the horizon. There was just bear cactus and buffalo grass and sky. There weren't no place for shade, and there weren't nothing but grass, grass, grass in every direction. No buttes, no mesas, no volcanic cones, no cottonwoods— nothing but grass and more grass as far as you could see. That was Comanche land.

I traveled all that day and the next. By nightfall the horses was getting thirsty and restless again. We rested a while after sundown and at midnight started again. I tried to give 'em a little sip of water from the canteen, but not too much, figuring that if worse come to worst I might have to do some walking.

When dawn broke, I couldn't see nothing again but what I'd been looking at all the day before. I looked back occasionally and seen we was making as straight a track as we could. It was a mighty discouraging sight, but we moved on all through that day.

'Fore sundown that evening I thought I seen something different on the horizon to the south. Even with my sharp eyes I couldn't tell for sure. There was one thing that brightened my thoughts a little, and that was the gathering of a few thunderstorms that was scattered and moving east in a line. They was like big sentinels rumbling and threatening their way ever so slow 'cross them prairies. I was hoping we'd be in line with one of 'em, but we didn't have that kinda luck. Them horses was 'bout as nervous as I'd ever seen 'em and was stepping real stiff. Their nostrils was wide open and they was puffing, with their eyes rolling and their tongues hanging out and their lips all caked with grime. I weren't much different.

When the sun went down and it got dark, we rested a little bit, 'cause there hadn't been no place to stop during the day. I only had 'bout half a canteen of water left. I took a good swig myself, then stuck the end of the canteen in the horses' mouths and give 'em each a little flush. They rolled it 'round on their tongues and went almost crazy trying to get some more, following me 'round and nudging and pushing. I sure had to be rough to spread the water 'tween the three of 'em. They'd left a tiny little slush in the bottom, just enough for me, and I reckoned I'd save it for the morning.

We rested 'bout three hours, then I mounted Warrior again and we headed off to the south, moving as best we could and watching the flashes of the thunderstorms. We kept ambling along and them horses finally got so's they wasn't holding their heads up no longer. They drooped lower with each step they took.

'Bout midnight, while I was watching some closer lightning flashes off to the west, a slight wind sprung up. It swooped up big and begun to blow mighty good. The horses tossed their heads and turned into the wind and paused and sniffed 'fore they went on their tired way. 'Bout three or four minutes later I felt a light drop of water on my hand. then another one.

I got down off that Appaloosa and held them three horses facing head-on into the storm. It was coming our way at last, and if we didn't gather much water, at least it'd cool us down. Using my knife, I dug as good a hole as I could. I didn't know if we'd get enough water to do us any good, but it was worth a try. Then I laid out my blanket roll, hoping it'd catch some water. If nothing else, we could wring it out and suck on it.

The drops started coming faster, then it begun to rain for sure. Them horses was tossing their heads and holding their noses up towards the raindrops, licking and whinnying and blowing a little. Then the rain begun to come down in sheets.

I stooped down on my knees again and dug out the sides of that hole to make it wider. In the darkness, I could reach down and feel where water was gathering. There was already a half inch of it on the bottom. I wished I still had a hat to catch a refill for the canteen.

In five minutes the storm'd passed and we was soaking wet. All my clothes and the hides of them horses was steaming with the water. Where I'd dug the hole, they was able to get a fair drink. It was like handling a wild horse herd, what with all of 'em wanting to stick their noses in at once, but at least they got watered enough to last through the night.

When we was through, I climbed up on the mare and we headed south again. The stars come out and there was a gentle prairie breeze. It was kind of cool. As a matter of fact, it felt plumb chilly to me in my wet clothes, and I started shivering like I had a fever.

When the first streaks of light come up, I strained my eyes looking south to see if I could make anything out. As the sun climbed higher, it lit up the welcomest sight I'd ever seen in my life. There lying 'bout fifteen miles ahead of us was a fine long line of solid cottonwoods. I knowed I was looking at the North Canadian River.

One thing I had to check out for sure was that there weren't no Comanches 'tween me and that water. It sure'd be hell if I got there and run into a nest of 'em, 'cause me and the horses weren't in no shape to do nothing 'bout it.

As the sun come on up I realized we'd have to cross that last fifteen miles in the brightest part of the day, and there weren't no helping it. We finally got to it in the early afternoon, and glory be to God, I never seen nary a sign of Comanches. We pushed on through the trees and come to the edge of the water. I had to be real careful of quicksand, and them horses was hard to control, 'cause they sure was determined to make for the water. We was in luck there and got down to the edge of the muddy stream without having no trouble, 'cept them horses sinking in up to their fetlocks.

I remembered the bad time that Michelle and me'd had on the Arkansas when we'd got so sick, so I was careful how much water I let them horses drink at first, and went sparing myself. Back in the cottonwoods I found a good place to camp, and as I was looking 'round, I was glad to see the first sign of game in many a day: the tracks of a doe and a fawn—what looked like white-tailed deer. If'n I stayed 'round there a little bit I might do some fancy eating and refill my pemmican supply. I picketed the horses and spent the rest of the afternoon scouting 'round, then went down along the river for maybe four miles on foot, keeping my eyes sharp open for any sign of either game or Indians. There was some more deer tracks, but even if I'd seen the animals, I weren't gonna risk taking a shot 'til I made sure there weren't no Indians thereabouts.

I come back and made a cold camp that night. At daybreak I climbed the small bluffs that was to the north and east. I didn't see a living thing—no buffalo, no antelope, no Indians. Nothing but wide-open flat country with only the dark line of the North Canadian River running through it. Yet, somewhere out there in all that vastness, the land harbored bands of the toughest, cruelest savages that ever lived—horsemen that was among the best in the world and as deadly as snakes. But right then there weren't nothing in sight as far as I could see.

I knowed full well that it didn't pay none to look at a piece of country for five minutes and think you'd seen what's in it, so I stayed there and spent most of the day just watching. Once or twice I seen a hawk circling far above the cottonwoods way down the stream. But that was the only movement I seen during the whole afternoon.

Then, in the low, slanting rays of the setting sun I caught a glint of movement in an open park maybe a mile away to the east. A couple of white-tailed deer was moving cautiouslike but easy and feeding gentle. I knowed there couldn't be much activity in the area, 'cause them animals was so calm.

I went back to the camp, but I didn't light a fire. Instead I took the stallion to water and picketed him in another area. The two horses in hobbles seemed to be hanging 'round in good shape. When it got dark I bedded down in a soft pile of grass and lay peeking up at the prairie stars through the gaps in the cottonwoods while I made my plans for the next day.

I got up 'fore daylight and watered the horses. Then I worked my way 'bout a mile downstream towards that open park where I'd seen the white-tails. I moved real cautious. When the first light of day showed, I was mighty pleased to come up on a herd of five of 'em still feeding in the same park. One of 'em was a barren doe and I knowed she'd be the best eating. Taking careful aim, I put her down.

The rest of the herd run outta there and I thought how different them white-tails run from mule deer, taking big jumps and flashing their white flags, while them mule deer just keep hopping stiff-legged. The white-tail's more graceful and lots faster, and I think the meat's better, too. I think it depends on what the animals is feeding on.

The only advantage to killing a mule deer is that mulies is 'bout twice as big, so there's lots more meat to be had. Seeing as how I was the only meat eater in our outfit, I reckoned that white-tailed doe was plenty good enough. She was in real good condition, and I cut the back strap off'n her in a hurry and took some pieces of her hide, figuring I could use the doeskin for something down the line.

I made it back to camp fast and put the raw venison out to dry in the sun. I weren't about to build me no fire in the middle of the day. I also weren't aiming to stay in that country another night. We'd all had enough water and food to last us for a stretch.

I got the animals ready in the early afternoon, then I climbed back up that little bluff on the north side of the river and took a last good hard look all 'round. There still weren't nothing moving in all that vast land. It was 'bout a hundred miles due south to the main Canadian, and I figured if we traveled hard all the rest of that day and night, we could be there 'bout daylight the next day.

I kept up a steady jog all that afternoon, swapping horses every hour or two. When the sun went down, we paused to rest a little and I rubbed old Warrior down a bit. He was carrying most of the load, so's I give him the best treatment. During the early part of the evening, when it was cool and too dark for anyone to see the dust we stirred up, I hit out into an easy lope. During the day I hadn't noticed no prairie dog holes nor nothing like that, so I didn't worry 'bout them horses sticking their feet into one and taking a spill.

We kept on at an easy lope through most of the night. When it got light enough the next morning, I could see the long line of cotton-woods of the Canadian off to the south. We got there by midmorning without incident. I done the same camping arrangements there that I'd done on the North Canadian.

I surmised that during the night I might've rode over some of the country near the cache, but I really didn't feel that was the case. I thought I was now a little east of where we'd done our buffalo hunting. The thing to do was to find where we'd crossed the Canadian from the south to the north side, and try to backtrack north from there.

Even though it was late August and I might never see the tracks of the crossing we'd made in March, I thought I could locate the place or something that looked familiar. From there I figured I'd be able to work north following the hunt we'd made.

I spent the next week all along the Canadian River and never seen no sign of life 'cept an occasional deer or big bird whirling 'round. I also didn't see any signs of our crossing nor any familiar places. I reckoned I must've been farther downstream on the Canadian than where we'd crossed before, so I moved on west.

Then I begun to get into country that really looked familiar, the way the cliffs was shaped and the way the river changed direction. After a week of fooling 'round, I come to a place where I was dead sure. It was a kind of draw in the low cliffs on the south side, and the ground on the north side sloped gently away out to the prairie.

I remembered us coming down that draw and hitting the river with the wagon and them mules all churning in the current. The river'd been fairly shallow then, being early in March with no floodwater coming. Dubeck'd been driving, with them skinners riding the spare mules alongside. Pedro'd been out in the lead on Blackie, plunging into the water, grinning that old grin of his, waving that black hat and shouting and laughing and having hisself a helluva time.

I looked 'round for some tracks, but there'd been so many prairie storms that there weren't the slightest trace. The only thing I could do was go on from memory.

I crossed the Canadian right there and let the horses drink for the last time to fill theirselves up with water. I done the same myself and filled my canteen, then climbed slowly outta the riverbed onto them dead-flat plains of the northern Llano Estacado. I headed due north and tried to repeat them first days of the buffalo hunt. We'd carried water barrels, heading out into country that just plain didn't have no water in it. We'd only made 'bout sixteen miles a day, traveling steady, and there was lots of times when we'd stopped and camped when we got near the herd.

So I figured where it'd taken us two weeks to travel north, I might be able to do it in three days. But I was still taking a chance—I was gonna need water somewhere. There'd been a water hole or two in some patches of snow on the prairie that early spring, so's it hadn't been no problem for the herds nor for our stock. But by God, at the end of a dry, hot summer it was a different story.

That trip was a real nightmare. I couldn't ride at night 'cause I had to be able to spot the pile of hides. If and when I did see 'em, they'd be the tiniest little dark bump far out on the flat plains. During the day, things weren't too comfortable. It was hot and dusty, and there was a ceaseless wind blowing. The plains ahead danced and shimmered in the summer heat. The sweat run down my face and I kept wiping the dust away from my eyes and looking out over the prairie, wondering if my eyesight was going bad or if I was going plumb crazy.

I had one big advantage—the flatness of them great plains. I reckoned I could see a band of horsemen twenty miles away. I made up my mind that I weren't gonna take no chances trying to find out whether they was Indians or white men. I'd just stay away from anything I seen.

I kept switching horses and give 'em a lick of the canteen every few hours. That second day was the toughest, all the plains around shimmering in the heat. It seemed hopeless, like them horses was riding on some kind of big turntable that was flat as a pancake and met the sky in all directions. Their legs kept on, but the distances didn't seem to lessen.

I found lots of old buffalo chips and a few wallows where there'd been some water in the spring of the year, but there weren't no sign of living buffalo in any direction, and there was nothing else to give me a clue.

In the late part of the second afternoon, dust was searing our throats and thirst was beginning to mount up to the choking point when I seen a cloud of dust in the far distance to the northeast. After watching for a while in the glaring sun, I come to the conclusion that it couldn't be nothing else but horses—maybe a good-sized band of Comanches or a remuda of wild mares run by their stallion. There was a big enough cloud that it couldn't have been a cavalry detachment. A cavalry bunch wouldn't have been that big. I turned to the west to avoid 'em and pushed along at a mighty good clip.

I reckon that was the thing that saved our lives, since if we'd kept on in the direction we was headed, we would've had to go all the way back up to the North Canadian 'fore we hit water. I rode 'til sundown and then a little distance farther into the night. I figured that was good tactics, as I could still see ahead maybe ten miles and I couldn't see no sign of the cache.

It was plumb lucky we made them ten miles in the cool of the evening, 'cause by the time we got ready to camp, the horses started acting like they smelled fresh water. I didn't want to risk missing too much of the country, so we stopped right there. I kept what was left in the canteen for me, and we started again a little 'fore daybreak, heading due west.

After 'bout an hour I looked back to check for dust on the horizon to the northeast. Not seeing a thing, I reckoned it was safe to start heading northwest again and tried to turn the animals that way, but all three refused me. They was dead set on going west, and by that time I'd learned enough to let 'em go.

'Round eleven o'clock I seen some cottonwoods in the far distance, and a couple of hours later we come up on 'em. It was the east arm of the Rita Blanche Creek and it was a lifesaver. I learned later that there sure as hell weren't no water in the direction I'd tried to head.

That creek was near dry, but there was pools of water along some of the clay banks and more seepage underneath the sand. Them horses got to digging right away, and they was soon filling up. I done the same, getting the cleanest water I could, which weren't saying much, filling myself and then the canteen. We was due for a rest, so I worked upstream to a big bunch of cottonwoods and camped there for the night.

AT LONG LAST

The way the East Fork of Rita Blanche Creek run north and south through the country, I figured I could make me some big loops out over the plains and come back for water every few days, but I sure as hell had to get a way to carry enough water during the loop, so I picketed the horses and went deer hunting.

I spent a little time getting into position 'bout a mile from where I'd made camp in them cottonwoods running along the creek that evening. There was a trail where them white-tails'd been coming down for water.

It was starting to get dark when I seen a movement in the trees. It was four white-tailed deer—three little bucks and a larger one. I was real quiet. The wind was outta the northwest, so with me being south of 'em, I figured I was all right. They moved slow—walking, stopping, listening with them cocked ears, looking up and sniffing the air, moving and taking ever-so-dainty steps—making their way towards the water hole. I kept looking at 'em, watching and waiting breathless for 'em to reach just the right place. The one thing I'd had to sweat out was whether they'd close the range enough 'fore it was too dark to see my sights. I needed to wait 'til they crossed maybe seventy-five yards away.

I was sure thankful that when they got in close, I could still see. I drawed down on the big buck. My rifle crashed and he went down with a grunt. I had another shell in the Winchester in two seconds, but them smaller deer was running like hell. I let drive just as the closest one sailed over a log, and he went down easily.

Then you know what I done? I didn't move. I stayed right there and waited, remembering the time that I'd made my long shot at the mulie 'cross that canyon and got up and started running down, whooping and hollering like a damn fool kid. The scar on my neck helped remind me.

I didn't move for almost a half hour. Then the new moon come up over the plains to the east and there was a little bit more light. I got up and crept forward real cautious. I didn't have much trouble finding where that big buck was lying in the brush. I skinned that critter out in short order, being careful not to poke any holes in the hide while I was working.

I had to hunt 'round a little to find the second buck. He was fairly cold and the skinning didn't go so clean, but I fixed him up the same way.

I spent the next day working on my buckskin water bags. I didn't have no salt for curing, but I found an outcropping of some quartz rock and sand. I used chips from it to scrub them hides clean the best way I could. I used the doeskin chunks I'd saved to make me some rawhide laces, then worked the fresh hides into two big bags tied together at the neck.

When I got through, I had made me a couple of half-assed water bags that weren't much to look at, but each'd hold 'bout four gallons of water. I planned to tie them water bags onto a rawhide girth 'round one of the horses. If we didn't travel too fast, and I could keep the bags from flopping and busting, our traveling range'd be a helluva lot bigger. The bags didn't hold quite enough water for three horses for two days, but it'd be enough to slacken their thirst.

It was getting towards the end of August, I reckoned, although I'd almost lost track of time. In places where we'd had good green buffalo grass before, there was just desolate plains. I weren't too worried 'bout seeing no Indians. Since there weren't much abundance of game, them varmints'd be too smart to be 'round there. They'd be up north with the buffalo herds.

I started out early the next morning and headed due east for 'bout thirty miles. Then I started swinging in a great loop to the north. By sunset we'd traveled maybe fifty miles. I let the horses drink outta the water bags when we camped for the night. When I stopped 'em, better'n half the water was gone. We continued on north the next day for maybe fifteen miles, then started swinging to the west again, moving real rapid.

'Long towards evening I sighted a few cottonwoods, and that night we come up on Rita Blanche Creek once more. We stayed there a day and rested, then made another loop north in the same way. I done that several times in a row and still didn't see nothing. That got me to wondering whether I might be too far north altogether. I thought that one over and figured out how far me and Pedro'd traveled that spring from where we'd crossed the Canadian, but I just didn't see how I could've got too far up. Maybe I was too far west of where we'd hunted, and them circles I was making was short of the distance.

The next circle I made I didn't work as far to the north, using the time to go way out east and back. I knowed that Coldwater Creek was way off to the east somewheres, but I didn't know how far. I plain didn't have the guts to take the chance of riding out beyond the limit of where we couldn't get back to the Rita Blanche. You can bet that both me and them horses was glad to get back to live water again, every loop we'd made.

At daybreak I rode out again. That time, instead of going out over the plains, I stuck to the east bank of the river and worked north one whole day's journey. I reckon we must've made fifty miles. I camped that night and the next morning and, after filling up, we started out on one of them big loops to the east again, figuring on coming back to the creek maybe twenty miles to the north.

I done that once and didn't see nothing. Then I done it again. On that second day of riding I come across a dry sandy arroyo on the way back to Rita Blanche Creek. There was something familiar 'bout it, but I couldn't quite put my finger on it—just something familiar 'bout the surrounding country.

I got back to the creek that night and slept kinda restless. I let the horses rest a day, then I headed out east again. When I struck the sandy arroyo ten miles out, I turned north and begun following it for a couple of hours. The country seemed familiar in a strange way, yet really no different from the rest. Then, where the dry sand creek wound a little more to the east, I knowed right where I was!

Somewheres right along in there, Pedro'd unloaded them hides to cross through tough going and soft sand. Sure as hell, I'd found it! There had to be water in them sandy creeks in the spring from the melting snows, and Pedro'd come to a sandy creek with water in it and'd had trouble getting across. Sure as hell, it had to be right along in there. I spent that whole day working up and down that sandy creek, looking for something that might tell me where Pedro'd crossed.

I didn't find nothing, and by the end of the day my heart was really down. I rode back through the night then and come to Rita Blanche Creek 'bout midnight. We stayed there watering and feeding for another day.

I could tell it was getting into the early part of September by that time, 'cause it was getting lots cooler and the traveling was easier. The horses seemed able to go longer without water, and I told myself that maybe it was 'cause I was training 'em not to drink. I got to laughing 'bout that. If I could train 'em so's they wouldn't never have to drink nothing a'tall, I'd have me a new kind of horse and we could cross the desert and never have to give a damn 'bout water. A man has to laugh and talk with hisself when he's all alone working the plains or the mountains. If'n he don't, he really will go crazy.

I remember sitting up there on my horse, stopping time and again, shading my eyes with my hand and looking out there as far as I could see in every direction, sweeping one great big circle 'round the horizon, lifting my eyes up slowly and following clear out to where the sky met the prairies. Once when I spied something off to the northeast that was humped up and dark, my heart jumped. For a few minutes I thought I was the greatest pathfinder in the world and'd found that cache. I whipped up the horses and went rushing in that direction, but after I'd rode a couple of miles, I could see that what I was looking at weren't nothing but an uncommon big tuft of bear grass.

Damn me if I ever knowed anything so tough as trying to find something out there on the Llano Estacado. It was one great big vast ocean of grass and sky and shadows of clouds, a flat universe filled with the moan of the prairie wind and drifting dust and fast-moving rain showers that chilled you to the bone, then blasted you with more shimmering heat. A man seemed helpless, all alone, wandering aimless out there like he was detached from the rest of the world.

It was a dismal camp that night, out there on the prairie with Warrior picketed to my wrist. When dawn broke, we started off again. Later during the day we was gonna have to turn west to hit water, so I headed out, bearing north and then a little northwest. I rode along kinda dreaming and trying to recollect the flat country of last spring and how it'd looked coming on that buffalo herd for the last time.

Then I jolted to the present and noticed the prairie'd begun to take on a slight roll. I remembered that, way back in the spring, there'd been two or three times when we hadn't been able to see no buffalo, just their dust cloud. It weren't that way down by the Canadian, but when you got a few hundred miles north it begun getting a sorta roll to it that hid things, and it stayed that way 'til you hit the mesa country.

We was going along at an easy walk when Warrior put down his head without breaking his stride or nothing, and sniffed at the ground. He'd do that every once in a while when he seen something that was strange, something that he wanted to examine a little closer—a chuckhole or a dried rattlesnake skin or a buffalo skull or the bleached bones of an antelope. I'd got used to his ways.

But that time when he sniffed, I looked and didn't see nothing but that patch of ground that passed under his hooves. I was sitting there swaying with the rhythm of his walk, and I turned and looked behind to see if I'd missed something.

I brought that stallion up with a jerk, whirled him 'round on his haunches, and leaned over to take a closer look. I let out a whistle, for lying in the buffalo grass, scattered over a couple of square yards, was about two dozen green, weather-beat shell cases from a Sharps rifle.

I slipped down off'n Warrior fast enough to make him shy back a little. I knelt down real quick to see for sure, with my hands trembling. Yessir, it was that big .50 ammunition from last spring. It was right there where we'd got that first big stand of buffalo. Sure enough, a little farther along beyond a gentle rise, the prairie was dotted with buffalo skeletons.

Then I'd knowed right away where I was. 'Bout fifteen to twenty miles to the northwest was where I'd got my last stand of buffalo and that's where we'd made the cache. What a piece of luck! How in hell could a man wander over thousands of miles of prairie and then look down and see his dead partner's shells from six months before? It was no art; it was just pure ass luck—a piece of luck I weren't gonna forget.

I went back and gathered up all them shells as if they was my best friends. I didn't know what I'd use 'em for, but I weren't willing to let 'em go. They was green, but they hadn't got almost black, the way they do when they've laid out for several winters.

If I hadn't knowed better, I would've guessed they'd been out there five years, but since then I've learned how fast they lose their shine lying out there in the open.

I climbed back up on Warrior and headed northwest, just 'bout the angle I remembered going on that hunt. I was looking back and reconstructing how it'd looked and how far we'd gone. I kicked the horses up to a lope and, following an old trick of mine that I'd used on the Chisholm Trail while looking for cattle, I slipped myself up to a standing position on the stallion's rump, where I could get a better view of the prairie. With them moccasins I wore, I could feel his muscles moving with a nice easy rhythm, and I knowed him well enough by then to tell how to handle him. I felt like a circus clown, but I could see a helluva ways.

I rode standing up for the most part of an hour, shading my eyes and scanning in every direction. Then my old fear started rising again. Somehow, in spite of the luck of finding them shells, I might not find that cache 'fore we'd have to return for water. It sure would be a bitter pill to swallow.

I was getting more anxious by the end of the second hour. Then, real suddenlike, a new idea come to me. God almighty, how could a man get so dumb so quick? How in hell could I've forgot? I remembered so well them last days, sitting 'round that cache of hides looking towards the west waiting for Pedro and his wagon. There was one thing that we'd always seen in the far distance to the northwest.

There'd been a couple of mesas, and when the light'd first come up on the prairies in the morning, you could easy mistake 'em for wagons. Then, as the light got better, you could see it weren't nothing but them flat-top mountains.

I stopped and done some figuring. According to the sun, it was the second hour of the afternoon. We was almost outta water and we was at least thirty miles away from Rita Blanche Creek, maybe more, and that was if the Rita Blanche's headwaters weren't turned off farther towards the west where it'd give us a real fit finding it. I could turn back and head south-southwest to be sure of hitting it and then try to come back and do it again. But it'd be damn hard to retrace our tracks what with them early fall storms. I couldn't take no chance like that. There was just one thing to do—hit right along to the northwest and keep driving 'til them mesa tops come into sight.

Then I sat back down and kicked my stallion up to a nice lope and urged the other two horses along. They obeyed reluctant-like, pulling and showing their teeth at the lead line with them empty water bags flopping and banging on the withers of the gelding. We kept up that lope for 'bout an hour and a half and must've covered the best part of ten miles when two mesas begun to appear.

Outta all that flat nothingness of sky and vast stretches of prairie grass glimmering in the heat, it was a wonder that I could just ride a measly ten miles and look up and see the first two mesas right there against the northwestern sky where they was supposed to be.

I hopped up to stand on Warrior's back again. To the southwest, 'bout three and a half miles away, I seen something interesting, but it didn't exactly look right. When me and Pedro and them skinners'd stacked them hides, we'd covered 'em with brush to disguise what they was. What I was looking at was a kinda round, sandy pile. I thought at first it was a big bunch of buffalo grass or maybe a natural earth mound. I started to look away to search the rest of the horizon, but something brought me back. I looked at it again long and hard, then all of a sudden I seen what it was and why it looked like it did.

I kicked up them horses with a wild shout and we come in on a dead run. Sure enough, there it was, a pile 'bout seven feet high, maybe twenty feet long and ten feet wide—a pile of 'bout a hundred fifty buffalo hides. But it was covered with a layer of dust and mud driven by hundreds of summer winds and caked with dozens of summer rains. It looked like one big dirt hump lying out there in the prairie, the same color as the soil.

When we drawed up close, Warrior got hisself plenty nervous. He sure didn't like the looks of that big brown bad-smelling heap, and when he spooked, he spooked good. He put his ears forward and bulged his eyes out, and went to snorting and rearing and whirling, letting me know he didn't want no part of it. I managed to work him up sorta close, then I slid off, patted him a little, and quieted the other two of 'em down. I eased on forward. I had to pull hard on the reins, and two or three times Warrior braced his feet and stretched his head out stubbornlike, showing his teeth and dancing away from me.

I finally got close enough to reach the pile, and I stretched out the top hide and flicked some of the dust off'n it. It was decayed beyond hope. I pulled off the first three or four hides and got to them that was turned right side up, thinking that maybe they'd lasted better. They wasn't worth a damn, either.

The only thing I done by casting aside them hides was to spook the horses, so I had to calm 'em down again. Then I went back to them hides and slowly unpiled 'em. The summer heat, the dryness, the winds, the dust, the rain—they'd all done the job. Them hides weren't worth the powder to blow 'em up. The hair on 'em had slipped, making them beautiful buffalo blankets useless as hell. I looked out in the distance and seen spottings of white buffalo bones and couldn't help but think that them big old buffalo that'd wore them hides last spring'd all died for nothing.

Well, my attention turned back to the ammunition I'd come for. I begun a furious fit of slinging them hides aside and trying to hold the horses, but they got so excited I had to slow up and take it easy. Finally, there they was. Them shell cases was lying there 'bout like they was when we'd took 'em outta the wagon. I reckoned there was twelve hundred rounds of the Sharps and at least six hundred of the .44. That was plenty enough 'til the snows come. Then I could go into the settlements and sell the Sharps load for good money.

It was getting real late in the afternoon. 'Fore long it'd be dark, and I knowed we had many miles to go 'til we'd make it to water. I hobbled the mare and the gelding and turned 'em loose to graze on the prairie. Then I hobbled Warrior and took one of my rawhide ropes and tied it from his left back leg to his right foreleg and drawed it up real tight. That fixed him so's he couldn't go nowhere. I weren't taking no chances. I knowed only too well that to lose my horses then'd mean death.

On several of them hides, even though the hair'd slipped on 'em, the hide itself was still tough. I cut up some strips to use for laces, then I cut holes in the edges of two hides and folded 'em up to make 'em into a bag, and run the laces through and bound 'em tight. By sundown I had a couple of bags that I could load up with the ammunition.

I picked the gelding to load first, figuring that he'd prob'ly be best for starters. I sure did cuss myself for not having made a cross-tree packsaddle when I was down in them cottonwoods. Out there on them plains there weren't no timber to make nothing with, and the only thing I was gonna be able to do was tie my ammo bags to the rawhide girths that I'd made for the water bags.

By the time I got the little white gelding loaded, we'd had our own private rodeo out there on the plains. There weren't nobody watching, but it was really something. Although I packed him while he'd still had his hobbles on, he spooked and whirled and twisted and throwed hisself down half a dozen times, with me cussing at him and jerking his jaw rope and once or twice kicking him in the guts.

I finally got to talking to him real soft and stroking his neck 'til I got him quieted down. He sure didn't want no part of them smelly buffalo bags. I made up my mind that he was gonna have to pack 'em and I didn't care if we stayed there for a week. He was either gonna die of thirst or pack them bags. He finally give in.

'Fore I slid them cases of .44 shells into the pack bags, I broke one open and put thirty rounds into the loops of my belt. That sure made me feel better. That give me 'bout fifty rounds real handy—enough to give a big band of Comanches a helluva bad time.

When I finally got them bags all packed and took the hobbles off'n the stallion, it was almost dark. I passed 'round what was left in the water bags and we set out and kept on traveling all night by the stars. By early light I could see that we was right up to the edge of the mesas. First there was the two that I'd seen in the distance. They was on either side of me, maybe five miles apart, standing up like thousand-foot giants rearing outta the plains. In back of 'em and beyond—towards the north and northwest—stretched countless others as far as I could see.

When we come up on the crest of the first rise 'tween the mesas, the long, dark line of cottonwoods that marked a running creek was running along real nice and beautiful. Them horses got all stirred up and started tossing their heads and snuffling. Just a short ride and we was right up on the creek. It was the coolest, sweetest water I'd tasted in a long, long time. I didn't know it then, but that was the headwaters of Frisco Creek, and it was a mighty good place to camp.

I went through the usual unloading and hobbling the horses and picketing the stallion, then I moved off a safe quarter of a mile and rolled up in some leaves to hide away while I slept. We'd had a good march, so's we stayed there two days just taking it easy. I weren't sure where to go next, but instinct told me to keep heading northwest. We went up through the valley past them two mesas and didn't travel more'n thirty miles 'fore we come up on another good-sized stream, fresh and nice as you'd like to see. I later found out that was the South Fork of the Carrizo, way up 'round the headwaters. We stopped there overnight.

During all that time I hadn't seen no Comanches, but I'd had lots to think on. There I was with them three horses, one of 'em always carrying me and the others carrying the load. Part of the load weren't of no immediate use. Twelve hundred rounds of big .50 ammunition weren't no help to me then, but it was as valuable as gold, and there sure would be one helluva market for it if I could get it to the Santa Fe Trail.

I could pack it back to the settlements along the trail, but if'n I done that, I was gonna miss my last chance at Comanches for that season. I knowed what'd happen at the first snow. The buffalo herds'd move down south towards the Canadian and beyond, and them Comanches'd be with 'em, a hundred miles to the east of the trail, along the east side of all the mesas. They'd spread out and fan into that limitless plains country—a hopeless place to find anything.

No, I'd catch 'em as they went by 'fore they got out into that big country. It struck me that I was ambushing a migration. When I was drifting with Daddy up and down the Mississippi, I recollected some of them old mountain men talking 'bout trapping way up north where the caribou lived and how the Indians was always depending on the caribous' southern migration in the fall. They'd lie there watching for 'em and if them caribou didn't show up, them Indians was doomed to starve to death.

I'd hide out in that mesa country. From the top of some of them flat mountains that was three or four thousand feet high, I could see for a hundred miles out on the plains. If I seen any buffalo dust clouds, then I'd know there was prime game headed my way.

I also expected lots of them Comanches'd see them mesas to the west and come in there to camp close by. That was their favorite place 'cause there was always lots of springs nearby. It was real natural to come on in and camp where there was good water and grass for their ponies, and where they could watch for the herds. As a matter of fact, that was what the band of Comanches was doing that'd picked up me and Michelle.

I broke camp the next morning, crossed the South Fork of the North Carrizo, and went maybe ten miles upstream. Then I come to a mesa that had mighty nice rock forms and seen it'd be a cinch to find it again. From a distance it had what looked like a pinnacle sticking up, and I nicknamed it "Big Thumb." I picked a place on the south side of Big Thumb, right in the oak brush beside some white rocks, where I could mark it real easy. I took good careful notice of the distance from the stream and from the pinnacle. I made a crude pick outta oak brush limbs, loosened up the soil, then lifted the dirt out with my hands. I unloaded them cases of .50 shells and buried 'em deep. I left half of the Winchester .44-caliber stuff with 'em, figuring I couldn't lug it around everywhere. When I was through I didn't leave no sign that anything was buried there.

It was kinda like hiding away a hoard of gold, and I got to laughing when I thought about it. By God, as far as most of the plainsmen was concerned, them shells was gold. Any time you was out in the open country, or anywhere on the frontier for that matter, ammunition was as good as gold and sometimes better.

After I made that cache, I worked on along the edge of the mesas to the northeast for a day and a half and reached one that was outstanding for its size and height. I picked out a good way up through the oak brush to a place on the cap rock close to a gentle ravine where we could go clear to the top. We made it up easy.

The top of that mesa was covered with open, flat grasslands occasionally broke by patches of piñon pine, juniper, cedar trees, and every once in a while a few ponderosas. The grass was as high as a man's waist, 'cause there hadn't been no buffalo up there, and what few elk and deer there was couldn't begin to eat out the range. I was plumb enchanted. It was real beautiful.

There was one place where I found a big hollow with a shallow lake surrounded by rocks. Why it hadn't evaporated out there during the summer, I couldn't say, but maybe it was filled by rain showers or an underground spring. It sure was nice—the sorta place that makes a man think twice 'bout what he wants in life.

I worked along to the east side of the mesa by a good-sized clump of trees where I could look out far across the plains. It sure seemed like a perfect place to me, and I figured if I could stay there and keep on making a cold camp, something'd show up. I had plenty of pemmican and there was lots of grass and water for the horses.

The whole thing run out east on a long tongue of rock that made a natural fortress. My lookout point was at least three thousand feet above the plains that spread to the eastern horizon. It was a grand and glorious perch, cool and pleasant with an easy breeze blowing. The whole place on top of that mesa sometimes seemed to me like a lost spirit world. I reckon that's the way the mesa tops struck the Indians, too. The Utes used to bury their dead on mesas for just that reason.

There sure was something beautiful and mysterious 'bout that place, and for the first time in a long while, I was content to sit and watch and bide my time. I stayed in that camp for two to three weeks. I scouted out a good place nearby to hide my extra .44 shells, and once in a while I went out and killed a deer, which weren't hard a'tall.

The mulies mostly fed down in the ravines below us. Wherever there was a slice in the cap rock I could see 'em working along, feeding in the thick brush below—the sage or the serviceberry bushes or the mountain mahogany or oak brush. From where I was, I could pick 'em out below and it was an easy stalk. But every time I killed a deer, you can bet I hid silent for a while to see if anything else was moving.

It was 'bout as pleasant a life as I'd enjoyed in many months, and I couldn't help but remember that the last time I'd really felt that way was when I was sitting 'round the fire with Michelle on the upper part of the Cimarron. That sweet girl was just ashes blowed away with the wind. But she was still there with me in a way, 'cause I thought of her often, and in my dreams I held her in my arms warm and soft. It was times like those when I'd wake up, with the white cold hell of rage that'd fill me, and I'd swear to murder the whole Comanche nation. It used to take me a spell to cool down, fight back the tears, and think on a cold and deadly revenge.

It was then that I'd seek high places where I could lie way up there on the cap rock, looking out over all the world around and cool my soul. I'd get in the shade of one of them juniper trees four or five feet from the edge of the cliff and spend them daylight hours looking out over the edge to the far horizon of them Staked Plains. I could see

everything that was going on and nothing could see me. The lair of
the big cat, that's what it was, and I knowed, like any cat knows, if he
lies in wait and is real quiet, that given time, his prey'll come by.

Each day was a make-believe scene to me, like something being
played in a great big theater. First it'd start out with the faint light of
dawn. Then, maybe if there was a cloud or two on the horizon, the
backdrop'd turn pink and then red. Then it'd go to silver. Then later
the shining ball of the sun'd send streaks of gold 'cross the prairies. As
the sun rose farther, a soft haze'd form to the east and I could turn and
look far off to the west and see the tips of them snowcapped peaks of
the Sangre de Cristos peering up above the edge of the mesa. I could
see 'em real clear, even though they was more'n a hundred miles away.

Then, as the sun rose more and more, all them shadows in the cuts
and cliffs in the cap rock of the mesas nearby'd begin to change colors
and sizes. There'd come a warmness mixed with the cool sweetness of
the morning air, and the haze in the distance'd thin out.

It was often still, without a breath of wind, and lying on the grass at
the edge of the cliff, three thousand feet above the plains, I could hear
the twitter of birds in the trees and the hum of bees, mixed with the
soft chatter of squirrels and other little critters as they started 'bout
their day's business.

Along 'bout midmorning, a patch of clouds'd gather in the blue sky
and a warm gentle breeze'd sweep 'cross the grasses of the mesa and
sigh through the needles of the piñon trees. Then them clouds'd begin
multiplying and casting shadows out over the plains so that, in the
bright noon sun, their shadows'd hide the wandering course of the
riverbeds far away. I liked to watch them shadows as they moved
'cross the plains, looking like dark, flat, creeping monsters.

By late afternoon some of them clouds built up into huge towering
castles, tall piles of golden fluff, and always they was flat on the
bottom. On occasion, I'd see a long veil of wispy rain showers drift
with an easy curving flow across the prairie. Sometimes in the early
evening I'd hear the rumbling of distant thunderstorms. Then it'd
soon grow dark and cloudy as them big black giants gathered, and
there'd be flashes of lightning that'd run down from the clouds to the
prairie grass.

I was always on the lookout for a fire, so's I could be sure to mark it,
and check to see that it weren't made by nothing but the forces of
nature. Once or twice I seen fires started by lightning strikes and

they'd smoke for a day or two. Seemed like they moved 'cross lots of land, but they was so far off in the distance I couldn't tell much about 'em. Then, in a day or two, there'd come a shower drifting 'cross where they was and they'd be gone.

Evenings was usually the nicest time of all. As the sun went down in the west, it broke through the clouds with one last burst of flame and the whole prairie'd light up like a fiery red carpet. That's the way it was in the early part of September. As the days drifted by and the nights got crisp, the oak brush turned red and the quakie trees in some of the ravines and hollows turned all bright yellow, and the cottonwoods out along them dry creek beds become yellow-gold strings stretching far out on the prairie. On some of them fall days the skies'd stay clear and I wouldn't see a cloud all day.

I felt like the king of all I surveyed, and I didn't mind waiting for my prey. I knowed they'd be coming my way—it was just a matter of time. One day soon I'd see the dust of buffalo herds and I knowed that there'd be roaming bands of Comanches following 'em. If I give 'em time, they'd come for water and I'd sure see 'em then. Meanwhile, I'd been looking over the mesa nearby, as well as the one I was on, marking a few places covered with green that meant springs that they might choose to camp by. I measured 'em by the size of the greenness and checked the area around to see if there was grass for ponies and whether there was any firewood about.

Maybe it was the piñon nuts, not just water, that they'd come for. There wouldn't be many places around where they could get a good supply. They used them piñon nuts to make their pemmican. Maybe that's why they'd come my way, or maybe they was just out over the prairie to the west, and them tall mesas held an enchantment for 'em like they done for me.

I weren't keeping real close track of time. It was on a day in maybe mid-October when I seen what I was looking for to the northeast—a rolling cloud of dust. It was near midmorning when I first seen it, something denser'n the eastern haze. By the time the sun got in back of me, I could see better. There was a vast, moving black shadow maybe sixty miles away. It had to be buffalo, and with 'em'd come bands of Comanches. I lay quiet and waited.

The first Comanches I seen, strangely enough, weren't the ones that was coming from a buffalo hunt, but quite something else. It was the middle of the next afternoon and I thought I'd get up and walk the northeast rim. I weren't too far from it, so I left my lookout place on the east end of the mesa, taking my Winchester with me.

I eased back from the edge maybe two hundred yards towards the tall grass of the mesa, turned all gold with autumn, and checked the ponies over to see that they was doing all right. Then I headed in a northwesterly direction, figuring I'd reach the north edge of the mesa after 'bout a mile and a half of jogging.

It was getting on towards midafternoon, in the cool air of fall, and there weren't nothing but clear blue skies in every direction. Jogging along up on the flat top, I was running in a world by itself, a kind of spirit world, an upland of beauty all its own. It was like you was looking out on an unreal place built on a platform that was way up there in the sky and might've once been the home of the gods.

In a short time, jogging along through knee-high grass, I come up on the north side of the mesa. I was able to see the next mesa to the north maybe three or four miles away, and as I got close to the edge, I could see down the slopes of the opposite mountain more and more. Finally, as I come to the edge of the cliff, I could see down into the valley and I got a helluva shock. I ain't never forgetting how quick I stopped in my tracks.

Far out in the valley, maybe a couple of miles to the northwest, I seen the dust cloud kicked up by a long line of ponies, and on each of 'em was an Indian warrior. The whole column was moving at a real good clip. Judging by the length of that line there must've been three hundred of 'em—the biggest war party I'd ever seen in my life.

I knowed it was a war party, 'cause there weren't no travois nor squaws nor nothing going with it. Maybe it was others gathering with the warriors I'd seen headed northwest when I'd crossed the Cimarron last spring. Maybe they'd been ambushing along the Santa Fe Trail, or maybe they'd been pushing the settlers and miners up north of the Arkansas. I couldn't tell for sure. All I could see was a long line of horsemen.

I watched for a while 'til I could make out their horned buffalo war helmets and once in a while see the flash of a feathered lance or the white of a shield, or maybe the glint of the setting sun on the steel barrel of a rifle. It was a breathtaking and barbaric sight. They'd pass by going east maybe a mile and a half to the north. I knowed they was riding with some purpose in mind, 'cause they was all in single file. If Indians was working 'cross the country, they'd ride in bunches, maybe side by side, talking with one another or something. But that band was headed out in a straight line and it looked like they knowed what they was doing.

I dropped down in the grass and eased my way towards the edge of the cap rock, not wanting to skyline myself. I crawled out to where I could see the whole valley below.

I lay there for a few minutes looking hard at the scene and trying to figure what it was all about. I reckoned that a war party that big was more'n Cat Brules wanted to take on, but I knowed there weren't no chance that they'd see me. They'd likely go on through the valley and maybe out to the plains to some camp, or on down through Comanche land to the Canadian and beyond.

While I was staring at 'em in the distance, I heard some rocks crackling down below and to my right. I slid over to where I could look down off the cliff in that direction. There was a long narrow ravine, a kind of natural stairway leading up through the oak brush and the cap rock of the mesa and opening onto its top. It'd be possible to ride a horse up through there. There weren't no good footing—nothing but slick rock—but the slope weren't so tough that a horse couldn't make it, 'specially if he had a little help. The sound of grinding rocks come echoing up that ravine.

There was a bend in the passageway where two great big boulders and a pine tree made a small gateway into the edge of the oak brush. I looked up again when I heard more of that rock crackling and damned near froze cold. Scrambling through that opening and starting up that rock ravine come a line of Indians.

At first I was scared cold blind that they'd seen me and was coming up to get me. Then the thought come that they prob'ly weren't looking for me a'tall, but was coming up to perform some kind of ceremony or other. Maybe the mesa I was on was sacred to 'em. It was prob'ly that stairway that made it so—a stairway to their gods.

They was all dismounted and leading their horses, 'cept for one at the rear—a rare thing for Comanches. The rock was steep and slippery, like a huge trough or slide. It looked like it'd been cut smooth by the rains of thousands of years. It was obvious to see by the way them ponies was humping and struggling that their footing weren't no good and that the only way they was gonna make it to the top was by being led. If they was made to pack a man on their back, chances was they'd slip and fall and slide all the way back down the ravine clear to the narrow gateway made by them two boulders and the big pine.

I could see right away what it'd be like. If one of them horses was to slide down there and jam against the boulders, it'd be like closing a trap. My heart started pounding. Yessir, just as plain as could be, that tree and them boulders'd form a closed gateway if a horse's body was jammed 'cross 'em. There wouldn't be no going back down for nobody else. The only way to get outta there'd be to struggle on up, and Cat Brules'd be waiting for 'em at the top.

Not one of 'em had any idea that there was a white man within a hundred miles, let alone Cat Brules inside a hundred yards. The nearest one to me weren't more'n forty yards away, and the one at the bottom of the line'd be 'bout ninety-five yards away when he come through them two boulders and the pine tree.

After the last one passed 'tween the boulders, I counted eleven warriors and their ponies, all but one of 'em pulling and straining at their lead ropes, while the ponies was slipping with their heels clicking on that slick rock, trying to make their way up that giant staircase to the top of the mesa.

I took one more good look at them eleven braves to fix their positions in my mind. All of 'em was dismounted 'cept the last one, and he was pumping and kicking and whipping at his pony to make him hump up there, like he was too stubborn to get off—a typical Comanche.

Now, it might seem silly as hell for me to have even thought of starting to shoot at those eleven bucks, what with more'n three hundred of their clansmen four thousand feet below. They was sure to come up to investigate if they heard shooting. But, if you think 'bout it, you'll see why I done it: I'd had no other choice! Those eleven bucks was getting in real close. If I'd turned and run they would've seen me when they topped out on the mesa. I couldn't have possibly made it to my horses at a dead run 'cause they was too spread out. If I'd let those eleven bucks get after me in the open, I'd have been a goner. If I'd turned to hide from 'em, they'd have seen my horses and searched me out. Nosir. I took the lesser of two evils—kill those sons of bitches 'fore they saw me and take my chances on the three hundred below hearing the firing. I figured there was plenty of ways to avoid 'em if I could only get my horses put together in time. 'Course there might've been more bucks following them eleven, but if I could plug that gateway, they'd never get up. It was a calculated risk, but I summed it up in a flash and decided to take it.

I took real careful aim on that last rider and shot his horse right through the front of the neck. The noise of the Winchester echoed up and down the rockslide like it was multiplied a thousand times. The results was as spectacular as anything I'd ever seen in my life.

When the slug hit that old pony, he reared back on his haunches and fell over backwards on top of his rider. The whole kicking carcass of horse and rider went sliding downhill and jammed up solid against the two boulders and the pine tree, just like putting a cork in a bottle.

I didn't have no time to fool around after that—I had to keep the action going. I swung the barrel uphill and shot the lead horse, almost straight below me, in the head. His hind legs give out on him and he crunched down on his haunches and then peeled over backwards and piled up against all the rest of them Indians and their ponies as they was heading up the slide. That was a beautiful sight: a thousand-pound pony rolling and sliding and banging down against the rest of 'em. That whole bunch collapsed and rolled downhill like a giant snowball—a collection of kicking, screaming horses and Indians crashing and rattling and piling up at the bottom where the stopper was jammed up against the boulders and the tree.

When the lead buck's horse went down, the rider let go of the rope when he seen he was caught in a trap and made a quick dash to try to reach the top of the slide twenty yards from where I was. I knowed that if he made it, I was a dead man, so I made sure he didn't. My bullet went through the side of his head when he was ten feet from the top. He rolled all the way down to join the mess at the bottom.

Then I sat there and had me some fun with the Winchester. I took my time watching them horses kicking and thrusting 'round and left 'em alone, but every time I'd see one of them redskins coming out from under the pile, trying to make a move for somewhere, I'd shoot him through the head. Ninety-five yards ain't no distance a'tall for a dead gun, and a target as big as a man's head was something that Cat Brules weren't gonna miss on that beautiful fall afternoon. It was as fine a turkey shoot as I ever seen. I s'pose I didn't kill 'em all, I only shot about nine times, but the rest of them horses was broke up bad by their fall and the Indians under 'em had to be crushed plenty.

When I knowed that there weren't no more Indians coming outta that mess, I took my gaze off the pile and looked out 'cross the valley and saw exactly what I'd feared. The long line of warriors'd broke ranks and was galloping hell-bent towards the mesa. They couldn't have knowed what'd happened, but I reckoned they figured the few warriors that'd branched away from 'em to come up on the mesa had run into trouble.

Them Indians was certainly coming to rescue or to back up their own kin and must've thought they was coming after a few enemies, not just one lone man working fast. Whatever it was they thought, I knowed it weren't time for me to sit up there and try to fight off a hundred warriors. The way I covered the ground back across them mesas towards where my horses was picketed was just about the same as flying. I scarce touched the ground.

While I was running, I was thinking fast, too. I knowed that band of Indians riding them ponies'd come first to the rockslide and find the big jam-up. There wouldn't be no way they could get by that, any more'n the ones up above could get down—it was a natural dam of horses and Indian bodies. They'd have to start fanning 'round the mesa in both directions to try to find a way up.

I figured that by the time they reached the lower slopes of the mesa, I would've just 'bout reached my horses. I could ride hard and fast to the southwest end of the mesa, which was maybe five miles away, but then I'd have to pick my way slowly down off the cap rock. Meanwhile, them hard-riding Comanches'd be galloping like hell back down to the open country below the oak brush to surround the mesa. It was gonna be tight and I knowed it, but I didn't have no choice.

When I hit the picket line, I cut the stallion loose with one quick slash of my knife and vaulted onto his back. Then I rode past the mare and the gelding and cut them loose, too, leaving their picket ropes behind. We took outta there with me yipping and yelling and driving them two in front of me, then we cut across the tall grass of that mesa with the breeze in our teeth and run like we had the devil hisself behind us.

I could feel the stallion's rhythm settle down as he stretched out. There ain't nothing finer in the world than the feel of the action of a good horse 'tween your legs when he's running full out, and there's something 'bout a stallion with Arab in him that's the best thing in the world. It's like he's got the power of wings. Every drive seems like it makes him a part of you and you a part of him. There was something real smooth and strong 'bout them arched-neck Arab and Spanish horses and what was left of their blood in the Indian ponies that made it real easy for a man to sit on their back and stay with the rhythm of the gallop.

I'd been riding Warrior without any saddle for quite a long time. I could tell by the feel of him that he was pulling his heart out and he was gonna give me a run that I'd never forget. It seemed like he was drinking the wind through them wide-open nostrils of his, sucking his breath to the rhythm of his pounding hooves. I done some mighty yelling at the gelding and the mare to make 'em keep ahead, even though they weren't carrying no load. They was caught with the excitement of the run and was having a helluva time staying with the stallion.

I didn't need no rein. I just sat there with my knees clamped 'round the stallion's ribs and my whole body in motion with every jump he made. I was holding my Winchester across my lap, and as I rode with the wind fluttering my clothes, I was taking out shells from my cartridge belt and squeezing 'em into the magazine. One thing I knowed, I might have a repeating rifle, but it weren't worth a damn less'n it had all the shots in it that it could take. If you want some sport, try this sometime: Set astride a horse without no saddle when he's at a dead gallop and try taking one shell at a time outta the loops of your cartridge belt and putting 'em in the magazine.

I covered the distance to the southwest corner of the mesa in record time, and I didn't have no trouble finding the ravine where we'd come up—the horses seemed to know it. I slowed the stallion to a trot as we went down through there with the gelding leading and the mare following, blowing hard. I sure didn't wanta lose 'em, 'cause I knowed I had to go back sometime and pick up the rest of the .44 ammunition. We went stumbling and banging down through there, hit the oak brush in a hurry, and then begun dodging and twisting and working our way out to the open plains. There was at least a half hour left 'fore the sun went down, and I knowed we had to do some real traveling if we was gonna stay outta trouble.

As we broke through the last of the oak brush and started out over the buffalo grass, I heard a wild yell behind me and above me. I twisted 'round to take a good look back and seen a long column of thirty or forty of them painted varmints working their way 'round the west end from the north through the brush. They must've been figuring on coming 'round and up the mesa behind us to make some real sport, and spotted me running. They seen that the trap'd been sprung too late and paused for a minute.

I could guess what they was thinking. All they could see was three horses and only one man running across the open prairie to the west. They must've wondered whether the main party was still up on the mesa, or whether them two horses was all of what was left of three men that'd been shot out, or just what was going on. They made up their minds in a hurry, though, 'cause about two-thirds of 'em'd started down through the brush after me. I had maybe a half to three-quarters of a mile lead and I aimed to keep it that way.

I kept yipping and yelling at the gelding and the mare to keep up, and they was racing as best they could, but they weren't no match for that stallion. The hard thing to do with horses is to keep 'em bunched up and running. They have to have some reason to think they're running, although when horses get real spooked and there's a lead horse that seems to know his direction, the rest of 'em will stay with him—least ways 'til they start tiring.

By the time it got halfway dark, them three horses was all beginning to show some signs of wear and tear. Even old Warrior's nostrils was standing out and his breath was coming a little bit short, but a stallion like that don't know his own strength. If you carry on with the whip, you're gonna get every extra ounce he has, and he'll gladly give it to you. I hated to rawhide him that way, but it was a matter of life or death, and I could see that the gelding and the mare weren't gonna be able to keep up.

I didn't know what kind of mounts them Comanches was riding, but they must've been awful fine animals. They was showing good signs of staying with me, but that's 'bout all. It become real apparent after we'd been running for 'bout twenty minutes that them horses weren't gonna catch up with my stallion less'n he put his foot in a hole or something. If he kept flying 'cross the grass the way he was going, I was as safe from them Comanches as if I'd been in the arms of Jesus.

Them braves was still in hot pursuit when the last light of day faded and I couldn't make 'em out no longer. I kept on for a while at a mighty good clip, then slowed down to a trot and changed direction real sharp to the west, figuring to hold out in that direction for a while and then cut up to the northwest and ride through the night. I'd lost all track of the gelding and the mare, but all I could do was sit there and cuss at them horses that hadn't stayed with us. I sure needed 'em, but I didn't dare turn back and hunt for 'em.

I eased the stallion down to his easy-riding, mile-eating single-foot. I was grateful that it was a night with no moon, and I kept my ear peeled for any noise that might give me a hint of Indians. I hoped and prayed that them heathen bastards'd give up when it was too dark to see my trail.

I rode steady all through the night headed northwest. When dawn broke, the early sun begun tinting them snow-clad peaks of the Sangre de Cristos. The Santa Fe Trail was only 'bout two miles in front of me, and beyond it the big basin 'tween Raton and Wagon Mound stretched away fifteen miles to the foothills of the mountains.

That Appaloosa was a mighty tired horse when we crossed the Santa Fe Trail in the early light. I reckon the thing that saved his life was the coming of dawn, 'cause if he'd had to keep up that pace it would've killed him. It's a helluva thing to run a horse to death, but sometimes a man ain't got no other choice. The sad part of it is, you can only do that with a spirited horse that's really worth his salt. You take an old jughead and he'll just slow up and quit on you.

With the coming of the early light, I kept looking back to see if anything was following me, but I knowed in my heart that I'd left them Comanches behind. I was out two packhorses, though, and I was gonna have to think of something else if I was gonna get back my ammunition.

I crossed the Santa Fe Trail as the sun was coming up. It was near midmorning 'fore we'd covered the fifteen miles west to the timber. I turned the stallion up a little valley that had a creek running through it, and it sure was great to hear the murmur of the water and smell the shade of the quakie trees and, before long, the sharp scent of pine.

When we hit the pines, I done something I always done whenever I was being followed. I cut back on a diagonal, gaining altitude outta the valley and coming out on a ridge. It was covered with heavy timber, but I rode along it 'til I broke out into a clearing that allowed me a good look at the little valley below and the great open plains and mesas in the distance.

I must've stayed there an hour, shading my eyes against the morning sun, but I didn't see nothing. The best thing I could do was stay put and keep watching 'til nightfall. Me and Warrior needed the rest anyway, and I reckon I was a little saddle sore, if you can get saddle sore when you ain't riding with no saddle.

Towards nightfall we headed up into the higher spruce-covered slopes. I made camp 'bout midnight, picking myself a good hiding place where I could keep an eye on things. I stayed there for three days and didn't see no action a'tall, 'cept for a fine little forked-horn buck that run across ahead of me into the timber when the sun was coming up the second morning.

I brought him down quick and spent most of the day curing the meat, figuring on taking as much with me as I could. I remember that batch of venison 'bout as well as anything, 'cause I was hungry and cooked some over a small fire that night.

I didn't see no special reason for moving. I wanted to go back for my ammunition, but I had to give the country 'round it time enough to cool off. I reckoned them Comanches weren't gonna stay around long. They needed to move on for hunting and to get to their winter quarters down to the southeast. I decided to give it a week—by then I reckoned the country'd be clear. Meanwhile, camping out in them high glorious mountains of blue spruce was as good a way to pass the time as any, and I thanked God that them Comanches'd give up the chase.

One afternoon 'bout a week later, I worked down outta the high country so's to come out onto the open plains at nightfall. I moved along down the basin to the cut of the Santa Fe Trail, and on across into the mesa country of the east to a place on the side of one big hill where there was enough trees for me and the stallion to spend the new day concealed. At daybreak on the second day, riding concealed all the time, I topped out on the sacred mesa where my .44 ammunition was. 'Bout nine days'd passed, and it was still a little creepy working 'round that country.

I picketed the Appaloosa and went on foot to see what I could make of things. I walked all the way 'round the rim of the mesa that day, keeping a sharp watch and stopping every so often to take a good look far out over the plains and 'tween the valleys and mesas nearby. I had the place all to myself. It was a relief that them warriors'd moved out, but my Comanche hunting weren't gonna go too good if'n things stayed so quiet.

Seemed like the best way to make up for the lack of activity was to get busy myself. I rigged some extra rawhide thongs to tie off my blanket into a pack that I could sling over my shoulders. Then me and Warrior made a few trips back and forth to Big Thumb, bringing all the .50 Sharps boxes back to our camp. I left the rest of the .44-caliber stuff undisturbed out by the Big Thumb, 'cause I figured I could come back to it easy anytime I needed it in my private war with the Comanche nation. Right then I had all the .44 shells I needed— nearly fifty altogether. There was still no sign of migrating Comanches, and I thought about the possibility of taking them .50s on into Taos for trading.

I could pack half of it on the Appaloosa and walk and make two trips of it, but somehow that didn't appeal to me. I reckoned it was a two-weeks' walk to Taos and back, and two loads'd take a month. By then the snow'd be flying good and I weren't aiming to walk over Eagles Nest Pass in anything very deep. There'd be fresh packhorses easy at hand if I could just find me a small party of Comanches.

I started taking little short scouting trips on the stallion, part to keep us in condition and part to sniff around for any fresh Comanche sign. During the second week one of them early fall snowstorms hit and blew up like hell. It was a quick one and didn't leave more'n three inches of snow on top of the mesa, but it showed I was right.

That first snow turned my thoughts more and more towards loading up as much ammunition as I could and heading for Taos 'fore the winter snows piled up in the mountain passes. I finally got Warrior loaded and settled down after burying the ammunition he couldn't carry. Then I started off on foot with him following me. We walked towards the southwest corner of the mesa—a pathway me and Warrior'd covered so many times. We made it down off the mesa okay and started heading due west for the Santa Fe Trail and the Taos cutoff, traveling all that night. At daybreak I watered him and tied him up. I didn't let him feed much during the day, 'cause I knowed he'd get too feisty and I'd have trouble loading him again that night.

I did lighten his pack load some, although I didn't take everything off. I just left him standing there in a clump of trees part loaded. I was dealing with a stallion—an almost wild stallion at that—and there weren't no use in pampering him, 'cause if I did I'd be sorry for it. He might throw off the whole works and run away and leave me on foot with my ammunition scattered all over the prairie.

The next night, we made the distance across the Santa Fe Trail and reached the heavy timber of the Sangre de Cristos by daybreak. We rested half the day and then moved on. It was never my custom to stay right on one of them trails if I could help it. The Taos cutoff over Eagles Nest Pass and on to Ranchos de Taos was ideal for traveling my way. I could stay in timber and off to the side so's not to encounter nobody and yet keep along the route.

We was four days making it over the mountain and the fourth afternoon broke out of the thick timber overlooking the beautiful Taos valley. Off in the distance I could see the Indian pueblo with blue smoke curling up from cooking fires, and there to the southwest of it, the little Spanish town nestled in the cottonwood trees.

18

A Blind Guitarist and
Two Beautiful Young Whores

It was late afternoon and there weren't no traffic as I walked by the mission church of Ranchos de Taos south of the main settlement. I'd dropped down to the trail leading my tired horse and his heavy load. I was getting in among the farms with their adobe walls and it felt strange being back among civilized people, although I hadn't spoke to a single person. I kept on going and a little bit later I seen a donkey coming down the lane between the walls, loaded with wood, and a woman with a shawl on her head walking behind driving the donkey with a stick. We passed and I didn't say nothing. Her, acting real shy, turned away rather'n meet my eyes.

When I was 'bout a quarter of a mile beyond the old mission church, I come up on the adobe walls of an old building that had big wooden doors opening out onto the street. I peered inside as best I could, half-timid, holding my Warrior on a lousy rope. I could hear the soft strumming of a guitar. It was real dark inside, but there was a couple of old chairs and tables sitting around and a kind of a bar. Pretty soon I could make out a Mexican man sitting there in a corner. I made a hand sign to him, but he was staring in the distance, his eyes sunk in and kinda milky-looking. He just kept playing that guitar and singing in a soft, beautiful voice.

Two señoritas come out from in back of the cantina and walked 'round and took me by the arm. They was jabbering away in mixed-up Spanish and English and I couldn't understand everything they said, but there weren't no doubt what they done for a living. They was young, maybe fifteen and seventeen, and sure was pretty to look at. I tied my tired horse to the hitching rail and, carrying my rifle and all, I went into the building. They set me down in one of them chairs and got me a jug of tequila.

It all come to me real clear. I'd found me a quiet Mexican cantina, a blind guitarist, and two beautiful young whores. It seemed like a great place to spend the winter, so that's what I done. I spent the winter of 1868 in that cantina, a quarter of a mile north of Ranchos de Taos and south of the main town. That was one of the great times of my life.

It didn't take me long to get situated. That afternoon I took the Sharps ammunition to Plaza de Taos and sold it to a dealer for five hundred dollars. Like I'd figured, it was worth its weight in gold out there on the frontier. A week later, after a little friendly arguing, I sold old Warrior to a horse dealer. I done right well and didn't have no more money worries.

Emanuel was the blind minstrel's name, but everybody called him Chico, and he become one of the three or four real friends I ever had in my life. There was some rooms in the back of the cantina where customers could take the girls or travelers could spend the night, but I didn't stay there, preferring to head out under the stars every night. I reckon I'd spent too many months in the open to be confined under a roof when it come sleeping time. I didn't mind using a bedroom when I was having a good time with the girls, but I didn't see much use spending the night there when I could have that canopy of stars hanging over me and the sounds of the night critters for company.

I made my campsite up on the mountain where there was a little spring. I made a little lean-to that was real peaceful and fine and slept there in the wintertime rolled up in my blankets. Many a night the snow was a foot deep and it was real peaceful. I didn't like staying 'round human habitation too much. It was better for me to be up in the timber and only go down to the town when I needed something for excitement.

I'd stay up at my place a week or two at a time, and when I'd come in, Chico and them two pretty gals'd treat me like a long-lost friend. I always tried to bring 'em something that'd be useful, like a good piece of venison or a fresh-tanned hide. I lived good up in them hills, there being lots of deer around. I killed an elk one afternoon. Once, in midwinter, when I was roaming through the mountains in back of my camp, I come across a bear den. I kicked the old sow out and killed her, and when I come back to town, Chico was sure glad to get that bear hide.

I never did stay 'round the cantina when it was crowded. There was some old mountain men who stopped there, and lots of times some of the soldiers from Fort Garland'd come through. Everybody got to raising hell on some of them festive nights, and it was too much noise and confusion for me. It was nicer when the gals and Chico was there alone. Oftentimes that was in the middle of the day. Later in the afternoon, when it got too loud, I'd slip out and ease on up the mountain.

I didn't talk much to folks. Mostly I liked to sit back in the quiet shadows of the cantina and drink a little tequila, or maybe some Mexican wine, and listen to 'em talking and later think 'bout the things they'd said and stories they'd told. If people'd come up and say hello, or go shouting 'round drunk or something, I wouldn't pay 'em no never mind.

Early one evening a bunch of them soldiers was sitting at another table. One of 'em glanced over at me and I heard him say to a young recruit, "Oh yeah, it's that mad mountain man, the one they call Cat Brules. They say he's real strange. He isn't s'posed to be nobody to mess with."

Hearing that made me feel so queer that I got up and eased out. After that, it was nigh unto two weeks 'fore I come down to the cantina. It didn't seem to me that I could ever get adjusted to the civilized folks' way again. To be real truthful with you, I reckon I never did.

I felt like my only friend was the blind guitarist, and I sure did like the company of them two cute little gals. Once I tried 'em both. I liked to think 'bout 'em as I was lying up there in the camp, wondering what they was doing, longing for 'em. Thinking like that one afternoon, I'd gone down there and walked by the cantina to make sure it was real quiet and there weren't no one there. Then I eased in and sat down beside Chico and listened to him strumming away.

It seemed like that man was always playing. I reckon that life for him, being blind, didn't hold too much excitement, but it was with his ears and his fingers that he seen and heard and spoke of the world. He had the damnedest collection of songs. Some of 'em was in his native Spanish, but lots of 'em that he'd got from the cowboys and the soldiers and the other customers was in English. He sang them words with a strong accent, but you could sure tell what he was talking 'bout.

One of the little whores—Juanita, the oldest—could speak a good bit of English and often she'd sit and tell me what the songs was about that Chico was singing in Spanish. They sure had a great wide range. I reckon some was the songs that come clear from the time of the conquistadores, and maybe even from the old times in Spain. Them's the ones that made me think 'bout Pedro Gonzales and what a fine man he'd been.

Juanita told me the words to the songs of horsemen and Andalusia. Some others was songs of them hidalgos that'd come outta Castile, some was songs of them conquistadores that was in Mexico and others that'd gone to Guatemala and all the countries down south, and some was songs of the Indians that was there. All of 'em was 'bout deeds of bravery or love, 'bout having a good time at a fiesta, and all them things that's important to any of us.

One thing 'bout them songs. Through all of 'em, whether they was in English or Spanish, there was a kind of sadness, a note of longing—like there was a dream out there that the singer could never find, like there was a goal that he could never really reach but was always dreaming 'bout, like somehow or other, things was gonna end in some kind of tragedy.

Damned if it didn't seem it was that way in life, too. Lots of times when I was lying out there under the stars and thinking 'bout what made the world work, I used to dream over them songs that Chico sang and what the meaning of 'em was. It seemed funny that those words and music'd been made up by people that was always with people, where I was a loner out there in the forests, wanting to be by myself.

Yet I had the same kinda feelings—the same kinda longings and ambitions—as them folks that wrote them songs. Seemed like, somehow, life had lots of promise and held out some kinda hope, but you was never gonna get there. It was always just beyond your reach, no matter what you done with your life.

There was always longing and a hope of something that hadn't been quite reached. I don't know what it was, but it seemed to me that them songs was expressing the real meaning of life—that life was, in a way, a wonderful thing but yet a dirty trick. That it always held out something for you that you knowed was there, just on the horizon, that was really worthwhile going for, but when you got there, you looked 'round kinda lost, and found a new longing.

Another thing them songs seemed to say was that you couldn't go talking 'bout the things of life without talking 'bout death, too. Yeah, you sure as hell was gonna die sometime, and no matter how you worked it, it was a tragedy. So how could you say anything was coming out right? How could you say anything was gonna be great? All them damn fools working and striving to build ranches, or them that was building cities or conquering nations and fighting like hell among theirselves for all kinds of things—what the hell was they working for? They weren't gonna end up with nothing but a grave.

Seemed to me that the thing for a man to do was to live out in the forests under the stars and listen to the rushing of the streams and the song of the wind in the pines. He could watch the prairie grass moving with the rain shower, and the shadows of the clouds as they swept 'cross the flats, and the circles of the eagles as they flew 'round in the blue, blue sky, sailing with their wings on currents that no man'd ever know. Those was the things that was worth living for.

I used to like to sit there and listen to Chico and hold hands with Juanita, less'n she was away and busy. I enjoyed being with her or her little sister, Ramona. It was all the same. Chico didn't seem to care much 'bout making love to the girls, and I wondered if that part of him'd died with his eyes.

Sometimes I'd walk away and leave 'em, telling 'em I'd be back sometime. Seemed like they all thought of me like a mystery man, although Juanita was always telling me how handsome I was and how I had a fine figure for a man. I kept myself as hard as nails and quick as a cat, but I never thought of myself as being handsome. I had me a big beard, which was too much trouble to shave, and left my hair long, 'cause it was easy to keep it tied back outta my eyes that way. Whether I was handsome or not, we sure had ourselves a nice winter, and I felt plumb reluctant when spring come and I knowed I had to move on.

The snows begun to melt in that spring of 1869, and then the quakie trees greened up a little. The oak brush started showing signs of budding and the grass in the valley 'round Taos sprouted up with young shoots. Occasionally I seen long lines of geese working their way north from Mexico, and I knowed it was time that I got on the trail again.

I come in one afternoon and spent some time with Chico and the girls. I still had 'bout two hundred fifty dollars, and I left it all with Chico. I knowed he needed it more'n I did, although he swore it'd all be there when I come back next winter. I went to bed with both of them girls for the afternoon and they cried when I kissed 'em good-bye. At daybreak the next day, I headed east on foot again for the mesa country, the Comanches' spring and summer hunting grounds.

That's the way I lived, pretty much without no change from 1869 to 1873. I hunted them Comanches for four more years, all through the mesa lands and even down as far as the Balcones Escarpment, way south of the Canadian, and up as far north as the Arkansas. I spent the winters in Ranchos de Taos, sleeping with them two little Mexican gals and listening to the songs of the blind Mexican minstrel. Chico and Juanita and Ramona—they was my family, and I knowed if anything happened to me, they'd take care of me, and I sure as hell'd take care of them.

Out there on the prairies, things stayed the same. The same kind of ambushes, the same watching from the top of them mesas, me traveling on foot, hoarding my ammunition, and waiting for my chance to spring on 'em—keeping my supply of pemmican up and listening and waiting and watching for the excitement that goes with the hunt. I done the same kind of ambushes, the same attacks on Comanche braves, and left the same cat signs. Every year 'fore winter'd come, when I'd make the same long trek back to Taos, I usually had a couple of stolen Indian ponies to trade when I got there, so I done real good for money.

The first time I went back to Pedro's grave I found it, by God, by a white reflection shining out there on the prairie. When I got close I found it was them Comanche skeletons that I'd piled up there so long ago. It was a fine white monument commemorating old Silver Pete. I went by Pedro's grave many times in four years, and I'd always give a wave and a salute to him. A few times I stopped on my way back to Taos and told him a story or two 'bout how I'd evened the score that summer and what I'd done in the way of cleaning out a few more

Comanche families or busting up a war party. I'd tell him how I'd messed up a buffalo hunt or how many horses I'd stole, so's he'd feel better.

Then I'd talk to him 'bout life in Ranchos de Taos, and 'bout Chico and some of the songs that he'd sing. Once I even sung him a song as best I could remember it, 'bout horsemen back in Andalusia. I liked the tune and I'd learned them Spanish words, although I didn't know the meaning of 'em exactly. Anyway, I sung it to old Pedro just for the hell of it, 'cause I knowed he'd like it.

I sure was glad that I'd piled up them skeletons. They was so white and clean you could see 'em from twenty miles away, so's there weren't no way for me to forget where Pedro's grave was.

There was one thing I kept noticing that was different on the prairies. I didn't ever find them Comanches in their old camp-grounds. When I'd scout out the sites, I'd find my cat sign but no fresh Indian sign.

There was one other thing I'd noticed: There weren't never no Comanche pony tracks nowhere near Pedro's grave. It seemed like when Cat Brules went through a place, them Comanches didn't wanta come back.

One summer morning, when I was sitting up on a mesa, I seen a cloud of dust and I reckoned it either had to be buffalo or Indians or horses. I watched it for a long time, and the dust cloud kept moving along its west-northwest course, approaching a mesa to the north. I thought I might find me some happy hunting, so I set out 'cross the valley in a steady jog and made me a little altitude when I covered the foot of that mesa.

In the late afternoon I seen that it was a band of horses, maybe thirty or forty, and there weren't no riders with 'em—it was a wild horse herd. I felt foolish that I'd done so much traveling trying to get close to 'em, but I sat and watched 'em as they come in closer. When they was 'bout a mile away, I seen something that almost made my hair stand up—the leader of the bunch was a black and white stallion, and there was something real familiar 'bout him. His black and white coat stood out real clean and you could tell from the way he was moving that he was the master of the herd and weren't taking no sass from none of the others.

If there was any young stallions in the bunch, they must've been awful young and in no position to challenge that old boy. Yessir, he was a black and white stallion, the kind they call a piebald. Right then it come to me. God almighty, he weren't just any old piebald, he was *my Piebald!* I like to jumped outta my moccasins. I watched and kept thinking I had to be wrong, that he couldn't be no such, but as I studied the familiar markings and everything 'bout him I knowed that I hadn't made no mistake. How he'd ever got loose from them Indians and gone wild and collected him a bunch of mares was more'n I'd ever know, but I was sure glad in my heart.

By the time I'd identified him, that remuda weren't much more'n half a mile away and I decided on something real bold and crazy. I walked through the oak brush and straight towards the herd as it was feeding and moving along the prairie grass. I hadn't gone a hundred yards 'fore one of them mares spotted me and raised her head and let out a snort. The whole remuda started staring at me with their tails streaming out and their ears cocked. The stallion—God bless him, old Piebald—trotted 'round in front, getting 'tween me and the mares.

Man, he was a magnificent sight! He was my Piebald all right, but there was something 'bout him that breathed out the air of freedom, like he was master of his whole domain, like he was beholden to no man. That makes any man or animal beautiful to see. He just stood there, so I put my fingers 'tween my teeth and let out a whistle, like I used to do when I'd call him. Piebald stomped his foot for a minute, then raised his head and whistled back. He come trotting a little closer, looking things over, and I spoke to him in a nice steady tone like I'd always done.

"Hey, Piebald. It's your old buddy. It's your ol' friend. Don't ya remember haulin' me up the Chisholm Trail? Don't ya remember when we crossed the Smoky Hill an' the Arkansas? Don't ya remember how ya carried me an' Michelle along? Don't ya remember, ol' man? Don't ya remember Cat Brules?"

I whistled to him again. He kept coming closer and closer, always looking. He stopped to paw and snort and toss his head. The mares stood off in the distance and watched their lord coming up to something human. They must've figured he was awful brave. Piebald arched his neck and rolled his eyes and pawed the earth, and then he come a little bit closer. I called him again. He come up real slow to within 'bout fifteen feet of me and sniffed and snorted and looked at me while I stood there talking to him. I could see by his scars that he'd gone through lots of fights with other stallions protecting his mares, but he was in beautiful shape, his hide shining and slick, his eyes bright, his ears up, and his mane flowing in the prairie wind. I figured that's 'bout what anyone wants—to run free and go wild. That's what's deep down in all of us and there's always something spoiling the dream.

I took two steps to get close to him, just itching to put my hands on his mane. I got to within a foot of doing so when he let out a snort and whirled and flew away like lightning. He whistled to his mares and they took off and went racing 'cross the plains at a dead gallop, with him nipping and snorting at their flanks.

Well, you know, in my day, I done lots of cussing at horses simply on account of 'em running off, but I couldn't do no cussing at Piebald for taking off then. I tipped that sloppy old hat of mine as a salute, then waved it as I watched him go. I wished him the best of luck, for he was doing what I liked best, running in the wind with his freedom, and my heart went with him all the way.

One day early in the summer of 1873 I was riding along hearing the hum of flies and looking at the shimmering haze on the prairie. In the distance behind me and to my left, stretching up to the north, was a long line of mesas that seemed to stand like sentinels on the edge of the plains.

Then I seen something at the base of a hill and a little bit back from the Cimarron River. It was black, and at first I thought maybe it was a bear or two. It didn't move none, and as I rode up closer I seen it was a burnt-out wagon train. Two wagons. It looked like two families'd come that way 'bout three or four days before. 'Course there was Indian sign all over. Them two families'd started 'cross the Cimarron cutoff just like I'd done with Michelle. Like me, they didn't have no more sense than to cut right through Indian country, prob'ly thinking they'd save a few miles and make the rest of the trip shorter. Well, they made it shorter all right, shorter by the rest of their lives. Only I reckon it was a helluva lot longer for the womenfolks that was with 'em.

Everything was burnt and scattered from hell to breakfast. The charred spokes of them wagon wheels and the tongues of the wagons was sticking up outta the mess, and the frames and all the canvas was burnt out, but I seen a wagon seat or two and some metal pieces that'd been took off to make some lance heads. There was the reins of the mule harness and a couple of whippletrees and a half-burnt barrel for water or flour. And there was scattered bits and pieces of torn clothing—mostly women's and children's. When I come up close, the vultures got up and circled away from what was left of the festering bodies of two men. Their clothes'd been picked from 'em, and I seen that they'd died of gunshot wounds, then been scalped and left where they lay, up close to one of the wagon wheels.

The women and children'd been carried away. Though I've killed a lot in my time, the looks of what happens when a bunch of Indians goes through one of them family wagon trains is terrible to see, and it made me feel plumb sick.

Without coming too close, I worked 'round the wreckage of them wagons in a big circle, my horse sashaying sideways to get away from what he seemed to consider bad business. On the far side of the circle, I seen what was left of a little baby. It was lying on the ground and a stick'd been drove through its chest. I reckoned that the spearing hadn't hurt it none, though, 'cause it looked like its brains'd been bashed out 'fore it'd been impaled on the ground.

That's what they called "Indian paling" and I reckon they done that for some spiritual reason, something 'bout their not wanting the ghosts of anything they'd killed to come back. But I reckon that baby's ghost, if there is such a thing, must've come back to haunt that brave.

When I'd see something like that skewered white baby, it made me think that maybe some of them Comanches weren't as tough as they thought they was. Maybe they was physically, but mentally they wasn't. When it comes to spooks and spirits, I reckon the white man—'specially one like me that didn't give a damn 'bout nothing—was every bit as tough as any of them Comanches, and maybe tougher.

I hit off down along the Cimarron, 'bout a mile from the cottonwoods, and rode for maybe half an hour 'fore I seen some buzzards circling over a bend in the river where the cottonwoods was thick. I reckoned there was something I should investigate. I drifted down and found what I'd expected—folks that'd been in the wagon train—three full-growed men, two women, and a girl that I reckoned was 'bout twelve or thirteen years old who'd had a leg broke bad and couldn't travel. At least I guessed that from what was left of 'em.

Their bodies was hanging upside down from a tree and there was the ashes of two or three small fires that the Indians'd prob'ly used to get their knives red-hot for the torture.

The whole mess set my stomach to churning and my mind to spinning. It served to remind me of the horrible things them Comanches done to my Michelle and Pedro, and the white-hot hatred that'd been cooling in my belly flared up all over again.

I spent the rest of that summer racking me up a real nice Comanche kill.

SLIM PICKINGS

I went on down to the plains country real early in the spring of '73. I left Ranchos de Taos on foot like I'd always done, crossed Eagles Nest Pass, and hiked 'cross the basin south of Raton at night, going over the Santa Fe Trail in a place where I knowed I couldn't be seen. Then I headed east to the end of the mesa country and spent a week or two just wandering up and down.

I got a little bit impatient when I didn't see no sign of Comanches. I even went back into all the old encampments where I'd once found 'em and left my sign, but I still didn't find no sign of Comanches.

Funny thing was, I didn't see no sign of buffalo that year neither. That was strange, but then buffalo was strange creatures, moving 'bout according to their own notions. Sometimes they might be late for maybe a month or two for some reason a man'd never know. 'Course it might also've had something to do with the fact them railroads kept pushing farther and farther west and more'n more buffalo hunters'd begun pouring into the country 'round about.

I'd been down in Taos when I'd first heard 'bout the Union Pacific joining up at Salt Lake in '69, and the Kansas Pacific that I'd seen stop in Hays City back in '67 was clear out to Denver by '74. And they was building another railroad up on the Arkansas and I reckoned it was gonna go on past old Bent's Fort and on into Pueblo 'fore too much longer.

Anyway, not seeing no sign of Comanches 'round there, I figured maybe I'd better go on down to the Llano Estacado and see what it was all about.

One day, 'bout midmorning, I seen something real strange off in the distance. It was a funny-colored speck on the prairie and I kept watching it real careful as I moved towards it. I finally seen what looked to be a man lying down, only he weren't moving none. At first I thought he might be an Indian, but then I seen that he had more clothes on the upper part of his body than an Indian'd be wearing. There was a buzzard or two circling round in the sky overhead, but they didn't come down to feed, so I figured whoever was lying out there was prob'ly still alive.

I weren't gonna get suckered by no Indian trick, though. I come up on him real slow and careful. The prairie was flat, so's there weren't no place to spring an ambush. I figured whoever was lying out there couldn't be planning nothing I couldn't handle. As I walked up on him, I seen he was a white man lying flat on his face with his hands throwed out, and a buffalo Sharps lay on the ground a few feet away. There weren't no doubt in my mind that he was a buffalo hunter alone out there on the prairie who'd run outta steam one way or other.

I could tell he was still breathing, 'cause the back of his chest rose up and down real slow. I went up to him and rolled him over real easy and his eyes opened just a little, showing he was conscious. I looked him over real good, but couldn't see no sign he'd been shot. Then I thought that maybe he'd been throwed off'n a horse and'd busted his head or neck, but that weren't it neither. Finally, I seen that his tongue was all swole up and his ribs was showing and I reckoned that he'd run outta food and water.

I put my canteen to his lips and give him a little taste of the water. That got his attention. His eyes scrunched up tight and he grabbed the canteen and started sucking at it like a baby at its mama's breast. I pulled it away real quick. The fastest way to kill a man who's dying of thirst is to pour water into him as fast as he can take it. So I held back on the canteen. "Now wait jest a minute, pardner," I said. "Take it easy. Slow's the way. Ya ain't gonna live long if'n ya make a hog a yerself."

He opened his eyes and looked at me real fearful 'til he

comprehended that I was one of his own kind. Then I give him the canteen again, making sure he drank real slow.

It took most of the afternoon to bring that old boy 'round enough to where he could sit up and make a little sense.

He kept talking 'bout his partner, Yoder. Yoder done this and Yoder done that, he kept saying over and over. It seemed he was a buffalo hunter who'd come out of Fort Dodge 'bout the time old General Miles had. "If I was going buffalo hunting, I believe I'd go where the buffalo was," Yoder'd said.

The old man explained that everybody knowed the buffalo was all in Indian territory, and that land was protected by a treaty with the Comanches. But them army boys was all for cleaning out the buffalo, knowing that they was a moving commissary for the Indians. They knowed that was the only way they was ever gonna get them Indians slowed down.

That's all I got outta him then. Along towards the end of the afternoon I persuaded him to quit mumbling and rest so's we could travel in the cool of the night. He was still real weak and I had a helluva time helping him walk.

He seemed like a square enough fella, although I didn't cotton to many white men and no Indians. He was an old-timer who should've knowed what he was doing. By bad luck or a mistake in judgment he'd got hisself off in the predicament I'd found him in. That can happen easy enough to any of us if we ain't careful.

I didn't ask him no questions. I let him talk whenever he felt like it—which, I must say, after he got his senses 'bout him, weren't too often. I kept feeding him pemmican. He weren't no stranger to it, so he got along fine. On our second day on the North Fork of the Canadian I shot a small deer, so we ate real good for the first part of the next week, and the old boy gained his strength back fast. He mentioned a couple of times that he had to get hisself back to Fort Dodge to claim Yoder's things, so the parting of our ways was in order. I didn't question him no further, figuring that if'n he felt it was any of my business, he'd tell me.

We'd only covered a couple of miles a day. Fortunately there'd been a few of them evening thunderstorms, so we had enough water 'til we got to the North Fork. As we was resting there on the banks 'round the campfire that last night together, he told me his story. He told me his name was Shellabarger or some such and that him and his partner, Yoder, had teamed up with a bunch of wagons and left Dodge City 'bout five weeks before. He spouted off a bunch of names, but I couldn't remember most of 'em, 'cept that there was a man named Hanrahan and two others named Tyler and Leonard.

Them fellas'd hired that grand old scout and frontiersman Billy Dixon to guide 'em from Fort Dodge over to a place on the Canadian River where they could set up stores and a supply depot for the buffalo hunters that was coming into the Indian territory after old General Miles'd cleared the way. I never did meet Billy Dixon, but I'd sure heard lots 'bout him round the frontier. All the men that knowed him said he was a helluva man. One reason I cottoned so much to listening 'bout Dixon was 'cause folks claimed he was a dead gun, and I liked to compare some of the things he done with what I knowed I could do.

Shellabarger and Yoder went along with this gang 'cause it was a good way to get into Indian territory and kill some buffalo and be supplied while they was doing it. They weren't under no illusions 'bout how dangerous it was, but they figured there was quite a few of 'em and they was all good shots. Chances was they'd make a real good showing of theirselves if the Comanches got waspy.

Be that as it may, Billy Dixon done guided 'em down to a place that he knowed 'bout on the north side of the Canadian. It was a real good layout—a nice creek coming in from the north feeding into the Canadian with good meadows and good water. The creek was called Adobe Walls Creek, and it must've been a good place, 'cause Shellabarger told me that Kit Carson'd built a fort out there 'bout twenty years before when he was buffalo hunting with the Indians. Carson didn't do nothing that didn't make sense, so it weren't no surprise that Billy Dixon'd picked a good place like Adobe Walls Creek for his setup.

Leonard built a shelter outta cottonwood logs and set up a general store there, and Hanrahan fixed hisself up a saloon. After they got the depot set up and them fellas went into business, Shellabarger and Yoder, with 'bout thirty other buffalo hunters, broke up and begun spreading 'cross the plains north of the Canadian, looking for buffalo herds.

They'd had some mighty good luck hunting, and Yoder and his partner ended up on Chicken Creek, where they put down a lot of animals and got busy skinning 'em out. They needed more salt for the hides and tossed to see which one of 'em was gonna travel the seventy-five miles back to Adobe Walls for it. It fell to Shellabarger and he'd headed out. He was a day and a half making the trip in, and when he hit Hanrahan's, he poured hisself three fingers of whiskey as a starter. Being tired from a long day's riding, and of course a little drunk, he passed out real calm 'fore the night was too far along.

He said he remembered hearing somebody telling of two men who'd been killed by the Indians the day before on Chicken Creek, but he was so boozed up that it didn't bother him none, and he holed up for the night on the floor of Hanrahan's. 'Bout three o'clock in the morning, there was a sound like a pistol shot and Hanrahan jumped up and said, "Damnit boys, clear out, the ridgepole is busting."

Everybody got up real groggy and staggered outta the place. Hanrahan rummaged 'round out in the woodpile and found a stake pole he could shove under the ridge. By the time they'd all finished fussing 'round, it was starting to get daylight and Hanrahan offered to pour another round of drinks.

I reckon that's what saved their lives. Billy Dixon was out at daybreak putting some of his gear in a wagon when he looked up towards the east and seen what he thought was buffalo. It later turned out to be a Comanche war party of seven hundred thundering down on that little depot with all the speed their ponies could muster.

Well, Billy Dixon took one shot at the bunch and then run for the saloon and dove in. Things was hot and heavy there for the next hour or two. Them buffalo hunters was fighting off an army of Indians that was determined to wipe out that depot that'd been set up in the middle of their buffalo hunting grounds.

Shellabarger said it was 'bout as sporty a time as he'd had in his life. At the end of 'bout two hours, the attack slowed. Dixon was really a dead gun and so was two or three of the other hunters. They'd raised hell with them Indians with their big .50 Sharps. Many of the horses them fellas had, along with lots of Indian ponies, was shot up. The stench of dead Indians and dead horses got mighty bad, 'til a lull in the fighting on the second day give 'em a chance to bury or drag away anything that was too near the saloon. Shellabarger said that fifty-six dead horses was counted and at least thirteen Comanche bodies that hadn't been drug off. He reckoned they must've killed or wounded damn near a hundred warriors, most of which'd been carried off.

Years later, there was a lot told 'bout the four-day fight at Adobe Walls and Billy Dixon's mile-long shot. Shellabarger was a man who didn't talk much, but when he did, he had plenty to say. That's why I reckon most of it was true. He said they outgunned and outfought them Comanches.

Only four white men was lost in the fight—the two men sleeping outside in a wagon at the first attack; Tyler, who'd stepped outside to get a better shot and took a bullet in the lung; and the cook, Bill Olds, who was killed by accident. He'd been in a loft over the saloon and was leaning on a barrel as a lookout for his shooting. Mrs. Olds, a stout old gal, was down below loading his rifles and passing 'em up to him as fast as he could shoot. In the excitement he must've leaned down and took one of them rifles by the barrel just as she was passing it up and the hammer must've hit something. Anyhow, the rifle went off just below his chin and blew the top of his head clean off. He come tumbling down outta that loft, and Mrs. Olds was plumb broke up 'bout it.

The fighting eased off on the third day. The Indians seemed to've growed plenty weary of them Sharps in the hands of the buffalo hunters. In the late afternoon a string of five or six warriors rode out on the top of some sand cliffs 'bout half a mile to the east. Everybody knowed that Billy Dixon was by a long ways the best gun in the bunch and begged him to try a shot. Old Billy was somewhat reluctant—the distance being so great—but he finally climbed up into the loft with the best Sharps available, took careful aim, and knocked one of them Indians plumb off'n his horse.

'Bout two weeks later General Miles come in there with a column of troops. He had a surveying team with him and Miles had 'em measure the distance of that shot. It come out to 1,538 yards! It seems almost impossible, I know, but the shell of them big .50 Sharps was 'bout six inches long and packed one helluva wallop.

That night 'round the fire, I got my curiosity up enough. "Friend, I can't quite get it through my head why ya took it ta come up this way, right through the heart of Quohadi Comanche country, when ya could've gone down through the Canadian an' crossed back over ta the Cimarron an' the Arkansas, lower down where there's better water an' where ya would've been closer ta the reservations. Now, I know it ain't none a my business, but seein's I found ya out here, I'm real curious ta know why ya took it ta go the long way."

Shellabarger kept looking in the fire, kicked one of them burning logs a little, and when the sparks flew up he drawled, "On account of the Kiowa medicine man." He didn't say nothing more for a minute or two.

"I don't reckon you'll believe this," he continued, "but I knowed I wouldn't run into no Comanches up this way. I figured it was a long ways between water and maybe added a hundred miles between Adobe Walls and Dodge City. I didn't know where the water holes was, and that's where I come to grief. But I knowed if I wanted to stay away from them Comanches, the only thing for me to do was to strike north from the Canadian 'til I hit the east end of them mesas between here and the Cimarron. All I had to do was to stay right along there 'til I crossed the Cimarron and I wouldn't see nary a Comanche."

I was sure surprised and amused to hear that. I'd been hunting Comanches all through there for the better part of six years. I looked real doubtful. "Well, I ain't fer changin' your mind much, but I spent a mite a time myself all through this country, dodgin' in an' out amongst them mesas an' watchin' whole parties a Comanches, an' I can tell ya there ain't been no shortage ever up there 'cept perhaps this year. But then, the buffalo ain't comin' up yet, so's I'm not too s'prised that I ain't seen any."

He looked up from the fire right at me. "Well, you ain't gonna see no more either, even if and when the buffalo comes. I'm telling you that right here and now. My partner, Yoder, got it straight from the Kiowa medicine man. Yoder spoke good Kiowa and he never told me nothing but the truth, so I believe it. Stranger, I think you really got some more information coming."

That really got my dander up. "Kiowa medicine man? What'n the hell does a damn Kiowa medicine man know 'bout the Comanches out in this country anyhow? Where's this medicine man? When did he tell your partner all this?"

Shellabarger shrugged. "Yoder used to haul freight between Kansas Landing and the Indian agent at Medicine Lodge. He got to know them Kiowas real well—he took up with a Kiowa squaw for two winters—and spoke some of their language. Last winter he got to talking to one of his squaw's relations that was a Kiowa medicine man. Did you know them Kiowas is friends to the Comanches? That old medicine man told Yoder that the Comanches'd quit going to that mesa country—them Quohadi Comanches, the wild ones. Yessir, they blowed clear outta that mesa country and they ain't hunting there no more, all on account of the Cat Man."

"What's that?" I kept my head down.

"There's a white hunter up there. The Indians believe he's a devil. I heard tell all the way from Dodge City to Kansas Landing, even down in Hanrahan's Saloon, that there's this man working all through them mesas. The last three or four years he's been playing bloody hell with them Comanches. He's s'posed to be as slick and quiet as an Indian, and just as fast. He's been knowed to wipe out a whole village. Now the Indians ain't working that country no more. The Kiowa medicine man said it's all the work of the Cat Man. He leaves his cat's-eye spirit sign as a warning."

He took a hard look at me and then shifted real uncomfortable-like. "Say, now that we're talking about it, I was noticing your eyes. They's kind of like a cat's." He paused and stirred up the fire with a stick. "You ain't by any chance the Cat Man, are you?"

I almost busted out laughing, 'cause he'd had a scared look. I wondered if he believed them Kiowa medicine tales—that the Cat Man was a kind of ghost spirit.

I smiled. "My name's Brules. I ain't no cat, but I'll tell ya this much. I spent a little time the last few years killin' Comanches on account of a personal reason that I ain't gonna bother ya with. I'm hopin' that what ya tol' me ain't right, an' it ain't gonna turn out that them Comanches has quit comin' through the mesa country. If they have, I'm in a bad way with nothin' more ta hunt."

Shellabarger stood up and laughed. "By God, I want to shake your hand. There ain't nobody out here on the frontier that's done folks a better turn than you. I sure heard lots about you and what you been doing. I believe, just looking at them eyes of yours, that you're the dead gun they say you are."

It was the last he said about it. The day was breaking and we kicked out the fire and had us a little more pemmican.

When it got good and light, the old buffalo hunter picked up his Sharps and his canteen, throwed his blanket 'round his shoulder, reached out his hand and said, "Thanks, Cat Man. Best of luck to you." Then he turned and started walking off to the northeast. I stood there watching him 'til he'd passed over one of the bluffs. Then he disappeared, and I never seen him again.

I never knowed whether there was any truth to the story of the Kiowa medicine man or if the reason them Comanches'd never come back was 'cause the buffalo was gone. It was the time of the last of the big herds and the hunters'd pretty well killed off all the buffalo on the plains, so's that could've just as easy been why.

Whatever the case, it weren't 'til early December that I crossed over the pass and dropped into Ranchos de Taos. It was real lonely there that year and not near the fun I'd had in the winters before. Them two pretty gals, Juanita and Ramona, had left and been replaced by a couple of ugly Pueblo squaws that I plumb didn't take to. Chico told me that Juanita'd gone south to El Paso del Norte, for reasons of her own, and Ramona'd married a rich rancher up in the San Luis Valley. Chico weren't feeling too healthy hisself, so he didn't sing much no more. It was a bad winter.

When spring come matters got worse. In early '74 I heard some shocking news. The Kiowas and Quohadi Comanches'd been rounded up and put back on the reservations. Old Chief Quanah Parker'd give up, and that meant there weren't gonna be no more Comanche hunting for me.

I'd been hearing some interesting stories 'bout them Mormon folks out yonder in the Utah Territory. It seemed like them Mormons'd knowed what they was doing when they'd broke from the United States. Anyway, with them Comanches tucked away on the reservation, there didn't seem to be no good reason for me to keep hanging 'round Ranchos de Taos. 'Sides, I sorta had a hankering to go on out and have me a look at that Mormon country.

My money was getting short, so I figured that I could swing through the San Luis Valley and visit the Valdez spread and see if old Señor Valdez'd maybe give me a horse or two for my trip out west.

I set off during the late winter of '74 and finally come up on the Valdez ranch in the south end of the San Luis one evening early in March—same's I'd done nearly seven years before when I'd escaped from the Comanches. Only thing different was that I was coming up from the south.

When I come up on the hacienda it was just like the first time: a dog barked, a light come on behind the window shutters, and the old man stuck his gun out and hollered to see who was there. I'd managed to pick up enough Spanish so's I was able to answer in such a way that I didn't take no chance getting my head blowed off.

I told him it was Cat Brules, the amigo of our dear departed Pedro Gonzales. Them words was the keys to the kingdom. The old man flung open that big wooden door and, along with the señora, rushed out. Both of 'em throwed their arms 'round me like I was the prodigal son the Bible talks 'bout. Far as they was concerned, there weren't nothing to do but to bring me in, light up the fire, set candles all 'round, and fill me up with coffee and chili. I sure welcomed that chili, 'cause I hadn't had nothing but pemmican in my belly for a long time—'cept a bit of that hot Taos lightning.

'Course they was all for questioning me. They'd heard 'bout my spending the winters in Taos and it seemed like they was hurt, 'cause I hadn't come up to see 'em. I explained to 'em that I was really a wild man and not much given to visiting civilization. To tell the truth, it'd made me feel ashamed of myself that I hadn't come to see them good folks, but me being a lone wolf and shy was prob'ly the real reason I'd never stopped off. There was only the old man and the señora around. The sons was off buying some cattle, and I found out that the daughter'd long since got married and moved off to the south with her rancher husband.

They begged me to tell 'em the whole story of Pedro's death, so I started with tracking Silver Pete's wagon and finished with how he'd broke loose with his stallion and run him 'til he were gutshot and collapsed. I seen the old man's eyes glint hard as steel in the firelight. The way his jaw muscles tightened every now and then, I knowed he would've give his lifeblood to've been with Pedro when all of that was going on. I could see the fighting spirit shining in the old boy, and it warmed my heart.

He give me a big shot of wine and I reckoned that loosened my tongue a little more. I went on to tell 'bout how I'd found old Pete strewed out there, or at least what was left of him, and what them Indians'd done. By then the old man's eyes'd begun flashing like steel.

When I told him 'bout how I'd dug Pete's last resting place, he broke down and wept like he was mourning for his long-lost son.

It was a heart-stirring thing, and something made me go on telling him 'bout how I'd tracked that Comanche band up into the mesas where I'd shot 'em up and then suckered 'em into charging me on the open plain, and how I'd massacred them in his honor and left their bodies laid out 'round old Pedro's grave.

Then I told him 'bout my years of wandering in Comanche land, how I'd ambushed 'em, and left my cat sign along the mesas. The old man'd rub the arm of his chair with the palm of his hand and say, "Good. That is magnificent! You have the good kill!"

It was just like them Spanish folks, it seemed, to have that kind of a feud. You was either their great friend and they'd die for you, or you was their enemy and they'd hunt you down to the hinges of hell.

As I told Valdez and the señora what I'd done the last several years, it seemed like a big burden lifted off'n their hearts. True, Pedro was dead and gone, but they still felt something of his presence. Now, even more than that, they felt he'd been revenged proper and fittinglike. By my count, at least two hundred thirty-four Comanches'd paid with their lives in tribute to Pedro's memory. I didn't think that was near enough, and I told old Valdez that. I told him that if I was to kill a thousand of em, that still wouldn't be near enough.

After we was all finished talking 'bout Comanches, I looked real sorrowful and sorta run the brim of my hat through my fingers. I told him that I was in bad need of his help.

"Ah, my son," he said, "just tell me what it is that I can do for you. Whatever it is that you wish that my house can give, you know that I will help."

"Señor," I said, looking straight into them sharp old brown eyes of his that made me feel as if he was looking right through me, "I need some ammunition fer my Winchester, some supplies, an' a horse so's I can head off fer Mormon country. What with all the time I've been spendin' huntin' Comanches, I ain't been makin' me no money ta buy nothin' with."

He nodded kind of thoughtful. "Why is it, my son, that you wish to go to the Mormon country?"

"I heard tell that even though them Mormons're s'posed ta be back under government control since the railroad's been built through Salt

Lake, there's lots a country down in them canyons a the Colorado that no white man's got ta yet. That's the kinda place fer me."

"I see, my son. Well, that is good, and I wish you Godspeed. But you will stay here tonight, no? Let us take care of you. We can give you what you need in the morning—ammunition, clothes, some food, and a good horse. And now let us do something about the way you look. You are a mountain man with a big beard and buckskin shirt and pants that are all covered with dried blood and grease and full of bad smells. Come, why don't you shave that beard that is like a bush and I will give you some new clothes. You will feel much better then, no?"

I had to admit he was right. It'd been so long since I'd had clean, new clothes and a face free of whiskers that I couldn't remember what it'd felt like.

What come next was some of the hardest things I'd done in many a year. First I had to set still while Señor Valdez's manservant, Pepe, took some sharp scissors and cut away most of my beard and long hair. Then he shaved off the rest of my beard. I must say that when old Valdez'd give me a mirror 'fore Pepe'd started, I'd realized how tough and dirty I was looking. Then, when he showed me how I looked after the shave, I didn't know it was the same man. I was thin in the face and pale, it seemed like, although I had to admit that the skin 'round my eyes was more dark and leatherlike than most.

Then I had to take me a bath—something I hadn't done for a long time. I'd swum in the rivers once in a while out in Comanche country, when it was real hot and I'd cross a running stream, but I hadn't took what folks call a real bath in so long that I couldn't remember. It sure was a funny feeling when old Pepe took me to the tub of water that was ready out on the back patio of the hacienda.

I shivered, cold and naked, when I got outta that tub, and was glad for the towel and the nightshirt they'd give me to wear. Then the señora took me into one of them rooms where there was a fancy bed laid out with blankets and even a sheet. Pepe made the motions to show me that that's where I was to sleep that night, and with that, he blowed out the candle and went out, shutting the door.

I felt all cooped up and almost panicked when that door closed, but I knowed I could trust Valdez. As long as I had my guns by me, I could stand it. I overcome that cooped-up feeling, but trying to go to sleep on the bed was something else. Now, I don't reckon it was as fancy as the beds that folks have nowadays, it being made up of a straw mattress on slats with bedclothes on it, but it was way too fancy for me, and I plumb didn't feel right. I must've stayed there almost an hour trying to sleep. When I seen that I couldn't, I rolled up on the floor with a blanket. I took my Winchester in my right arm and laid my .38 right where I could reach it with my left hand, and I slept that way real sound all through the rest of the night.

Next morning, Pepe tapped on the door and come in carrying a steaming bowl of chili. It sure smelled good and I set up to eat. He went off and pretty soon he come back with an armload of fancy clothes. They was the damnedest-looking things—a big, wide sombrero and a black silky head bandanna to wear under it, a soft-looking white shirt with a black string tie, a black vest with fancy-colored stitching, and some black leather pants that worked as *chaperos* and trousers at the same time. There was also a pair of shiny boots with the biggest spurs I'd ever seen. They looked like they'd gut a horse the first time you touched him with 'em. Pepe made me understand that the stuff was a present from the old man and that he wouldn't hear of nothing but me accepting it. I didn't know if they was some of his own going-to-town clothes or maybe extras from the boys, but they sure was fine. I was gonna look like a regular hidalgo in that getup.

I had a helluva time making up my mind to get into them clothes, but that's what I figured I'd better do. When I put on that rig and looked at myself in the tall glass mirror that was in the room, I almost fell clean over from the shock. I would've no more said that I was Cat Brules than anything in the world. I looked more like some of them Mississippi gamblers, or maybe them rich Mexican ranchers that come up to trade from south of the border. I could hardly get them boots on, and when I did, with them high heels, I felt like I was tipping forward. They fit real snug but didn't pinch none, so I went ahead with it all just to please the old man.

When Valdez seen me for the first time in my new getup in the living room of the hacienda, he started laughing out loud real gleeful-like, then he danced 'round and clapped his hands and called for the señora. She come running outta the kitchen, and when she seen me she screamed with delight. She throwed her arms 'round me and give me a big kiss and told me in Spanish, which I'd begun to understand real good, that I looked like how old Valdez'd looked when he wore them same kinda clothes to come courting her. That made the old boy frost up a little bit and he spoke to her sternlike, but right away he seen the funny part of it and started laughing again hisself.

Then the old man took me out to the corral and showed me the horse that he'd picked for me. It was a big black stallion that reminded me of the one that Pedro'd rode, only this horse had a white forehead and two white fetlocks on his hind legs. Soon's we got out there, Valdez spoke to one of the vaqueros. That boy swung his rawhide lasso and it whistled out and settled 'round the stallion's head. A few of the other cowboys got on the line and dug in their heels and then all hell broke loose. The stallion went to plunging and milling 'round, kicking the hell outta things, and all the rest of them horses jammed over on the other side of the corral, staying away from the show.

While all that was going on, old Valdez, with a twinkle in his eyes, said, "That is your new horse, my son. I call him El Cimarron, the wild one."

It didn't take me long to see why. As I sat on the corral rail, I could see that stallion had lots of fight in his eyes and kept bellowing and bucking while them vaqueros dug in and hung onto the rope. I must say, it warmed my heart to see the way that horse was acting, 'cause he looked to me like the nearest thing to Piebald I'd seen since I'd parted company with that old horse. I still missed him after all those years, but I had a proud memory of him with his band of mares out roaming the mesas.

Them vaqueros finally got the stallion quieted down and he stood trembling where they held him at the edge of the corral. It took a little time 'fore they could get a blindfold on him. Valdez called to one of the young men and he went to a shed and come out with a mighty nice-looking Mexican saddle, some of it fancied up with pretty silver workings. He throwed it over the stallion's back and cinched him up quick. That saddle was even finer'n the one I'd had such a hankering for all them years back in Albuquerque.

I could see from the way the stallion stood when the saddle went on him that he'd been rode before. He weren't exactly a wild horse, but he was one that weren't given to being overly gentle when you first got on him. I figured, too, that maybe he hadn't been rode much.

They brought out a Spanish bridle that had a pretty wicked-looking bit, and got it onto him okay, although they had a helluva time parting his teeth. When they was finally ready, Valdez motioned with a generous smile and a proud glint in his eye for me to take over. I could see from his look that he didn't have no malice, like lots of cowmen do, watching somebody climbing onto a horse and hoping to see him get bucked off in a hurry. That weren't his attitude a'tall. He was presenting me with a fine horse that was a little green and plenty spirited, and he knowed I was rider enough to handle him.

I slipped down off the corral fence and walked over slow. Them vaqueros was holding the stallion, still keeping the blindfold on him. I put my hand on his neck and stroked him easy and felt how he was trembling all over. I got up next to him and let him get a good smell of me, although I reckoned that after that bath and putting on them fancy clothes I was disguising the real Cat Brules. But I figured that somehow, when I got back into my greasy buckskins out on the trail, he'd know me for sure and'd prob'ly like the smell of me. I rubbed my hands all over his back, down his rump, and 'round his legs, and slowly the trembling begun quieting down. Real easy, one of them cowboys turned the rest of the horses out into the pasture, and me and Cimarron was left there in the corral alone.

When I thought he'd calmed down enough, I slipped my foot into the stirrup and eased up slow and steady and took a good seat in the saddle. I nodded to one of the vaqueros sitting on the fence and he reached out and pulled off the blindfold and let him go. It must've been beautiful to watch. He took one look 'round and then reared up and really started to plunge. But he didn't have no mean buck, just lots of spring and twist to it and a nice rhythm with everything he done. 'Course he done lots of bellowing and flinging his heels up pretty high, but it was easy riding and I played with him. We went 'round the corral three or four times, then he started spinning 'round easier out there in the middle and finally he quieted down.

I motioned to the vaqueros to open the corral gate, and I eased him out real slow. When he got clear of the gate, he started to bolt, and I knowed I had a real horse under me. I couldn't hold him back at first, so I let him spread hisself out and showed him I could stay right with him. Even running flat out, it felt like he was sailing on the wind. It was a joy to have a fine horse like that under me again, and I remembered that no matter how good them Comanche ponies was, there weren't none of 'em that had old Cimarron's lines and breeding.

When he'd run 'bout three miles out, I turned him 'round and we come dusting back partway. Then I quieted him down and got him into a walking trot and we made friends. I kept talking to him and running my hand up and down his neck, stroking his mane, and patting his withers good, and I was real careful to go easy on the spurs.

By the time we come back to the ranch house, we was old buddies and I got off'n him without no trouble a'tall. I seen that him and me was gonna get along just fine.

Valdez had a few steers out in a pasture north of the ranch house and I rode out there to see if the horse knowed how to work stock. He was a natural for cutting, and when a steer'd light out, he'd put me right up where I could rope good. I didn't want to rope none of Valdez's stock, it being impolite to be handling another man's critters if'n there weren't no call for it, but it was easy to see that I could've done a good job of roping off'n that horse. I must've worked with him for an hour and a half while old Valdez set there on the corral railing, watching us with pride. He stayed there all the time, smoking his pipe and once in a while making a few jokes and laughing with the vaqueros.

I come back after a bit and walked Cimarron around to let him cool off from the lather he'd got into. When we come back into the corral he was acting gentle as a kitten.

"Señor," I said, "I shore wanta thank ya plenty fer this great horse. I got ta tell ya right now that I don't need no mule ta go along as a packhorse."

He started to protest and I told him that I was planning on traveling real light and really preferred to only take Cimarron. Besides, lots of the time I'd be doing some walking and one horse was all I wanted. He finally shrugged and smiled and said that he'd always s'picioned I was loco and this just confirmed what he'd always thought. Any man that was offered a present of stock animals and only took one of 'em had to be soft in the head, but if that was what I wanted, that was okay with him.

Old Valdez couldn't understand why I took my buckskin pants and shirt and them high Comanche moccasins, rolled 'em all up in my bedroll, and tied 'em on the back of my saddle. He thought I was through with them clothes forever, but I had plans for 'em sooner'n he figured.

I put the ammunition he'd give me in my saddlebags and tied the rest of my gear on top of the bedroll. The saddle come with a real first-class rifle scabbard, so I was all set to travel in comfort and style. As far as I was concerned, I was ready to go clear 'cross the continent. Seems funny now, being an old man and needing lots of extra things, how in them days I could get along with next to nothing.

I stayed for supper and then bade them folks farewell, hugging the señora and old Valdez like they was my own mama and daddy. The old man tried to persuade me to stay another night, but he knowed I was wanting to get on my way.

There was a little quarter-moon high in the night sky when I finally lit out, and I pushed off to the northwest, staying east of the gorge of the Rio Grande and working up towards the headwaters.

When daylight come, I'd rode far enough north to where the Rio Grande weren't in a canyon no more but was out on the flats of the San Luis Valley. I picked me a good bunch of cottonwoods, something I'd been doing for a long time, and set up camp. It didn't take me long to get outta them fancy hidalgo clothes and crawl back into my good old homey-smelling buckskins. I was real glad to notice that my face was gathering a little stubble and I reckoned that it wouldn't be too long 'fore I'd have me a good beard again. I rolled my blanket under some bushes that still had a nice cushion of leaves and slept me a good sleep.

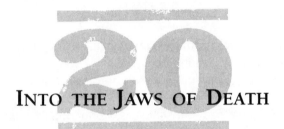

Into the Jaws of Death

$\mathbf{A}$s I rode along the foothills of the range that lay to the west side of the San Luis Valley, I come across a kind of an old Indian trail. I'd expected it. It was the one that led over Cochetopa Pass and down into the Gunnison River. I turned and followed it 'til sundown to the top of the pass, where I couldn't help looking back over that great broad valley to see them beautiful peaks of the Sangre de Cristos off to the east. Old Blanca Peak was sitting down there to the southeast like a fine sentinel all by itself, and south of that stood all that range that I'd crossed more'n seven years before when I was getting away from them Comanches. Seemed like lots of water'd gone over the dam since then. I'd come to know a helluva lot more since then and was much tougher.

Watching the sun go down, shining its last light on all them sawtooth peaks to the east, and seeing their snow-covered tops turn crimson against the purple sky gladdened my heart. I knowed right then and there that most of my life'd be spent out in the wild country. I wouldn't go taking up with no men and getting into lots of stinking messes like it seemed I done whenever I got into a town.

I made a good camp that night up on top of Cochetopa Pass and built me a fine, crackling fire. There weren't nothing in that country to see it but an odd Ute. I set there looking into the flames and musing, resting against a rock, with the wind singing through the pines and the smoke of the fire drifting by.

There wouldn't be no more Indian hunting—that part of my life was over forever. I set there staring at the fire and listening to the crackling and popping of the pine logs, wondering what was in store for me. I didn't know much about the far west country, mostly what I'd picked up in the cantinas from trappers who'd come way down from Jackson Hole.

The next morning it turned bright and beautiful and I pushed on off westward and down into the valley of the Gunnison. I seen deer and elk everywhere I looked. A couple of times that day, across the meadow towards the river, a movement caught my eye and I looked over and spotted a bear moving along just outta hibernation, looking for his spring feed.

I didn't hit the Gunnison River 'til nightfall. It was the early spring of '74 and the leaves on the quakies hadn't come out yet. I was glad to see there was plenty of green grass, although the nights was still sharp. I slowed down and took my time, enjoying the sights of all that vast and wild country. I made a couple of camps on the south rim of the Black Canyon of the Gunnison where I could look down into its black and shimmering depths and listen to the thundering of the river below. I followed the river on down to where the North Fork come in, and then 'bout forty miles below that I hit the junction with the mighty Colorado River.

I left the river at that point and hit out due west into the red canyon country. I could see the snowcapped La Sal Mountains in the distance. I didn't wanta stay too near the Colorado 'cause I was getting close to them Mormon settlements, and I didn't have no hankering to be 'round those folks just then.

So what I done was to work my way due west to where I crossed Dolores Creek at the east foot of the La Sal Mountains. They was beautiful, towering 'bout twelve thousand feet in the sky. I then climbed up a ways to where I could swing 'round their north face and see the Colorado 'bout a mile below, rushing real muddy due west and then southwest to a deep canyon country forty miles away. I knowed that from there on it was at least four hundred miles to the Grand Canyon, through a labyrinth of pinnacles and depths—most all of it unexplored.

I decided to stay up in the timber country of the La Sals and work my way 'round to the northwest corner of the mountains and then on over to the west side of 'em. I was in big blue spruce all the way.

Finally, after a couple of days of easy and slow travel, I come to a point where I looked down through the timber at the little Mormon town of Moab, hidden in a green valley 'tween red cliffs and the river four thousand feet below.

At that point the Colorado River, by then a brown shining ribbon, was flowing almost straight to the southwest into a red canyon wilderness, a maze of turns I could see extending for nearly a hundred fifty miles to the Henry Mountains. It was a mighty impressive sight. It made you wonder 'bout the meaning of things—of all this creation and how unimportant man really was—and yet it stirred a sense of yearning to see what was out there beyond all them canyons and mountains.

I decided that them Mormons was real smart folks. I'd heard tell that they was hard workers and'd carved theirselves something permanent outta the wilderness. The only thing different 'bout 'em was that each man had lots of wives, but I couldn't see nothing wrong in that. It seemed to me that a man having more'n one wife'd come under the heading of his business. Me—I didn't want to get tied down to even one woman, let alone four or five.

I didn't have no intention of going down to that town. So I worked my way 'round the slope of the mountain to the southeast side through the timber at the top edge of the quakies 'til I come to a place where a little stream was running past a perfect campsite. I stayed up there four or five days, turning things over in my mind 'bout them La Sal Mountains I was in. The old French trappers'd called 'em the Salt Mountains, "La Sals," and I reckon that was right. There was lots of salt in them hills judging by the amount of gray-white gravel pits around. Then, too, I'd say them mountains was a real game paradise. I reckon I'd never saw so much game in one patch as I done there on the south side of them La Sals.

There weren't no mining booms in that country like they'd had back in the early seventies in Ouray, Durango, and Telluride. There was just a few scattered ranches around and some cattle grazing on the hills. There was mule deer everywhere and I seen hundreds of elk and lots of black bear and something else besides—the tracks of a big grizzly.

'Bout four years before, I'd spotted two grizzlies a long ways off in the Sangre de Cristos, but I reckon there'd been enough hunting by the Spanish ranchers and the old freighters so's most of them grizzlies'd cleared out of that country and worked their way west. I'd heard that in the old days along the Arkansas there was grizzlies 'round there as thick as flies. But that was fifty years 'fore my time, when them boys like Zebulon Pike and the Bent brothers and Frémont'd come through that way.

While I was sitting there by that campfire way up on the side of the mountain away from Moab, I done a lot of thinking 'bout grizzlies. They seemed like exciting animals and I decided I'd stick around a while and try to find me a few of 'em. I didn't have no real idea in mind 'cept that I'd like to track one down and study what it acted like and maybe get me a grizzly hide to tan. I reckoned that after hunting Comanches, it'd be a cinch.

At daybreak the next day I threw my saddle and bedroll on old Cimarron and moved on 'round the side of the mountain to the southeast. I figured to scout 'round 'til I seen tracks—several of 'em. When I was hunting Comanches, I'd try to think like one, so when an Indian'd naturally go somewhere at a certain time, I'd be there ahead of him.

I got to thinking that way 'bout the grizzly. What would I do if I was one of them big bears waking up after sleeping in a hole for five winter months and being hungrier'n hell? I knowed right where I'd go. I'd hurry to the edge of them rockslides to look for varmints, and perhaps along the bottom of the cliffs I'd find where some of them bighorn sheep might've slipped on the winter ice.

I guessed that many a grizzly'd got his first spring feed on a bighorn that'd fell off an icy ledge during the winter. After a sleet storm, I bet them rocks that some of them bighorn'd been jumping 'round on would be slicker'n hell. Even as surefooted as them animals all was, some of 'em was bound to miss a jump and fall to their death.

Oftentimes later, I'd watch them grizzlies in the spring. They'd come down outta their holes up on the side of a mountain where they'd been hibernating and they'd work along them rockslides, turning over rocks and looking for ants and varmints, sniffing away trying to find out where the next meal was coming from.

When the animals that'd come to their death in the wintertime begun to thaw out in the spring, they'd get to decaying and stink like hell. Lots of deer died during the winter—them that was heavy with

fawn and running poorly—and it was the same way with cow elk.
The grizzly'd smell 'em from miles away and make right for 'em.

After he'd cleaned out most of what was lying 'round, having lots of
competition from other grizzlies, he'd move on down into the low
country and begin killing hisself some fresh game. Sometimes he'd
get the whistle pigs moving in and out of the rocks, and once in a
while he'd run into a prairie dog town and raise hell. Many times,
them grizzlies'd lie in wait and kill 'em an elk. A full-growed grizzly
can kill a big bull elk with one swat. In the spring, when the elk has
shed their horns and growed them velvet stubs that become the big
antlers of late fall, them bulls is unarmed and easy prey.

I spent the whole day working my way up through the blue spruce
towards timberline, always on the lookout for grizzly sign. I didn't see
nothing. I made me a cold camp that night. It was a tough picket for
old Cimarron, there not being much feed among them needles under
the blue spruce. But I told him that the next morning we'd be up in
the tender grass of them high meadows.

The next morning I pushed on up towards the edge of timberline.
Just 'fore breaking out of the blue spruce I come across one of them
torn-up logs, which is a sure sign that a grizzly's been 'round, twisting
and turning things, looking for ants. It was the damnedest thing—a
log 'bout three feet thick and maybe fifty feet long that some old
grizzly'd moved 'round and tore apart like it was a matchstick. I could
see where he'd been scraping for ants and I was heartened to be in
good grizzly country.

When we come up to the shoulder of one of them tundra ridges
along the timberline, I turned Cimarron loose to let him fill up on the
high mountain grass. He was real hungry and'd also took a real shine
to me, so I knowed he wouldn't go far.

I set there looking far away to the south at the lower part of the
Colorado River stretching towards a maze of red canyons. Due south
was a dark blue line of mountains and to the southeast there was still
snow on the top of old Lone Cone Peak. Farther to the southeast was
the San Juans and I could see 'em clear as anything. Due east was that
mountain they call the Grand Mesa, and to the southwest, in the haze
of the morning, I could see the peaking tips of the Henrys. Far away
south of them I could make out, but just barely, the round, smooth
haystack curve of Navajo Mountain.

Yeah, it was a grand view, and I was sitting up there enjoying what the world was all about. El Cimarron munched away not far from me, just swishing his tail and eating his fill. I leaned back in the grass and started to doze away when Cimarron suddenly stopped his munching and put his head up. I had my hat pulled over my eyes, but when he done that, me having been so long in Indian country, I woke up real quick. I looked at him outta the corner of my eye and seen he was holding his ears up and looking down the mountain to the east of us. Three hundred yards to our left and a little bit down the slope was an old mama grizzly and two small cubs.

The old sow'd already smelt Cimarron and was reared up on her hind legs, paws bent and balanced in front of her, sniffing the breeze. I reckoned she hadn't seen me yet, but even with her bad eyesight, she couldn't miss something the size of my horse. She sure looked huge, outlined against the sky. I reckoned she must've weighed eight hundred pounds, which is big for a sow.

I was always in the habit of pulling my rifle out of the scabbard whenever I got off'n my horse, knowing it was a good way to hang onto it in case the horse got spooked. It was beside me and I grabbed it up and made a quick dash to catch old Cimarron, but I was too late.

Cimarron let out a snort and went off 'round the mountain like he was carrying the mail. The old grizzly dropped down on all fours and took off the other way, batting her cubs along in front of her. She didn't look back any and I guess, as far as she was concerned, she weren't taking no chances. That's the way it is with a grizzly. If you come up on 'em real close when they're tending cubs, they'll take you, but if you're far enough away, they'll run for cover.

It was like seeing a great big steam engine go pumping down the mountain. I never seen such muscles, and the hump on her back stood up real plain. Even though I knowed I was gonna be all day catching up with Cimarron, I couldn't help standing there and admiring her as she made for timber. It must've been a quarter of a mile, but she covered it in nothing a'tall and disappeared in a hurry.

Then, cussing and swearing, I started back 'round the side of the mountain to the west, looking for Cimarron. Soon I come to where I could see him 'bout a mile away, still trotting up a hill. I whistled and hollered at him, but either he didn't hear me or he didn't pay no attention. So I spent the rest of that day following him. Just 'fore dusk I found him stalled up on a rockslide clear 'round to the west side of that mountain.

I eased up to him and got hold of the bridle and give him a good cussing for running off. He understood plenty but paid me no mind. I rode him on down to timberline and set up another camp near where some water was trickling out of the rocks at the bottom of a ravine. Knowing Cimarron'd been spooked plenty by the grizzly, I reckoned he'd be restless, and I took care to see that he was picketed good so's he couldn't run off. Then I lay back and done some thinking.

Why hadn't I pulled off a shot at that she grizzly? I could've hit her easy. I guess there was something 'bout the way she was herding them cubs along that kept me from hammering her.

Come to think of it, many's the time I watch mountain lions lying up on a ledge looking at something, and sometimes they'd let game go right by 'em and never make a pass, 'cause they weren't in the mood for no hunting. That's the way I was with that grizzly sow—real amused at watching her run down the hill with them cubs scampering ahead of her. I knowed that when I finally got onto the trail of a big boar, things'd be different.

I got to thinking 'bout all the trouble Cimarron'd been, and I reckoned it'd be same old story again. Whether I was hunting a Comanche or a grizzly, I could do it better on foot than I could on a horse. That horse wouldn't do nothing but give me away most of the time I was stalking, and he prob'ly wouldn't be around when I needed him for transportation.

In the morning I hit back up to timberline on old Cimarron and rode 'round the south side of the mountain. That whole day I didn't see nothing—not a single sign of grizzly. I felt kinda discouraged. The same thing happened again the next day. Then for almost a week I kept riding all through that country with the idea that if I found something, I'd picket Cimarron and do the stalking on foot.

That week it seemed like I was wasting my time. It weren't as if I hadn't seen no other game. I run across plenty of elk and deer, and one morning I seen some black bear. For a minute they'd kinda give me a start when I looked over across a slope and seen 'em maybe half a mile away. I thought they might be grizzlies, but after a good look I could tell they weren't nothing but little blackies. Some of 'em might've run to 'bout five or six hundred pounds, but they just ain't the same breed as a big grizzly.

I weren't gonna waste no ammunition busting black bears way up on the side of the mountain. They was too easy to come by down in the valleys where packing 'em out wouldn't be near as tough and where I could use the meat. Nope, by then I had my heart set on getting me a grizzly hide.

Then one day, along towards evening, I come up on the damnedest-looking place. It looked like a bunch of angry Goliaths'd been working along the edge of a rockslide. The ground beside it was tore up as if there'd been a war going on—logs, pieces of dirt, and rocks was throwed all over the place. A couple of big holes'd been dug like some big giant of a dog'd been looking for a bone.

I knowed it was grizzlies, but I was plumb amazed at how strong they was. I seen where one of 'em'd moved a big rock 'bout twenty feet from where he'd dug it outta the ground. I went up to it and couldn't quite get my arms 'round it. I tried with all my might to move it, but it wouldn't budge. There was bear tracks all over the place, and in a couple of soft places I seen footprints as big as my hat.

Them bears must've really been grubbing 'round for anything they could find to eat—ants, grasshoppers, whistle pigs, squirrels. The trail they'd made tearing and ripping up the grass and the rocks run all the way down along the rockslide to where it went into timberline beyond the blue spruce. We followed it down, and I seen where logs as big 'round as small wagon wheels'd been moved 'round like matchsticks.

You sure know it when you're in grizzly country. 'Sides all hell getting tore loose, you can really smell 'em. There was bear droppings all over the place, and them pies was as big as a buffalo's. You could sure tell they weren't laid by no black bears, 'cause there ain't nothing that stinks as much as grizzly shit less'n it's a man's. The whole place smelt like some big outhouse.

When we come close enough to get a good whiff, Cimarron started snorting and rearing, keeping his ears straight up. He arched his neck, his nostrils got all expanded, and his eyes flashed wild. I could tell he didn't like bear country worth a damn and I seen it was time to find a good safe place to set up camp and picket him out. I rode him back up along the edge of timberline and 'bout a mile 'round towards the south side of the mountain, where I'd seen a little rivulet running down outta the high snows way up at the peak.

I pulled off the saddle and bedroll and shoved 'em under a big old spruce tree that was leaning way over. That was a good place to hide the saddle away and keep it outta them afternoon thunderstorms. I didn't see no sign of porcupines around and figured that the saddle'd be safe from getting chewed up too bad. I jerked the blanket loose and made a cold camp, 'cause I didn't want to make the bears curious with a fire.

I was mighty tired and slept good that night, waking up just 'fore dawn. I got out a handful of pemmican and soaked it in the stream and chewed on it a while for breakfast. I weren't as careful 'bout keeping track of my ammunition as I'd been when I was hunting Comanches, but I guess my Winchester had 'bout sixteen shots in the magazine. I figured that was more'n enough to bag me a grizzly. I thought 'bout taking the .38 and putting it in the belt 'round my waist, but finally I figured I might have to do some belly crawling, so I put the .38 under the saddle. Old Cimarron seemed happy enough feeding away at the end of the picket line, so I took my Winchester and started on 'round the mountain.

I made fast time and 'fore the sun was up I was at the rockslide where them grizzlies'd been working. I followed the slide down to the timber and tracked 'em to see which direction they was heading. I couldn't see how many there was, but I knowed there was several. When I got down in the darkness of them blue spruce, I begun to move plenty cautious.

I'd never really come close to grizzlies before, but I'd heard 'bout their reputation from lots of old-timers. They sure had an unsavory one. Fact is, I don't know nothing that could put the fear of God in them mountain men more'n a grizzly done. I'd had several of 'em tell me that they'd rather stand off a handful of Blackfeet warriors than one grizzly. Well, I'd had my share of Comanches, and it was hard to believe that a grizzly could be much tougher'n three or four of them bastards coming at you full tilt.

I followed the tracks as they angled back up towards timberline. When I broke out into the clear, the sun was maybe half an hour above the horizon. That upland grass was shining, with the morning dew sparkling on every blade.

I kept working up, with the air getting cooler and fresher all the time. I didn't wanta spook them grizzlies like I'd done that old sow, so I was moving more and more cautious. When I come to a ridge, I peeked over easy and could see the sign that them grizzlies'd left going through the dew grass.

I sneaked up to the top of the next rise, but there weren't nothing but a small ravine in front of me, and I could hear the soft trickling sound of melted snow water running over the little rocks in its path. I jogged down the slope and climbed up the other side, stopping just below the ridge to lift my head up for a slow, easy look. The sun was shining bright by then, throwing sharp shadows off all the ridges and ravines and highlighting the stands of timber below. I was looking over into a small glacial valley 'bout four hundred yards wide at a scene plumb likely to gladden the heart of any hunter.

It seemed like the whole side of the mountain was crawling with grizzlies! I counted nine of 'em in what I reckoned was less'n half a square mile, and there weren't no she bears or cubs in the lot—they was all boars. Down off to my right was four more of 'em maybe a quarter of a mile away. Most of 'em weren't too big. I reckoned they was prob'ly three-year-olds, run off by their mothers the fall before. At first I thought they was big blackies, their hides shining in the morning sun, but there was no mistaking that hump on their backs.

Then I looked back up the side of the mountain and seen two good-sized boars, 'bout even with me and a quarter of a mile away. They was turning over rocks right and left, looking for their early-morning meal.

Farther on up the mountain, maybe half a mile away and on the other side of another little valley, I seen some of the biggest animals I ever seen in my life: three great big bears that I reckon must've weighed near a thousand pounds apiece. One, even bigger'n the other two, was working high up on the hill above the others. I guess it was kind of befitting his position.

I've hunted lots of grizzlies since that time, but I never did see none bigger'n him. The sight took my breath away, and for a few minutes I lay there watching as he lumbered along on the side of the mountain, taking slow, steady steps. He was tossing his head from side to side in a slow rhythm, pausing now and then to put that keen nose of his to the breeze. He moseyed on 'round the mountain like a lazy giant, stopping here and there, using one paw to move boulders that would've took five men to lift.

Prettiest of all, he was a true silvertip. The light from the morning sun made the tips of his hair shine real beautiful. I lay there for a long time, taking things all in, watching them boars move along real slow, rolling their heads and sniffing the breeze. I kept noticing the way the wind was blowing and how often it'd change. Every now and then a little breeze'd pass 'cross the high mountain grasses and move the heads of them wildflowers that danced to a gentle morning song. A patch of clouds'd cast a shadow for a few minutes and move on to the east, leaving behind the shining hillside and the steady movement of the feeding grizzlies.

I kept thinking 'bout how I was gonna get at that big one. Oh, sure, I would like to've had a hide off'n any of them other big boars all right, but that old one sitting way up there on top of the mountain like he was the king—he was the one for me. I'd have to figure the wind just right so's I could sneak past all them others to get to where I could do something 'bout old Silvertip. From what I knowed of the grizzly's vitality, his awful strength, and his will to live, I figured I'd better shoot from good and close.

I must've stayed there near an hour watching things. I could've gone right up the ridge I was on, staying outta sight, but the wind was blowing from the southwest and I knowed that as soon as I got up higher on the mountain, them two that was feeding 'cross from me'd catch a whiff of me and take off, spooking the big one.

As it turned out, I should've chanced it and come up on Silvertip from above. That's the only way to hunt grizzly on a steep slope—it's crazy as hell to come up on one from below. If you don't kill him with the first shot, he'll come downhill and be on top of you 'bout four times as fast as if he had to go uphill to get to you. But I'd been more concerned with the wind and with not spooking 'em. That was a big mistake.

I finally decided I was gonna have to work my way downhill, keeping outta sight in the ravine, and go way out 'round that hillside full of bears and climb up the other side. It looked to me like a good two-hour trek, even as fast as I figured to make it, but I couldn't see no other way for it, the way the wind was blowing. I stayed up there a little while longer, trying to judge how fast that old griz was moving and in what general direction, 'cause I was gonna be outta sight of him for the best part of an hour.

He weren't making no time in particular, just stepping from one rock to another and turning 'em over and sniffing 'fore he'd move on to the next one. Sometimes he'd scratch 'round a little bit and dig, come up again and look 'round and sniff, then he'd move on real slow and careful. I reckoned by the way he was moving that he wouldn't cover more'n two hundred yards in an hour.

I eased on down the ravine, making real good time. I reckon I weren't more'n twenty minutes getting to timber, and I made it without spooking any of them bears. I dropped down maybe three hundred yards into the spruce 'fore I started on 'round on the off chance that there might be some more of that bunch feeding at timberline. I was moving as fast as I could, but the going was a little tough. The trees'd growed real thick and there was lots of deadfalls and ravines.

I reckon it was better'n a hour later by the time I'd worked 'round and up to timberline again. I eased up over a ledge and couldn't see nothing. It worried me that maybe them bears'd spotted something and moved off, but after a few minutes I seen them three or four small ones that'd been in the rocks above the timber. I knowed they hadn't been spooked 'cause they hadn't moved much, and I was in good shape downwind from 'em.

From where I was I couldn't see the middle bunch, or them three big boars way up the mountain. I had another thousand-foot climb to get up to where I figured they'd be. I worked 'round a little farther 'til I was outta sight and then started up the steep grassy slope above timberline, plugging my way up there and keeping my eyes peeled for one of them big humps on the skyline, but I didn't see nothing.

Every now and then I'd come to a wall of rocks that run for fifty to a hundred yards or so 'round the mountain, and I'd have to work on 'round it 'til I could climb any higher. It was a good two hours 'fore I was high enough to work back 'round the mountain on about a level with them three boars.

I went at it real cautious, crouching low and moving slow and steady, raising my head to peer 'round the curve of the mountain as I made my way. The three or four little ones was almost eight hundred feet below me, still working away among the rocks by timberline. My heart was pounding like a war drum.

A few minutes later, two hundred yards ahead and a little below, I seen a medium-sized grizzly. I figured I must be getting up close to where them big boars was, but a sharp shoulder of the hill kept me from seeing 'em. I figured that maybe I might not be quite high enough, so I turned and started straight up the ridge. I climbed fast for maybe a hundred feet and was puffing hard when I seen a slight movement against the sky 'bout fifty yards above and a little to the left.

Like I said, my heart was pounding, but it got to going double when I seen the hump of a grizzly just over the skyline, moving so's the top of his fur seemed to be skimming along 'cross the blades of grass. I hesitated a second. I didn't quite know what to do—climb up and get to him 'fore he went the other way, or just stand there and see what was gonna happen.

It turned out I didn't have long to wait. I crouched down low and in a couple of seconds I seen the grandest sight in all the world. Right out against the horizon come old Silvertip hisself. I'd never seen nothing like him in all my life. The muscles in his rippling shoulders and his long white teeth would've made any Texas longhorn bull alongside him look as dainty as a dancing girl.

It'd been a long time since I'd been real scared—way back on the Cimarron River in 1867 when I was out there with Michelle and I'd knowed that them Comanches was working up on us in the moonlight. Even now, thinking 'bout the sight of that old grizzly still sends chills clear through my heart. The old mountain men used to say that them bears looked as big as a horse and could run like one—only a horse don't have five razor blades on each hoof. Well, I reckon this one had twice the strength of a horse and a disposition that was real vicious. Standing there fifty feet below him, I was scared. I reckon that's what caused me to make my mistake.

At first he didn't see me, him not looking 'round or nothing—just sniffing along the ground. Then he got a whiff of something and turned and stopped short in his tracks. He was as s'prised as I was, and couldn't seem to make up his mind right at that second what to do. He raised up on his hind legs to get a better look at me and, my God, he looked ten feet tall!

It's now or never, I thought. Placing lots of confidence in my ability, I throwed up that Winchester. It come back in a hammer cock as it settled into my shoulder. I was sweating, but I took cool aim at his throat. I'd heard that if you could get a front shot at a bear and shoot him in the neck just under the jaw, that was the best place to kill him dead.

I don't rightly know what happened, but I reckon that bear moved slightly to one side just at the second I pulled the trigger. I seen the shock when the bullet hit him and he humped and twisted a little with the blow. Then I knowed instinctively that it weren't fatal, 'cause he just shook and arched. I seen that I'd missed the jugular and the neck bone by a fraction, shooting him in the shoulder muscle where it meets the neck.

There was "dead gun" Cat Brules slightly missing by less'n an inch the most critical shot of his whole danged life, and all 'cause he'd turned yeller and got scared. It takes cold nerve to be a dead gun and I knowed it. Hell, I would've been long dead in Comanche country if I'd ever lost my nerve like that. But there I was—I'd done it, and I had to face the consequences.

A lousy shot is a helluva thing when you've got a thousand-pound grizzly fifty feet away from you up a hill. The next thing that happened come so quick I can't hardly tell you in words how it worked. Such a roar come outta that animal that it seemed like it shook the whole mountain. And the way he looked. . . . I've seen some grizzly heads that was stuffed and put on a wall and had them glass eyes that they put in, but there ain't no glass eye in the world that gets the wild look that's in a wounded grizzly's eye.

There was streams of spit running off'n his teeth—teeth that was better'n three inches long—and he come at me with jaws wide open. I got off another shot that took him in the chest just 'fore he got to me. When that second shot went into him, he couldn't have been more'n fifteen feet away. Christ, this is the end! I thought. I'm gonna dive ta my right side an' try ta get outta his line, but I don't think I'm gonna make it.

I was quick as a cat on my feet and could move fast when it come time for moving, but I weren't quick enough to get past that grizzly. All I remember was seeing the whole mass of him diving for me while I leaned hard off to the right with my rifle balanced in my right hand.

I felt a sledgehammer blow followed by a terrible pain. The rifle went clattering outta my hand and slid down the rocks and moss on the mountainside. Silvertip went crashing down behind it. The force of his blow'd throwed me over backwards, partway down the hill and off to the right. Looking down, I seen that the grizzly's left shoulder was hurt bad and he'd lost the use of that leg. He couldn't check hisself and'd gone reeling on down the slope.

He kept tumbling down to maybe forty to fifty feet below me 'fore he got his balance, gnashing his teeth and roaring all the time. Then he got hisself stopped in a spread eagle, growling and snarling to beat hell, and swung back up the hill after me. I was half-stunned by the blow he'd give me—the top of my left arm was hurting something fierce and the lower part was numb.

It was plain to see that I was in terrible trouble. My gun was way down there by the grizzly, and I weren't so sure it was working anymore even if I could get at it. I grabbed hold of the grass on the steep slope with my good right hand and pulled myself to my feet, then I started to claw up the slope as fast as I could go, glancing over my left shoulder to see what was happening.

It was like I'd figured. There was the grizzly coming back up the slope, but I could see that he was hurt bad and having trouble with his left shoulder. It was dragging and he almost hit the ground every time he made a lunge with it. His chest and belly was all covered with blood. Every movement he made was plunging forward, and although he was tearing up the ground, his forward motion weren't as good as it should've been. It sure weren't nothing like it would've been if he weren't shot up real bad.

My idea was to scramble on up the hill and move as fast as I could, giving due care not to run into them other two boars. I didn't know how they'd act, but I figured that the sound of the shot and their curiosity might get the best of 'em and they'd come over for a good look.

There prob'ly ain't no more terrible animal in all the world than a man with a rifle in his hands. And there ain't nothing more helpless than a man without one. It's the difference 'tween having brains and weapons, and having only your teeth and fingernails, and maybe a skinning knife. They ain't much of a match for a grizzly. Them kind of thoughts was going through my mind as I pushed up that hill, and I can't describe my feelings in no other words 'cept pure terror.

I reckon I moved as fast as I've ever moved in my life, and a good thing it was, too, 'cause I was just able to stay ahead of that grizzly. It sounded like he could reach out easy and bite a chunk outta me, but he was really 'bout thirty or forty feet away.

I didn't waste no time trying to decide whether I should look back at him or keep churning. I kept my eyes on the hill in front of me and kept pushing ahead, having to use my good arm every now and then to keep from slipping. All the time I heard that roaring and snarling behind me and wondered when them awful fangs was gonna chew into my legs, and when one good forepaw was gonna deliver a swat that'd break my back.

I must've traveled three or four hundred feet up the mountain, puffing and blowing enough to make my lungs burst, when I heard the roaring slack off. I seen it was my one real hope for life and redoubled my efforts. I kept on going for another couple of hundred feet 'til I knowed I had enough room to look back.

That old bear'd slowed down and was floundering and pitching forward on his chest, rising up only to pitch and fall again, roaring and groaning all the time. I rested for a second, my chest heaving and blowing, then kept churning uphill to put as much distance 'tween me and that animal as I could.

It was a good thing I done that, I reckon, 'cause 'bout the time I got to the shoulder of the ridge that I was climbing on, them other two great big boars come 'round the face of the mountain. They was moving along at a slow amble with their heads up, listening to the old boy's roaring. They was down below me a couple of hundred feet, 'bout even with where the big grizzly was floundering and still tearing up the grass all 'round. They was so busy looking at him that, being crosswind from me, they never spotted me. They ambled slowly over to see what was wrong with the king of the grizzlies they'd been hunting with a little while before.

I didn't wait to see what'd happen. I popped outta sight over the skyline of the ridge and started off at a good jog 'round the mountain. My aim was to put as much distance 'tween me and them grizzlies as I could. There weren't no use going back and looking for my rifle, not with one wounded bear nearby and them other two big ones hanging 'round.

At that minute, my feelings 'bout hunting grizzlies took a real turnabout. I kept looking back as I jogged along, to see if anything was following me. Half-afraid there might be, I couldn't help but take stock of things. I'd started out all bright-eyed and bushy-tailed, planning to raise hell with them grizzlies and get me a real nice hide. Instead I'd got the hell knocked outta me by the first one I'd come across.

My arm was broke or something. Just how bad I didn't know, but it was hanging limp and blood was dripping down off'n my fingers. The upper part was hurting like bloody hell and the lower part had no feeling. Worse'n that, though, was having my gun knocked outta my hand. I knowed damned well from the blow that it took and the way it'd bounced down the side of the mountain that it was likely all busted to pieces.

That was the worst thing that could happen to me—to lose my Winchester. I knowed I'd have a hard time getting a new one out in Mormon country. I might have to journey back to Fort Garland, and that was one helluva ways to go.

Right then, though, my job was to put as much distance 'tween me and them terrible animals as I could. I didn't ever figure I was short on guts, but I'd never been through anything like the charging of that grizzly. I sometimes have nightmares 'bout it to this day.

Anyway, I figured to keep moving on down to where Cimarron was picketed and get my Smith & Wesson as quick as I could. As I was trying to jog along and fight down the pain in my arm, which was getting worse and worse, I got to wondering how I could've been so sloppy as to miss killing him with that first shot. I thought back and I knowed I hadn't missed, he'd moved some was all. I'd done him lots of damage, but I hadn't finished him. That was unforgivable. Then, too, grizzlies is just extra hard to kill. Even though the second shot I put into him went dead into his chest and blowed his lungs all to hell and prob'ly even got near his heart, he kept on coming. He sure was one tough animal.

I slowed down to a walk 'cause I got winded pretty easy at that altitude. I knowed I needed to attend to my arm, but I didn't feel I could stop even when I crossed a couple of little streams where I could've washed things off and got me a little drink. I made up my mind that I was gonna get back to where I'd left that Smith & Wesson .38, and once I got it stuck in my belt, I weren't never gonna let go of it again.

It took me 'bout two hours to get far enough 'round the mountain to where I could look down and see old Cimarron munching away a thousand feet below at timberline. It hadn't been all easy going. I'd had to cross two or three rockslides and my arm was paining me something fierce. I kept looking back, fearing that them grizzlies was still following me, kinda tracking me down to finish me off.

That was a helluva thought. I couldn't believe no bear could ever do that, but my imaginings was wild right then. Maybe I was half-delirious. I don't know, but I kept on looking back and I sure felt scared, prob'ly with good reason, 'cause since then I've heard tell of bear that've done just that—tracked a hunter down for miles and killed him.

It didn't take me long to hop and slide and skid and twist down over the grass and slick rocks on the mountainside to where old Cimarron was picketed. He looked up when he seen me coming and cocked his ears and snorted, looking at me as if I was the devil hisself. I guess I weren't a pretty sight and, as I come a little closer, he got a whiff of the blood and maybe some bear smell on me. He stamped and twisted and went out on his picket rope as far as he could.

I went right on by him, paying no attention to him a'tall, and dropped down to where my stuff was stacked under the tree. I reached in and took hold of the Smith & Wesson and held it up, flicking loose the chamber and spinning it and flopping it back in again, checking to see if it was loaded. It was full 'cept for the one chamber that I always carried empty when I had the hammer down. I debated whether I oughta put in another round, did so, and then stood there and got to laughing at myself. It seemed like when I touched the Smith & Wesson life and confidence come back into me. That's the way of a true gunman, he's not happy without a gun. He knows that's his big advantage, whether it's over man or beast. When he's without a gun, he ain't much, but give him one and he feels good.

I went on down to the little glacier stream that run past where I'd picketed Cimarron. I knelt down beside it and wet the sleeve on my bum arm and begun pouring water over the wound. There was a big tear in my shirt, along the outside of my arm from the shoulder clear down past the elbow. I was still bleeding a mite and felt a little weak from the loss of blood. I couldn't quite tell if something was broke, not knowing none 'bout them things, but there was a lump at a bad angle just below the elbow. It still hurt like hell and my fingers was plumb numb.

I went on into the timber and cut me three sticks off'n a spruce tree. I smoothed 'em off good and went back to my bedroll to get some of them rawhide thongs that I always carried with me. I fixed up a crude splint and it seemed to give me some support and eased the pain a little, 'specially when I moved around. Then I tried to think what to do. I weren't too keen on the idea of going down to find a doctor. The nearest town was Moab, twenty-five miles away, and I weren't sure there'd even be a doctor there anyhow. What's more, I really didn't wanta go no place where there was very many folks around.

I decided the most important thing was to keep the arm from moving and let things take their course. I knowed 'bout lots of mountain men that'd got bad mauled or hurt a long ways from any help, and they either got well or died, as nature willed. I figured that's the way it'd prob'ly be for me. I sat there for a while in the sunshine and a new thought come to me, real strong and clear. I'd come to hunt grizzly, I'd got in on a hunt that'd turned sour at the beginning, but that didn't mean Cat Brules was gonna quit. I'd learned that you never took a grizzly from downhill—always above him. I decided to change my shooting tactics, too. The next time I'd hit him right 'tween the eyes. To hell with going for the throat.

Then I thought 'bout old wounded Silvertip. He was at least bad hurt if'n he weren't dead, so I figured I'd go out there to check on him and pick up my rifle. It might be worth fixing. How in the hell was I gonna know how bad busted it was 'til I seen it? The idea of going back up there among them bears was spooky at first, but the more I thought about it, the more I knowed that was what I was gonna do. The Smith & Wesson weren't much of a gun for grizzly hunting, but it was still a gun, and it'd still kill anything if you hit it in the right place.

I felt weak and shaky and didn't have no hankering to walk that far, so I got hold of Cimarron and tied him up to a spruce tree. Somehow I got him saddled up with my one good hand. I had a helluva time getting the bedroll up and tied on tight, but I finally got it done. Then I swung up on that horse real easy and headed him along the side of the mountain towards the rockslide where I'd first spotted them grizzlies.

My left arm was hanging there in its splint and pounding like hell. My fingers was still numb, and every now and then my head'd swim a little and I had to grab the saddle horn to keep from slipping off. When we come to the rockslide and dipped down back into the timber, the only thing that kept me from passing out was when Cimarron'd start snorting and spooking from smelling the bears.

We worked 'round the bottom of the rockslide through the timber and then come up the other side and busted outta timberline into the mountain grass that run clear up to the snowbanks. I kept the stallion working up and over the ridges that I'd crossed on foot. It was real steep and the mountain grass was slippery in places, but he kept climbing in a zigzag.

I worked Cimarron 'round the mountain real cautious. I kept expecting to come up and see some of them old grizzlies, not knowing whether they'd charge us or not. I was half-scared that Cimarron'd spot 'em first and rear up, and me, in my condition, would get throwed off. I didn't reckon I could take too much of that. Anyway I moved Cimarron real easy and gentle 'round each ridge and kept watching from up in the saddle to see what was ahead 'fore he could get a look. By that time, the wind was blowing pretty stiff from behind us, and I worried that it'd change and old Cimarron'd get a good whiff of grizzly and that'd be the end of the show.

There ain't hardly no way to explain how a man feels coming up on a wounded grizzly, 'specially one that's already mauled him good. Sometimes it takes all the guts he's got to keep going, 'specially if'n he's alone and weak with loss of blood and armed only with a handgun. Sneaking up on Comanches is a cinch compared to coming up on a wounded grizzly.

Several times I thought 'bout getting off and walking, but I felt too unsteady for that. I had to hang tight and ride it out. The distance seemed endless. More'n two or three times I thought we'd gone past the place where Silvertip and me'd had our problems, but I didn't see nothing. I couldn't believe that grizzly weren't hit hard enough so's that once he lay down, he'd stay down.

I kept looking 'round to make sure I weren't too high or low, and that no other bears'd come wandering over the hill to give me a bad surprise. I'd begun thinking that maybe I'd better give up. Then, as we topped a steep little draw coming up 'round the curve of the mountain, I drawed old Cimarron up short.

Lying fifty yards away was the biggest pile of silver-gray fur you ever seen, hunched up in a mound. It looked like a giant porcupine, sleeping there in the afternoon sun. I damn near stopped breathing when I took a closer look—the wind was blowing the fur, making it look like the carcass was breathing. Old Cimarron hadn't seen it yet, and I weren't aiming to be on him when he did. Thanks to the wind being behind us, he hadn't got a whiff of that old bear yet, either.

I pulled out my Smith & Wesson and balanced it in my good hand, twisting the reins 'round the numb fingers on my left. Then I sat there in the saddle, watching a long time to see if the old boy was really breathing. I sure weren't hankering to make no mistake, and in my imaginings it seemed like he was lying there waiting for me. But all I could see after a while was how the waves of wind run through the mountain grass, then through the fur, and passed over the ground beyond to sail off into the blue sky.

No, there weren't no movement from that old grizzly. There lay the king and I was sure he was dead. Finally, real easy, I slid off Cimarron on the uphill side. The excitement in me was building up and I didn't feel so faint. With the gun in my right hand, and the reins still wrapped 'round the fingers of my bad left, I started to move up slow and steady.

When Cimarron had a right fair view of what I was heading for, he gave a snort and a jerk, and a terrible pain shot up my arm and all through my body. I quick grabbed the reins with my pistol hand and hung tight while he reared and plunged, with me cussing and yelling at him and trying to hold with each jerk. Even though I was trailing my left arm, it felt like a red-hot iron was working on me all the time.

I finally got that son of a bitch under control 'bout fifty yards on down the slope. He still couldn't smell the bear, but what he'd seen he didn't like none. I weren't gonna get any nearer without lots of trouble, so I clawed back up on him, rode 'bout four hundred yards over to the timber, and staked him out on a picket line. I waited 'til I got some of my strength back and started walking back up towards the carcass. Even knowing that grizzly was dead, the way the wind was blowing his fur made me look twice to make sure he weren't breathing.

The closer I got, the more I marveled at the size of that monster. I didn't want to waste no ammunition, but at the slightest movement I was gonna put a bullet through the back side of his head, right where the skull joined the neck. I worked up within a few inches, debating whether I should give him another shot. I stayed froze nigh unto a minute and then, slow and steady, I eased on 'round to where I could get a look at his face head-on.

Them terrible eyes had the dull glaze of death. Just to make sure, I touched an eyeball with the barrel of the .38. It didn't move. Then I sat down and looked at him real close, amazed at the size and strength of the thing in front of me. I'd seen a few bear in my lifetime, big ones and little ones but I hadn't seen none that compared to that grizzly.

His head was as wide across as my shoulders. His teeth was two and a half to three inches long. I touched them terrible claws and it felt like they was as sharp as razors. His paws was as big as my hat. It was all I could do to pick up one front leg, and I reckoned that his elbow was as thick 'round as my waist. I tried to pry him up to where I could roll him over, but I didn't quite have the strength to do that. He must've weighed more'n a thousand pounds.

I could see where my second rifle shot'd bored through his chest. It'd made a helluva mess. The first bullet'd come out the left shoulder and tore all the bone and muscle. I was real grateful 'bout the way that front leg was knocked outta commission, 'cause I wouldn't be here telling this story otherwise. Looking at him lying there so magnificent even in death, I had a sense of respect and awe that he could've took that pounding from two bullets and still shagged me up a real steep mountain slope for more'n a hundred yards.

While I was sitting there looking, I come to my senses and realized I'd been so took up with that bear that I'd clean forgot 'bout retrieving my rifle. That's saying a lot when old Cat Brules is so impressed with something that he forgets to recover his gun. I begun casting my eyes around and seen the rifle lying quite a ways down below. I got up and walked down there, fearful of what I'd find.

When I first got close, I near jumped for joy. That rifle didn't look like it'd been hurt none a'tall. But then, when I picked it up, I seen it was scratched along the barrel and there was a big crack running down the narrow part of the stock from the trigger guard to the cheek plate. Something had to be done 'fore that rifle was fired again, but I thought I knowed what I could do, so I lugged it back up by the bear.

Then I took a few minutes to look 'round careful to make sure there weren't no other bears around and there weren't something coming over the hill to see what was going on. As a matter of fact, I guess the shooting and the excitement'd caused 'em all to run off. Anyway, everything looked real calm and peaceful.

After that I set to work. I took a look at the bear hide. Although it weren't in prime condition like it would've been in the fall, it still looked good enough for me. 'Sides, it was something I wanted more'n ever after the fight that bear'd showed, so I whipped out my skinning knife and went at the job. I started with the left paw, the one that was on the busted shoulder side. Then I went to work on the pads and fingers 'til I got the hide peeled off'n the paw. Funny thing 'bout a bear, 'specially a grizzly—when you pull the claws and hide off'n the paw frame, what's left looks like a human hand, kind of naked, with the fingers and thumb pointing at you and asking you why you shot 'em.

I kept at it but it was tough work, 'specially with my bum arm giving me pain all the time, sometimes to the point where I near fainted. I labored all through the afternoon, pausing now and then to sharpen my knife on the whetstone I always carried. I'd spit on the stone and grind the blade a while and then go back to skinning. It was slow work that you had to do real steady. I weren't 'bout to ruin that hide.

I had a tough time rolling the carcass around. It was all I could do to get some leverage on one of his legs and turn him belly side up. I moved real careful, peeling the hide away from the nose and back over the head, then working the whole thing back and up the sides, fleshing as I went. By sundown I had him all skinned, although it was one helluva job to roll his big greasy carcass off'n the hide so's I could peel it off'n the middle of his back. I finally done that by using both feet and bracing my back against a rock. Just 'fore the sun went down I was able to stretch out the hide over the grass and flesh off most of the meat that was still on it.

Then I rolled up the hide real careful, tied it up with a strip of rawhide, swung it over my back, and balanced it while I picked up my Winchester with my good hand. That hide, not properly fleshed and still wet, seemed to weigh the better part of a hundred pounds even without the skull, and I was staggering under it. There was a cold wind blowing, and my left arm was anchored down still useless and giving me lots of pain as I started making my way 'round the mountain where old Cimarron was picketed.

The moon'd begun to rise in the east behind me and every now and then a gust of cold evening breeze'd come whistling past, hissing in the grass. I reckon that coming up on Cimarron with the moon behind me, carrying a big load of stinking bear hide, was enough to scare the daylights outta anything, let alone a spooky horse. I was a hundred yards away when I heard him snorting and pulling the picket line. I figured I'd better drop the hide right where it was if'n I was ever gonna reach him 'fore he throwed hisself someway and got all snarled up in his rope.

I worked up to him, talking gentle all the time. He stood there in the moonlight, spread-legged and wild-eyed, looking at me with his ears up. He sure didn't like that bear stink that was clinging to me and maybe coming in on the breeze from where I'd dropped the hide. It took me a good while to ease up to him. I put my hand on his trembling neck and talked to him real soft 'til he seemed to feel better.

I loosened the picket rope with my good arm and slowly led him back to where the hide was. I got to within twenty or thirty yards from it 'fore it must've smelled so bad to him that he wouldn't do nothing but just balk and twist, pulling away and rearing up. I give him a helluva cussing and jerked and pulled, but it didn't seem to do no good.

That was one rough night. I must've been three hours trying to get that horse calmed down to where I could tie the bear hide onto the saddle good enough to get back down to timberline. Finally we was loaded up and I eased him on down off'n the hill. I unloaded old Cimarron in a likely place, jerking the hide and the saddle off in one quick motion, and picketed him out again some ways off.

Then I made me a good fire—that's tricky with only one hand—and it warmed me up a little. We was camped right by a high-running trickle coming down off'n the snow, so I was able to mix a little pemmican and water to fill up on. I'd had a long day and I don't mind saying I was plumb wore out. I rolled up in my blanket under a spruce tree and went to sleep, despite that pain in my arm.

I didn't wake up 'til near noon the next day. It was one of them warm, beautiful summer days in the high country, so I decided to stay right where I was and finish scraping the hide. I staked it out in the sun and went to work on it. In 'bout two hours I had it in fair shape.

Like I said, there's lots of places in the La Sals where little springs and riverlets come from the base of rocks with some kinda salt in 'em to form natural salt licks. I'd seen two or three of them places nearby where deer and elk had been licking on the rocks, so I knowed there must be enough salt there to serve my purpose. I went back to one and gathered a bunch of that salt-lick gravel up in my shirt. It weren't sharp salt, mind you, but if'n you put that gravel in your mouth you could taste a little salt and that's all it'd take to keep the hide from spoiling and slipping. It took all that day 'fore I got the job done to my satisfaction, and when the sun went down I was ready for sleeping. I didn't have no trouble going to sleep again, although my arm was still hurting me real bad. By that time it'd steadied down to a dull ache and I was tired enough not to care.

The next day I decided to do some work on my Winchester. I dug out my scraps of rawhide and set to fashioning a snug brace, which I wrapped 'round the small part of the stock where the crack was. Then I took the whole thing over to the spring and soaked the rawhide good, working it up as tight as I could. When I set it out to dry, it begun to draw up real well. It dried out completely by the following day and I reckoned I had a girdle of rawhide 'round that rifle stock that was tight enough and strong enough to keep the crack from getting outta hand. A rifle with a cracked stock can be a dangerous thing to fire, but that soaked and tightened rawhide made a helluva reinforcement. I'd often heard tell of the old mountain men doing the same thing with their Hawkins muzzle-loaders.

The weather was still good, and I got to thinking 'bout what I was gonna do next. The thing that appealed to me most was doing a little more grizzly hunting. Maybe I wanted to prove to myself that I weren't no coward. I don't really know. Maybe I figured if I could get the big, old granddaddy of 'em all, I could prob'ly pick off a few more. Maybe them hides wouldn't be total prime, but when I come down off'n that mountain I aimed to have enough grizzly hides to take into Moab and maybe get enough money for 'em to make it worthwhile.

I hung my prize hide up in a tree where I figured nothing could get at it. Then, taking the rest of my stuff, since I didn't know how long we'd be gone, I piled on old Cimarron and started working 'round the mountain again, looking for grizzlies. In them days, if you got into good bear country, you was apt to see at least two or three a day. True, you could go long stretches at a time, like I done at first, without seeing any. But if'n you got 'round to where they was, you'd find 'em thick enough to keep you busy.

I didn't do no good that day, but the next morning I run up on an old sow working a small rockslide. She was so busy turning up rocks looking for grub that she didn't see me coming up on the downwind side. This time I took it real easy and calm. I didn't get above her, but stayed on the same level, and after I drawed a bead with that Winchester, I shot her right through the back of the ears. She dropped in her tracks and never moved, and I went right to work skinning. After that, I done some more real good hunting.

I don't remember how many days I went on like that, but my

shooting eye was as good as ever. Pretty soon I had six more hides hanging in the trees by that campsite. I'd killed one more sow and four more big boars, although there weren't any of 'em as big as old Silvertip. One thing you can sure count on—I come up on all of 'em either at their level or from above. Cimarron'd got better 'bout carrying them hides, too, and we had ourselves a real nice time. It was beautiful country and I sure liked the views from up there on that mountain. I loved looking out over the desert at them red cliffs far below and watching the shadows of the clouds easing out over the canyons of the Colorado and the flats of Disappointment Valley. In the distance I could see the snowcapped peaks of the Uncompahgre and the San Juans, and my favorite of all was the snowcapped crown of old Lone Cone in the distance to the southeast.

I loved to hear the sound of the wind blowing through the high mountain grasses and smell the fresh perfumes of the bright-colored wildflowers. Seems funny now, remembering all the times when I'd look south and admire old Lone Cone Peak. Back then, I never dreamed that I'd spend the last years of my life in a log cabin up here on its high, spruce-covered slopes.

I could've stayed up there all summer hunting grizzly if my arm hadn't started troubling me. First I thought it was gonna be all right. The pain seemed to get less after the first couple of days, and by the fourth or fifth day, I figured it'd get well by itself. But a few days later it flared up again, and places started turning a blue-green where the flesh was tore, and the whole thing got sore and painful and pussy as hell.

Soon it'd swole up to where I couldn't touch it or nothing. I tried soaking it in a cold mountain stream and that seemed to help some, but as soon as I'd move 'round a bit, it'd start bothering me again. I didn't know what to do. I'd never been to see a doctor in my life, and the only ones I'd ever met was a couple of 'em that was drunk in saloons. I didn't have no hankering to go back to where very many people was, but something started telling me to get down off'n that mountain and let somebody look at my arm.

I hadn't seen no grizzlies for several days, so I saddled up Cimarron and piled on the flat bearskins, saving the hide of old Silvertip for last. I made me a makeshift diamond-hitch pack setup using the picket rope so's them hides wouldn't go sliding off every five minutes. It weren't a real good packing job, but it had to do.

I led Cimarron down through the blue spruce and made right good time, 'cept for some places where we hit deadfalls and had lots of going 'round to do. We was in the quakies by noon, and by late afternoon'd hit the oak brush. By that time I was half-mad with pain and I reckon I was a little outta my head. A big mule deer jumped up outta its bed, and as I watched it run off, bouncing away on them stiff legs, it kind of turned into two animals. Then I knowed that my eyes weren't seeing right and that I was going plumb bleary from whatever poison was in me.

I kept touching my arm every now and then and it felt like I was wearing a big leather boot on it. It was 'bout the same size and hardness and had 'bout as much feeling. I knowed I had to keep going. I felt a little better after I'd laid down in a rushing stream to soak my arm for a spell and drunk some ice-cold water. 'Long 'bout sunset I looked towards the west and it seemed like the sun'd become a hot fiery ball eating away at my eyes. It'd grow and then shrink and then start to pulse. I blinked my eyes and it seemed like it split into two suns.

'Bout that point I realized I didn't have no idea which direction Moab was, but I knowed I was coming down off the south side of the La Sals. Dimly, through all the shimmering and doubling that my eyes was doing, I could see a real green valley far below. It run 'tween some high red cliffs and when I could focus, it looked like there was open meadows down there amongst the trees.

As darkness come up, it begun to get awful cool. I was glad, thinking that maybe the coolness'd ease the throbbing in my arm. God almighty, how I longed for another drink of water! But there weren't any water. We was down into dry country. I reckoned we wouldn't get nothing to drink 'til we got down to where the creek was that run through them green flats I'd seen. All I could think 'bout was water. My tongue was parched and'd growed thick in my mouth, and everything kept swimming in front of my eyes. I weren't even think-ing good, and it was getting darker all the time. The only thing that kept me going was the rhythm of the pause and tug on Cimarron's halter rope.

I don't know when I lay down again, but it must've been several hours after dark. The next thing I knowed there was that great fiery ball standing right out in front of my head. Every time I'd open my eyes, it tried to sear 'em. I groaned and rolled to try to turn away from it. After a while I got the idea that maybe it was another day and time for me to get up and get going. I managed to stagger up and work along again with that lead rope still wrapped 'round my good hand. I don't remember much that happened next. Things was hazy. I must've fell down on my back, 'cause I faintly recollect half-waking up a couple of times and seeing that same ball of fiery sun dancing in front of me, and thinking that maybe I was on my way to the deep raging of hell.

The sound of running water kept coming back to me, but I reckoned it was just a dream. Finally, I couldn't stand it no more. If it was running water, I had to get to it somehow. I tried to get up again, but couldn't make it, so I begun to crawl on my hands and knees towards that rippling sound. I couldn't hold Cimarron no more, so I let him go. Then I got to something that seemed like sand and rocks, but it was cold and wet and I could tell I was lying in a small mountain stream. That's all I can remember, 'cause I collapsed right there.

WILD ROSE

There's no way a telling how long I was half-lying there in that stream clutching that wet rock and sand, 'cause the next thing I seen was that red glare that'd been burning me so bad, 'cept there was a lot of twigs and things 'tween me and that fiery ball. I was under some bushes or trees and it weren't as hellish as it'd been before.

I still couldn't see nothing or think too straight. I was lying there on my back like I was tied down. My left arm was swole up and hurt real bad. It felt like it was a big wood club, or maybe it just had a bunch of wet gunny-sacks tied on it. All I knowed was I couldn't move it much.

Then I tried to move my right arm and felt something real strange, like two hands was holding me down. I struggled to open my eyes. Things was hazy and twisted 'round. I slowly begun to make out small pieces of light that turned into something that I could recognize. It was something I sure as hell didn't wanta see. It was the sleeve of a beaded jacket. Then I seen what looked like a buckskin skirt 'round the knees of a kneeling squaw. My heart just plumb sank, 'cause I knowed what it was all about. Kneeling by me was one of them damned Comanche squaws! I was staked down again like I'd been before, and my left arm was tied so tight it was all swole up.

The squaw was leaning on my right arm with all her weight on her arms and hands so's I couldn't reach for a rock to brain the guard with. I'd been caught by a Comanche squaw while I was trying to get loose, and she was holding me while the guard was gonna tie my arm again. They must've brained me or something and that's why I couldn't get my eyes focused. I reckoned I was still staked out, waiting for the torture. All that business 'bout escaping, fighting off the Comanches, going into the San Luis Valley, old Pete showing up again, going to Taos and Santa Fe and Albuquerque, and going out on that buffalo hunt . . . Hell, that was all just the mad dream of a fevered man who was 'bout to die.

The thought took the heart outta me. How could I have thought I was free? How could I possibly have got away from being staked out like that. Never a chance. Then another thought come to me: Maybe there was no one else around. Maybe the guard'd gone off somewhere. Brules, are ya gonna let a squaw hold ya down like that? Ya'd better fight back. Now's the time ta do it, 'fore that guard comes back ta help her. Ya got one hand loose, man, an' only she's holdin' it down.

With that, I made a real effort to shake that squaw loose, to lift her up off'n the ground with my right arm, but she seemed awful strong, or I was awful weak and couldn't budge her. I couldn't move. I struggled and twisted, but she kept holding me tight.

"*Ka hav-y, ka hav-y,*" she kept saying, over and over again.

I wondered what in the hell she was trying to tell me. I was so exhausted I finally give up and tried to concentrate on opening my eyes, trying to see more, but it didn't seem to work.

Then I felt cool water on my face, and a hand going over it and dabbing at it. My eyelids was being fingered with cold water. I didn't understand. What the hell was going on?

I lay there a bit and realized that the water was clearing my eyes, so I opened 'em and seen the outline of things. I seen the blue sky and the shape of a woman's head. I seen shadows and leaves and twigs and then some long, dark hair and that beaded jacket again. I heard the sound of a calm voice. After that, there was more water dabbed on my face. When the picture come clear, I just couldn't believe it! My God, I couldn't believe it! There in front of me was the most beautiful sight in the whole wide world! Yessir, there was the face of the Sky Woman again, looking right down on me, looking down as if she'd come right outta the sky like she'd done seven years ago.

Once more I seen them soft doelike eyes and kind smile. I felt the easy stroke of her hand on the side of my head and chest, and heard soft words—not harsh, raspy Comanche talk, but soft, soothing words, almost like a baby's lullaby.

Maybe it's true, Brules, I thought. Maybe ya done died. Ya ain't on earth no more. Ya died an' went through that fire an' ya come out here in heaven, an' the Sky Woman's tryin' ta bring ya 'round.

Even though I was tired and dizzy, somehow I didn't have no more fear. My heart'd stopped pounding and begun to take up a quiet pace. I laid my head back and passed out again, but I kinda think there was a smile on my face.

The sunlight was gone the next time I woke up, and I seen a fire burning a few paces away. At first it frightened me, 'cause I'd begun thinking 'bout the torture again. Then I realized that weren't so, 'cause, sitting there by me, her face shining in the firelight, was the Sky Woman. When she seen me open my eyes and come 'round a little, she smiled. She ran her hand 'cross my brow and through my hair, and then she felt both of my cheeks with the back of her hand and quick and graceful-like got up and fetched a bowl of water and put it to my lips. It was delicious and cooling, and I thought maybe there was a chance that I'd live.

She kept talking to me in a low voice, with a kind of crooning sound, but I couldn't make out nothing she said.

I reckon I stayed awake for a half hour and then was gone again. Sure enough, the next time I woke up, I was well shaded by the twigs and trees that seemed to be 'tween me and that burning ball of sun. And there, again, was the Sky Woman, kneeling by my right side and gently rubbing my cheeks and forehead, speaking to me in some strange language, all soft and kind and crooning.

She was so beautiful! Her long hair was like a wave of black velvet flowing over her shoulders and down the middle of her back. She had clear, light suntanned skin that was soft and perfect, and none of her features looked like any of them Indians that I knowed. Them high cheekbones meant she must've been an Indian for sure, but she was much lighter skinned and it seemed that her nose and mouth and even her ears was finer looking.

She had nice, clean, straight, mild lips—not the thick-lipped look of the Comanches. Her teeth was small and even and well set—not the big, heavy jaws and widespread teeth of the Comanche squaws. Then there was her eyes. They weren't like no Comanche's eyes; they was soft and gentle, like a doe's.

She come over again and held up my head and give me some more water. It was then that I noticed the smell of her was like pine needles and green grass and flowers and maybe piñon smoke. It was a wonderful clean and clear smell, like the great outdoors. Tears come to my eyes. I just couldn't reckon with it.

After a while I tried to sit up again, but she put her hands on my shoulders and arms and shook her head no, saying "*ka hav-y*." I knowed she meant I was supposed to lie back.

She went over to get some leaves and mud from the riverbank and then come back and put it on my sore arm. Somehow it seemed to ease the pain. I don't really know what she used, but it was like a mud poultice, or something that was covered with herbs—something she knowed about. Anyway, it made things feel better—so much better, in fact, that I begun looking 'round and taking stock of where I was. I seen a lot in a very short time.

I seen that the leaves hanging over me on the branches weren't no natural bushes, but was a kind of wickiup the Sky Woman'd made to shade me from that fierce red sun. I reckoned it'd also serve at night to keep the rain off if'n she put buckskin hides over it.

I noticed the sound of running water, and I realized that we was in a dry creek bottom right near the stream. I wondered if maybe it was the same stream that I'd seen when I was up on the mountain, trying to get down to water. It could be that stream running through the center of Hatch Gulch. I remembered then that when I'd last fallen it was on some wet sand and rocks that was along the edge of running water.

I later found out that's exactly where she'd found me, lying face-down. She couldn't lift me up and carry me away from the edge, so she'd drug me far enough so's I could be outta the dampness. Then she'd built the wickiup to give me some protection. She seen right away that I was bad hurt and knowed it was gonna take a long time to get me back on my feet, but for all I could tell she'd set to it with a will, and it was the one thing she was thinking 'bout more'n anything else.

I seen by her sad smile and her bright, soft eyes that she knowed that I was suffering and'd been on the edge of death, and even then had knowed I might not make it. I could tell by the way she was working on me that she was doing her level best to see me through and was gonna use every bit of Indian medicine in her power to get it done.

I kept watching her going 'bout the camp and doing the things that needed to be done. Truth was, I couldn't keep my eyes off'n her. I never seen such a beautiful creature in all this world. She had a graceful, beautiful form and seemed to glide along instead of walk. Her arms was so perfect in the way they carried her hands, like waves describing the things for which we had no language 'tween us.

It seemed she was making the best of what food we had. She had some pemmican and I reckoned we'd been getting along right well with that. I noticed, too, that she had a string she was using in the creek and I looked close to the fire and seen fish bones. She'd been fishing and'd prob'ly caught some trout. Squaws is awful clever with that—using a handline with a fish-bone hook and something on it.

Fact is, I think that the Sky Woman'd been feeding us for several days on just that kinda thing. I seen the skin of a rabbit and figured that she'd prob'ly set a snare. But we weren't eating like no king and queen. We was closer to starving, but I could see that, starving or no, she weren't gonna leave me no matter what happened.

I felt a swelling joy in my heart. For the first time since I'd been hit by the grizzly, I figured there was a real reason for wanting to live. I seen her working 'round the fire, her beautiful face all lit up and red with the firelight. Her lovely eyes was always looking at me—first at the fire, then back at me, then at the stream, and back at me, then up at the trees and at the sky, looking for weather, and then back at me.

I thought my feelings for Michelle'd been powerful strong, but I never had no idea 'bout another woman like I had 'bout the Sky Woman. I thought she was a goddess. I figured she was untouchable. I thought she was not only the most beautiful thing I'd ever seen, but the most kind, most able, the wisest, and the most watchful. I closed my eyes and just kinda daydreamed 'bout her.

The fire went low in the darkening night and she took a blanket and set it over me. Then she crawled down beside me and made like she was gonna keep me warm and protect me. There weren't a single move that she made that give any indication that she was interested in a man-woman way of things. It was just that she was a kind person, like a guardian, and there weren't no monkey business a'tall.

The second morning, I was conscious of the light of dawn and then the sunrise, and a lot of nice things 'round me. I watched the Sky Woman as she went about her work, listening to her crooning some Indian tune that was real strange and soft and wavering and beautiful.

'Bout the middle of the day, I decided to try to communicate with her. I couldn't understand that Comanche language she was speaking, and I didn't have no idea how to make her understand English words. I was plumb tongue-tied. Then I got the idea of using a little sign language with my good hand, so I started with the easiest thing I knowed—the sign for water. When I made that sign, she nodded right away, jumped up, and run and got me some water.

I weren't really asking her for none—I was just making the sign—but I knowed real quick that she seen what I was talking 'bout. Then I done what I thought was the next obvious thing. I pointed at her and said, "Comanche, you Comanche."

A look of disgust come over her face and she shook her head violently. She kept saying, "Shoshone, Shoshone," pointing to herself.

'Course she weren't no Comanche! Noway! She didn't look like it, she didn't smell like it, and she didn't act like it. She may have spoke their language sometimes, 'cause I'd heard her do that, but she weren't no Comanche. She come from a different tribe, the Shoshone.

Now all of us on the frontier knowed 'bout the Shoshone. Americans'd been told by Lewis and Clark when they'd come back from the Pacific what a wonderful people the Shoshone was: how they was tall and handsome, how they had lighter skin than most of the tribes, how their women was the most beautiful of all the Indian nations. Looking at the Sky Woman, I sure could believe that!

I'd also heard how virtuous their young girls was. You couldn't roll no Shoshone girl outta her blankets like you could a Minnetaree or a Mandan squaw.

Everybody knowed how it was that a Shoshone squaw named Sacagawea guided Lewis and Clark to the Pacific. If it hadn't been for her they all would've starved to death on the Lolo Trail in the mountains 'tween the Lemhi and the Clearwater. They knowed how Sacagawea found the roots and herbs that the men could boil and eat to keep alive. She was the one who was always pointing out things when they was crossing the Shining Mountains that give them some kinda decent direction.

There was other things that folks knowed 'bout the Shoshone, too. They was 'bout the only Indians that never resorted to torture. Far as I know, they never went to war 'cept to defend theirselves. Whether that's true or not, I later found out firsthand that they was a wonderful people. 'Course I was prejudiced as hell, 'cause I'd first learned 'bout 'em from the Sky Woman.

One day, when I thought I knowed enough, I begun trying all sorts of ways of communicating with her. I was eager to learn all 'bout her and to try to tell her 'bout me. The first thing I done was point at myself and pronounce my name.

She looked surprised and repeated, "Brules, Brules," and shook her head. Then she pointed at me and said, "*Tababone, tababone.*" Fortunately I'd spent time as a kid hanging 'round them river joints in St. Louis, so I knowed that *tababone* was the word for white man. I remembered the story when Lewis'd first tried to explain to a Shoshone squaw that he was a white man. He'd opened his shirt and showed his white skin and said that word. It was 'bout all the Shoshone I knowed, but when I seen she didn't get the idea that my name was Brules and she was trying to tell me I was a white man, I let it go at that.

Then I took another tack and begun pointing at other things all 'round the camp. I pointed at my rifle and said, "gun." She nodded and said "*hi-tah.*" We went through the whole camp that way, pointing at the fire, at the creek, at the trees, at some horses that were picketed out in the flats. In looking at the horses, I seen with satisfaction that she had my horse Cimarron well took care of. I also seen that she'd pulled them bear hides off'n him and had 'em hung on the branch of a tree. Weren't that just like a good Indian squaw! You never get her away from her horses and she never leaves 'em saddled or packed up. Little did I know what a wonderful horsewoman that Shoshone girl really was.

After we'd pointed out every object that we could think of, including the La Sal Mountains, and used the English and Shoshone words for 'em, we found that we could repeat 'em and be reasonable correct after a few tries. I seen she was as eager to learn English as I was to learn Shoshone.

I remember the cowboys in San Antone saying that if you ever wanted to learn a language, you'd better pick a girl to teach you. If you wanted to learn Spanish, you'd better take up with a señorita. Well, it looked like I'd made the right beginning taking up with a Shoshone maiden.

Then I begun a kind of tricky experiment. I pointed to myself and said, "*Tababone*, white man, Brules." Then I pointed to her. "Shoshone, Indian," and left the third name blank.

She caught on quick as a flash. She seen I was asking for her name, so she repeated, pointing to herself, "Shoshone, Indian, Che-ah."

I repeated everything she said—"Shoshone, Indian, Che-ah." It weren't 'til quite a while later that I found out the name Che-ah meant Wild Rose, and it ain't a name I'll be likely to forget. Fact is, I quit thinking of her as the Sky Woman. Wild Rose was good enough for me, and a lot closer to what she really was.

Matters went on like that and we was there together and spent hours every day doing that kinda thing. It got to be a fun game, and we was both learning quick. One thing I remember right clear: I was puzzled and a little miffed that every time Wild Rose'd point at me and say "Brules," she'd shake her head and laugh. Later I learned that she had a reason for doing that.

As the days went on, my arm seemed to be getting better at a rapid rate. I was beginning to get some feeling in my fingers, and I got so's I could move the elbow just a little. The swelling'd also gone down and that green and black look that it had for so long was slowly disappearing. Wild Rose'd bathe it regularly in her mud and medicine poultices and make a clucking sound all the time she was doing it. I gathered that she was very concerned and was giving a hopeful sign that it was gonna be better.

One of the things that we had a difficult time with was the shortage of grub. True, Wild Rose'd been able to get rabbits and trout, but not often enough to keep our bellies full. I'll never forget one morning when I was still bedded down and unable to rise, how I just set up halfway with the saddle in back of me for a pillow. Wild Rose was by the fire making the most of what little food we'd had. I happened to look up the side of the sagebrush slope just north of our camp and seen two little buck mule deer poking their way along, ducking their heads here and there and raising up and listening with their beautiful ears to hear if there was anything going on that might spook 'em.

The minute I spotted their white rumps, I give a low hiss. Wild Rose looked at me and I pointed to the hill. She turned quickly and her eyes opened wide. Then I seen something I couldn't believe. My rifle was leaning up against the tree 'bout ten feet away by some saddlebags. In one motion that girl left the fire and crossed to the rifle, crouching low and moving just like a panther. Since I was very strong on appreciating cat movements, that filled my heart with delight. It was less'n three seconds 'til she was back with me and'd put the rifle stock in my right hand. I made a quick swing towards the nearest buck on the hill, which I reckoned was 'bout three hundred yards away.

It was too far for me to hold steady without my left hand for support. 'Sides that, I needed to lever a shell into the chamber. I motioned quickly for her to cross over me and kneel down facing the deer. Then I rested the rifle on her shoulder, levered the action, and after taking careful aim, fired a fine shot. The buck leaped high and fell dead.

Wild Rose screamed with delight and, grabbing her knife, rushed up the hill like another deer. In a few minutes she come back with back straps and a haunch and started slicing things up and putting 'em on sticks over the fire to be cooked.

Wild Rose was happy as she could be. After we'd ate our fill, she made two or three trips to the buck's carcass and brought the other haunch, the rib cage, and the front quarters down to our camp. She set 'em up in a shady place for our commissary. There weren't no flies that early in the spring, so it seemed like the meat'd last for two or three days, 'specially if we kept it in the shade and poured water on it at times to keep it cool.

Wild Rose made several other trips to the carcass and cut big strips of deer hide and brought them back to the camp. She knowed she could make lots of good things outta the hide, and rolled it up in small rolls tied with rawhide to keep for good purpose later on. I tell you, I knowed then that she was some gal.

After that time, my progress got real rapid. It got so's I could sit up and stand and walk some. The swelling'd almost completely gone down on my arm, but it was still black and green in places, and my fingers weren't moving as well as they should.

By then we'd knowed enough of each other's language to make some reasonable communication, so I begun questioning her 'bout how she'd come to find me in that godforsaken place.

She started to tell the story and I realized it was a long and sad one. It was like this.

The Shoshone tribe lived up there in the Wind River country in northwestern Wyoming and there they was noted for raising their elegant paint horses. They had some Appaloosas, too, that I reckon they got from the Kutenai tribe way down in the Appaloosa Valley on the lower Columbia.

Whatever that may be, they sure was knowed for their prized horses, and they'd made a good living trading 'em to other tribes. The Comanches, it seems, was the most interested. They loved paint horses but didn't really have many of their own. The Comanche horses'd come from the mustangs, which run off from the great ranches of Pedro's native Chihuahua.

Them horses was descended from the conquistadores and was a cross 'tween an Arab and the Castilian knights' horses. Neither the Castilians nor the Arabs liked paint horses. Frankly, if a foal was born paint, they destroyed it right quick. So when the Spanish come into Mexico they didn't bring no paint horses. Some claim they did, but what they'd really brung with 'em was dapples.

Anyway, what them Comanches wanted was the paint horse of the Shoshones, and they paid a good price. It's always been a mystery to me how them Indians living in the Columbia Valley, and the Shoshones and the Blackfoot living up in the Shining Mountains of Wyoming and Montana, should have paint horses when the southern tribes was so short. What's a real mystery is where them damn paint horses come from. If they didn't come from Mexico, where in the hell did they come from?

In any case, that don't make no difference here. What's really important is that the Shoshone'd lead a small string of paints and make the long trip from the Wind River Mountains to south of the Arkansas, and sometimes clear down to the Canadian—almost a thousand miles. They was able to trade with the Comanches on the basis of four to one. They'd have a string of eight or ten horses tied head to tail coming down, but when they made their trade, they'd have four times that many going back, so it weren't practical to string 'em out like that. It was much better to herd 'em along in a bunch.

I reckon that trading'd been going on for a couple of hundred years—at least as long as any of the Shoshone tribesmen could remember. It was on one of those trips that Wild Rose come along with her two brothers and four other warriors. I reckon she was 'bout fourteen or fifteen years old at the time. It weren't unusual for a squaw to accompany warriors on a trip when all they was really doing was some peaceful trading. The presence of a squaw showed other tribes that they was on a peaceful mission and not a raid. That's one of the reasons why Lewis and Clark took the Shoshone squaw Sacagawea with 'em to the mouth of the Columbia. She'd helped calm the fears of the tribes that the Lewis and Clark boys met.

Well, it was on the first trip that Wild Rose and her brothers come to the camp of the Comanches at the foot of the Sangre de Cristos near the head of the Cimarron, where I was staked out waiting for the torture. It was her first time among the Comanches and, as I learned from her, she was shocked and frightened by the ways of that tribe. She didn't like 'em a'tall. Although the Comanche and the Shoshone spoke the same language, their habits and ways of doing things was a long, long ways apart.

I guess the trading expedition she was on at that time was real successful and she and the boys returned with a bunch of good horses and decided to do it again. Apparently they'd done it three different times after that. The last time, they run into disaster. When I asked her where her brothers was, she started to cry, then made the sign for brother, then the sign for scalping, and said, "Mescalero." I knowed right quick what she meant. The Mescalero Apaches'd attacked her party somewhere along the route. I didn't know just where, but I was gonna find out. Apparently everybody but her'd been killed and scalped. It was totally beyond my mind to understand how that little girl, bent on returning with her string of horses to the Shoshone reservation at Lander, Wyoming, found her way through that lonely desert waste two hundred fifty miles up to Hatch Gulch, where she found me.

In trying to figure out where she'd first been attacked, I begun to think 'bout the Mescalero Apaches: where they was located and what I knowed 'bout 'em. I knowed that they'd been took by the dragoons in the late fifties and stuck down on a reservation at the Bosque-Rhedondo on the Pecos River right near Fort Sumner. It'd been real tough for 'em to run sheep and cattle and try to make a living there, and it got a lot tougher in '63 when Kit Carson brought the whole Navajo nation in. He'd whipped the Navajos in Canyon de Chelly earlier that year and their price for surrendering was to be moved to the new reservation at Bosque-Rhedondo.

As it turned out it was a damned poor plan. Even the Navajos couldn't make a living there, and they was in terrible shape all during the time from 1863 'til about 1871, when everybody give up on the

Navajo plan. The Navajo wanted to go back to their homeland, naturally, and the Bureau of Indian Affairs and the military seen that the Bosque-Rhedondo experiment was a dismal failure. So it was agreed that the Navajos should go home if they'd lay down their arms and never fight again. They made a long procession back to their own country and kept their promise, but in the midst of the confusion, the Mescalero Apaches, without permission, just plumb packed up and cleared out as well and went down to their old country near Ruidosa in their mountain stronghold they called the Home of the Mountain Gods. After that nobody bothered to go back in and get 'em. I reckon they stayed outta trouble most of the time and was allowed to exist the way they did.

However, they used to cross the Rio Grande from the east and pay visits to the Chiricahua Apache Indians way west on the White River. I also knowed that along that route, between Ruidosa and Fort Apache, there'd often been fights with other Indian bands. The military, having enough trouble with the war with the Confederacy and trying to protect the white people, didn't pay much attention to the Indian fights. That was understandable, but why in hell did Wild Rose and her brothers ever go over in that country when they was headed back to the Shoshone reservation and should've gone back the way they'd come, by way of Fort Lupton and Fort Laramie east of the Rockies?

I was gonna have to find that out from Wild Rose. I also promised myself that I'd learn all I could 'bout her brothers' massacre, where and when it'd took place, and how she'd got out of it alive. Funny thing, but it just seemed that I had to know all I could 'bout her. She was just taking up my thoughts so much every day and every night.

I kept exercising my arm and the muscles started to get better. Finally I got so's I was taking some longer walks each day. One of the great joys of that was not only getting to feel better all the time, but having Wild Rose go with me. She insisted on it in case I might get to feeling bad or lose my balance and fall on my bad arm. But I also got the feeling that she wanted to go with me anyway, and that pleased me more'n I could say. The truth of the matter was that something was happening to both of us.

On every one of those walks I tried to talk with her more and more and she made the same effort towards me. We learned how to put sentences together so's they made some sense, although I had to admit that I was sure clumsy with the Shoshone language compared with the way she was making progress with English. Both of us'd burst into gales of laughter when we made some stupid mistake.

Language, of course, is a dangerous thing and you can say stuff that you don't mean a'tall and get yourself in real trouble. Well, we never got into trouble with each other 'cause we had too many kindly feelings and it was easy to laugh anything off that was kinda ridiculous. I loved to hear Wild Rose laugh. She had the most perfect laugh I ever knowed. It was plain she was enjoying life and it made me feel good just to be with her.

Sometimes she'd say my name over and over again, and then she'd laugh. I never quite knowed what she was laughing at and sometimes I'd get a little embarrassed, but I never got mad. I'm glad I didn't, 'cause way off in the future I found out why she was laughing and it meant a lot to me to know.

During all that time I couldn't help watching the habits of that wonderful woman. She was as clean a person as I'd ever knowed. 'Fore she'd start to cook any food, she always went down to the creek and washed her hands, then she'd wash 'em again after we'd ate. She was so clean that I was embarrassed that I hadn't been more like that in my rough years as a lone hunter. I sure took to copying her.

Every day she'd go off for a while to take a bath and I was real careful to busy myself 'round the camp while she was bathing and never tried to get a look at her. I made a big effort never to have her feel uncomfortable 'bout my being 'round, 'cause I damn well weren't gonna embarrass her while she was bathing.

One afternoon I went out to gather some firewood. I kinda felt like it'd help my bad arm more and more to be using it in hard work like that. It was when I topped a little knoll and looked 'bout a hundred yards upstream that I seen Wild Rose coming outta the creek. She weren't wearing no clothes. Instinctive-like I turned away 'cause I was ashamed to look, but I have to admit that at the same time I was stirred and my heart jumped a bit. She was so beautiful.

Among the things I most enjoyed was the way she kept telling me that I was getting better and better looking all the time. I felt she was trying to make me feel good, but the truth of the matter was that I was getting stronger every day.

Another thing I liked so much 'bout being with her was the stories she'd start telling me 'bout her life with the Shoshone people, what she thought of various warriors and the old men of the tribe who were so wise and had things figured out, and what she thought 'bout the country and the Indian agent that was there on the Shoshone reservation.

I kept asking her questions and she'd answer and make the funniest descriptions of people and sometimes the saddest ones, and she'd tell me how much she loved somebody. Maybe it'd be another girl that was a cousin, or maybe a friend or even her father, that she seemed to sorta like but thought was full of funny ideas that could sometimes make things difficult.

I'd stayed away from the topic of her brothers and tried not to ask any questions, 'cause once or twice when the conversation drifted that way she'd got real sad and wouldn't talk for several hours. That was a situation I never liked to have happen.

The other thing that amused me so much 'bout Wild Rose was when she got to talking 'bout an old lady that she called great, great grandmother. I thought that was funny 'cause I know there ain't no grandmothers that live that long and go that far back. She explained that the woman weren't her real grandmother, just someone that everybody in the village called great, great grandmother. Wild Rose told me that she was the same woman who'd gone with the "Red Chiefs" to the "great water" at the mouth of the Columbia. When she said that, my eyes nearly popped out.

I remember she was quite surprised when I asked her if the woman's name was Sacagawea.

"Yes, how you know her name?"

"Why, everyone knows 'bout Sacagawea, the Bird Woman that led Lewis an' Clark 'cross the Shinin' Mountains. I knowed it when I was a little boy 'cause my daddy always talked 'bout it, an' everybody up an' down the Mississippi an' the Missouri couldn't talk a'tall 'bout things without mentionin' Lewis an' Clark. Do ya really know this woman? Does she really live in your village?"

"Yes, she lives on the reservation there and Agent Irwin is kind to her." Wild Rose said she liked Irwin very much, but she liked Sacagawea best of all the people who was there, whether they was cousins or friends or others on the reservation that she'd spent her girlhood with. She just loved to hear old great, great grandmother tell the stories of where she'd been and what she'd done.

Wild Rose told me once that there was only one thing that she ever thought was wrong with great, great grandmother. When I asked her what it was, she said, "Well, she is such a liar. She is just a terrible liar."

I laughed. "Sometimes ol' ladies get that way. What'd she tell ya that was such a big lie?"

"Well, she talked about when she went to the 'great water' at the mouth of the Columbia and seen a fish as big as a house."

Then it was my turn to start laughing, and Wild Rose asked me what was so funny. "*Ka-nung-en*—I don't understand. Am I so foolish?"

"No, but great, great grandmother ain't the liar ya think she is. That big fish she seen was a beached whale."

With that, Wild Rose made the most peculiar noise. It was sort of an "eeeee." I didn't know what to make of the sound at first. I knowed it was something she was expressing, but it was something full of wonder and pleasure. Something like we'd say, "Is that so?" or "Oh, wonderful," or "Tell me more." I heard that expression many, many times afterwards, and it always pleased me.

"Do you really mean there are fish as big as houses?"

"Yah, they's called whales."

"What are you saying? Whales?"

"Yah, whales." 'Course we was using our pidgin English and pidgin Shoshone and making lots of gestures in between. It weren't a smooth conversation like I'm telling it, but we still knowed what the other one meant and that's how we got along.

But when I begun talking 'bout the whales, Wild Rose took on a whole other look at things. She got real interested. "Do you mean that great, great grandmother is not a liar?"

"More'n likely. I mean, the very fact that she mentioned such a thing makes me think *fer shore* that she went with Lewis an' Clark."

Wild Rose nodded. "There are many people who doubt that she ever went on a trip and everybody laughs at her because she is such a liar, but maybe she really is telling the truth and they are the fools."

"Sounds like that ta me. I'd shore like ta see the ol' girl someday."

That remark opened up a whole new line of conversation. Wild Rose took me by the hand and walked me to the fire and had me sit down, then she sat down across from me.

"It is to the Shoshone people I must go. That is my home. I have been gone a long time and I am very sad for my family. I was all alone and very frightened after my brothers died, but now that I am with you, I no longer feel frightened. I know you are a mighty warrior and there is no one among all of the tribes and all the land that you need to be afraid of, for you are better with the gun than any of them. All the nations now know that when the guns of the Cat Man speak, they speak with the tongue of death.

"Do you know how I know this? I remember how I hated those Comanches when my brothers and I came to them to trade horses for the first time. They are so dirty and so cruel. I remember when I was there in the village how they tortured some people. I do not know who they were or why they were tortured, but I could not stand their screams. I ran down the river so I would be away from what was going on, and I used to weep a great deal for things I did not understand.

"When the warriors brought you into the camp they had your hands tied behind your back and you wore a black hood over your head so you couldn't see. I could tell that you were suffering a great deal. When they took the mask off of your face, I saw you had been struck by trees or branches and that you were bleeding along your nose and mouth.

"I saw that you had whip marks on your back and shoulders and I knew you had to be very thirsty. I watched them as they pulled off your clothes and staked you out on the ground.

"I could see by the muscles of your arms, your chest, and your legs that you were a mighty warrior. I knew you had to be strong and swift, but I did not know about your greatness with the gun, nor had I seen your eyes.

"I remember too how bad it was that you were to be tortured to death. It seemed like such a terrible end for such a brave warrior and that no man should have to face it. I went to the stream with the clay bowl and came back to give you water. There was no way with that hood that you could have had a drink all day. The sun was hot and the ride was long.

"I was lucky, for the guards were busy with their packhorses when I came to you. Your eyes were shut and your lips were moving just a little. I lifted your head and gave you water, although you seemed to resist.

"I remember thinking that perhaps you thought I was one of the Comanche squaws who liked to tease the prisoners by pouring hot coals on their bodies. Such a horrible thing I could not understand. What I wanted you to have was a drink of cool water.

"I remember how you resisted me and then how you swallowed the water and how it seemed to be so good for you, because it was then that you opened your eyes. I was so shaken because I had never seen eyes like that on any warrior. They seemed to look straight through me like the eyes of a cat, a big cat, the cat we call the *to-ye-ro-co*—the panther. I did not know then how important those eyes were. I just remember that they made my heart beat faster.

"When the guards discovered me and drove me away with bad words and blows, it hurt, but it hurt more to see you there helpless, and to not be able to give you more water. I cried, not because I was hurt by the guards' blows, but because I thought I would never see you again. I was sure they would torture you to death that night. All I could do was to run down the river and be a long ways off so I couldn't hear you scream.

"When I came back at noon the next day, I was half in dread of seeing your charred remains. It was then that I heard you had killed a guard and escaped and that the warriors who had gone to hunt you down hadn't yet returned. My heart gave a leap because maybe you had got away for good, but I dared not be too hopeful because prisoners do not escape from Comanche tracking parties. When the warriors did return late the second night, there were only half of them, and you were still gone. My heart jumped for joy and pride for I knew it was the great warrior with the cat eyes and the repeating gun that had broken a tracking party in half.

"Now, that is why I say that you need fear nobody. Your name and your deeds have been told throughout all the Indian nations, and the sign of the cat which has marked your revenge on the Comanches is known and feared by every tribe. That is why I know I will be safe if you will go with me to my people. In your hands I have no fear. I beg of you, will you take me home?"

I didn't have to think twice. I would've gone to hell and back for her if she'd wanted me to. I broke the silence to tell her just that. If she wanted to leave for her people tomorrow, I was ready to go with her.

I'm sure she'd been real concerned 'bout trying to go home all alone. It made me plumb terrified to think of that young girl traveling alone through country where there was wild tribes and white settlers and where there was the transcontinental railroad to cross with all the towns and people that'd be along it. There'd be a lot of cold and lonely nights and a good chance she'd starve on the way, 'specially in the red desert country, where game was scarce. It was unthinkable, and I aimed to see that she was escorted proper all the way. You could bet your life on that.

Well, I near lost my senses when I seen what she done next. Perhaps a white woman in the same situation would've throwed her arms 'round a fella and give him a big hug and kiss, but an unmarried Shoshone Indian girl couldn't possibly do such a thing. In the first place, she didn't even know what kissing was. The Shoshones and most other Indians didn't ever kiss. To show affection once in a while, they'd rub noses, but only when they was married. It was real bad form to do it at any other time. In fact, it seemed to me it was hard for Indians to show any emotion, one way or another, 'cept for laughter or anger. 'Course in them two cases they weren't a bit backward in letting you know how they felt. But Wild Rose done something that surprised me, kind of embarrassed me, and in the end, was over-whelming.

She got up, come over in front of me, stood there a minute, then she dropped to her knees, put her head down, touched the earth with her right hand, and touched her forehead. Then she done the same thing with her left hand. Then, without lifting her eyes, she gracefully rose from her kneeling position and walked off and started attending to things 'round the fire and left me standing there with my mouth open.

It was obvious to me that what she was doing was expressing deep thanks and sealing it with the Earth Mother. It was like saying, As I come from the earth, I am grateful to you. Well, I've heard a lot of speeches 'bout how people feel, and most of 'em run off me like water off'n a duck's back, but that simple gesture stirred me to the heart.

Next morning, even though my arm weren't completely well and I was still a little weak, I asked, "Are ya ready ta go ta your people today? If ya are, I'm ready ta take ya."

I thought she was gonna cry. Instead she smiled and looked at me for a long time, and I knowed how much she wanted to go home.

"You are a kind and trusting man, Brules, but we cannot leave here now. You are not well yet. We will stay. I will tell you when we can go."

She was right. I knowed I needed more time to recover, but I was a man who had all the world to live for—and a will to live.

That afternoon we had plenty of food again. Wild Rose kept showing me different roots and herbs that you could dig up and boil to make a good soup. With venison meat it made a dandy meal, and we was eating good again.

When Wild Rose told me that we weren't leaving yet, I knowed who was running things in camp. I just figured that whatever she wanted, that's the way it'd be. It's a good thing I listened to her, 'cause moving my arm made it sore again and I had a relapse. She got worried and went to work again with the poultices, but in another week I was all right.

It was getting towards the end of July. I was feeling a lot better—not quite up to what I should be, but I had plenty of energy and could use my left arm enough to do some hunting. Wild Rose went with me all the time. After we'd done some considerable walking for several days, back and forth to the camp, we decided to do some riding.

That's the way it worked. July passed into August and August into September. We didn't keep track of the calendar. One thing I noticed when we went riding was that Wild Rose had a way with horses the likes of which I'd never seen. She was gentle by nature and the horses sensed it. Half the time she didn't need a lead rope, 'cause they'd just follow her 'round like she was gonna give 'em something good, even if she didn't. They'd come up and rub their noses on her shoulder, and she'd talk to 'em using Shoshone words that I didn't understand, but them horses seemed to savvy.

The way she'd talk to a horse, the way she'd feed a horse by hand whenever she got the notion, the way she looked over horses' hooves and felt their legs to see if they had any injury, and the way she'd take care and time to rub their backs with a bunch of leaves and twigs and comb their manes, you knowed she loved 'em. She always used a blanket on 'em under her saddle, which most Indians didn't seem to give a damn about.

To my knowledge, she never did use a quirt on a horse and she didn't wear spurs. She had very light hands and reined the horses real gentle. Sometimes I seen her doing maneuvers with a horse without showing any motion a'tall with her hands or knees or feet. She must've been putting pressure on the right spots, but you couldn't see it. She was a great horsewoman.

Anyway, day after day she'd check my arm and rub it often, using some tallow that she'd got off'n the hides. It felt real good.

It was the happiest time I knowed, but I begun to worry 'bout what was gonna happen when we left. Something had to change. That paradise couldn't last. 'Sides that, there was a strange longing in my heart that I couldn't explain. It was something that was growing stronger all the time, yet I kept denying it.

We talked every chance we had and got better at it. It was a mixed-up jumble of English and Shoshone words, but we had no trouble getting our thoughts across. Once in a while we'd get into some pretty complicated thinking, but we still made out all right.

Sometimes there'd be a pause—a question that weren't clear—then the thing'd be explained in a different way. In the end we got it right and we understood each other. Once or twice, when we skirted touchy questions, she'd give me a strange look and I couldn't tell what to make of it. I couldn't tell whether she was saying to me, Come on, Brules, why don't you act a little bolder; or maybe she was saying, Stand back, boy, you're getting on dangerous ground.

Whatever it was, I kept my counsel and put on my best behavior. I never wanted to make Wild Rose angry. I never did, and I can't imagine what I would've done if I had, but I know I would've been sick at heart.

She was pleasant all the time, always bouncy and full of questions and laughter. Once in a while she'd tease me 'bout something and I'd laugh good-naturedly. I didn't care how much she teased me, just as long as she was around.

I remember when I first seen her how I'd thought she was a goddess, an angel of mercy that'd come outta the sky and helped me when I was in desperate need. But even I could see that she weren't no goddess, just a beautiful Indian girl, and I worshipped her for what she was.

One afternoon Wild Rose looked at the clouds and the angle of the sun and then looked at my arm. She turned me 'round to face her, put her arms on my shoulders, and announced, "Tomorrow we go." That was all there was to it.

I watched Wild Rose make the preparations for travel. She took the back straps of the last deer I'd killed, cut 'em into long pieces for jerky, and set 'em out in the sun to dry. I knowed then that our time in paradise was running short.

22

THE LONG JOURNEY BACK

The morning was bright and clear the day we broke camp and headed for Shoshone country. Wild Rose'd made a lot of pemmican and we had a haunch of venison, a brace of ribs, and some back straps hanging from the back of our saddles. We knowed it wouldn't last very long in the heat of the sun and the riding we had to do, but at least we had some supplies to start with. 'Sides, there weren't nothing to stop me from killing a deer or two along the way.

We left with high hopes and headed north, crossing the lower Dolores River 'fore we come to the edge of the Colorado in the middle of the big loop that it makes 'tween Grand Junction and Moab. I'm glad we hadn't had to try crossing that thing in early May with the spring runoff. It was late September and still a helluva river.

We rode up and down 'bout five miles each way 'til we found a place where we thought we could cross. Me and Cimarron led the way and the rest of them horses come along.

I was leading all them horses, each one tied to the tail of the next. Wild Rose was on her paint, following right behind the whole string. Her horse was a dandy, a strong gelding, but it was the way she rode him that made him look so good.

Suddenly the rear packhorse begun to lose his footing in the swift current and started to drift downstream. It was then that Wild Rose really showed her horsemanship and the kinda stuff she was made of. Yelling like a warrior, she swum that paint of hers to the hindquarters of that rear packhorse. Like a flash she reached down in the water and come up holding his tail. With a wild Indian yip and yell from her, and me cussing, we headed up into the current, kept the horses from drifting downstream, and made it to the other shore, but it was a real maneuver. Half the time that big gelding of hers was so far down-stream that he'd gone off the ford and was swimming.

We was soaking wet when we come outta the river, particularly Wild Rose, who was in the ice-cold water up to her waist. I can tell you we was a bedraggled sight. I looked back at her expecting to see her scared outta her wits, 'cause there'd been a good chance the whole bunch of us might've drowned. But there she was, laughing and thinking it was the funniest thing that ever happened.

From there we headed 'cross the White due south of Sleepy Cat and then turned north so we'd strike the Yampa just below its junction with the Williams Fork. I didn't want nothing to do with them Utes, 'specially with that Shoshone girl with me, and I kept my rifle real loose in the scabbard. We traveled at night 'til we crossed the Savery Branch of the Little Snake and passed east of Baggs Ranch—far enough from Ute territory to where I felt we was safe. It was late September when we headed out into the desert country of southern Wyoming. Two days later, bearing straight north, we struck the Union Pacific Railroad.

I ain't never forgetting how in the afternoon we topped a rise in that barren red desert and seen lying 'cross our path in the distance the long, level roadbed of a railroad that run as far to the east as the eye could see and stretched the same way to the west. It was the first railroad I'd seen in the seven years since I'd left Hays City in October of 1867.

It was a strange feeling. I'd been so much by myself in them seven years and got so s'picious of people that I looked on that railroad with mixed feelings. On the one hand I knowed that men'd built it there in the last six years and maybe it'd spoil the wilderness. On the other hand, there was something 'bout railroads that I liked, but I couldn't tell you just what it was. Them two ribbons of steel reached out 'cross the whole stretch of America from one ocean to the other, and I knowed that when you went to it and stood on the track and looked along it, it seemed like them rails come together in the far distance.

That railroad made it feel as if there was some kinda steel bond 'tween me and a better world. There was something strong 'bout it, something that said that at last the West was being conquered.

We rode straight ahead and when we come up on the railroad bed, I realized we was 'bout seven or eight miles west of Rawlins. Along the railroad tracks was telegraph poles with wires strung out. Wild Rose called 'em the "*we-he-tim-oke*"—the talking wires. Them wires'd sorta whisper in the wind, and you could imagine that what was going on was the whispering of the messages as they was traveling 'cross the continent. Wild Rose insisted on getting off her horse and listening against the telegraph poles to see if she could hear the palefaces talking.

I later made some friends among some cavalry scouts that told me they'd seen all the Indians—the Arapaho, Shoshone, Pawnee, Sioux, Cheyenne—do the same when they'd come to them telegraph wires. They'd look on with some mystery in their eyes, often getting off their ponies and leaning up against them telegraph poles, listening to see if they could hear the white man talking.

I knowed that Wild Rose'd feel plenty uncomfortable in a white man's town. Rawlins being a rough old railroad stop anyway, she'd be real unhappy, so I never planned to take her there.

We crossed the railroad and went on up a draw where there was some cottonwoods. I knowed we'd find a spring there. It was 'bout a half mile from the railbed and real hidden and comfortable. We made camp, picketed the horses, and got a fire going. We was sitting 'round it when I told Wild Rose, "Now, little lady, tomorrow I'm gonna take them grizzly hides inta Rawlins an' sell 'em ta get money fer ammunition."

"Oh, no, you are not to do that. I want one of the grizzly hides for my father. He will be so pleased and he will have great respect for you because few men kill the big bear. I also want to make a nice coat for you so that everyone may know what a hunter you really are. I will need one more hide to make a nice robe for myself. I would be the envy of every Shoshone girl with a robe like that."

"That only leaves four hides, don't it?"

She looked at me coyly. "You can do what you wish with the other four hides."

"Well, I reckon what I'll do is go on inta Rawlins. I'm shore there's a tradin' post there an' I'll trade somebody outta some ammunition fer them hides. I know I can do that."

She smiled. "Yes, you will need ammunition and there are no more hides that we need. I will wait for you here in the camp, Great Warrior, and I will have something for you to eat when you come back."

I packed up the next morning and headed into Rawlins. As I rode along I seen a tough-looking crew along the tracks and I felt uneasy 'bout Wild Rose.

When I got into Rawlins, I was a little shy myself and I understood how Wild Rose felt. I'd been alone all the time, 'cept for that wonderful Indian girl, and I'd only been with her for maybe three months. I'd been a lonely man during the last five years, making my way alone everywhere I went, and I was uncomfortable with lots of folks around. But it couldn't be helped. I had to grit my teeth and go on into town and get my job done. I needed more ammunition for my Winchester.

I didn't have no trouble finding the general store. When I rode up to it, leading the packhorse with grizzly hides on it, I caused quite a commotion in that small place. The trader come out and looked at them hides. "Boy, you've got something there, ain't you?" he said.

"I hope so."

"Grizzly hides ain't worth much these days."

"Oh, yeah? Where ya gettin' 'em?"

"Well, there's a lot of Indians that's hunting grizzly."

"Come on, don't try ta kid me. First place, ya have ta have a hunter that has the guts ta go get 'em."

That trader was pretty sharp. When I said that, he started to laugh as though it was easy to kill a grizzly.

He weren't an Indian agent or nothing like that. He was just a fella running a general store on the railroad. Folks come in all the time to trade for one thing or another. Maybe they was trading arrowheads or Indian jackets or something that had to do with pieces of ore or something to do with the West, and a fella like him'd buy it. When the trains'd come in, passengers'd come over and look at them trading stores, and that's how the old boy'd do his business.

Well, he weren't working for his health, and he was gonna trade hard. He was gonna knock down the price as much as he could, but I knowed them grizzly hides was worth at least a hundred fifty dollars apiece for a full-growed one, and maybe seventy-five dollars for the cub size. 'Course Rawlins weren't the best market you could find for selling things. I would've done better in Cheyenne or Denver, but I didn't have no inclination to go to either of them places.

The trader looked at me. "Come on inside, fella, and we'll go to the back room and sit down and have a talk."

As we walked through the store, I seen that he had all kinds of things. There was folks in the store trying to buy stuff, but not very many of 'em. Some of 'em was settlers and there was a railroad worker or two, but I didn't see no Indians. We went into the back room and he drawed up a couple of chairs to the table and we sat down. He got out a jug of whiskey and wanted to give me a drink, but I told him that I'd pass on that. I weren't running no risk of coming back to my Shoshone lady smelling like a brewery. I knowed that even though I weren't drunk she wouldn't like it. She'd had a lot of trouble with whiskey and the braves on the reservation. To her, liquor was the kiss of the devil, so I figured I'd damn well better steer clear of that. As a matter of fact, I didn't have no liking for it anymore. When I did take a drink, it was only for the hell of it.

The trader seemed disappointed when I passed up his whiskey. I reckoned he was fixing to warm me up that way. Then he started asking me lots of questions 'bout where I'd got them hides and how come. I told him that I'd been way down in Utah in the La Sal country, and he seemed to take some interest in that, but didn't seem like he was overly impressed.

He figured what them hides was worth and I knowed how much I had to give up to get them sold in Rawlins. But 'fore that, I wanted to find out if he had any ammunition. There weren't no use selling hides less'n he had ammunition I could buy. He didn't know if I had a lot of money on me and could buy without selling the hides or not, and I sure as hell didn't let him know. He took a look at his stock and said he had some cartridges that'd fit my Winchester fine. Then he quoted me a price for the shells that was higher'n a cat's back. He weren't no fool. He'd buy cheap and sell expensive. But I could see that even for a few dollars I was gonna get an awful lot of ammunition for the price of just one of them grizzly hides.

The conversation lasted a long time and I got nervous thinking 'bout Wild Rose. Then I remembered I had old Cimarron and the packhorse tied to the hitching rail outside the store and somebody just might come along and relieve me of all them hides while I was talking to that knothead. So I made out that I weren't interested and started out the door. I told him that if he didn't want to pay a decent price, it was okay with me.

When I come out I seen something that give me a big shock. Standing there right beside my horse was a man looking at the hides. I swear I nearly jumped outta my skin, 'cause he looked so much like Pedro. He was 'bout the same size, dressed a little different, but he sure looked like him from behind. He was talking to another man and the voice and accent was just a dead ringer for my old friend.

I listened for a minute or two, and I seen there was some difference. I turned to the trader. "Who in hell's that big man standin' by my horse fingerin' them hides?"

The trader grinned real smartlike. "That's Baptiste Pourier, General Crook's French scout. They tell me that Crook thinks as much of him as Custer thinks of Charlie Reynolds."

I could hear there weren't much difference in the accents 'tween that big fella and Pedro when they was talking English, 'cause there weren't much difference in the accents of a greaser and a Frenchie. But I sure did like the cut of the man's chin and the way he was looking with interest at them hides.

As for the trader, he seen him in a different way. He seen that maybe I didn't like nobody looking at them hides or fingering 'em, and that I was going over there to pick a fight. He was looking for a little fun.

I stepped over to the old boy. "Well, mister, do ya like 'em?"

That old Baptiste rolled 'round like he'd been shot, took one look at me puzzled-like, and then a grin come over his face that was just as infectious as hell. It was just like old Pedro's grin—lots of teeth. I liked that fella right away. I don't take to many men, but that one, I could see, was my kinda man. He looked me up and down and seemed to get the same idea. "By gar, you him that kill these grizzly?"

"Yeah, an' two or three more of 'em."

"Why, goddamn." He grinned all over. "There are some men that hunt all their life and kill one grizzly and they's real proud. Now, you said you killed 'bout seven? Where are the others?"

"I give 'em to a friend a mine."

"Give 'em away? What the hell. Them hides are worth two hundred dollars apiece."

With that it was my turn to grin, and I looked at the trader, who was giving Baptiste dirty looks and signaling him to shut up. I started laughing. "This gentleman here just tol' me that they was real cheap nowadays an' when I asked him fer seventy-five dollars a hide, he backed off real fast."

"Oh, Bill Peters always was a goddamn thief," said the big guy. "Bill, you know those hides is worth a helluva lot more'n you offered. You can take 'em back to Chicago or Denver and sell 'em for six hundred dollars each. You know that!"

Bill Peters wormed around. "Don't think I could get that much," he said.

"Come on, cut the bullshit," Baptiste said. "You know goddamn well these hides are worth a lot of money."

I could see that old Bill Peters was getting a little hot under the collar 'bout the way Baptiste was spending his money for him. But there's one thing for sure, he weren't gonna challenge old Baptiste. That big boy could make mincemeat outta Bill Peters faster'n you could say Jack Robinson, and I bet he was just about as good with a knife as old Pedro. Maybe not, but I wouldn't wanta try it. Anyway, Bill Peters said to me, "Come on back in and we'll bargain a little more for these hides."

"Well now, my new friend," said Baptiste, "I come with you."

I could see that old Baptiste'd had a drink or two, but that didn't spoil his personality none, and I sure as hell liked him. So I said, "C'mon in here and help me deal with this border thief."

Old Bill Peters give me a hard look, but I looked him right back just as straight and hard. Then he looked kinda s'prised when he seen my eyes. Then he done like all men do. He dropped his glance and swallowed. We went on in the back room where his office was. He got out the whiskey again and old Baptiste had a drink.

That damn Peters paid me two hundred dollars a hide straight across—cubs or full-growed—and then I turned 'round and bought a hundred dollars worth of ammunition from him, which added up to 'bout two hundred rounds. Then I bought a *bandolera* that I could load the shells in to take the place of the one that them Comanches'd relieved me of when I was down on the Cimarron.

"I bet you are a good shot," Baptiste said. "You do a lot of shooting? Can you shoot pretty good?"

"Fair."

"Well, come on. We go on out there and have us a shoot. I get a gunnysack full of bottles from the bar next door and we hunt 'em."

I knowed I needed to practice some, as I hadn't been shooting much since I'd been laid up. I figured it'd be a good idea if I warmed up some.

"You go get the sack full a bottles, get your gun, an' I'll take these horses down an' put 'em in the corral," I said. "I like ta keep 'em in the shade. I'll do that just as soon as I unload these hides. They's pretty heavy, an' I don't like the packhorse havin' ta stand there all the time, just 'cause Bill Peters is tighter'n a bull's ass at fly time."

Old Baptiste busted out laughing and laughed hisself silly. When he quieted down, he said to me, "Tell me, you scout? You have Comanche moccasins."

"Nope, I'm no scout. I never done no scoutin' fer no one."

"You have Comanche moccasins. You fight Comanches?"

"No, hell no. I don't fight 'em, I hunt 'em."

With that, old Baptiste exploded again, laughing and hitting his thigh and all. "Boy, you scout. You plenty scout. You come with me. Crook send me now to meet Custer in Black Hills. Custer, he hunting grizzly out there."

"Grizzly?"

"He also going out there on big expedition to see if he can get the miners out of there, but what he really is looking for is gold and I think Custer would like to start another war with the Sioux and give 'em a bad time. Anyway, he is out there hunting and you could go with me."

"There's nothin' I'd rather do. I just cotton ta grizzly huntin'. Shore I'd like ta be one a Custer's scouts or Crook's scout. Who wouldn't? That's a fun job. But right now I got some important business that needs attendin' to an' I can't discuss it none."

"Okay, okay. You do as you like, but someday you may want to be scout. Then you look for old Baptiste. I get you fixed up good."

"That'd be fine." We shook, and my hand just passed outta sight in that big paw of his.

To make a long story short, we got our chores done. It was getting on towards the middle of the afternoon and the sun was still fairly high in the western sky, it being only late September. Him and me started outta town, which for Rawlins weren't very far. Go three hundred yards and you're out in the prairie. We started to look 'round to see what we wanted to do. Baptiste was carrying a bag of empty whiskey bottles that he'd got at the bar, and I was just carrying my rifle and my revolver and the *bandolera* full of cartridges. When we'd picked a likely place, he said, "Now, you see that kind of sand bench over there? Why don't you just go over there and put up two bottles and maybe I shoot and you shoot. No?"

I looked him square in the eye. "Whaddya mean? Ya want me ta walk all the way out there just ta put some bottles down ta shoot at?"

He give me a funny grin and shrugged. "Well, monsieur, okay, maybe I go out there and put 'em down."

"No, that's not what I mean. Hell, I don't mind goin' out there, but what's the use a walkin' clear out there just ta put out a couple a bottles. Take that bottle ya got there an' just throw it up in the air."

He looked at me real puzzled. "No. I throw him up there and he gonna bust when he hit the ground."

"It ain't gonna hit the ground," I said as I levered a round into the chamber of my Winchester. A glint come into his eye and he leaned back and threw a bottle as hard as he could, a long ways up in the air. I hadn't done much trick shooting for a long time—just once when I was messing 'round with a fella down in Albuquerque, but my shot broke that bottle 'bout three quarters of the way through the down drop. That was the hardest thing to do, but I wanted it to be spectacular. I reckon I was just showing off.

Baptiste told me that he'd done lots of shooting in his time, but he hadn't never seen nothing like that. I handed him two more bottles and told him to throw both of 'em. He took 'em in those big paws of his and wound up and throwed 'em as hard as he could. The bottles spun over and over and went separate ways. I shattered 'em real quick up in the air. When Baptiste turned to look at me that time, I could see the approval. "By God, that's damn good shooting, monsieur. Can you do that with the pistol?"

"I don't hardly know. Maybe ya oughtta try me, but right now, throw two more bottles fer my Winchester. I need the practice."

He took two more bottles and slung 'em not quite so high and I broke 'em easy. Baptiste shook his head and turned back towards town, leaving the rest of them bottles right there in the sack.

"Just a minute, Pourier. Hold on there, pardner. Now, take two a them bottles in each hand an' I'll use the revolver an' see if'n I can do any good."

He looked at me with his mouth open. "You mean I should throw four bottles up?"

"Two an' two makes four, don't it?"

He grinned again and took the bottles outta the sack. Then, crouching down on his knee and leaning forward, he pulled up in a big haul and swung 'em underhanded up in the air. I fanned the hammer on that Smith & Wesson and hit every one of 'em.

He just stood there and looked at me wide-eyed and shook his head. Meanwhile, I took some of the bottles outta the sack and laid 'em right there on the ground and throwed the gunnysack down with 'em.

Baptiste stopped grinning. He put his arm on my shoulder. "Yes, my friend, someday we go for the Sioux. You are already in the company of the scouts. Whenever General Crook or General Custer see you shoot, you ain't never gonna get home again. They are gonna keep you there all of the time. Now I know what you mean when you say 'hunt Comanches.' "

I felt real good 'bout that shooting, and that man made me feel better'n I'd felt since I'd been with Pedro. I don't know, but at that minute I felt that I could maybe lick the world. For the first time in a long while I begun to feel like my old self again.

Just as we were ready to stroll back to town, I took a wild notion to do something. Baptiste had his right arm 'round my shoulder and I reckoned we must've been all of forty yards away from the bottles that I'd left standing on the ground. Big Baptiste told me later that what I'd done was faster'n anything he'd ever seen. Even though he'd had his hand on my shoulder, he really didn't know what happened. I jumped sideways at least six feet, whirled 'round at the same time, and landed in a crouch, firing off all six shots in the cylinder. My gun made one steady roar, and when the dust floated away, all that pile of bottles was broke flat.

That did it. I never had to show Baptiste or any of the other scouts my shooting or even any of the officers or soldier boys in Crook's or Custer's command, but that was years later. Baptiste'd spread my fame ahead of me by then.

On the way back to the corral where I was fixing to get my horses, Baptiste kept trying to talk me into going out with Custer in the Black Hills. It was getting kinda dark, but we was walking along pretty good, and while I was reloading my revolver he put his arm 'round me again and said, "Yes, we go to Cheyenne in six hours and from there ride four days to Blackfeet."

"What the hell're ya talkin' 'bout? Six hours ta Cheyenne? That ride's a helluva lot longer'n that."

"Oh, we put the horses in the boxcar and we go on the train."

And then, by God, it struck me! What a railroad really meant was that a three-hundred-fifty-mile ride—'bout a week's travel riding fifty miles a day and moving right along—could be done in six or seven hours on a railroad without sweating. I begun to see what it meant to have steel rails spanning the country.

I would really like to've gone with old Baptiste, but I told him, "No, not this time. Maybe when I get squared away I'll come look ya up. You'll be with Custer or Crook, won't ya?"

He nodded. "You come to see me. I am your friend."

That was kinda nice. Just as I was shaking hands with him, we heard the shriek of a locomotive whistle maybe a mile down the track. I almost lost my hat. Everybody come running outta their houses, stores, and bars, and yelled that the evening express was coming through from the East. All the folks run up to the railroad station and Baptiste and me both got the fever and we run, too. Hell, I hadn't seen a locomotive in so long I couldn't remember what it looked like. We got to the station platform and kept watching the engine's headlight coming up the tracks. It growed larger and larger, like some monster from a distant land. I ain't likely to forget watching that locomotive coming 'cross the prairie—that lantern up in front that lights the tracks, and sparks flying from the stack. It sure was a sight: awesome and noisy as hell and full of pride and strength! That big black locomotive was almost like a living thing, puffing and blowing as it thundered into the station and slowed down to a stop, its bell still ringing, like a relay horse waiting to be resaddled to go out again.

I stood up by the edge of the platform and listened to the engine while the passengers got off and a crew reloaded the mail and freight. The locomotive was panting like a beast getting its breath again 'fore it made another one of them long dashes 'cross miles and miles of track and prairie clear to the Pacific coast. Yessiree, it seemed hungry to get to the western ocean.

I couldn't help but think how the Indians called it the "iron horse." Yeah, I knowed it was made of iron and steel and it was fired by coal and steam, but it sure seemed like it was alive.

Pretty soon the whistle blowed again, so close to me that it damn near blew my eardrums out. Then, with lots of chugging and puffing and blowing and the steam busting out the sides, that locomotive went to work and started hauling the train out again on its way to California. We stood watching the lights disappear in the distance along with the noise of its going and the singing of the rails.

We went back to the corral after the train'd gone and I got my ponies and said good-bye to Baptiste.

"Don't you ever forget, I am your friend. You come be scout. Plenty fun. Hunt Sioux. Hunt grizzly," he said.

I laughed and thanked him. Then, feeling a sense of urgency, I pulled on outta there and hurried alongside of the tracks, headed west for a seven-mile ride to get back to my little Shoshone lady.

I rode along thinking 'bout this and that and the other thing that was going on in the world, but I couldn't get those steel bands outta my head. I couldn't figure out what was gonna be the result, 'cept it had to be more people coming in, things opening up, farms and such, and it had to be sure that the wild Indian'd seen his day. Weren't no way that he could keep supplying hisself in the summer and winter and keep fighting the white man when the white man had a thing like the railroad. The white man could ship horses and ammunition and supplies and Gatling guns and everything else and just keep on hammering him.

The moon come out and I could see good. I kicked old Cimarron into a good lope and we was moving out. I reckon I rode for the better part of a half hour 'fore I come up on what looked like the east ridge of the draw where our camp was. I thought how nice it was gonna be in that warm camp with the fire going and the meal cooking and that beautiful Wild Rose waiting there by the fire. How could a man ever want any more'n that? I was glad I hadn't had no whiskey. She wouldn't have liked that.

I was kinda musing along, wondering what she was thinking 'bout and what she was gonna do when she got back to the reservation and just how that was gonna work out. I was a little fearful that I weren't gonna see her again.

I was dreaming along like that when I heard a wild scream that cut right through my heart. God, it was a yell of terror that was 'bout half-scream and half-Indian yell, but I knowed right away what it was, and I kicked old Cimarron into one helluva run and angled off towards what I figured'd be the head of the spring. The country was a little rough and we had to pick our way, which weren't too easy at a dead gallop, but I didn't spare nothing.

I let go of the packhorse's lead rope. He weren't carrying nothing anyway, but he couldn't run as fast as Cimarron, and fast riding was what was needed most. I sure as hell knowed that. My heart was sinking fast. I come up over the top of that ridge and looked down on the camp. The fire was going and the kind of wickiup that Wild Rose'd made was there, just like it oughta be. I could see the rump of Wild Rose's paint horse in the light of the fire. But the worst thing I seen, something that almost drove me crazy, was Wild Rose writhing in the arms of two big, burly men—prob'ly railroad workers. They had her damn near naked and they was wrestling her down to the ground, although she was fighting like a wildcat. I could hear 'em cussing her and slapping her, but I didn't hear that for long. I rode down off'n that slope in a dead run, jumped right over the fire, and dismounted running. I grabbed one son of a bitch that'd already piled on top of her and pulled him off and whirled him 'round and hit him so hard in the face that I smashed most of his teeth. He went down in a heap, kinda fumbling. Then the other one started cussing and come after me hard. He only had 'bout five steps to take, but I seen a knife in his hand and I kicked his wrist and broke it as he come at me. Then I hit him twice, once with a right and once with a left, and he went down, too.

Then them damn fools done the wrong thing. Both of 'em reached for their guns. Them two muckers was spread apart a little bit, which made it a hard draw against two guns, but they was no match for Cat Brules and I destroyed 'em both in a roar of gunfire.

When the noise cleared, I rushed over to Wild Rose. She was lying on the ground leaning up on one arm, sobbing and shaking, and her dress was all tore up. I seen she had a real bad bruise on her cheekbone where them sons of bitches'd slapped her when she was trying to defend herself. That beautiful beaded shirt of hers was ripped open bad, and one of her breasts was showing. It looked like it was bruised.

From what I knowed of Wild Rose, she was a levelheaded girl, but that experience, plus losing her string of horses, which them bastards'd run off, just shook her to pieces. I kept holding her while she sobbed and finally asked her if she was in any real trouble.

She shook her head. "No, but if you hadn't come just then, two or three minutes later would've been too late."

I picked her up and carried her over near the fire, then put a pot of water on and made some coffee. I didn't know what else to do.

While she sat there sipping out of a cup and staring into the fire, I begun collecting our gear, went after the packhorse and found him grazing fifty yards away, and brought him into the firelight. Wild Rose looked at me kinda puzzled.

"We gotta get outta here," I said. "When they find these two dead men, they're gonna accuse us of murderin' 'em ta rob 'em. We'll never be able ta prove that this was attempted rape. There's no jury in this country that's gonna convict a white man fer rapin' an Injun girl. Far as I'm concerned, they'd look at me as a squaw man. Yep, they'd see us as just a squaw man an' his squaw who killed two fellas ta steal their payroll money. There won't be no argument strong enough ta stop 'em from lynchin' us both.

"We've gotta get outta here tonight an' put a hundred miles 'tween us an' this situation 'fore we can rest. We're gonna cover our trail the best way I know how. We're gonna ride hard ta get ta the Shoshone reservation. We'll stand a lot better chance there with that agent ya say is a good fella than we will with some mob a railroad workers here in Rawlins."

Wild Rose was no fool. She seen I was right. She begun to pull herself together and we started packing what gear we had, which weren't much. I was real proud of her, though. She'd got over her hysteria and was working steady.

We saddled up our horses and packed outta there that night. I was careful to do a good job of covering our tracks. I took a narrow ravine that I'd seen earlier. It was filled with hard rock shelves that wouldn't bear too many marks and we climbed up outta there going north.

Afterwards I went back out in the moonlight and took a willow branch that I'd cut and tried to destroy all the tracks I could find. That ain't easy in the moonlight and I'm not sure that I was successful. But there was another thing we could count on: I figured that it'd be two or three days 'fore somebody'd find those bodies, what with them being almost a mile north of the railroad tracks and up in that cottonwood draw near the spring. 'Course that was assuming none of those men's buddies knowed where they was going. There weren't no guarantee of that, but it was the best we could hope for.

Meanwhile, we had to do some hard riding. It was a little more'n a hundred miles to the Shoshone reservation from Rawlins. Both of us stretched out so's to put lots of mileage behind us. The horses done real well, being in good condition. We'd watered 'em 'fore we left the spring and again when we'd crossed the Sweetwater at dawn.

By that time the Wind River Range was towering way up there ahead of us, and by that night we was in sight of the cooking fires of the Shoshone reservation. We rested for a few hours 'til dawn broke and then saw a kind of a fort, which they called Fort Brown, and a bunch of tepees 'round it. It was nestled right at the foot of the Wind River Range and sure looked beautiful. In fact, the whole country around was some of the most beautiful I ever seen. The peaks of the range towered straight up outta the fertile plains like giant sentinels. They was great for protecting the Shoshone reservation from the howling westerlies in the wintertime. Thanks to them mountains, the wind at the Shoshone agency was practically nothing, while Casper, just a hundred miles to the east, had the highest winds in the United States.

There was lots of heavy snow on the reservation in the winter, and there being almost no wind, the moisture just sunk into the ground. During the spring thaw it made for the greenest meadows you ever seen.

The skies stretched big and blue overhead. Wild Rose told me that the streams of the Wind River country was full of trout, and that one of the creeks that run through Sinks Canyon went underground for several miles and then come out again. The hills was dotted with bighorn sheep, and the elk played in the meadows. There was lots of deer around and wild geese and ducks and prairie chickens. It was an Indian paradise, ideal for hunting and fishing.

When we got near the village, the dogs begun to bark and people come out to see what was going on. Normally there'd be some warriors move out with some firearms, but it was easy to see that there was only the two of us on horseback leading a packhorse. That hardly amounted to anything that'd be dangerous. When we got in close, Wild Rose begun to call out in Shoshone and pretty soon she was getting an answer, and then a lot of happy voices and other signs that she was recognized.

I guess out of some sort of modesty she asked me not to mention nothing 'bout the incident the night before. Maybe women are funny 'bout such things, but I respected her wishes and never made a peep.

I asked her how she was gonna explain that awful bruise on her cheek and she said I shouldn't worry 'bout that none. She said she'd tell 'em she'd had a bad fall off her horse, then she looked at me with a wry smile.

When we got closer, Wild Rose was calling back and forth to others and it was plain they was real happy that she'd returned home. I reckoned they'd give her up for being lost after she'd been away so long with her brothers. It was gonna be great for her to be home, but there was gonna be some sad moments when she told the whole story.

When she come in close to the village, she slipped off her horse and begun hugging everybody. There was lots of screaming and laughing.

When she begun to explain 'bout me, she talked so fast that even though I knowed a good many Shoshone words by that time, I couldn't get very much out of it.

I made out something 'bout a friend and 'bout guns and one or two other things, but they didn't make a lot of sense, 'cept I knowed that she was telling 'em that I'd been taking care of her, and that I was a respected friend. I knowed that for sure, 'cause they was real friendly with me, smiling and shaking hands and doing lots of good things.

After a bit, a tall, good-looking warrior come up and I gathered he was one of Wild Rose's cousins. She tried hard to tell him all 'bout me, 'cause I could see she was glancing at me, and then she brung him over and we shook hands. I could see he was appraising me all along, and I got the idea that I'd passed the inspection. He was a fine fella hisself, and if'n he wanted to be friendly, I did too. I figured he was the kinda man who could be a real friend. Wild Rose said his name was Wesha and that he was the favorite son of Chief Washakie, who was famous all over for his statesmanship.

All the time we was coming up from the camp at Hatch Gulch, I'd had a very strange feeling 'bout Wild Rose. Although it was fun being with her, and we'd had a wonderful time, I kept looking at her and wondering what was gonna happen when we got her home to the Shoshone people. I did lots of thinking 'bout whether I'd ever see her again, and the thought of it made my heart ache.

Every step we got towards the reservation was putting me into deeper and deeper gloom, 'cause I felt that when we got there I was gonna lose her. I didn't expect I'd have much luck talking marriage, 'cause the Shoshone was noted for being awful particular. They seldom, if ever, married out of the tribe.

'Sides that, there'd be plenty of warriors looking for a girl as beautiful as she was. I prob'ly wouldn't have a chance even if Indian law permitted it.

I'd asked Wild Rose several times on the ride what she was gonna do when she got back to the reservation. I had a hard time making her understand what I meant. What I was trying to find out was if she was gonna be living with other friends, or her old man, or if she was gonna get married. When she found out what I was talking 'bout, she told me in a pleasant and lighthearted way that she was going back to her father's tepee and she'd wait there for some warrior. She'd live with her father 'til someone courted her and took her away. She said that her father'd never give her to no ordinary warrior. He'd have to be very special and, looking at me coyly, she said the bride price'd be very, very high. She said she didn't know of anybody right off who could pay it.

That afternoon I found out what she'd meant. She took me to her father's tepee, and I seen right quick that he was a grumpy kinda person. When I met him, Wild Rose was talking all the time and I could tell she was kinda building me up, saying how many things I'd done for her and how she'd never've made it without me.

The old man seemed like he weren't gonna give me credit for much of anything, and was real casual 'bout welcoming me or being glad of something I'd done for her. To be real honest, I didn't take to him, either. I begun thinking of a name for him in my mind, and I decided to call him "Old Stoneface."

That's what the homecoming was like. Fun for everybody and sad for me. I didn't know how I was gonna get along without seeing that Shoshone girl every day like I had for the last several months.

I had to say good-bye to Wild Rose in a very formal way in front of everybody, and make a formal presentation of the grizzly skins to her and to her father. She took the one she'd kept for me and told me she was gonna make me a coat as a present for escorting her back home. She seemed all light and happy that she was back, but I sure didn't feel that way myself. It become apparent that I weren't gonna be too welcome 'round her father's tepee and that I prob'ly weren't gonna see much of her from that time on. That made me plenty downhearted.

After a while Wesha come up and Wild Rose interpreted and said that I was to go with Wesha to meet his father, Chief Washakie. We went down through the camp and all of the warriors and squaws we passed was nodding and smiling and being very pleasant. I guess word'd traveled 'bout all I'd done for Wild Rose and that I was a friend of the Shoshone.

Wesha took me to his father's lodge and we stood and waited to be called inside. I reckon you don't just enter a chief's lodge without plenty of ceremony. When the chief come out, I could see why everyone, including his son, held him in such great respect.

He was one of the finest-looking men I ever seen. I reckon at that time he must've been seventy years old. He had snow-white hair and piercing black eyes that seemed to take in everything. I never did know exactly what the old man said, but from the few words I picked up, it sounded like he was saying that they rejoiced at having one of their daughters back. The man who'd took care of her during that time, and seen to her safety 'til she was home, was a friend of the Shoshone and was welcome in their village.

Wild Rose got the word out to some older squaws that we was both as hungry as could be, and she took me over to a place where they'd feed me. Then she excused herself and went off. I wondered if I'd ever see her again. I kept thinking all the time, Brules, ya gotta be a damn fool. Why'd ya bring that girl back here? Couldn't ya've found some excuse ta keep her out in the rain? Ya would've had her fer the rest a your life but, no, ya dang fool, ya done walked inta the trap, brung her back ta her father's lodge, an' now she's gonna marry some young Shoshone buck.

It was them thoughts that made me feel low when Wesha come back to see me after I'd been fed. He invited me to come to his lodge and meet his family. He had two wives and they was good-looking girls. I sat over on the male side of the lodge and they sat on the female side. They didn't pay no attention to me. Everything was for Wesha. Meanwhile he was gracious and we smoked the pipe together. He invited me to stay and said I could put my things on the male side of the lodge and that I'd be welcome there.

We smoked the pipe a little more 'fore I finally answered, being real careful so's not to offend him. I explained that I'd been riding and hunting on the plains and in the mountains for the last six summers and winters and I'd been sleeping in the open for so long that I wouldn't be nothing but real uncomfortable in a house—even a home as nice as his. I realized that it was an unusual invitation and I'd had to be real gracious in my refusal, but I had to tell him the truth.

Wesha had a great reputation and he lived up to every bit of it. He was a tall warrior with a wonderful-built chest, shoulders, and arms that was just as solid as a rock and shaped real graceful. His manners was graceful, too, befitting the son of a chief. He smiled at my explanation and nodded as if he understood. It was like him saying that he used to do that and if he hadn't had a couple of wives, he'd do the same thing.

He told me that he'd heard all about my shooting ability and he'd like to see some of it. Not wanting to waste much ammunition, and having a bad feeling 'bout showing off in front of strangers, I suggested that we go hunting together. He went for it like a trout'd go for a fly. He said that right then was as good a time as any. It was early October, and them elk cows was still in heat and the bulls was bugling all through the mountain valleys.

When he said that, it cinched the deal. I asked when he'd like to go and he give me to understand that he'd be ready by dawn the next day. I told him I'd be camping at the entrance to Sinks Canyon and if he'd just come by, I'd have my horse ready and we'd go on from there. There was something 'bout the way he responded to me and the way I liked him that I figured we'd be good friends.

Sure enough, Wesha was there at dawn and I was up and ready to go. He was a fine-looking Indian, sitting on a fine-looking paint horse. He rode like he was part of the animal. I felt like I could do the same, and after watching me, I think he come to the same conclusion. I rode Cimarron with one of them little antelope saddles with just loops of hide for stirrups. I tied a bag of pemmican, a rifle scabbard, my ammunition *bandolera*, and a rolled-up blanket to the back of the saddle, and we headed up towards the high country. That was the beginning of my friendship with Wesha, one of the finest men I ever knowed.

We hunted real casual the first day and killed a couple of young spikes for the meat. We dressed and butchered 'em out and hung the meat on the limbs of a tree that we marked pretty good. Wesha worked right along with me, 'cause he knowed the value of keeping the meat fresh—even though he regarded what we was doing as squaw's work.

Late that afternoon I killed a big bull with a long shot way up on the side of the mountain. It was near dark when we reached him, but we could see that he was a dandy. He had a fine spread and a thick boss and six points on one side and seven on the other. Wesha weren't inclined to dress him out 'cause it looked like a lot of work, but he did take some back straps off and I took the cape and head and horns.

That amused Wesha, 'cause Indians aren't trophy hunters as a rule. I knowed someday I'd want that trophy in a cabin if I ever had one. When I'd done what I needed to preserve the animal, I volunteered to stay up there on the side of the mountain with the dead bull and camp all night and have him pretty well butchered by morning. Wesha nodded his approval and told me he'd go down to his tepee and bring up one or both of his squaws with his son and some packhorses and let 'em finish the job in the morning. 'Sides that, he said, his son needed hunting experience and it'd be good if he went along. I was pleased 'bout that, but I knowed that Wesha was really going down to the village to get help 'cause he'd told me in no uncertain terms that skinning and butchering was squaw work. Then, too, I reckon he'd wanted a reason to go down and see one of his young squaws that night.

I couldn't blame him one bit. They was real pretty girls. Fact is, they was more'n pretty. I didn't like to let myself think that way, 'cause I knowed it was poor business for me to conduct myself in a bad way 'round that village and get a poor reputation. As a matter of fact, even though I was there for quite some time, I kept my eyes to myself and never tried to approach none of them Shoshone girls.

Wesha brung his squaws up the next morning just like he'd promised, and they set to work on what was left of the bull, but I'd had most of it done and hanging on a tree. Anyway, they packed it on the horses and went off. Wesha said he'd send his son back to the village to guide the squaws up to where we was located as soon as we made another kill.

We done good the second day. We killed five elk and a nice mule deer. We gutted 'em and let it go at that. Wesha sent his oldest boy, who was 'bout eleven, down to get the squaws and they was up there early the next morning going to work.

We was out maybe a week altogether on that hunt and come in
with enough food to feed half the village. Everybody was impressed
and Wesha kept telling 'em 'bout the kinda shooting I done. To be
truthful, I did make several long shots that I wouldn't normally try,
but in the interest of getting meat for the winter, I went at it as if it was
just plain business. I killed two fair-sized bighorn rams and a couple
of mule deer bucks, but most of it was elk. I don't remember how
many animals we brung in, but I got fancy with my shooting. Every
time I did, Wesha'd raise an eyebrow, stop and fill his pipe, sit down
and smoke, say nothing and think it over—typical Indian style. He
knowed a good gun when he seen one and he knowed a valuable
friend. He seen both in me.

That fall, me and him hunted the Wind River reservation from one
end to the other and brung in lots of game. As time went on, Wesha
had a lot more squaws working on picking up the meat and a lot of
young boys running as messengers from everywhere we went.

The squaws seemed to think it was great fun when they'd come out
in groups after we had a few animals down. They'd sing and rejoice
and act as if they was going to a picnic. I s'pose that did break up the
monotony of village life. They got to ride way up in the high mountains, see more game, and look over the kills that we'd made. All that
time I never seen Wild Rose once. She never come out with any of the
other squaws to join in the fun. I knowed she weren't a loner and that
she was real sociable with people of her kind, but since I never seen
her I wondered if maybe she was avoiding me.

Now that she was back in her village and going her way, maybe
I'd served my purpose and she didn't need me no more. Bitter
thoughts like that went outta my mind real quick when I stopped to
think 'bout the kinda person she was. She just weren't that way. If
she was your friend, she'd be your friend forever. But I sure missed
seeing her.

As for Wesha, I liked him more and more. He seemed to know that
I was a wild man, born to the mountains and forests and the roaring
streams and the wind on the prairie. Him being an Indian with a soul
close to that, he didn't have no trouble understanding my ways. Fact
is, I think he admired me, maybe more'n most whites, for the way
I was.

'Course it weren't too long 'fore the word of my shooting ability got 'round that Shoshone village. One day Wesha told me in the best way he could that the Indians wanted to see me do some shooting. Wesha seemed proud that my skills was the curiosity of the village at that time. I protested that I shouldn't waste ammunition, there being a shortage. Then Wesha took me to meet Doctor Irwin.

We walked into the agency and old Doc Irwin greeted me like he'd heard all 'bout me. I liked that old man. He was different than most Indian agents. I reckon the average agent was always working the Indians for everything he could get out of 'em—cheating 'em outta rations and all that stuff. That weren't Doc Irwin's way. Him and his wife'd always had the Indians' interests at heart and they was trying all the time to see that they got a square deal. Irwin was working to keep the government in Washington, with all them blowhard congress-men, off'n their backs and was making a real effort to jack Washington 'round to make good on the promises made to the Shoshone people.

Doc Irwin was full of information. He'd seen it all happen, from the time the Shoshone reservation was forty-four million acres to when it was cut down to 'bout three and a half million. It later got cut to half of that. All that time, Irwin told me, Chief Washakie'd been a friend of the whites. The one thing that the chief always bragged about was that no white man's scalp ever hung in a Shoshone lodge. The chief was smart enough to see that he couldn't buck the white man and he decided real quick that he'd better get on their good side. By doing that, he'd made some powerful friends. 'Course the pressure of all them land-hungry whites moving west kept crowding his people into a smaller and smaller space, which I reckoned was gonna happen anyway, yet he'd managed to keep his people in better shape than most of the Indians, some of which'd been plumb wiped out. It was easy to see that the Shoshone had one of the very finest reservations in the country, unlike them vicious Comanches.

I remember how when we went to see old Irwin he'd spoke real kind with me 'bout the Indians asking to seeing my shooting. He told me he'd like to see it, too. When I said my piece 'bout ammunition, he told me he'd just received a shipment of Winchester .44 stock and that he'd advance me some against a fur trade, which I could pay back later. I reckon that was real neighborly and right of him, but I also think he had in mind the interest of the Shoshone Indians, 'cause he wanted to show 'em that this white man, who was Wesha's friend, weren't all useless and might be handy to have 'round the next time the Blackfoot or the Arapaho raided, or the next time people begun getting hungry and game was scarce. Him and Wesha talked a minute and decided to set up a kinda show, picking a special day and planning a feast afterwards. Then Wesha left, and me and Doc Irwin started talking 'tween ourselves.

"I heard you once did some fighting with the Comanches south of the Arkansas," he said.

"Yessir."

"Well, I never had any contact with them, even in their heyday, when they were the toughest fighters on the plains. But I certainly heard about the ferocity and the unspeakable atrocities they committed for so many years along the Texas-Mexico borderland. I guess they were the most cruel, backward, and desolate of all the savage tribes."

"Could be."

"Yes indeed. I'm sure it's true, yet it seems so strange."

"How's that?"

"You see, a long time ago they were once a part of the Shoshone nation."

"The hell ya say!" I stood bolt upright, plumb shocked and indignant. "That can't be. There ain't no way these beautiful, gentle Shoshone is part an' parcel a them stinkin' Comanche skunks. They's as different as day an' night. I lived among 'em both an' there ain't nobody can tell me that."

"Well," said Irwin, "did you know that they speak the same language?"

"Yah, I did, come ta think of it, 'cause Wild Rose an' her brothers was talking to 'em an' they didn't seem ta have no trouble. But I didn't give it much thought at the time."

"Yes, that's right." Doc Irwin paused for a minute. I stood there swaying, trying to collect my thoughts.

"Of course," he went on, "there is a difference in dialect, like between a Scotsman and a Connecticut Yankee, but the basic language is the same."

My thoughts was in a whirl and I could hardly believe my ears. Yet somehow I seen that perhaps there might be something in what Irwin was saying. The language being the same'd account for me feeling uncomfortable when I'd first heard all them Shoshones talking in their village. At the time, I couldn't put my finger on it, but I seen that was what it was. Sounding like Comanche, it'd raised my hackles, yet how in the hell could that be?

"You see," Irwin continued, "about a thousand years ago the Comanche branch of the Shoshone tribe left this beautiful Wind River country and journeyed far to the south to central Texas. I often wondered myself how they could have become such horrible savages when they came from the gentle Shoshones. This was a long time before any tribe had the horse. Perhaps life was so hard in that bitter country, or perhaps they came into contact and mixed with the Tonkawas and the Karankawas, those fierce cannibal tribes along the coastal plain and the mouth of the Rio Grande. Or maybe they came under the influence of the Toltec or Aztec tribes in Mexico. Anyway, in a thousand years they were molded into a far different culture, and I agree that it is now hard to believe that they could have been related."

I declare, I was a most disbelieving and bewildered man when I left Irwin's office. There was nothing I could say, 'cause he seemed to have all the facts, but they sure went down hard.

I wandered off and done lots of thinking, but I don't reckon I solved much. To me, the Shoshones was a beautiful people, and whether or not I was a friend, and whether or not I was in love with a Shoshone girl, I had a high regard for them. I thought I knowed 'em right well, and I sure as hell knowed the Comanches. Putting them two together was like pouring poison on honey. I just couldn't get it through my head. After a few days, I turned my thoughts from that puzzle and begun to think 'bout the coming shooting exhibition.

It was a clear fall day when we done it. The light was good and there was no wind blowing, which always helps. Since Doc Irwin was careful 'bout seeing that there weren't no whiskey 'round the reservation, there weren't no whiskey bottles to use for targets, but they had some old tin cans and some medicine bottles that'd come outta an old apothecary chest. I had Wesha put 'em 'round in position where I had the sun to my back and a real clear look at everything in front of me, where there weren't nothing but rolling prairie and bright blue sky. That sky made a good background for any target. If you're trying to get off a lot of shots, throw your target in the air towards the prairie and for quite a long time it won't fall below the horizon, where it's harder to see it. If you get your shots off fast and you know what you're doing, you'll do a good job of scoring.

Everyone from the village and the agency'd gathered 'round behind me and I started first with the medicine bottles. I had Wesha throw up a couple at the same time and I busted 'em both with the rifle. We done all of them bottles that way, watching 'em shatter in the bright sunlight. I never missed and the crowd cheered.

Then I had two braves fill some cans with dirt so's they was steady and could be throwed good and high. I had 'em throw four cans up at the same time. I fired four shots with my revolver, but I knowed that I was late on my fourth one. When the young Indians run out to pick up the cans, there was holes dead center in three of 'em and the side of the fourth one was nicked. That was something they hadn't seen before.

I took an old tin plate 'bout a foot across and set it up maybe four hundred yards away. It was shining bright in the afternoon sun, and I could see it well, even though at that distance it was just a speck. I put a little spit on my thumb and rubbed my Winchester sight on the bead so's it'd glisten. Then I fired six shots freehand as fast as I could. One of the Shoshone boys run out and got the plate and brung it back and there was five holes in it—three of 'em near the center. There was one nick on the outside of the upper edge where I'd pulled the sixth shot a fraction too quick.

Then I put six cans in a row on a log at forty yards and fanned off six fast shots using my Smith & Wesson. There weren't no cans left standing.

Then for the last thing, I done the old rolling trick with the .38 and the can on the ground at twenty-five yards away, keeping it hopping and never missing a shot. That ended the exhibition and we had ourselves a fine old time feasting that night.

After that, there weren't no doubt in the tribe 'bout the kinda shooting I was able to do.

All that time, I never seen Wild Rose but twice—once when she come out for the shooting and sorta stood aside, and then once when I was down by the river and I seen her come for water. I tried to go over and speak to her, but she quickly shied away and went down and filled her jar and come up by another way so's to avoid me. I figured what'd happened was she'd just gone back to the old Indian ways, and an Indian maiden weren't s'posed to have nothing to do with a buck 'til he'd made his intentions knowed.

THE BRIDE PRICE

The next morning I went to see Wesha. I let it be knowed that I wished he'd join me in a hunt. He didn't take much persuading. He'd rather hunt than eat, same as me. Weren't long 'fore we packed our way up into the hills. It was gonna be just him and me and we was gonna be real choosy 'bout what game we took. We wandered up past Crow Butte up on the Wind River and crossed over to some wild rugged country south of the Yellowstone that they call the Thoroughfare. We got into a bunch of elk and five days later come back triumphant with our packhorses loaded down. It was during that time that I made it knowed to Wesha by sign language and the best Shoshone words I could dig up that I was interested in marrying Wild Rose.

It was then that Wesha showed hisself to be a true friend. He seemed real pleased and told me that we ought to go right away to her father and ask him for her. I wondered if my being a white man'd go against me. He said it might, but on the other hand I was knowed as a mighty warrior and the best shot in the West, and there was an awful lot of girls that'd like to be my squaw. That was comforting, but I didn't want an awful lot of girls. I just wanted Wild Rose. So I had to ask him again what I should say to her old man. He told me I'd better be prepared to part with my best horse.

During the time that I'd been staying there, I'd seen some nice horses and, using some of the money I'd got from them grizzly hides, I bought a couple more horses 'sides old Cimarron. They was good horses, but nothing like my old pal.

At first I made the mistake of thinking that the hardest thing a man had to give up for a squaw was his best horse. Then I realized just how bad that thought was. I would've given up a hundred horses for Wild Rose. I'd fallen into the old trader's habit, and it weren't worth a damn in that case.

I was even so dumb as to tell Wesha I'd give my second best horse, 'cause I didn't want to give up old Cimarron. But Wesha kept shaking his head and pointing towards my favorite horse, signing that he thought the father would consider him the right bride price for his daughter. After I happened to see Wild Rose that night, I decided I hadn't better take a chance on getting turned down.

I took Cimarron, saddled him, and picked up a dozen beaver pelts that I'd collected earlier in the fall when I went out with Wesha to Jakey's Fork. I threw 'em in a bundle on top and then, with Wesha's help, I led Cimarron over to Wild Rose's lodge and tied him outside. Then, like Wesha told me, we stepped back a ways and stood there real silent, waiting for the father to come out and cinch the deal.

Old Stoneface come out in due time and stood there pompous as Sitting Bull hisself, crossed his arms, and looked at me as though I was nothing more'n a lowly coyote. In my mind I called him Old Stoneface, but his Indian name was Never Gives, and I figured it suited him better. He looked over the horse, running his hands over the withers and the flanks, checking the legs and the belly, the chest, the throat, taking a hard look at the teeth, then stood facing us with folded arms, saying nothing.

I was getting anxious, wanting to know when we was gonna close the bargain, but it didn't seem like we was getting nowhere. I started to move and Wesha motioned for me to freeze. Both of us stood there for a long time.

Old Stoneface finally started talking Shoshone, and I couldn't understand a word he was saying 'cause he was talking so fast. He kept on in a singsonging way and, after a while, Wesha answered him. Then Wesha took hold of my shoulder, turned me 'round, and shook his head. He walked up and untied Cimarron, handed him back to me, and led me back to his lodge. It was real simple to see that we'd been turned down, and I was having a helluva time trying to find out what it was all about.

Wesha got the idea across to me that the man'd claimed that I thought his daughter was kinda worthless, just offering him one lousy horse and a few pelts. Actually, Cimarron was the best horse in the whole damned Shoshone camp and prob'ly was the best one I'd ever owned, 'cepting old Piebald. I reckoned he was prob'ly worth any Indian woman that ever lived. But according to Wesha, it weren't enough to close the bargain, maybe 'cause she was his only daughter.

Naturally, when I said "worth any Indian woman," I was excluding Wild Rose. She was something else. I thought it over for a couple of days and told Wesha that I wanted to offer my two best horses. We done the same thing again: tying the ponies outside the tepee, waiting for the father to come out, standing there in silence, listening to the old boy singsonging for a half hour, saying nothing, and then having to walk away with them two horses. I got a little mad when Never Gives done the same thing a week later with *three* horses.

In sheer desperation—after I'd done lots of thinking 'bout it and even gone off by myself for a day or so trying to get over my mad and seeing if'n I could get that girl outta my mind—I offered him all four of my horses and them pelts.

Damned if old Never Gives didn't turn me down again. He come outta his tepee real haughty, looked them horses over real contemptuous-like, pulled out his knife and, with four surly strokes, cut their lead ropes and turned 'em loose. It couldn't have been a bigger insult.

By that time I was real mad. It seemed like I wanted that Shoshone girl more and more each time I got turned down, 'cept I wanted her more'n anything else in the world to begin with, and I damned well knowed it, and I damned well knowed that old man had me by the throat.

I couldn't get much of an explanation outta Wesha. Every time I'd ask what I was s'posed to do next, he'd shake his head and shrug his shoulders.

I spent another two or three nights out on the prairie, looking at the stars and thinking 'bout it, rolling 'round in my blanket and not getting much sleep. Then I formulated a plan and told it to Wesha. The gist of what I said to him was that I was gonna have that girl if I had to get a whole herd of horses to buy her, and I knowed that there was two ways of doing it. One was to go out and try to round up wild horses, and the other was to go raid the nearest Indian village and steal some.

The nearest big village was some Blackfoot lodges located on the Stillwater north of the Absaroka Range. The Blackfoot Indians was the blood enemies of the Shoshone, and horse stealing is one of the finest games that Indians play. Wesha was all for it, and him and his younger brother volunteered to come along. It was late November—the time of year when Montana weather could turn fast from Indian summer into deep winter.

'Sides the village on the Stillwater, there was several villages farther up in that country all the way to the Canadian border, and we thought for sure we'd find at least one with a big horse herd.

We started out at daybreak one morning and followed the Wind River to the Big Horn Basin. That took us two days. On the third morning, when we was rounding the end of the Absaroka Range east of Granite Peak, we seen an enormous black cloud up near the Stillwater. Wesha pointed towards it and said "*tock-op.*" Although we was still in the sunshine, we knowed what it meant—one helluva snowstorm. If we was out on a raid and got caught in a blizzard, it'd not only blow the raid, but we might have a mighty hard time getting back home ourselves.

But my desire for Wild Rose was so strong, and Wesha was such a faithful and gutsy friend, that, even knowing the risks, we decided to go on and take our chances. I urged Wesha and his brother to continue on for a few miles, telling 'em that it might be just a bad squall and we'd be all right the next day. Wesha shook his head. Being the kinda man he was, loyal to his friends and understanding what I was going through, he agreed to go on for a ways, but we soon come to realize that was plumb foolhardy.

At first it started with just a few snowflakes and a cold wind blowing, but it soon got real furious. It weren't long 'fore the snow was coming down as if the clouds'd opened up and dumped the whole load on us. It was freezing cold. The temperature must've dropped thirty degrees from what it'd been just an hour before, and I could see that it was hopeless. I was real reluctant to turn back, but my Indian friends was looking at me in a way that said I must be crazy, so I finally give in.

We turned 'round and headed back as fast as we could go. We

knowed that in about six or seven miles we'd find a tributary of the Big Horn with some cottonwoods along its banks, and that was where we was gonna have to get some shelter and some wood for a fire if we was gonna survive and last out that blizzard.

By the time we reached the tributary and its cottonwoods, the blizzard was in full blast and we had a helluva time seeing more'n fifty yards ahead of us. We ducked down into the banks of the river there and quicklike got into a grove of cottonwoods and made us a fire. Knowing it was gonna be a helluva storm, we cut down some saplings and made us a kind of lean-to, or spike camp, and it was there that we stayed and lasted out that blizzard, which sure as hell would've destroyed us if we'd been out in open country. It must've deposited 'tween two and three feet of snow on the level, and we realized we was in deep trouble.

We'd give up all thought of raiding. How in hell could you drive a herd of horses through deep snow and try to keep the Blackfoot from tearing your butt off as you went? They'd be on you like a pack of wolves and you'd end up lying out in the snow without your scalp. Our problem was to get back to the Shoshone reservation, and that looked like it was gonna be awful tough.

When the blizzard cleared off the second day, it was a sparkling and beautiful morning, and we started out plowing our way through the snow. It was easy to see that the horses was gonna give out 'fore long, but we had no choice but to keep going. We finally come up on another small branch of the Big Horn that had another camping place with cottonwoods. We done the same thing as before, only we made us a better shelter 'cause we planned to stay there for a few days, waiting for the snow to melt down some, and perhaps blow off the ridges and give us some kinda chance to travel without wearing out our horses.

We did a little hunting in the cottonwoods near the stream and found some animals doing the same thing we was: getting down in them cottonwoods away from the storm. I killed a small buck early in the morning of the first day. That give us enough to eat for a couple of days. After that we begun hunting again, and Wesha killed another doe with that old single-shot cavalry carbine of his.

Unfortunately, a second storm hit us 'fore we'd really got over the first one. It was beginning to look like we might have a helluva time getting back to the reservation that winter.

We was in that camp for damn near three weeks 'fore the weather finally broke and turned fair for maybe a whole week, and we figured that the traveling'd be good enough so's we could make decent headway. By that time we was damn hungry. We'd run outta venison a couple of times and had to get by with killing anything we could— squirrels and a muskrat or two.

We started off again to get back to the Shoshone people. It was a hard two-week trip to cover something that we'd made in four days on the way up. That'll give you some idea of the conditions.

When we arrived in Wesha's village, the people come out and seemed overjoyed to see us. We looked like hell, what with being pretty ga'nt from starvation and suffering a little frostbite. Indians don't carry much hair on their face, and my beard was sticking out like a cocklebur and was froze stiff most of the time.

Wesha, instead of being disgusted with me as a friend who'd got him into a lot of trouble over his longing for some squaw, showed what kind of a true brother he was by asking me to come in and share the men's side of his tepee. Since I was in no condition to go out and camp at the mouth of the Sinks River like I'd done before, there being maybe two feet of snow around, and me with no supplies or equip-ment 'cept what I had on my back, I was more'n glad to sleep in a warm lodge and have something to eat.

Boy, Wesha's two beautiful wives was sure glad to see him. They'd been worried plenty, and I reckon they weren't looking at me with much favor for dragging him off on some crazy horse raid. 'Course I'd not let out nothing 'bout what we'd had in mind, and Wesha hadn't told 'em neither. But they knowed just the same that I'd been the influence that'd pulled Wesha away from home.

While I was there they done some mending on my moccasins and fixed some of my other clothes, which'd took a big beating for a long time. They seemed to say that if I was Wesha's guest there was nothing too good for me, and they'd do the best they could to see that I had the necessities.

On the other hand, neither one of 'em'd look me straight in the eye. Their eye contact was all for Wesha, and when they looked at him, you knowed they thought he was standing on the right hand of the Great Spirit.

It took about a week 'til the weather eased off enough for me to pack up and move out of Wesha's lodge. I thanked him very much and went back to the mouth of Sinks Canyon and took up my old camping spot. I built a lean-to shelter that was good enough to last me through the winter. I had a good place to make a fire and a place to hang game.

I had my rifle and fixings, and that was all I needed—'cept for my beautiful Shoshone girl, but that was another story. How in hell I was ever gonna make contact with her, I didn't know. But I figured that as long as I was 'round there, I'd make some attempt.

I tried to be everyplace I thought Wild Rose'd be, but she didn't come down to the river when it was froze in the wintertime. It was easy enough to get water from the snow, and I couldn't stand by her tepee and make a damn fool of myself in front of that whole village, just waiting to see her come out for anything. 'Sides, I'm sure she wouldn't have liked it.

I just couldn't figure out how come she was treating me that way. I didn't get no message or nothing. Worse yet, I didn't know but that some other buck was courting her and maybe giving me the kinda competition I could do without. I asked Wesha, and he inquired around and found out that nobody'd come to offer any horses for her. If old Never Gives's treatment of me was any example, I didn't think there was no other buck rich enough to offer more'n what I had. But I did have some bad thoughts—that maybe with me being a white man the price'd be double or triple what it would've been for a Shoshone warrior. Wesha told me that he didn't know for sure, but he didn't think so. That made me feel a little better.

Now, I did do one good thing that winter: I made a good friend outta Doc Irwin. He was a fine man. I didn't normally take to folks, but he had so much information I wanted to know 'bout that I used to stop in and see him quite a bit. We talked a lot 'bout Shoshone history and Comanche history and we made our guesses as to why they was so different in their ways.

He told me some of the problems they was having with the Bureau of Indian Affairs. He was real worried 'bout two things. First off, he didn't want to see the pressure of all the whites moving west and cutting down the Shoshone reservation, which'd already been stripped from an enormous area to 'bout a tenth of what it was. The second thing that worried him was that he'd heard some rumors 'bout there being no place in Colorado to handle the Arapaho. Some of those damn fools in Washington was talking 'bout maybe moving the Arapaho onto the Shoshone reservation.

What them bureaucrats didn't understand was that the Shoshone and the Arapaho was mortal enemies. What mixing two hostile tribes together amounted to was cutting the Shoshone reservation in half. Irwin, being the agent, didn't look forward to the kinda trouble that dumb plan'd produce.

That's what we hacked over for a time, but I didn't tell him nothing 'bout Wild Rose or my feelings, 'cause I thought maybe it was too personal and I didn't want to drag him into it. I had to talk to brother Wesha on that subject.

One day I approached Wesha's tepee and waited to be invited in, which happened in quick order. I sat there and told him that I'd been wintered up for two months and I hadn't seen Wild Rose a'tall. I had no idea what she was thinking. I didn't know whether she cared for me and, if she did, whether she'd give up since I'd been unable to come up with the bride price.

I was plumb fed up with the whole thing and sick and worried. I figured I weren't doing no good 'round there, so I thought 'bout maybe heading south. I figured I'd go down and winter in that beautiful country 'round the redstone canyons of the Colorado. Maybe I could pick up the Green River where it crossed the railroad west of Rock Springs and follow it on down into that country 'round the Bow Knot and perhaps even farther down to where the Colorado and the Green come together. I thought that'd be a great place to winter over.

There's lots of scrub timber in them canyons, they didn't usually have much snow, and there was protection from the wind by the warm cliff walls. There was all kinds of deer in there, too. I'd seen that once before, and I thought maybe that'd be a good place for a wild man like me to lay up and see what was happening.

From there I could go on down south—maybe clear into Mexico, I didn't know. The way it was then, I weren't doing no good a'tall. I reckoned I was gonna have to get farther away from the Shoshone camp in order to forget that girl and my desire for her and all the trouble I was bringing to everyone.

Wesha listened and smoked his pipe with me and then he said that whatever I wished to do, I would always be his brother. He understood my wanting to go a long ways away and it was too bad when a squaw spoiled things for everybody.

On the other hand, he pointed out, there'd only be maybe two or three more moons 'fore spring'd break and then we could try the raid for horses again. Well, that's the kinda man Wesha was. Lots of fellas would've said that we tried it once and it didn't turn out so good and I don't believe I want to help you out on this again and you don't seem to have your medicine together. Not Wesha. If I wanted to go on a horse raid, he was ready to go, providing that conditions was practical. He well knowed that a man could get killed real easy on them raids. That was part of the Indian way of life. On the other hand, he knowed he was gonna get a cut of the spoils. He also prob'ly knowed that I'd go by myself, 'cause I was going whether anybody went with me or not, and he weren't gonna allow that.

All the time I was talking, them two beautiful squaws of his was sitting over on the women's side of the tepee, sewing moccasins and minding their own business. When I mentioned I was going south— maybe clear to Mexico—I seen the oldest look up quickly and then turn her head right back to her work. No Shoshone wife'd give more'n a side glance to a male guest in the tepee.

While we was smoking the pipe and mulling over what I'd been saying, there was a call outside the tepee. Wesha got up and went out. I figured it was one of his relatives, and they was speaking fast in Shoshone. I couldn't make out what they was saying, so I just sat there smoking my pipe and meditating on what he'd said.

The squaws was busy, their fingers flying as they done their sewing. Then the damnedest thing happened. I guess it never would've happened under normal circumstances in a Shoshone home. The older of Wesha's two wives, who'd had her head down working hard, spoke slow and distinct, "She waits for the sign of the Cat!"

I damn near jumped outta my shoes when I heard that. She'd spoke slow and deliberate and I knowed enough Shoshone so's I hadn't missed the meaning. Right then and there I wanted to start a conversation with her and get more information as to how she knowed that and what she really meant, but I knowed that was futile. If I started talking to her she'd keep right on working and pay no attention to me and never say another word.

By that time my heart was pounding. I knowed I'd got a signal. Somewhere along the way one of Wesha's wives and Wild Rose'd had a conversation. If I was so dumb as to not take up that hint, then I deserved to lose that girl. Right then and there I give up my plans to go south, but I didn't say nothing to Wesha 'bout it. When he come back in, we sat smoking for a while, and then I bid him good-bye and went out to my diggings up at the mouth of the Sinks.

From that time on I made up my mind that I weren't going nowhere. I was gonna stick it out right there all winter. It weren't too bad, either, although my longing for Wild Rose was sometimes beyond bearing. But Wesha and me went hunting a lot during the winter and had lots of fun together, and that took some of the sting out of it.

Meanwhile, I done everything I could to be in a position to see Wild Rose, but I only managed it twice. Both times was under circumstances that didn't give either one of us no privacy. She just passed right on by as if I weren't around. Once I seen what I thought was a kinda quirk to her mouth which could've been the beginning of a smile. I knowed that Wesha's oldest squaw hadn't got that information outta thin air. She'd got it straight from Wild Rose, 'cause it was the kinda communication she wouldn't give less'n she knowed what she was talking 'bout. Since I'd knowed something 'bout Indian ways by then, that was good enough for me.

That winter of '74–'75 passed faster'n I figured it would. After the first two storms, the weather begun letting up some. Me and Wesha done some real hunting, but it weren't 'til early spring that conditions was such that we could go anywhere.

Then one morning Wesha come to my diggings and didn't even get off'n his horse. He just stopped long enough for me to stand up from the fire and greet him.

"Tomorrow, we leave," he said. "We must raid the winter village of the Blackfoot on the Stillwater before they fold up their tepees and move away for better grazing. They have been there most of the winter months and the feed for their horses must be short. They will have to move soon. If we do not go now, we will lose our chance."

That was just like opening the door and letting in the summer sunshine. I put on a broad grin and told Wesha, "My brother, it's good news ya brung. Tomorrow mornin' at sunrise I'll be at the north end a the village ready ta ride. I'll wait fer you an' your brother."

We met at dawn and left outta there following the Wind River down to the Big Horn Basin. We stayed west of the Big Horn River and headed for the country north of the Absarokas, where we picked up a heavy Blackfoot trail and followed it 'til we spotted a village on the Stillwater with a good horse herd.

We done a nice job of sneaking up on that camp at night and running off most of the horses. We kept 'em moving all through the night and all the next day. Time and again Wesha and me'd ride to a height and look back for the Blackfoot pursuit we figured was sure to come.

In the middle of the second day we seen a dust cloud in the distance behind us and knowed right away what it was. It was old stuff to me and I told Wesha just what I wanted to do. If he and his brother'd keep moving the horse herd on, I'd ambush them Blackfeet and give 'em something to think about—something that'd discourage any more of 'em from coming after us.

I found a nice spot where two mesas come close together with a peculiar formation of rock pillars on both sides that made a natural gateway. We run the horse herd right 'tween 'em and Wesha and his brother kept right on going. I tied my horse outta sight in some trees, and climbed the side of the bigger pillar and settled down to wait. We was in Crow country, but the Blackfeet didn't give a damn. They wanted them horses back.

I'd picked my place well, looking down on a narrow defile where there weren't no easy way for a chase party to scatter and hide 'til long after I'd got through shooting.

Then I begun thinking 'bout it. There I was with a repeating rifle and a *bandolera* full of cartridges: old dead gun Brules setting in perfect ambush with them Blackfeet coming after their horses. It was gonna be one helluva slaughter.

I felt kinda funny 'bout that. I didn't have nothing against them Blackfeet, not like I'd had against the stinking Comanches. Blackfeet never done me no harm, and all they was doing was coming after them horses we'd stole from 'em. You couldn't hardly blame 'em for that. It didn't seem really right that I should kill maybe a dozen or so just on account of they was eager to get back what they figured was rightfully theirs. Sure, I could do it easy, being the rifleman I was, but just 'cause I could didn't seem to make it right.

I pondered some more. Hell, I thought, I gotta kill 'em. If'n they keep on coming an' catch us, they'll tomahawk the hell out of us an' take their horses back. That's what they come fer. Horse stealin's just a game with Injuns. They know all 'bout it from both sides. If'n it was the other way 'round, they'd shore as hell kill us.

Yet, somehow it didn't seem right. Unbeknownst to them, they was up against the best gunman in the West. I thought 'bout it a little bit and then remembered something Wild Rose'd told me: "You are a legend. It is known to all tribes that when the gun of the Cat Man speaks, it speaks with the tongue of death. This is not hidden. All Indian nations know this."

I could hardly believe that my reputation'd spread that far, but there might be a bit of truth to it. If so, I could just possibly do something to save a lot of Blackfoot lives, providing I weren't risking my own too much. I sure as hell was against that. Anyway, I decided to be a little merciful. Indians always had spirits that could do all sorts of things. They was suspicious and fearful by nature. Maybe if the knowledge of the Cat was knowed throughout all the tribes like Wild Rose'd said, the Blackfeet'd take some heed of it.

I knowed by the position of the dust cloud that them avengers was still maybe twenty minutes away, so I rounded up a few little pieces of wood and two or three sticks that was 'bout two inches thick and maybe four or five feet long. Then I done a foolish thing, but I thought it was right. I started a fire right quick and burned them sticks 'til they was charred. That took 'bout ten minutes. I was getting a bit twitchy, 'cause I didn't know how far away them avengers was. I only knowed they was closing the distance fast.

When I had my sticks charred like I wanted 'em, I stamped out the fire. Then I run on down to the entrance of the ambush place 'tween the two mesas and, right there on the big pillars of rock on both sides, I painted the sign of the Cat. I done a good job. I made a big eye and all the rest of it that goes with the Cat. Them signs on both pillars looked like the gateway to hell.

If Wild Rose was really right 'bout all them tribes knowing the sign of the Cat, then they knowed not to trespass no farther, 'cause back of that sign was the stiffest shooting rifle in the West and it couldn't mean nothing but death to them that passed.

'Course them damned Blackfeet might've been so stupid they'd never heard of it. Prob'ly they'd just come pouring through and I'd have to do something 'bout it. I was prepared either way. I set myself down in a nice little hole with my rifle barrel leaning on a ledge of rock and measured the distance to the open gap where them two pillars stood, knowing it to be 'bout a hundred thirty yards. I just lay there quietlike, got my breath steady, and settled down like I always done when I was ready to do some serious shooting.

Pretty soon I could hear the thundering of the ponies, first kinda far off and then coming on fast. I could hear lots of yipping and yelling. Then it seemed the rush stopped and they was milling 'round, yelling and arguing among theirselves. When the yelling and the hollering quit, I knowed they was talking it over. I had to sit there and wonder whether they'd take my advice—whether they'd pay attention to the sign of the Cat—or whether I was gonna have to kill 'em all.

My question was soon answered. There was a big yip and yelling again and then through the gap come three warriors riding like hell, rifles held high in their hands, naked to the waist, their ponies pulling for all they was worth. They hadn't gone thirty yards past the opening when I killed all three of 'em. They peeled off'n their horses and bounced into the bushes. The horses went one way and another and I don't rightly remember how they passed by, but they was riderless.

Suddenly all the noise on the other side of them pillars stopped and there was just a murmur. Then there was some more stomping and some more horses neighing and puffing, but pretty soon that sound begun fading away. After a while it was almost completely gone. I moved up real easy alongside of the hill away from the narrows. I could still protect it if they wanted to come back, but mainly I could see what was going on outside of the ravine. I soon seen what I'd wanted, and it made my heart real glad. There was a whole line of Blackfoot riders trotting away to the north, going back to where they'd come from. They was giving up their horse herd. They was so spooked by the sign of the Cat that they hadn't even bothered to come in and get the bodies of their friends I'd killed. That was most unusual and I felt real spooky 'bout it. Maybe it was a trap. Nobody figured an Indian was a dead Indian 'til he was sure, and that usually took 'til the next afternoon.

Anyhow, it'd worked. It seemed to do the job. I lay real quiet for a long time, watching them Blackfoot ponies going off in the distance on the same trail they'd come in on, headed north to their home range. Their actions almost said to the warriors they left behind, If you three hadn't been so stupid, you'd never've defied the sign of the Cat. That's a powerful evil spirit that no man can challenge.

'Course I don't know exactly what they'd said, but there was no doubt that they was going home. I lay still for a half hour, then, real cautiouslike, I crawled down to the bodies of them three slain warriors. One of 'em was carrying a lance, but the other two had rifles and I almost jumped with glee when I seen they was 1873-model Winchesters, the newest rifles in the country. They was the finest things Winchester'd ever produced. How those savages'd got them new weapons when our cavalry boys was still shooting single-shot carbines is more'n I can say, but they'd prob'ly got 'em from the traders on the reservation. There was lots of crooked stuff going on in them days on the reservations and lots of people was filling their pockets in the process.

It didn't make no difference to me. Them rifles was priceless. They was the first 1873 Winchesters I'd ever laid hands on. I'd heard tell they shot the same caliber bullet as mine, only with a larger load. That meant you could only get thirteen shots in the magazine and one in the chamber, making fourteen instead of the seventeen that my gun had. But they shot a faster bullet that flew flatter and had a longer range. That I knowed, but the thing I didn't know 'til I felt it was what a different gun it really was.

I reckon that my 1866 Winchester was more akin to the old Kentucky rifle and later the Hawkins. The 1866 Winchester simply hadn't got rid of the nose-heavy barrel. When you'd throw the gun up, you had to use extra muscle to keep it up and steady. With the 1873, the balance 'tween the barrel and the stock was just 'bout perfect. The gun come up as nice as anything you ever felt and slipped right into place on your cheek and shoulder. It took 'bout half the effort to hold the sight on target.

I searched the body of the first warrior and found something I didn't like much: a cavalry cartridge belt carrying maybe twenty rounds that the varmint was wearing 'round his waist. It had a cavalry buckle made in London. I took it and moved to the next Indian, who was only 'bout six or seven yards away, and took his '73 as well. His cartridge belt had six rounds.

It was pitch-dark by then, but I still kept crawling, dragging all three rifles as I worked my way back outta there. I kept on like that for a while 'fore I eased up into a low crouch, moving as silent as I could 'til I come to where my horse was tied in the trees.

It didn't take me long to mount up, although it was real awkward packing them rifles without no scabbards or slings. I hung tight and rode hard through the whole night. At daybreak I seen a dust cloud

maybe thirty miles away. I figured it was the horse band that Wesha
and his brother was herding.

I could see that Wesha'd kept dropping back from the herd of
horses and looking for me at every rise. When he seen me the first
time, I was 'bout three miles away, loping along on a floundering
horse. It weren't long 'fore we was united and he went into a war
dance when he seen them rifles. I give him one of the 1873s and you
would've thought I'd give him the sun. He knowed it was the best rifle
on the frontier, but the Shoshone'd never been able to get any. I heard
that he kept his 'til he died.

When Wesha and his brother and me rode up towards the Shoshone lodges, the whole place went crazy. Most Indians like to lie
'bout their hunting parties and their war parties, but the one thing
they never do among theirselves is take credit from one brave to
another for their deeds. Right quick Wesha told the warriors and the
squaws that'd gathered 'round 'bout the horse raid and that it was me
that'd done the rear guard work of stopping them sixteen Blackfoot
warriors and that I'd done it single-handed. They'd all saw me shoot
and knowed I could do it.

There was lots of excitement and everybody run off to prepare for a
big victory dance that night. Me and Wesha, 'specially me, had much
more important business. With the help of a couple of young bucks
and Wesha's brother, we'd been holding the horse herd out away from
the village while Wesha'd been giving the explanation to the elders.

Now me and Wesha, whooping and hollering, come riding in back
of the horse herd right through the middle of the Shoshone village. All
hell broke loose: Squaws and braves and everyone else come running
outta their tepees, wondering if they'd been caught in a charge.

We yipped and ki-yied our way right on through, stopping them
ponies right in front of my Shoshone girl's tepee. Old Stoneface come
outta the tepee with lots less dignity than he'd showed before. The
thundering of all them horses whirling 'round, and the yipping and ki-
yiing, got even his curiosity up. Maybe he was even a little spooked.

Old Stoneface's Shoshone name, Never Gives, sure suited him. He
was the stingiest old man I ever knowed in my life, and he was also
greedy. When he seen all them horses milling 'round, his eyes bugged
out. Wild Rose come out, too, all flushed and excited and clapping
her hands.

By then I was able to talk to Wesha right good and I asked him to tell Never Gives, "Here's a whole bunch a horses—the bride price a Wild Rose."

Old Never Gives could tell by the look on my face that he was either gonna accept 'em or I was gonna drive the whole herd over his tepee and take his daughter anyway. My blood was up and I figured I was the toughest, wildest man this side of the Missouri. There weren't nothing gonna stop me. I wanted that girl bad, and I was gonna bed her that night.

Wesha was caught up in the excitement as well, and I reckon he told the old man a thing or two, 'cause he sure rang out in Shoshone loud and hard. He kept shouting and whooping and hollering all through his talk. Then he made me show the rifles, and that 'bout cinched the deal. Wesha later told me that Never Gives didn't want to give up his daughter less'n he found someone who was a real warrior. That's what Wesha said, but I didn't believe him. I think Old Stoneface was greedy and knowed he could get a big bride price for a girl as pretty as Wild Rose.

It didn't matter noway, though, 'cause I got the girl—although I didn't get to bed her that night. The deal was made then and there, and it was all set for her to become my wife the next day. Wesha saw to all the ceremony. It weren't much of a wedding, 'cept that Wild Rose was dressed in her best white buckskin and I had to ride in with Wesha and his brother and formally present the horses.

We didn't let Old Stoneface have the whole bunch of 'em. I took enough to make a good pack string and let Wesha pick a few for him and his brother. Since I didn't have no tepee to take Wild Rose to, I mounted her on a good horse and we headed up-country with me leading the pack string.

It took three horses to carry all our stuff. It seemed like Wild Rose'd gathered all kinds of things that she wanted to have with her, and I got to wondering whether she'd been anticipating this day for a long time.

I led the first horse on our pack string and she rode beside me. When we was outside of the village and far enough away, what she considered a decent distance, she reached over and we rubbed noses. Then we laughed and sang and hugged and rubbed noses again, and then I told her that I was gonna show her the white man's kiss. She blushed and giggled for quite a while, but I finally got her to put her lips against mine and she seemed to come alive and get interested.

We rode up the Wind River to 'bout where the town of Dubois is now. We found a stream there that made a beautiful waterfall and we camped in the green meadow. She made camp as quick as anything I ever seen. We didn't have a lodge with a travois 'cause things'd all happened too fast and there weren't no way for us to collect one, so I promised her we'd have the nicest one in all the land when we come back from our honeymoon.

Meanwhile, she made out real good with what we had. She made a respectable wickiup outta alder branches and got a fire going while I unpacked the horses. When she finished she called to me to bring the bear hides over to the fire. I seen that she'd made a coat out of each of 'em—the small one for her and the big one for me. She said she'd give the biggest bear to her father to try to persuade him to give in to my bargain. She was afeared I'd get discouraged and never come back.

"Oh, Brules, you don't know how I missed you!" she said. "When I came to the village of my people, I knew that I had to go back and live in my father's lodge and act like a young maiden waiting for some warrior to come and get her, but there was only one warrior in all the world that I wanted to touch me.

"I didn't understand why it took you so long to decide to bargain for me. When you didn't come around, my heart ached and I kept wondering what the matter was, what I'd done wrong, or whether you'd seen some other girl that you liked better.

"I remember we saw each other once or twice, but it was not my place to make any sign that I knew or liked you. No Shoshone maiden would ever do that. If she did, she could never expect to be married, and I couldn't bear the thought of that.

"How much of our custom you knew and understood I could only guess. It seemed to me you took a long time to do anything, and sometimes I got very angry with you, but I could do nothing about that. I wanted no one else and I could only wait. Oh, Brules, my heart was breaking. Then when I found out that you were bargaining for me with my father, I was so thrilled I almost died. I kept watching through a hole in the tepee to see what was going on between you and my father. I could hear my father's voice and all the terrible things he was saying to you, and you and Wesha could say nothing. But my father berated you in every way. Perhaps you didn't understand, but he said what a stingy poor man you were to offer him only one horse.

"I knew what you thought of Cimarron, and I knew what a fine horse he was, and I knew if you would offer your best horse, that meant that you loved me better than you loved him. That is something any Shoshone squaw would be proud of. I was very angry with my father when he refused your offer, but he was stubborn and told me to be silent and to behave like a proper Shoshone girl.

"I didn't know if you would come back or not. I was afraid that you were glad to get Cimarron back and not have to give him away for just an Indian girl. When you came with all your horses and some beaver pelts as well, I was so proud and pleased that I was beside myself. Then I heard my father call you all kinds of names, saying what a poor suitor you really were and how worthless your gifts were and that if you thought you were going to get his daughter that easy, you must be crazy.

"I'm sure you couldn't understand everything he said, and I was grateful for that, for if I had been you, I would have been so angry I would have gone away and never come back to our tepee again. I was so afraid of that that my heart almost burst. I pleaded with my father again and then got angry and said some very bad things. He told me to be silent or he'd give me a whipping, but I knew he was just talking, for he'd never do that. I was more afraid that he would treat me like he did my older sister. She had a terrible time trying to reason with him to accept a bride price for her.

"I did not want that to happen with me, so I had to be very careful and say, 'Yes, father,' whenever he would lecture me, but I'd made up my mind that if you came back again, and I surely hoped you would, and my father didn't accept your offer, then I'd run away. Even if I was a shameless Shoshone girl, I'd throw myself at you and beg you to take me away. I was even afraid of that, because then you might discard me and never come back. Then I'd have no home and no husband."

When she got through telling me all that, I couldn't help thinking 'bout what would've happened if she'd come to me that way. You couldn't have parted me from her with wild horses, and I would've told her father to go to hell. But that weren't Shoshone custom and customs are strong among people. You have to be very careful not to disturb 'em too much or you may put troubles in your way that'd stop you from ever getting what you wanted.

Wild Rose kept on talking and telling me all kinds of things. She said that the last time I was away with Wesha and his brother, she didn't think I was going after more horses. She thought I was going hunting and that prob'ly she'd never see me again. She said she stayed in her lodge and cried her heart out for many days and didn't stop 'til she heard the thunder and the drumming of many horses coming through the village. That's when she run outside and screamed and danced with delight.

She was so proud that everybody in the village could see the kind of bride price I was willing to pay for her. She knowed then that her father could never refuse, 'cause if he did, he'd be considered the biggest fool in the village. But she also knowed that she didn't have to worry 'bout that, 'cause he was greedy and all those horses was certainly the finest offer he'd ever get for her.

Then she told me some wonderful things. She said that after we was together that night, we'd be as one person and that we'd go together not only all the rest of our lives, but all through eternity. No matter what happened, our spirits could never be separated. She wanted me to know all kinds of things 'bout her feelings that maybe I wouldn't understand if she didn't explain 'em to me.

"Men call you Brules. I remember when you told me that, how I laughed and laughed, because I thought of another name for you at the same time. You were looking at me very steady with those eyes of yours which are so beautiful and yet so strange. Yes, the palefaces call you Brules and some of them call you Cat Brules. Indians call you *to-ye-ro-co*, the big cat of the mountains—the panther. As for me, when I am around palefaces I shall call you Brules. When we are alone, I shall call you Cat, and when I want you to make love to me, I will call you Gray Eyes. It fits you well. Now, Gray Eyes, show me again how white men kiss, and I will show you how a Shoshone girl loves."

There was no other woman in all the world like Wild Rose. She stole my heart from the very beginning and she still has it and will keep it forever.

Next morning we headed for the West Fork of the Donner. Camping as we went, we crossed to the East Fork and from there up over the Shoshone Pass and down into the South Fork of the Shoshone.

We hunted and fished for three whole months there, just the two of us. I was sure that Wild Rose was as fine an Indian wife as any man ever had. She could ride as good as any man and could make and break camp in jig time, start a fire in a sleet storm, and gather roots and herbs and make stew better'n any white man ever tasted. She could cure hides and sew buckskin and gather wood, pack horses, skin a bear, and shoot a rifle. Her laugh was like sunlight rippling on water and she could keep the silence of the stars so that nature wouldn't be violated. She was obedient, faithful, sweet-smelling, clean, and made love like she was grasping for the fountain of life itself. I never knowed the equal of her and never expect to as long as I live. By any man's standards, she made a fine wife. My happiness was complete.

That country of the South Fork was wild and beautiful in them days—loaded with moose, elk, deer, and grizzly, and the streams was teeming with trout and beaver. Any man that couldn't make a good living there just weren't no kinda man.

It was during one of those evenings 'round the campfire that Wild Rose turned the conversation to a very different line.

"Now we are one, Cat. It cannot be otherwise. I know it and you know it. It is therefore proper and necessary that we know all that has passed in each other's lives. We now know how we feel and how much we love each other, but we do not know very much about either of our lives before we met, or how we lived during the six years from the time of your escape to the time I found you almost dead from the grizzly.

"You know that I am a Shoshone girl, the third of three sisters. You know that many summers ago—more summers than you can count on the fingers of one hand—I rode with my brothers on paint ponies for many moons to the south, to the headwaters of the Cimarron River, the favorite buffalo-hunting grounds of the Comanches.

"You know that it was there that I saw you helplessly stretched out on the ground, naked and defenseless. It was there two nights later that I learned what a great warrior you really were, how alone you destroyed half of a Comanche pursuing party. That is a deed for all men to remember.

"Six years later, I found you dying by that stream in the canyon below the great Salt Mountains. When I saw you there, I knew you were the same warrior of my girlhood dreams. I thought surely the Great Spirit had put us together for a purpose. I was overjoyed. I nursed you with all my heart, because I gambled my life that you could overcome the terrible sickness you had as the result of the grizzly's vengeance.

"During all the years since I first saw you staked out waiting for the torture 'til I found you by the stream at the foot of the Salt Mountains—all that time I dreamed of you. In my heart you were the greatest of all warriors. You were my man and my dreams. Now we have lived and loved together for three moons, so you must know that I always speak the truth.

"When a Shoshone girl gives herself, she does so with all her heart. There is no man in the world that will ever be as the man whom she first loved. In this beautiful meadow with this winding stream and so much wildlife around, we are the most natural things in all creation. At night when you hold me under the stars, we are the world."

She laughed lightly. "But you need to know more about me— where I came from, who my family is, who my ancestors are, what they did and why they died for their own reasons. You must know all of this, and I insist that you tell me where you came from.

"I knew you as you lay in the clutches of the vicious Comanches, and I knew you as a dying man at the foot of the Salt Mountains. But I need to know all about where you came from. I need to know what happened to you from the time that you escaped from the Comanche camp—and showed how one man, with a repeating gun, could defy the whole Comanche nation—to the time I found you.

"In order that we may learn these things, when we leave here, I want you to take me back to my village for a short time. I will tell you all about my girlhood: where I spent my time, where I sang my songs, where I made my prayers and who my friends were. I will tell you about great, great grandmother, who is to me a spirit in herself. She is a wonder. She is something that tells me a little bit about who I am because once she was somebody like me. She knew that she must do something, and she did it. And I know that I must do something and I am going to do it. Gray Eyes, my beloved Gray Eyes, you must help me.

"Let us go while the sun still crosses a little high in the sky. For this will be a great autumn season. This will be an open time of the descending sun. There will be no storms and when the leaves fall, only their sad flutter will wound our hearts. There will be no snow, no bitter cold. It will be sunshine and beauty, and you and I will ride together.

"Then we must go from my family's village on the Wind River back to that place in the little valley by the stream at the base of the Salt Mountains where I found you. We must take all our horses, for I, too, have a few beautiful paint mares and stallions that I have collected from childhood, and of which I have said nothing to you. I am very proud of them and I beg you, let us take them with us, along with your horses, because they are part of a plan.

"We will go back to where we found each other, where I crawled under the blanket to keep you warm, to hug you and to feel you beside me. I longed to have you take me then, but I dared not show the slightest sign of my longing, for if I did I would spoil the real way that I wanted you. I was a Shoshone maiden, brought up in the Shoshone ways, and I had to give myself as a Shoshone girl should do.

"I love you with all my heart and soul. It is not possible that I could ever love anyone else now that I have loved you, because you have all of me. I am exhausted in my promise to you. There is nothing left for others, so now I must know all about you. I must climb with you up into the high country to see where you first began the grizzly hunt and where you were finally struck and how you worked your way back to your horse, and then how you went back and killed the other grizzlies.

"We are the envy of the Shoshone village! The mighty hunter, *to-ye-ro-co*, has provided for his squaw a grizzly robe, then one for himself, and one for the father of his wife. What other Shoshone girl can boast of such a thing? I am so proud, Gray Eyes! Now I must see where you fought the grizzly. Then we must go across the mountains to that wonderful place which you call Brules's Fort, where you handled the Comanches so well.

"I must see all of this. I will do anything that you command, my wonderful Brules, but please, take me to the southland."

I s'pose in that way I was her slave. I was her slave 'cause she made me feel like I was her king. She made me feel that any wish that I commanded she'd obey. But, in doing that, it was the other way 'round. I'd go to the ends of the earth for her. As long as she was there

I'd be in harmony with the universe—with the forest and trees and fields, the running streams, blue skies, clouds and mountains, and all of the wild and beautiful things that run through the land. It'd be just me and Wild Rose. If I was to be a slave to that, I'd be the happiest servant in all the world.

I was so excited with what she told me that I promised we'd start on the journey the next day. After a wonderful night of lovemaking, we slept well, then we woke with the dawn, packed our horses, and rode hard, returning to the Shoshone village in just two days.

Right away we went to see her great, great grandmother, Sacagawea. She lived in a little lodge slightly north of the Shoshone village. I was in awe of that great lady, and was struck with something very strange 'bout her. She had a presence, a way of letting you know that she knowed things which most people didn't. She weren't overproud 'bout that, though, she was just deep about it.

When I seen Sacagawea she was a little old crone, regarded respectfully by the Shoshone as a great, great grandmother and laughed at for her lies. She was an old wizened thing, with pure white hair. Her skin was wrinkled, and her form was bent. Her voice come as a crackle, but I knowed that somehow I was standing in the presence of history. She was the greatest Indian woman in the land. I was thinking all the while that prob'ly her effect on the people of our country'd never be understood. A few people might try to show their appreciation, but the meaning of what she'd done'd fade with the sun.

One thing I noticed 'bout her was her flashing eyes. They might've been old, but they was a long ways from dead. Them eyes'd seen so much—more'n all of them Shoshones in the village put together. You got the impression she didn't care a damn what they thought 'bout her.

Her eyes blazed when she seen me, and she turned to Wild Rose. "So this is your man? He is the one that I hear is so great with the gun? I can see why, because he has such eyes, because he is straight and tall. He reminds me of the Red Chief of long, long ago."

When she said that, I was as proud as if I'd been complimented by the president of the United States. What she was talking 'bout was that she thought I looked like the explorer Clark, and there ain't no greater compliment to be paid a mountain man than that.

In the minds of a million Americans, Clark was the greatest of all explorers. Everyone knowed it. Talk 'bout a leader! That tough old redheaded Captain Clark and his partner, Lewis, had held a rough bunch of men together. They was some of the bravest fighters, best hunters, and hardest workers in the territory, and they traveled eight thousand miles through unexplored Indian country clear to the mouth of the Columbia and back. They had to be some men to do that!

So when she was telling Wild Rose what she thought 'bout me, I puffed my chest out and right there the old girl sold me on her being what she said she was.

She seemed on real good terms with Wild Rose. They spoke friendly, and she kept asking Wild Rose 'bout her seven horses. That made my ears perk up. Wild Rose was a smart girl and a modest one. I already knowed that, but to think that she'd put away for her own keeping a bunch of horses all by herself and never said nothing 'bout it 'cept to me and Sacagawea was something special. I could see that Sacagawea thought so, too, 'cause she smiled and hugged Wild Rose and made a big fuss over her.

When we left Sacagawea, I told Wild Rose, "Honey, it's a wonder your father weren't so anxious ta trade ya fer one or two horses. He already had seven of his daughter's. If'n his daughter didn't leave, he'd still have seven horses."

She laughed. "Yes, but he made a good trade. Now he has six times two hands of horses that you brought from the Blackfeet. I am very proud of my warrior."

Then Wild Rose took me out to the pasture east of the village down by the Wind River, and I understood what she was talking 'bout. She had two paint stallions and five paint mares that was the prettiest things I ever seen. She was a great judge of horseflesh. When she said she had ponies, you could bet they was the best. I didn't know how well mannered they was, nor how their gaits was, but they sure looked good on the hoof.

Then come the real nature of Wild Rose. She took me by both arms and looked me straight in the eyes. "Now, Gray Eyes, give me the paleface kiss." So, I obeyed. She seemed kinda shy, but then she said, "Here is what I want to do. I want to make you a present of these horses."

I could've fell over dead. They was all that girl had in the world, and to an Indian they was a small fortune, but she was giving 'em to me. It was a kind of love I just couldn't believe. But, on second thought, I s'pose I could. That was the way that little Shoshone girl was, through and through. She was the most loving, most unselfish human being that was ever my good fortune to know. I would've lived for her or died for her, whichever was necessary, no matter how things turned out.

After that, we stayed in the village for two more nights. There was drums beating and there was singing and dancing, which made things nice and made us feel welcome.

Wesha wanted me to go hunting again but I told him, "No, not this time. I'll come back next year. Right now, I aim ta please my new squaw and take her on a long journey."

Wesha laughed. I told him we'd most likely spend the winter somewheres down south and I'd be back next summer. Then me and him could go hunting a-plenty. He nodded and smiled and give me the "brother" sign, and I was proud to return it to him.

The next morning we started out with our packhorses, Wild Rose on her dandy paint and me on my Cimarron, driving seven beautiful paint horses as well as several head of Blackfoot ponies that was my share from the raid.

STARTING A NEW LIFE

We headed due south and made mighty good time, keeping the outfit moving right along. I fixed it so's we crossed the Union Pacific Railroad at night, far from any towns and where there weren't nobody around. We went on down through Brown's Hole, keeping outta people's way and not visiting any ranches.

We finally crossed the White west of Meeker and kept moving 'til we hit the Colorado. We laughed when we seen it, 'cause by then the water was so low that things'd become real manageable. We weren't gonna have no trouble crossing like we'd had the year before.

I was always amazed by some of the things that Wild Rose said. It was plumb fascinating to see how her mind worked. She was so much in tune with all that was going on 'round her that I just watched her in wonder.

"You know, Cat," she said, "these months of the falling leaves are going to be warm and nice this year. It will be pleasant 'til the time of the shortest day. That means we have three moons in which to see the things you told me about."

It was a stirring day when we come in sight of Hatch Gulch, where she'd found me after the grizzly mauling and brought me back to life. Because it meant so much to us and 'cause it was such a great place to camp, we spent two nights there. We laughed and joked and made love and talked 'bout how much better it was than when she was just taking care of me and I was worrying 'bout whether I'd ever see her again. That was all done, though, and we was back as man and wife.

Early the next morning we started on up the mountain, and I took her everywhere I'd been on the grizzly hunt. It was a long ride and she wanted to see everything.

As we rode through them mountains it seemed like I was living it all over again, only I gotta say that I was having lots more fun than before. Instead of a fierce grizzly bear, I had me a beautiful Shoshone wife, though in many ways that could've been just as tough to handle.

We went on climbing up that southeast face of Mount Peale, the southern peak of the Salt Mountains, traveling above timberline in that beautiful tundra that supports so much game. We stopped at noon, dismounted, and sat down to eat some pemmican. Wild Rose looked across the valley in the distance to the southeast. "Look at that beautiful, beautiful mountain," she said.

"Yeah, little lady, that's Lone Cone Peak. It's the most western of all the peaks in this part a the Colorado Territory."

She asked if I had ever been there.

"Yeah, but I've just skirted 'round the bottom of it. I always wanted ta take a look at that mountain high up. I kept tellin' myself I was gonna come back here someday an' do it. This's as good a time as any."

She jumped up and down and clapped her hands. "Yes, we are going to explore the Lone Cone Peak. Is that not what you called it? The Lone Cone?"

"Yep, that's it. Just ta the southwest of it ya can see a mountain called the Sleepin' Ute. It belongs ta the Mountain Utes. All this land that ya see east a here is the Ute reservation, an' it's enormous. The Utes have two different tribes—the Northern Utes live up at Meeker on the White River, an' the Southern Utes live up 'round Montrose. The Southern Utes have a smart chief. His name is Ouray an' he knows how ta get along with white folks. He's not so dumb as ta think that he can beat the paleface, what with all the paleface's machinery like railroads an' cannons an' all different kinds a things."

"I suppose that is so. Our Chief Washakie says that it is so. We must learn to live with the white man, although sometimes it is very hard." She looked straight at me. "Isn't that right, Gray Eyes?"

I looked at her sideways and she jumped up and started to run away, so I run after her. 'Course she didn't run very fast. She slowed up on purpose so's I could catch her. I was her man, and when she called me Gray Eyes I didn't aim to disappoint her none on that wonderful afternoon up on the southeast slope of the Salt Mountains.

When we was through with our lovemaking she said, "Let us go tomorrow. Let us go explore the mountain they call Lone Cone."

We went back down the slope and set 'round the campfire that night singing and talking and hugging each other. It was our place, the place where the Great Spirit had brought us together.

Next morning we started out for the Cone. I figured it was 'bout a two-day ride, but we'd have to keep moving. We stayed to the east of the Mormon town of Monticello, at the foot of the Blue Mountains, and kept going 'til we come to the San Miguel River. It run deep down in the canyon and had its headwaters up where Telluride is now. I believe there may've been a few prospectors up in the Telluride Valley at that time, but the year 1875 was pretty far back and there weren't a helluva lot of things going on in that part of the world.

The Mormons'd been there since the time of the Forty-Niners, almost twenty-five years before. But they'd kept pretty much to theirselves and stayed west of the Colorado-Utah line. The only spoiling done in that part of the country by white men was for mining purposes, and once in a while there'd be a lone hunter. But whether they was prospectors or hunters, they was always a little spooky 'bout working in the western part of Colorado, which was then Ute country. The Utes weren't knowed for their peaceful ways. On the other hand, they weren't near as tough as the Apaches—not by a damn sight. But when you're in wild Indian country you don't know whether they're hostile or not, and you wouldn't know 'til you met 'em. If they was friendly, it couldn't do you much good less'n you knowed it ahead of time, and if they weren't friendly, you was damn well outta luck.

Far as I was concerned, I weren't never afraid of Indians as long as I had my guns with me. I weren't looking for trouble, though. I knowed that if you kept on picking fights with 'em, there'd come a time when there'd be more numbers than you could take care of, and they'd bury their hatchet in your skull. So I kept watch all the time for Indian sign and Mormon sign, but we was lucky and didn't see nothing that bothered us none.

When we come to that canyon of the San Miguel, we went down its steep sides for almost a thousand feet. It weren't a cliff or anything like that. It was just a very steep slope with lots of piñon and cedar and rocks, and you had to be careful how you picked your way, 'cause you could injure your horse if'n he was to get sliding on some of that shale.

Anyhow, we crossed the San Miguel with no problem 'cause it had real low water. As I recall, it weren't as big as its sister river, the Dolores, which was way over on the other shoulder of the mountain, maybe fifty to seventy miles south. It was still a pretty good gorge to get in and out of, and our horses labored mightily coming up the southern slope.

We burst out onto level country that was mostly all sagebrush with not much grass. I reckon we crossed over where the town of Norwood is now, but in them days there weren't nothing there 'cept some places with ponderosa timber. Old Lone Cone Peak just to the east of us sure was majestic. There weren't no doubt 'bout that! It stood by itself like a sentinel a long ways west of the main range of the San Juans. Better'n thirteen thousand feet high, it plumb dominated the sagebrush plains all 'round it. It was a big mountain by any standards. I reckoned it'd take three days to ride 'round its base, and it was a cinch we weren't gonna see all that mountain then, nor for years to come.

It was mid September when we reached old Lone Cone, and the first snow'd yet to fall, just like Wild Rose'd predicted. Still, I figured it'd be safer for us to explore the mountain from the south, so we maneuvered 'round that way. On the second night we found a small stream coming outta the timber at its base, so we made camp there.

The next morning we rode along 'til we seen a part of the mountain that we really liked and started climbing, picking our way up through the oak brush and then through patches of quakie aspens and green meadows to the beautiful blue spruce forest that covered the upper slopes.

You can have the ponderosa, the lodgepole pine, the piñon trees, or the Engelmann spruce, but give me that beautiful tree called the Colorado blue spruce. Down there in the southwest they grow big and high and they got plenty of room underneath the lowest branches so's a man can ride a horse under 'em real easy. There ain't hardly no underbrush—just pine needles. When you're riding along through there you experience a deep, dark, quiet, mysterious sorta thing that makes you feel you're in a real forest. Once in a while you might see a deer or an elk move quickly through the shadows and be outta sight 'fore you know it, but mostly it's just peaceful and beautiful.

With every step the horses took, we moved higher and higher on the mountain, and Wild Rose begun making that high "eeeee" of hers. We kept on that way 'til we got far enough up to where we could see for a hundred miles around. Then she fell silent. It seemed like the beauty of the whole thing was sacred to her, and she didn't want to spoil it by talking. Feeling the same way, I rode right along with her, leading that string of paint horses.

We must've been a sight—a bearded Indian fighter and a beautiful young squaw, both of us mounted on paint horses and working our way up that mighty mountain and drinking in the beauty of all God's world.

It was 'bout three o'clock in the afternoon when we come over a ridge on the south side of Lone Cone and seen spread out before us a valley that was, I reckon, the best place in the world. From where we was you could look south down to the Sleeping Ute, southwest to the high rocks of Monument Valley a hundred forty miles away, and west to the Blues. If you was to swing 'round to the northwest, you'd see the La Sals, and in back of you to the northeast was the high peaks of the San Juans, the most noble of all them mountains in Colorado Territory.

I tell you, it was breathtaking. As we brought our horses to a standstill and gazed out over the country, I could see the mounting excitement in Wild Rose. She turned to me with that wonderful, natural, mysterious look that she so often had when she seen something that stirred her.

"My man, this is the place for our home. This is the most beautiful place in all the world. That lovely stream that runs down through the meadow of this valley will give us plenty of water, and these high mountain grasses are just the sort of pasture that my precious horses would enjoy so much. Here, I think, is where we should build our home."

I couldn't add nothing to that, my feelings being exactly the same. I'd wandered all over hell and creation in my young life and never seen nothing like it. You couldn't improve on it, and if my beautiful little Shoshone girl wanted to stay there, by God, that was where we was gonna stay. There weren't no mistake about it.

Since then, in all the years I've been 'round here, I've seen the different colors of the rising sun and the gold of the late afternoon. I've seen the fiery sunset in the western desert, and the stars overhead at night so clear it seemed you could pluck 'em outta the sky with your fingers. My Shoshone girl was right: This is the most beautiful place in the world.

We didn't waste time getting things in order. We hobbled our horses, put 'em out in the green grass to feed, and picked us a good campsite by the running stream. Wild Rose had a wickiup in place in short order.

I got a fire going and looked 'round to see where there'd be the best chance for nice fresh meat for the evening meal. I picked up my rifle and told Wild Rose that I was just gonna take a look southeast 'round the shoulder of the mountain and that I wouldn't be gone long.

I moved rapidly 'round the shoulder of the hill and seen a small spike buck standing just long enough for me to draw a bead. Half an hour later I was back in the camp with some fresh venison. Wild Rose was by the fire with a knowing smile. She'd already rigged up a spit where we could roast the meat. Her smile said, I knew you wouldn't be gone long. You can't fool me. You're a great hunter. When I heard the rifle crack, I started the fire going in a strong way.

I went over and kneeled beside her. "Wild Rose, I wanta whisper a secret ta ya." She tilted her head in a coy way and put her ear up to my lips, waiting. "Do ya know what I wanta do? I wanta give ya another lesson in paleface kissin'." With that, I give her a big hug and kiss and our hearts begun beating again, way outta tune with anything but the excitement of love.

There was a little delay in making our dinner that night, but it really didn't matter none, 'cause nothing mattered as long as me and Wild Rose was together. That was the way it went.

During the many nights that followed, as we sat by the campfire talking to each other, I was amazed at how much she knowed 'bout nature. She seemed to know instinctive-like what was going on 'round her and why. She had a natural way of convincing me that whatever she said was so, particularly when it had to do with the things of the natural world.

I watched her face while she told me stories 'bout the different animals and how they'd come about. They was stories her Shoshone ancestors'd used to explain to the little ones how matters come to be and why the Great Spirit made things the way He did.

We also begun talking 'bout plans for our life together. I pointed out to her that this beautiful valley was a natural pasture and could hold many cattle and horses. The stream that meandered through it traveled 'bout half a mile and then disappeared over the horizon. What we was looking at was a shelf on the side of the mountain, a shelf that seemed to stretch out to the edge of the world and then disappear. Where the stream went outta sight, there was a gap 'tween two great cliffs of rock. Beyond that, we could only see the mountains in the far distance—the Sleeping Ute and the Blues. It was as if we was looking out on the edge of the world. It was the kinda place that the Utes called the Spirit Land.

One morning we took a long walk beside the stream. As we come upon pool after pool, the trout darted with lightning speed under them overhanging banks. Near the end of the meadow we begun hearing the sound of falls. Sure enough, when we reached the edge we looked down on a sparkling scene. The stream was falling with a foaming roar into a pool 'bout thirty feet below and then out and down the mountain through the pine trees. In the distance, 'bout three thousand feet below, we could see where it went far out into the sagebrush flats that lay 'round the skirt of the mountain. It flowed south to the Dolores and on to the Colorado and over to the western ocean.

On either side of the falls was red rock ridges that run up the slopes of the mountain on both sides of us. When we stood down there at the brink of the meadow with the thunder of the water in our ears, we looked back and seen what we should've seen long before—a great big beautiful meadow, better'n five thousand acres, and on both sides of it, stretching way to the north and up the mountain, was walls of red rock called the Red Rock Cliffs.

Timber lay there along the base of the rock walls and on the mountain slopes above 'em, but the important thing was that them walls enclosed the valley so's nothing could get in or out 'cept from the north—the way we'd come. At the head of the valley was a long ridge and more steep cliffs, but in places there was broke openings much different than the walls on the sides.

Suddenly I turned to Wild Rose. "My woman, we've found a wonderful place! We've found a great ranch where it's a simple matter ta fence off gaps that we see up ta the north an' the trail that we come in on from the west. We can make a worm fence outta lodgepoles cut from quakies an' with them cliffs an' this waterfall, we can enclose the whole valley. It'll be ours, an' our cattle an' horses'll graze in here without no trouble a'tall. No cattle nor horses'll try to go out through this gateway to the south 'cause of the falls. In a few days, workin' hard together, we can make us a nice ranch outta this valley. It'll only take a couple hundred yards a fence."

Wild Rose seen it the same way I did and expressed her delight with that wonderful "eeeee." Right then and there it become our home, the home of Wild Rose and Cat Brules.

Then a strange and wonderful feeling come over me. I suddenly realized what it was I wanted to do with my life: I knowed then and there I didn't wanta keep on being nothing but a Comanche killer or grizzly hunter or even a scout for one of them bigshot generals. No, I didn't wanta do none of them things no more. What I was gonna do was settle down. I had me a fine girl and we was gonna raise us a big family.

Yessir, I was gonna be a rancher, a real one—a great one! In my mind I was looking out over our spread, seeing the thousands and thousands of head of cattle that'd someday be ours. People'd come from a long ways away to see our fine stock and learn just how a real cattleman carried on an operation. Why, we'd be shipping cattle clear back to them eastern markets, 'round Ohio and such. We'd have us the greatest spread the country'd ever seen.

I was thinking, too, of the big house that we'd have someday. It'd have all kinds of fancy things that Wild Rose'd be needing. I pointed up to a little timber-covered hill sitting close to the stream on the west side of the valley. "That's where we're gonna build our home. It ain't gonna be no more'n just a cabin fer now, but someday we'll have us a big house with a beautiful view of all the mountains fer more'n a hundred miles ta the south an' west. Ta the east we'll be able ta see our valley an' our ranch an' it'll be a helluva sight."

Wild Rose jumped for joy. I'd never seen her so excited. She hugged and kissed me and said all sorts of things in Shoshone so fast that I couldn't understand her. Then she throwed her arms 'round my neck and I begun hugging and kissing her like I'd never let her go.

She finally stepped back and smiled shyly. "How bad it is for me to do what I have just done," she said softly. "I am not acting like a good

Shoshone wife, but I am so happy with you, Gray Eyes. When we are together there are so many ideas we share. Now I know that the Great Spirit has picked this place to be our home for many years. We will have many sons and daughters. The boys will be great hunters and herdsmen and the girls will be the most beautiful in all the land. I will teach them well how to behave themselves and how to do all the things that are necessary for young girls to do. You, my man, will teach the boys how to hunt and raise cattle. You will no longer be the Cat Man making war. There has been too much war in your life. We will call our home the Broken Arrow Ranch and it will be a place of peace."

My heart filled with joy, 'cause it was plain she understood the kinds of thoughts I'd been thinking during our travels together. But I seen one thing that she didn't, so I tried to explain it to her.

"My woman, our sons must be more'n hunters an' herdsmen. They'll need ta be educated. There's a time comin' when we'll have ta foller the white man's ways. We'll have ta send our young 'uns ta good schools so's they can learn ta be ladies an' gennelmen. They'll have nice clothes an' they'll marry good an' go on ta do all kinds a things. Maybe one of our sons'll grow up ta be president someday. Who the hell can tell? Anyway, that's what we'll need ta be aimin' fer."

Yessir, I thought, we was gonna be somebody. Folks's gonna tip their hats ta me an' my lady. There ain't gonna be no slouchin' 'round. We ain't gonna slouch 'round like some mountain man an' squaw that folks's afeared of an' don't wanta have no part of. Nosir! We was gonna be part a what's goin' on in the world—an important part.

That was the beginning of our plans for the future. We went back up the stream and selected a homesite on that timbered hill and decided where we was gonna place everything.

"The corral will be over there," said Wild Rose.

"The gate ta go out ta the valley'll be over there," I said.

"Where will you build our lodge?"

"We ain't gonna have no lodge." Her smile faded. "Wait a minute," I said real quick. "Lodges're made so's ya can follow the game. We're not gonna need a movin' lodge 'cause we're gonna live in this valley all the time. We'll raise cattle here an' we won't have ta go huntin' every day just ta get somethin' ta eat. There'll be lots a game that'll come in an' outta here. We'll get our share an' we can live well. But your beautiful horses'll be here all the time. Ya don't have ta worry 'bout nothin'. I'll build you a cabin right here overlookin' the stream."

She looked at me real quiet for a whole minute. "You mean I am to have a white man's house? I am going to have a house with walls and a roof?"

"Yep, an' maybe a fireplace an' a nice stove an' a table an' bed."

"That may be too much to take care of."

"Naw, you'll get used to it, my woman. You'll learn; it'll be easy. I'll be here ta help ya, an' we'll be warm an' snug in the winter. We won't have ta worry none 'bout the winds an' the snow."

A cold gust of wind come along and I shivered and pulled Wild Rose into my arms. "We must build our cabin now," I said, " 'fore the snow falls, so's we'll be ready fer winter. After that we can finish our travelin'. I'll take ya then ta see the place I call Brules's Fort, where I killed all them Comanches. But first, we must do our work here. Even though I know yore a great one ta tell what the weather'll be, no one can be absolutely shore. We must have a cabin ta come back ta, an' that'll be impossible if'n we have ta build it in the snow."

Wild Rose pulled free and jumped up and down and clapped her hands. "We must start right now. No more do we sit in idle talk."

I laughed. "Okay, girl, that's the kinda thing I like ta hear."

I went over to our camp and took the ax outta the pack outfit and walked over to the aspen grove. I started cutting down poles to make our fence. I cleaned off the limbs and tips and worked with as much speed as I could muster. When I'd cut and trimmed a few, I said to her, "Get one a the horses an' drag these poles over there, an' over there, an' over there," pointing to the different places. "String 'em out so's I can make a fence." I used my fingers. "There should be four in each place. That's the number a poles that I'll need ta make fence rails. We'll lay 'em out zigzag an' I'll notch 'em an' lock 'em together. Then we'll put 'em up an' it won't take long fer us ta make a worm fence that the horses'll respect."

I knowed that by then the grizzlies'd gone into hibernation, and I weren't worried 'bout no cougars, 'cause no self-respecting cougar'd take on a full-growed horse. That was too much of a job. A cougar'd pick on a colt, but we didn't have none of them yet. The horses'd be fine and safe for the winter and we'd have us a cabin.

We worked real fast. I cut down five-inch quakies at a quick rate.

Wild Rose, being as skillful as she was with horses, would take her lariat and tighten a loop 'round the log end, take a turn 'round the saddle horn and drag them fifteen-foot logs into place. She laid 'em out real beautiful, as if somehow she was a natural builder, and I just kept cutting and cutting and cutting that timber. At the end of two days we had the logs laid out for the fence, and by notching and weaving we built us a worm fence zigzagging 'cross every opening in the valley. It didn't seem possible to me. We couldn't have built more'n a furlong of fence, blocking off maybe ten different gaps, yet we'd closed that whole wide valley so's not a critter could get in or out 'cept through our gate by the homesite.

When it come to building the cabin, that was a different story. We couldn't use quakie logs, so we cut us some pine timber. You wouldn't think two people could do that in the short time that we done it in with just one ax, but we was pretty fast, and I was real pleased to see that Wild Rose could swing that tool just about as good as me. She was real handy 'bout lots of other things, too, which made the work easier.

Being good with horses, she didn't have no trouble sliding the logs up to where we was gonna put up the side of the cabin. I didn't have nails, so's I had to notch all the logs at the corners. Plenty of other men'd built cabins 'round America with nothing but an ax, so I didn't see no reason why we couldn't do it, too. When it come to the roofing, I just made a frame. I figured that first winter we'd get by with some lodgepole pine laid on close together, covered with twigs and leaves, and then sodded over. I could sod the roof easy, 'cause I had a shovel in my pack outfit. You never wanta travel cross-country without a good ax and a good shovel.

Well, anyhow, we got it done in jig time.

We didn't have no way to swing a door or nothing, so I went out and killed me two big bull elk, skinned 'em out, and sewed the hides together in such a way as to make a usable door. I fastened it to the top of the threshold on the outside and inside and let it hang down. Then I tied it to the door frame with rawhide laces. It took a little while to get in and get out, 'cause you had to undo the laces, but it pretty much kept the wind out.

When it come to the fireplace, there weren't no way to make that without no mortar. A stove was out of the question. Where in the hell was we gonna get a stove in that country?

What I finally done was to make another door that went out from that part of the cabin that we was gonna use for whatever food supplies we had. I made a little passageway 'bout three feet wide, dug a trench, and then made me a nice big pit in the ground and banked it up all 'round. Then we screened it up, including the passageway.

What we done was drive two rows of stakes in the embankment, mostly quakie stuff, and fill 'tween 'em with leaves and dry dirt and whatever we could get, then covered over part of the passageway. That left an open-air pit that had a screen 'round it to keep the wind out. We was able to make a kind of bench outta the embankment. In that way we could have us a pit fire. If we didn't let it get going too good, it was 'bout as good as having a fire in the house. We knowed we weren't gonna keep the house warm using that pit, but we could cook over it without going out in the wind. Even better'n that, we could hang some of the meat supplies in the passageway.

It got so cold at night that we had our own icehouse. The cabin was colder'n an iceberg, but that didn't make no difference to Wild Rose and me, 'cause we had plenty of buffalo robes. We just took off our clothes at night and piled in there together as naked as the day we was born. There we'd stay all night long, just as warm as could be. Hell, that's the way a man and wife oughta sleep anyway.

To be real honest, 'cept for the fire, the whole 'commodations was better'n any damn Shoshone tepee. It ought to've been, 'cause it weren't movable.

Although we hadn't completed it, we'd done most of the rough part within three weeks' time. That may seem impossible, but I seen two men put up a good cabin in two weeks by staying right with it. I believe that Wild Rose was every bit as good as any man, 'cept for maybe strengthwise, when it come to lifting heavy logs. Even then she didn't shirk none.

It was early October when we had it mostly all done. Wild Rose looked over what I called "our spread," and said, "We have our winter place now. There will be no snow for almost two moons. Let us go to Brules's Fort, for it was there that you showed what a mighty warrior you really are and where you punished the Comanches for their cruel handling of you. It is also where I learned to stop pitying you and began loving you."

I told her it'd take many days of hard riding, but we could do it. If we took just one packhorse and a spare we could move fast. With the fence built, I figured we could leave the rest of our ponies there. I pointed out to Wild Rose that being on the south side of the mountain, and the sun being as fierce as it normally is in that country, we wouldn't have too much snow anyway. I figured if we had a big storm it'd melt off fast and the chances of our horses getting short on food in the winter'd be very small.

'Sides that, we weren't gonna be gone all winter. If things looked tough when we got back, we'd figure a way to get out and down to where the horses could make a good living.

Later on, when we'd run cattle, it might be a different thing. Cattle can't dig for feed as well as horses, but we could make 'em a hay meadow to take care of that. There was part of that valley that we could fence off someday that'd be just fine for that. Then we could put up some hay for the cattle for the toughest months of the winter.

THE RIDE TO BRULES'S FORT

One bright sunny morning me and Wild Rose, her riding her favorite paint and me riding Cimarron, set out for Brules's Fort with the old packhorse and a spare following behind.

We started off down Lone Cone, zigzagging through the blue spruce 'til we was among the quakies, then we took a game trail that made a turn or two and finally ended down in the sagebrush.

We made it all the way to the Dolores Canyon the first day and dropped down into it. That canyon is 'bout a thousand feet deep, but it ain't sheer cliff. It's sloping timber and rocks just like the San Miguel. It's steep and tough, but you can ride a horse down there if you take your time and pick your way.

The Dolores was low when we got there and easy to ford. On the south bank we set up camp for the night and the next day traveled on 'round the southern tip of the La Plata Mountains. We cut 'round the San Juans just south of the little mining town of Durango. I was careful to avoid all mining towns. I sure as hell weren't gonna go into one with my Indian wife, 'cause I'd prob'ly have to kill some drunken son of a bitch to get outta there. I weren't hankering to cause no trouble.

I was enjoying life more'n I ever had at any time before, meandering 'round on good horses with a great girl. There ain't no way to beat that combination. Every day our love for each other just seemed to grow. There never was an unpleasant word spoke 'tween us. We never seemed to get irritated 'bout nothing. We just laughed and played and talked and looked at the scenery and watched the animals and rode them horses that we loved to ride so much.

I couldn't help remarking that it was getting pretty dry. We hadn't had no moisture since early fall, but that didn't seem to upset Wild Rose none. "It will stay nice for a long time," she said. "Perhaps in the winter big snow . . . maybe." She was my weather prophet, and I seldom seen her be wrong.

It was in that fashion that we moved on down towards Cumbres Pass. It was nice country to travel in—real easy slopes. When we topped the Cumbres, we done so just 'bout at the headwaters of the Conejos. Not many people know 'bout the Conejos even today, but it's gotta be one of the prettiest streams in the Rocky Mountains and plumb loaded with trout. Wild Rose had lots of fun with her handline and her bone hooks and we had plenty to eat.

When we come outta the Conejos Valley, Wild Rose seen the great San Luis Valley. She made another one of them "eeeee" sounds like she was having the greatest pleasure. As a matter of fact, from the west side looking east, it's a fantastic sight. You're looking at the high Sangre de Cristos and the towering battlements of old Blanca Peak, and the yellow sand dunes at the foot of the mountains called the Crestone Needles just north. Them Crestone Needles is a sight, 'specially when they're covered with snow and their jagged tops stick up in the blue sky. As for the San Luis Valley, just the size of it takes your breath away—a hundred twenty-five miles long and seventy-five miles wide. It's kinda like you're on top of the world.

We crossed the San Luis in two days. That part of the trip was a boring ride, 'cause the bottom of the valley is as flat as a pancake. When you start going 'cross there, them mountains stand up in front of you and they stand there for two days. You keep looking at 'em over your horse's ears and they don't seem to get no closer. It's not 'til the last afternoon of the second day that you begin to get close enough to see that the mountains are real and not just something painted on a screen that's leading you on.

We cut 'cross the Santa Fe Trail 'tween Valdez's ranch and Fort Garland just after dusk. We stayed outta sight and watched the traffic that afternoon and didn't see nothing that was real important and knowed we'd be all right in the evening.

We camped high up in the Sangre de Cristos that night, and the next morning crossed over the divide where I'd passed through coming the other way eight years before.

That night I told Wild Rose that we'd come to Brules's Fort the next morning when the sun was halfway up. She got mighty excited and kept telling me that I was the greatest warrior that'd ever lived, and that she was gonna be my wife forever, and if there was any other woman that come anywhere near me she'd make mincemeat outta her. She kept up that kind of chatter all night long, 'cept when we was making love.

Two or three hours 'fore dawn we fell asleep and woke up late that morning, but that didn't make no difference 'cause we weren't on no schedule. We finally got moving and crossed over to where we could see in the distance the whole of the western plains—the Comanche country that I'd come through the first time when I was an uncomfortable prisoner. I told Wild Rose all about it and she didn't say nothing. She just stared at the prairie. In another hour I seen the beginnings of the rockslide and soon we was coming up on it. I told Wild Rose that the rockslide'd come from the crumbled cap rock that run along the top of the mountain.

Wild Rose made me show her everything. We spent the rest of that day and all of the next going over the ground where I'd fought them Comanches.

When I'd finished telling Wild Rose how I'd bested them Comanches with my Winchester, she stood there for a long time looking out over the plains at them big fluffy clouds in the sky, just as I'd done.

Then she turned to me. "Oh, Cat, I am so glad that you did not die in this battle. I am so glad that you are here now and that I am here with you."

"D'ya wanta go down into the flats where the Comanche village was an' see where I was staked out an' where ya brung the water ta me?"

"No, I do not wish to see that. That is an evil place. This is a place of honor for you and me, but that is a place of evil. Once I wished to go out in those great plains with you, but it would be meaningless now. I would like to have hunted Comanches with you. It would have been exciting, and I would have been proud and felt safe with you. But now it is meaningless, for what is left of them has long since drifted away.

That is what comes of being cruel and fierce. No real good comes from that.

"Our great Father, Chief Washakie, boasted that no white man's scalp had ever hung in the tepee of a Shoshone and that was right. Never, never, never did we torture prisoners. That is a horrible thing to do.

"Because the Shoshones were the friends of the whites and because they acted in a peaceable and lawful manner, they came out of the Indian wars with a great reservation. The Comanches were sent like sulking dogs to Indian territory, and they are scattered among the reservations of the other tribes—Pawnee, Shawnee, Creek, Cherokee, Seminole, Cheyenne, Kiowa, Choctaw, and Fox. Now they have no nation of their own. They are gone.

"The Apache had better watch out. They had better be careful because some of their young men are still wild and fighting. If they continue to do this, the palefaces will destroy them like they did the Comanche!"

With that she turned and we jumped from rock to rock, working our way outta the rockslide to where the horses was tied.

"Now, take me over the divide and back into the San Luis Valley so I can see how you came out of this fight and where you went down to the Valdez ranch. I do not wish to go there, but I would like to see it from a distance. After that, let us make our way home. Let us go to that beautiful place on our own side of the great mountain."

It was like our hearts welded together at that moment. Now she knowed how I felt and what I'd done, and I knowed how she felt and what she'd done, and we was at peace.

Five days later, we crossed the San Luis Valley and made camp on a stream on the eastern side of Cochetopa Pass. The next morning, with the sun at our backs, we made our way to the top of the pass and stopped to look out west over the Gunnison Valley. Beyond it in the far distance was the peaks of the Salt Mountains and the tip of Lone Cone.

Wild Rose turned to me with real soft eyes and put her hand in mine. "Cat," she said, "there is something you must know. Six moons from now there will be a little one with us. That little one will be the first child of our love."

When she told me that, I damn near busted with joy! I jerked off my hat, let out a war whoop, pulled out my Smith & Wesson, and fired off every shot in the cylinder. The horses skidded 'round and very near went berserk, but Wild Rose was laughing at the top of her lungs.

I reached over and touched her knee. "Now you have to be very careful."

She started to laugh again. "Cat, you are a crazy man. You are a silly boy. I am glad you are so full of joy that you act like you have lost your head. You must not worry about me being careful. I am not a paleface woman. I am an Indian woman that holds this child of yours. I will keep it and when I bear it, it will be easy. The child will be healthy and you will be proud. If it is a boy, he will grow up to be strong and have a keen mind like his father. If it is a girl, she will be beautiful, for look at the father who gives her beauty."

When she said that, I turned to her and looked her straight in the eyes. "That's the only foolish thing I've ever heard ya say. Yeah, our daughter'll be beautiful. She'll be very beautiful. But the reason'll be 'cause a her beautiful mother, not her bearded ol' mountain man father. Now, give me a kiss, ya Shoshone beauty."

She stopped laughing then and put her hand in back of my head and give me a long sweet kiss. "Yore learnin' the paleface ways real quick," I said.

It was a happy journey that we made down the valley of the Gunnison. It was as if we was heading west again and the whole new world was opening up for us. We knowed a lot about it, but we didn't know what our lives was gonna be like. We knowed it was gonna be a wonderful and joyful time. The idea of raising a family with this magnificent Indian girl just filled me with pride and joy.

We left the banks of the Gunnison River when we come to the Black Canyon country and worked our way across the Cimarron River, which pours into the Gunnison from the south. We crossed over the hills and dropped down into that desertlike valley at the headquarters of the Southern Ute Indian Agency at Los Pinos on the Uncompahgre River. Los Pinos Agency was just a small community, but it was a place for me to buy supplies and to trade hides, and I thought it proper that we stop there for the better part of a day.

While we was there, something caught my eye. I was standing on the front porch of the general store right by the agency when I first seen it. By God, it was a wood stove. It was flat on top, with some of them iron plates you can lift off with a handle so's you can use the stove for both cooking and heating. That started me to thinking.

All the way down the Gunnison I'd been turning over in my mind something that I didn't like 'bout the cabin. At first, I hadn't been able to put my finger on it, but I knowed something was wrong. It was all right for me to dig that trench out in the back and then make a pit for handling a fire and then put a windscreen 'round it, but that wouldn't do the house no good in the chill of a real hard winter. At eight thousand feet, it'd be mighty cold.

Me and Wild Rose'd be fine while we was there together in them buffalo robes, but we wouldn't be worth a damn doing anything but sleeping or making love. Knowing that a baby was coming got me to thinking hard. That stove was the difference 'tween a tepee and a cabin. You could make a fire in the wintertime right in the middle of a tepee, 'cause the smoke'd go up through the hole in the roof, but you couldn't have a hole in the roof of a log cabin and have it work any good. In the first place, the smoke wouldn't feed out that way. Most likely it'd circle all through the cabin. A tepee—which was made to fold up and put on a travois and get going to the next place in short order—had a kinda fan at the top that drawed the wind and sucked the smoke out. The trouble with a permanent dwelling was there weren't no way to make a fire in the middle of it. It'd burn the place down right 'round your ears. That's why a man had to have a stove.

I'd built that whole cabin without no nails, no hammer, and no saw—nothing but an ax. But I couldn't build a stove that way. There was one sitting right in front of me, and I made up my mind in a hurry that I was gonna buy it. I still had quite a bit of money that I'd got from trading them grizzly hides. I hadn't had any way to spend it on a Shoshone reservation nor up in the thoroughfare of the North Fork of the Shoshone when we was honeymooning. I went right in that general store and bought that stove and some stovepipe to go with it and a piece of tin that I could put 'round the roof to keep it from catching on fire where the chimney went out.

Wild Rose didn't really savvy what I was doing. She kinda knowed what a stove was, having been in Doc Irwin's house. She weren't too sure 'bout just how it worked, though, and the rest of the things like the stovepipe she couldn't make out a'tall. I told her not to worry none—that we was gonna get it all done and she'd be real pleased.

We packed up the stuff on one of the packhorses—stovepipe and all. I thought for a while that that horse looked like a Mississippi steamboat. We made it out of Los Pinos and climbed 'cross the Uncompahgre Plateau right by Dallas Pass, then we camped on the San Miguel below Telluride and went on up to the southwest slopes of Lone Cone. 'Bout midafternoon of the second day, when we come over the hill and through the gate of our little ranch, we was both beaming with pride. There was a little snow on the ground, but it was just like Wild Rose'd predicted—there hadn't been much.

First thing she wanted to see was how our horses'd done while we was away. She run on down into the meadow and begun counting 'em and looking at 'em. When she come back she said they sure looked good.

Meanwhile, I was unloading the stove and working it into the cabin. I couldn't get the whole stove set up 'fore dark that evening. When it got kinda cold and we had to go out to the fire pit, Wild Rose begun to get the idea. I had the stove in the next day by noon, with the stovepipe sticking outta the roof with tin all around it.

I cut some small logs, just enough to go inside the stove, and lit her up. In a few minutes the whole cabin was cozy warm. I tell you, that made a big difference with Wild Rose.

Then I showed her how to work them steel plates on the top of the stove to get the most heat for cooking. When she seen how she could get the cooking done and heat at the same time and not have smoke in her eyes or flames to bother her, she started appreciating again what a white man's world was all about. I didn't do nothing with the fire pit. I just blocked it off so's we could use it in the summertime.

I got up early the next morning to go hunting and it was good. I shot 'bout two weeks' supply of meat and then sashayed 'round the country to get the lay of it and see if I could find anything of special interest—like deer or elk runs or anything else. I didn't see no bear tracks, but, hell, they'd gone into hibernation long before, so I weren't surprised.

On the third day, 'bout noon, I was riding in from an exploring expedition when Wild Rose come outta the cabin, looked 'round at the cloudless sky and other things, and said, "Snow come tonight."

There was one thing 'bout that little Indian girl you could count on—she sure was right with nature. How she was able to smell bad weather I could never figure. She was uncanny 'bout that kinda thing, and 'bout finding game, too. She just seemed to know how they thought, or she thought the way they did when she was hunting. I don't know, but she never failed to do something astounding like that. When she said there'd be snow the next day, I didn't doubt it.

Sure enough, even though it'd been as clear as a bell all that day, in the middle of the night a blizzard come up. When we woke up in the morning, unlaced them hides on the door, and looked out, we seen a winter wonderland. The blizzard raged for two days and left 'bout two feet of snow in front of our door. I was kinda worried 'bout what the stock'd do in that flat meadow, but then I seen that they'd got into where the willows give lots of protection and they was eating them willows and pawing up the ground to get at any grass that might be left.

I figured that if them horses could winter in the Wind River Range, they sure as hell could winter off of Lone Cone Peak. I figured that with us being on the south side, it wouldn't take long for that snow to melt down a lot faster'n they'd starve. So I didn't worry 'bout it none.

It was clear and beautiful in a couple of days, and then the snow come again and it kept getting deeper. It was that way for the rest of the winter. Wild Rose made us each a couple of snowshoes and although I'd never used 'em before, she showed me how to tie 'em on. They made a big difference and we got around just fine.

The game was still plentiful. If'n we had a bad storm and the snow was too deep, I'd just put on the snowshoes, go downhill a ways, and get outta the blue spruce and into the quakies. If I didn't do any good there, I'd go clear down into the oak brush. But I always found game. I never had no trouble getting us something to eat, and I always had a few pieces of a haunch or rib cage or front quarters hanging up someplace so's we'd have plenty of spares. They kept real good in that cold—just like in an icehouse.

One day Wild Rose produced a great big beautiful red woolen Hudson Bay blanket outta her pack. It sure was a piece of warm-looking stuff. She announced that she was gonna make me a capote.

All I'd heard 'bout capotes was that the French trappers outta Fort Assiniboine on Lake Winnipeg had used 'em all the time and that they was real handy to make, 'cause the squaws just made 'em out of a Hudson Bay blanket. A capote was a wool coat that come to 'bout the knees and was tied on with a wool belt, or maybe strapped in by a leather one. It was made with a hood that you could pull over your head even though the collar of the coat itself was up tight 'round your neck. If a fella wore warm gloves and warm shoes and a capote, he was in right good shape in almost any kinda stormy weather.

It took Wild Rose damn near three weeks to make that coat, but it was the most comfortable thing I ever had on in my life. It wore like iron and she kept telling me it was the best-looking thing she'd ever seen on me. I told her she'd seen me with nothing on, and everything else from there up, and finally come out with a capote that covered everything and made me feel real good. If she thought I looked fine, that was good enough for me.

She laughed 'bout that and then called me Gray Eyes again. We spent a wonderful winter in that cabin and our happiness was just as it'd always been since we'd been together. It was complete.

Spring come a little earlier in '76 and the snow begun melting on the lower slopes. Each day got warmer and the herds begun moving up the mountain. Even though there was ten horses out in the big pasture, the deer and elk come through there like they owned the place. I s'pose in a way they did. They'd been there long 'fore we was. There weren't no use in arguing 'bout that. Anyway, me and Wild Rose both loved to see 'em 'round.

Pretty soon there weren't no more snow in our pasture. A little bit higher up than us, at the ten-thousand-foot level, there was the snowcap that went all 'round Lone Cone Peak, but that was all.

'Bout that time Wild Rose and me begun to feel restless. We could see the signs of spring more and more every day. First there was buds on the trees. Then we heard the geese calling and watched 'em as they flew north in great long *Vs*. An Indian understands them things better'n a white man, although I must say I was in tune with it as much as anybody, and we both loved it.

As we watched the seasons change, Wild Rose'd hold my hand and say, "We're coming into spring, Cat. The little one will be here before another moon. That will be a fine time to be born. You and I are going to have a wonderful summer!"

I believed it.

MOUNTAIN GODS AND BROKEN ARROWS

One beautiful day in late March I proposed to Wild Rose that we saddle our horses and ride 'round the whole of Lone Cone Mountain just below the snow line. That high up I reckoned it'd only be 'bout a six- or eight-hour ride, whereas if you was to ride 'round the base of that mountain, it'd take three days.

She went for it like a piece of candy, even though she was so far along in her pregnancy. You really can't blame her none, though, 'cause she'd spent most of the winter in the cabin. A few times she'd gone down on snowshoes to look at the horses and we'd gone on a couple of hunts that way, but most of the time she'd just been holed up. I kinda had cabin fever, too.

'Fore we started out that morning, I give her a choice. I asked if she wanted to go down and look through the oak brush and see if we could find some wild game that'd wintered down there, or if she'd rather ride 'round the Cone. She weren't long in answering. "Let us stay high on the mountain," she said.

We took the halters and walked down to the pasture together. I whistled Cimarron in and she done the same thing with three or four of her horses. When we begun to look 'em over, she seen the big, dark roan that we'd been using as one of the packhorses. Why she ever picked that animal I'll never know.

"Why d'ya wanta ride that horse when ya've got so many beautiful paints ta ride?" I asked.

"Well, I have been looking at him. He is a strong horse. He is a big horse. He can do many things if he is just taught some manners. I don't like him nearly as well as I do the others, but all horses have a place. This one can be made to do very well. When we have to pull heavy logs and do some hard riding on the steep slopes of the mountains and when we have long distances to go, I believe that this horse is strong and willing and that he can go a long ways."

I'd never argued with Wild Rose 'bout nothing. When she said she wanted to do something, it was okay with me. I just shook my head and thought, I don't know why this girl comes out of a long winter with cabin fever an' don't take her best horse an' ride 'round like she's a queen. She's takin' a big roan with a head like a gallows tree an' prob'ly a mouth as hard as steel an' maybe a heart a hell, too. I don't like the look in his eyes.

On the other hand, Wild Rose knowed lots 'bout horses that I didn't. She was a better rider'n I was, too, although I considered myself 'bout as good as any other rider I knowed. It weren't that she was any stronger, or even as strong as I was, and it weren't that she could maneuver her horses any better, but she had a way with horses that no man could match. I've seen women like that. Wild Rose was particular so. When she got next to a horse, even though the horse was rambunctious and might have strong men trying to calm him down, she'd walk up and touch him and talk to him. He'd quiet right down and do pretty near what she wanted him to.

In a way, I could understand that horse's behavior. When she wanted to get me to do something, all she had to do was be nice to me and I was ready to break my neck to please her. Maybe that's the way horses felt. I don't know. Still, I didn't like the looks of that big roan. When she saddled him up and got on, I had a funny feeling. She was big with child and weren't quite as well equipped to maneuver herself, let alone the horse, as she would've been a year ago. Still, I give up thinking 'bout it and we started.

We had one wonderful ride. We stayed 'bout two hundred yards below the snow line where it was wet from the melting and the runoff, but we was still way up on the mountain—I guess 'round the ten-thousand-foot level. The timberline in that country is clear up 'round thirteen thousand feet, not near as low as it is farther north, but still in big blue spruce country. Every now and then we'd break out into parks and have a view where we could see all of the world.

We hadn't gone halfway 'round the mountain, in and outta them spruce trees, when we come to a big open park. 'Bout three hundred yards below us was a big grove of aspens. Aspens don't come up as high as blue spruce and they're a different kinda tree by a long ways. The blue spruce is an evergreen. Aspens, of course, shed their leaves every fall.

When you ride among spruce, you got no underbrush and your horse can see what he's doing and you don't have to duck under no limbs. The quakies, with lots of ferns 'round 'em, cover everything down below. Quaking aspens live a very short time compared to blue spruce. Living that short time, they have lots of deadfalls 'round 'em, and them groves are just the worst kinda thing to get a horse tangled up in. You can't see them dead trunks, 'cause they're lying underneath the brush. When a horse goes to take a step over 'em he goes clear down and locks into two or three crisscross logs. Then, when he goes to get out, he gets excited and plunges 'round, getting hisself in worse shape than ever. A horse can break a leg real easy that way. Every mountain horseman knows to stay outta quakies less'n he wants trouble. You can always ride in blue spruce and sometimes in oak brush, if'n you have a pair of chaps. But quakies is poison.

We come outta that big clearing and sat there for a few minutes looking off towards the San Juan Range to the east. The sun was high in the sky and I judged it to be close to noon.

Everything was peaceful as could be. Suddenly Wild Rose pointed to the left and up the hill. 'Bout four hundred yards away was a grizzly family—a big sow and two cubs. There ain't no more fun thing than to see a grizzly mother with her cubs. But you don't want to get too close, 'cause she's as protective as can be. A mother grizzly with her cubs is 'bout the meanest thing you can come across.

We reined our horses and stood real still. The gentle wind was blowing from us to her, and she was below the snow line and turning over rocks looking for varmints. We sat there for a few minutes and I was wondering when she'd start smelling us. If the wind'd been blowing the other way, our horses would've been raising hell.

We certainly had a grandstand seat, watching her toss around small boulders, prob'ly looking for groundhogs. They was boulders me and you together couldn't begin to lift. She kept on doing that and we just waited. Sure enough, she finally got our scent and whirled 'round and sat straight up. The cubs paused and looked where she was looking. Bears don't have very good eyesight and I don't reckon she seen us on our horses at the edge of the timber, but she could smell us. Then she started cuffing her cubs into action, moving 'em outta danger. She kept them little rascals going downhill 'til she got to the timber 'bout a quarter mile away. They didn't bother looking 'round; they just kept going 'til they disappeared into the forest. That big sow mother looked sorta like a big gorilla. Boy, she had all kinds of power and motion. A grizzly on the move is an impressive sight.

After they disappeared, we congratulated ourselves on not having our horses pick up the scent and give us a bad time. I asked Wild Rose if she wanted to go back or on 'round the mountain.

She just smiled. "We are going around."

We started off again and'd traveled maybe two or three hundred yards when the wind shifted and a strong smell of bear—strong enough for even a man to smell it—come our way.

All hell broke loose. Our horses begun rearing and plunging and twisting and snorting, 'specially Wild Rose's big roan. He begun bucking and raising hell and then stopped stiff-legged looking down the hill with his ears standing up and his eyes bulging out. Wild Rose was yelling at him in Shoshone and reining him back hard. She'd rode out the bucking in good style and I thought she had him stopped, but he whirled and took off again, running back down the hill in big jumps heading for the aspen groves. My heart sank.

By that time I had Cimarron calmed down and started after 'em. I was riding for all I was worth, but always a little behind. I knowed that the roan had the bit in his teeth and there weren't no way Wild Rose was gonna hold him. I was racing to catch up and get hold of his bit and yank him 'round, but I couldn't reach him. He went tearing into the quakies and down through a bunch of deadfalls and 'bout five inches of snow, a-clammering and crashing and banging.

It happened just the way you'd expect it to. Damned if he didn't catch his foreleg on a big deadfall and go over in a somersault—right straight over just as clean as could be. Them big hindquarters come clear over his head. There was a terrible crash and Wild Rose was underneath it all. I started to draw my rifle to kill him, but then stopped myself for fear I might hit her. I piled off old Cimarron and lit out running through the aspen grove as fast as I could, but there was deadfalls all over the place and I was having to stop and jump and run and twist and turn to get over to where Wild Rose was lying like a bird that'd fluttered down in the snow after the life'd been shot out of it. The roan'd managed to get up and wandered over to where Cimarron was waiting. Miraculously, he weren't hurt none.

For a minute all I seen was a stretch of raven hair and a little color on that beaded jacket of hers. When I got closer, I seen blood on her face. I lifted her head and shoulders and held her tight. She was pale and her eyes was turned back. I was sure she was dead. In deep despair I put my thumb up against the side of her neck and felt very careful. God almighty, there was a heartbeat! She was alive! If I could just keep her going. If I could just somehow keep the life in her, maybe things'd be all right, even though I knowed she must've been hurt awful bad.

I kept talking to her, crooning and holding her and bathing her face with some snow so's to bring her around a little. Then her eyes flickered and finally come back and tried to focus. After a while I seen she recognized me.

She tried to whisper and I had to lean down real close to pick up her words, but when I heard 'em they was clear enough. "Ah, my man, I am bad hurt. Yes, very bad. I think now the little one is coming. My legs do not seem to move and my side is giving me great pain."

I looked closer and seen she had blood on her lips and tongue. Since she'd told me her side hurt, I figured she must've broke ribs all along there and maybe one of 'em'd punctured a lung.

I asked her how it was to breathe. "Oh, Cat, it hurts, but I will breathe because I must open my eyes and see you again."

I got all upset. "C'mon, baby, yore gonna make it. Yore gonna be all right. Yore not just gonna see my ugly ol' face once, yore gonna see it a lot. Now take it easy, just rest easy. I'm gonna take ya back ta the cabin."

With that I lifted her real careful outta the snow and deadfalls of the aspen grove.

It was the deadfalls that'd spilled that roan all right, but then again it was the deadfalls that prob'ly saved her life. In that terrible crash the whole weight of the hindquarters of the horse'd come down and smashed her to the earth. If it'd been completely flat ground, she would've been dead in an instant, but she survived 'cause her body sunk down 'tween the quakie logs. They was what took the main blow of the horse's fall.

She was easy to lift, although she was heavy with child. I reckon her normal weight would've been maybe a hundred twenty pounds, but she weighed close to a hundred thirty-five or forty by then. She gasped a couple of times. I knowed things was really hurting, but I couldn't let her lie there and freeze to death in the snow. I had to lift her. It's bad to move somebody when they're hurt real serious like that, but there weren't nothing else I could do. I was frantic, so I carried her, gingerly working my way through the snow and dead-falls, lifting my legs up and climbing over the logs as best I could. Finally I reached the edge of the quakie patch, where old Cimarron and the roan stood looking at me with doubtful eyes, trying to figure out what was wrong.

Cimarron was well trained. Another horse would've run off and I would've been helpless, but he stood there as I come swinging 'round, using the tips of my fingers to get his reins up 'round his neck. I worked him into a position where I was above him on the steep hillside. Then, still holding Wild Rose in my arms, I managed to get my foot in the stirrup and hoisted both of us onto the saddle. Leaning way down, I kind of rested her in my lap, gathered the reins and started moving out. The roan followed along behind us.

That old horse Cimarron had a wonderful single-foot pace. It was just like riding on a river raft in smooth water. He stepped out real nice and we didn't feel the slightest jar. Nonetheless it was a tough ride back to the cabin, not 'cause there was anything wrong with the trail or Cimarron's gait, but 'cause we was holding each other, and the shadow of death was hanging over us. I could see that Wild Rose was cold and shivering and pale, and during that last mile I could feel her getting fainter and fainter.

We come to the cabin in 'bout an hour. I slipped us both off the horse and went through the door and laid Wild Rose down real gentle on our straw bunk. No matter how gentle I was, though, just moving her caused her to gasp. But there weren't a cry outta her. She just weren't gonna give no sign of pain.

When I laid her down, she looked up at me with a sad smile and them gentle eyes. She reached up with her good hand and stroked the side of my cheek. "Poor Cat, I make so much trouble for you."

There was trouble all right, real terrible trouble, but it weren't anything she'd made. I run around there fast, getting the fire started and lacing up the door so's the cold wind couldn't come in. Then I put a water bucket on the stove. I didn't quite know why, but I *knowed* somehow that we had to have some hot water.

When that cabin begun to get warm and cozy, Wild Rose come to pretty good and told me what to do. I made some venison soup for her and covered her with buffalo robes and just sat there and waited for her orders. I could tell she was in labor, and I knowed something real important was gonna happen to both of us.

She labored all through the night and I done what I could to help her. It was most unusual for an Indian woman to be in labor that long and we both knowed it. Most likely, if she'd been well and healthy and the baby'd come three weeks later like it should have, she wouldn't have had no trouble a'tall. But she sure had trouble that night.

The cabin was warm and I kept it that way, only occasionally going out through the door to get more snow to melt for water. It was a good thing there weren't no blizzard blowing. It was a clear, starry night.

Just as the sky begun to show the first crack of dawn, the little one come. I ain't never forgetting the bursting squall when that little girl took life and begun to breathe. Wild Rose coached me on what to do and soon I had the baby up in her arms. The squalling stopped when she started to nurse. I seen real quick that Wild Rose was bleeding bad. She looked awful pale—I knowed she'd been fighting all the time to keep her strength—but it looked like a losing battle. I knowed I had to do something fast to stop her bleeding.

I looked all around to see what I could use for some packing, knowing that if I could just get the blood flow stopped, it'd dry and heal. What to use was a helluva problem. Hides or skin weren't no good. There weren't no leaves or nothing around, and we didn't have no cloth I could use. Then I suddenly thought of the capote, that beautiful red coat made outta the Hudson Bay blanket. There's wool in that, I thought—that'll do the thing right. I run over to it and pulled off the belt to cut into cottonlike wads. I packed her with 'em as best I could, and the bleeding finally stopped. She kept on nursing the baby, but she was drifting back and forth 'tween being conscious and being in a dreamworld.

One time when she come to, I was sitting there holding her hand, and she looked at me. "Oh, Cat, I am so glad we have the little one and that we now live together with her. When you opened the door to go out to get snow for water, it was then that I saw the morning star. It is such a good sign. We shall name the baby Morning Star and she will bring much joy to us. When I am gone to the spirit world, she will remind you of me."

"Now look here," I said. "Don't go talkin' like that. Ya ain't goin' ta no spirit world. Yore gonna be just fine after a while. Ya just need a little rest an' some care, an' I aim ta give ya that. In a little while yore gonna be up an' around an' you'll be fine. We're gonna raise us a family just like we planned. Ya mustn't talk 'bout goin' away no more 'cause I'm right here with ya an' our baby's here with us, too. There's three of us here now, where just a short time ago there was only two."

I took my wife in my arms and held her and the baby. I can't describe my feelings. Wild Rose just looked at me and smiled sadly. Then she closed her eyes and didn't say no more.

I hung 'round all that day and all night and all the next day, doing everything I could for both Wild Rose and the baby. I done some praying, too. I ain't no religious man, and I don't know a lot 'bout praying, but I prayed to every god there was, whether it was a Shoshone god or whether it was the Christian god, or whatever gods there may be. I just prayed and prayed for help to get them two human beings, who was the dearest in the world to me, back on the road to health.

Well, things move along whether you like it or not, and it seemed like Wild Rose was getting a little better each day. Maybe it was the praying, I don't know, but I kept it up. Morning, noon, and night, I sat by my darling as long as I could stay awake, and when I went to sleep I went to sleep beside her like she'd done with me a long time ago.

Every now and then the little baby'd wake me with her bawling. When Wild Rose wanted something real bad, I'd feel her reaching over and squeezing my hand. I'd wake up and want to know what I could do for her.

Like I say, it seemed like she was getting better. She'd smile and sometimes talk, but God, she looked awful pale. I kept trying to get her to eat as much as possible, but she didn't feel like it most of the time. I'd give her stuff that I thought'd go down the easiest—some nice thick venison soup or whatever I could lay my hands on.

Some days she was better and some days she was worse. By and large, though, I'd say she improved right noticeable over the next two weeks. One thing she was able to do all along was feed the baby. That little rascal growed almost while you was just watching her. Every so often Wild Rose'd have me bathe the child, and I could do that real good with a bucket of warm water. I'd get her nice and dry with a beaver skin towel and then give her back to her mama, who never failed to smile when I'd bring the baby back to her.

I took care of Wild Rose that way, too. I'd sponge her off as best I could, though she seemed to hurt real bad. When I tried to roll her over on her stomach, she had lots of pain. She'd also talk to me sometimes 'bout her breathing: "When I take a deep breath, my whole side aches." I felt 'round her ribs and it was easy to see that they'd been pretty well banged up.

Sometimes, when she coughed, there was blood on her lips. I was sure she'd punctured a lung. How in the hell could she help it, having the whole weight of that big thirteen-hundred-pound horse somersaulting right on top of her with his hindquarters coming down and crashing her into the earth. It was a damn wonder she was even alive.

Time passed like that for three weeks. I'd only go out to get water. Then I'd be back tending to my family. A couple of times I walked over to the side of the hill and looked down into our big meadow, counted the horses, and seen how they was doing. Everything looked all right, so I'd fill a bucket with water and come back into the house and tell Wild Rose.

Morning Star kept growing and growing. You could almost see it happening. And she could really yell. When she woke up hungry, she had the strongest lungs of anything I'd ever heard. You'd know what was the matter with her real quick, and you'd better do something 'bout it in a hurry.

I made a little crib for her. I'd gather her up and bring her over to her mama, who'd smile and take her in her arms and feed her. Then Wild Rose'd look up at me and say something real nice. She seemed to be doing better and looked forward to holding her child, even though feeding the baby was real uncomfortable 'cause of the way she hurt.

Progress was slow. There was times when she was real peppy and others when she'd lapse and sleep a good part of the day and night. I really had hopes for her, but I just couldn't figure out some things, like why she was hurting so bad on one hip and didn't have no feeling in her legs. She didn't try to get up and walk none, which was real strange for an Indian squaw. They're usually walking four or five hours after birth. It was plain she'd been hurt bad. I just hoped it weren't her spine. Only time'd tell.

Her breathing was real bad, too. She said that every time she took a deep breath it hurt, 'specially on her right side. One morning she begun telling me that she was hurting in the lower part of her belly. It got worse, and I done what I could for her, but I couldn't see nothing 'cept that her belly was real swole up. Then I realized that she prob'ly had some deep trouble there—maybe some infection. I was afraid that it come from my packing her. Maybe I'd done it all wrong. All I knowed was I'd done my best and if'n I hadn't stopped her bleeding, she would've died right there three weeks before.

She kept getting lower and lower each day. She still took the baby to feed and'd spend some time with me each day, holding hands and talking 'bout nice things, but it was easy to see that she was sinking fast. I was getting real worried. That night it seemed like she was having bad dreams and she begun to talk weird. I stayed up with her and she fed the baby in the middle of the night.

The next morning turned out bright and beautiful. It seemed like she was getting better again. She even laughed some when the baby started squalling and I took our daughter to her. She was a little better then and when she was through she handed the baby back to me.

I took Morning Star and put her in the cradle, which was lined with the warm beaver hides that I'd trapped in the meadow stream during the winter. The cradle was warm and smooth and felt good, and she settled down and went to sleep.

Then I come back to Wild Rose and she took my hands in hers and looked at me sadly. "Gray Eyes, my love, remember the baby's name is to be Morning Star. When she was born that is what I saw. You must promise me that she will always be called Morning Star."

"I told ya 'fore an' I'm gonna repeat it again, my woman: Yore gonna see that she's called that. Ya don't have ta worry 'bout what I'm gonna do."

She shook her head. "No, Gray Eyes, no. I am going to the Spirit World."

"No ya ain't. Yore gonna stay right here an' yore gonna get well. You an' me an Mornin' Star are gonna be the beginnin' of a big family."

She just made that sad smile of hers and looked at me with her soft doe eyes that I can't never forget—eyes that I'd first seen when I was waiting for the torture and then again when she'd watched over me so careful and'd nursed me back to health after that grizzly'd mauled me. Then she squeezed my hand and drifted off into the dreamworld again.

I stayed up with her all that night. Sometimes she'd wake up and we'd talk. Once we even sang a little. But she was sinking fast. When the bright morning sunshine come, she pulled me close to her and whispered, "Now, my man, I am going, for the Great Spirit is calling me. I must leave you, my brave, beloved warrior, you and my little Morning Star. Keep her well, for she is both of us."

I took her in my arms and whispered my love and begged her not to leave us, but she only sighed, squeezed my hand, and turned her face away and died.

I grabbed her 'round the shoulders and hugged her and lifted up her head and shook her violentlike. "No! No! Yore not leavin'! Wild Rose! Ya can't leave us! Fer God's sake, don't leave me an' Mornin' Star! There's three of us! Ya can't go! Wild Rose! Wild Rose!" My voice faded to a whisper, 'cause I looked at her again and knowed she was gone, gone forever. Forever and ever. That truth was an unbearable pain.

It ain't good to see a strong man cry, and I'm glad that no one was 'round, just the little baby sleeping in the crib. But I want to tell you, my whole body shook with the sobbing. I couldn't control myself. I was a broken man setting there, hugging my beautiful Wild Rose, my beautiful Wild Rose who was gone. It's times like them that shakes a man clear to his soul, and he gets to thinking what it's all about. How come he's here. How come he's had such joy and sorrow while he's here. How come the great God, whoever He is, wherever He is, how come He'd just snatch a life away like that.

THE RIDE

I don't know how long I was there holding Wild Rose, but her body begun to get cold. I suddenly woke up to reality when Morning Star busted out crying to be fed. Then the whole horror hit me again. How in hell was I gonna feed that little baby? What was I gonna get for her to eat? What in God's world was I gonna do? I guess the shock of realizing what a bad fix I was in brought me to my senses. There I was all alone eight thousand feet up on the slopes of a big mountain, miles and miles from any help, with just a baby that was the only living link 'tween me and my beautiful Wild Rose.

I picked up the child from the crib and set her up on the table and started warming some water on the stove. I got me a little tin pan and put some sugar in it and warmed the water to where it was just 'bout the same temperature as my hand. I put my little finger in it and put the finger in the baby's mouth while she was a wailing to beat the band. She stopped for a minute but real quick started up again. That made me panic. Brules, I thought, ya can't lose your cool now. Ya've gotta hang tight. If this baby's gonna live, it's gonna be 'cause a you an' you alone. Ya'd damned well better think 'bout what ta do.

I kept feeding her that way and she'd stop crying for a minute to suck the sugar water, then she'd bawl again, so I'd stick my finger back in the pan. She ate some, but it didn't seem to do much good. Once in a while she'd stop for a few seconds and I'd have a chance to gather my wits. Then I seen it right away. It was simple. I had to get the baby to a woman, and I had to get her to a woman that was wet from having her own child. How in the hell am I gonna do that, I thought. There's no way I can cross Dallas Pass an' take her ta the Southern Ute nation in Montrose ta get some help. The snow on the pass this time a year'd be ten feet deep.

There was a dirty little mining camp at the head of the Telluride basin, but there'd be nothing but tents and maybe a shack or two. There certainly wouldn't be no women 'round—less'n there was an old whore who'd set up her business in a shanty someplace, and she sure as hell wouldn't be no woman with a newborn child.

There was only one way I could go. I had to make it down to the southwest, down into the desert where it was warmer, so's I could travel fast to someplace on the Navajo reservation and find me a Navajo woman. If I could just get the baby there in time.

The nearest point that I knowed of was Mexican Hat, at the ford of the San Juan River. From Lone Cone Peak to Mexican Hat is a hundred twenty-four miles as the crow flies. I was gonna have to travel more'n that, 'cause I couldn't make no straight path. God! That seemed like a helluva way, but there weren't no helping it. I knowed the baby was early born and couldn't stand what most babies could, but I still figured that if I could get her there in twenty-four hours, she'd have a chance. When I thought 'bout riding a hundred twenty-four miles in a day, a lot of it mountain riding, I was near appalled. Fact is, I was outta my mind for a little bit, 'cause I sure rushed 'round there and done everything I could think of in a hurry.

First thing I done was get me a fresh halter outta the cabin and run down to where the horses was. I seen that they was bunched 'bout a half mile away, and I made it there as fast as I could. I was thinking 'bout using that Appaloosa stallion that Wild Rose was so proud of— the stallion she'd called Spotted Chief. He was a big horse, 'bout sixteen hands, and was muscled as hell and strong as a bull. 'Sides that, he had them wide-open nostrils that I liked so much. For sure he was gonna have to be a "drinker of the wind" if he was gonna hold up. He was young and he was Wild Rose's favorite and that was good enough for me. I needed the best horse in our remuda for what I had in mind.

When I got in close, I whistled 'em up just like I'd seen Wild Rose do a hundred times. You know, you can take the best and tamest horses and have 'em come to you on call daily, but when you let 'em run wild most of the winter, it ain't always for sure they'll come. If they'd run off, I would've had a helluva time catching 'em. Hell, it might take hours, and all the while that little baby was starving. But Spotted Chief raised his head and looked around. The rest of them cayuses done the same, and some of 'em started ambling towards me, including my old Cimarron. But, damned if old Spotted Chief didn't come a-running. I don't know why, but he sure come quick. It seemed like he knowed I needed help bad.

I slipped the halter on him and swung up bareback, expecting the worst, but he didn't buck a bit. I didn't waste much time. I rode him to the corral, tied him to the hitching post, and saddled and bridled him in a hurry. I filled two canteens that I'd always had for Wild Rose and for me. I took a small bag of oats, some fire steel, a bag of pemmican, my knife, a little ammunition for my Smith & Wesson, and rolled all that stuff up in my blanket and tied it on the back of the saddle.

Then I noticed that old Cimarron'd followed us up. Seeing him reminded me that I'd best take a second horse in case I needed a remount. I quick throwed a halter and a lead rope on him, too. Then I headed for the cabin. I went in and looked at Wild Rose, and the awful thought come to me that I should bury her right then. But the ground was still froze and I knowed it'd be pure hell trying to bury her. I figured it'd take hours—if I could do it a'tall. In the meantime, the baby was starving. But ya can't leave Wild Rose in this cabin, Brules, I thought. The wild animals'll break in. The bears'll be comin' outta hibernation an' ya'll have nothin' but ruination when ya come back—*if* ya come back. Ya can't leave your wife like this. Either way my mind was tortured.

Then I got a good idea: Maybe I could put Wild Rose up on a scaffold away from the animals like the Shoshone done. But the idea of leaving my wife out there in the wind and the rain and all that was something I couldn't stand. Then I got a better idea. I wrapped her up in a buffalo robe and tied it all 'round her real tight and nice and pulled part of it over her head and tied it up so's no one could see her face. I took one last look at her 'fore I done so, 'cause I knowed I'd never ever see her again. I had some rope that we was using for lariats, so I tied 'em 'round both ends of her body 'bout midway along. I climbed up and put the ropes over the main beam of the ceiling. Then I jumped down and pulled on 'em equal-like, moving her body to where it was hanging up there just below the roof. She'd be safe there. She'd be outta the way, yet she'd be protected from the wind and the snow and the rain and all the bad things that come with the weather. She'd be in our cozy home and she'd have an Indian burial when I got back.

I was gonna ride like hell for Mexican Hat. When I got back I'd dig her a grave after the frost was gone outta the ground. I'd put her where she'd be looking out over the desert and mountains like she used to do. I knowed right where it'd be. But right then I had to get help for Morning Star if I was gonna save her life. I took off my shirt and made a kind of sling out of it with the sleeves and some rawhide buckskin laces. Then I put the baby in it naked. I tied that 'round and over my naked shoulder and 'round my waist with long strings of rawhide. I put my capote on, and I fixed it so's the baby's head was just by my neck and shoulder on the left side. She could look forward just like a papoose. Then I pulled the hood up so's it was over both of our heads, and I tightened the neck string so she could still look out and breathe, but it'd keep her warm.

She was bawling quite a lot 'fore we started, but when she got next to my shoulder, the warmth of our bodies together seemed to quiet her down. I went out and grabbed Cimarron's lead rope and then swung up on old Spotted Chief and we was off.

It was 'bout one o'clock in the afternoon. We started down off'n that mountain in a hurry heading southwest. There was a game trail part of the way and we kept working it. It kept cutting back here and there and we finally made it outta the gloom of the blue spruce and down into the quaking aspens—down, down, and down through the rough limbs of the oak brush. I didn't have no chaps, but I had a good pair of leather buckskin trousers and they served just as well. I wore fur gloves and had real heavy Comanche moccasins that give me lots of protection 'cause they was clear up to my thigh. I was ready to ride.

By midafternoon we was off the mountain and out onto the sagebrush flats. I put old Spotted Chief into an easy lope and didn't rush him none, knowing that I had to save him for a long ride. Every time you mount a horse and head out on something like that, even with a remount along, you wonder whether you can make it. I kept patting him and talking to him and telling him to take it steady and easy, that we had a long night's ride ahead of us. He tossed his head a few times and blowed out his nose like he understood.

On that late May day, the sun didn't go down 'til pretty well in the evening. It was still shining some when we come to that great canyon where the Dolores River roared a thousand feet below. We'd come more'n forty miles in five hours and had to cross the canyon with still eighty miles to go, but the stallion was running strong. He had all kinds of bottom and he seemed to know that he was on some sort of special mission.

The Dolores Canyon is really something. It runs in a great bow, cutting right across the route 'tween Lone Cone Peak and Mexican Hat. It don't have no sheer canyon wall, just a real steep slope of rocks and piñon trees and cedars and patches of grass and then more rocks. It's tough enough in broad daylight, but as the descending sun throwed dark shadows and gathered the canyon in gloom, I become more and more fearful of what we was doing. Hell, I could survive anything. I weren't bothered none 'bout that. But I was thinking 'bout how the baby was gonna make out. I had to get her to Mexican Hat within twenty-four hours. If that horse slipped or stumbled and broke his leg, the baby was gone. Me, I could scramble out, but not Morning Star. That baby's life hung on the surefootedness of that horse as he kept his nose lowered a-sniffing and feeling his way down that canyon slope.

He done a great job of it, mostly sliding 'round and zigzagging on his haunches, and we finally got to the bottom. He stood there a minute looking at the roaring torrent of the spring flooding of the Dolores River. It was bigger'n the San Miguel and there was a lot of difference crossing it in the spring rush than crossing the San Miguel in the fall when it was damn near dried up. I could hardly hear myself think above the roaring of that river.

What's more, I was dismayed to see that them boulders in the creek was as big as kitchen tables. I could easily see a horse jamming up his foot somewhere in there and getting twisted 'round and pulled by the current, perhaps pulling a ligament or breaking a leg, and I wouldn't know what to do 'bout it. The only thing I could think of was to give the horses a little rest for a few minutes on the north bank and then try to find a good place to cross and have a go at it.

I slid off old Spotted Chief and pulled the saddle off'n him. I rubbed his back and legs and let him rest a minute. I done the same with Cimarron. Then I got the idea to pull out the oat bag. I let 'em take turns. They went for that and had theirselves a nice quart of oats each.

Oats to a horse is like whiskey is to a man. It's like having a shot of Yukon Jack 'fore you go into some tough thing. That's the way it worked with old Spotted Chief. He picked up his head fast and nickered as though he was saying, Hell, the last forty miles ain't been nothing, boss. Let's see what we can do here. That horse was just getting going. Cimarron still looked okay, but he begun balking bad when we got to that roaring stream, so I decided to leave him there rather than risk losing him in that raging river. If he went down, he might just drag us down with him, and I weren't going to risk that.

I saddled Spotted Chief up again and eased onto him, being real careful of the baby. I begun thinking out what I'd do if the horse spilled and we went underwater: how I'd get back out, which bank I'd claw for, and all that. I figured I'd have to get a fire lit quick and get the baby all dried out from the ice-cold water, or she'd never make it. I was just having bad thoughts ahead of time.

I needn't have fretted none. Old Spotted Chief picked his way 'cross just as nice as you please. He floundered some a couple of times and lost his footing and the current moved him a little, but he kept heading upstream all the time. That's the way you keep a horse if you don't want him to get lost in the heavy current, only I didn't have to do that none with him. He done that natural-like. He just kept heading upstream to where he could get the drive of his legs against the current and keep his balance and feel and fetch his way along with his front feet. We labored and belabored our way across to the far side and he scrambled up and took off like he was fresh as a daisy. By God, I just had to take my hat off to him. What a helluva horse!

I patted him on the neck and leaned down and give him a few real nice compliments. You know, it's a funny thing, but sometimes a horse knows what you're talking 'bout.

I headed him up the steep south slope of the canyon and we wove 'round in the darkness trying to pick our way 'round them rocks and trees. It was a tough climb, and when we got near the top we come into the worst part of all—the little rim of cap rock that runs all around the edge of the canyon. There weren't no way to get 'round that. You had to find some kind of a ravine, some kinda draw that split that cap rock so's you could make your way up through it. It was pretty dark and hard to find, even with my sharp eyes.

There was a sickle moon and the stars was out bright, but it was still tough trying to pick out details in the shadows of them ravines. There was 'bout four of 'em above us, and I tried to choose one that looked good. When I did, we got a third of the way up and seen it was blocked by a rockfall, so we had to back off and do it again. We done that twice more. The last time we picked the right ravine and started up and kept churning. It got steeper and the rocks kept sliding out from under that horse's feet, and it got tougher as we neared the top. Spotted Chief was plumb exhausted. It was a helluva thing to put a horse to. It was the cruelest kinda slope. If he'd slipped and fell, we would've slid halfway down the canyon, and God knows what would've happened. We prob'ly would've rolled over a couple of times. "C'mon, boy. C'mon," I told Spotted Chief. "We're near the top. C'mon, just give it a little bit more. C'mon, boy. C'mon. Here we go!"

We almost made it when we had a bad moment right at the top. That ravine was so steep and the footing so bad that I could feel Spotted Chief struggle close to the limit. It was touch and go, and I knowed that if he lost his footing and started to slip, he'd go over backwards and kill us all, and I could feel him starting to do just that.

All of a sudden I realized it was my weight on his back that was ruining his balance, and I pulled an old trick just in time. It was a trick I'd learned from talking to cavalry troopers. They sometimes used it when they was swimming their horses 'cross a big river and clawing up steep mudbanks. I slipped my feet outta the stirrups and, lying on my belly, slid back right over his hindquarters and dropped like a cat to the rocky slope of the ravine. With one hand I grabbed at the rocks for balance, and with the other I grabbed the horse's tail and give a war whoop. All I could see was the horse ahead of me outlined against the night sky, lunging for his life and ours. He just did make it, dragging us all out into the starry night at the top.

I stopped. I knowed how that horse felt. He was trembling all over. He'd just give everything he had and was blown. That pull up the canyon was like giving him forty miles of riding. He'd just 'bout had it. His legs was shaking and he was puffing and wheezing. His belly and lungs was as if they was just burning out. Old Spotted Chief was standing there with his head down a little, and that ain't good with a horse. I knowed he needed some special treatment right away if he was gonna go on. I took off his saddle, then I pulled out that oat bag and give him another shot while his flanks was still heaving.

Now, you ain't s'posed to do that when a horse pulls his guts out coming up a hill or nothing. You're s'posed to let him have an hour or two 'fore he feeds, but we didn't have an hour or two to give. Anyway, I knowed I'd like to've had a swig of whiskey after I'd gone through something like that. That horse seemed to feel the same way, and damned if he didn't just go right to them oats! It worked wonders. I could tell he felt lots better. His head and ears come up, so I throwed the saddle back on him and tightened up the cinch.

Then I done something real special that I do with horses when I try to give 'em the best break. I just took his reins and started walking ahead of him. I didn't get on him a'tall. I let him get along without my weight. We was both in this together, and I'd weave along packing the papoose. I walked for pretty near two miles that way, and it seemed to help his breathing some and settle his legs. When I'd go back and feel 'em occasionally in the starlight, I could just make out that he weren't shaking no more and that he weren't puffing or blowing.

He seemed to be all right, but I walked ahead of him a little more. Then I could tell he was feeling pretty good, 'cause he got up behind me and kinda rubbed his forehead against the middle of my back and pushed me along and unbalanced me a little. When a horse does that you know he's doing all right. It's his way of saying, Come on, boss, come on. Get on my back and let's get going again.

I swung up in the saddle and we started out. I walked him for maybe two or three more miles, then I got him into a slow trot and we kept on that way. We must've trotted for 'bout an hour, maybe two, I don't know. But it was a bright starry night and them stars stood out like they was all watching to see whether that little baby was gonna make it or not.

After a while I brought Spotted Chief into a slow lope and he took it nice and easy. He got to breathing good and you could tell by the way he was lifting his front feet and the way he was rocking along bending his knees that he had a lot of spring left. Things was going good. Gradually, as we went on through the night, his loping begun to get faster and faster. He finally broke into a full gallop like he'd got his second wind. After eighty miles and one canyon, that was hard to believe.

I tell you, I ain't likely to forget that night's ride. There was a stiff, cold wind on my face and I could smell the sage. I could feel the power of that great stallion 'tween my knees as he lunged along with more drive at every jump. There was the stars and the sickle moon in the sky and the sudden thunder of coveys of wild grouse busting loose from the sage as the stallion sped by. We went on like that, hour after hour.

I marveled at the power of that horse. It seemed like he knowed how important this trip was. He seemed to be saying, It's okay, boss, we're gonna make it. Come on, you keep that little baby tight. We're gonna make it.

I talked to him a lot, telling him he was the greatest horse in all the world and that we was winning. I kept calling to him, "Go, boy! Go!" Then I got to talking to myself. I was getting tired and sore, but I kept saying, "Damn your hide, Brules, ride! Ride, Brules, ride! Damn your lousy hide, ride!"

All night long there was the drumming, drumming, drumming of the stallion's hooves under the sickle moon. There was just me and the baby and the horse—running for the baby's life. Only one time could I feel him check his pace, breaking the stride of his gallop and beginning to gather hisself. He seen something I didn't see, and when I finally seen it, God almighty, it was a big dry arroyo. It must've been twenty-five feet deep and twenty feet across, one of them washouts that happens along the sagebrush country from cloudbursts. When we come up on that, I thought, oh, God, here we go! We're gonna have us a pileup.

But the stallion gathered hisself and sailed 'cross it as if he'd had wings. You know, I kinda believe he did have wings, 'cause he picked up the pace again and held it all through the night. I was picturing little prairie dogs that heard him coming and stuck their heads up above their mounds and then ducked down as the stallion whirled by. He knows he's gotta get the little girl where she's goin', I thought. He knows! He just knows somehow! I don't know how he knows, but he damn well knows. We was just ridin', ridin', ridin'. God, that stallion really had bottom! His power seemed to gain at every jump.

Then I got to thinking, what's this all about? A ride, a ride. I've got a little naked baby on my shoulder, a baby that's sometimes sleepin' an' sometimes cryin', an' the stallion's pullin' his guts out, an' I'm ridin' like I never rode 'fore. What're we doin'?

It seemed like Morning Star's heartbeat was going down through my heartbeat and down into the heartbeat of that horse. Then I realized we was riding for a life! We was fighting for life! That was all there was to it. That's all it was. That's what the meaning of life is, to keep living, to keep on, and keep going.

That little baby with me was all that was left of the life 'tween me and Wild Rose. If that baby died, our love'd die with it. Then I reached down and patted that horse. What good is a man without a horse? I loved him so. How I loved that horse! He kept pulling and pulling. God, how he was going! He was doing it for my little baby and for my dear Wild Rose who lay up there on the mountain all by herself, watching us go.

I knowed Wild Rose was watching us, 'cause she told me just 'fore she died, "You must not weep for me. You must not be sad, Gray Eyes. You must not grieve for me, because I won't be there to be grieving about. I'll be out there in everything. I'll be in the sound of the wind in the trees. I'll be the sheen of the sun on the rippling streams. I'll be the smell of the wildflowers and the song of geese when they're going north in the spring. I'll be everywhere, Gray Eyes. But most of all, I'll be with you and I'll be watching you all your life 'til you join me. Grieve not, my man. Grieve not, for I will be there always, always, always. . . ."

Spotted Chief kept up the pace 'til dawn broke, but then there was something different. He was just a little slower. He was unwinding, but it didn't make no difference. In the early light I could see the San Juan River winding through its valley ten miles away.

It must've been right 'bout noon—the time of the shortest shadows—when me and the baby and old Spotted Chief come stumbling into the trading place called Mexican Hat. We was a beat-up outfit and covered with dust. Spotted Chief's head hung low, and he shuffled along at a walk like a horse that'd come to the end of his rope. I was riding with my head down in a state of near exhaustion. My legs was so sore and stiff I didn't think I could get off the horse. The little baby'd been crying a good part of the time, but she hadn't cried a'tall since the early hours of the morning. A few times I was worried like maybe the whole thing'd been too much for her and that the life'd slipped outta her tiny body. But that weren't true. If I was real careful, I could feel her heartbeat against my naked shoulder. Still I knowed she couldn't last much longer.

Mexican Hat was right at the ferry and the ford of the San Juan River, and there was some Navajo hogans around—maybe three or four. There was some corrals and a shed and something that looked like a store or trading post. The street was dusty and wide, and there was chickens running 'round and a pig or two, and there was a sorta roadway that run down to the ford.

The sky was blue and it was a warm morning in the sands of the desert that spread all the way southwest to Monument Valley and south to Canyon de Chelly.

When old Spotted Chief come shuffling in, people begun to gather 'round to see what was going on. Here was a rider half-asleep in the saddle and a horse with his head down just a-shuffling along, all ga'nt and covered with dust. From what anyone could see, we must've had one helluva ride, and I was wondering if Morning Star was gonna come 'round. She'd been real silent for the last six hours and if she was in some kind of exhausted stupor from lack of food and sleep, it was a stupor she might not come out of.

Some squaws and kids begun gathering 'round and old Spotted Chief, sensing it was the end of the road, stopped for a minute and stood there. Then I heard the most glorious sound in the world. Morning Star burst into a loud hungry wail. There was excited chitchatting among the squaws. They looked at each other and then gathered 'round real close. Painful-like, I slid outta the saddle and stood unsteady on the ground. I pulled off the capote and they seen the child hanging by the shroud that held her to my shoulder.

I made the sign for mother and for death and them Navajo women knowed real quick what it was all about. There was lots more chattering. Then the squaws lifted the baby off'n my back and, holding her in their arms, started shuffling towards one of the hogans, talking and cooing to her. They took her inside—she was screaming and crying and hollering the whole time. A minute later there was silence, and I knowed that some Navajo woman'd become a new mother for Morning Star.

I stood there in the bright noon sun and glanced back at old Spotted Chief. He shook the dust from his head and then walked 'bout twenty or thirty yards and just fell over. I don't mean he lay down, he plumb fell over—stiff legged. He hit the ground with a thump that made the dust fly. God! I thought, he's dead. I run over there and dropped on my knees and put my arms 'round his neck and patted him and started talking to him. I felt for the blood vessel on his throat and found it. Thank God! The faint beat of that great heart was still there.

I took one of the canteens and put it to his lips. He licked it and tried to make something out of it. I poured it into him, but he was too tired to drink much. Then I swigged what was left and jerked the blanket roll off the back of the saddle. Then I lay down with my head on Spotted Chief's neck, spread the blanket over me, and passed out cold.

Me and that horse slept together right there on the dusty main street of Mexican Hat all that afternoon and through the night. 'Course there weren't much traffic through that little town—maybe a mule train every few days—so we slept undisturbed while the chickens pecked 'round us and the pigs grunted by.

I was woke up the next morning by the horse hisself making up his mind that he was ready to get up. When a horse wants to get up, there's no holding him, so's I rolled off and grabbed my blanket at the same time and stood up. When he was all erect and standing, he held his head only halfway up, but his ears come up a little. He was looking 'round, seeing where he was and what was going on. Then he shook hisself all over and I come over close to his head and he rubbed against me, scratching his nose and forehead. Then I stood away for a minute and looked at him. He appeared mighty stiff and tired and sore. He seemed to be saying, Boss, that was one helluva ride. We ain't gonna do that again today, is we?

I just laughed at what I was thinking: No, old buddy, we ain't gonna do that again.

I don't know what horses think, but maybe they know something that me and you don't. Anyway, I took him by the lead rope and we went real slow down to the San Juan River and he had hisself a long, long drink.

After I'd swabbed him off and rubbed his legs, I took him up to the corrals, pulled the saddle and bridle, and turned him loose. He just kinda nosed 'round and stood there for most of the afternoon, eating on some oats I put in the bin for him.

Later some of the Navajo women come out and one of 'em had

Morning Star in her arms. She was sleeping real good and looked happy. The women was all smiling and laughing. It give me the idea that things was just fine. That's all that made any difference. I got to working 'round in sign language and, with the few words of Navajo I knowed and what English words them squaws knowed, I was able to get across a few ideas. I had to think 'bout the future of the baby.

I found out that the nursing squaw was the wife of a young buck that was down at Canyon de Chelly and'd be back the next day. She was nursing not only her own child, who was 'bout two months old, but taking care of Morning Star as well. That was a good deal by me. I just let it be that way. How could I do otherwise? I expressed to her that when her husband got back I'd like to talk with him, 'cause I had a real proposition for both of 'em.

I went up to see if there was a trader in the tiny store, but there was only a young Navajo woman inside. The trader'd gone down to Monument Valley for a few days.

There weren't no use in my worrying 'bout nothing 'til that Navajo buck arrived. I just moseyed 'round some. There was an old cantina that had some tortillas and other stuff, so's I got me something to eat.

The buck come in the next morning and I talked with him and his wife. I told 'em that my little girl's mother was dead, lying up there on Lone Cone Peak. She was a Shoshone woman and it was necessary for me to take the little girl back to the Shoshone people in Wyoming. I knowed that there'd be someone there who'd take care of her and that she'd be among kin. As for me, I was just a wandering hunter and had no place for the baby and nothing she could make good use of.

I proposed that if they'd take my baby and their own papoose and ride to the Shoshone reservation with me, a matter of maybe twenty suns, I'd pay 'em real handsome. I offered 'em a hundred dollars in cash and two of the finest paint horses they'd ever seen. I told 'em I'd give 'em a mare and a stallion.

We struck us a deal pretty quick, 'cause I could see that in spite of that buck being real cunning and cute 'bout trading, he wanted a pair of paint horses worse'n anything. Who the hell wouldn't? All Indians wanted 'em.

Once I'd made the deal, I felt kinda comfortable, but I knowed I had a big job ahead of me. I let old Spotted Chief rest for five days 'fore I saddled him up again and took off real slow for Lone Cone. Having a lot more time to spare, I was able to take it easy. We crossed the Dolores farther downstream near where the town is now located. 'Course there weren't nothing there then, but the sides of the canyons weren't as steep, and it was better going.

In six days we made the same trip that I'd made in less'n twenty-four hours going the other way. Old Spotted Chief was doing all right, but I think that the ride that night was the peak of his physical ability. I kept telling him he was coming back to a beautiful pasture with a lot of pretty mares, but he didn't seem to listen. I think from that time on, he prob'ly took it a lot easier and done things a bit more ordinary.

When I reached our cabin, I turned Spotted Chief into that five-square-mile pasture with the rest of the horses. Then, real reluctant-like, I unlaced the cabin's hide door and looked in to see what was going on. I was half-fearful that something might've happened to spoil the arrangements that I'd made for Wild Rose. But she was suspended up there under the rafters in peaceful silence, and I knowed then that she'd had a decent Indian burial, so I could give her a proper burial according to the ways and customs of her husband.

I went out to pick a spot for the grave. I walked maybe a hundred yards through some timber and out into what was a nice open meadow sloping down the mountain to the southwest. It was a beautiful spot. From it you could see in a big arc all the way from the La Plata Mountains in the southeast, past the Mesa Verde and Sleeping Ute clear on across to Monument Valley, then west to the Blues. If you really twisted your neck 'round, you could see the tips of the Salt Mountains to the northwest. I could see the beginnings of wildflowers coming up on the crest of the meadow, and I knowed it'd be a pleasant place for a grave—a place that Wild Rose'd like.

By then I'd been gone almost three weeks. The warm spring sun'd done a lot to the earth. The digging was a lot easier, and I quickly made a nice grave.

I went back to the cabin and talked to my sweetheart for a little while 'fore I climbed up and eased her down. It'd been cold as could be in that cabin. There'd been no stove going, and she was froze stiff in her buffalo robe. I took her in my arms out into the sunshine and down through the woods. I laid her in the grave facing towards the southwest, 'cause that's the way she told me she always wanted to be. That's the way she'd gone with me.

I put some things in the grave that I knowed she'd want—stuff that I'd bought here and there on our travels, like a Navajo squash-blossom necklace and a bracelet. I took the red capote, tattered and torn, but something that was a token of the love 'tween us, and I laid it down around her so's maybe it'd keep her warm. 'Course another reason I done it was I couldn't bear to wear it no more. It belonged to me and Wild Rose and to our baby Morning Star. It belonged in this place—our ranch. This is where Wild Rose'd made it and this is where it should stay.

Well, I'd done it all. It took the whole day. Then I sat there in the evening when the sun went down and talked to her. I told her what she meant to me. I told her what I thought she was really like. I told her I'd always see her with her beautiful hair waving in the breeze while she rode. I told her that I'd hear the sound of her laughter for the rest of my life, and I told her that I knowed she'd be watching over me and Morning Star, and I'd be waiting 'til my time come to join her.

The next morning I cut some heavy aspen logs and used Cimarron to drag some logs over to cover her grave. He'd made his way back to the ranch after I'd cut him loose at the Dolores. I made a good-sized pile, big enough so's nothing could get at her less'n it was a grizzly, and he'd have to do one helluva lot of work. I didn't think that it'd be worth it to him. I would've put stones on top of her grave, 'cept there weren't none—not there—maybe way 'round the other side of the mountain, but not where she was buried. It was all soft dirt. That's why stuff growed so good and why there was nice trees and deep green grass and wildflowers in the summertime.

I didn't spend that night in the cabin. I couldn't bear to. I made me a fire and slept out in the open. The next day I took that big roan out and packed him with whatever I felt'd be useful for the journey. I left a few things in the cabin, but they weren't too personal to Wild Rose. The things that was personal'd been buried with her. I picked the lesser of the two paint stallions and a mare that was 'bout average and tied 'em to a lead and started off back to Mexican Hat. I left the gates to the pasture open so's the paint horses could run wild if they wanted to, although I figured they'd stay in their own meadow for a long, long time, since it was the best feed around. But I left the gates open anyway so that if they wanted to get out they could.

I knowed it'd be a long time 'fore I'd come back. The hurt in my heart'd have to be gone. It was a beautiful place and I loved it, but I loved it 'cause my wife'd also loved it. To be there without her at that time in my young life would've been bitter beyond measure.

I was another five days getting back to Mexican Hat. I wanted to take it easy on them horses and not have the Navajo buck back outta the bargain. He didn't. A day later I pulled outta Mexican Hat heading for Shoshone country with him and his wife, each with a saddle horse and pack mule. I was riding Cimarron, with Morning Star on my back and leading the big roan that'd fallen on Wild Rose as a packer. He seemed docile enough, and I was glad that I hadn't lost my temper enough to kill him. After all, a horse is just a horse and don't really know what he's doing and don't do it on purpose most of the time. Anyway, he kinda acted like he was sorry that it all had happened, and the part he took in it was something he was real ashamed of. Well, you know me. I was always thinking that horses got feelings and thoughts beyond what they ever had. I'm sure of that, but there's been times when somehow I knowed they was thinking right and far beyond what you figured.

We made it to the Shoshone reservation in twenty days without no problem. We arrived there sometime the first week of June. I don't rightly remember the date. Most of the time I couldn't figure dates nohow. I remember it was June for a special reason. As soon as we arrived the whole place turned out and looked us over. It weren't every day they seen a man carrying a papoose and a Navajo family trailing behind him.

I looked up Wesha right away. He seemed powerful glad to see me. When I told him the sad news, he turned away and hid his sad expression from me. Then he put his hand on my shoulder and made the sign of the Great Spirit and let it go at that. I knowed what he meant. He was kinda saying maybe it was God's will.

We had to find a wet nurse for Morning Star again. Wesha's sister, the one called White Antelope, was a great friend of Wild Rose when they was young girls. She was shocked and saddened to hear of her death, but more'n anxious and loving to adopt Morning Star and care for her along with her own daughter of 'bout the same age. The whole thing was a big relief to me, 'cause I knowed that Morning Star'd have real good care—the kinda care that I could never give her.

Then Wesha said to me, "It is fortunate that you come, for tomorrow we are leaving to campaign against the Sioux. We are to meet General Crook and his pony soldiers at his camp on Goose Creek near

Cloud Peak. There will be a hundred of our warriors. Our friend Tom Moore will go with us with the pack train. Brules, my brother, you must come. Your wife, who was dear to your heart, is no longer with us. You have nothing to think about. What you need is a good war, and we have one for you. You and me, we love to hunt and have done so with each other for many moons. Now our young men are going to war and I wish with all of my heart that you would come with us. It will be exciting and there will be many brave deeds done. You, with your rifle that speaks so deadly, will be of much importance."

I got to pondering 'bout it and couldn't think of nothing else better. I weren't going back there to Lone Cone. I'd go crazy. I figured that I had to do something to get my mind off the terrible sadness that was weighing down my heart. So it didn't take me very long to tell Wesha that I'd be honored to go with him. I wanted to pay the Navajo man and his woman and baby and send them away. Then I'd be ready to go.

The Navajo already had his horses down in Mexican Hat, but I give him the hundred dollars more that I'd promised him, and he headed for home. I departed the next day with the Shoshone warriors to join General Crook on Goose Creek and to fight against the Sioux.

That's how I begun ten years of Indian wars. I was with Crook at the fight on the Rosebud and, 'cause he sent me as a messenger, I was with Custer's scouts at the Little Bighorn. Later, I joined Crook again and seen all the fighting at Slim Buttes and other places. I scouted some for General Miles against the Nez Percé and done some of the work rounding up Crazy Horse. Then I followed General Crook in 1881 when he went back to his old stomping grounds down in Arizona and the Mexican border warring against Geronimo. He'd been there ten years before when they called him up to Wyoming to fight the Sioux, and when he went back to Arizona to finish the job, I went with him.

It took five more years to finish the Apache wars in Arizona. I followed 'em all over. I was there when Geronimo surrendered for the first time to General Crook in the Sierra Madres. He and his people were taken back to the San Carlos Indian Reservation, but Geronimo moved up towards Fort Apache, got restless and dissatisfied and broke out again about a year later.

Crook was in Washington at the time and took a couple of months to get back, but in 1885 he started a new campaign with about six thousand troops and one of them newfangled heliograph signal systems. He also had him about three or four hundred Apache scouts. Crook was a good Indian fighter and knowed that that was the way to dig Geronimo out.

Progress was slow, and I guess Crook took a lot of political heat. Anyway, he eventually resigned after 'bout a year loaded with trouble, and General Miles took over. Maybe Miles had something to do with his resignation, I don't know.

I was there when Geronimo surrendered again, this time to General Miles in Skeleton Canyon sometime in the fall of '86.

Before Crook retired, he give me a medal and made a personal gift to me of a .50-caliber buffalo Sharps. Both he and I knowed that the buffalo was gone and there wouldn't be much use for that Sharps, but I was pleased to have it. As a matter of fact, afterwards I made some long-range kills on elk with that gun.

I lay around Fort Bowie for about three months waiting for my discharge. During that time I got to thinking a little bit 'bout all that'd happened. I'd been so damn busy in the ten years of Indian warfare, 'tween '76 and '86, that I hadn't given much thought to lots of personal things.

I'd left the cabin to take Morning Star up to the Wind River reservation. After I'd done that, I hooked up with Crook and all that hell fighting during the Indian wars kept me real busy. Seemed like whenever I thought of my little girl it only made me grieve more bitterly for Wild Rose. It was more than I could bear, so I buried myself in my work. By golly, it was a real shock to me to suddenly realize that she was a ten-year-old kid now and hadn't seen her old man in all that time!

I resolved right then and there to go back and find her on the Shoshone reservation and, what with her being pretty well growed, maybe she'd come with me and we could make a new home somewhere together. I was most grateful to Wesha's sister, who'd raised her, and I knew that she'd been in good hands, but after all, she was my daughter and maybe she'd cotton to coming with me.

I had all kinds of fancy thoughts 'bout that and often wondered what she'd look like. Would she have Wild Rose's beautiful eyes? Would she have her mother's long black hair? Would she someday be the raving beauty that her mommy was? Would she be kind and gentle like Wild Rose? It all got me kinda excited and, though I hadn't done nothing for her for ten years, I was finally ready to do what I could for my little girl. I'd have to settle down and quit scouting and Indian fighting, but things was clearing up with the Indian trouble and it looked like I'd have to do that anyway.

I'd got a clerk at San Carlos to write me a letter to Agent Irwin on the Shoshone reservation, telling him what was going on. I also sent a pair of little cowboy boots with a lot of nice silver trimmings that was made up by the Navajos. I thought that'd be a great present for a little girl and told Irwin to be sure and see that Morning Star got 'em.

I told him that just as soon as my discharge come through, I'd be on my way up there and we'd all be joined together. I asked him to tell Wesha as much and also Wesha's sister and we'd all have a happy time when we got together.

I got a return letter from Agent Irwin 'bout a month later and it was a shocker! It shattered all my dreams in one blow. He told me that he'd received the boots and they sure was wonderful-looking things, but the trouble was that Morning Star weren't there to receive 'em. She'd left the reservation 'bout five years before.

He said that Wesha's sister, White Antelope, had been taken ill with tuberculosis and, like all Indians that didn't have no resistance to that disease, had passed away. Then my little girl had been kinda bounced from pillar to post among the squaws without really getting another mommy. Irwin told me that she was a beautiful child and just as bright as a dollar, but that he was worried 'bout her 'cause some terrible things was happening there on the Wind River reservation.

The Indian Bureau, in its infinite wisdom, had moved the Arapaho tribe onto the reservation right on top of the Shoshone without asking their permission. What it'd amounted to was to really reduce the Shoshone people's holdings by one-half, as they'd had to split it with the Arapaho, their blood enemies. All hell was breaking loose, traders was selling whiskey on the reservation border and fights was breaking out everywhere. Murders was common and it weren't no place for a little girl who was half white to be raised.

Irwin told me that he'd written his sister in Granville, Ohio, to ask if she'd be interested in adopting Morning Star. His sister was in her early thirties and was married to a banker. She'd been married more'n ten years, but was childless. When she heard 'bout this little girl that might be put up for adoption, she wired her brother that she'd be real happy to have such a child in her house.

Irwin said that his sister was a fine lady and he knowed she'd give Morning Star a wonderful start in life. She'd have a nice home, would be sent to good schools, perhaps even to college, and that she'd have the kind of background and training that'd give her an opportunity to lead a happy life when she was out on her own.

He said that at the time all those arrangements was being made, Morning Star was only 'bout five years old. He arranged for her to be taken back on the train to Granville by two nuns from the Convent of the Sacred Heart in Rock Springs. He also said that he'd registered the adoption at the Rock Springs Courthouse.

As to the boots which I'd sent her, he said he forwarded 'em to Granville and understood from his sister that Morning Star was real happy to get 'em. But Irwin said that he hadn't mentioned that they'd come from her real father. He said the boots had come from an old family friend and let it go at that. He said it was pretty difficult business to have a real parent show up after a child had been adopted. It confused the child and the adopting parents as well and it never seemed to work out for the best. After all, the child had been given away in good faith, and there weren't nothing that nobody could do about it.

Irwin also said that he hoped that I wouldn't press the matter of seeing my daughter, as the poor kid'd be very much upset and have many conflicting emotions that'd only make her life difficult. She was happy where she was and well cared for and had every chance of leading a good life. He thought that I'd understand the situation and said he was sure that I'd want everything for her to be just great.

Well, I read 'tween the lines and it was real simple to see that that child'd be all upset by having some rough old mountain man and gunfighter come waltzing into a real fancy home back in Ohio and try to make up for ten years of lost time. I could see the trouble it'd cause if a rough old hoss like me, chewing tobacco and cussing, with no real table manners nor nothing that was required—wearing dirty old buckskin clothes and just looking plain horrible—come along and told her he was her dad.

I just couldn't do such a thing to my little girl—it'd be a terrible shock to her, something that she didn't deserve.

So finally I decided I'd swallow my pride, bury my own sorrow, which, when you come right down to it, was really of my own making, and give that little kid a chance. I put her outta my mind and resolved to never think 'bout it again. That was a damn hard thing to do. I had the clerk write a letter to Irwin accordingly and described my feelings and what I thought was best.

Everybody I knowed agreed, so when my discharge come I lingered 'round the southwest a little and then headed back to Lone Cone in the summer of '88. In all those years, I'd growed more and more lonesome for Wild Rose. I just couldn't seem to be happy nowhere. I grieved for her often, and I believed it was time that I went back to see her.

When I got here, things was 'bout like they'd been, 'cept some of the roof of the cabin'd caved in and there was the natural mess of things that you'd expect after twelve years. The first thing I done was to go to Wild Rose's grave. Most of the timber'd rotted away, but the grave was intact and nothing'd bothered it.

Thinking that there was no other place I wanted to go in the world, I rebuilt the roof on the cabin. The horses, of course, had long gone outta the pasture, running wild somewhere up there in the mountains. I was real glad for that. Twice I seen the band running with a big stallion and I knowed that they'd multiplied real good during the time I'd been gone. But they was running wild, and them being Wild Rose's horses, it was best to let 'em be that way.

I'll tell you a real strange thing. I thought a lot 'bout Wild Rose and mourned for her many times during the campaigns of the Indian wars, but I only seen her in my dreams a few times. Yet the first night that I come back here and slept in the bunk where me and Wild Rose'd spent so many happy nights, she come back to me in a dream. Even though it was twelve years later, she was just as young and beautiful as I'd ever seen her. She talked to me, but I couldn't hear her very well, though I could sense what she was saying. She said she'd been watching me and that she was glad to see me back. Her voice was very faint and she smiled her sad smile and looked at me with them soft eyes, and then she was gone.

I've been here twenty-eight years now, and she comes to me often in my dreams. You can tell I'm an old man now, and she's been gone forty years, but she still comes as a young woman. She's so beautiful.

She's real and I know she's here. Oftentimes I go out in the evening and sit by her grave. There's no marker there, but you know the place, 'cause a deep bed of wildflowers grows over her grave in the spring. It marks her sweetness. I think the aspen logs made good soil through the years.

I don't want to go nowhere else now. I only want to stay here and see Wild Rose when she feels like coming. At different times she tells me that she's waiting for me to join her, and I know that won't be too long. I can tell you that all my life since she left, I've wanted to be with her again. It's with real joy that I look forward to the time when we'll be together.

These mountains are beautiful. The desert is beautiful. The sunsets are like red glory. Summer has its green and winter has its white mountains blanketed with snow, but it's all meaningless without my Wild Rose. I must go to her, and I'll do it soon.

Now, let me tell you another strange thing. Maybe you won't believe me, but it's true. Many years ago I saw Wild Rose once and she was real. She weren't no spirit. It was down near the foot of the mountain in a big meadow and she was gathering wildflowers. It was in the afternoon and it weren't no dream. I seen her! I absolutely seen her! Strange as it may seem, she weren't wearing her beaded head-dress and her Shoshone buckskin skirt. She was wearing white woman's clothes. I think that was very strange. I called to her and she seen me, but she didn't want to speak with me. She just mounted her horse and galloped away. I ran after her, but I was old and on foot and watched her go, my heart broken. I just dropped to my knees and put my head in my hands and bawled.

That was almost twenty years ago. I don't know why she run off, but I'll ask her when I go to her soon.

A NAVAJO BLANKET

The old man drew the pipe from his mouth and spat into the fire, the light and shadows flickering on that leathery old face and in those strange eyes. While I watched, it seemed as if those cross-hairlike pupils grew smaller and tighter as they gazed into the firelight and, somehow, Brules's soul receded behind their inscrutable light.

The old man remained silent and, although we both sat there for nearly an hour after he'd stopped talking, he never opened his mouth again.

The first faint streaks of dawn lit up the eastern sky as I rolled away from the fire into my blanket. I gazed at the fading stars, trying somehow in my mind to put all of these things together, to picture and memorize the life of that strange old man who had wandered the whole face of the West in the half century before.

It seemed as if I were reaching for a sort of spirit world, a will-o'-the-wisp, the shadow of a cloud passing over the ridge of a mountain—so unreal and yet so vivid, but so far away. Finally my exhausted mind slipped backward into a deep slumber and the scene was gone forever.

It must have been midmorning when I awoke, because the sun was shining overhead, brightly. It was one of those gorgeous fall days in our western country when the world seems freshly painted all around. I sat up and shook myself and wondered whether what I'd heard over the past three days and nights was a dream or whether it was indeed real.

The cabin stood there stark and silent in the shadow of the pines, outlined against the distant view. The cold ashes of the fire lay gray-white on the forest floor. The cabin door was open, but the old man had gone. Somehow I knew and respected that he wanted to be alone again. Perhaps he had gone to sit by Wild Rose's grave when the fires of his own story had burned out and there were no embers left to stir.

I saddled my father's horse while the fresh, gentle wind blew through the pines. For some odd reason—I suppose it was curiosity—I walked over and took a look at the inside of the empty cabin. It was strange, but I realized then that I had never been invited in. I had always spent the time around the fire with old Brules and then, when the time came to sleep, I'd roll up in my bedroll. I was never interested in seeing inside, but I was now.

When I looked in, I was immediately struck by its neat, clean appearance and the sense of order that seemed to prevail in the small space. The floor was made of shining adobe that looked as if it had been swept and mopped a thousand times. Beside the old potbellied stove with a bucket on top was a wood bin. On the other side, against the wall, was a wide wooden platform made of planks laid over log supports. It served as both a storage shelf for supplies and as a table. A wolf skin hung on one wall and the only window presented a small but beautiful view of the distant Sleeping Ute. An impressive set of full-curl mountain bighorns was nailed to one wall, and on the other side the tines of a trophy elk horn served nobly as a gun rack for two old rifles—an 1873 Winchester and a big .50-caliber buffalo Sharps, undoubtedly the one General Crook had given him in the spring of 1885.

A rim of low logs containing clean straw served as a bedstead in the southeast corner. Spread upon it was a comfortable, well-cared-for buffalo robe, but I was immediately aware that it served as the only covering that the old man had to weather out the deadly cold of a Rocky Mountain winter, where, if the stove went out, the temperature inside could easily drop to forty degrees below zero.

On the table rested a poignant touch—a piece of Indian pottery. It was a bowl that I recognized had Shoshone patterns, and it contained a group of late summer wildflowers, whose beauty and brilliant colors were startling. Their significance was obvious to me.

I stood there for a minute before I decided what to do next. I stepped out of the cabin and walked over to where Father's horse was tied. I quickly undid the oilskin slicker from the back of the saddle and rolled out the Navajo blanket that I had purchased at Mexican Hat six days before.

It looked fantastic in the bright morning sunshine. The gorgeous red, blue, yellow, and brown colors—conformed into the figure of the thunderbird—made it perhaps the most beautiful man-made thing I had ever seen. I hesitated for a minute and then strode over to the cabin, entered, and spread the blanket onto the bed. It was like magic. It brightened up the whole interior of that lonely mountain home, giving it a sense of warmth and color.

Feeling immensely pleased, I stepped back out of the cabin door and turned to take a last look at my farewell present to old Brules—my outlaw, the mountain man, the hero of my boyhood dreams.

I mounted up and made my way on down out of the blue spruce, through the quaking aspen, and off the great skirted lower slopes of oak brush to the lush meadows of our ranch.

Two days later one of the cowhands drove me over to Rico in the buckboard and I caught the train for the East. A week later I entered an eastern college and a different world.

It was all new and exciting, but it was a long, long way from the cattle country of the Southwest, from the towering, sentinel-like slopes of old Lone Cone Peak, where one could look south for more than a hundred miles past Sleeping Ute to the Lukachukai Mountains.

It was, indeed, a far cry from the country that had a domelike sky stretching from one horizon to the other—a country that had tall blue spruce and golden aspen trees that whispered in the western wind, a wind that promised many things.

It was a long way, but my memories of old Brules the mountain man, even across that distance, have remained with me for all my years. I still see his strange eyes shining in the firelight and hear his toneful words—words that told of the days when the Old West was young. In them I still hear the voices of the prairie wind. I listen to the distant war drums beat. I hear the thunder of the buffalo herds and the wild shrill cry of the Comanche charge. I hear the crack of rifle fire and the soft sweet notes of a Shoshone maiden's love song.

The memories are all there and the words are as clear today as when I first heard them, lying by the fire, high, high up on the mountain that men call Lone Cone.